Praise for Nick

THE GONE-AWAY WORLD

"An epic, stupendous outburst of a book. . . . It's about the end of the world, the perils of thinking too hard (about anything), and friendship, family, and love. In that sense, it's a lot like *War and Peace*—huge, unexpected, and written by some guy you probably should have read already and can't wait to hear more from. . . . Harkaway's absurdist humanism reads like a surrealist smashup of Pynchon and Pratchett, Vonnegut and Heller, but his voice is his own. . . . *The Gone-Away World* is a flat-out ferociously good novel, and Harkaway has heralded his own coming with one hell of a bang." —*Austin Chronicle*

"A gripping, satirical, post-apocalyptic war epic populated with mimes, ninjas, bureaucrats, chimera, and gun-toting nerds."
—*New York Magazine*

"A stunning debut." —*Scotland on Sunday*

"[A] magnificent, sprawling, epic work . . . Could easily become a modern classic. Its scope and ambition are extraordinary, its execution is often breathtaking, and its style is by turns hilarious, outrageous, devastating, hip and profound. . . . Throw in some perfectly plotted revelations, an unforgettable finale and a life-affirming and thought-provoking denouement, and you've got a tale which will live long in the memory, and a writer destined for great things." —*Independent on Sunday*

"Harkaway delivers plenty of action and surprises. . . . Likely to be this season's major conversation-starter."
—*San Francisco Chronicle*

"[A] post-apocalyptic triumph. . . . Immensely rewarding. . . . genuinely terrifying. . . . Has the pace and action of an episode of *24*." —*The Times*

"Vivid and exciting. . . . Harkaway manages to meld a vision of war more germane to today's world, and take it to its most horrifying, apocalyptic conclusion." —*Charleston City Paper*

"A debut novel of the kind that comes along only once every couple of years, overflowing with imagination. . . . A master storyteller. . . . It has the scattergun inventiveness and confident, extended comic riffs that you'd find in Douglas Adams or Kurt Vonnegut. . . . If *The Gone-Away World* reads just like a dam-burst of dreams, then that might be because that is literally what it is." —*The Scotsman*

"Breathtakingly ambitious. . . . A sprawling odyssey of a novel. . . . A bubbling cosmic stew of a book, written with such exuberant imagination that you are left breathless by its sheer ingenuity." —*The Observer*

"Hits exactly the note of dazed and comic awesomeness. . . . There are delightful moments aplenty. . . . Any author who has come up with the beautifully silly plan of melding a kung-fu epic with an Iraq-war satire and a *Mad Max* adventure has to be worth keeping an eye on." —*The Guardian*

"Leaves the reader gasping for both adjectives and description. . . . It's a powerful and accomplished first novel that weaves elements of romance, mystery, SF/F and—yes—thriller together." —*January Magazine*

NICK HARKAWAY

THE GONE-AWAY WORLD

Nick Harkaway was born in Cornwall in 1972. He studied philosophy, sociology and politics at Clare College, Cambridge, and then worked in the film industry. *The Gone-Away World* is his first novel. He lives in London with his wife.

www.nickharkaway.com

The Gone-Away World

The Gone-Away World

A NOVEL

NICK HARKAWAY

Vintage Contemporaries
Vintage Books
A Division of Random House, Inc.
New York

FIRST VINTAGE CONTEMPORARIES EDITION, SEPTEMBER 2009

 Published in the United States by Vintage Books, a division of Random House, Inc., New York, and in Canada by Random House of Canada Limited, Toronto. Originally published in hardcover in Great Britain by William Heinemann, a division of Random House Group Ltd., London, and subsequently in hardcover in the United States by Alfred A. Knopf, New York, 2008.

The Library of Congress has cataloged the Knopf edition as follows:
Harkaway, Nick.
The gone-away world / by Nick Harkaway
p. cm.
I. Title.
PS3608.A7425G66 2008
813'.6—dc22 2008008701

Vintage ISBN: 978-0-307-38907-7

Book design by Robert Olson

www.vintagebooks.com

Printed in the United States of America
10 9 8 7 6 5 4

For my parents.
You know who you are.

The dreamers of the day are dangerous men,
for they may act their dream with open eyes; to make it possible.
This, I did.

—T. E. Lawrence

The Gone-Away World

Chapter One

When it all began; pigs and crisis;
close encounters with management.

THE LIGHTS went out in the Nameless Bar just after nine. I was bent over the pool table with one hand in the bald patch behind the D, which Flynn the Barman claimed was beer, but which was the same size and shape as Mrs. Flynn the Barman's arse: nigh on a yard in the beam and formed like the cross-section of a cooking apple. The fluorescent over the table blinked out, then came back, and the glass-fronted fridge gave a low, lurching hum. The wiring buzzed—and then it was dark. A faint sheen of static danced on the TV on its shelf, and the green exit lamp sputtered by the door.

I dropped my weight into the imprint of Mrs. Flynn the Barman's hams and played the shot anyway. The white ball whispered across the felt, came off two cushions, and clipped the eight cleanly into a side pocket. *Doff, doff, tchk . . . glonk.* It was perfect. On the other hand, I'd been aiming for the six. I'd given the game to Jim Hepsobah, and any time now when the power came back and everything was normal in the Nameless Bar, I'd pass the cue to my hero pal Gonzo, and Jim would beat him too.

Any time now.

Except that the lights stayed out, and the hollow glimmer of the TV set faded away. There was a small, quiet moment, the kind you just have time to notice, which makes you feel sad for no good reason. Then Flynn went out back, swearing like billy-o—and if your man Billy-O ever met Flynn, if ever there was a cuss-off, a high noon kinduva thing with foul language, I know where my money'd be.

Flynn hooked up the generator, which God help us was pig-powered. There was the sound of four large, foul-smelling desert swine being yoked to a capstan, a noise pretty much like a minor cavalry war, and then Flynn let loose some of his most abominable profanity at the nearest porker. It looked as if it wanted to vomit and bolted. The others perforce followed it in a slow but steady progression about the capstan, and then pig number one came back around, saw Flynn ready with another dose and tried to stop. Lashed to the crosspiece and bundled along by its three fellows, it found it couldn't, so it gathered its flab-covered self and charged past him at piggy top speed, and the whole cycle accelerated until, with a malodorous, oinking crunch, the generator kicked in, and the television lit up with the bad news.

Or rather, it didn't light up. The picture was so dim that it seemed the set was broken. Then there were fireworks and cries of alarm and fear, very quiet but getting louder, and we realised Sally Culpepper was just now turning on the sound. The image shook and veered, and urgent men went past shouting *get back, get clear,* and *ohshitlookatthatfuckerjesus,* which they didn't even bother to bleep. In the middle distance, it looked as if maybe a figure was rolling on the ground. Something had gone absolutely, horribly awry in the world, and naturally some arsehole was present with a camera making himself 10k an hour hazard pay when he could have been rolling up his arsehole sleeves and saving a life or two. I knew a guy in the Go Away War who did just that, dumped the network's prized Digi VII in a latrine trench and hauled six civilians and a sergeant from a burning medical truck. Got the Queen's Honour back home and a P45 from his boss. He's in an institution now, is Micah Monroe, and every day two guys from the Veterans' Hospital come by and take him for a walk and make sure the medal's polished on its little stand by his bed. They're sweet old geezers, Harry and Hoyle, and they've got medals of their own and they figure it's the least they can do for a man who lost his mind to giving a damn. Harry's kid was in the medical truck, you see. One of the ones Micah couldn't reach.

We stared at the screen and tried to make sense of what was on it. It looked, for a moment, as if the Jorgmund Pipe was on fire—but that was like saying the sky was falling. The Pipe was the most solidly constructed, triple-redundant, safety-first, one-of-a-kind necessary object in the world. We built it fast and dirty, because there was no other way, and then after that we made it indestructible. The plans were drawn up by the best, then checked and re-checked by the very best, and then the checkers themselves were scrutinised, analysed and vetted for any sign of fifth columnism or martyr tendencies, or even a serious and hitherto undetected case of just-plain-stupid, and then the contractors went to work under a scheme which emphasised thoroughness and adherence to spec over swift completion, and which imposed penalties so dire upon speculators and profiteers that it would actually be safer just to throw yourself from a high place, and finally the quantity surveyors and catastrophe experts went to town on it with hammers and saws, lightning generators and torsion engines, and declared it sound. Everyone in the Livable Zone was united in the desire to maintain and safeguard it. There was absolutely no chance that it could imaginably, conceivably, possibly be on fire.

It was on fire in a *big* way. The Pipe was burning painful white, magnesium, corpse-belly, nauseating white, and beside it there were buildings and fences, which meant this wasn't just the Pipe, but something even more important: a pumping station or a refinery. The whole place was wrapped in hot, shining smoke, and deep in the heart of the furnace there was stuff going on the human eye didn't know what to do with, weird, bad-news stuff which came with its own ominous soundtrack. On the screen something very important crumbled into noise and light.

"Fuuuuuuck," said Gonzo William Lubitsch, speaking for everyone.

It was a funny feeling: we were looking at the end of the world—again—and we were looking at something awful we'd never wanted to see, but at the same time we were looking at fame and fortune and just about everything we could ever ask for delivered by a grateful populace. We were looking at our reason for being. Because *that thar on that thar screen* was a fire, plus also a toxic event of the worst kind, and we, Ladies and Gentlemen, put your hands together, were the Haulage & HazMat Emergency Civil Freebooting Company of Exmoor County (corporate HQ the Nameless Bar, CEO Sally J. Culpepper, presiding) and this was the thing that we did better than anyone else in the entire Livable Zone, and therefore anywhere. Sally was straightaway talking to Jim Hepsobah and then to Gonzo, making lists and giving orders. She set Flynn the Barman to brewing his chews-through-steel espresso, and at last even Mrs. Flynn was up off her on-board cushions and moving at flank speed to make provisions, prepare tallies, and take letters for loved ones and estranged ones and people glimpsed and admired across the floating ash of the Nameless Bar. We ran to and fro and bumped into one another and swore, mostly because we didn't have anything important to do yet, and there was hubbub and brouhaha until Sally jumped up on the pool table and told us to shut up and get it together. She raised her phone above our heads like the thigh bone of a saint.

Sally Culpepper was six feet tall and much of her was leg, and on her right shoulder blade she had an orchid tattoo inked by some kid a quarter-inch shy of Michelangelo. She had strawberry lips and creamy skin and freckles across her nose where it'd been rebuilt after a bar fight in Lisbon. Gonzo claimed to have slept with her, to have had those legs wrapped around his hips like conjoined Italian calf-skin boa constrictors. He said she left him all but dead and grinning like a crescent moon. He said it happened one night after a big job, beer running from the rafters and everyone shiny as an egg yolk with success and soap-scoured skin. He said it was that time when Jim and Sally were trying not to be a thing, before they just gave in to the inevitable and got a place together. Every time we all met up, me and Gonzo and Sally and Jim Hepsobah and the others, Gonzo'd throw her a wicked grin and ask her how her *other* tattoo was, and Sally Culpepper would smile a secret smile which said she wasn't telling, and maybe he knew what that other tattoo looked like and maybe he didn't. Jim Hepsobah just pretended he hadn't heard, because Jim loved Gonzo like a brother, and love like that recognises that your buddy can be an ass, and doesn't care. We all loved Sally Culpepper, and she ruled us with her transparent lashes and her milkmaid's face and her slender arms that could drop a punch on you like a steam hammer. So there she stood, and there was a reasonable facsimile of calm and attention, because we knew that if the call came it would come on that phone, and we knew she had five-of-five reception here, and that was one of the reasons why the Nameless Bar was our place of business.

So we stopped hunting for lost socks and packing bags, and fretting that we'd somehow miss the starting gun, and settled in to Mrs. Flynn's provender. After a while we got quietly chatty and talked about small domestic chores, like cleaning gutters and chasing bats out of the loft. When the phone did ring (any time now), we could go and be heroes and save the world, which was Gonzo's favourite thing, and perforce something I did from time to time as well. Until it kicked off, we might as well not fuss. And then the Nameless Bar went quiet again; in little groups and one by one we fell silent as we beheld a vision of awful destiny.

The vision took the form of a small child carrying a snot-crusted and elderly teddy bear. It marched out into the room with much gravitas, surveyed us all sternly, then turned to Mrs. Flynn the Barman to gather in details for the prosecution.

"Why was it all dark?" it demanded.

"The power went out," Mrs. Flynn the Barman said cheerfully. "There's a fire." The child glowered around the room.

"These are loud men," it said, still annoyed, "and this one is dirty." It indicated Gonzo, who winced. It considered Sally Culpepper.

"This lady has a flower on her back," it added, having found conclusive proof of our unsuitability, then sat down in the middle of the floor and helped itself to a cheese and bacon roll. We goggled at it, and tried to make it go away by rubbing our eyes.

"Sorry," Mrs. Flynn the Barman said to us in general. "We don't let him in here normally, but it's an emergency." She eyed the child without approval. "Sweetie, you can't eat that; it's been on the floor near the dirty man."

Gonzo would probably have objected to this, but he didn't seem to hear her; he was still gazing in mute horror at the kid in front of him, and so was I, and so was everyone else. It was unquestionably a human toddler, and from the context certain conclusions had to be drawn which were uncomfortable and even appalling. This infant, swaddled in a bath towel and presently attempting to jam a four-inch-diameter granary bap into one ear, was the Spawn of Flynn.

Now, the fire on the Jorgmund Pipe was deeply unsettling. It represented danger and opportunity and almost certainly deceptions and agendas and what all. It was, however, well within our common understanding. Things burned, things exploded, and then we came along and made them stop. A breeding population of Flynns was another proposition altogether. We looked on Flynn as our personal monster, a safe, disturbing ogre of corrosive profanity and sinister glassware. He was ours and he was mighty and we grew great by association with him, and proof of his dangerous overmanliness was to be found in his fearless sexual trystings with the vasty Mrs. Flynn, but we didn't really want to live in a world entirely composed of Flynn-like beings in their serried ranks, vituperative and grouchy and unwilling to take an IOU. That was a new order even the bravest of us would find inhospitable, and the glimmer of it, the Spawn of Flynn, was even now throwing pieces of mushed-up cheese at Gonzo's boot. Mrs. Flynn the Barman, oblivious, finished whatever domestic task she was about amid a flurry of folding cloths and wiping, and trotted out. The Spawn of Flynn blithely ignored his mother and took a chomp from the side of the soiled roll.

"Crunchy," said the Spawn of Flynn.

Sally Culpepper's phone made a little chirrup, and everyone pointedly didn't look.

"Culpepper," Sally murmured, and then, after a moment, snapped it shut. "Wrong number." We all made faces to suggest we weren't fussed.

For a while, the Nameless Bar was filled with the sound of a small child eating and a lot of rough and tough-talking men and women thinking perturbed and unfamiliar thoughts about time and mortality and family. Then the quiet was broken, not by a phone call but by a sound so deep it was very nearly not a sound at all.

You heard it first as a kind of aggressive quiet. The whoosh and snarl of the desert all around us was still going on, but somehow it was subsumed by this deep, bass silence. Then you could feel it as a coldness in your knees and ankles, an unsteady, heart-attack feeling of weakness and vibration. A bit later it was audible, a thrumming *gnognognogg* which echoed in your lungs and let you know you were a prey animal today. And if you'd ever heard it before you knew what it was, and we all knew, because when we'd first met it was the noise we'd made together: the sound of soldiers. Someone was deploying a decent-sized military force around the Nameless Bar, and that meant they were emphatically not kidding about security. Since it seemed unlikely that they were deploying in order to arrest us, and since in any case if they were there would be absolutely nothing we could do about it, we all crowded through the big pine door of the Nameless Bar to watch them arrive.

Outside, it was cold and dry. The night had set in, witching-hour black, and the sands had given up their heat, so a chill wind was gusting across the wooden rooftops of the bar and the outbuildings, and the gloomy shacks and clapboard homes which made up the no-hope town of Exmoor, pop. 1,309. Off against the brow of Millgram's Hill was our section of the Jorgmund Pipe; a single shadow-grey line lit by Flynn's bedroom window and the work light in the paddock, and every now and again by the gleam of another lonely little house along the way. It ran in both directions into the dark, and somewhere on the other side of the globe those two lines met and joined, surely at a place which was as vibrant and alive as Exmoor was not. On the top of the Pipe, every few metres, there was a little nozzle spraying good, clean FOX into the sky; FOX, the magic potion which kept the part of the world we still had roughly the same shape day by day. No one quite knew where it came from or how you made it; most people imagined some big machine like an egg with all manner of wires and lights condensing it out of air and moonshine, and drip-drip-dripping it into big vats. There were thousands of them, somewhere, vulnerable and vital, and let them never stop. I'd once seen some of the machinery involved: long black lozenges with curved sides, all plumbing and hoses, and rather eerie. Less an egg than a space capsule or a bathyscaphe, except this was the opposite; not a thing for journeying through a hostile place, but a thing which makes what is outside less hostile.

Most people tried very hard to avoid noticing the Pipe. They had euphemisms for it, as if it were cancer or impotence or the Devil, which it was. In some places they painted it bold colours and pretended it was an art project, or built things in front of it or even grew flowers on it. Only in pissant remora towns like this one did you get to see the thing itself; the rusty and despised spine of who we were, carrying vital solidity and safety, and the illusion of continuance, to every nook and cranny of the Livable Zone.

In truth it was not a loop at all, but a weird bird's-nest tangle. There were hairpin bends and corkscrews, and places where subsidiary hoses jutted out from the main line to reach little towns on the edges, and places where the Livable Zone pulled close about the Pipe like a matron drawing up her skirts to cross a stream, where the weather and the lie of the land brought the outside perilously close; but taken all together it made a sort of rough circle girdling the Earth. A place to have a home. Get more than twenty miles from the Pipe (*Old JP,* they called it in Haviland City, where the Jorgmund Company had its headquarters, or sometimes *the Big Snake* or *the Silver*) and you were in the inimical no-man's-land between the Livable Zone and the bloody nightmare of the unreal world. Sometimes it was safe, and sometimes it wasn't. We called it the Border, and we went through it when we had to, when it was the only way to get somewhere in any reasonable length of time, when the alternative was a long drive around three sides of a square and the emergency wouldn't wait. All the same, we went in force and we went quickly, lightly, and we kept an eye on the weather. If the wind changed, or the pressure dropped; if we saw clouds on the horizon we didn't like, or strange folks, or animals which weren't quite right, we turned tail and ran back to the Pipe. People who lived in the Border didn't always stay people. We carried FOX in canisters, and we hoped it would be enough.

Rumour had it some of the outlying towns had been sacked recently, split open and burned to the ground by people—or nearly-people—from beyond the Border, from the shifting places where bad things were. So the myrmidons of the company were patrolling a bit more and asking more questions, and people were sticking close to the Pipe, where it was safe. Step off the path, and maybe you'd get back and maybe you wouldn't, but you would be changed. Which sounds like strange and awful until you realise that that's actually pretty much how it's always been, and if you think any different, it's because you've never left that little stretch of comfort and gone someplace where what you know gets a bit thin on the ground.

The roar of the convoy was close now, and the big spots from the command car were sweeping back and forth, sometimes lighting us up and sometimes showing us the sand and grit all around. Deserts in wildlife shows are sweeping, noble places of savage majesty: photogenic ants and awesome spiders, all clean and sheer, because at that magnification the dirt looks like boulders. Our desert was kind of a dump. When the wind blew from the west, it carried the smell of hot metal and diesel and combat-ready men. When it blew from the east, it carried the distinctive flavour of recently exercised pig. Neither was the kind of smell anyone was going to put in a bottle with a flower on it and market with an expensive and strategically-not-quite-nude supermodel. They were real smells, living and nasty and oddly comforting on a night when the world was on fire. So we stood there in the dark, away from the TV and the Spawn of Flynn and the pool table, and we all breathed in and grinned at one another and we were us, very *us.* Jim Hepsobah took Sally Culpepper's hand and we pretended we couldn't see. Annie the Ox murmured something to Egon Schlender; Samuel P. cursed and muttered; Tobemory Trent did nothing at all, still and silent like a grave marker. I thought about my personal version of heaven, which is small and calm and features only one angel, who cannot sing.

Close your eyes and think of a house on the side of a mountain, made of stone and wood. The air is clear and cold and flavoured with snow, and the sounds you hear are the sounds of real people working hard on things they can hold, eat and use. There is woodsmoke, and that woodsmoke is touched with tonight's dinner and an open bottle of the good stuff. The woman in the doorway wears blue jeans and a white shirt and a pair of cowboy boots, and she has eyes the colour of lake water. This is my wife, and yes, she is as beautiful as all that surrounds her. This is my heart, and it is the one thing I have that Gonzo Lubitsch does not.

The convoy roared in, big and loud and adolescent, and everyone was trying very hard not to snigger, because under the best circumstances you don't really want to snigger at a full armoured unit, and this was an emergency and these were some nervous young men and women with guns. So we looked very serious and churchy and respectful and wondered what the hell was going on. And then the lead tank stopped in the "reserved" parking space and the lid flipped up, and instead of some grizzled bastard with a regulation sneer there was a pencilneck, a slender, coiffured sonuvabitch, and you could smell his come-fuck-me cologne and the hand-tooled leather briefcase he was carrying.

"Hi," the pencilneck said. And then, because it wasn't enough that he should be a management guy, he had to be a doofus as well, he added, "Could someone give me a hand here? I'm stuck in the porthole!" and laughed.

When they send you an escort, it means you need to be somewhere fast, and that's not so bad. When they send you your own personal pencilneck, it means blame and skulduggery and contractual folderol, and everything you should be able to count on will be all screwed up. It means they intend to lie to you, and they want one of their own on hand to emphasise how open and truthful they are. Sally Culpepper went to condition red, and Jim Hepsobah let go of her hand so that she could go back to being a CEO and a player and not a girl from Darzet who's waiting with surprising patience for her big, loving lug of a boyfriend to get down on one knee.

The pencilneck rose slowly into the night like the villain in an old spy movie on some kind of personal elevator, except that when his shins were about level with the rim of the hatch (not "porthole") you could see a couple of nobbled hands, and then forearms almost as big as Jim's, and then Bone Briskett's ugly face came in sight, so there was a grizzled bastard in residence as well. He put the pencilneck down on the front of the tank and didn't say anything, in such a way as to imply that he, Bone, thought the pencilneck was seriously pointless, and would happily run him over if we gave the word. We could all pretend it was an accident and there'd be one less layer of bureaucracy between us and whatever we needed to get this job done.

The Jorgmund Company spanned the world, and it was old and wise and cautious, evolved out of other companies from back before the Go Away War. That meant it took care of itself, protected itself, and that was annoying but probably necessary. There were mayoralties and city states and the like, making up a mosaic of power we called the System, and the idea was that they upheld the law and maintained the army—the people like Bone, who patrolled the edges of the Livable Zone and chased off bandits and worse things than bandits. But in the end Jorgmund ran the show, because Jorgmund had—was—the Pipe, and that was the thing we couldn't do without. The circle-snake logo of Jorgmund was everywhere, or at least everywhere that mattered. So here we were, and here was this guy, the pencilneck: he had a boss, sure as anything, because men without bosses do not come to Exmoor, not even when the sky is falling. And in the interest of his boss, and his promotion, and all good things, he was out to screw us.

The pencilneck landed on the sand like he was expecting it to swallow him, and it flipped up and over his brogues as he walked and got inside his shoes and dusted his silk socks, so by the time he reached us and looked at Jim Hepsobah and stuck out his hand, and Jim kept his arms folded and Sally shook hands with the pencilneck in a way which said "strike one," the man from Haviland City looked as if he'd been bleached or whitewashed to the knee.

"Dick Washburn," the pencilneck said, and right away we were all trying to smother a laugh, and Samuel P. bustled forward and leaned over his paunch and stuck out his hand and said "Dickwash what?" which didn't faze the pencilneck at all. Richard Washburn, Snr VP i/c whateveritis, gave his name for a second time, clear and sharp, and nailed Samuel P. with a look which said he could take a joke as well as the next man but don't think he was gonna laugh that one off, and we all revised our opinion slightly upward. Pencilneck, perhaps, but not invertebrate. If Dick Washburn could show some iron here and now, then back home he was near enough an alpha male, and one of the ones the silverbacks kept an eye on in case they caught him sizing up their offices and nodding at the view. In fact, they probably had, and here he was, pointman and focus of all and any ensuing litigation in the matter of the *People vs. the Jorgmund Company*. A prince who becomes too popular is best destroyed with insoluble opportunities.

We all went inside while the troopers did their hard perimeter thing, and did it pretty well, although they looked confused and unhappy about taking up defensive positions around a building which appeared to be made from cardboard and snot, stuck out on the edge of the civilised world and populated by folk like us, and which would probably be rendered unto box clippings by the recoil from one of the big guns mounted on the armoured personnel carrier. There was a bad moment when four large shapes showed up on the infrared, moving in a rapid arc towards the rear of the Nameless Bar, and two sets of heavy weapons came online and tracked them: *shwoopHUNKdzzzunnn!* and *Sir, contact, sir!* followed by *Soldier, if you fire that weapon I will stick it up your* and *guboozzznn* as the turrets moved, probable field of fire going through Flynn's living room and the saloon. Of course, the enemy was the desert pig generator system, currently labouring to produce enough power to run the kitchen and the TV all at once. So the pigs hovered on the brink of spectacular annihilation for a few seconds, and then were classed as zero threat, the guns went *zugug-slrrrmm* and back to first positions. Bone Briskett (Colonel Briskett) handed over to his second, a scrawny bloke who was probably as dangerous as the whole rest of them put together, then followed us in and shut the door.

Dick Washburn stood in the middle of the room, and we all looked at him. He tried to look back at everyone at once and bottled it. He was surrounded. He looked at Bone Briskett, but

Bone was contemplating the awful reality of the Spawn of Flynn and having some kind of godforsaken epiphany of his own. He glanced at Sally, but she was paying him back for the handshake thing and waiting with everyone else, so he stood there in his ruined mortgage-your-house shoes and his manly yet sensitive yet raunchy aftershave in a room flavoured with stale beer and the aroma of drivers and cheese rolls and pig power, and tried like hell not to look like he was out of his depth.

Consider this man, Jorgmund's most expendable son. He wears his second-best suit (or third-best, or tenth-, who knows, but he's surely not risking his Royce Allen bespoke in a tank, not for any kind of promotion) and his face is smooth with Botox and lotion. Without genetic engineering, without intervention or expense, the Jorgmund Company has remade him, barracked him in some halfway *ville dortoir* and stripped him of his connection with the world in a crash course of management schools and loyalty card deals, surrounded him with pseudo-spaces, malls and water features, so that he is allergic to pollen and pollution and dust and animal fibre and salt, gluten, bee stings, red wine, spermicidal lubricant, peanuts, sunshine, unpurified water and chocolate, and really to everything except the vaccum-packed, air-conditioned in-between where he spends his life. Dick Washburn, known for evermore as Dickwash, is a type D pencilneck: a sassy wannabe paymaster with vestigial humanity. This makes him vastly less evil than a type B pencilneck (heartless bureaucratic machine, pro-class tennis) and somewhat less evil than a type C pencilneck (chortling lackey of the dehumanising system, ambient golf), but unquestionably more evil than pencilneck types M through E (real human screaming to escape a soul-devouring professional persona, varying degrees of desperation). No one I know has ever met the type A pencilneck, in much the same way that no one ever reports their own fatal accident; a type A pencilneck would be a person so entirely consumed by the mechanism in which he or she is employed that they had ceased to exist as a separate entity. They would be odourless, faceless and undetectable, without ambition or restraint, and would take decisions entirely unfettered by human concerns, make choices for the company, of the company. A type A pencilneck would be the kind of person to sign off on torture and push the nuclear button for no more pressing reason than that it was his job—or hers—and it seemed the next logical step.

Dickwash cleared his throat and unrolled the Mission like he'd ever done this stuff himself, spewing officer-grade profanity because, I suppose, he thought that's what Real Men Do.

"I guess you all know there's a fire on the Jorgmund Pipe," he said, giving us a determined frown. "Well, it's more than that. It's a pumping station, a major one. There're thousands of barrels of FOX there and it's going up like kerosene, burning a *hole in the fucking world.*" He nodded ruefully. I think he was trying to do serious, but he just looked as if he'd dropped a load of red wine on the carpet: *Christ, Vivian, what can I say? Totally my fault. No! No salt. If you just leave it they can get it out, AMAZING chemical stuff, kills all known vintages stone dead! It's the VX gas of stains! Yah, I know, I thought so too. But helloo-oooo, sailor! That's the most gorgeously risqué dress when you're in that position!* He didn't get any bounce out of the audience, so he tried again, this time with emphatic clichés.

"We've gotta go down there and *put that fucker out,* blow it out, uh, *like a fucking candle,* otherwise . . ." At which point he trailed his voice and let the breath flow out of him and he paused to let us construct our own metaphor for catastrophe. And that right there is what you call a rhetorical ellipsis, the cheapest device in oratory and one of the hardest to do well. An ellipsis is like a haymaker punch you throw with your mouth, and the only tricks more low rent than that are making fun of your opponent's ugly puss and bringing up something by saying you won't mention it. We all stared at him for a minute, and he went sort of pinkish and closed his mouth.

"Explosives," Gonzo said, and Jim Hepsobah nodded.

"Have to be," Jim said.

"Make a vacuum?"

"Yup."

"Is that going to work with FOX?"

"Ought to."

"Need a very big bang," Annie the Ox pointed out.

"Oh, yeah," said Gonzo.

"Can't have it catch again after," Annie went on. "Helluva big bang. Can we get that big of a bang?"

Annie the Ox was a blunt-fingered woman with big cheeks who knew about explosives. She had narrow, solid shoulders and heavy forearms and thighs, and she collected puppet heads. It was impossible to say whether Annie collected these things because she liked to have soft, plush friends to talk to, or if they were faces for the people in her life who were Gone Away. I had never asked, because some things are private, and Annie was not the kind of person who answered questions about private things.

She looked at Jim and Gonzo. They looked at Sally. Sally looked at Dickwash.

"Yes," Dickwash said, with absolute certainty. "I can fix that."

It always creeps me out being with pencilnecks. Anything over a type E and you can get the feeling what you're talking to isn't entirely human, and you're not entirely wrong. A guy named Sebastian once explained it to me like this:

Suppose you are Alfred Montrose Fingermuffin, capitalist. You own a factory, and your factory uses huge industrial metal presses to make Fingermuffin Thingumabobs. Great big blades powered by hydraulics come stomping down on metal ribbon (like off a giant roll of tape, only made of steel) and cut Thingumabobs out like gingerbread men. If you can run the machine at a hundred Thingumabobs per minute, six seconds for ten Thingumabobs (because the machine prints ten at a time out of the ribbon), then you're doing fine. The trouble is that although in theory you could do that, in fact you have to stop the machine every so often so that you can check the safeties and change shifts. Each time you do, the downtime costs you, because you have the machine powered up and the crew are all there (both crews, actually, on full pay). So you want to have that happen the absolute minimum number of times per day. The only way you can know when you're at the minimum number of times is when you start to get accidents. Of course, you're always going to get *some* accidents, because human beings screw up; they get horny and think about their sweethearts and lean on the Big Red Button and someone loses a finger. So you reduce the number of shifts from five to four, and the number of safety checks from two to one, and suddenly you're much closer to making Fingermuffin's the market leader. Mrs. Fingermuffin gets all excited because she's been invited to speak at the WI, and all the little Fingermuffins are happy because their daddy brings them brighter, shinier, newer toys. The downside is that your workers are working harder and having to concentrate more, and the accidents they have are just a little worse, just a little more frequent. The trouble is that you can't go back, because now your competitors have done the same thing and the Thingumabob market has gotten a bit more aggressive, and the question comes down to this: how much further can you squeeze the margin without making your factory somewhere no one will work? And the truth is that it's a tough environment for unskilled workers in your area and it can get pretty bad. Suddenly, because the company can't survive any other way, soft-hearted Alf Fingermuffin is running the scariest, most dangerous factory in town. Or he's out of business and Gerry Q. Hinderhaft has taken over, and everyone knows how hard Gerry Q. pushes his guys.

In order to keep the company alive, safeguard his family's happiness and his employees' jobs, Alf Montrose Fingermuffin (that's you) has turned into a monster. The only way he can deal with that is to separate himself into two people—Kindly Old Alf, who does the living, and Stern Mr. Fingermuffin, factory boss. His managers do the same. So when you talk to Alf Fingermuffin's managers, you're actually not talking to a person at all. You're talking to a part in the machine that is Fingermuffin Ltd., and (just like the workers in the factory itself) the ones who are best at being a part are the ones who function least like a person and most like a machine. At the factory this means doing everything at a perfect tempo, the same way each time, over and over and over. In management it means living profit, market share and graphs. The managers ditch the part of themselves which thinks, and just get on with running the programme in their heads.

So this almost certainly wasn't going to be easy. But unless there was an earthquake or another war, Gonzo was going, which meant I was going, and if we were going, the chances were the crew would come with us to make sure we were okay, and incidentally to make sure we didn't do something amazingly cool which we could then rag them about, and finally to make sure we didn't come back zillionaires and rub their noses in it before setting them up for life. Gonzo Lubitsch is addicted to playing the lead. I work for a living, I take my bonus home to my wife, and we get drunk and naked and we act like teenagers and feed each other pizza.

Back to the bar: Sally had Dick Washburn penned up in a farmhouse with the entire Mexican army coming down on him. He'd come in rock 'n' roll, thought he'd wrap the truckjocks by five and get his aerobicised backside back to the city and sink a few martinis and *My God, Vivian, the place was a hellhole!* But Sally has negotiator *gong fu* of the first order. In the small world of civil freebooting companies, she is the go-to girl, the top cat, the queen bee and the *wakasensei,* and her eyes undress the fine print and her fingers trace its outlines and she knows it, owns it, makes it sit up and beg for her touch like a happy gimp. The pencilneck was watching his Christmas bonus shrink like a white truffle in January, and the reckless testosterone feeling he had come in with was fading with it. Vivian's body in its Lycra workout gear was vanishing and being replaced by the possibility that Sally was handing him his head. So Dick Washburn dug deep and dark into his management-school magic set and tried an end-run, a wicked, one-pill-for-all-ills solution, which is maybe what he intended to do all along: isolate Sally and get us to make the deal for him. A type D pencilneck has *vestigial* humanity, which is the kind you can fit in a cigarette case and offer people at parties.

"The trucks," Dick Washburn said.

"What about them?" asked Sally.

"At the end of the run," the pencilneck said, "you can keep the trucks. They're amazing trucks." He hit the word "truck" just a little harder each time, and when he said it the third time, everyone in the room heard it above the ambient bustle. Jim looked up and Sally looked back at him like she knew there was a thing happening, but she didn't know how to stop it.

"Really *amazing,*" the pencilneck repeated.

Sally pointed out that we had trucks; that our possession of and facility in the handling of trucks was central to our professed identity as truckers, which in turn was key in regard to the pencilneck's presence in our midst, that presence being a consequence of his desire to deploy those talents in the service of the populace and the enterprise for which he was plenipotentiary spokesperson, ambassador and man on the ground, and in whose short-term interest he now sought to bilk, cheat, con and bamboozle us out of due legal and contractual protections in line with industry practice and good solid common sense, but whose shareholders would, like the aforementioned wider population, unquestionably look with disfavour and consequent litigiousness upon the inevitable wranglings and disputations resulting from said rooking, hornswoggling, grifting and humbuggery, should any ill befall in the due exercise of our discretion and judgement in the course of whatever hare-brained adventure the party of the first part (the pencilneck) chose to inflict upon the soft skin and girlish charms of the party of the second part (the naive and open-hearted drivers of the toughest and most competent civil freebooting company in the world).

"We can fix all that," the pencilneck said. "You have to come," he leered, "and see the *trucks.*" And that time he made it sound like your first orgasm, or maybe your last.

So we did. Sally reluctantly, Jim calmly, Gonzo eagerly, Tobemory Trent sidewise like a crab and all the rest of us according to our lights, we went out of the Nameless Bar and into the Nameless Parking Lot. The pencilneck waved his arms, and forward they came with a grumble and a clatter, with a great white light and the smell of fresh rubber and vinyl and engine, and lo, there were trucks indeed.

But not trucks as we knew them. These were the trucks of legend, the trucks every vehicle with more than six wheels dreams of being. They were black and chrome and they stank of raunchy fuel consumption and throbbing power. If these trucks could have sung, they'd have sung bass, deep and slow and full of the Delta. They had leather seats and positioning systems and armoured glass. They were factory new and they had our number plates already on 'em, and there was a hula girl on the dashboard of Baptiste Vasille's, and a stack of pornographic images in Samuel P.'s, and Gonzo's truck had flames on the side and Sally Culpepper's had a red suede dash. Someone out there understood us, our needs, our mad little schticks, the things without which we weren't the Haulage & HazMat Emergency Civil Freebooting Company of Exmoor County (CEO Sally J. Culpepper, presiding), we were just guys and girls in pound shop clothes.

In other words, this was a honey trap. If you're giving guys like us kit like that to do a gig like this, it's because either 1) you're going to make a ton of profit or 2) you don't think we have a rat's chance of coming back alive. Most like, it's both.

But then again that was hardly news. If they could have done it themselves—if they hadn't been too damned scared to take on what needed to be done, for fear of their silk-socked lives—they never would have come to us. The Free Company was on the clock and there were only three commandments: look after your friends; do the job; come out richer. To these the pencilneck was adding an apocrypha of penalties for excessive damage and materials overspend which we fully intended to ignore, because he was the tool of a litigation-wary softass outfit and they were afraid not only of death but also of flesh-eating lawyers and class actions and angry investors and anti-trust and whatall, and the first and second commandments forbid stinting during a run. Thus we gazed upon his many provisos and codicils, and we said "bah."

Basic plan:

1. go to place A (depot) and pick up item X (big box go boomboom)
2. take it to place B (the pumping station), which is undergoing state Q (on fire, *v. v. bad*)
3. introduce item X to place B (big box go boomboom, burning pumping station; burning pumping station, big box go boomboom. *Shake hands. Didn't we meet once over at van Kottler's place? Gosh, darn, I believe we did!*) and instigate reaction P (boomboom, bang bang-a-diddly, BOOM) and hence state R (oxygen deprival, pseudo-vacuum, *schlurrrrrp!*) thus extinguishing B (~Q, ~P, *so sorry, dear old thing, have to go, children have school tomorrow, ciao-ciao mwah-mwah*), thus
4. making enough money to buy a small nation-state, farm watawabas and eat mango all day long (*boo-yah, sing hallelujah, we didn't die*).

The question I should have been asking all this time—the thing which we all should have been wanting to know, pressingly and insistently—is this: how the hell did part of the Pipe, the all-ways-up most enduring and secure object ever manufactured by human hands and human engineering; the triple-redundant, safe-tastic product of the most profoundly dedicated collaboration in history; how did this invulnerable thing come to catch fire at all? And when you put it like that, the answer is obvious:

Someone made it so.

But hey. We're not those kindsa people. We are can-do, not what-about—except for me, maybe. The pencilneck smiled at Sally Culpepper, and his victory grin went a bit slack as he realised we'd never had any intention of saying no, and we knew that he knew that we were expected to lose people. Just for a second I thought perhaps he was ashamed. And then he looked down at his feet and caught a glimpse of his messed up year's-salary shoes, and he hated this stupid, ugly and above all *cheap* place, and his pencilneckhood rolled back as he found that part of himself which was indifferent, and he slipped gently into the warm water of not giving a damn.

Look at him again: this is not Dick Washburn you're seeing, not exactly. Dick has vacated possession for this bit of chat. Standing here is not Richard Godspeed Washburn, who sustained a nasty concussion on his fifteenth birthday, the very eve of the Go Away War, and who spent his next weeks in darkness and candlelight as the hospital he had gone to slowly shut down and ran out and fell apart, then grew to manhood in the new, broken world. This is not Quick Dick of the Harley Street Boys, who—before the orphanfinders came and settled him in a home of sorts and things got somewhat normal once again—could open the rear door of an army truck and pinch a pound of chocolate before the soldiers ever knew. This is Jorgmund itself, staring through Dick's eyes and measuring things as numbers and profit margins. Of course, Jorgmund is nothing more than a shared hallucination, a set of rules which make up Richard Washburn's job, and every time he does this—slips away from a human situation and lets the pattern use his mind and his mouth because he'd rather not make the decision himself—he edges a little closer to being a type C pencilneck. He loses a bit of his soul. There's a flicker of pain and anger in him as the animal he is feels the machine he is becoming take another bite, and snarls in its cage, deep down beneath his waxed, buff pectorals and his second-best (or ninth-best) suit. But it's really a very small animal, and not one of the fiercer ones.

And then it was over. Deal done. Job on. I sidled over to Sally and murmured in her ear.

"So, before Dickwash showed up . . ."

"Hm."

"Phone call."

"Yes."

"Wrong number?"

Sally shook her head. "I lied," she murmured, just as quiet. "It was a woman. Didn't know her."

"What did she say?"

"She said not to take the job."

"Nice."

"Yeah."

"Anything else?"

"Yes," Sally said. "She asked for you, in particular."

And Sally didn't say "Keep your eyes open" because she knew me, and that was fine. She nodded once and took the keys to her new truck from the pencilneck's unresisting fingers.

Sally and Jim in the first rig, me and Gonzo in the second, Tommy Lapland and Roy Roam in the third, and on to the back of the line. Twenty of us, two to a cab, ten trucks of bad hair, denim and spurs, with Tobemory Trent wearing his special-occasions eyepatch bringing up the rear. Trent was from Preston, born and bred in pork pie country with coal dust in his blood. He lost that eye in the Go Away War, had it taken out in a hurry so he wouldn't die or worse. Trent spat on the road and roared, Captain goddam Ahab of the new highways, harpoon rack over the driver's seat in case of trouble. He vaulted into the big chair and slammed the door hard enough to make the rig rock, and there was only one really important thing left to do. Sally and the pencilneck shook hands, Sally turned to look at us from the running board of her truck and there we were, proud and wired and dumb with eighteen-wheel delight. And Gonzo William Lubitsch of Cricklewood Cove, five foot eleven and broad like a Swiss Alp, dropped his trousers and pissed on our front right tyre for luck. Annie the Ox and Egon Schlender hollered and hallooed from number six, and Gonzo dropped his shorts too, exposing a muscular arse in their direction, then leaped into the truck and punched the starter. I had my feet on the dash and I was sending up a tiny prayer to the God who ruled my personal heaven.

Lord, I want to come home.

MOSTLY when we left the Nameless Bar, we headed westwards along the Pipe. Exmoor was a mile or so south of the main trunk road, and the mountains kicked up funny weather, so eighty or ninety miles in the other direction was one of the pinch points in the Zone where you paid close attention to the people you saw in case they weren't really people at all. Every so often, traders came through town, and there was a special guesthouse in the back of the Nameless Bar where Flynn put the ones he wasn't sure about. It was comfortable and safe, but it was further from his family. Flynn's a decent man, but a cautious one.

This time, we went east, very fast. Bone Briskett's tank was the kind with wheels which can do a decent speed, and he was getting everything he could out of it and asking for more. We drove through the night, and either they'd cleared the road or no one was coming the other way. We hurtled through a steep-sided valley and on along the pinch. The wind was blowing in our favour, off the mountains and away, but even so you could see a broad misty curtain to the south, maybe five miles distant, strange shadows twisting and turning. In a few miles, we could turn left, under the Pipe, and there was a loop of road which would bring us north-eastwards fast. I waited. We didn't take it.

Instead we drove on, and on, and on, and the dawn was building in the sky, and I started to get that feeling which says "Be ready" because there was one route out here which would bring us over towards Haviland City and full onto a big thick section of the main Pipe. It was an old road, and it would get us there damn fast, but we'd never taken it before because it went through Drowned Cross. I nudged Gonzo and he glanced at me, then shrugged. Drowned Cross was bad country, the far edge of the Border. That was why it was empty, and dead.

We rolled out onto a flat meadow, and there was no more desert. A wide green plain stretched into the distance in front of us, cut by a grey line like a dowager's eyebrow which departed from the main trunk and headed south. Bone Briskett's tank took the corner without slowing, and Gonzo tutted—whether at this haste or at our destination, I didn't know, but I could feel him paying more attention, looking at narrow places on the road and measuring them with his eyes, checking the escort and wondering whether they were good enough.

Right after the Reification and the Go Away War, there was a period of what you might call undue optimism. One particular town was built with two fingers up to the recent past, first of a new breed of bright, safe places where we could all get on with real life again, pay tax and worry about our hairlines and middle-aged spread, and is the guy next door flouting the hosepipe ban during the summer heat? They called it Heyerdahl Point, and they sold it as an adventure in neo-suburban frontiersmanship. About five thousand people lived there. It had its own little capillary of the Jorgmund Pipe making it secure, and it perched on a hilltop so the people there could look down on the valleys below, and out into the dangerous mists of the unreal, and know that they were pushing back the boundary just by being here.

"One day," they could say to one another over decaf, "all this will be fields."

Now it was called Drowned Cross.

We came around a curve, and there it was, tucked up on its little hill and dark and empty as your dog's kennel after you take him to the vet and say goodbye. The road went straight to it, and so did Bone Briskett, and so did we. Drowned Cross got bigger but no lighter, jagged and sprawling across the sky. The big broken tooth over the whole place was the church spire, and the rough-edged thing it had fallen against was the town clock, stuck at five fifteen for evermore. The houses were clean and pale, with terracotta roofs. The windows were unbroken. A couple of cars were parked neatly in the main square, and one had the door open; the kind of town where you left the keys in the ignition while you bought your paper. Birds flew up out of the sunroof as we went by, grey and black pigeons with mad pigeon eyes. One of them was too stupid to dodge in the right direction and bounced off the windscreen. Or maybe the others had pushed him—it's not hard to believe in murder among pigeons. Gonzo swore. The stunned bird tumbled away and lay in the road. If it was still there when Samuel P. came by, he'd drive right over it.

No one really knew what had happened in Drowned Cross. There weren't any survivors. No one showed up, addled and desperate, at the next town along the way; no lonely shepherd saw the whole thing from an adjoining hill. Whatever it was, it made no noise, in the grand scheme, and left no image of itself. Something came up out of the unreal and swallowed the place. Perhaps the hill under Drowned Cross eats villages. I heard a story once, on the radio, in which a group of sailors cast adrift came at last to an island where they moored for the night. They had not expected land, so far off course and bewildered by foreign stars; they had anticipated thirst and madness. They wept and kissed the ground and lit a fire to cook their supper, and at last fell into a fitful sleep. Of course, in the middle of the night they woke to a dreadful howling, and the isle on which they stood began to shake, and then great, boneless arms reached from the water to snatch at them, and they realised they had sought refuge on the back of some horrid monster of the deep.

I loved cautionary tales like that when I was a child, but sitting with Gonzo and looking down on the clean, vacant houses of Drowned Cross, I kept thinking of clams slurped with garlic sauce, and the shells thrown back into the bowl. What had happened there was nasty, plain and simple, and there'd been others, since. In the still hours of the night-time in houses all around the Pipe, people woke, and listened, and were afraid of things from beyond the Border. Somebody out there ate towns, whole, and went on his way. People said it was the Found Thousand. I hoped that wasn't true.

The Cross itself—our road and the other one, the east–west road which went through the town and headed out into what they all figured would be the next slice of reclaimed land—was on the far side of the square. We went slowly, partly because the cobbles were slick with dew, and partly because you don't squeal your tyres in a graveyard, no matter how much you want to leave. Something glimmered in the dust where the roads met: a silvered piece of metal engraved with what could have been a new moon or a bowl of soup with a spoon in it. It looked expensive, and I wondered how long it had sat there. Since the day Drowned Cross got its name, most likely. It could have been a cuff link, or a bracelet. It seemed sad that someone was missing it—maybe it was one of two, and he still had the other one—and then I felt guilty and crass because whoever owned it was almost certainly dead, and his missing watchstrap whojimmy wasn't bugging him any more.

And then, as swiftly as it had come upon us, it was gone. A small place, after all. Gonzo turned the wheel, bringing the truck in a wide, powerful turn, and the last empty cottage vanished behind us. Bone Briskett's tank went roaring out ahead, and Gonzo rapped his hands on the wheel, *papapapahhh!*

"The open road!" I shouted into the radio.

"Oh, ecstasy!" cried Jim Hepsobah and Sally Culpepper.

"Oh, poop-poop!" yelled Gonzo Lubitsch.

Bone Briskett didn't say anything, but he said it in a way which made it clear he thought we were mad.

Please, dear Lord.

I want to come home.

Chapter Two

At home with kid Gonzo;
donkeys, girls, and first meetings.

"IT'S time to eat," Ma Lubitsch says, a broad expanse of apron topped by a summit of greasy peanut-coloured hair. Old Man Lubitsch doesn't hear over the buzzing of his hives, or he doesn't care to join us, because his baggy white figure remains out in the yard, tottering from one prefab bee house to another with a can of wispy smoke. Ma Lubitsch makes a noise like a whale clearing its blowhole and sets out knives and forks, the delaminating edge of the table pushing into her belly. Gonzo's mother is big enough that she takes up two seats in church and once near-killed a burglar with a rolled-up colour supplement. Gonzo himself, still able to count his years without resorting to two hands, has his father's more sparing construction.

One of my first memories, in all the world: Gonzo, only a few months before, staring into my face with a stranger's concern. He has been playing a game of indescribable complexity, by himself, in the corner of the playground. He has walked from one end of the sandpit to the other and rendered it flat in a particular place, and he has marked borders and bridges and areas of diffusion and lines of demarcation and now he needs another player and cannot find one. And so he turns to look about him and sees a small, lost child: alone in a moment of unfathomable grief. With presence of mind he directs his mother's attention to the crisis, and she trundles over and asks immediately what is the matter and am I hurt and where are my parents and where is my home? And to these questions I have no answer. All I know is that I am crying.

Gonzo answers the disaster by approaching the white ice-cream truck at the far gate, purchasing there a red, rocket-shaped ice with a sticky centre, and this he hands me with great solemnity. Ten minutes later, by the alchemy of sugar and artificial flavours and the security they represent, I have joined Gonzo's incomprehensible game and am winning—though perhaps he is going easy on me—and my tears are dry and crusty on my smock. During a momentary ceasefire, Gonzo informs me that this afternoon I may come to his house and meet his father, who is wise beyond measure, and partake of his mother's cooking, which is unequalled among mortal men, and even feed biscuits to the Lubitsch donkeys, whose coats are more glossy and whose eyes are more lambent than any other donkeys in all the wide world of donkey-kind. Ma Lubitsch, watching from a small distance, recognises by the instinctual knowledges of an expat Polish mother that her family has grown by one, and is not perturbed.

In her oven gloves and enveloping apron, Ma Lubitsch gazes through the French windows a bit longer, but Gonzo's father is now chasing a single errant bee around the hives with the smoke gun. Political dissent among the bee houses is not permitted. Ma Lubitsch makes a seesaw turn, stepping from one foot to the other once, twice, three times to bring herself back to the table to dish up, swearing the while in muttered Polish. The infant Gonzo, mighty with filial affront, dashes out to rebuke and retrieve the Old Man; I follow more slowly, five years of age and cautious with brief experience; appearances deceive. Honest faces lie and big boats sink where small ones ride out the gale. But ask me how I know, and I will not be able to tell you.

"Ma says lunch," Kid Gonzo says firmly. Old Man Lubitsch holds up a single gloved hand, a sinner lost to apiarism, requesting indulgence. The bee is on the flagstone in front of him, presumably coughing. It appears for a moment that Gonzo will stamp on it, rid himself of this impediment to family harmony, but his father is fast for all that his face looks like faded wool, or maybe it is just that Old Man Lubitsch understands the value of strategic positioning: he swoops, his body blocking Gonzo's line of attack, and, lifting the bee in gentle fingers, he pops it into hive number three.

"Lunch," Old Man Lubitsch agrees, and for a moment I believe he smiles at me.

We return to the house, but Gonzo's mother is not mollified. Things are strained. They have been strained since before I arrived, since Gonzo's older brother Marcus went to soldier, and neglected to duck on some forgotten corner of a foreign field that is forever Cricklewood Cove. Lunch is Ma Lubitsch's small white witchery, her article of faith—if she can provide Gonzo with hearty nutrition and a solid, dependable centre, he will be well-fitted to the world. He will conquer, he will survive, he will feel no need to seek adventure. He will not leave her. For Ma Lubitsch, lunch defies death. Old Man Lubitsch, however, knows that sometimes, for reasons which are obscure even to bees, the hive must disgorge its children and see them set upon the wind. And so he prepares for the moment when this son either finds a queen and starts a family, or flies and flies until he cannot continue and falls to the dirt to become once again a part of the mossy meadow carpet all around.

Ma Lubitsch doesn't speak to her husband during the meal. She doesn't speak from the first potato to the last flake of chocolate icing, and she doesn't speak over coffee, and she doesn't speak as Gonzo removes himself to the creek to fish. It seems that she will never speak to him again, but when I return unannounced for a forgotten tackle box, I glimpse her, the enormous body racked with sobs, cradled in the arms of her tiny mate. Old Man Lubitsch is singing to her in the language of the old country, and his shadowed, sharp little eyes lay omertà upon me, dark and deep; *these are secrets between men, boy, between the true men of the heart.* I know it. I understand.

It is this image which comes to mind later whenever Gonzo is about to embark on some act of unconsidered heroism: a bird-like man in white overalls lending his strength to a shattered mountain.

Gonzo fishes. He catches two tiddlers of uncertain species, and throws them back when they appear unhappy. I never tell him what I have seen, and when I turn around, five years have passed.

GONZO LUBITSCH at ten: a ringmaster and a daredevil, he leads with the chin, gets back on the horse, hates rules and is the object of a thousand crushes. Lydia Copsen holds hands with him in public, making Gonzo the most envied boy in the region, though none of us is able to source our bitter disappointment, and collectively we put it down to the fact that Lydia's mother is free with her sweet jar. Lydia is a tiny, imperious girl, proud owner of a selection of dresses with fruit patterns on them. She is also, it is clear to me from this distance, the daughter of Satan and the Wife of Bath. By turns haughty and adoring, Lydia dishes out featherlight kisses with an instinctive political acumen, and she deploys her ready access to confectionery to create a powerful and loyal clique of girls who yield secrets and obeisance to their mistress of the watermelon frock. At nine years of age, Lydia Copsen is somewhere between a tabloid editor and a Beverly Hills madam. Her admiration for Gonzo is matched only by her scorn for me, but Gonzo, loyal friend, will not ditch me, and thus I am gooseberry on their daily walks around the playground, and chaperone as he escorts her home. At Lydia's insistence, I walk ten paces behind them, but here she scores her own goal, because my only wish is to be as far from the loving couple as possible.

It is around this time that I lose, absolutely, my faith in a merciful deity, through the agency of the headmistress of our school. Her *real* name is the Evangelist, and it is thus that God and his angels and Yahweh and his angels and Allah and his angels and all the other gods of the world and their angels, demons, avatars, servitors, minions and mugwumps know her, and it is thus that she is inscribed in the hundred lists of the living and the dead that they all carry around like so many celestial bookkeepers. She masquerades, however, as Mrs. Assumption Soames, of the Warren, Cricklewood Cove, where she is headmistress of the eponymous Soames School for the Children of Townsfolk. She is small and slim at an age which has never been disclosed, but any child with access to a Bible (and all children at the Soames School have plentiful, even overwhelming, access to Bibles) would confidently date her from the tenth chapter of the Book of Genesis as coming somewhere between Aram and Lud. It is rumoured among the brave and foolish who speculate on such matters that she may be as old as fifty. Mr. Soames, whose father's father's father founded the school, died sometime back of a marsh fever, and the tacit consensus among the parents is that it was with a considerable sense of relief. Mr. Brabasen even suggested that Mr. Soames's sole intention in his frequent and prolonged fishing trips to the darkest and most pungent area of the Cricklewood Fens was to infect himself with said disease, a virulent virus which in 80 per cent of cases claimed either the victim's hearing or his life, either sad outcome being, in Mr. Brabasen's opinion, reason enough for Mr. Soames to seek it out.

If Assumption Soames's nickname sounds sophisticated for our infant wit, the reason is that it originates among the teachers, a flea-bitten and secular motley of brilliant minds culled from institutions too prissy to put up with their foibles. To the Evangelist, these weaknesses are burdens given by Providence along with their gifts to test their mettle. In accordance with the perfect wisdom of the divine plan, failure in these trials serves only to bring them into her healing and censorious arms so that they can teach her charges and atone and learn restraint. More than one of them has a nervous collapse during my time at school, and at least one of those surviving is heavily medicated purely as a result of Gonzo's inventive deployment of a thirty-foot spool of number seven line, a plastic skull and a ragged horse blanket. For all this, they're a solid lot, and despite the Evangelist they push the educational boat out further than they otherwise might. Mr. Clisp the gambler teaches us not only mathematics but also materialist ethics, setting logic puzzles on the board which appear to be value-neutral but which, when resolved, condemn the vituperative harridan in ringing tones. He also explains the rudiments of poker and the business of making book. Ms. Poynter (whose precise sin is whispered to involve negotiated services of a physical nature) includes in her biology classes a smattering of first aid and natural history, and also sexual education of increasing sophistication as the years pass, so that by the age of ten we can recite a list of erogenous zones and appreciate the difference between primary and secondary sexual characteristics in humans, and by the onset of puberty no one is in fear about the inevitable swellings and expulsions. Later, Ms. Poynter is temporarily relieved of duty by the Evangelist before the Board of Governors can object to her decision to teach a class on sexual technique to the girls and impart a stern lecture on mores and self-restraint to the boys (spiced with a brief but memorable digression on the theory and practice of cunnilingus). Mary Jane Poynter takes two weeks in Hawaii with Addison McTiegh, the PE teacher, and both of them return quieter and less twitchy and when the exam results come in with a near-perfect pass rate, the Evangelist elects not to fire her on the condition that no more parents are given cause to complain. The Board, who would for the most part have liked to see Ms. Poynter burned at some form of wooden upright, are too busy battling the Evangelist's blazing determination to ban on religious grounds several of the texts students are required to study that year. *Gulliver's Travels* survives the scissors, as does *A Christmas Carol*, but *Modern Short Stories in English* is consigned for ever to the forbidden zone. Sadly, it is so dull that not even this recommendation can make any of us read it more than once.

My loss of faith is sudden, and it's not so much a conversion as a reappraisal. Children are still modelling the world, still understanding how it works; their convictions are malleable, like their bones. Thus, I experience no sudden horrible wrench as my belief is uprooted, but rather a feeling like the right pair of glasses being put in front of my face after some time wearing someone else's. The Evangelist brings me to her study to tell me off for one of Gonzo's outrages, and I sit waiting for a higher power to intervene and tell her that it isn't my fault. I look upward, naturally, to the place above my hairline where adults come from, the place where, broadly speaking, heads can be found and persons in authority exert their will in the name of justice. There is no one there. It is unclear in my mind whether I am looking for God in person or a more earthly parent as his instrument, but neither appears. The Evangelist adds a charge of "rolling your eyes at me" to the sheet, and I spend a week in detention after school. Gonzo is mysteriously unwell for the period, with a vile sore throat which is probably infectious but doesn't stifle his ability to loaf, and which Lydia Copsen also develops. They convalesce a great deal together, feet touching under the blanket as they sit at opposite ends of the sofa and choke abominably.

Spring becomes summer, summer becomes autumn, and Gonzo and his beloved part company over her inability to comprehend the importance of muddy walks and frantic leaf-kicking. She takes the opportunity to inform him that she went with him only to gain access to his parents' donkeys, to which Gonzo responds that the donkeys loathe her, despise her silly hair and stupid upturned nose, and they have asked him, by means of sign language, to convey to her their deepest and most unalterable disdain for her opinions in all matters of consequence. Thus avenged, the wretched girl departing in a frozen fury, Gonzo retires to the riverbank and we fish in silence, and this time Gonzo catches a decent-sized trout with his new rod, although it is left to me to kill the creature and present it to Ma Lubitsch, who dutifully guts and cooks it for dinner. Though fortunately it is served alongside a more enjoyable dish of meatloaf.

Gonzo is not the only person with relationship issues. At Old Man Lubitsch's insistence, we sit in Ma Lubitsch's parlour one night in lonesome October, watching the world have something of a tizzy. Ma Lubitsch's television is very much a curiosity—a wood-panelled thing with chunky buttons which whines and gutters alarmingly and occasionally overheats and has to have a rest. But on the screen, all the same, are more people than I have ever seen in one place, and half of them appear to be very pleased about something and the other half extremely cross, and neither side has a great deal of patience about it. Old Man Lubitsch explains that this is normal in what is called *politics,* which is essentially the business of countries and big groups of people trying to make everyone see things their way. Since no one ever does, very little is achieved and practitioners are voted out and others voted in who reverse the process, so government (as Old Man Lubitsch explains it) is not so much a journey as a series of emergency stops and arguments over which way up to hold the map.

What has happened today is therefore something of a shocker. An actual decision has been taken, in the face of all the odds, and it is one which absolutely no one saw coming. It is also, to use a technical term deployed by a chortling analyst, something of a corker. The island of Cuba, which is a long way away, has thrown off its communist rulers (who were in fact *not communists* but *totalitarians*—and here Old Man Lubitsch looks as if he may spit, but Ma Lubitsch gives him a totalitarian look of her own and he subsides) and has chosen a somewhat improbable route to enter the modern world. The people of Cuba have petitioned the United Kingdom of Great Britain and Northern Ireland (which is not really a *kingdom*—that would be another form of *totalitarianism*) for admittance, and been accepted. The resulting entity is the United Island Kingdoms of Britain, Northern Ireland & Cuba Libré, and is already being referred to by the wits as Cubritannia.

As an introduction to *politics,* this is pretty much in at the deep end, but Old Man Lubitsch is well-informed and patient, and by the end of the night I understand that I have seen a historic thing and that the people of Cuba have opted to join a nation of shopkeepers because they want *infrastructure* (roads and sewers), *freedom* (not being beaten up for pulling faces at politicians) and a decent injection of cash and junk food (this is called *standard of living*). The people of Britain have accepted them because they relish the notion of an influx of well-trained, educated people of pleasing physical appearance who *have rhythm,* and because their national psyche needs somewhere to replace another island called Hong Kong which they apparently lost somehow and are still sulking about. Mostly, however, it seems they have accepted this arrangement because it has *put the wind up* the rest of the world, and that pleases them greatly. The people who seem most upset are elements of the *global business community* based in distant places like Johannesburg and New York and Toronto and Paris, who basically assumed that Cuba belonged to them, and was on lease to the *communist totalitarians* all this time.

This intelligence means very little to me, but Old Man Lubitsch insists that the time will come when I am glad to have seen it, and proud to remember it. And while Gonzo finds this unlikely, and sees in his mother's eyes a deep patience with her husband's folly, I believe it. The silent bristling heat of conviction is in Gonzo's father, and it passes in some small measure to me. I carefully store Cubritannia away in my mind's attic, and throw a blanket over it for good measure, and the next day is a Wednesday and our first lesson is history and the Evangelist puts her head around the door to tell Mr. Cremmel specifically not to talk about it, and she sits in to make sure. Mr. Cremmel dutifully teaches us about the Industrial Revolution instead, but he makes some kind of innocent error when it comes to homework, and the page references he gives us are for Cuba after all.

SNOW comes to Cricklewood Cove that winter. It is early December, and the temperature rises from below zero to a comfy one or two. There is a strange, crisp smell of pine and woodsmoke and something clear and different. A wide, low cloud settles over the cove and over the Lubitsch house and (thanks be to the God I no longer believe in) over the school. The cloud does not loom, nor does it threaten. It is warmer and deeper than a rain cloud and has a definitely benign feeling, and when it is finally ready it unburdens itself of a vast quantity of white flakes, which fall straight down. They are not the thick wet flakes of spring snow, which are sort of misplaced, like confused geese. They fall in an endless flow, small and dry and floating evenly and covering everything, and when they go down the back of your neck and chill your spine, they are still solid when they reach the waistband of your trousers. This is real, bona fide snow, come down from the high mountains and stabling the sheep and visiting the saloons, and raising a ruckus over a girl in little frilly trousers (the blizzards strand me inside and I discover the Western, and John Wayne is my hero for evermore, although a hero of admiration rather than emulation because he always ends up dead—Gonzo plays at being the Duke and lies dramatically and probably auto-erotically splayed upon the hall carpet, gasping out his last).

When the clouds clear, it does not get warmer. It gets much, much colder—cold to cause glaciation and kill mammoths and drive migrations in the Neanderthal men whose existence the Evangelist denies, thus inspiring a brief but frantic exploration of the library for malprinted or heretical Bibles and fierce debate about the nature of Esau. Children, bored and opinionated, are scholars of the most dogmatic stripe.

The alcohol thermometer in Gonzo's garden cracks, and Old Man Lubitsch has to arrange a curious external heating system to preserve his bees, which he does using piles of compost which are in the grip of an *exothermic reaction* (although Gonzo's father calls it an *eczozermic ree-ekchon*), which means that the process of decomposition is generating heat. Old Man Lubitsch carefully creates piles of warm rotting garden goo around his bee houses, and the smell is curiously pleasant and grassy rather than rotting and deliquescent, but Ma Lubitsch does not approve and mutters darkly about dratted bugs and how much honey can one eat in a lifetime anyway? But Old Man Lubitsch takes this in good part and hugs her—he actually gets his arms around her and lifts her off her feet—and she swats at him and demands to be put down before he does himself a harm. The Lubitsch house retains its unorthodox external heating arrangements (although Ma Lubitsch extracts a promise that they will be gone when the spring comes, so as to avoid any possibility of explosions). On the following Sunday, and for the first time ever, Megg Lake freezes over.

Megg Lake is an oxbow, a hoop of water named for the Greek letter Ω, one of the few Greek letters of which the Evangelist approves, the others being in some mystical way *gateways to licentiousness.* It is constantly refilled by an underground river which flows down from the Mendicant Hills, and when there is a great deal of rain, the lake bubbles over the rocks at the western end and finds its own floodways to the sea. At any time, Megg Lake is a choppy and turbulent body, ripples sprinting out from the centre where the water boils up, and reflecting off the craggy shores to make (according to our geography textbooks) a pattern of *constructive interference* where the splashes collide and produce waves, and *destructive interference* where their interaction yields little patches of calm. But now it is frozen, a broad grey-blue crescent of bowed ice, thick and growling.

Ma Lubitsch parks the car. It is a 4 × 4, and it is completely forbidden to Old Man Lubitsch, who (on the occasions when life's exigencies place him, against his spouse's better judgement, behind the wheel) drives it like a racing car, in a pair of nasty shades, and draws admiring glances from women younger than his suit. Ma Lubitsch brings the beast to a halt by the lake, and Gonzo scrambles over me or possibly through me in his urgency, and then we are all unloading the car. Tackle box, check. Rugs, check. Charcoal burner, check. Ice saw, check. This family—extended family—is going Eskimo fishing, something Old Man

Lubitsch and Ma Lubitsch used to do back when she was a sylph-like thing with no hips and he was a bull of a man, short and powerful as a tropical storm, and my, how she adored him. And from the immodest twinkle in her eyes, at least as much of them as I can see through folds of skin and squint and woollen comforter, she still does, and shall do evermore. It is only the ghost of one soldier that stands between them, and even this is not a separation, but a strange sad bridge and a deep mutual knowing like nothing else. Marcus Maximus Lubitsch, tennis player and able cook, laid to rest now, and visited sporadically in a well-kept corner of the churchyard at the edge of town. At this moment, Marcus is present. Even Gonzo, thigh-deep in snow, and flailing gleefully at the powder, quiets his voice and shares the solemn smile which passes between his parents.

Ma Lubitsch lights the burner, but she uses somewhat too much fluid and the thing fairly erupts, singeing her muffler. She gives a great shout of Polish obscenity and then looks guiltily around, but there are no linguists within thirty miles, and she giggles (more *constructive* and *destructive interference,* no doubt, in the pattern of her wobbling fat, but this is concealed), and Old Man Lubitsch goes to get the ice saw.

Megg Lake's ice is not lightly to be cut. It is oddly clear and hard, more like glacial ice (which is pressurised and squeezed over thousands of years) than lake ice (which is fraught with cracks and rivulets). Gonzo's father assails the ice with the saw—initially near the shoreline, but latterly further out when it becomes apparent that there's no earthly danger of it breaking—but to little effect. Old Man Lubitsch hacks away, but this is serious frozen stuff, ice like Arctic ice, with a bad attitude and a stubborn mien. It is ice, in fact, a lot like Old Man Lubitsch himself, who was hounded from his home town for being cheeky to the communists, and then refused return when he was cheeky to the new fellas in much the same way. Perpetual exile, letter-writing malcontent, "Furious and disappointed of Cricklewood Cove," Gonzo's father will not concede. He will get through this ice if he must declare an eternal feud upon it. And so it is that Gonzo comes to his aid with a plan.

In the normal run of things, I am Gonzo's plan-confidant. It is to me he brings his worst ideas, and it is my job to squash them and propose, as an alternative to connecting an electric torch directly to the mains power so as to make a lightsabre, some activity less mortally perilous. Today, however, Gonzo's plans receive an audience less jaded and, perhaps, less sensible. Parents dote. Fathers, in particular, indulge their sons in matters of manly comportment and tasks which approach the sacred duties of the heteropatriarch, such as shooting enemies, blowing things up and hauling mighty armfuls of dead animal across the white wastes to feed the tribe. This situation—the possible defeat of the clan hunters by an inanimate icecap—falls broadly into these categories, and thus it is that when Gonzo proposes a simple solution, swift and sure, Old Man Lubitsch gets a look in his eye. It is a look which says that, when he was Gonzo's age, he had some idea of similar magnificence, and this jewel was crushed beneath a weighty grown-up heel. But here he, Gonzo's father, is in a position to carry through the deed, and in one stroke to avenge himself and demonstrate a more enlightened understanding of his son's unbridled genius than was shown to him. Grizzled and rugged, red flannel shirt and preposterous fur hat upon his head, Old Man Lubitsch looks down benignly on his child.

"Say it again!" says Gonzo's father proudly.

"We should use the lighter fluid," says the infant anarchist, "and *burn* a hole in the ice!"

Ma Lubitsch sighs a little sigh, but trapped within the matriarch it seems there is still a breathless groupie falling for her husband's wild eyes and floating hair (such as remains) because there's a sparkle about her which says loudly she does *not* approve, does *not* think this is wise, will *not* be held accountable, but is absolutely dying to see it happen and will reward most richly whatever prince of men can carry off this splendid boast.

This tacit complicity established, my formless worries are brushed aside, and an order of service is drawn up as follows:

1) a spot will be appointed, no less than thirty metres out, where this conflagration may safely be begun, and where fishing may latterly occur;
2) Old Man Lubitsch, and he alone, will walk out to the spot thus designated and deploy the matériel, in quantity. He shall do this by:
    i. hollowing out a small basin
    ii. pouring thereinto a large quantity of flammable stuff, leavened with such kindling and fuel as may be garnered from the rear of the car and the ground nearby
    iii. making, by means of more stuff, a fuse or trail back to the lakeside, where
3) we shall await him and when he is safe,
4) jointly ignite the furnace.

This all duly done, a strange and beautiful thing happens, which is absolutely not what we had in mind.

The thing begins as advertised, with a bright flame licking smartly across the ice to Old Man Lubitsch's reservoir. That reservoir, lighter fuel with an admixture of dry wood and charcoal, and a couple of rags from the back of the 4 × 4, catches and burns well, a five-foot-high column with its feet in the ice. A certain amount of smoke goes up, which may also be steam. The whole thing seems to be doing very little in the way of melting the ice, but perhaps it's early days. And indeed, it *is* early days; the next stage is somewhat more dramatic than we had envisaged. There is a noise as of incoming mortars or a train crash or the steeple of the church falling into the vestry. It is a vast, tectonic, tearing noise which seems to come from everywhere. In truth, it is probably none of these things, but it is very loud, and I am a small boy.

The ice has split, as it does when you put an ice cube in your drink on a hot day. The fissure is narrow, but it is lengthening at speed, and other cracks are forming, and something vast is shrugging underneath. Ma Lubitsch, with a mother's sense of threat and consequence, perceives the shape of things to come. As dinosaurs battle beneath the icecap, she throws her beloved, idiot family into the car and takes off at a clip Old Man Lubitsch himself finds somewhat startling. Gonzo and I stare back at Megg Lake, fascinated, through the rear window. Thus we alone in all the world are positioned to see what happens when the runoff of an entire range of hills is pent up for several days beneath a plug of ice and air, and then released by a rebellious sexagenarian with a yen to relive his glory days in front of his family.

The icecap gives a final wriggle, and goes *"shhOOOMF!"* and a frothing eruption boils up and out. The plume of water reaches higher than the high trees by the lakeside, and lumps of ice like Sunday roasts fall ahead of us on the road. The full weight of water from the Mendicant Hills, thwarted these many days in its passage to the sea and gathered underground in a column of pressure two hundred feet high, is at last released.

A duck, knocked unconscious by a bit of ballistic slush, tumbles to the ground in a field to our right. And then, extremely locally, it rains. It rains sleet and snow and ice, and a small number of unhappy frogs.

Old Man Lubitsch looks back down the road at the devastation, and he starts to laugh. It is not a hysterical laugh, but a genuine, delighted, belly laugh at the view, the madness, the gorgeousness of the cock-up. Ma Lubitsch calls him a string of names, but her face is flushed and she, too, is laughing, and it seems likely that if ever Gonzo is to get a younger brother, it will be tonight.

The Cove Cold Snap ends a few days later, as if by sympathetic magic we have broken the grip of winter on the land. The snow melts overnight, and there are little green things eagerly yammering for attention shortly after. The Lubitsch donkeys, cause of great and now-forgotten turmoil, are led reluctantly from their winter accommodations and told to start thinking of themselves as outdoor beasts again. Their mournful and utterly mendacious cries of distress are responsible for some sleepless nights in the Lubitsch house, but Ma Lubitsch keeps to her iron rule and the donkeys get the message, and are content.

THUS GONZO, incendiarist and leader of men. And Gonzo's inescapable hanger-on—the kid no one notices? He also grows up. Not even last-picked for football teams and athletic tryouts, the perpetually benched; he is Gonzo's shadow and occasional conscience when the Plan—be it raiding the kitchen for food or escaping this borstal to live with Gypsies in Mongolia (described by the Evangelist as "a festerance of Sin and Capitulation," on what evidence I cannot guess)—calls for excesses in excess of what the authorities will accept as demonstrating that boys will be boys. Outwitting the librarian and purloining banned books is almost expected; releasing the inmates of the ant farm along a trail of purloined sugar leading to the staff showers is ingenious enough to merit wry applause from the science master along with a string of punishment duties; making and testing explosives with cheap domestic ingredients I veto, not out of any dislike for the splendidness of the concept, but from a natural awareness that there are borders everywhere, and sending the football pavilion—even empty—four hundred feet into the air using homebrew nitroglycerine is on the far side of both what would be tolerated and our own alchemical competence. I remember, where Gonzo does not, the safety film featuring scarred and rueful victims of their own hubris urging us against such ventures. We settle instead on a concoction intended to induce percussive internal combustion in the rumina of cows, but the test subjects are unaffected by the stuff, save for a minor increase in distraught mooing.

At fourteen, Gonzo discovers martial arts movies: the oeuvre of Messrs. B. Lee and J. Chan, along with assorted other players of greater and lesser talent. The martial arts film is a curiously sentimental thing, fraught with high promises and melodrama. Those of the Hong Kong variety are frequently filled with untranslatable Chinese puns delivered in a bout of sing-song badinage. The plots are moral, Shakespearean, and have a tendency to charge off in some unexpected direction for twenty minutes before returning to the main drama as if nothing has happened.

Inspired by these, Gonzo commences to study karate. He is the ideal candidate: fearless, physical and delighted by the changes wrought in his body by multiple press-ups, his only disadvantage that he comes late to the party. Had Gonzo begun his training younger, he might one day be a true master. As it is, he must content himself with being merely an excellent student. For the weedy sidekick (whose *yokogeri kekomi* is indeed the weediest in the school's catchment area), karate is another arena in which life's beatings are legitimately delivered, but he struggles on. He has—I have—despite a long-nurtured understanding that he cannot equal his friend's achievements—never learned to quit, one virtue he possesses which is utterly alien to Gonzo, whose effortless rampage through life has never required him to consider it.

And then one day the universe decides that I am fledged, and accordingly demands of me my first solo flight; Mary Sensei leads me from the tatami to examine my now-familiar bloody nose. It has never broken, but—unlike my hands, which remain fragile despite hours of training at the bag—it must by now have developed a mighty sheath of calcium. I wonder if I can shatter boards with it. Mary Sensei replies that this is unlikely, and she would prefer that I delay the experiment indefinitely. Five foot three and fifty-four kilos, Mary Sensei tells me I'm not cut out for karate. But my dedication is sufficiently impressive that she can suggest an alternative: another school.

I object that Gonzo won't want to change schools.

"No," Mary Sensei explains. "Not Gonzo. Gonzo will do fine here. Just you. Without Gonzo."

This is a new concept, but not—oddly—an unpleasant one.

"Another karate school?"

"No. Another style. Maybe a soft form."

"What's a soft form?"

She tells me.

The upshot is a tour of the local schools of soft-form pugilism, and the first thing which becomes apparent is that the term "soft" is misleading because it is relative, the comparison being with men and women so desperate to turn themselves into machines of empty-handed demolition that they have spent hours and days and months striking wooden boards and sandpapered target dummies to condition their fists, and who consider an hour ill-spent if they have not driven one foot through a pile of bricks. It is not a question of whether the style is *violent,* but of whether that violence is direct and forceful or subtle and convoluted. To the eye of a novice, soft forms appear delicate, baroque and artistic, while the hard forms are brutish and merciless. The truth is that the soft forms are more considered in their application of pain and damage to the body. Which is more unpleasant to the object of their attentions is an open question—and which variety attracts more dangerous lunatics in the suburban setting is also unclear. I rapidly reject the smiling, flinty *aikidoka,* whose expressionless perfection informs the opponent that his life or death is irrelevant, and whose motions include a sword-cut twist at the end to provide the coup de grâce. Their modern, street-fighting cousins of European and Brazilian ju-jitsu are also unsatisfactory; the former are cheery, laddish men tending to be under five foot six and almost the same across the shoulder, the latter are chuckling lunatics with a fondness for submission holds and women in impractical swimwear. Puritanical and sovereign, I stalk from their classroom without a second look—but this leaves me with a problem. Judo is as much sport as self-defence. T'ai chi is fluid and elegant but requires an entire lifetime to be usable in combat. More esoteric—and, to be honest, no softer than karate—escrima and silat are not taught anywhere within an hour of Cricklewood Cove. I look in desperation at Mary Sensei, and perhaps, this once, my need is enough.

"Yes," Mary Sensei says, "there's one more thing we can try."

Which is how, for the first time *without* Gonzo Lubitsch, I come to be standing on the doorstep of Wu Shenyang, seeking admittance to the House of the Voiceless Dragon.

"Wu like *woo,*" Mary Sensei said two minutes ago, strangely breathless in her aged VW Rabbit as we sat waiting for the precise appointed hour, "and then Shen and Yang as if they were separate, but they're not. And you don't call him Wu Shenyang, anyway, you call him Mister Wu. Or Master Wu. Or . . ." But she could not think of anything else I might call him and anyway it's time. The door opens. An excited voice says "Come, come!" and I watch my feet take me across the threshold.

Mister (Master) Wu is the first teacher of whatever sort to ask me to his home, and he is the first martial arts instructor who has wanted to know me off the mat before seeing me perform on it. According to Mary Sensei, if he does not find what he is looking for in my heart, there will be no point in testing the rest of me. I inspect my heart, and it seems an impoverished organ for such a big task. It is the right sort of size and located not as moviegoers believe in the high left side of the chest (that is in fact a lung) but just off centre and further down. It beats approximately seventy times a minute and pumps vital nutrients and oxygen carried by haemoglobin around my body in the approved fashion, but it conceals as far as I can tell no mysteries, and is devoid of secret heritage or supernatural skills. Having thus ascertained by introspection that I lack whatever it is this gentleman is seeking, I feel able to observe his living room, which is itself remarkable. It is, as well as being a place to sit and read and eat cake, a treasure house of oddments and curiosities—a gold statue of a war-like pig in one corner, a pair of Foo

Dogs on the mantle, standing lamps from various periods of design, weapons and china ducks on all the walls. Wu Shenyang is still assessing me—I can feel the stress of his regard—and so I begin to catalogue the contents of this place with an eye to returning perhaps as a cleaner or a general dogsbody.

Item: two armchairs, split in various places and of considerable antiquity, but also to all appearances monstrously comfortable. These are positioned loosely on either side of an open fire at one end of the room, along with a coffee table whose clever construction allows books to be stashed willy-nilly beneath the tabletop.

Item: with its back to us, a leather sofa of similarly advanced age, showing signs (to wit, a pillow and a blanket) of having recently been used as a camp bed. Indeed, there appears to be a person camping on it still, because a pair of white-socked feet, slender and almost certainly feminine (by the pattern of the weave) and perhaps my own age or a little younger, protrude from the western side.

Item: a grandfather clock, running smoothly if somewhat previous, in dark and gold-leafed wood with a fine, painted face. The panel door is open and the pendulum is visible as it makes its long, slow strokes from left to right and back again, producing a steady and undeniable *tock tick* noise in defiance of convention. This *tock tick* also reassures me that the person on the sofa is alive and not dead, because her northernmost foot *tock ticks* along with it from time to time, and then returns to a state of rest.

Item: one desk and chair, both liberally covered in cake crumbs and paper. The desk is functional rather than impressive, and surmounting the piles and stacks of letters and drawings is a single sheet of blank paper and a pencil. Mister (Master) Wu does not use a pen for casual work, because where—or maybe *when*—he comes from, ink is expensive. Thus, the softest of soft leads, because Mister (Master) Wu is writing in Chinese.

Item: an ancient gramophone, literally; not a stereo or a turntable, not a CD player, but a scratched and whistling construction with a chrome arm and a huge flower-shaped horn and a thick, blunt needle making music from brittle black discs which turn at 78 rpm. The entire trick is accomplished mechanically, without electricity or transistors or silicon.

To me, a child of the digital age, this is a great white magic, so awe-inspiring that I forget for a moment to be nervous of Wu Shenyang. It is in any case hard to remember that he is a person of dread solemnity and pomp, because he seems to approach everything as a kind of game. He is even now leaping over to the gramophone to display it in full glory: winding it, picking out an old record by the Fisk University Jubilee Singers and grinning widely as he waits for my reaction to his fabulous trick. I am too lost in the crackling perfection to smile, until the record comes to an end and his deft fingers lift the needle away. He drags out from beneath the machine a bag of yet more impossible records and presses them upon me. I leaf through them with aching concern that I will shatter one, and finally play the adagio from Mozart's Clarinet Concerto in A, listening until the very end. Mister (Master) Wu's gaze lights on my fingers as I lift the needle just as he did, because this thing is too perfect, too carefully preserved and lovingly made, to allow it to be injured by carelessness. And then finally I am looking at the man before me.

Wu Shenyang is tall and thin. He does not look like Buddha, he looks like a ladder in a dressing gown. Time has polished him, abraded him and passed on, leaving him nearly eighty and stronger than a brace of college athletes, though he favours his right leg just a little. His wide, umber-coloured face is not impassive like that of Takagi Sensei, who once visited Mary's dojo and grunted meaningfully as I launched weak and indicated attacks at a girl from Hosely; despite the bristling brows in shock-silver above his eyes, he is not stern. Wu Shenyang laughs loudly—alarmingly—at inappropriate moments, and seems to take joy in inconsequential things, like the colour of the window putty and the slipperiness of the carpet in front of his desk. The latter he demonstrates to me by standing square in the slick patch and gyrating wildly, waggling his whole body, sliding his slippers on the spot as he shifts his weight rapidly from one to the other and twisting his hips. When he has finished, nothing will do but that I take a turn. I am immediately concerned that he will think I am mocking his game leg, but again I copy his method exactly and he registers his approval by laughing and shouting "Elvis Presley! Graceland!" When he tries to say "rock and roll" he gets into a terrible tangle because his English is, even after many years speaking it, gently accented with his mother tongue—but this also doesn't worry him in the slightest, and so it doesn't worry me either. We pass on to further matters of consequence: he likes my trousers, but he thinks my watch is too young for me, because it features a smiling cat whose whiskers indicate the hour and minute. He also thinks I need a new barber, and though loyalty prompts me to defend Ma Lubitsch's kitchen table cut, I do so in the knowledge that he is right. Wu Shenyang apologises—to me and to Ma Lubitsch. There is a snort from behind the sofa, but I am immune. An elder stranger, without irony, treats me as a being of equal worth—if of lesser experience and discernment in the matter of timepieces. In the course of the watch discussion we compare forearms, and it is established that mine is actually as thin as his, which for some reason is hugely pleasing to him. Only when I explain why I am here—though of course he must know—does he recover his composure. He peers at me gravely and ponders, and I prepare myself for the inevitable, the impossible testing and the sorrowful rejection. He turns to the wall and selects from amid the ducks a short fat sword with a single edge and a sharp point. Holding it carefully in one hand, he removes the sheath and turns to me.

"Tool of war. Very respectable. Man's work." He grimaces. "Or you could say, a butcher's knife! It is very sharp," says Wu Shenyang, "and very old. Take it and tell me what you feel." He steps towards me, extending the hilt, and somehow his bad leg slips as he moves across the slick patch of carpet. The Tool of

War is launched into the air, slowly rotating around the point where his hand released it, until (I am relieved to notice, though I have not yet had time to move) it points away from me. Wu Shenyang's body hurtles forward, almost a dive, and I realise that the hilt of the weapon, striking my chest, will propel the blade into him. It is therefore incumbent upon me to move, and I do. The sword's top edge is blunt, so I stroke it with my right palm, pushing the point outside our circle, and step forward and bend both knees, back straight, to support the old man as he tumbles.

He does not tumble. His bad leg stretches out and takes the weight easily, and the blade, recaptured without fuss, *swooshes* through the air in a fluid, whirring spiral and returns to the sheath. Instead of his weight falling across my arms and being absorbed—somewhat—by my legs, the barest of contacts bespeaks his passing, and he emerges from the swirl standing by the door. I look down. My feet are spread in what is called a horseriding stance, my arms are extended above them, palms up and bent at the elbow.

"It is called Embrace Tiger, Return to Mountain," *Master* Wu says after a moment. "Practice." But it is only when the girl emerges from behind the sofa and with enormous gravity shakes my hand that I realise I have been accepted as a student, and that somewhere, somehow, it all went right.

"Elisabeth is my secretary," Master Wu says, without a hint of laughter. "She is quite stern, but as long as you are well behaved, you will get along fine."

And so it proves. Elisabeth is a small blonde person who rarely speaks, but she orders the arrangements of the House of the Voiceless Dragon with the absolute certainty which is the preserve of ladies of that age, and she studies the forms with the other students and lives on the couch because her mother is too busy to take care of her. Master Wu is utterly obedient to her tyranny and she, in turn, takes care to exercise her power with great subtlety and discretion and even—amazingly—mercy. And sometimes, when Master Wu is lonely or homesick or simply tired, she makes spiced apple cake or Char Siu Bao, and we all eat them together, which helps. Together, because somehow or other I have been adopted again, and now I must split my time between Gonzo and Master Wu.

Voiceless Dragon is taught every morning and evening at seven, and at weekends all day, and students come when they can and stay for at least an hour. During the week, Master Wu composes calligraphy and reads a great many books, so that he knows a great many higgledy-piggledy things about a great many subjects, and some of these things are useless and some are not, but almost all of them find their way into the lessons. Thus along with the Elvis Walk, we have Lorenz Palace Step (mathematical *gong fu*) and Vetruvian Fist (da Vinci *gong fu*), and—until Elisabeth intervenes—Fallopian Tube Arm (the name culled from a diagram in my biology textbook, chosen for the shape of the elbow in the final posture, but rather alarming). I study whenever I can, and for some reason however much time I waste when I should be doing homework, my school grades go up rather than down through my association with Master Wu. I worry at first that Gonzo will be resentful of my absences, but he is busy with other matters, and certain of his activities require personal space.

In March, Master Wu has an unwelcome visitor, a man called Lasserly who travels all the way from Newport. Lasserly is a forceful person with a big, florid head. His arms are very thick, and he smells of old canvas. He wants to learn the Secrets. Every student of any martial form knows about the Secrets. They are rumoured and scorned across the world. Students are encouraged by some teachers to believe that knowledge of the Secrets will allow a practitioner to defeat age and death, hold his breath for hours on end, and project his spirit out of his body to smite his opponents like a Flash Gordon ray gun. Other masters, more down-to-earth or more honest, aver that the Secrets are symbolic, representing way stations on the journey of the self, or particularly important stylistic elements for the advanced student. Master Wu tells Lasserly that there are no Secrets.

"Come on," Lasserly says. "Of course there are."

No, Master Wu says gently, really, there aren't.

"You know things," Lasserly says.

That is undoubtedly true. And almost certainly, Master Wu allows, he knows things—even *gong fu* things—which Lasserly does not. But he doesn't feel inclined to talk about these things with Lasserly, because Lasserly is somewhat abrasive and even rude, and Master Wu has nicer people to spend time with.

"Well, okay then. Let's fight instead."

This is preposterous, on the face of it. Lasserly outweighs Master Wu by a hundred pounds, and his hands are thick with calluses from long practice.

No, Master Wu says after a minute or so of silence. No point.

Lasserly walks out. On his way, he puts his immense finger on my chest. I feel the solidity of him, his body lined up behind the touch. He could channel his whole weight through that finger, probably punch it right through me. I shouldn't have let him get that close.

"You're wasting your time," Lasserly snarls. "This guy doesn't know any Secrets." And he walks out, slamming the door so that the china ducks wobble against the plaster.

We practise in silence. Master Wu looks very sad.

On the night of this dark day, when Master Wu has finished wrapping himself around his third slice of apple cake, and is contemplating the advisability of wrapping himself around a fourth, Elisabeth is moved to ask him about Lasserly. The question starts as a curiosity, but by the time she has finished asking it her voice has risen because she cannot hold in her fury any longer, or her shame.

"Why didn't you *fight* him?" And then she hears her own question and is abashed.

Master Wu shrugs. "Mr. Lasserly wanted to know if I knew Secrets," he says. "He wanted to fight me so that he could find out. And now he thinks he knows the answer. He knows that I was so absolutely sure of which way it would go that I didn't want to fight him."

"But he thinks he would have won!" And this, in the end, is the heart of the matter, because in Lasserly's certainty our own is eroded.

"Oh, goodness me," says Master Wu, with vast sincerity, "I didn't mean for him to have that impression at all!" He opens his eyes very wide, as if realising for the first time how it must have looked. "Oh dear! I am so *clumsy*! Do you think I should call him and tell him that I would have beaten him because he has stiff legs, moves like a cow and tenses his shoulders? But," says Master Wu happily, "he didn't leave a number. Well, never mind." And he laughs. "There are no Secrets," he says, "but there are lots of things I don't feel like telling someone like Mr. Lasserly. That's not how you keep Secrets at all—not," Master Wu says, with great delight, "that there are any."

"Are there? Secrets?"

"Secrets?" Master Wu says, as if he's never heard of any such thing. Elisabeth looks at him sternly.

"Yes," she says. "Inside-the-door. Inner Teachings."

"Oh," says Master Wu, "those Secrets." And he smiles.

"Those Secrets," Elisabeth repeats a moment later, when Wu Shenyang's eyes once again roam in the direction of the apple cake, and she realises that the expression of deep division on his face relates to it, and not to the arcana of the chi.

"You mean like the Internal Alchemies? The Iron Skin Meditation and the Ghost Palm Strike?"

The Iron Skin makes a warrior immune to physical weapons; the Ghost Palm passes through solid matter—it cannot be avoided or deflected. I have seen them in movies. I did not know that girls watched those sorts of movies.

"Yes," says Elisabeth.

"Well, no," says Master Wu, "there aren't really any of those."

This is what he tells everyone who asks, and everyone asks sooner or later. Master Wu has few students, but some of them have students of their own, and one or two of those also have students, spread out across the globe in a great tree of tuition and discovery and experimentation and instruction, but the root is here in Cricklewood Cove, and here it is that every student of whatever level eventually comes to meet Master Wu. Each generation of student is supposed to acknowledge a kind of family relationship with the ones around—we have Voiceless Dragon elder uncles and aunts from Eastbourne to Westhaven, and countless brothers and sisters and nieces and nephews. Some are brash and some are deferential and almost all of them, when they come here, are looking for a saint or a warrior, or a demigod wrapped in mysteries, and Master Wu takes care to relieve them of that illusion in the most painless way.

"No magic," he tells them stoutly. "No Secrets! No 'inside the door.' The truth is not hidden. It is simple. Just very difficult—but I am stubborn!" The laugh, too big for him, and then a little grin, just for you: "And I am lucky! I started early," by which he means that his father whispered the training songs over his crib in Yenan.

"No," Master Wu says now, "there are no Secrets. None at all. Would you like me to teach you one?"

"One what?"

"A Secret."

"You said there weren't any."

"I will make one up for you. Then the next time someone asks, we can tell them we do know Secrets after all. Although it might make Mr. Lasserly very cross if he ever found out." This fearful drawback clearly does not alarm Master Wu at all. He ponders. "Okay," says Master Wu, after a moment, "a story and a Secret. Are you ready?"

We nod.

"Once upon a time," Master Wu says, "in the days when your mothers' mothers were young and attractive and before the wireless carried the voice of England to the corners of the world, there was a boy who could hear the sea from a thousand miles away. He could stand in the dry mountains and hear the sound of breakers on the beach. He could sit with his eyes on the mountains and listen to the storms crashing against high cliffs he had never seen. The salt water was in his veins, and in his heart.

"It made him very bad at many things. He was a bad farmer, a bad hunter, a bad cobbler and a very bad musician, because the noise distracted him and made him play the notes at the wrong time, and in the wrong place—and worse, when he played false, everyone else got drawn into the great ebb and flow of the sea and even the cheeriest music slowed down and sounded like a funeral song: deep, long breaths trailing away into nothing and then rising up again like tears.

"You might think he'd be unpopular, but he was a good-natured boy and his people were good-natured too, and as long as he worked hard and didn't break things very often, they were happy with him. He moved in a graceful, liquid way, stepping from one foot to the other and back, in and out, back and forth, but of course not every shape in the world lends itself to someone who walks like a rocking horse, so even though his touch was light and his grip was strong, he snapped the ends of things or jostled people from time to time. It balanced out, maybe. In the morning, he worked with his father making things out of leather—his father had set aside a place in the workshop where he could sway without knocking anything over—and in the afternoon he worked with his uncle making bread, which doesn't care if you roll it and twist it like seaweed on the beach. In the evening he sat and he closed his eyes until he could feel the spray washing over him and he breathed in time to the waves hitting the rocky cliffs he had never seen. And always, always, at dawn, he and his father and his uncle and all their family—even the women, which was most unusual—practised their *gong fu* together, because they knew they would have to fight one day, somehow. And of all of them, the young man trained the hardest and studied most deeply, because his patience was like the sea which whispered in his head.

"One day, a great master of *gong fu* came to the town. He was a fat man, and a mercenary. A soldier for hire, without an employer, and that is a dangerous thing. There were many great masters then, and some of them were very great and some of them were only a little bit great and some perhaps were only great as a courtesy. This one was of the middle ground: he was quick like a cat, but not like lightning; he was strong like a river ox, but not like a mountain bear or a giant; he was clever, but not wise, and he enjoyed his strength and his speed and his power over other people. And so this great master, who was really not a nice man, grew very drunk in the village saloon and laid about him with a broken spar of wood, and he struck the owner of the saloon between the eyes and cracked his skull so that he died, and then he set about the customers and the saloon owner's family too.

"So the leatherworker and his brother—our young man's father and uncle, you remember—went in to meet him and tell him to behave himself like a master and not a thug, and he cast his eyes downwards and acted most contrite, then when they relaxed, he knocked them head over heels out through the door with his broken spar. The young man's father had a bruise on his head and his uncle had crossed eyes and was bleeding from one ear. And so the young man, who had never been in a real fight before, walked into the saloon and told this old, accomplished master of *gong fu* that he was a small man, a miserable creature, a weak, drunken oaf with no conversation and no chance with any lady he did not pay for. And while the master was still staring at him, he added many other things less polite which were perhaps unfair, but still most efficacious in attracting the master's attention. And so, they fought."

Master Wu smiles, and he stretches his narrow shoulders and they pop, and there is a little shine in his eye as recollection takes away his years.

"It was a great fight. Many buffets. Perhaps a hundred. They leaped and they struck and the young man broke the spar with his foot and the great master hurled him back and the young man rolled to his feet and attacked him again, and so on and so on, until the saloon funiture was all matchwood and they were both shaking and bruised, but the great master was still on his feet and his opponent could not prevail. The young man was covered in cuts and bruises, and his mouth was swollen. And the great master said:

"'You have done very well, young man, but now I see that you are tired, and I am older and stronger than you are. Retire, and I will not hurt you any more, but if you remain, I will break you as you broke my spar, and your mother will weep for her wasted years.' But the young man did not reply. He smiled as if he were just now understanding something, and he shut his eyes, and he listened to the sound of the waves. And he began to move. He moved in step with the slow, inevitable rhythm in his head, and the storm lent strength to his tired limbs and the ebb and the flow of the sea washed away his hurts and doubts, and soon the whole room was filled with the rush of the tide. The great master fell into that same rhythm and their footsteps moved as one, until the young man heard a great wave come roaring in from the deep, and it bore down over the great master with the weight which shatters stone, and the great master fell to his knees with a shout, and the fight was over. The master lay gasping on the floor of the saloon and spent many weeks in a cot recovering from his wounds. And then he left, after paying for the damage, with great humility. It is rumoured that thereafter he became a baker, and married, and had many children, and was a better man.

"And the young man was nicknamed Ocean thereafter, and he was still a terrible farmer and very bad dancer, but his father and uncle and his mother and all his family were very proud, and he was content. And the Secret is this . . ."

Master Wu screws up one eye and opens the other very wide. He crooks his hands and lisps. This is presumably an appropriate face for imparting Secrets.

"*In unifying your chi with that of your opponent—in aligning the breath of your life and theirs—you will storm the strongest fortress.* There! Is that a good Secret?"

I have no idea. It sounds as if it might be really profound. It also sounds like baloney. It is, therefore, the highest-quality *bull-shido,* or martial arts hogwash. I don't know whether to commit it to memory and study it or consider it an object lesson in the ease with which you can counterfeit ancient proverbs. Old Man Lubitsch once worked in an auction house in far off New York City, and is very fond of a saying he heard there regarding the provenance of religious iconography from eastern Europe: "Seventeenth century, but the artist is still alive."

"What does it mean?" Elisabeth says.

"No idea. It's a Secret. Means what you need it to mean. But now we have one, we can refuse to tell anyone about it!" He laughs. Wu Shenyang of the Voiceless Dragon, making up fairy tales like Lydia Copsen.

And then he puts another record on the gramophone (this one is Ella Fitzgerald, who—according to Master Wu—knew a great deal about chi), and Elisabeth and I are the first of his students ever to know the Inner Teaching of the Voiceless Dragon School.

THE SUMMER of that year is abnormally hot, and it is dry. The soil of Ma Lubitsch's garden turns to dust by degrees, and the lawn cracks and fades. It doesn't seem to matter how much water she sprays on it, the earth is so thirsty it can't absorb moisture any more, and the sun slurps it all up into the air before the plants can drink it. In the end, she takes to hosing the whole place down at night, and Old Man Lubitsch makes a huge white tent from spare bedsheets to shade the entire garden during the day. Gonzo, aside from occasional trips to Angela Gosby's house to use the pool (and fall in frantic lust with his young hostess), remains in the shade and pronounces himself unable to move.

When the temperature goes up another degree, only the bees are happy, and even they must make allowances. The central chamber of the beehive cannot be allowed to rise above thirty-six degrees. A humming flight path reaches from the Lubitsch house to Cricklewood Creek, the inbound traffic carrying individual drops of water in gentle bee-fingers. Air-conditioning by slave labour, if you believe that a hive is run by an autocrat, but Old Man Lubitsch has long ago explained that the Queen is an asset, cherished and nurtured but not obeyed, and that the hives are a functioning biological machine. He cannot decide if they represent an eerie social harmony or a grim nightmare of mechanistic subservience to a purposeless and endlessly repeating pattern. In the heat, he muses on this imponderable aloud, until Ma Lubitsch pronounces it unsuitable conversation to go with lemonade, and her husband gratefully abandons political philosophy for citrusy relief.

Then September comes, and torrential rain. There are dry days after, of course, even barbecue days, but the flat-iron summer has been lifted and set aside. We go back to school and I find, briefly, a fresh tormentor among the new inmates who have arrived to receive the Evangelist's curious wisdom.

Donnie Finch is a Big Bad Kid. This is to say he is strong, sporty, delinquent (in a very minor way) and antipathetic to anyone who pays more attention in class than he does. He is instantly well-liked, instantly obnoxious, instantly aware of his social inferiors. He backs me against the wall between French and biology and announces that I will henceforth call him "sir."

This is the thing that I hate above all others. Donnie Finch does not know me. He has no reason for his animosity. He just knows that it is the Done Thing. He is Donnie Finch. I am not. He is a football hero, a smoker and a joker. I am not. Therefore, in the only mathematics which interest him, I am to be despised and picked on. He presses his thick damp hand in the middle of my chest and sneers. (I think of Mr. Lasserly.) This is habit. It is literally mindless: Old Man Lubitsch's horrible determinist bee society writ large and sticky-fingered. There can be no discussion, no nuance, because either of these asserts a world which Donnie Finch's picture of life denies. He eschews these things and chooses instead an off-the-shelf alternative.

In my mind, there is a calculus of risk and reward playing out. I am not helpless. I could kill Donnie Finch. I would quite like to, at this moment. His body is fragile. There are four targets in reach of my hand which would end this discussion in no small way, although three of them (temple, larynx, nose bone) require for a deadly blow more strength than I can easily bring to bear, and would most likely only incapacitate and terrify him. The other one (carotid artery) is something of a lottery. A smart tap will probably knock him out, but might dislodge a clot or cholesterol smear and cause an embolism in his brain. Killing him *by mistake* is not the point.

But satisfying as mayhem and (short) combat might be, these are not solutions. They are just reactions—as idiotic as Donnie himself. Thus I am paralysed, and upset. I want to unleash my anger. I do not believe that I *should.* At sixteen, it is a terrible thing to be hog-tied by conscience. I gaze at Donnie Finch's pink face and his nasty freckled mouth and wonder what to do, and what he will grow into when he's older. Maybe he will always be a thug. He shunts me against the wall, and I breathe out and am preparing to test my less lethal options, which are by definition more difficult because fending off an opponent without seriously damaging him requires a level of skill vastly greater than his, when Donnie Finch is mercifully eclipsed. Planet Gonzo's orbit has brought him to the east corridor, and the gravity of my situation has pulled him in. He doesn't say anything. He just steps firmly between us and closes his hand over Donnie Finch's, and squeezes. Donnie Finch lets go. I am not sure whether to be relieved or not.

Christmas brings ribbons and pine trees and Ma Lubitsch's

memorable cake. The Evangelist, driven by a wretched fear of hormonal wrongdoing in the Season of the Lord's Birth, pronounces that dating is forbidden by scripture. This is so remarkable that there is a queue at the library to read the Bible for anything we may have missed. A theological debate is set in motion which lasts into February and beyond.

Master Wu's daughter moves to Lindery, which is just along the coast. She is Ma Lubitsch's age but looks mine, and she is very tiny and very beautiful. Her name is Yumei, and her daughter—who is two—is called Ophelia. Ophelia watches me gravely as I practise my Embrace Tiger, and her little hands bat insistently at my hip. It is sticking out. I try harder. Ophelia consults with Master Wu, and approves the change—and Master Wu smiles hugely as his assistant moves to her next student.

One of the donkeys develops a case of halitosis beyond what can be tolerated even in a donkey. The others ignore him, giving rise to great mournful honks of loneliness and betrayal until the vet arrives and performs some abscess-related miracle and all is well again.

In April, I walk along Cricklewood Creek with Penny Greene, who does geography with Gonzo and wears a plastic butterfly in her hair. It is cold and very beautiful. We are looking at the water and talking about ducks, and she sort of lunges. I think for a moment that she has fallen, but her arms are slim and strong around my back and she eels up over my chest and plants a smacker on my mouth. She is very soft in some places and very bony in others, and the difference between her body and mine is like switching a light on in my head. We kiss for a very long time. She is pleased. She goes home. I sort of expect this to lead to an official date, but it doesn't. We remain friends. I find that this does not bother me. Penny Greene falls in love with a boy called Castor, and the whole business looks—from the outside, at least—utterly desolate. I go on a date with Alexandra Frink instead, but she is monumentally boring, or perhaps I am, and we part chastely and with a measure of relief.

And then there comes the day when Master Wu and I are mixed in a blur of limbs and actions and reactions ("Newton! *Very* good *gong fu*!") and I see an opening and I strike sharply into it and even as I do so I am thinking that I have made a mistake, and of the gramophone and my horror at the notion of harming it, and at how ghastly and impossible it would be if I struck my teacher and damaged him, even to the extent of a bruised head, and God forbid I should break his skin. At which point his left hand gently but firmly captures my fist, and his right, driven by the same motion turning around the fulcrum at the base of his spine, borrowing my force for his purpose, propels me through the air and into the ornamental fish pond, which causes Master Wu and half a dozen senior students to laugh so hard they nearly rupture, and my relief and my delight at the cheeky old sod are so great that I have to be helped out before I drown. But Master Wu is more delighted because he is also proud.

"Excellent! You won!"

"I fell in the pond!" I object, but he shakes his head.

"You made me misjudge! You were fast! I had to do something I did not intend!" He grins. "Do you think you found out what the Secret means? Maybe you very nearly merged your chi with mine! Then you'd have to teach me!" He laughs, and he is glowing, and so am I. From the sun deck, Elisabeth is watching, her face completely still, and she fetches a towel for me, which I know is a high honour indeed.

"Does anyone ever really win? Do they even get close?" I ask Master Wu that evening, as he swings his legs over the edge of the little bridge at the bottom of his garden and cools his feet in the water.

"Oh, they get close all the time," he says, "but they never know that they are close and I never tell."

"You told me!"

"Once! Not again. Now you must work it out like the others! Yes? Yes! For everyone the instruction they need, all of it, but no more." He smiles. "I have one student who might beat me. But he doesn't."

"Why not?"

"Maybe he thinks that's what *I* need—and what the other students need: for me to go to my grave as the teacher who couldn't lose." He grins. "But more likely he is too scared to try in case he is wrong." He laughs, loudly, and splashes me with his foot.

A week later, Alan Lasserly's teacher knocks very politely on the door of the House of the Voiceless Dragon, and watches Master Wu teach Ophelia for half an hour. He watches Master Wu's feet and his hands and the way he steps, and he watches Master Wu's index finger touch Ophelia behind the knee so that her whole body falls into line and she looks like a little fighting woman and not a small girl playing at *gong fu*. When Yumei reclaims her daughter and takes her off for milk, Mr. Hampton bows very low to Master Wu and thanks him for the lesson. Master Wu says Mr. Hampton is very welcome, and Mr. Hampton says that he wishes he had known Master Wu when he was Ophelia's age, to which Master Wu responds that when Mr. Hampton was Ophelia's age, Master Wu was a wild and intemperate youth much given to drinking and taking off his trousers in public places. Mr. Hampton smiles and says that he supposes this is not impossible, and Master Wu avers that there are photographs to prove it, although no one will ever see them. Mr. Hampton says that is probably for the best. They drink tea. After enquiring as to the good health of Mr. Hampton's family and friends, Master Wu asks after Mr. Lasserly. Mr. Hampton says that Mr. Lasserly is sadly still an idiot, and they both find this lamentable and extremely amusing.

IT IS on the evening after Mr. Hampton's visit that I notice the bells for the first time. Seeing them, I realise they have always been there, that they are as much a part of the room as the china ducks—but they are different from the ducks because they are very deliberate. Amid the clutter of Master Wu's life, the bells stand out because they are *structured.*

Elisabeth and Master Wu and I are loafing. We have eaten a muddled sort of meal, cake and cheese and fruit, and slices of salami, and Elisabeth and Master Wu are discussing the matter of China's space programme. The discussion is quite animated. They have co-opted the butter dish (the Moon), the cake plate (the Earth) and a mango (the Sun, acknowledged to be much further away and not to scale, but equally a necessary component in their orrery), and currently Master Wu is waving a spoon, which symbolises the Apollo rockets. The gist of his argument is that the Moon is *up* in the sky, and America (as evidenced by European and American maps) is *on the top half* of the world. The journey from the United States to the Moon is therefore *considerably shorter* than the journey from China, which is (as evidenced by European and American maps) *on the bottom half* of the world. It is therefore *absolutely consonant* with his contention that China, despite her flaws, is the most advanced nation on Earth, that the Americans should reach the Moon before the Chinese. They simply did not have to work as hard.

Elisabeth is stumped by this contention on two fronts. In the first place, it is balderdash, of a sort which is so fundamentally wrong-headed as to be hard to argue. In the second, she cannot shake the nagging suspicion that her revered teacher knows full well the measure of this wrong-headedness, and is gently stringing her along to stretch her cultural preconceptions, is in fact *taking the piss.* She sputters for a moment.

Initially, this whole thing was grand sport. I tuned back in for a while and even suggested that the American rocketeers were at a disadvantage because the Earth was spinning, and they had to build a ship which could go really quickly so as to reach the Moon before it passed by overhead, whereas the Chinese had longer to make course corrections, owing to the greater distance.

Master Wu brushed this aside as a minor consideration and Elisabeth seemed to regard it as treachery, and back and forth they went, Master Wu twinkling and vexatious, and Elisabeth in one of her moments of doubt. These are fun to watch, because they are extremely rare. Elisabeth's fundamental attribute is certainty. However, after the debate over the positioning of the mango and whether it should affect the arrangement of the cake plate and whether in fact the mango should be replaced with an object several miles away and about the size of a house, I sort of drifted off again and I am now viewing the room with new eyes, or at least, with eyes which are paying attention to the detail.

Everything is familiar, of course. I have sat here countless times since I first saw the overstuffed furniture and the weapons on the walls, and fell in love with the gramophone. At this moment, I am looking at the window frames. I have not, until now, spent a lot of time doing this, but a long day and a lot of *gong fu* followed by cake (planet Earth) and tea (either a non-relevant experimental error or a terrifying cosmological event even now threatening to upset the gravitational balance of the solar system) have produced in me a state of contemplative calm and watchfulness. I have studied Master Wu's mouth, and concluded that the occasional twitch of his upper lip is in fact a *quirk,* and evidence in favour of the supposition that he is winding us up. I have studied Elisabeth's upper lip and concluded that it is a fine specimen of the kind, slender and pale pink and slightly masked by a wisp of icing sugar. And so now I have turned my attention upward and outward.

The window frames are made of a darkened wood, which has a fine sheen of varnish over it, and the edges are crusty with yellow, resiny stuff. This is probably where the treated wood has sweated over the years. If I were to touch it, it would feel smooth and shiny and slightly flexible, and then it would snap like crystal sugar. The glass is old and ever so slightly distorted. Glass is mysterious. I once heard Mr. Carmigan, the chemistry teacher, discussing it with Ms. Folderoi, the art mistress. Mr. Carmigan asserted that glass is still technically a liquid, slowly but inevitably obeying gravity as the years pass, while Ms. Folderoi said it isn't and it doesn't. Mr. Carmigan replied that neither of them would live long enough to make a personal empirical observation. Ms. Folderoi hit him with an oil sponge. The debate—like the one unfolding in front of me now—was irascible but good-natured. Also like the one in front of me now, it was one in which I took scant interest. I ponder the window again.

Master Wu has eclectic taste in curtains. The window immediately beyond Elisabeth's blonde head has drapes of white cotton with cherries on them. They are not lined, so the Moon (the actual one, not the butter dish) is visible in the sky beyond. The window behind Master Wu possesses thick, green velour things, winterish and warm, with a pattern of gold coins woven in. I turn my head. The window over by the desk has brown curtains. They are made of rough silk, and probably were at one time quite expensive, although they are strikingly dull.

Something else, however, has now attracted my attention. On each window, there is a run of bells. They are small, but not so small as to produce a little tinkling noise. These bells would make a shrill, sharp clanging. Each bell hangs suspended on a separate length of thread, and each thread is fastened at the top to a thicker line, which in turn falls from a slender shelf tacked to the frame. Knocking one bell would cause it to ring, but might not disturb the others. Removing one bell, conversely, would almost certainly set off the whole lot. Opening the window even a little bit would sound like the percussion section's after show party. I turn round and look at the door. The bells there are set up slightly differently. There is also a cat's cradle arrangement on the fire guard. In fact, when Master Wu goes to bed, putting the guard in front of the coals, he will be surrounded by a low-tech burglar alarm. I realise that I have looked at the bells and the windows any number of times without actually seeing them. How odd.

Master Wu and Elisabeth are still discussing the planetary

question, but Master Wu, at least, has lost interest—or rather, he has found something more interesting. My discovery has woken me up. I was sort of cow-like, placid and digesting (or, in fact, ruminating). At some point during my examination of the bells, as I became more intent and focused, the impact of my presence in the room changed. Master Wu clocked this immediately, and is now watching me while he explains that *even if the Moon were low in the sky, the Chinese would still have to go up to it, while the Americans could simply drop on it,* and Elisabeth has noticed her teacher's divided attention and followed it back to me, and so they both put cosmology on the back burner on hold, and Master Wu asks me what is wrong.

"Nothing," I say. "Nothing's wrong. I just noticed the bells. On the windows."

"Oh, yes!" Master Wu nods. "Very important. I am the Master of the Voiceless Dragon, you see. Many enemies."

"Enemies?"

"Oh, yes." He smiles genially. "Of course."

"What kind?"

"Oh," says Master Wu, matter-of-factly, "you know. Ninjas."

And he shrugs. He takes a bite of his cake, and waits for one of us to say "But." He knows that sooner or later, one of us has to. Elisabeth and I know it, too. Just hearing Master Wu say "ninja" is like hearing a concert cellist play "Mama Mia" on the ukulele. Ninjas are silly. They are the flower fairies of *gong fu* and karate. They can jump higher than a house, and burrow through the ground. They know how to turn invisible. They have mastered those elusive Secret Teachings (like the one we now know and no one else does) and can do things which are like magic. And that, surely, is Master Wu's point. He is making with the funny.

Before I can feel the wash of embarrassment which is rising up my spine, Elisabeth says "But." I love her for ever.

"But . . ."

"Ninjas are silly?" asks Master Wu.

We nod.

"Yes," he says. "Very silly. Black pyjamas and dodging bullets. I know. But the word is not the thing. And the word is wrong, anyway." He stops and leans back. His voice deepens, losing the cheery crackle and the old man's roughness, and he looks bleaker and much older.

"The night I was born, my mother hid in a well, under the stone cap. I was born in lamplight. The first thing I smelled was mud and soot and blood. My father and a cattle man attended my birth, because we had no doctor. My uncles beat a pig to death in the square of the village we were resting in. They made it scream for seven hours, until the morning came, so that no one would know a woman was giving birth, so that my mother did not have to stifle her cries. For four days, my uncles carried her on a stretcher, and told everyone their friend Feihong was sick. They'd been pretending she was a man, a fat man, for three months. She carried a sack of stones on her belly, and as I grew, she threw them away, one by one, so that people who looked at her would just see Fat Feihong, with his funny arms and bandy legs, and his small feet. My mother had unfashionable feet. Too large for a woman. Still tiny for a man. But after four days, they couldn't carry her any more, or people would notice, would ask whether maybe Feihong had something serious, whether maybe they should leave him behind. Then she got out of the stretcher and she walked, and she carried me in her sling, the way she'd carried the rocks. I learned to be a quiet baby. I hardly ever cried. When I did, she sang, very loud, very squeaky, like a man trying to sing like a lady, and they called her Squeaky Feihong, and my uncles and my father sang along with her. Catscream Wu and Monkey Wu and Goatbleat Wu, you could hear them coming for miles, and the farmers claimed we turned milk. We were hiding, always. Last of the Voiceless Dragon, running and hiding, by being as loud as possible.

"Why? Because of ninjas. Not ninjas like in Hong Kong movies. Couldn't fly. Dodge bullets hardly at all. But . . . strike from the shadows? Kill in the darkness. These things they did *very well indeed.* And sometime, long time ago, someone paid them or ordered them to kill everyone in my family, and make my father's father's father's *gong fu* disappear. They never quit. They just keep trying. It's what they are. War—for ever. My father's oldest brother. His children. Their mother. All gone before I was born."

Master Wu sighs.

"Lots of people were at war in China then. Chiang Kai-shek was chasing Mao all over the country. We hid with Mao's people on the Long March. Thousands of miles, mountains and lakes. Our war just disappeared into theirs. And when they died—when maybe ninjas killed them instead of us—that just disappeared too. Everybody was dying then." He shrugs at the wall, the weapons in their racks. I had assumed he was proud of them. Now I think maybe they are there to remind him. I think he is prouder of the extremely ugly ducks.

"Their war," Master Wu goes on, "was about who was in control. Ours was about staying alive, of course, but it was also about *choice.* Very much the same thing. We teach *gong fu* so that you have a choice. Otherwise . . . the man in charge has all the power. Yes? And . . . what if he is not a man? A hundred people all bowing down to a child who does anything he pleases. No responsibility. Just power. No wisdom. Just actions. As if the throne were empty. China had too many child-emperors already.

"Whoever paid the ninjas believed we are wrong. Power belongs in one place. Nothing should disturb the way things work. No alternatives. Or maybe it was just them: the Clockwork Hand Society, ninjas, call them what you like. And us: Voiceless Dragon. Them and Us. For ever. So my mother carried me to Yenan on a bed of rocks. My father taught me my *gong fu* when I was three. I learned in Yenan, which is a hard place. But I learned about silence before then. My first teachers were ninjas."

If Master Wu were a grizzled, elderly trucker, or a veteran of more familiar wars, he would light up a cigarette or grab our hands and tell us we were lucky kids. He does not. He just sighs again, and somehow when he does this, the regret which ripples out from him is a physical thing. I have heard of people who fought with their anger, who made rage into a physical force. I have never heard of anyone doing it with sorrow.

I look around. The night has drawn in while he was talking. The window onto the veranda is open, and I am listening for stealthy feet on the boards outside. In the brush at the bottom of Master Wu's garden, something snuffles. I do not know whether ninjas snuffle. It seems to me that a very subtle sort of ninja might snuffle so as to make you think he was a neighbourhood dog, or just to let you know he was there and yet leave you guessing. On the other hand, maybe a ninja would regard this kind of trick as amateurish.

I try to relax my shoulders so as not to be caught tense by the attack which might be coming. This is extremely difficult in a big soft chair, and I feel like an idiot for choosing the lounger. Elisabeth is sitting on a more upright thing with hard cushions, and consequently need only roll forward or leap up to be ready for anything. Master Wu's chair is a rocker, although he has stopped the motion with his cane. The opportunities for fast deployment from a rocking chair are many. Only I will be caught double-weighted (stolidly caught between one foot and another, and therefore immobile), or worse, on my fat arse. I have not been mindful. On the other hand, if I am honest, the two better fighters in the room are well-placed by virtue of my choice. Perhaps I am subconsciously a master tactician.

"When I was five," Master Wu goes on, "I built a ninja trap." The sorrow recedes and something warm fills him: a weathered pride held close across the years.

"I had been out in the forest collecting game from snares. Rabbits. In the mud, there were footprints. The ninjas came out of the forest and watched us in the night. They liked us to know they were watching, all the time, so that anything you did after dark, you were afraid. It was daytime now. And I thought if I made a big snare, a strong one, and laid it on the path, I might catch a ninja, and make my mother less afraid. I might see approval in my father's face, like when I worked well in his tannery, or when I practised my forms one more time after he had told me I could stop. He might grunt. My father laughed when he thought something was funny, and he smiled when he was happy, but he only grunted when he was impressed. I made him grunt very seldom. So I borrowed some tools, and I made a big, wide snare out of wet leather, and covered it in mud leaves and attached it to a big old log so that when the snare was touched the log would haul the ninja up in the air, and left it there."

He shrugs.

"It was a very bad ninja trap. Possibly an old, fat, stupid ninja might have tripped over and fallen on his stomach because he was laughing so much at this trap, and injured himself. If he fell in the right direction, he might have put one foot in the snare at the same time and been caught in it. But when he had finally caught his breath and finished laughing, he would just have cut himself down and gone away. Ninjas are not like rabbits.

"But that night, I woke up, and there was a ninja in my room. He was staring down at me. And he said:

"'My name is Hong. You may call me Master Hong. What is your name?'

"So I told him my name. And he said:

"'Do you know who I am?'

"And I told him he was *xiong shou,* an assassin, because I had never heard of ninjas, then. And he laughed.

"'I am Sifu Hong of the Clockwork Hand Society. We are the sons of tigers. We are the hope of China—of the world. We are order. And you—you are the little boy who sets traps for us.'

"I didn't say anything, because I was afraid. And he said: 'Children don't hunt tigers, boy. Tigers hunt children.' Which is actually not fair to tigers. It's only ninjas which hunt children. I didn't say anything. I was too scared to move, or cry out, or even to pee, which was something I very much wanted to do. He said:

"'So now we have come for you, because of your pride. Because we always come, in the end. You are lucky. We have not made you wait. Because we always come, in the end.'

"And he drew out a knife, suitable for hiding under clothes at a very expensive banquet, or for opening the veins of a small boy. I prepared myself to feel the grating of that blade against my bones, the swift warm rush of my life, and then to find out what was the fate of children in the world beyond. And then—you understand, I was *very* surprised, and I thought for a moment this was part of his preparation to kill me—his left foot flew up in the air and he flew out into the hall, and the knife fell on the floor in my bedroom. There was a terrible cry, and silence. And my father came into my room, and carried me out into the hall, and there was my ninja, hanging by his foot, with a huge leatherworking awl buried in his chest. He was hanging by the twine from a ninja trap just like mine. And my father held me by the shoulders and he made me look, and he said: 'What did you do wrong?'

"I thought about it, and I thought about saying I had been foolish to involve myself in grown-up things, that I should have asked him before trying to catch a ninja, or that I had not considered the nature of my prey and should have made the trap to kill rather than to capture, or maybe just weeping because I was so relieved. My father asked again. And finally I said I had made a functional trap, but I had put it in the wrong place. And my father thought about this, and he thought long and hard, for he said nothing while we cut the ninja down and dragged his body into the main square. And then we walked home, and finally he looked back at the square and down at me. And he grunted."

Master Wu smiles, and raises his hands like Bruce Lee, and says "Heeyayayay-HAI!" and throws his paper napkin at Elisabeth. She deflects it with the flat of her hand, and says "Pffft!" which is the noise hands-like-lethal-weapons make in movies, and she rolls off her chair and throws a pillow at me. I decide to let it hit me, and fling my arms wide to indicate that I have expired. Master Wu grins.

"He is faking! His dead-appearing *gong fu* skill is weak!"

And after that, it's a merry evening, and much fun is had by all before we must wash up the teapot and go on our way. And by then we have just about persuaded ourselves that, like the mango sun and the Chinese space effort, Master Wu's ninjas are one of his goofy jokes.

I AM so engrossed in my small world that I entirely neglect the bigger one, with the consequence that, when it comes time to look for a job or a place to continue my studies, I am utterly unprepared. The rest of the world is facing graduation and university. I am, again, tail-end Charlie. I do not know the language and I seem to have missed the deadlines and there's no space for me on the forms. Elisabeth is going to a place upcountry called Alembic, having quite naturally sorted everything out last year, and it is she who galvanises me, sets me on course again, stamps her foot until I pay attention.

"No!" she says.

"I'll—"

"No, you won't!"

"But—"

"No!"

She stares at me. At eighteen she is not pale or albino or that weird Scandinavian superblonde, but close on translucent, like something living in the dark of the sea. Almost, she is drawn in black and white, and this colouration is so strange that it distracts you from her face, which is strong, perhaps a little too broad, with features which lack the perfect symmetry of the *beautiful* or the mediocrity of *pretty,* so that she is *striking,* maybe *attractive,* but definitely *unique.* Until this moment, we have never had a conversation about anything which wasn't part of life in the Voiceless Dragon, and we are both confused and a little alarmed by this sudden shift. She frowns.

"Right. Go and see my mother."

"I—"

She holds up one finger like a dagger.

"Don't make me stamp!"

At which point I have to confess that I have no idea who her mother is. Elisabeth looks at me as if I have grown an extra head.

"I'm Elisabeth Soames. I'm Assumption Soames's daughter."

And now I know who she looks like, although it's too weird to think about it because Elisabeth is my own age and not a lunatic, and her mother is my headmistress, the Evangelist. I gargle at her.

She stares at me fiercely until I concede that I will talk to Gonzo's parents and ask them for advice, and if that fails go and talk to "Assumption," and then she kisses me once, on the right cheek, and flees, to say her *au revoir* to Master Wu. I feel a curious lurch as she closes the door, and set myself firmly on track for the Lubitsch residence to talk about Embarkation.

Students at the Soames School do not merely graduate; the school's founders were secular men of rationalist bent, and they considered that the young persons entrusted to them for broadening and preparation were not going on to some higher realm of adulthood or finishing their studies, but merely changing venues in their search for truth. For this reason, and also because the Evangelist holds anything old as a natural good, as if a practice could acquire holiness with repetition—in which case certain sins she has forbidden in strident tones must surely by now qualify as redeemed and even redemptive—those leaving the school each year are said to be Embarking, and they are referred to not as Embarkees, which carries some stain of steerage class about it, but as Embarkands, which is both suitably academic and ineffably superior.

I do not feel like an Embarkand. I feel more like a castaway. Around me, young men and women are preparing for places at exalted colleges and working part-time or sponging to pay for them. They buy new clothes and pack suitcases and talk in a strange code about bunking and halls, freshers, gyps, mats and frats, about Noughth Week and courts and moots. When questioned, they fall silent and look embarrassed, which I take to mean that if you don't know already, there's no hope you'll be going. It is like a midnight feast to which only the cake-bearing elite will be invited, and I have no cake, no cake tin, and no book of recipes. Even if I did I lack means to purchase flour. Gonzo has naturally secured a scholarship to study Land Management and Agricultural Economics at a university called Jarndice; "naturally" because while it is absolutely forbidden to offer scholarships on grounds of sporting prowess alone, fortuitously LMAE seems to require a certain cast of mind whose academic virtues are not readily subject to conventional testing, but which is strangely and happily consonant with that required to grasp instinctively the tactics and strategy of a number of competitive field enterprises. Some students of LMAE, regrettably, become so immersed in this alternative use for their talents that they never, in fact, obtain a degree at all, choosing instead to enter the arena of professional sports. Jarndice University's horror at this waste of young minds is somewhat offset by the fact that these same sad failures often provide the best captains and star players for the university, and honour the Dear Old Place with small thanks such as libraries, pavilions, and (in one case) a painting by Van Gogh. Gonzo was interviewed for the scholarship in the LMAE admissions office, just off the rugby pitch, and after they'd talked about cows (Gonzo displayed a detailed knowledge of their digestive processes and expressed a hope that he might, working with a particularly comely member of the vet school, be able to discover a cure for the plague of flatulence and burping which had afflicted the university herd since his arrival on Thursday) and loams (Gonzo averred that he had no outstanding debts) and crop rotation ("My mother told me never to play with my food," at which Professor Dollan nearly swallowed his pen lid and had to be carried out), the interviewees were invited to pop out onto the field for a friendly, informal, entirely optional *Interviewees vs 1st XV* match, in which the interviewees were thrashed 73–14, the visitors' points coming exclusively through the efforts of G. William Lubitsch. A post-match tally of incidents and accidents also revealed that Gonzo had legally but savagely incapacitated two members of the home team and taken significant hurts to his person without noticeable diminution of his ability, viz. a minor concussion, a briefly dislocated shoulder, three stitches over the left eye, two cracked ribs, and assorted bruises and impact marks which, on removal of his shirt, caused the physiotherapist to insist that he accompany her instantly to her office, where she could tend to his hurts more thoroughly.

It is not that Gonzo could not have found a place to study using his brain. He is more than capable. It is that this would have involved more effort than he cares to expend, or has ever needed to. Sport is just plain less taxing to him than chemistry or geography—two subjects he enjoys and excels in when he can be bothered—so sport he chose. I have somehow missed learning what questions I should be asking. And so, to my own surprise, I visit my headmistress in her study.

I am surprised at how small the room is, and indeed at how little is the Evangelist herself. I stare across her neat, filed, indexed, labelled and categorised possessions, past the pens in colour-coded groups and the little roll of paper stars used to indicate good work and the thick black-on-yellow TOXIC stickers for very bad work, at the staunch opponent of evolution who runs the school. It occurs to me that she looks a lot like a macaque monkey, which—on so many levels—is such a disastrous line of thought that I shut it down immediately. Instead, I wish her good morning, and she smiles thinly.

"I want to go to university," I blurt, because with the Evangelist I have discovered that it is best to get the awful truth out in the open as quickly as possible and give her less time to pour out her acid wit. "Elisabeth said I should come and talk to you. At

Master Wu's." Because I wouldn't wish her to think, at this moment above all, that I was trifling—in a physical way, beyond the physical contact necessary to be thrown on the floor and immobilised in a leg bar, and considering the intimacy of physical intertwining implied in that position, which is suddenly sexualised beyond measure, I am bewildered at how I have survived it without either blushing or exhibiting other autonomous physical responses less ambiguous, and push this entire chain of thought from my mind lest I say it out loud—with her beloved (neglected) daughter.

The Evangelist doesn't answer directly. Instead, she leans back in her chair and steeples her hands. She purses her lips and touches each narrow line to the tips of her index fingers and closes her eyes. She inhales deeply and sighs, no doubt directing a prayer in the direction of her vengeful, arbitrary, prohibitive, humourless deity. Then she scowls at me from beneath lowered eyelids, reaches into her desk and produces a packet of cigarettes ("cancerous, blasphemous, steeped in the blood of slaves and mired in the culture of sin and sensuality which pervades this modern world") and fires up a chunky Zippo lighter one-handed. She cocks the gasper at a jaunty angle in the side of her mouth and draws sharply through it.

"Alllll right, then," says Assumption Soames finally. "I can fix that." She sucks more carcinogenic sin into her mouth and expels it, dragon-style, from her nostrils. "Close your mouth, man, you look like a letter box."

This is entirely likely. Until this moment I have assumed that Assumption Soames sets an extra place at table every night for God, sings hymns in the bath (which she takes dressed so as to avoid arousing anyone's erotic lusts, unfeasible as that seems on the face of it) and eats only gravel and oatmeal in order to avoid inflaming the senses. More recently, on realising that her daughter is the slender, elegant child/woman with whom I have been practising lethal and exacting modes of pugilism, and who seems like me to have no home to go to, I have envisaged a silent, crypt-like dwelling place of grey stone and burlap. Meals in my version of Warren are announced by a tolling of heavy bells, and the floors are made of bare pine which Elisabeth must sandpaper each morning so that they do not attain the voluptuous sheen of trodden wood. I have totally bought into Assumption Soames's public persona. This, it now appears, was naive.

I close my mouth, but don't know how to address this rather significant discrepancy, and the thought has occurred to me that this is some warped Evangelical testing process to determine whether I am worthy to receive the help and succour of her Church in my educational hour of need. The Evangelist I know is utterly straightforward in the most devious possible way, a subtle bludgeon like those computers which play chess by going through every consequence of every move there is. The Evangelist, when manipulating, plays across a broad field, takes advantage from every setback and emerges victorious in the micro by pursuing the macro at every turn. I dare not trust this new face. Assumption Soames glowers at me for a moment, then sighs more abruptly, and knocks her ash into an ashtray in the shape of a cherub. She wriggles, as if this is something she has been impatient for. It dawns on me that she is prepared for this moment.

"You want to hear a story?"

I nod, cautious. The chair I am sitting in is the chair in which I lost my faith in God; it reeks of lonely realisation. Only now I seem to be finding a friendly face where I least expected it. The chair and I are reassessing our relationship. This is far safer than reassessing my relationship with the Evangelist, who has clearly lost the plot and may at any moment begin frothing at the lips or singing bawdy show tunes. She wriggles again, down into what must be a cushion (it looks like a *luxurious* cushion, rather than one full of rocks or razor blades, as I might have expected). Content with the position of her backside, Assumption Soames begins. The story is by way of being a parable.

"A traveller on the road one night misses his turning and finds himself lost in a forest. He has a dog, but the dog is doing the dog thing, can't seem to decide which way is home. Perhaps he's in a car, and the dog doesn't know. Anyway, when he's totally and irredeemably lost amid the trees, he comes to a fork in the road. He has his faithful hound, so he isn't afraid, but he *does* want to get home"—she waves the cigarette in a narrow circle—"so he's pleased when he sees that there's an inn at the fork where he can ask directions. A hotel, maybe, with a bar. No one really has inns any more, right? So he comes to a hotel. A nasty, sawdust-on-the-floor kind of place. The kind of place where *you* should not go. Okay?"

I nod.

"So, sitting at the bar are three scary old hags so ancient he can't see their eyes. Their faces are that wrinkled. Hmm?"

I nod again. This is the first time ever in conversation with the Evangelist that I have had a sense that my consent and even participation were a necessary part of her game plan, and the discrepancy is making me tense. Assumption Soames, on the other hand, is shedding tension from muscle groups as if she's been unplugged from the current. She waves her arms, taps her feet, and stabs the cigarette through the air to make little glowing full stops when she gets to the bits which are important.

"So the traveller goes up to these ladies and asks them, polite as can be, how best to get home. And the oldest one—in the middle—she grabs her forehead and parts the curtains and glowers at him and she says she *don't answer questions no more*!" Assumption Soames hits the desk with her hand and her voice for a moment is scratchy and back-country and alarming. "And she points at her sisters on either side of her and she says *one of these ladies always tells the truth and the other always lies, and they only answers one question between 'em*!

"So if he wants directions from these ladies, he's got to ask a pretty sophisticated question. But fortunately, our traveller—Evander John Soames of Cricklewood Cove—is a teacher. He knows just what question to ask. *Right,* says Dr. Soames, looking at the hag nearest to the gin, *then my question to you is this: which of the two roads would the other of you tell me is the way home?* Because Dr. Soames is no slouch with the logic, and he knows if he's talking to the truthful sister, she'll tell him truly which the wrong road is, because that's the road her sister would choose, and if he's talking to the liar, she'll tell him that the right road (which her sister would tell him to take) is the wrong road—so whichever answer he gets, he knows to take the other road. So the hag tells him to take the southern road, and off he goes, north."

Assumption Soames takes another draw on her gasper and frowns across the desk. It would be unsatisfying if that was the end of her narrative, but this pause has the feel of an audience participation moment. I cast around and ask a question.

"Does he make it home?"

"No."

"What?"

"No. He does not make it home to his wife and baby. Nor does the dog. Dr. Soames goes along the north road where he is waylaid by the many sons and daughters of the three hags, who are all *anthropophagi.*"

"Um."

"Cannibals. With man-eating, and sadly also dog-eating, dogs." She leans forward. "They make Soames pie, and *they* all live happily ever after until they are wiped out by an outbreak of kuru, or possibly by the marines. And the moral of this story?"

"Don't leave the path."

"No. The moral of this story in so far as it has one is that cannibals can study logic, and that *if* you are going to leave the path, you better have your wits about you and know better than to trust the first scary old lady who talks to you in a public place. 'One of my sisters lies and the other tells the truth!' What a load of crap. For God's sake, why doesn't he ask the barman? Or just retrace his steps? The man's an idiot." She sighs. I adjust the angle of my jaw again, bringing my lips at least near enough to one another that I will not be mistaken for a tea chest. It must be moderately obvious to the Evangelist that I have no earthly idea why she is telling me this, or what is happening in this room if it is not the case that I have gone totally batshit or she has, or the Devil has come and stolen away her soul and left in its place that of a New Orleans brothel madame. She makes a circular gesture with her hands, an inviting twitch which I recognise from her occasional interventions in my education as meaning "*Think,* boy, the Lord gave you grey matter between your ears for something other than ballast." I answer as I generally do—with a sort of hopeful hiccough. There is a resigned pause.

"Your pal Gonzo," says Assumption Soames, "does not leave the path. Not ever. He does everything from the shelter of the path, and the path kind of takes him where he wants to go because he's cute. You're sitting in my office now and you can't figure out how you never saw I wasn't just a crazy Bible lady or why I was so goddam mean to you for fourteen years, and the answer is that I'm a very good liar and that is the only way I can make sure to be allowed to teach you the stuff you need to know. People don't want children to know what they *need* to know. They want their kids to know what they *ought to need to know.* If you're a teacher you're in a constant battle with mildly deluded adults who think the world will get better if you imagine it *is* better. You want to teach about sex? Fine, but only when they're old enough to do it. You want to talk politics? Sure, but nothing modern. Religion? So long as you don't actually think about it. Otherwise some furious mob will come to your house and burn you for a witch. Well, hell. In this town, the evil old lady who tells everyone what they can and can't read because it isn't decent is *me.* So I can hire whoever I damn well like to subvert my iron rule and they can teach evolution and free speech and the cultural bias of history and all the rest. And I do this because you, you *are* going to leave the path, however much you want to stay on it. And if that's going to happen, you better damn well be prepared!" She slumps. "Man's an idiot," she mutters. "I'll take care of Jarndice for you. It is Jarndice you want, I take it?"

Yes, it is. She makes a note, and we sit there, exhausted, and she's wondering whether she's gotten through to me and I'm wondering whether I can trust her and we're both wondering in shy, weird little ways whether we've made a friend today or whether, if we offer the hand, it's going to mean laughter and a bit of hurt before we can slam the shutters down again. And then, because I have never learned to quit, most especially while I am ahead, I ask if it's a true story. Assumption Soames does not immediately say anything. She puts her hands back in their church steeple position and she draws a breath of clear air and thinks about it. And she puts out her gasper a bit solidly and draws herself in sharply as if she's getting ready to jump off the top diving board.

"No," says Assumption Soames. "The true story is that Dr. Soames managed to persuade the cannibals to let him go, under certain conditions. And then he used their phone and called a bunch of breakdown services and taxi companies and had them send drivers out to the little cannibal town where they were killed and dressed and served up with apples, and the cannibals and Dr. Soames all had a big meal together and Dr. Soames fed bits of some telecoms engineers to the big evil cannibal dogs under the table and to his own dog and then the stupid sonuvabitch came home and died of kuru in my house. Even the dog died, because one of the big, evil cannibal hounds took a fancy to dessert." She shrugs. "Get out of here. I have calls to make. And take care of my kid." Which I would, but she doesn't need me to. Assumption Soames waves me away.

I go tell Gonzo the good news, at which he roars skyward like a great ape and beats his chest with delight, because Tarzan is showing at the drive-through and Belinda Appleby has developed a burning desire for Johnny Weissmuller and Gonzo desires to be the nearest available approximation by the time he happens to meet her in the Crichton's Arms this evening.

"But," Gonzo says, with one index finger loosely held to his lips. I know this "but." It is the precursive "but," the "but" of truly terrible plans and splendid coups. The "but" of boy/boy dare-making and the finish-my-sentence double act which is our friendship. "But," says Gonzo, "we should *entirely* go out there and see."

And I know what he means, without asking. He means that we—and possibly Belinda Appleby and any of her slender, becleavaged, feminine, supple friends who happen to be around when we later have this brilliant notion out loud—should pile into some form of car or truck, most likely Ma Lubitsch's moody 4 × 4 with its ancient green metal flanks and dinted grill and boxy workhorse shape, and go out to the inn and see whether there are really cannibals at the crossroads in Cricklewood Marsh. And when there are not, but we have startled a few screech owls and seen a badger and the ladies have imbibed all the safe scariness they can, we should proceed in an orderly fashion to our mutual place of reclinings and partake of lusty private delights and serious physical celebration with one of those fine examples of enthusiastic early womanhood.

Which is how I come to be riding shotgun with Gonzo Lubitsch, with Theresa Hollow's face next to my ear and her fingernails lightly scratching my neck with each jounce of the jeep, almost by accident—except that every time I move to point the heavy torch at some suspect shadow and Gonzo yowls and the girls shudder and laugh and hit him, Theresa's hand resettles in the exact same place and commences to raise all the hairs on my body, in a ripple which spreads out evenly from that single point of contact and collects hotly somewhere between my knees and my heart in a kind of writhing, pleasurable knot.

THE NIGHT is not actually spooky. It's summer and there's no mist and there are animals grunting and gurgling all around, and off away to the south there are lights and a murmur of traffic. Somewhere out to sea there's an ocean liner having what is most likely a shuffleboard competition, lines of elderly orgiasts tossing their car keys into the hat in the hope of spending a night of Zimmer-frame lovin' with the winner of the round (they won't be disappointed because the cruise companies always make discreetly sure everyone's sexuality lines up nicely; I spent a month balancing the applications one spring, and it was hellish tough allowing for seasickness and cancellation and catalepsy, but they had a formula and we got the job done). There's a disappointing lack of mist and sadly no howls, though a dog at one of the farms on the other side of the delta is barking at something, fit to burst. Gonzo has the windows open to push some cool air into the back of the jeep and induce the ladies to a little close contact with the manly radiators in the front seats, and they're nothing loath.

Theresa's fingernails have just slipped under the double-stitched neck of my T-shirt when we round the corner and there actually is an inn, burned out and broken down and covered in vines. It isn't marked on the map; there's no signage. If you weren't looking, you'd just see trees and a few boards, but since we *are* looking, my torch picks out a doorway still standing and a flight of two or three steps and Belinda Appleby, damn her unto a thousand hells, murmurs "We can't go in there" and Theresa's fingers stiffen on my skin and her breath catches. Everyone knows there's only one possible response to that.

"Of course we can," I say, because Gonzo is already slowing the jeep. Theresa exhales softly, in admiration or alarm, I cannot tell.

Silence should not frighten you. In silence, even the slightest sound can be heard. The beating of your heart and the sound of your breathing become audible because you strain to hear what is not there. When Gonzo stops the truck, it is not silence which claims the crossroads, but a humming sound of presence. There are a hundred other things going about their business in the night around us: tiny rodents and the flapping nightbirds that hunt them; shrubs whispering and rustling as the wind stirs them; wild pigs grating their tusks against the trees and shaking loose their fruit, which drop like stealthy footsteps on the ground. Somewhere, a small mammal has just been caught and eaten by a larger one. The barking dog across the delta is still going, and the sound of pensioners getting jiggy with one another filters over the sand and through the woods and bounces around so that voices call softly all around, words just on the edge of hearing. In the darkness, things go *crack* and *tssssht.* Theresa's high heels sink into the turf. Belinda leans on Gonzo. I draw the torch in a slow circle around us, scrutinising every metre of the darkness for watching eyes and predatory smiles. There cannot possibly be cannibals here. There never were, and if there were, they died. Even their pets died. I have no doubt about this at all. None. At all.

Gonzo leads us in.

Dust and dirt, rags and cracked mirrors, bottles broken and bottles filled with off-colour booze. A small space, maybe a snug or saloon, bare walls gone to cracks and shadows. A ripe, musky smell of animals. Someone has made a fire in the middle of the room, and smoked, and gotten drunk, but not on what was behind the counter. They brought their own: some previous expedition, come and gone. Perhaps Marcus came here, before he went to war.

We look around. Wood. Linoleum. Cheap chairs. Gonzo writes his initials in the dust on the bar, grins a *veni vidi vici* and turns to go—and stops as a deep growl vibrates in the dark. It is not a human noise. It is a predator noise of another variety, a feral, challenging, no-messing rumble which hits your brainstem and says *fight or flight.* We all look towards it.

There is a monster in the doorway: a big, fat, ugly canine with a head like a basketball and too many teeth. It is ludicrous to imagine that this might be an actual cannibal dog. Even a descendant of cannibal dogs. Clearly, it is a pit-fighting dog or a bear-hunting dog or the kind of dog an idiot thinks would be really cool, which then eats his hand and runs away to live in the forest or hunt wild horses on the moors. The kind of dog which gets very territorial and would choose to live in an abandoned bar. I push Theresa behind me, and at the movement the dog swings its heavy head in my direction and I have time to think "Oh, bugger" and it leaps.

I have some idea about dodging but I can't dodge with Theresa behind me and the thing is like a huge black torpedo. My right hand rises anyway, palm up, and I hope to God this is something Master Wu has taught me coming to the fore and not just a lousy bite-my-head-off-I'm-prey reflex. And then there is Gonzo's broad back and his leg is braced on the floor and he catches the dog as it falls on me. It scrabbles at his chest with its hind paws and snaps at him, but Gonzo holds it by both front legs and wrenches them apart. I see his trapezius muscles labour, and release, and I hear the crack of the dog's ribs and I hear it scream and then hit the ground, broken.

Gonzo's face, when he turns, is filled with revulsion which only I am allowed to see. And then he grins lightly, like he does this every day. It would be callous except that if he did anything else it's possible Belinda would actually pass out from horror.

"Reckon it's time to go," he says. He ambles out. Belinda follows. So does Theresa. I look down at the monster, and I wonder whether my hand was coming up to slap it over me, or whether I was just going to get savaged. And then I realise the dog is not dead. It's not going anywhere; it's not about to rear up and assail me. It will die soon. It just hasn't yet. Gonzo's dog-destruction technique, culled from survival manuals and rumours of burglary, is unpractised and imperfect. Wrenching open the forelimbs should burst the heart, but it hasn't. The job is unfinished.

Black, reproachful eyes accuse me as I walk to the door. And then it whimpers. The sound is small and desperate and it ought to come from a dog you'd trust with your kids and which would bring you your slippers and carry cats around in its mouth without ever even contemplating a feline snack. It has no business coming from this thing which just now tried to rip a new orifice in my chest. From which Gonzo saved me. I turn and look at the dog again. There is pain obvious in its posture, and helplessness. It jerks, sniffles and hauls itself over to expose a patch of white fur at the neck. If there is a language shared by mammals, it is the language of pain. Dominance is clear. Only the question of relief is open to discussion. I am asked to finish what Gonzo has begun.

I step closer, half-expecting vengeful snapping. There is none. The dog just waits. I give the only help I can. It does not take long. And then I emerge into the dark, and try to smile and be relieved.

Gonzo does not, in fact, sleep with Belinda Appleby that night. She is too distraught, and he is gashed in a way which exceeds manly and becomes messy. She tends his wounds, but insists on a suspension of familiarities. I take Theresa to my room and make up a bed for myself on the floor with some extra cushions while she is in the bathroom. She emerges, and I take her place, washing for longer than is strictly necessary because I cannot quite get the smell of dying dog from my nose. When I return, she has folded my makeshift bed into a neat pile, and the single sheet which covers her in no way conceals the fact that she is naked. We give Ms. Poynter's lessons a thorough testing. It is not, technically, a first for either of us, but it is the first time the results have been so utterly, back-archingly, desperately enjoyable. Fear and danger, perhaps, but also maybe just a kinship of sorts; I am Gonzo's shadow as she is Belinda's. There is no suggestion of consequence to our encounter. We go our separate ways in the morning.

Gonzo picks me up the following morning, and we do not talk about cannibal dogs until breakfast is nearly over, and then all my nervousness pours out and I confess I have no idea what I would have done had he not been there. Gonzo shrugs. Without me, he says, he never would have gone in. I stare at him.

"You were stopping," I point out.

"I was turning the bloody car around," he answers, and then stares at me right back. "No way," he begins, but I am already howling with laughter because neither one of us wanted to go into that bloody place and both of us went because the other one was determined. The death rattle of the monster is fading in my memory. I tell Gonzo he saved my life, and he grins and says maybe yes, maybe no. And so we dawdle our way home.

After lunch, I receive a call—the *gong fu* of the Evangelist is strong—from Dr. Fortismeer at Jarndice University, who is delighted to tell me (he sounds genuinely delighted, and before I can stop myself I have arrived at the theory that he and the Evangelist are lovers, and that my entry to the place has been bought on a promise of physical delights untold, a prospect which appalls me because it entails a brief and hastily suppressed vision of their coupling) that I have been selected for a new programme called the Quadrille Bursary, which seeks to ameliorate the relationship between the arts and the sciences by creating a Generalism Degree. Dr. Fortismeer sounds like one of those bluff, turbulently fat individuals who take the virtues of manhood to be found in hunting and fishing and a collection of activities falling under the general heading of "roistering," and his explanation of the programme is punctuated with guffaws and snortings to indicate that he too was young once, and that indeed his heart and other parts still are. The Quadrille will comprise four segments (hence the name), these being I. Art and Literature; II. History, Anthropology and History of Science; III. Mathematics and Physics; and IV. Chemistry, Basic Medicine and Biology, in the style of a Renaissance autodidact, save that there will be no "auto" about it. I will be expected to show up for four years of my life and I would do better to avoid (*snort snuffle*) too much in the way of partying, entertainment and, above all (*ho ho, my boy, I think we all know how much notice you'll take of this*), girlish distractions, which are (*fatal to the mind, delectable to the juices*) apparently a frequent cause of lower grades and personal heartbreak. Dr. Fortismeer pauses at this point and apparently expects me to say something, so I say thank you, and he laughs so loudly that the phone cannot convey the signal and distorts it, then tells me to remember to pack warm clothes as Jarndice can be damned chilly at night if you haven't got company (*hufflehuf-flesnort!*). I assure him that I will, reflecting that I am delivered by one bizarre character into the hands of another and that this should not surprise me.

I'm a-goin' to college.

Chapter Three

A university education;
sex, politics, and consequences.

THE MAN whose head occupies my attention is called Phillip Idlewild, although I know him (as of an hour ago) as *Lay Chancellor* Idlewild, PhD, professor of Greek and nominal top dog at Jarndice University. It is a blusterous October evening; the sky is a deep blue-grey made popular by an artist named Payne. We do have those days, and this is one of them, but for the most part the place where I grew up—bounded by Cricklewood Fens on one side and Jarndice on the other—basks in a gentle climate which favours delicate flowers and happy short-haired dogs. Tonight, though, the wind is whipping in across the ocean and bringing a tang of salt, spume and tar, and there's a bass note of corruption: a huge dead sea creature floating on the forty-foot swell, picked apart by gulls. It is the perfect night to be a young man; it is a night to tear off your shirt and howl at the sky and run, to feel the moisture on your skin and not care about the cold. It is a night when wine and whisky will flow and a roaring fire and a wild dance will find you in the arms of that girl or this one or making friendships which will last for ever.

Unfortunately, I am at a function. I arrived at my set (not digs, please, or rooms, or even accommodation) and opened my suitcase and set up my music, which is pretty much all the unpacking I needed to do, and went directly from there to Matriculation Dinner, which is the first in what is an almost inexhaustible list of traditional Jarndice occasions which are best discreetly ignored. Almost no one ever knows that about the

Mat Dinner and so they end up, like me, staring at the bald patch on the top of Phillip Idlewild's head and wondering whether the pale, scabrous material which is fluttering from it as he rubs his hand through the two or three remaining hairs is in fact a contagious disease, a harmless consequence of advanced age or the residue of something he accidentally dipped himself in at lunch.

Professor Idlewild cannot speak unless he is horizontal, or at least unless his head is horizontal. When he wishes to emphasise a point, he twists his face up towards you like a passionate piebald owl and nods, and the tendons in his neck stand out amid the wrinkles, but for the most part he addresses his eloquence to the patina of the dining table. A vertical cross-section of Lay Chancellor Idlewild, taking its plane from the line of bilateral symmetry between the eyes of the normative human figure, would likely reveal a distorted set of interior organs and bones in the shape of a question mark, which seems mysteriously inappropriate in a man whose entire conversational armament consists of exclamations. As the butler (who is a postgraduate student in Industrial Conflict Resolution Theory) brings the fish course, Idlewild looses another flurry of dermis or necrotic fungal spores into the butter dish and, by means of a series of puppet-like twitches, turns to me.

"Mr. Lubitsch! Welcome to Jarndice. I'm told we should expect great things." He smiles. "Do try to make a gesture in the direction of LMAE, won't you, it makes them happy!"

I realise that I will have to tell him I am not Gonzo. I do so. To my surprise, he hoists a horizontal smile at me.

"My dear fellow," he says, "I'm most terribly sorry." He thinks about it for a moment. "Oh, you're the other one!"

Yes. I am. Of all the students here, only I am the other one. Idlewild grins and turns back to his prior interlocutor. I look for Gonzo in order to hate him, and find him for a moment silent and bereft, two chairs away and across. On his right is a glowingly beautiful girl who appears to be genuinely interested in the conversation she is having with her opposite neighbour and his companion about crystal structures, and on his left is a hard-eyed dame of the Evangelist's type who announced herself to him audibly as they sat down as "Doctor Isabel Lamb, and I loathe attractive young men." Whether this is in fact true (I suspect it is not, and that Gonzo was supposed to take it as a challenge) it wrong-footed him and he simply edited her out of his world. Dr. Lamb is now holding forth to the man beside her on the subject of catastrophic failure in suspension bridges, and Gonzo is almost switched off. Without an audience to verify his magnificence, Gonzo has to look deep inside to find himself. He is looking now, but amid the clutter and the obvious sociableness of everyone around him he's having a hard time. I can do nothing for him from here, not directly, but if I can find the right moment to butt into the conversation on my left and drag it into more promising fields, Gonzo will be able to unleash his charm on the situation and will stop looking so horribly empty and insufficient. Ma Lubitsch did not say to me, as we left Cricklewood Cove, that I was to take care of Gonzo. Old Man Lubitsch did not, as he dropped us at the train station, lay upon me a burden of fraternal care and support. They did not do these things because there was absolutely no need. I understand my obligations. After a moment, I beg my neighbour for the salt, and in passing ask why powdered salt is so different from crystal salt and why no one cooks with it, and the conversation roars off at a tangent and Professor Idlewild wants my attention again and Gonzo is debating spices with the numinous girl. Idlewild's conversation takes the form of a lecture, and I consider this new world and take care to avoid eating any small pieces of him which make their way onto my plate.

Jarndice University is not large, but nor is it new. Its proper name is the Jarndice-Hoffman Metanational Wissenschaft-u. Kulturschule, from which it is possible to deduce that although Mr. Jarndice was what is usually for the sake of brevity known as English (i.e., possessed of a genetic heritage including the DNA of warring Angles, Normans, Saxons, Jutes, Picts, Celts, Kerns, shipwrecked Catholic Spaniards, fleeing Sephardi Spaniards and curious Moorish Spaniards, and also mercantilist Burgundians, Viking Scandawegians, rampaging Goths, sullen Vlams and the occasional dislocated Magyar) his fellow rationalist and educator was a pure German (specifically a Teuton-Tartar-Turkic-Russ-Ashkenazi-Franco-Prussian). These two individuals determined not only to found an institution of higher learning and scholarly debate free of the wranglings of academic strife, but also in doing so to create a place apart from the petulant squabblings of national entities. They therefore required in the *Ordinanses of ye Univarsitie* (which also decree that all students shall live within a *myle radiusse* of Jarndice Library, a regulation which became impractical in 1972 when the faculties, sports fields and lecture halls came to occupy most of that space, but which could not be repealed and was instead reinterpreted as referring to a league, which in turn is three English nautical miles, which is 5.55954 km, rather than 5.556 km, which would be three international nautical miles, a distinction chosen to honour Palgrave Jarndice's nationality in spite of his dislike for all forms of patriotism, but which also serves the useful purpose of obfuscating the precise terminator line of that great circle and allowing everyone to live where they damn well please) that anyone who comes to Jarndice in whatever capacity make oath to the effect that they will *looke upon ye world with an eye to ye proper managemente thereofe, ye goode conducte of ye businesse of livynge and ye keeping of ye pease, and that all magisters will give heede to ye thoughts one of another, and not take untoe themselves an excessive pryde.* As a consequence, Jarndice University is a hotbed of cordial scholarly loathing, departmental vituperation and ecstatic political extremism. It is also infamous as the "U of Ye," short for "University of Ye Ordinanses," in reference to the eponymous document, and pronounced by detractors and Matriculats (first year students) as "yee," whereas the letter *y* in this context is in fact the Anglo-Saxon symbol for *th,* a point the lay chancellor does not tire of explaining in exhausting detail to whoever sits upon his left at Matriculation Dinner.

And here I sit, longing to be up and roaringly drunk, instead clad in a rented blue velvet gown with silver trim which scratches at the back of the neck and smells strongly of elderly cat. Dressed thus like a bargain basement Polonius, but with the manners I learned at Ma Lubitsch's table too firmly ingrained to do anything so uncouth as interrupt the flow of nested histories regarding the Great Vowel Shift and the decline of classical scholarship since Hadrian, I endure the stewed beef and smile at the fine-featured woman opposite me and wait for Professor Idlewild to run out of breath. This he does, as dessert arrives, not slowly, but all at once. He stops, and shivers. He compresses himself against the dining table as if looking for a particular fragment of his head which he has decided he will want later. His nose grazes the polish, and two ragged cones of mist appear beneath it—uneven, because his head is turned somewhat towards me. His hands grip the edges of the table. I look across at the fine-featured woman on Idlewild's other side, but her face shows only chiselled bewilderment and the beginnings of the same concern which must be showing in my own. It strikes me as entirely conceivable that Professor Idlewild is having some form of heart attack, or is about to have one, and I realise that I know nothing at all about what to do if this should prove to be the case, nor even how to determine if it is. Part of me also is unthrilled at the notion that he has elected to expire right here in front of me, of all people, at this time, which will inevitably scar me in ways I cannot envisage.

Professor Idlewild throws himself back from the table in a cloud of dandruff, and sits bolt upright, staring and shock-headed. He gurgles a bit, then curls himself around his chest, hands and arms contorting, and gives vent to a kind of bark or yawp. He is either dying or being possessed by the divine animus; the former would be tragic, but also frankly a bit weird, and the latter leads one to contemplate the nature of a deity who might select as his messenger, even his vehicle in this world, an academic bore with a minor but revolting skin complaint and mushroom breath. I glance around a bit frantically for someone who has a clue about what to do next, but no one is paying any attention at all. This complete absence of anyone paying attention—anyone from Jarndice, that is, as the new arrivals are all sharing a moment of unease up and down the table—is a big hint. I find the butler at my elbow wearing an expression of absolute blandness. Since his master is, at this moment, grabbing both his ears and pulling hard, so as to produce an effect not unlike the wings of a fruit bat held up to a bright light, and since this appears to discomfit him not at all, I deduce that Lay Chancellor Professor Idlewild of Jarndice is subject to some form of seizure disorder and it is polite to ignore it. It is in fact polite to the extent that no one would ever consider mentioning it in advance, or commenting on it to anyone who might leap up and do something about it. I am deeply thankful that I am sitting here and not Gonzo, who, having just cottoned to the situation, is preparing a savage lunge down the table to perform a tracheotomy, but has the native intelligence to note that I, who am closest to the emergency, have taken a serious decision to do nothing and that there must be a reason for this. I am therefore spared the spectacle of my best friend sprinting pell-mell along an oak banqueter, spraying nineteenth-century china in all directions, and plunging a silver port funnel from the Arts and Crafts period (probably late 1890s, well made, although not a very attractive example owing to a series of nicks and dents resulting from careless use) into the throat of Professor Idlewild in order to facilitate his continued access to oxygen.

In all of this confusion—like Harry Callaghan—I forget myself sufficiently that I accidentally chat up and make friends with the fine-featured woman sitting opposite me, and it emerges that her name is Beth, and that she is from Herringbone and that she has just left her boyfriend because he was seeing a dancer named Boots on the side. By the time Professor Idlewild has sufficiently recovered himself to break into the conversation, I have even managed to make some forays into the knotty problem of what we will talk about when we go for a drink later in the week. The answer, of course, is politics.

POLITICS IS very much in fashion at Jarndice, because—aside from being a topic specifically frowned upon in Ye Ordinanses—it is also one which provokes lively debate, passionate shouting matches and wildly inconsistent positions, and is therefore ideal for student posturing and social one-upmanship. The flashpoint of the day is the Addeh Katir Problem.

Addeh Katir is a small nation rubbing shoulders with a variety of big ones. It is temperate and tropical both, richly colourful, lush and splendid. A great chain of lakes runs along its spine (the largest of these being Lake Addeh, quietly famous because its water was for many years reckoned to be the last word in teamaking) and this fertile interior is wrapped in sheltering peaks, the eponymous Katirs, which jut eastwards from the Himalayas and have embraced Lake Addeh and its smaller companions as if determined to keep them.

Politically, the best description of Addeh Katir might be that it is broken. There are many failed states, but this one has rather been vandalised. The place has no inherent ethnic tensions owing to the somewhat unique circumstances of its creation: the people of today's Addeh Katir are descended from assorted thoughtful souls who grew bored with the endless pendulum of massacres and treaties in their own countries, and also with a curious ban on fermented beverages being then imposed by party-poopers of the Buddhist, Muslim, Christian and Hindu faiths, and also by various other sects and cults with a me-too approach to religious prohibition. They therefore hoofed it from what are now China, Tibet, Pakistan and India, and headed to the Katir mountains to hide out and (to be honest) get drunk. Arriving on the shores of Lake Addeh, they found that the entire indigenous population had been wiped out by a variation of rubella to which they were by and large immune.

Thus presented with a nation ready-made, they proceeded to divide the overlarge parcel of land as equitably as they knew how, and set about living as quietly as they could. They selected as their leader a minor noble expelled from his home for unrecorded but minor sins and basically told him not to bug them too much, and he didn't, and nor did his son, or his son, and so on, a tradition of benign indifference which has endured into the present. Their languages blended together, and so did their genes, and after a few generations they forgot they'd ever been from anywhere else. The British conquered Addeh Katir as a matter of course, looked at the infrastructure and established that the Katiris were quite content to fly any damn silly flag as long as they were allowed to get on with it. Bored ladies and jaded gentlemen of the Raj spent a certain amount of time chasing nubile Katiris up and down wooden staircases and along polished verandas, and that—along with the adoption of English as Addeh Katir's second tongue—was by and large the full extent of the Imperialist Yoke. The colonial project is considerably less enjoyable when you can't think of any improvements and the place runs itself so well that you feel rude making suggestions. When the British departed the subcontinent in 1947, there was a brief period of unrest brought about by a cartel of opium traders seeking to move their product along the waterways of Addeh Katir. The reaction of the lake-dwellers was sufficiently emphatic that the project was abandoned.

In 1966, however, the All Asian Investment & Progressive Banking Group—under the great Developmental Initiative which was begun in that year with a view to raising the entire world beyond the reach of poverty through triumphant large-scale capitalism—made a loan to Addeh Katir. It was a most curious loan in that it was not requested and the nation never drew on it. It sat in an account and accumulated a certain amount of interest. Strangely, however, the incurred debt accumulated interest more rapidly. Thus, in 1986, when the loan was due to be repaid, the bank was in fact owed several tens of millions of dollars in addition to the original enormous amount. Addeh Katir was called to account. The maharaja pointed out that he hadn't asked for a loan, didn't need it, had entered into no contract with anyone and had never benefited from the money. The All Asian Investment & Progressive Banking Group responded that while this argument was not without *intuitive appeal,* the situation was now ipso facto a *counterintuitive* matter, in that it dealt with the intricacies of the economic system, which often defied common sense, and that the nation of Addeh Katir had benefited from a perception by investing businesses that the loan was there to be drawn on at need. The maharaja responded that no businesses had invested in Addeh Katir. No businesses, in fact, had been invited to do so. Addeh Katir was just fine, thank you. The All Asian Investment & Progressive Banking Group got snarky and told the maharaja to pay up. The maharaja, very politely, told the All Asian Investment & Progressive Banking Group to stick this suggestion in its ear. The All Asian Investment & Progressive Banking Group alerted the members of the North Atlantic Treaty Organisation to the now-obvious truth: the maharaja was a cryptocommunist.

The maharaja was overthrown during an extremely expensive and well-organised insurgency of questionable representativeness and replaced by one Erwin Mohander Kumar, an Anglo-Indian immigrant, former drug-smuggler and noted syphilitic, who under the banner of the Katiri Provisional Authority was detailed to bring Addeh Katir into the economic fold. He immediately signed a document committing the nation to paying its debt, and followed this up by according himself certain seigneurial prerogatives regarding the women of the locality. Addeh Katir collapsed into civil war, but at least there was no danger of it falling into the hands of the communists.

The Addeh Katir Problem of the new semester is a consequence of this sad chapter. Erwin Kumar's depredations have created a resistance movement. The lakes of Addeh are now home to a kind of buccaneer named Zaher Bey, reportedly a giant warrior, a militarised Gandhi, who has been acclaimed ruler of the islands and of a nation of piratical revolutionaries. This Colossus, clad only in traditional sailor's trousers and brandishing a great cutlass in either massive fist, absolutely rejects the Katiri debt, and has inspired in the womanhood of Addeh Katir and the surrounding nations a twittering of fraught sexual fascination. A Bollywood film has been released which features a marriageable girl falling into the Bey's awful clutches, and (through the media of dance numbers, upbeat love songs and demure glances) taming him so as to make of the monster an ideal husband. It is a weird combination of *Beauty and the Beast* and *My Fair Lady.* The racy subtext is that the Bey is something of a wild man in the sack, and one of the numbers was adjudged too fruity for domestic circulation, assuring instant distribution in electronic samizdat form through the sprawling internet/sneakernet of southern Asia. The Zaher Bey of this snappy piece of political commentary makes no mention of elections or responsible democratic government, but is not in any sense a diseased maniac with (as now turns out to be the case with Erwin Kumar) a foot fetish. The question under discussion in the halls of Jarndice—where, quite clearly, secret opinion-seekers wait around every corner to rush convincing students to the halls of international policymaking—is whether the mysterious Zaher Bey should be supported as a friend of all mankind or reviled as a terrorist.

Alas, it emerges that Beth believes the latter, and I the former. Our date is a bust, and she leaves me at our table to talk to a portly third-year named Dhugal, with an *h.*

Furious and hairy in cheap cowboy boots and a chequered red-and-black workshirt, I am the very model of modern disaffected youth. I am the spectrum of discontent, and each colour takes me far less than a whole winter. I wear a baseball cap and low-slung jeans and shout abuse at the smart set. I wear skintight black PVC and white foundation and I glower and mourn the death of Byron in the back of the bar. From there I discover punk, and briefly have no hair at all, then am mistaken for a fascist by a group of businessmen who proceed to celebrate my bravery and drink my health, and driven by this horror I grow it out again. I go yuppie, briefly, when I get so angry at the world in general that I reject my own generation and its pathetic caring for this vile planet, and then I rediscover radicalism by sexual transmission. My co-revolutionist's name is Aline.

Aline of the tangled dark hair and the improbable lips; Aline of the Roman nose and the pasta chef's fingers; Aline of the astoundingly loud orgasms. She corners me after a study group and demands that I account for my ill-considered and old-fashioned views. She pins me to the wall and sets an arm on either side of me to prevent my escape, then lambasts me with referenced and footnoted counterpoints, and when I splutter my best high male affront, she leans closer and parts her lips, and silences me with a lush and frankly erotic kiss. Her mouth tastes of coffee and cigarettes and chewing gum, and she has thought this out (the politics and the kiss) far better than I. I am, however, just smart enough to respond by wrapping my arms around her and making the whole thing my decision, in so far as that is still possible, which is a delusion she allows me to keep. When we come up for air, it is time for dinner, and she knows just the place: an unlikely club tucked between a bank and a post office, a narrow corridor of tables opening onto a smoke-filled lounge at the back. It is called Caucus (definite and indefinite articles denote a bourgeois need to distinguish a favoured locality from one which is accessible to the lumpenproletariat, and hence Caucus—known like a dear friend as *Cork*—eschews them, and indeed the inadvertent use of articles on sequential occasions can be grounds for suspension or some form of forfeit) and it is an old and respected bastion of radical opinion. I eat at Cork for months, and Aline feeds me sexual ecstasy and political agony, and I become, if not a man, at least a reasonable facsimile thereof, and there is a bounce in my step, and a swagger, and I grow familiar with the faces around me and gradually even understand something of what they talk about.

The denizens of Cork go by names like Iggy, Quippe and Brahae—this by choice rather than because their mothers called them such things—and they lean heavily towards black jeans and leather waistcoats. They will argue about almost anything, at any time, but mostly they argue about the Global Open Market Agreement (which is not exciting) and the Eurasian Economic Partnership (which is even less so) because these unexciting things govern who is rich and who is poor and who starves and who survives, all of which are rather more interesting.

"GOMA will fall," Aline asserts one afternoon, "because it depends on constant correction by the government—that's not an invisible hand, it's a glass fist, and sooner or later it will shatter and the whole illusion will come—" And surely she intends to say "apart," but she does not because Quippe, who is meaty and a cheat at cards, flings up his chubby hands and cries out that she is insane, that GOMA is perfectly balanced on the moralistic spike up its own arse, and nothing short of revolutionary surgery will get it off.

"Poppycock," says Sebastian, and there is silence. Sebastian does not speak on small matters. Like Aline, he is somewhat Italian, and like her also he has served time in the student brigades. He has been struck repeatedly by oppressing policemen and once set fire to a barricade in Amsterdam. Sebastian can quote a string of revolutionaries from Socrates to Lenin to Michael Moore and knows the numbers on any claim you care to make. He knows how much the sea level has risen and which nations are most at risk. He knows the precise atmospheric projections for the next ten years, the next twenty, the end of the century. He knows the GDP of Uganda and the percentage of the total global economy which is derived from drugs and prostitution. He knows all this, or can make it up so smoothly and uncheckably that the difference is moot.

"Revolution," Sebastian says, as if we should all have known this already, "is *reaction.* It's the body politic in spasm. When was the last time you saw someone in the throes of an epileptic fit?"

No one mentions Lay Chancellor Idlewild, but his dandruffed head hangs like a collective hallucination before us.

"So," says Sebastian, "would you choose that moment to ask the patient about taxation? Or, would they mind holding your newborn child? No? So why on Earth would you imagine that a revolution would be the ideal moment to propound a better way of living?" He rolls his eyes, which by coincidence draws everyone's gaze to the narrow and very fetching scar which marks his otherwise flawless brow—courtesy of a Dutch riot policeman whom Sebastian later befriended.

"The problem isn't *who* is in charge. It's *what* is in charge. The problem is that people are encouraged to function *as machines.* Or, actually, *as mechanisms.* Human emotion and sympathy are *unprofessional.* They are inappropriate to the exercise of *reason.* Everything which makes people good—makes them human—is ruled out. The system doesn't care about people, but we treat it as if it were one of us, as if it were the sum of our goods and not the product of our least admirable compromises. The only revolution which matters," Sebastian concludes, "is the one where we stand up and do it for ourselves."

When he doesn't get much in the way of response, Sebastian shrugs and returns to his magazine and his vodka tonic. Aline picks up the conversational ball and runs for the scoring line. Quippe and the others are still goggling a bit at the idea that revolution might be a bad thing, and she touches down with ". . . and *that's* why the means of production [citations, quote] is teleologically orientated towards penetrative modes [citations, data], which entails ambient and inherent injustice on a monstrous scale!" And everyone nods. Aline glances at me and licks her lips, because political discussion leads inevitably in one direction for her, and we leave and go to my apartment. Society may—or may not—be teleologically oriented towards penetrative modes, but there's no question about Aline.

Sex and politics and a free passport to cool are all a growing boy could wish, and the high is compounded when we demonstrate and shout and flee the myrmidons of the law and steal a policeman's helmet and mount it over the bar at Cork. When the drunken conga line of victory is over and we adjourn to Aline's flat, it transpires that the helmet is not all she has stolen. I emerge from the shower to find her nude and wearing nothing but a pair of service-issue handcuffs and kneeling, breathless, on her own bed. Fortunately, she has also stolen the key.

THE PHONE CALL comes the following morning. It is Elisabeth Soames, but she is crying and speaking almost entirely in a foreign language. I try to slow her down. I ask her, very gently and simply, to be calm, and to speak English—or at least I attempt to do this, but some transference has occurred and I cannot actually say anything, because my throat has closed and my mouth is full of salt and water. When I've dealt with that, my nose starts running and I find tears on my face. Elisabeth rants at me, or rather she screams and rages in general and I am the person who is witness to it. The whole time, she keeps lapsing into her alien tongue: strange, hard syllables which have no place in my head, which make no sense. And still, perhaps because she is so upset, I cannot stop crying and my throat is raw. At some point in all this, I look for Aline, but she has left for an early lecture. I am not sure whether this is desertion or mercy. I am not sure whether she was here when the phone rang.

Elisabeth is silent for a while, or at least she doesn't talk. She rasps down the phone, and when I listen I realise that I am hearing my own breathing as well, phlegmy and uneven. We have been doing this for over an hour. And finally I can hear what she has been saying. I can remember the conversation, the endless, circular awfulness of the last sixty minutes, and I know she has not been speaking a foreign language at all. It's not the words which are the problem, it's the thing itself. She has been telling me that Wu Shenyang is dead. And with that understanding I lose track of however long it takes until I am standing outside what used to be his house, and she is sitting alone on the kerb, with her feet in the gutter, and that is how I spend my day.

Ma Lubitsch taught me there was only ever one truth. That was how you knew it; it was unique. There were no multiple versions of events, there was no "from a certain point of view." Ma Lubitsch is above all a mother, and motherhood is not a binary state. But here, by the roadside, in front of the smouldering char which was the House of the Voiceless Dragon, there are two truths. Both of them acknowledge certain facts. This house is number five in the street. It was inhabited by an old man of Chinese origin, and contained a collection of antique weapons, a lot of geriatric furniture and an antique gramophone. Sometime between six and midnight, when they returned, a fire started on the garden side of the house, which swiftly consumed the place.

So much is, as it were, the skeleton. The fire, however, has consumed the flesh, and so the skull of truth has two faces. The first is simple and bleakly comfortable. Yumei and Ophelia were staying with Master Wu while their home was being redecorated, but were out that evening at a puppet show. Alone, and perhaps lonely, Wu Shenyang went to bed late, having consumed a certain amount of brandy. He neglected to place the guard in front of the fire, and thus a stray spark emitted from green logs crackled across the room and ignited the mismatched curtains. The house was filled with paper and wood, and the blaze was rapid and very hot. This would be a hard truth. That kind of grief is of a commonplace sort, and it is cool enough to hold.

The second face is fanciful. There is no evidence for it. It is a hero's death. It goes like this:

The big clock is *tock tick*ing and the fire is low. Master Wu is eating spiced apple cake—Elisabeth has sent him one in a Tupperware pot. Master Wu is fascinated by Tupperware. The variety of it, the fabulous utility of reusable, sealable plastic containers pleases him. This box is the new kind with the little wings which clip down over the side to make the boxes airtight. He is holding the box loosely in one hand and flipping the side up, *clack,* and down again, *plick plack;* there are two fastenings on each side—they open as one, but you have to close them individually. *Clack . . . plick plack.* The plastic is cool, but still ductile or elastic (this part of my mind doesn't have full access to my education, isn't sure which word is appropriate). It is bendy, anyway, bendy enough that old fingers can open it without catching fingernails or abrading skin. *Clack . . . plick plack.* The apple cake is very good. It is fresh and sweet, with moist bits of apple and the applegoo which happens when you make a cake like this and get it just right. There are none of those awful retch-inducing bits of core which some cooks insist are an important part of the apple, presumably out of a false sense of parsimony, because those bits ruin perfectly good mouthfuls and therefore consume scarce apple cake resources. Elisabeth is an apple cake perfectionist. *Clack . . . plick plack.* Master Wu's fingers trace the smooth curve of the Tupperware box. It is a largish one. This particular model, he knows, comes with two segmented trays, so that you can store different but related foodstuffs in it. You could keep, for example, two portions of chicken, two of rice, and two of vegetables in oyster sauce. He does not actually like oyster sauce. It always tastes of oysters. *Clack . . . plick plack.* The box lid is a smooth quadrilateral with stubby wings. It is reinforced across the top with flanges or stanchions, injection-moulded as part of the lid form. It is not heavy, but it is strong. The base is more flexible, possibly so that it can absorb little shocks and knocks, possibly to allow for food and liquids which contract on cooling. The plastic is also resilient to being cut, almost sucks together around the small nicks and scars where someone has cut a cake *inside* it—something Master Wu would never do. *Clack . . . plick plack . . . tink.*

Master Wu does not change his position. He does not tense. He is exactly as he was a moment ago. And yet everything is different. The noise *tink* is a specific thing. It has implications and layers of significance, like a sort of deranged domino game spread out across several floors of a mansion house. It is the sound made by the leftmost bell on the middle line. It means that a small amount of pressure has been applied to the middle window. The fact that only one bell sounded means that it was a very, very slight pressure, and it has now been withdrawn. It is as if a butterfly took off from the window. At this time of night, of course, it would be a moth. *Clack . . . plick plack.* So. The moth has departed. However . . . *tink.* It has a somewhat heavier-handed friend, perhaps a boy-moth chasing a girl-moth. If so, he is doing so just by the window on the right. And . . . *tinktink* . . . the girl-moth is a game lass, and she is running him all around the house and all the way over to . . . *tink* . . . the window on the left.

Master Wu is sitting in the rocker. He is an old man. He has eaten a lot of cake and drunk some tea, and he's been playing with a Tupperware box for half an hour. If the cause of the bell ringing were not a pair of randy moths—if, for example, someone were thinking of entering his house with a view to assassinating him—they could not fail to see that he is over the hill. A harmless old geezer who is now falling asleep, lulled by the rhythm of his own fidgeting and the gentle movement of the chair. Perhaps he has chosen this fraught moment to enter a second childhood. His eyelids droop, but do not quite close. He is so old that the difference is hard to detect.

The man who comes through the leftmost window is big, which makes his silence all the more scary. He is in amazing shape; in order to step through as fast and quietly as he does, he has essentially to do the splits while standing on one leg, hold it, extend himself into the room and never lose his balance or his control as he moves onto the other foot. All this he does in a fraction of an eyeblink. The bells on the window make one more *tink* noise before he stills them.

Master Wu does not wake. He mumbles something, paws at his Tupperware. The intruder freezes. Two more men enter the room through the same window. More wait in the garden. There is an army out there. The ninjas—the foot soldiers of the Clockwork Hand Society—have finally come for Wu Shenyang. And as they look down at the old fart dozing in his chair, and as they realise that they have come all this way in such numbers and with such caution to deal with one octagenarian has-been, the leader gives a soft, unpleasant chuckle.

The lid of the Tupperware box hits him squarely over the eye. It's not a dangerous cut, but it makes his forehead bleed and he can't see clearly. He loses depth perception almost immediately, and so he cannot defend himself as the rocking chair flings Master Wu forward and almost into his arms. He thrusts and twists with his longknife, and it finds a target, but that target is the base of the Tupperware box. Master Wu twists it sharply. The plastic clutches around the knife blade, and the other man cannot easily withdraw it or hold onto it and consequently is in danger of being disarmed. His decision to cling to his weapon is instinctive, given that he has already been partially blinded and is not yet caught up with events as they are unfolding. Master Wu does not attempt to take the knife away. He accepts the direction his enemy has chosen, and flows with it, continues it and suddenly owns it. The other man finds his hips out of synch with his feet, his hands too far away from the centre line of his body for his arms to bring their strength to bear. The cycle ends with Master Wu in possession of the longknife, and the big man on tiptoe with the razor's edge under his chin. That's what you get for ignoring the beauty of Tupperware.

Master Wu chooses not to kill the man at this time. That is, in a sense, the definition of being a good guy. He knocks him out and hopes, very briefly, that his enemy will reconsider the path his life has taken. Then he steps smoothly between two more opponents and redirects their attacks towards each other. Regrettably, they are trying very hard to kill him and one of them therefore sustains a nasty wound high in the chest. This distracts his partner, and Master Wu takes advantage of this, propelling him backwards into two of his friends who are preparing an attack of their own.

The fight scene goes on, and it is fluid and magnificent, but at some point Master Wu realises something. He is getting tired, and they are not. He is unscathed, but by the same token he cannot sustain injuries, or he will lose. He has to be perfect; they only have to be persistent. He realises that even if he can beat all these men—even if he were to kill them, one by one—more will come, at a time and place not of his choosing. If he continues this battle much longer, the likelihood is that Yumei and Ophelia will come home, and even if they are not killed, they will be exposed. At the moment Master Wu could well be a bachelor. The ninjas have no knowledge of his family arrangements, because they haven't had the opportunity to look around inside the house, and that's where all the family photos are. They've seen only this room, and they've been kinda busy. Similarly, they do not have any idea who his students are. All that information is in the desk. Thus, he is the weak link in his enemies' chain. Without him, they simply cannot find the Voiceless Dragon. It will be not only silent, but invisible. That's the kind of situation which makes a ninja's shoulder blades itch. It will be interesting to see how they like having the shoe on the other foot. And it is at this point that he makes a decision.

There are three men coming for him now. They approach slightly out of time with one another, which makes dealing with them exponentially more difficult, and by-the-by implies that they're very good. It's hard to avoid accepting the rhythm of those around you. Master Wu steps to meet one of his attackers, then slides through the space another is preparing to occupy, and slams the second man into the first. Both of them tumble into the fireplace and ignite. The third man hesitates, then breaks off to haul them out. Master Wu takes the opportunity to open the liquor cabinet and select two bottles. He smashes them over his head, creating two extremely unpleasant weapons and also drenching himself in alcohol. He steps to one side, allowing a fresh enemy to destroy the cabinet, breaking more bottles, and then he moves around the room, leaving a trail. He ducks and bobs, slices and scores, his arms whirling and twisting around his body. As he passes the fireplace, he shuffles, splashes booze into the flames. An instant later, fire laps at his feet, following him as he continues around the room. The curtains catch, and the painted walls start to smoke. The ninjas pursue him; blades slash past his back and over his head, heavy hands clutch at him and stamping feet thunder against the ground where he is no longer standing. They cannot touch him. Wu Shenyang is made of water.

And then, amid the chaos, there is a single perfect moment of stillness, as all the actions and reactions are held in balance. Master Wu smiles, reaches out to the flames and catches fire. He is still smiling as he turns to the remaining ninjas, a glass razor in each hand, burning arms spread wide. Every single one of them will remember this feeling for the rest of their lives, in quiet moments and in the cold, truthful hours of the night, and every time they see Tupperware. They will remember the terrible old man with placid eyes who stepped nimbly towards them while his skin blistered and his hair fizzled away; who advanced as they fell back. They will remember that he forced them out of his home into the night, and that he followed them, and kept them at bay until the house and all its contents were beyond salvation, and then kneeled down neatly to expire, at peace, while they cowered in the dark. They will remember it as the moment they discovered fear.

MASTER WU's funeral is surprisingly large. It seems he knew nearly everyone in Cricklewood Cove. Every tradesman, every family, every teacher from the Soames School, everyone from every beach house and second home, all of them arrive to see him off. People bring cakes and tea, and we all stand and raise them in salute—I had no idea he knew so many people. I mention it to Elisabeth.

"I asked them to come," she says. "It's traditional to have a lot of guests. And I couldn't—" Her mouth gets very tight, and her hands clench in her pockets. I know what she is not able to say; I too am disappointed. The people we could not find—despite great efforts—are Master Wu's other students. In every city, on every continent, the Voiceless Dragon has vanished—boiled away like steam. Or, perhaps, ashamed to have left him alone, they're just dodging our calls.

In the midst of the crowd, Yumei and Ophelia are almost invisible, two more guests at a big, bewildered show funeral for an old man. The urn is very small, so it's not clear who carries it as we walk solemnly out of town to the sea. We scatter Master Wu into the wind from a high place, and he drifts like a cloud until the breeze whisks him off on new adventures. Elisabeth embraces me, then turns away, and we grieve separately.

Gonzo and Aline, always uneasy in each other's company, take turns with me when I return to Jarndice. They get me drunk and make me forget or at least live through it all, until two weeks later I wake and discover that although the sky is grey and the world is dark, it is a dark which rouses my heart rather than subdues it. It is evening, and I am not hungover. I can function again, and indeed I am supercharged. The presence of death has woken me in some profound way, and I take great bites out of life. Aline and I screw like mink, and I leap from the bed as if sleep is for other people, and devour books and concerts and beverages and vast amounts of food. I put on several pounds of bulk. I wear my shirt open halfway down my chest without irony, and no one sees fit to mock. I am Tarzan, I am Long John Silver, I am *all goddam that.* Behold! Gonzo finds me alarming.

I reel from lecture to Cork to party to demonstration and the faces blur until the police are more familiar than the demonstrators, because although our comrades in linked arms and flowers are drawn from the same pool, we are always at the front, and spend more time looking through riot shields than back at our fellows. At one rally I am gashed by a falling stone, flung most probably from the back, but I am hailed as a hero and make the cover of the local news, and a genial letter arrives from the police superintendent saying he hopes I have sustained no lasting injury. To Aline's momentary disgust I reply chirpily that I am well and hope that he is too. She forgives me only when I point out that he has admitted tacit responsibility for something he almost certainly did not do, and when the scores are tallied this will count against him. I place telephone calls to Sweden and ask them to send a speaker to Cork, and when they agree (a tedious little man shows up from the embassy and tells us about mineral rights in the North Sea until we get him drunk and send him home with an ostrich feather in the back of his trousers). I call Moscow, Sydney, Rome (and the Vatican), Poland and even Addeh Katir in the hope of further coups.

Calling Addeh Katir is exciting and difficult because the dialling code is not listed and eventually I have to ask the caretaker at Cork, who once dated a woman from the Red Cross and knows a guy at the UN who has a number for the office the Katiri Provisional Authority maintains in New York, but when I ring, the receptionist tells me she hasn't been paid since November and she's damned if she's taking my message. I tell her she's doing a great deal for international relations, but she has already gone. I hang up and try something more daring.

I call a man who knows a man who once dated this girl whose address book contains reference to a person (gender unknown) who apparently has contact with a certain scholar. The scholar is close to the great Colossus, the destroyer of sound economic practice and layer-waste of treaty obligations; the ravisher of coyly willing maidens (and matrons); the master swordsman and gargantuan, fearless, indestructible freak of nature; the titanic warrior Fred Astaire of Addeh Katir himself, Zaher Bey.

This chain of loose acquaintance yields a cell-phone number with a Swiss area code, which is answered by a querulous individual of indeterminate sex.

"Konditorei Lauener, hello?"

"Hello? I'm looking for Zaher Bey."

"We have none. Only the hotel is now permitted to make it."

This response confuses me. I was not prepared for an exchange of sign and countersign. I grope for something suitably espiocratic, but the other person interrupts before I can assemble the requisite parts.

"There was a legal case, you see. The people at the hotel required an adjudication. It is their mark, you see. Anyone can make a chocolate cake *in the Sacher style,* ne? But only they can make *Sachertorte.* It's the law. But in any case," the personage adds, with some satisfaction, "we have none."

It appears that my interlocutor has misconstrued "Zaher Bey" as "Sacher Cake." I explain that I am in fact looking for the leader of a political movement arising in response to foreign economic imperialism and a puppet regime predicated on the lust of Erwin Kumar. There is something of a pause.

"You know that it's a cake shop?" the personage says at last, probably uncertain about whether to continue the discussion.

"This is the number I was given," I explain. My voice has slipped from professional and commanding to apologetic.

"You should give it back!" This with some amusement. "You have a bad number. This number, it's a cake shop. In Basel. That's in the north, huh? We have lots of cake. But no revolutionaries. Revolution, the shouting and breaking things. It's un-Swiss."

This information delivered, the personage politely disengages, and I sit by the phone trying to figure out what to do next.

Two days later, a dapper gentleman in his forties sits down at my table in Cork. How he has secured entrance I do not know, but he is carrying a glass of single malt from the bar and gives every evidence of being comfortable with his surroundings.

Mr. ibn Solomon (such being the name he gives me) has an almost unnoticeable pot belly and a fine blue suit. His skin is clear and fairly dark. He looks as you might imagine a Phoenician merchant or a Moorish market trader. He is clean-shaven and twinkly, and has well-kept hands. His voice is soft, and it is something of a surprise when he reveals that his full accorded title is Freeman ibn Solomon, Ambassador Plenipotentiary of the Bey's forces in Free Addeh Katir. Will he speak to the assembled thinkers and drinkers of the club? You betcha. It is his pleasure and his vocation. But Freeman ibn Solomon is a strict believer in single-level discussion and negotiation. No dais and no lectern; he will sit in this fine lounge and he will share in our conversation like one of us. And to demonstrate his willingness to be like us, he knocks back his Bruichladdich and obligingly fetches himself another.

"WE HAVE a gun mountain," says Freeman ibn Solomon. "You people are cursed with milk lakes and grain plains and all the rest. We have a gun mountain. We don't really mind having all your spare guns," adds Freeman ibn Solomon. "We just wish you'd put them right on the pile. They come into our country in little dribs and drabs. They go to Erwin Kumar and he loses them or he sells them and they show up all over the place. Only a week ago I found a whole crate of them in my kitchen, under the broccoli. And of course," he adds, without a trace of anger or irony, "very occasionally someone gets shot with them, which is so upsetting."

Iggy comes to the defence of the international system. It's very strange. Most of the time Iggy and the others bemoan the iniquity of the capitalist hegemony (that is, everything in the world). Now here is Freeman ibn Solomon, saying things they often say, but they are trying to persuade him it's not all that bad. This is probably because, when Freeman ibn Solomon says it, and puts it in context, you can't help but feel it could be your fault.

"You're not exactly representative, though, are you?"

"Good God, no," Freeman says, "we don't represent at all."

Iggy leans back, having established the fly in this dangerously perfect ointment.

"No," Freeman ibn Solomon continues, "we are a participant democracy. Everyone takes part of every decision, if there's time. Otherwise, of course, the Bey is afforded an executive right of action, so that we can't be caught sleeping. But we have no laws."

Iggy stares at him. Sebastian, behind a vodka tonic, opens his eyes and looks on with interest. Aline sputters.

"No laws?" she demands.

"No," says Freeman ibn Solomon. "Law is error, you see. It's an attempt to write down a lot of things everyone ought to know anyway. We don't have that. Every one of us is expected to act within the constraints of right thinking, and to be prepared to stand by the consequences of those actions. That is," he adds, "not as comfortable a position as you might think." And he takes another sip of his whisky.

"Doesn't that lead to corruption?" Aline wants to know.

"Oh yes," says Freeman ibn Solomon. "I mean, in a sense it's hard to tell. We're a pirate nation, so we have less formal administration. But yes, everyone feathers his own nest to some degree. On the other hand, anyone can be held accountable. There's always a person you can argue with." He shrugs. "With governments," he says, "you choose your poison. This is ours."

He looks so crestfallen that the discussion turns to other things, and then Quippe strikes up at the piano, and we are privileged to watch the Ambassador Plenipotentiary dance the cancan with Aline and a girl named Yolande who shaves one half of her head.

Once it gets out that we had a man from Addeh Katir on the campus, every other far-flung cause and dissident voice in the spectrum suddenly recognises our seriousness, and our importance as a free-thinking zone. I bring new causes to Cork, and new speakers, and some are friendly and some aren't, but I'm totally the man, and each speaker seems to make Aline randier and we all but wear out the oppressive manacles of the state oppressor and it's getting to the point where we'll have to pinch some new ones. Addeh Katir fades from the public view because the negotiations there are somewhat bogged down. The United Nations Security Council refuses to accept the request of Zaher Bey to send a peacekeeping force. Cork goes practically schismatic over whether this is a step in the right direction (away from quasi-totalitarian cultural hegemonising) or the wrong one (towards an isolationist economic imperium), but finally settles on having a foam party. Life goes on.

In Erwinville the great president continues his thirty-year rampage through the Kama Sutra.

Around Lake Addeh, Zaher Bey's faction maintains a semblance of order and infrastructure through a black market more efficient and humane than the legal economy.

Aline shaves her pubic region in protest against the fur trade. Despite this distraction, I manage to stagger through my exams.

Gonzo receives a care package from Ma Lubitsch which contains so much food and drink of such staggering richness that he can barely store it all in his accommodation. I am particularly fond of the oatmeal meringue with raspberries.

The idyll lasts until one morning, when I am sitting at the coffee table working on my biology coursework and not really listening to Sebastian telling Quippe that "the freedom of movement and the speed of communication intrinsic to the Late-Modern period entails but does not legitimate the demise of the Age of Presence," when guys in balaclavas explode—literally, explode, because their arrival is preceded by a blast of light and sound which makes my nose itch and my ears bleed—through the butler's pantry and the honour bar, and throw us all violently down to the floor and grind our faces into the threadbare carpet, so that I inhale an almost uncountable number of dust mites and the faintest odour of sexual congress. One of the balaclava guys yells somewhat redundantly that this is a raid.

I lift my head up. Aline is just across from me, dark hair charmingly and sexily askew, face utterly shell-shocked and afraid, and this in turn makes me afraid, because she's been through more revolution than I have and she never mentioned anything like this. I gasp her name and she doesn't look at me, and one of the shouting men comes and shouts into my face and I get lifted up and carted off alone because I am clearly more of a subversive than the others, or possibly because I have—equally clearly—been doinking the cute subversive in the skintight jeans and this is a very good reason for me to suffer.

The interior of a security services truck is a very bad place. It smells of fear and unwashed or unperfumed individuals and there aren't any cushions. My cuffs are linked to a big hoop in the floor and I envisage a sort of built-in padlock mechanism and wonder what would happen if the truck were to fall into one of the many rivers around Jarndice and conclude that there must be some kind of auto-release and then conclude that there probably isn't. I place my trust, and my hope, in the shaven head which is visible through the grillework, and try very hard to be a good convict and not a danger to society and also not to throw up, because being in the back of a windowless truck with your head between your knees in the Jarndice heat is conducive to nausea.

From the chatter on the radio and the exchange of monosyllables between the driver and his fellows, I glean the information that the guys in balaclavas are not technically soldiers. They are a nominally non-military task force for civilian defence and counter-terror. They are in fact an internal hire; the armed forces have loaned them to the security arm of the government, so for the duration of their present employment they are functioning as civilians. This means that they are trained as soldiers, beweaponed as soldiers, can fight and if need be *kill* like soldiers, but can be deployed at home and abroad without reference to annoying statutes like Posse Comitatus or the UIK's Bill of Rights. Curiously, *not* being soldiers frees them to be more unpleasant to people who are also not soldiers.

They march up and down the lines of hangdog detainees and scream that we are *quislings,* which seems like a particularly arcane thing to be upset about. Every now and again, they slap someone across the back of the head, or a detainee rashly objects and is silenced with a kick or a closed fist. Then they shout some more. We are *backstabbers, treasonists, collaborators, fifth columnists, turncoats* and *copperheads.* After we have been processed—this basically means taking our names, addresses and any confirmatory ID, and then sequestering our belts and shoelaces—a junior officer drops in to our cells to add that we may well be *Arnolds* and *Haw Haws.* I wonder, briefly, whether they're working from a thesaurus.

The holding cells are not high-tech. In some part of my head I was expecting gleaming corridors and bio-monitors and polygraphs. I was not expecting ad hoc detention facilities made by running chicken wire in a grid through the middle of a warehouse. I was not expecting single-bulb lighting and iron buckets to pee in. This place does not feel like my country. It feels like countries I have read about where things are very bad. It feels, in fact, like exactly the kind of thing we were protesting against, but we thought it was elsewhere. It is not heartening to find that it has come to us.

I am sharing my cell with Iggy and Sebastian and two or three persons I do not know who are obviously not students, because they are older and crustier and work for a living. They are unionists in the real sense, men who organise their work colleagues to stand up together to demand proper—but not outrageous—remuneration and safety codes. They are scared, which is scary, because they know more about this kind of thing than we do.

"Fucking Nazis," Sebastian says. Iggy isn't at all sure that's what they are—the frequent invocation of Holocaust imagery is counter-constructive because—

"If it puts you in a chicken-wire box," Sebastian says firmly, "and treats you like a sub-human, and it wears a sexy uniform and claims all this is for the greater good, it's a Nazi."

At which point they storm into the cell and pull him out and hood him, and Sebastian looks steadfast except that as he reaches the door I hear him start to cry. It's probably not the case that they "storm," not really. We can see them coming. They walk with purpose, and there are several of them looking muscular in their spiffy uniforms, but while they fling open the door, it is nothing when compared with their earlier entrance through the butler's pantry at Cork. They do not shout. There's no flash grenade, no barging and shoving. Still and all, they do what they do with the ease of long practice and a powerful kinetic energy, an odour of power which hurls us back from Sebastian and allows them to scoop him up as if weightless and carry him away. They do not bring him back. We keep expecting them to, but they don't. They do not bring anyone back, and gradually our warehouse gets quieter and emptier and more afraid.

I find myself talking. Almost everyone else is quiet, and most of them are sitting or leaning, but I cannot stop pacing and my mouth seems to be running by itself. I want to know if this can possibly be lawful, and if it isn't, whether that's better or worse for us. I ask if anyone has any experience with arrest, or any legal training, and Barry (the second unionist) points out that anyone who does might not wish to say so in a detention area which might well be monitored. That stops me asking questions for a while, but inspires me to search for listening devices until Iggy points out that they wouldn't have to be visible. I keep searching, in case they're there and I'm *supposed* to be able to find them, and Iggy starts to tell me to be quiet and sit the fuck down when the men come again. Barry walks towards them, offering his hands, but they ward him off. They step around him and past me, and they draw Iggy firmly out and cover him up, and when he stumbles they drag him along until his feet catch up.

"Not good," Barry says.

"Why not?"

"Well, if they want us in order, it follows they know who we are, doesn't it?"

And if they know who we are, or think they know, then this is at least not a simple mistake. They believe they have something. Barry shrugs and sits down. Clearly, he says, the ones they take away are simply placed in a separate area of confinement, so that they will not be able to prepare us for what's to come. It'll be fine. May take a bit longer to untangle, but it'll turn out right.

I preferred it when he wasn't worried enough to reassure me, and I wish he weren't shaking so much. I worry that I'm going to die here, disappear for ever. I tell myself this is part of the interrogation. It doesn't help.

The men come back, and the officer's boots are leaving little dark red prints. I hope to God he has walked through a freshly painted road sign, but know that he has not. They take Barry and he gives me a nod and says "Bear up" and this annoys them so they gag him before they hood him. Twenty minutes of eternity later there is canvas sliding roughly over my skin and it smells strongly of someone else's cheap cologne.

Walking hooded is a curious thing. I cannot see, cannot hear properly. The not-soldiers must hold my arms to guide me. I am dependent on them, but they in turn have to take care of me to this small degree. They are in loco parentis, and I am their ward for the journey from where I was to where I am going. The one on my left leans close. *Couple of steps, one, two, all right, stop . . . there's a good lad.* He seems genuinely pleased. *Turn around . . . now. Sit. There we go . . .*

They put me in a chair. It is uncomfortable, and it is damp. Someone has sweated a great deal in this chair, and possibly more—there is a lingering smell of bleach. They leave the hood on. The guy on the left—he's moved, actually, but it's the same voice—murmurs again: *Now then. You be well-behaved, all right? Much better off that way.* In the background, someone laughs at him and calls him Mr. Nice. *Yes,* he says, *yes, I fucking am.* From which I deduce that there is also a Mr. Nasty. Mr. Nice draws back from my shoulder. The air is just a little cooler without him. I wait.

Then I hear a loud scraping noise. The floor beneath my feet is your standard warehouse concrete, rough and porous, and so I realise that someone has drawn up a chair opposite my own. It is a moderately heavy chair, an office chair without wheels rather than one of those plastic disposable chairs they put in conference centres. The hood is whipped off with disdain for my nose and chin, which suffer minor friction burns, and I am eye to eye with a relaxed, bucolic geezer in a grubby general's jacket who seems to be in charge.

His face is not a surprising face, in the sense that it is big and red and somewhat covered with pale spiky stubble. His eyes are narrow and seem small because they are turned down at the outer corners, as if someone has stitched his eyebrow to his cheek. Part of me recognises this feature as an epicanthic fold, and helpfully supplies the information that it is common in persons of Asian descent, but rare in Europeans (what most Americans call Caucasians despite the fact that the peoples of the Caucasus mountains are a diverse bunch, and certainly not Anglo-Saxon) and sometimes associated with Down's syndrome. Since the man in front of me is clearly and inescapably not Asian, and since it is profoundly unlikely that a person with Down's syndrome could rise to this rank in the services, it seems the general is a minor biological curiosity—but that also is not the cause of the shock I experience on seeing him. I am surprised, even stunned, by the visage of this individual because his name is George Lourdes Copsen, and he is the father of Gonzo's donkey-loving princess bride, Lydia, and I know him and I know that he knows me. I last saw him across the table of a "guess the number of sweeties" stand at the Soames School fete. George Copsen did not guess well. He did not guess at all. Using a pocket calculator, he collated the guesses of the three hundred or so other entrants and produced an answer that was accurate to within the margin of error (i.e., when we came to count them we were unable to prevent one of the first-years from eating between five and ten sweeties). He eyes me with the air of a man who has already been briefed, has seen the file, knows the score, isn't tied to a soggy cushion and who holds a small remote control with a significant red button on it, all of which he is.

"How are ya?" says George Copsen conversationally, and I essay an insouciant nod to demonstrate how much I am in control of the situation despite the fact that I have just been abducted from a dining club by a paramilitary force and strapped to a chair. Unfortunately they have secured my head in some fashion and so I pull some muscles in my neck and look like an idiot. George Copsen grins in a friendly way and suggests I use words, so I tell him I'm fine. Good. A bit nervous, actually, and George Copsen says that I probably should be, but he's going to sort all that out now.

"All you need to do," George Copsen says, "is tell us who recruited you, and what the cell talked about, and what actions they engaged in, and who the others were." And he grins again.

Which is a problem for me because I was never actually recruited. I was signed up sight unseen and I was boned by a wild Italianate activist and I fell in love with her for what I now perceive to be less-than-highbrow reasons, but I was not in fact ever a member of anything more radical than a fraternity of windy drinkers and the rather large club of young men who have acquired radical opinions as a way of getting laid. George Copsen produces a file from somewhere out of my field of vision and leans close. He opens the file like a family Bible and proceeds. His voice is filled with reproach, as if I am a new puppy which has peed on his carpet.

"It seems many of you boys and girls of good family were very much influenced by one particular character. Let's call that person *Mr. A,* shall we? Hell of a man."

Sebastian. Christ. You are so fucked. And they want me to add to it. And what would Gonzo do? Gonzo would never be here. Gonzo is a track and field star, a footballer, a hero to the masses and a lover of profoundly conventional college girls. Gonzo is a free market, entrepreneurial, registered good guy. But

Gonzo would never turn on a friend. Not now, not ever, not for any price and not under someone's guns.

" '*Mr. A* was central to all actions carried out by the cadre at Cork.' " Since when did we have a *cadre*? I'm not even sure what one is. " 'He was a leader to us and a confessor to any who wavered. Without Mr. A, the thing could not have existed.' That's the one called Iggy. What's his real name?"

It's a harmless question. Iggy's clothes still have name tags from his schooldays. "Andrew," I tell George Copsen.

"Here's your man Quippe: '*A* taught us various techniques of subversion ranging from bribery and blackmail to sexual procurement and demolitions.' "

Quippe has clearly gone to town on fantasy. Mind you, perhaps he was encouraged.

"And then there's this little lady: 'I was recruited by one of my fellow students. I cannot overstate the power of his convictions or his resolve. In my case the avenue of approach was sexual; he seduced me and effectively addicted me to his physical presence. He inscribed himself upon my opinions at the same time, and introduced me to the club known as Caucus, which as I have already stated is a front organisation for the indoctrination and training of terroristic elements. I feel now that I lived between sexual obsession and physical fear of this man at all times. Thank you for' "—and here George Copsen's voice is suffused with some emotion which I take to be pity but which might in another setting be hilarity—" 'for *rescuing* me.' Sounds like quite a trip."

Aline, I think, has omitted to tell me that she was once a paramour of Sebastian, or that he exerted such a strong and lasting terror. Except that I have begun to realise that George Copsen is not talking about Sebastian, and this is confirmed when Sebastian's terse, punctuated statement also blames Mr. A for all the world's ills, and it is becoming very apparent that George Copsen is not looking for me to confirm this story, to add to the flames which will burn Mr. A on the pyre. Aline and

Iggy and Quippe are describing someone I do not know, someone I have never met until this curious proxy introduction. I am very much afraid, however, that they have dressed me in this bloke's coat and hung me out on the line. George Copsen shows me Aline's signature, flowing and elegant and somehow still wearing handcuffs in bed. And he nods and tells me yes, they all say I am Mr. A.

Even now, Gonzo would not give them up. He would not detail their transgressions, would not recall time and place or accuse them in turn. Gonzo would stand firm and demand a lawyer and his rights and he would *cast his despite* in George Copsen's face. I do my best, which is miserable, and I say that I don't know why they would have said any such thing, although I am bleeding within and only barely refrain from crying.

At this, the general's face goes a little grave and he suggests that I consider my position, so I tell him the whole story from start to finish and he listens attentively and then explains that he was not speaking figuratively. His recommendation was to be taken as a literal instruction. He produces a ladies' powder compact from his eminently male pocket and folds out the mirror, displaying to me between the spots of expensive cosmetic the full profundity of the deep shit into which I have gotten myself.

The sense of smell is deeply associated with memory. Old men, blind and senile in deckchairs on the lawn at Happy Acres, recall lucidly the things which happened to them around cut grass and in the flower beds of youth. This moment imprints on me in reverse, as it were: from the moment of revelation in that little room in Jarndice until this day I cannot smell that particular face powder without choking with fear. It is worn by dowager ladies with stiff manners and powerful personalities, which probably does not help, but I do not see them. Instead, I recall the slow process of putting together a picture from the two-and-three-quarter-inch mirror held in Copsen's hand. George Copsen's hands do not shake particularly, but he isn't a statue either, and so the mirror wobbles. This is not in fact a problem but an advantage; the mirror is too small to show me at one moment the nature of this chamber. My dawning horror relies on a phenomenon called image retention, which is also the basis for cinematic film: the human visual apparatus holds on to scenes for a moment after they are gone. A full representation can be assembled from disparate elements. A sequence of twenty-four slightly different frames becomes a moving image. And thus also I construct my predicament from a scattered series of circular reflections, and I have to concentrate to do it. Perhaps George Copsen knows this, and intends to focus my mind.

The reason this room smells of bleach; the reason the seat is damp and a little slippery; the reason my head is restrained and my hands will not move, is that I am in an execution chamber. I am sitting in an electric chair. A thick trunk of cable runs out like a rat's tail from the wall and connects to the base near my feet. If necessary, enough electricity can be run through this apparatus to set my brain on fire.

Lydia's father is considering whether or not to execute me on the spot, has his finger on the button, and in fact might push it by accident if I were to give him cause to clench his fists or even should he sneeze. This is highly illegal, and no doubt if anyone ever finds out, the general will be in big trouble, but this will (and it is plain that George Copsen follows every point and counterpoint of this debate) matter very little to the smoking, baked long-pig remains of a falsely accused undergraduate without the sense to appreciate when his arse is in a sling and when it is not appropriate to stand on constitutional ceremony.

Gonzo would call his bluff. Gonzo would be sure it *was* a bluff. *My* instinct is to explain the question of Mr. A in the terms I have recently been studying. This would mean telling General Copsen about Frege's notion of sense and reference, which is essentially that language and reality do not always match, and that it is possible to use words—such as "unicorn"—to denote an object which does not necessarily possess the qualities inherent in that description. The word "unicorn," for example, proposes a magical beast with a long horn sprouting from the forehead and a fondness for chaste women. This is the *sense.* The sense need not be an accurate description of what is actually there. That thing—the *reference*—may be something quite different; say, a grubby horse standing in front of a fence post.

Mythological beasts aside, the important and relevant point is that sense and reference can be quite independent of one another, can be *wildly* at variance, with the result that things you thought you knew from front to back and top to toe turn out to be different from how you understood them. At some point, for example, someone woke up, looked at the Morning Star, thought about the Evening Star and then looked through their telescope and saw what was actually there and realised that Phosphorus and Hesperus are both the planet Venus. *Two* incorrect senses with the same actual reference! What a day *that* must have been! A real eye-opener, oh, yes. How they must have laughed . . . *aha! A-hahahaha*! Something which everyone would have sworn an oath on, signed their name to, turned out to be completely untrue. Much as the mythical *Mr. A,* who does not exist, is a pure *sense,* a hallucination shared by the government and General George and latterly by Aline and Iggy and Quippe and all the rest, but whose *reference,* ludicrously, appears to be myself. We shall all laugh about it later. *Ah-hahahah! Oh, what larks!*

Something tells me that this line of exculpation will sit poorly with George Copsen. He may not have the patience for Frege *(pronounced Fray-guh)* and if he does not he may grow weary and press certain buttons just to see what happens. I do not want to know what happens, so I do not talk about Frege.

I do instead the first smart thing I have done in several months: I ask the general, very politely, to explain to me what it is he would like me to do, what he would do in my position and what, if I might press him for one further piece of information, would be the course of action I would wish *to have taken* were I looking back on this moment from the safety of advanced and healthy old age? And the general says that seeing as I am an old family friend, and I was never really part of this outfit, and seeing as how I have agreed to write down the names of everyone I can remember in the building and everything any of them ever said or did or even might have done, perhaps we might come to some arrangement—but if, *if* I get out of this alive, I should please study hard, play nicely, vote thoughtfully and with an eye to the patriotic good, and get my arsehole friend to apologise to his lovely daughter for that business about the donkeys.

I HAVE never written a confession before. Very few people, probably, ever have, until the time comes to do one for real. I have not been taught any kind of structure or template for admitting to treason (or admitting to having *been near* treason), but judging by the exemplars in front of me, confessional documents are somewhat inverted, having the good stuff up at the front in the initial declaration and the nitty gritty later down the line. Still sitting in the awful chair (they bring me a writing tray and a soft-point pen) I come up with the best I can do by way of a creditable first draft, always remembering that this is a work of fiction, a tissue of lies. Normally I would sit with a piece of paper and brainstorm first, but I sense that any departure from the appearance of remembering will go down poorly with George Copsen, and so I just scrawl it down. The only question, as I embark on the preamble ("to my enduring sorrow and shame I have been lured by persons more sophisticated than myself into the appearance of grave crimes"), is whom I shall indict. The spectre of Quippe hanging by the yardarm is a pleasing one, and the notion of Iggy sweating it out like this, confronted with his own undeniable wrongs, is another possibility. But they are buffoons, and I am looking for a scapegoat, not playing Smite the Iniquitous in the Evangelist's play group. And so it is Sebastian that I traduce, and I do it with seamless thoroughness, blending his life with my lies just as he has done with mine.

The magnitude of this deception is part of the power; I draw Sebastian carefully as an extremist, a fiendishly concealed spider in the midst of a balanced web of political sophistry. I imply that he is a hard-action man, but I do not say so. I quote him selectively to suggest that he is dedicated to change at any cost, revolution for the sake of revolution, not the measured, human variety he proposed over his vodka tonic, but the other kind, the tumultuous spasmodic variety which kills. I explain that he is not averse to drawing down the temple on top of himself, to fertilising the soil with his own blood and that of others, to bring about the new order. I do not attempt to define his ideology. I merely say that he is dedicated to it above loyalty to state, to human life, to his own survival. I leave the reader to fill in the blanks from the public record. This is an absolute calumny. It is a savage misrepresentation. Sebastian's credo—which he does indeed value above almost anything else—is that no single idea, no map of progress, no theory should ever advance in the world at the cost of a single human life. Sebastian loathes the statistics with which he is so able. He is interested exclusively in histories, because where numbers of the dead are only numbers, stories of them evoke tragedy.

According to Sebastian, ideas have run away with the world. He hates chain stores and fast-food restaurants, mass-produced items and fashionable clothes—any instance of something which is repeated across the world regardless of local context. These things deny the uniqueness of each moment and each person. They function as if we were all printed out of plastic, like egg boxes, and they try to make us function the same way. They are the intrusion of perfection into our grubby, smelly, sweaty living place.

I imply that he would therefore like to blow them up. But I do not say so. And nor, to my own surprise, do I do the same for Aline. I do not say that she is a siren and a Charybdis. I paint her as an innocent: a virginal, unsophisticated creature drawn to sex and somehow always making it her first time. And it occurs to me as I do this that perhaps it's true.

George Copsen reads this mendacious opus, and either believes it or believes something or somehow is served by it, because they let me go and do not kill me or even ever officially arrest me, although a burly non-sergeant leans towards me as I walk free from the internment building and murmurs ferociously the single word "donkeys."

Fortuitously, this part of the debt is easily discharged—Gonzo has recently re-encountered Lydia Copsen, and she appears to have blossomed into a very attractive, worshipful freshman of abundant cleavage and mightily pneumatic disposition, and the inevitable consequence of his taking her out to apologise is that the plaster falls off my wall and my paintings shudder and I miss Aline more than ever, as Gonzo and Lydia enjoy some after-dinner coffee in the adjoining room. This is almost certainly not what the general intended, but I have no intention of letting on and nor, apparently, does the much-pleased Lydia. Gonzo has that effect on some women. George Lourdes Copsen is satisfied as well (though not, I devoutly hope, in the same fashion), and I continue my studies at Jarndice with a deeper understanding of the nature of power and a degree of caution regarding my associations. The next time I see Aline's face is years later at a stag party. She is starring in a sophisticated picture called *Butt Before You Go,* a rendering into the erotic milieu of *Gone With the Wind,* in which the male protagonist (the renowned penile thespian Coitus Clay) subtly and tastefully coaxes a string of comely wenches to levels of bliss untold by means of non-standard penetrations. Despite being unashamedly pornographic, *Butt Before You Go* has a curious naivety about it, a kind of safety, perhaps in part because Coitus Clay seems genuinely affectionate towards his principal partner. Identification is difficult, because he is pictured mostly from below, but after a moment I am able to abstract the chiselled features of Sebastian from the lusty visage gurning before me.

More immediately, the product of my near-death experience in an electric chair is a large amount of hard work culminating in a considerable surprise when I receive my grades: I have scored in the top category. Gonzo, meanwhile, has achieved a middling result, which bothers him not at all. But here is another first time: in something which the world feels is important I am ahead of my best friend.

Chapter Four

Employment sought and found;
the nature of the universe;
Gonzo, again.

MR., AHMM, hello, right. I see. Sorry. Ahhh . . . Ms. Brent?" Oleana Brent is the third person to leapfrog me in the office of Tolcaster & Ream. Not that she has physically leapt over me. Oleana Brent is a dignified, skeletal creature who would not risk damaging her portable *froideur* by engaging in gymnastics in a corporate waiting room, even if it was the kind of corporation which rather liked that sort of thing. She sits, dour and forlorn with a cup of vending machine decaf and a magazine she brought with her which has no pictures in it. Her head comes up smoothly and she walks into the office as if she is expecting to be immersed in cold water and teased by kindergarteners.

Martin Raddle was kind enough to point out, when Susan de Vries (Asst. VP i/c Personnel@T&Rplc, but not SWALK, UNHCR or DOA, though she no doubt aspires) erroneously called him in advance of me, that I was on the list before him. Susan de Vries made a sort of flapping gesture to imply that this would all come out in the wash, and Martin grimaced an apology and went on in. De Vries made a similar wriggly motion when I politely attempted to prevent her from repeating this mistake with Govinda Lancaster. Now Oleana Brent marches into the inner sanctum and it is clear that the game is already over. Four years of student buncoboothing has taught me to recognise a rigged table when I see one, and this isn't so much a question of find the lady as lose her. And lo and behold, my interview (set for nine) is the last of the day, cannot be fitted in and will I come back next week?

I am the elite of the educational production line. There is no point in my coming back next week. I am being given the Spanish archer ("el bow," if you are wondering) and my return next week would probably precipitate a mass exodus from the back of the building. I have been weighed and found wanting, and I never even saw the scales. I know this because it is getting to be a familiar feeling. The fix is, for some reason, in.

At Brightling Fourdale Klember, I was nodded through an unexciting discussion by two bored execs who explained at the start that they had already selected their candidates this year—and then rushed me out so they could speak to a promising young man from the Lister School of Economics. Melisande-Vedette-Farmer Inc. did not answer my letter. Tolcaster & Ream do not seem to be interested in talking to me either. I depart, so as to avoid being carried out by security.

So it goes. Sempler & Hoit do not wish to employ me. Nor do International Solutions & Development. At Barnard-Fisch AG we end up talking about the weather in more detail than I expected, and I realise that the interview has in some sense gone off the rails when Mr. Lange-Lieman desires that I repeat the defining features of cumulonimbus and seems almost alarmed when I stray back to the topic of employment. Finally, at Cadoggan GMbH my interviewer has at least the decency to explain what is bugging her.

"It's rather unusual," she explains, "for a candidate file to have a secure annexe."

I was not aware that mine did, but she explains that this is why it is called secure.

"What does it say?" I ask. She does not know. This too is of the nature of the thing. It might say that I am an undercover operative. It might say that I am suspected of felonious activity abroad, or (and I am suddenly sitting on a slick, soggy cushion again) it might indicate that I have at some stage been associated with undesirable elements. I open my mouth to talk about Aline, but my interviewer shushes me. If I know the contents of the file, I should bear in mind that that information has been deemed classified, and she has no desire to be apprised of it in contravention of Section 1, para (ii) of the Information Act and 15, (vi) of the Dissemination & Control Act, and several assorted acts and orders which are themselves secret under section 23, (paras x–xxi) of a piece of legislation whose name is also too sensitive for general release. Unfortunately, with this significant question mark hanging over me, she also cannot offer me a job. And nor, as I have discovered, can anyone else.

Gonzo is unavailable, owing to a pressing romantic assignation with someone, or actually *someones*. Elisabeth Soames is my second call, and it transpires she is at home in Cricklewood Cove. I visit. I explain. Elisabeth wears the particular lack of expression I associate with rolling eyes and obvious answers, and then asks me which of my tutors at Jarndice best understands the real world. I ponder briefly—many Jarndice professors have worked in business and the law, science and the arts. None of them, really, gives the impression that they are world*ly*, save one. I say his name. Elisabeth nods. I cannot shake the feeling that she was waiting for me to catch up. I ask about her. She says she's now studying to be a reporter. She has the urge to travel. There are things she wishes to know. Her expression tells me that is as much information as I will get at this time, and so we walk, and I make her laugh, just once.

Before I leave, she kisses me lightly on the cheek. It is a chaste thing, of deep affection. I embrace her, and it occurs to me how slight she is, and how slender by comparison with my arms and chest. I am aware of these things because my arms encircle her completely, and while my left palm is pressed to her back to draw her close, my right hand touches my own shoulder. We draw apart, and she kisses me again, on the other cheek. There is just a trace of moisture on her lips, and they are very soft. The kiss lingers and tingles on me, but before I can look at her, examine her, she has turned and slipped away, and my train is coming.

"Bloody mess," says Dr. Fortismeer. He is not talking about my situation, but about his grouse, which has this minute arrived in the hand of a pretty Californian exchange student named Callista, whom Fortismeer has appointed his personal butler this year in a gesture towards equal rights for women. "Rebuke the kitchen, would you, please?" Callista favours him with a smouldering look, extremely fetching in her butler's uniform, and departs. The grouse looks much like any other, a sort of shocked pigeon with stunted wings, but I gather that Fortismeer's keener eye has spotted some deficiency.

"Potatoes," he says morosely. "All over the place, and covered in muck. I loathe gravy. Always tastes of horsemeat. Ever had horse?"

"No."

"Not bad, actually, bit horsey. Whiff of the stables, always."

He glares at the grouse, then pokes it dejectedly with a fork. It gives a wet little noise of crisp skin being rustled by a big gentleman, and somehow looks rather sad. Fortismeer is touched, and takes pity on it, and conversation is precluded for a while because Dr. Fortismeer's manner of eating, while scrupulously correct, is not quiet.

"You've got a problem," Fortismeer murmurs finally, and I realise that he has actually been thinking about this while he demolished the unhappy grouse. My heart lifts a little.

"Silly problem," Fortismeer murmurs. "Frightful girl, what was her name? Bloody Eva Braun waiting for Adolf. Not fair of me, of course, no destiny. Still, dobbed you in. Never liked her. Aline. Where is she now? Transferred. Buggered off. Say goodbye?"

"No," I respond, realising for the first time that this is so. Fortismeer nods.

"Took that idiot Sebastian Sands with her, of course. Small mercies. Gifted student. Frightful pain in the arse. Rather liked him. Always wished him on another university. Lo and behold . . . Time for a bit of pudding, I think." He rings the bell. Callista stalks back into the room with a vast bowl of rhubarb crumble steeped in cream. She has provided a second spoon, much smaller, for me. It is either a desperate attempt to prevent Fortismeer from rupturing or a backhanded comment on my relationship with him. She heaves a sigh in his direction as she puts the dish down and delivers a full-wattage pout. In Fortismeer's place I'd be having trouble sitting, but he seems not to notice. Callista straightens sharply and marches out.

"Rhubarb's the thing, you know. Increases circulation. Stimulates the sexual juices. Never know why they don't investigate it. Probably worth millions. Your friend must live on it. What's his name? Lubitsch. Eastern European blood, of course, goes at it like a weasel. Lubitsch, not Callista. She's furious with him, you know. Stood her up. Throwing herself at me by way of revenge. Silly girl. Couldn't be less interested. Too thin. Probably kill her if we got down to it. Snap her like a twig. She'd have to go on top. Hate that—always makes me feel like a whale being refloated. Need a woman of stature. Eh?"

Fortismeer draws an outline in the air of a woman constructed along the lines of a double bass. It is not a topic I wish to pursue, and so I remain strategically silent.

"Go and see Hoare. Knows things. Uncanny little sod. Too clever by half, and I'm so clever it's painful." His eyes glitter from his lax face, a fox in a thicket. "What will you tell him?"

"The truth."

Fortismeer thinks about that.

"Yes," he says at last. "Probably the best thing. Bloody deceptive, honesty."

Callista brings cheese.

. . .

AND SO I find myself approaching the place of work of Mr. Crispin Hoare, of the Office of Procurement, which unfortunate combination of names has already caused me to snuffle briefly on the telephone, but about which, I was informed in breathless confidence by the temporary receptionist, Mr. Hoare has exactly no sense of humour at all. Mr. Hoare, indeed, does not appear to get a lot of laughs out of anything. The building in which he works is a grey slab with stern windows and poorly chosen organic paint colours which are intended to produce a stable and relaxing working environment (as per directive Ev/9) but in fact cause the entire complex to resemble the messy interior plumbing of a sickly bison. The strip lighting (low energy as per directive Ev/6) is responsible for much of this, because it emits in the green and purple areas of the spectrum, which are not tints favourable to a feeling of general good health. Further, this illumination is produced by ultra-high-frequency discharges of an electric current through a tube of fluorescing gas, meaning that they flicker at a given (enormously rapid) rate, this frequency being one which sadly produces tension, annoyance and migraines in 81 per cent of adult humans, and has the interesting side effect of causing tachycardia in shrews. Shrews being very susceptible to stress, and having in any case ill-designed cardiovascular systems, it is safe to assume that any shrew entering Mr. Hoare's workplace with the intention of asking him for a job would be dead before it had gone five metres down the long corridor I am currently attempting, and would thereby instantly convert itself into organic waste and be disposed of by the sanitation crew. Should the shrew turn out to contain elevated or even toxic levels of chemical waste, or should there be cause to suspect, by reason of signs of aberrant and un-shrew-like behaviour or outward symptoms of transmissible disease such as, but not limited to, rashes, bleeding, elevated temperature and coughing, evidence of pre-mortem deliquescence, or petechial haemorrhaging, that the aforementioned shrew was in fact the carrier of a biological agent, the business of disposal would be handed over to a hazmat team trained in these matters, and the tiny body would be removed in a suitable container by men and women wearing spacesuits and taken to a place of investigation to ascertain the level of the threat and also to tease from the tiny, terrified corpse any forensic evidence suggesting that it might be involved in anti-statist activities, that it might, in fact, be a *suicide* shrew.

Since no shrew would in the normal course of events come anywhere near the Office of Procurement, the mere presence of the animal would have to be assumed evidence of abnormal activity, and a stray, confused and moribund rodent of this kind could reasonably be expected to close an entire government building for several hours and cost the taxpayer a cool quarter-mil. All of which goes through my mind as I trudge to Mr. Hoare's office in search of some way to earn money in what has turned out to be a hostile world.

The door is closed, of course, because men like Mr. Hoare do not emphasise their availability. In my dreams I have seen this door as grand and wooden, watched it swing open before I can knock. In these visions, the door itself was heavy, reinforced with strange materials spun off from space explorations and deep-sea diving, so as to withstand bullets, bombs and manual force for long enough to afford the priceless expertise contained in the person of Crispin Hoare ample time to summon assistance in the face of such outrageous assaults, or to take cover in the complex of tunnels spreading out from behind his study, or even to arm himself and personally repel the invasion by use of advanced weaponry and superior skill.

The door I am now approaching is mysteriously ignorant of this impressive ancestry, and seems determined to be made of a nasty prefab moulded stuff, and to have a grubby window in it, and "C. T. Hoare, i/c Proc't." stencilled or even transferred onto it in tatty gold leaf. I raise my hand, expecting to be pre-empted, and am not, which means that my first knock is rather muffled and ham-fisted, and I am forced to repeat the effort before a loud voice says "Come," and I struggle with the handle for a moment because my fingers are suddenly slippery and it is one of those round ones which are a bit stiff.

"Use a hanky!" cries the voice within. Since there is a box of them resting on a school chair next to the door, I do. The door—light and definitely not reinforced—opens onto a chamber the size of a concession stand.

Mr. Hoare is by any measure a tiny, rat-like bloke with ears like solar panels on a pink, nervous satellite, and he has been orbiting here for a while in the summer heat because his unique odour permeates the room. He smells of linen and mint and of damp, male civil servant, but is not thank God one of those men who produces a rich, salty mustard gas from their armpits, and so the effect is surprising but not revolting. He gestures me to a chair and leans forward curiously, and I have to shake my head slightly to dislodge the shrew comparison lest I say something foolish and (more crucially) unemployable. He asks what he can do for me and I tell him that I would like a job, which appears to surprise him.

"But my dear boy," says C.T. Hoare, "surely not with us?"

Yes, it has been my life's ambition.

"Do you know what we do here?"

This is something of a poser. It is either so obvious that it needs no explanation, or so secret that it may not be mentioned, because nowhere in the many pages of literature I have scrutinised in order to isolate the name of Crispin Hoare and obtain his coordinates have I been able to ascertain the precise function of his office.

"Looked at intelligently," I say, looking at Crispin Hoare intelligently, "this is the most important branch of the civil service."

"Oh yes, undoubtedly," says Crispin Hoare, very pleased, "but what drew your attention to us? Not a lot of people," he says sadly, "are even aware we exist. Necessary, of course, but sad."

I have no idea what ought to have drawn my attention, and no desire to lay claim to having had my attention drawn by routes either improper or unfeasible, so I agree with the necessity and dodge the question, and so it goes on, and with every one of my evasions Crispin Hoare seems to get a little more tired and sad, and each of my non-responses is a springboard into another question I cannot answer, and finally he holds up his hand for a halt and I know, absolutely clearly, that I have been busted wide open like a cantaloupe, and the only thing left is whether he takes pity on me or throws me out on my lying, untouchable arse.

Crispin Hoare looks at me across the desk and takes stock. He lets out a long, slow sigh.

"Forgive me," he says. "I think the reason you came to me is that you have no other choice. You are here," Crispin Hoare says, "because someone has given you nowhere else to go." He nods to himself, and I realise that his satellite head is not one of those ones which beams long-distance phone calls from Estonia to Kashmir, it is one of the ones which can photograph your hair follicles and read your mail from up there. C.T. Hoare is not someone you can kid with some unrehearsed blather and a Gonzo grin.

"There is an annexe attached to your record. I would imagine," C.T. Hoare says, over his cluttered, amiable desk, "that not one of the other people you went to for employment even talked to you about the job." He gazes at me steadily, with sympathy. "I would imagine that they talked about everything but the job. And despite some splendid prevarication, I would venture that you have no notion of what I do. Very good effort, though." At which point I nearly burst into tears, but manage instead a manly nod which is intended to convey that none of this is now or has ever been my fault, and yet I carry the cross without complaint or expectation of redress. Crispin Hoare opens a Manila folder and studies the single page contained therein. It takes him not very long at all. He reads it again, just to make sure. He shrugs.

"Would you like to see what it says?" And he slides the file halfway across the table towards me.

I consider several options, most of which are not options at all. I dismiss instantly all the ones which involve screaming, shouting or beating him to death with the heavy stapler by the window. Similarly I discard the possibility of kissing his hands and swearing my firstborn daughter to him as a handmaiden, or my son as a footrest. The only real question is whether I will reach across and accept the file and find out why I am unemployable, or leap to my feet and flee, and spend the rest of my life cleaning windows and wondering. It is a closer thing than you would think. The white page is mighty scary, and I glance down to assess its magic, only then realising that I have accepted it.

"REFER TO GEORGE LOURDES COPSEN" in large print, and then a note, in Lydia's father's wandering script: "Stat filler. Send him over if you like the cut." This last is a naval expression, the cut of a ship's jib being the angle of her foresail, the defining feature of her character as a vessel, hence also a man or woman's bearing, and thus by overextension possibly the jib becomes the nose. It seems improbable to me that George Lourdes Copsen is concerned with the formation of my nose, he being the possessor of a set of grade A epicanthic folds and hence a man well aware that the soul's complexion is not readily legible in the face. It seems more likely that he wishes Crispin Hoare to exercise his judgement, and that my future prospects hinge entirely on the decision of a man I have just failed to gull, who has seen through my impoverished blarney, who has no cause to love me and whom I have secretly likened to a geosynchronous shrew. C.T. Hoare looks at me, and allows the full weight of his intelligence to appear for a moment behind his genial, ugly little face, and like Master Wu he finds in me whatever it is that he is looking for.

"Stat filler," he says, sounding like the Evangelist (in her genuine, profane mode) talking about cross burnings. "Do you know what that is?"

I do not.

"Come with me." And Crispin Hoare gets up from his desk and leads me out of his office, down one corridor and up another, until we are in an office almost exactly like his own with a man named Pont. Pont has no first name, or no last. The little banker's plate on his desk reads "PONT" in capitals, so I wonder whether PONT is his title. Person Of Natural Talent. Political Organiser for Nebulous Treaties. Penguin Officer, North Territory. This last one sounds improbable, but it would explain why Pont's wallspace is covered in meticulous graphs and charts. I am looking for signs of Arctic birdlife and blubber studies, when Crispin Hoare speaks again.

"Pont," says Crispin Hoare, "I propose a Socratic sort of dialogue, culminating perhaps in a brief *excursus.*"

"Oh, right ho," says Pont gamely, and, laying down whatever data set he is reading for his personal amusement, he gives every indication of pricking up his ears. Pont, like my new friend Crispin Hoare, has a distinctly small-mammal thing going on. Unlike Crispin Hoare, he looks to be nocturnal. He blinks and rubs at his nose with a cupped hand, and communicates his readiness to proceed. Crispin Hoare leans against the wall next to the door and begins.

"Hobbes [the political thinker, not the rather delightful cartoon tiger of the same name] asserted that the natural state of mankind is war. What say you?"

"I say he was a pessimistic old fart with a bee in his bonnet about the need for big government."

"Pont . . ."

"All right, all right. The position is not utterly baseless. Proceed."

"I should be delighted. Thus, the creation of the state, with its first duty being essentially to prevent one man from preying on another. Yes?"

"Hnqgglflmmpf."

"I shall take that as a 'yes.' Now, are those engaged in the business of governing any different by nature from those they govern?"

"Yes. They're prideful and tend to sexual misconduct. Also, the situation of being in government tends to drive you mad."

"But are they more virtuous or more intelligent? Or more compassionate?"

"Ha!"

"Let's call that one a 'no.' So, in order to protect the populace from their own governors, the law must be universal. More, it must require transparent and consistent behaviour from those appointed to rule. Hence the rulers must function, not as individuals, but as applicators of perfect justice, the willing part (and here I use the term 'willing' meaning intending and asserting rather than merely accepting) of a machine for good government. Personal considerations are inadmissible, lest the whole structure be compromised by *privi lege*—private law. We are talking about a *Government Machine.* Yes?"

"I hope you're going somewhere with this, Crispin, because I've got a whole exciting pile of reports on potassium purchasing to get through."

"Trust in me, stout Pont. I am but a little way off my goal."

"Forge ahead, then."

"Such a mechanism cannot function without accurate information. Quite obviously, with every degree of imperfection in the *input,* the *output* will be wrong by that degree multiplied by whatever other relevant false information is already there, *and* by whatever drift is inherent in the system's construction (it being impossible according to the laws of thermodynamics to build any engine which does not dissipate energy in the process of performing its task). Since this machine is informational, of course, that loss of accuracy will not produce heat, but rather nonsense. Yes?"

"Garbage in, garbage out. Or rather more felicitously: the tree of nonsense is watered with error, and from its branches swing the pumpkins of disaster."

"Oh, my dear Pont, that's rather good!"

"Potassium-purchasing reports are so exciting, Crispin, that every so often I have to pull myself back down to Earth with a bit of hard labour at the creative coalface. But please, continue."

Crispin Hoare nods. "To recap: it is possible to put decent information into a Government Machine, have ordinary, good people running the thing, and a reasonable system in place, and still get utter idiocy out of the dispenser."

"More than possible. Likely."

"So let us look at a specific hypothetical case: let us suppose that the machine were looking for enemies within its own population."

"Well, inevitably it *will* have enemies. It's unfair, so people will inveigh against it. The question is how it perceives those enemies. Initially, it will see them as legitimate opposition, because that's written in. But each time it looks at them, the predisposition established in the last investigation towards the possibility of criminal activity will be emphasised."

"More plainly?"

"It's like taking a photograph of a photograph of a photograph. What's actually going on gets less clear. Shadows get darker. Faces are blurred. Eventually, it's all in the interpretation—but the interpretation is being done by people whose job is to look for danger. So they will err on the side of caution. Eventually, a photograph of a child's birthday party becomes a blurred image of an arms deal. The pixelated face of Guthrie Jones, under-nines balloon-modelling champion, becomes the grizzled visage of Angela Hedergast, infamous uranium seller. Each investigation of the same facts increases the likelihood that something will be found which is frightening—or rather something *will be found to be* frightening. Eventually, the mere fact that something or someone has been investigated eleven times becomes suspicious."

"And therefore the numbers of suspected enemies of the people?"

"Would explode. The Government Machine is looking at itself in the mirror, of course; it's seeing an image of its own weaknesses."

"So what, practically speaking, would be the upshot of this?"

"You end up with a machine which knows that by its mildest estimates it must have terrible enemies all around and within it, but it can't find them. It therefore deduces that they are well-concealed and expert, likely professional agitators and terrorists. Thus, more stringent and probing methods are called for. Those who transgress in the slightest, or of whom even small suspicions are harboured, must be treated as terrible foes. A lot of rather ordinary people will get repeatedly investigated with increasing severity until the Government Machine either finds enemies or someone very high up indeed personally turns the tide . . . And these people under the microscope are in fact just taking up space in the machine's numerical model. In short, innocent people are treated as hellish fiends of ingenuity and bile because there's a gap in the numbers. Filling gaps in the statistics . . . Oh. Crispin?"

"Pont."

"Did you just drag me through that entire fandango to get an explanation of 'stat filler' for one of your chums with a secure annexe?"

"I always enjoy our little talks."

Pont sighs heavily.

"Leave me, please, Crispin and friend. I have a futility-induced migraine."

"Thank you, Pont."

Crispin Hoare leads me back to his office. I sit.

"Is it true?" I ask.

"Broadly," says Crispin Hoare. "It's more nuanced, of course. The system is more reflexive than that. People are permitted a degree of freedom to express opinions. Usually the witch-hunt stops after a few iterations and we can all go back to what we're doing. Except for Pont, of course."

"Why him?"

"Oh, didn't I say?" Crispin Hoare smiles thinly, and there is a flicker of warning in his genial face. "Our friend Pont is the witchfinder general. The real one. He goes through the numbers. He reads the confessions. He tracks and he traces and he never forgets anything. Very clever man. He finds the really dangerous people and he deals with them."

"How does he find them? If it's all so messed up?"

"Sympathy, of course. Pont agrees with them. He loathes the Government Machine. Despises it. Anarchist, is Pont. But . . . he hates violence more, d'you see? Thinks it replicates and alienates. No answers in violence for Pont, just more rules, which of course he hates. So Pont . . . well, Pont thinks like the enemy, from our point of view. And from his, he turns in notional allies who think like us, and lets us deal with them. If you were ever thinking of getting involved in a real insurrection—not some student thing—you should be very afraid of Pont. He's never wrong."

Brrr.

"We tracked down your chum Sebastian, you know, offered him a job in Pont's office. No go. He and his wife—I think you know her too—are content with their new professional direction. One can only say it takes all sorts." He shrugs. I imagine vaguely that Sebastian and Aline must have opened an antique shop or started a business selling hand-woven linen goods.

"Sign," Crispin Hoare says. He slides a form across the desk. It is long and fairly complicated and it is filled out already. It is titled, with magnificent redundancy and majestic self-importance, "Form." At the bottom there is a space for the signatures of refugees from hostile interrogation who are lost at sea.

"What is it?"

"Only job I can give you. Only one you'll get. *George Copsen Wants You,* and all that."

"For what?"

"No idea." I stare at him. "It'll be all right," says Crispin Hoare. "At least," he adds, "I do hope it will be."

I sign.

THE PLACE is called Project Albumen. It has nothing to do with eggs. The designation was randomly assigned by a computer program which apparently was not instructed to avoid names which are unsettling or mildly disgusting. For all I know it is not in fact called Project Albumen at all, or at least not to anyone but me. It has that kind of feel about it, of secret operations and clearances and vanishing off the face of the Earth. It is therefore very much in line with my last George Copsen experience, although not with my childhood ones, which involved biscuits and orange juice and camping under canvas in his living room while Gonzo and Lydia played a variation of Doctors and Nurses whose convoluted rules seemed to require me to be the corpse most of the time and allow them both to heal me with improvised surgical instruments (a butter knife/scalpel, a handkerchief/bandage and a length of plastic tubing filched from the garage whose precise purpose was mercifully never revealed to me).

If you stand in front of Project Albumen and look up, you don't really see it properly. It is angular and stylish; the facade of the building follows a blocky in-and-out pattern like a ratchet or the tread of a sneaker. It has huge iron doors, burnished and sealed like a Greek temple with vague gestures in the direction of modernism. From close up, it's hard to get an accurate picture of it—it's just that big. If you go back along the road in order to look down on it, the sweep of the hill gets in the way. If you leave the road, against the stern advice of the signs reading "Danger—

mining" and climb the hill, you will almost certainly be blown up. The signage is accurate, but coy.

Even should you manage to reach the crest of the hill in one piece, you would not see the project itself, because it is at all times partly hidden by a flirtatious mist. A slice of the eastern wing tempts you to look one way, a flash of the rear court draws you back again. You could obsess over this building, grow frantic to unveil its mysteries and plumb its inviting depths. If you were that sort of person, you could start to feel that this building *wants it bad,* that it *deserves* to be the subject of a hostile military action, an espionage-driven commando raid, just to *teach it to behave.*

A few months ago three highly motivated gentlemen assailed Project Albumen in fine special operations style. They wanted the secrets this building so plainly keeps beneath its lush deco exterior. After weeks of planning, they got into their sexy black outfits and made their move. They blew open the back door and, no doubt with a grand sense of empowerment and dominance, thrust mightily inside.

Unfortunately, the entire main building of Project Albumen is a honey trap. The interior is very large and has intricate, folded metal all around the walls. This falsely gives the impression of a large number of secret doors and passages, so it took them twenty-nine or so minutes to establish that there are in fact no exits. Shortly thereafter they discovered that the sanctum sanctorum, the warm, secret heart of Project Albumen, is in fact rather cold and unwelcoming, because it floods on a half-hour cycle with liquid nitrogen. The motivated gentlemen were removed somewhat later in the day when they had thawed enough to be prised loose from the floor.

All this I learn by way of welcoming chit-chat from a man called Richard P. Purvis. *Lieutenant* Richard P. Purvis. He drives right past the car park and carries on down a small access road behind some empty gas cylinders and a water tank. He stops the car next to a run-down Portakabin with "Foreman" stencilled on the door, and leads me inside. It is, of course, not a Portakabin, but the real entrance to Project Albumen. When this is revealed, I very nearly make the mistake of asking Richard P. Purvis whether, somewhere near here, there is a tank containing man-eating sharks, into which enemy agents can be tipped by means of a trapdoor. I do not ask, because I am very much afraid that the answer will be yes. This place has no sense of its own ridiculousness, and that self-regard is fortified by the fact that it kills people.

The back of the Portakabin segues smoothly into a numinous creamy corridor with curved walls and a grillework floor which winds away into the distance like something from an all-too-optimistic science fiction flick circa 1972. A cheery woman in a uniform I do not recognise greets me and politely tells me to undress. I undress. The cheery woman does not look away. If my revealed genitals alarm her, she conceals her consternation very well.

She takes my clothes and wanders off with them and, when I remain where I am, patiently tells me to follow. I pass through a door and into a room full of clinical personages in masks and gowns, and I am examined with considerably more thoroughness; probed, X-rayed, shaved, showered, scraped, biopsied, deloused, disinfected, polygraphed, MRI'd and then given some new (nasty) clothes, and finally sent onward and inward to the place of business of one General Copsen, who is either my best friend or my implacable enemy and I am beginning to think the difference would be impossible to discern, except that maybe he would have pressed the button instead of just showing it to me in that room back in Jarndice. Lydia's father favours me with a piggy grin and says "Welcome to the strength" as if I'm not some kind of conscript.

"I guess you're wondering why I've called you here," says General George as we pass through a high-tech portcullis and into a hexagonal tunnel with something very like hair all over the walls, because he thinks he's seriously funny, and he wants me to think so too. I think so, at least enough that he nods in response to my wan little grin and doesn't have me put on a soggy cushion and strapped down.

"Truth is, you're one of my great white hopes. My boys. And girls, of course, but I call you all my boys. One of the best. Came through it all, head up, chin up, good kid. Crispin says you're clever, too."

I stare at him. George Copsen is misting up. The ogre of electrical death has a tear in his eye. He wants to be loved. He thinks bygones can be bygones and I can join his twisted research family and marry (not Lydia) one of his daughters. General George Copsen wants to play pater familias.

"It was bad back there," he says. "We had a quota. They said, 'Find us this many terrorists, we know they're out there!' So I was playing catch. Saving the best. You're one o' the best, of course. One of my boys." I wonder, briefly, what happened to the others. Tried? Held indefinitely? Released, forever suspect? Or just vanished? I'm furious with him for making me glad that I'm *one of his boys.*

He throws an arm around me like my skin isn't crawling and I don't want to be sick every time he twinkles at me, and he walks me along another big science fiction corridor towards whatever is at the centre of this spooky ant farm. The corridor is lit in some manner which defies my immediate analysis, and therefore I am unable to speculate what possible effect it might have on any shrews or shrew-like animals, save that I suspect they would be rendered placid and wide-eyed with wonder by the soft reassuring gleam of this walkway. It is devoid of right angles and has uneven foam spikes protruding from it in odd places to deaden the sound and make the whole thing undetectable to methods of espionage whose theoretical basis I am not cleared for, but which clearly require symmetry or solidity, a line of speculation I abandon in case I should figure out something I would have to be killed for knowing.

At last we round a corner and instead of another asymmetrical door or tangled staircase, there is an ill-proportioned room filled with men and women doing the kinds of things that produce grave expressions and thoughtful lip-chewing. Several of them, against the prevailing wisdom of the dental profession, are chewing pens or pencils, and of these one has a great smear of ink in the middle of his lower lip, and it is to him that General George is taking me.

"That's the guy," George Copsen says, all hushed and loved-up, "the number one. Clever like you and me and all these others together. He designed Albumen. Made this place. You're working with him!" This last as if this man were the Rolling Stones or this year's Audrey Hepburn. I'm underground in an insectoid, paranoid, futuristic maze, and my last encounter with my boss involved non-consensual torture games, but I'm going to be working with the man who created an entire architectural style for use as a lethal weapon. Yessir, George, that makes it all okay. Despite George Copsen's urgency, I stop to look around, and take in what is happening to my life. Perhaps he takes this as awe.

The room is painted in shades of grey, and the ceiling is covered in the same irregular foam spikes as the corridor. The desks, like everything else, have been shaped to avoid sharp edges, which unfortunately means they are uneven and the scribbled papers on them are all slowly falling off onto the floor. Research assistants bend and pick them up once every two minutes or so in a repeating pattern which I assume must be determined by the height of the pile of paper, the friction between individual sheets and even the amount of graphite or ink scrawled across them. In other words, the more prolific the boffin, the more likely he is to find his best idea under the leg of his chair. One genius (I have no doubt that they are all genii of one stripe or another) has hung her notes from clothes lines strung over her workspace. This solves the storage problem, but unfortunately she is short-sighted and can't see the ones at the far end from where she is sitting, so her day is a sort of geek version of a step-aerobics class: sit, work, check figures, stand, run to the far end, run back, sit. Repeat. *(Armageddonetics! Get healthy the super-weapon way!)*

In the approximate (or for all I know the mathematically exact) centre of the room there is a Perspex tank filled with a clear liquid, and at the bottom of it is a fake battleground with toy soldiers and artificial grass, and a collection of not-to-scale military vehicles like the ones I had when Gonzo and I played WWII in the garden of Gonzo's house, and chased the geese with firecrackers.

The guy with the inky lips—the only person with more paper and more space than the aerobics woman—is called Derek, or at least is *to be called* Derek, because this is etched on an oblong slice of metal which occupies the upper left panel of his white coat, thus: "Professor Derek." If this appellation seems truncated, appearances are quite accurate. A strip of white cloth tape or self-adhesive bandage has been applied with precision but without reference to aesthetics across the nether part of the badge. I am despite myself darkly fascinated by an organisation which requires its assets to label themselves, while at the same time demanding that they conceal this information from one another. Professor Derek looks at George Copsen and receives a genial nod.

"Okay, people, positions, please."

Like a rather sloppy chorus line in rehearsal, assorted people with bell curve–smashing brains take refuge behind screens and peer through scopes. Paper is shuffled to "safe" positions on chairs and in box files. Professor Derek glowers at everyone until they are all ready.

"Let's go . . . And . . . testing protocol: battlefield. The test area is flooded to allow precise measurement of volume displaced . . . Charging . . . firing." He ambles over to a small bank of switches and pushes one, then another, and finally—against a backdrop of spinning red lights and klaxons—a third. There is quiet. There is anticipation. There is a sudden wet splash.

The side of the tank is gone, a perfect circle bitten out of it, along with a slice of the mock battlefield and all the little soldiers. The water—or whatever it is—inside the tank immediately acts in accordance with physical laws regarding surface tension, fluid dynamics and gravity. My shoes get wet, and George Copsen, now the dampest general in the services, says "Oh, f'crissakes" and several words which he assumes Lydia does not know, although in fact to judge by my recollections of Gonzo's lengthy and in-depth apology, she not only knows them, but could teach a fairly advanced course in the particulars of certain subsidiary activities not actually an integral part of the original unmentionable verbs, but considered excellent accompaniments by those with relevant skills and experience. All this distracts somewhat from the realisation of what we have just witnessed, which is a magic button that can apparently destroy matter in a specific and alarmingly personal way. At which point George Copsen announces that I will henceforth consider myself in the unconventional weapons and tactics industry. He implies that this is a market sector which will shortly see some expansion, that I will be getting in on the ground floor of a pretty good thing. He further enthuses that, owing to my youth and resilience under pressure (having a bag put over my head and being told I may at any moment be used as the filament in a human lightbulb), I am also suitable for military training.

Without Ma Lubitsch to watch and guide me, and in the absence of good lunches, I have wound up in a dangerous place. I am gone to soldier.

"WHAT I AM about to tell you," says Professor Derek the following day, "may make me sound like a crazy person. So I need you to remember, to bear in mind very carefully, that I have an IQ of such monstrous proportions that if, for the sake of argument, I were *totally insane*—if the palace of my intellect were a scary ivy-covered mansion in Louisiana with peeling paint and dead flowers and a garden full of murdered corpses planted by a man named Jerry-Lee Boudain—I am so much more intelligent than anybody else you will ever meet that *there would be no way for anyone to tell.*" He glances around and finds that this comparison has not had the intended effect. He sighs.

"I'm not crazy," he says more directly. "I just deal with physics which is so complex that it basically sounds—outside of peer-reviewed journals—like nonsense. Like contracts and tax law." He looks at everyone again, and whatever he sees must be more to his liking.

"You are all familiar with geeks as a genus," he continues, "but what you need to get your heads round is that I am such a massive geek, such a totally terrifying concentration of nerdhood, that I have actually cracked the code for human social behaviour using mathematics. I am able to interact with people on what appears to be a casual non-scientific footing, and even get laid like a regular guy, because I made an intense study of behavioural and statistical ethnographics, and I am constantly running a series of predictive and quantitative calculations in my head, which provides me with acceptable human responses within the normative band and counterfeits qualitative judgement so well the difference is within the margin of error. On the most primitive level, for example, I know from the precise number of nods you are making and the muscles in your neck and face whether you are actually paying attention or whether you have decided that this part of the induction is not relevant to you personally and started thinking about something else. I know that I have a series of options regarding those of you currently thinking about last night's sexual adventures or the football game this evening, and that these include a) hoping you will get smart and pay attention, b) addressing the issue directly on an individual or group basis by pointing out that I am currently your only chance of a decent rating and hence a job at the end of all this, but more immediately of your physical survival should we go to war, c) mentioning the whole thing in passing as an organic outgrowth of my opening remarks, on the understanding that you are smart enough to take a hint and d) SHOUTING AT YOU, which I gather is the preferred military solution. You will note that I have in fact pursued all these options in a hierarchical progression, and I confess this is because the mathematics of that particular solution were especially aesthetically promising. I mention this not because it is important that you should know it, but because it is the only example of the scale of my IQ advantage over you that you actually may understand. Questions?"

There are no questions. Professor Derek has a very loud voice and his bearing (presumably chosen from a number of distinct ways of presenting himself to us) does not invite attempts at humour or suggest that he is particularly fond of the funnies. Derek is ageless and calm and it seems he may not strictly belong to the same species as the rest of us. It would be better if he were dumpy or badly groomed, but—no doubt resulting from a string of life/quality/work output formulae—he is rugged, in reasonable shape and has neat, ordinary hair. He looks like the kind of Rhodes scholar who could appear on the cover of both *GQ* and *Forbes.* Derek shoots me a glance which says that this is him going with option a) for the moment. I hasten to take notes in a bold, round hand which can be read upside down, but my writing deteriorates as I actually start paying attention.

"Did you know," says Professor Derek, "that we live in a narrow corridor of space? That if the Earth occupied an orbit only a little different from the one it does, we would not exist at all?"

I did know this, but Professor Derek was speaking rhetorically, or wants to be sure that everyone else knows too, because he goes on to explain. Essentially, what he says is that the Earth is a kind of estate agent's wet dream of happy location. It is close enough to the Sun to draw energy from it to power biochemical reactions such as photosynthesis, without being so close that it catches fire and explodes. At the same time, it is not so far out that the atmosphere freezes and falls to the ground, which is physically entirely possible, and a very nasty idea indeed, not least because it reminds everyone in the room of the middle chamber of Project Albumen, and the man called Tyler whose job is to go in there and scrape careless persons off the walls before they thaw out and go all slushy.

The world we inhabit is balanced between the Sun and the inky gulf of space. If we one day cease to exist, what will be remarkable is that we were ever here at all.

"Excellent. Then here," says Professor Derek, "is the hard part," and we lean forward and engage the last bits of brain-power we have left over and prepare for a real poser.

Professor Derek turns, and pulls down from the ceiling of the room a white projection screen. It is one of the modern perforated kind, not the old ones which doubled as flypaper, and the projector is sleek and small and expensive. It is therefore something of a let-down when the image projected on the screen is a red circle and a blue circle with a purple bit where they overlap.

"Red and blue," says Professor Derek, "on top of one another, producing purple. Yes?"

The next image is in fact two: on the left is a series of blobs and wiggles. On the right is a collection of blibs and woggles. Neither image is in any way a picture of anything. We wait for Professor Derek to say that this is a mistake, that these are finger paintings by his infant daughter. He does not. He presses a button, and the images slide together and become quite obviously a silhouette of a cowboy on a piebald horse.

"The world we see is a composite. It is an alloy. It is," says Professor Derek, in case anyone has not grasped at this point that our world is one thing made of several things, "one thing made of several things. Okay?"

It is a little annoying to be treated as a moron by this guy, but on the other hand he probably has difficulty distinguishing between people who are actually very stupid and people who are just significantly less intelligent than he is.

"It is not just *balanced between* opposing forces. It *is the overlap* of these forces. These things—what you might call elements or essences, if you were of a historical turn of mind—are on the one hand what we refer to as *matter* or *energy* depending on what shape it's in and how it is behaving at the time, and on the other *information.* Matter (or energy) exists. Information tells matter (or energy) how to behave and what to do. It *does* matter—"

Professor Derek pauses for a moment. "May I assume," he says, "that from this point on when I say 'matter' you will understand that I also mean energy?" We nod.

"Very well. Information, then, *does* matter—in the sense that it is the organising principle without which matter simply cannot exist. Without matter, there is no universe and there's no place to do anything. Without information, matter withers away. Vanishes. And gradually, even the memory fades. It won't dissipate entirely, of course. But it becomes . . . slippery."

Professor Derek seems to find that idea poetic. The guy on my left finds it "awesome." He is right, but I don't think he knows it. Information is what gives shape and stability to the universe. Remove it, and you get a perfect circle of absence, a space where there's nothing, because the matter (and energy) there doesn't know how to behave any more and (I cannot help but imagine it sulking) simply ceases to exist. Like the little toy soldiers in the laboratory downstairs.

Professor Derek and his team, by dint of his enormous intellect and considerable innovative powers and their collective technological know-how, have created a sort of Holy Grail of bombs. Or, at least, they have created the science necessary to create the bomb. The engineering, as ever, is playing catch-up—which is why they annihilated the side of the tank as well as the toy soldiers and why General George spent yesterday afternoon in his office wearing a uniform jacket and a pair of fluffy slippers. But any time soon they will be able to produce a controlled editing of the world within a discrete area, stripping out the information and leaving nothing behind—not even regret. They will have made the perfect weapon.

They will be able to make the enemy Go Away.

MY TRAINING turns out to be split between sessions with Professor Derek dealing with the necessary basic understanding of his theory (field radius, energy interactions, overlap issues, delivery systems) and learning how to be a military officer. The latter implies learning in the first place the rudiments of how to be a "fighting man"—military history being full of people who thought it did not, and these people quite often being associated with heroic, bloody idiocy and words like "rout" and "last stand." "Fighting man" rather than "soldier," because the term "soldier" is contentious. Several of our instructors are marines, who use "soldier" only to convey very deep contempt. A few others are technically airmen, in that they are high altitude low opening jumpers for the Special Air Commandos, and these regard the marines and the army with equal disdain because they don't include as part of their routine instruction any information about breathing in low-oxygen environments or what to do if your parachute doesn't open (I would have assumed there wasn't a great deal to do except pray for a subsequent failure of local gravity, but apparently there is a method for unscrambling a parachute which can actually keep you alive in 43 per cent of cases, which has to be better than the odds of not bothering to try).

These gentlemen and ladies take us out for extremely long runs and over assault courses, which are of course gruelling and cold and miserable. The chief misery is actually boredom. Wobbling legs and ravaged muscles become numb, even pain becomes commonplace, but the business of running miles and miles each day on the same track with the same bargain-basement insults flying at you is ghastly because it is dull like nothing else you have experienced. The instructors are probably bored too, and they channel that into clichéd aggression and obligatory howls of fury. And when we are bored into some kind of military shape, able to run in full pack without sinking to our knees, we are handed over to Ronnie Cheung, who regards everyone in the world apart from Ronnie Cheung as a total fucking idiot.

Ronnie Cheung grew up in Hong Kong when it was still part of Cubritannia, or rather when it was still leased by the United Kingdom from the People's Republic of China. He is to train us in all manner of combat. He is small and thickset and scowls at almost everything. He begins our lessons not with press-ups or running, but with a lecture in the same room which Professor Derek used to acquaint us with his genius. He leans on the lectern, doesn't like it and shoves it out of the way. He sits down on the edge of the plinth, so that we have to crane to look at him. Looking at Ronnie Cheung is never going to be a favoured pastime with anyone. He is not easy on the eye. He has broad shoulders and big, ugly knuckles and a wide, bald head. He cultivates a sneer. He has weighed us in the balance, and he is already appalled by the quality of the merchandise.

"What," Ronnie Cheung demands, "is the single most dangerous weapon used by most people in the course of a lifetime?"

"A gun," suggests someone immediately, and Ronnie Cheung makes a farting noise between his lips.

"A kitchen knife," someone else says. Ronnie Cheung shakes his head. By the absence of faux flatulence, we deduce that this is, although wrong, at least wrong in a good way. Domestic objects, then. Rolling pins? Cleavers? Axes? No, no, no. Someone gets lateral.

"The human body!"

Ronnie Cheung holds up his hand: stop.

"My body," Ronnie Cheung says, "is a lethal weapon. Yours is a sack in which you keep your vital organs." He flaps his hand. "You're right—the body has the potential to be very dangerous," and when this response elicits a triumphant smile from his interlocutor, he adds, "which is not to say I didn't notice that that was a suck-arse answer and that you are a suck-arse."

Ronnie waits. When it emerges that he has defeated us, he answers his own question.

"The automobile," says Ronnie. "A bludgeon consisting of several thousand kilos of metal travelling at speeds in excess of thirty miles per hour. Dangerous in unskilled hands, which is most of them, but bloody lethal if you know a bit about how to use it."

So, somewhat to our amazement, the first thing we learn is Automotive Tactical Engagement in Theory and Practice, suited to civil and urban warfare environments. It is an amazing amount of fun. We learn where you hit another car to make it spin out. We learn where to avoid pranging your own car in the course of an auto duel. We learn how to kill a car with sticks, chains, petrol, salt, guns and another car. We get jolted around and occasionally set on fire in our training suits, and we have a ball despite the injuries. Car combat is like sparring: it's about speed, distance and timing. And knowing what you have to hit to knock the other guy down. I am moderately bad at it, in a fun kind of way, and there are plenty of other people who are worse, including Richard P. Purvis and a woman by the name of Kitty who claims to have driven stick since she was nine. We demolish a small fleet of compacts and saloons, and two sixteen-seaters just for variety. It takes three days.

"Right," says Ronnie Cheung, when the last door handle falls to the dust and Riley Tench clambers victorious from a wrecked Nissan, "mêlée." Because most of the point of this, really, has been to get us used to getting thrown around and messed up and not caring about it. So we move on to hand-to-hand, which is more personal and more naked, because there isn't a three-foot crumple zone between you and the enemy. This is the bit where it's important that the project has a good dentist. It does, although I am fortunate enough not to need her services more than once before I get back into the habit of moving my head out of the way before doing anything else.

And thus life goes on for a while. I train, I learn and I live in a little green room at the bottom of George Copsen and Professor Derek's anthill. Ronnie Cheung lives on the level above, which is exactly the same, chair for chair, but he has two rooms side by side which he has kicked through into one. He does not invite us into it, but once in a while we are required to meet him at his door so that we can run somewhere or tackle the assault course under fire. Every so often I get a 48-Leave (mostly because it's my turn, and occasionally because I am on the winning team in one of Ronnie Cheung's bizarre exercises, such as the one where you are locked in a room with a selection of foodstuffs and required to make a weapon—the point of this is that a) a weapon doesn't have to be something you hit someone with, it can be something they slip on or which gets in their eyes and hurts, b) weapons are everywhere and c) sometimes weapons are not everywhere, or an improvised weapon is genuinely more trouble than it's worth, and you should just belt the other guy as hard as you possibly can in the head), and when this happens I go and see Gonzo's parents in Cricklewood Cove. Sometimes I bang on my own front door, or let myself into my parents' home with the hidden key. Sometimes there is a note for me or a meal in the fridge, or a brace of old airline tickets in the waste bin in the hall. Mostly, I seek Ma Lubitsch's kitchen and the buzzing of the bees outside. I talk to her and to Old Man Lubitsch about life, and things, and trivia, and I wander around the Cove hoping to meet Elisabeth by accident. Sometimes I stand on the bluff where we scattered Master Wu's ashes and drink tea from a Thermos flask. Once, I think I see her climbing up towards me, but she never arrives.

Gonzo himself is mostly absent, busy and productive with an ordinary life, and this gives me a warm feeling inside, as if it is something I have achieved; by straying from the path, I have allowed Gonzo to remain on it. It seems very odd to me that I am now part of the oppressive organs of state might, but I come to the conclusion that I am in fact investing in the defence of the conceptual framework of tolerance, and training for the last—rather than the first—resort to violence. If I sort of squint at this idea, I can almost believe it. Mostly, I do not think about it.

IN THE practice yard, Ronnie Cheung is sparring with Sergeant Hordle. I have watched Sifu Cheung for three months, but I have been careful in this context not to obtrude upon his notice. I have studied under Richard P. Purvis and alongside George Copsen's other minions. I have been outwardly an indifferent student, but not a bad one, in case bad students get personal attention from Ronnie Cheung. I have improved at about the same speed as Riley Tench, who is a narrow, whipcord officer with "career" all over him and a degree in military history. Riley Tench fights politely, as if it would be rude to surprise an opponent, but he hits hard and doesn't yield unless he has to. He's a by-the-book sort of a person, an uninspired, dedicated plodder, which is why I have picked him as my model. As long as I am on the same page as Riley Tench, I will probably get put in only moderately tricky positions and have to deal with the feasible sort of challenge. Riley Tench is not Gonzo.

In the time I have been here, I have never seen Ronnie Cheung as much as discomfited by an opponent; although the boys and girls of various elite units frequently hit him, it seems to have absolutely no effect at all—the blows are absorbed by his legs or his barrel chest and shrugged off his ugly bullet head. Ronnie Cheung is a hard-form stylist the way André the Giant was a kinduva big fella. His attacks are direct, powerful and very, very fast. They land softly on the head and chest of his opponent, because this is a practice bout and it would be improper to scar or break a student, even a soldier like this one.

Sergeant Hordle launches one last combination and Ronnie Cheung gently sweeps him off his feet and buries him in the dust. In this context "gently" means that nothing goes *crack* or *pop;* Sergeant Hordle hits the ground hard enough that I feel the impact in my chest. This would be fairly impressive anyway, because Ronnie Cheung is an ordinary-sized person at best, and Sergeant Hordle is a very big one, but Hordle is also a sergeant in 2 Para, which makes him just this side of tougher than an iron bar. Hordle bounces to his feet and grins.

"That was crap," Ronnie Cheung says, "it was *total* crap. Are you some kind of huge-testicled *ballet dancer* under that uniform? Are you a fucking *chorus girl* in a red beret? If I strip you off, Sergeant Hordle, and don't snigger because I can and we both know it, if I strip you down to your skivvies with my own two hands, which I wouldn't, because I don't know where you've been, *but I have thoughts,* will I find that you are wearing stockings and a bloody tutu? And lest you think, Sergeant, that I am impugning your *sexuality,* let me remind you that Billy Radigand from C Company was in here half an hour ago and nearly took my bloody head off and he is a *poof,* not to say a *homosexual,* not to say he sups on *sausage* rather than *fish,* but he is *hard as nails*! And *you* are softer than a baby's arse! Now fuck off and practise!"

This is Ronnie Cheung's version of the Socratic method. It is a powerful motivational technique he has developed over many years, which functions best when everyone ignores it outwardly while at the same time being shamed into applying themselves to impossible tasks and thus emerging (in his own words) absolutely top fucking banana. Sergeant Hordle ignores it. He gathers himself up and trots off to one of the groups of trainees and fits himself into the pattern, and it is shortly apparent that he is very, very good indeed.

Ronnie Cheung eyes him with great disfavour, then shouts at a few other people for good measure. Finally, he glances at our corner of the yard, and his gaze sticks. Reluctantly, his attention flickers in my direction, sums me up and doesn't see much to get excited about. He ambles over. He watches me closely and grunts. I am not using what I have learned from Master Wu. I am treating the whole thing as a new arena. I am learning a hard style as if I have never studied a soft one. Don't mix and match—learn and combine, but only when you are ready. I am currently punching a sackful of wire wool to toughen my fingers. I am doing so without enthusiasm, because in fact I am under orders to preserve my hands so that I can operate the weapons systems if ever I should be called upon to do so. That I am also under orders to train as a lethal mêlée fighter is a piece of inherently contradictory crap which I have come to understand is part of the functioning of the world as we know it.

"And who's this bumhole?" demands Ronnie Cheung.

"This is . . . ," Richard P. Purvis begins, a bit surprised that Ronnie doesn't seem to know my name after three months, but Ronnie Cheung is not watching me fudge hits on the target dummy, he is glaring at a pile of kit and supplies in the corner of the practice yard.

"No, not *that* bumhole," Ronnie says, "*this* bumhole!" He glowers at a box of blank ammunition and practice knives. "The bumhole who imagines he can hide himself in my yard with some piece of low-rent special forces turdmastery." And as he says it, he sticks his hands forward and into what I had taken to be the shadow of a packing crate, and emerges tangled in a furious exchange of blows with a broad, lethal figure all in black.

A lot of things happen very quickly. The man—it's absolutely a man—breaks out a sort of truncheon thingy with a gooseneck whip at one end, and starts belabouring Ronnie Cheung about the head, or what would be the head if Ronnie's hands weren't up around his ears, guarding the bits of his face which will have to be stitched back on if the whip connects too sharply. Ronnie doesn't seem to care that the skin on his forearms is splitting, and just keeps on blocking the thing and falling back. My choice would be to evade the whip and find a long, solid stick to use as a staff, but Ronnie is apparently either too proud to do this or doesn't give a rat's arse for staves and would rather suck it up and wait to get close, which he does now, moving as the guy in black makes a mistake with his whip-stick and bashing it out of his hand with a solid crunch which must hurt like hell. There is bone showing through Ronnie Cheung's skin on his left arm, but there's not really a lot of bleeding. This is the point of all the training he does: various bits of his body are now essentially impervious to normal injuries.

Ronnie launches a long, involved combination, arrhythmic and solid, with light skipping footwork to change the angle between them and move the centre line of his body out of his enemy's effective cone of attack. His lighter blows would knock me down, and the heavy ones would almost certainly finish the fight outright. The other guy wards them off, meets them with equal force, and lands a couple on Ronnie which actually seem to have some effect. Finally, though, Ronnie locks the guy's arms down and pummels him, then swings back and delivers a double-hand punch like the two prongs of a forklift truck hitting a corrugated iron wall, which sends the man in black through the air and onto his backside in a cloud of choking dust. Ronnie waddles over and glares at him.

The guy removes his black headgear.

"Gonzo," says Ronnie Cheung, "that was crap. You are a bumhole." He is extremely pleased, because his lips are swelling and he actually has a black eye. Gonzo grins. Then he coughs a bit, and Ronnie helps him up.

"I could have killed you, idiot boy," Ronnie says, and Gonzo replies that no, he couldn't, and Ronnie laughs again. Then Gonzo catches sight of me, and his bruised face lights up.

"Hey!" He leaps on me, delivers a great lunging hug, and I feel the muscles in his shoulders and chest. Gonzo was big a year ago. Now he is a titan. "Fuck, yeah!" says Gonzo, and because he likes to appropriate prowess by declaration he adds, "Have you seen this guy? Voiceless Dragon. Silent and deadly!" And Ronnie Cheung's unblemished eye falls upon me with cordial loathing.

"Kept *that* quiet," says Ronnie Cheung. "I thought they were all gone. Disappeared." And when he says "disappeared" he waggles his hands in the air to indicate mystery and fog. At the same time he is giving me a look, which I recognise as a look of *measurement.* I am saved from any questions he may have (and Ronnie Cheung is blessed with a fondness for gossip which would make a dowager duchess blush) by the agency of Riley Tench, who looks at Gonzo and finds it necessary to attempt some male bonding.

"Total fucking *ninja,* man," enthuses Riley Tench, slapping Gonzo on the back. He grins, and there's one of those *oh shit* silences where everyone wishes they were somewhere else. Gonzo looks sickly, and Ronnie Cheung goes completely still. He is not tense. There is no sense of doggish aggression. He's all relaxed and loose, the rooster strut falling away from him and being replaced by a perfect calm. This is a bad thing. It means he is absolutely ready to kill someone. He is five metres away from Riley Tench when he says "I do not train," and he is standing very close to him, having crossed the intervening space without appreciably passing through all the necessary points along the line, when he says "ninjas." He says this quite quietly and without particular emphasis, from a distance of about six inches. It is apparent that, even with Gonzo, Ronnie Cheung was holding back. He is faster and more dangerous than you would imagine is possible. He repeats himself, and Riley Tench sort of stops breathing and goggles at him. Ronnie Cheung says it again, turning his head slowly, so that when he says the full stop, which he somehow does, he is looking right at me.

"I do not train ninjas."

He nods once, very slightly, and I realise he is apologising to me for Riley Tench. I nod back.

"All right then," says Ronnie Cheung. "You," and he points at me, "and Spunkbubble here," and he indicates Riley Tench, who has just realised that he will not after all die today, and is measuring this glad news against the fact that he will hereinafter and for evermore be known as "Spunkbubble," "will now engage in a brief sparring match in which you will show him why soft forms are the dog's mighty mangrapes and hard forms are fit only to wash the back end of an incontinent cow. Make a space, boys and girls, for we shall see might and subtlety unleashed like my erection in the presence of a very expensive tart. Guard . . . Ready . . . Fight!"

Bugger.

So now I am in combat, not for real, but for a damn sight realer than I was twenty minutes ago. Ronnie Cheung watches me for signs of slacking, of holding back, and tells my opponent to make a bona fide attempt to injure me. Riley Tench, fair buzzing with fight/flight and desperate to regain some ground, charges in full weight. He almost makes it easy. He attacks high and hard, a basic opening, and I weave and step, brush and twist, and here's a lock, briefly, which throws him that way and then the other, and he is on the floor. He leaps up. Ronnie Cheung throws him a practice knife. Riley lunges for my gut, then turns the movement into a slash. I am inside it. I strike him with my hips, and he goes "Whuff" and tenses, so I wrap the knife arm around myself (incidentally crunching my shoulder into his chest so that he comes with me) and then unwrap and lock it against my chest. As he counters that, I follow his movement and wrap his arm around him so that the rubber blade brushes against his neck.

It is a distressingly intimate thing. For a moment, his face is layed over an agonised canine muzzle, coughing blood, in that tiny shack outside Cricklewood Cove. I ignore it, and flip him flat onto his back, following him down through the air so that the practice knife never wavers. He lands hard (which was admittedly the idea) and I move the knife lightly to indicate that Riley Tench has just joined the ranks of the honoured and exsanguinated dead. Ronnie Cheung calls a halt, and looks at me with distant interest, as if he has just found me on his sleeve and doesn't know from which orifice I have emerged.

"Volunteers?" he says, gesturing at me. Richard P. Purvis steps up and I win against him too, albeit it's scrappy and Elisabeth would sniff at me. Gonzo begs off. Ronnie Cheung shrugs, squares up to me, then beats down my defence and flattens me in about a second—but he does so, to be honest, with huge restraint, and when he says "Bumhole" it is in a thoughtful way. He hums and nods to himself, and the day comes to an end in a bar somewhere. Ronnie Cheung forgets himself as far as to buy the first round.

And Gonzo: what the hell is he doing there? How is G.W. Lubitsch, heading when last seen for a merchant bank with thunderous initials offering salaries like phone numbers—national dialling codes included after five years—and perks and possibilities beyond the dreams of mortal men, how is Gonzo William Lubitsch leaping out like a pantomime villain from behind a packing case? How does he know Ronnie Cheung? The answers are supplied over crisp beer and salty nuggets cooked in saturated fat. Gonzo has a uniform, although the precise name of his unit is classified. Gonzo is also in training, for tasks more direct and warlike than those General Copsen apparently has in mind for me. More cogently, Gonzo spent three weeks at his new job and decided, "If I stay here I will be found at fifty-five, naked under two secretaries with my feet tied to the bedposts and a lemon in my mouth, and I will be dead and fat and no one will cry except the shy woman living opposite who has always had a crush on me but could never tell me and who might have saved me from myself, but didn't."

By this strange logic, it seems reasonable that Gonzo would opt for a military life, and inevitable, once that decision was made, that he should seek the special forces and the dirty deeds done dirt cheap for the good of those who must never know. Gonzo could never be a line officer or a grunt. Gonzo could only ever be a Mysterious Stranger, dispensing justice and retribution in alleys all around the globe.

And with that, he orders another round and refuses to talk

about it any more, because he has not, as yet, done any of these things, he has only trained for them, and Gonzo hates to talk about himself in anticipation—it does not suit him to say he is, as yet, a rookie.

In my memory there are no strippers. Gonzo swears, the day after, that there were dozens.

Chapter Five

Un-war, hells, and cakes;
a date; the red phone rings.

GREY-BROWN EARTH and green mountainsides; misty air. In the distance one of the lakes of Addeh is giving up its moisture to the heat. When the wind comes from that direction, there's a smell of water, and diesel. When it flicks listlessly round, it comes off the Katir mountains, and carries pine and some kind of flower. Whatever direction it blows from, it doesn't make my tent any cooler or any less isolated in the middle of nowhere, surrounded by other tents and men and women just as lonely.

This is Freeman ibn Solomon's homeland, and the gunmountain he was so unhapppy about has turned out to be a volcano. The country is no longer even known as Addeh Katir; mostly people call it the Elective Theatre, which suggests in some way that there is a clear decision-making process behind what is happening here. That suggestion is extremely debatable.

In the distant past, in what might be described as the Golden Days of War, the business of wreaking havoc on your neighbours (these being the only people you could logistically expect to wreak havoc upon) was uncomplicated. You—the King—pointed at the next-door country and said, "I want me one of those!" Your vassals—stalwart fellows selected for heft and musculature rather than brain—said, "Yes, my liege," or sometimes, "What's in it for me?" but broadly speaking they rode off and burned, pillaged, slaughtered and hacked until either you were richer by a few hundred square miles of forest and farmland, or you were rudely arrested by heathens from the other side who wanted a word in your shell-like ear about cross-border aggression. It was a personal thing, and there was little doubt about who was responsible for kicking it off, because that person was to be found in the nicest room of a big stone house wearing a very expensive hat.

Modern war is distinguished by the fact that all the participants are ostensibly unwilling. We are swept towards one another like colonies of heavily armed penguins on an ice floe. Every speech on the subject given by any involved party begins by deploring even the idea of war. A war here would not be legal or useful. It is not necessary or appropriate. It must be avoided. Immediately following this proud declamation comes a series of circumlocutions, circumventions and rhetorico-circumambulations which make it clear that we *will* go to war, but *not really,* because we don't want to and aren't allowed to, so what we're doing is in fact some kind of hyper-violent peace in which people will die. We are going to *un-war.*

The first rumbling of un-war was nearly a year ago, when I was back in Project Albumen learning how to kill a car. Erwin Mohander Kumar, priapic president of Addeh Katir and stooge to the international financial system, defaulted on his obligations regarding the nation's debt. Rumour has it that he spent the last hundred million in Addeh Katir's bank account to obtain the services of every employee of a noted Dutch sex establishment for a three-year period. Almost everyone in the world now acknowledges that Erwin Kumar is unfit for dog ownership, let alone government. So much is obvious.

The difficulty is what happens next, which is that various nations and groups of nations who are notionally friendly to one another and here for identical, similar or compatible purposes get into disagreements. The good kind of disagreement comes to an end with harsh words and apologies, but disagreements between men and women trained to kill and armed with the best weapons available, who know that they are disagreeing with people who are similarly trained and equipped, are generally the other sort. Giving someone a jolly good talking-to becomes an exchange of warning shots and suddenly there's a minor battle going on. Minor battles become international incidents; international incidents foster distrust; distrust fosters conflict.

As a consequence of several small disagreements, we are now at un-war with:

- the Joint Operational Task Force for Addeh Katir (which is supported by France, Vietnam and Italy, and commanded by Baptiste Vasille)
- the Addeh Defensive Initiative (which is run by a frosty woman from Salzburg named Ruth Kemner and distinguished by a membership so varied and changeful that not even she actually knows on whose behalf she is fighting)
- the United Nations (white hats, sidearms, slightly less scary than an Addeh sheepherder, maintaining an airfield upcountry for the inevitable humanitarian disaster to come)
- the Army of Addeh Katir (Supreme Generalissimo Emperor-President Erwin Kumar commanding, largely concerned with draining the last dregs of prosperity from the national cup)
- the Free Katiri Pirates (Zaher Bey's collected thieves, patriots, arsonists and larcenists, who will steal anything from anyone at any time)
- the South Asian and Pan-African Strategic Fellowship (helluva nice people, actually, and fortunately camped so far away that we have only met them once since the initial misunderstanding and things are calming down a bit)
- and on several regrettable occasions also: ourselves, because accidents will happen.

It's almost as if, now that this place exists as a war zone, everyone feels it would be rude not to use it.

WHEN I WAS studying with Master Wu, I learned that his grandmother believed in a truly enormous collection of hells. In her mind the netherworld was like a great vizier's palace or hall of government, and every floor was given over to a different aspect of suffering. There was a Hell of Crawling Flies and a Hell of Scratchy Undergarments and a Hell of Lukewarm Soup and just about every hell, however vile or trivial, that you could imagine. There was a Hell of Standing in Line and a Hell of Loneliness and a Hell of Chattering Neighbours and a Hell of Silent Grief, all the way to a Hell of Boiling Pitch and a Hell of Smashed Fingers and other hells she declined to detail but delineated with significant noddings and rolling of eyes. These hells were arranged in no apparent order (except for a sequence of hells defined by their orderliness), presided over by guards of utmost probity and administered by sadists and reformers and all manner of intransigent folk, who absolutely would not be deterred from hauling or heaving or leading or shoving you into your appointed hell. There was even a Hell of Uncertain Anticipation where you simply sat around waiting to find out which hell you were eventually going to. For ever.

If there can be such a thing as the Hell of Not Getting Shot, I am in it. There is a war going on (or at least an un-war so much like a war as to be indistinguishable from the thing itself) and I am left out. I am in the thick of it, and yet I am not part of it. Men I know and men I do not are marching, patrolling, sometimes getting killed. I have trained and prepared for this, and still I am, as Ronnie Cheung would have it, a spare prick at an orgy. My moment has not come. I have been given subsidiary moments, auxiliary roles, because George Copsen does not waste resources, but these are sporadic and unsatisfying. Thus I wait and think about great and weighty matters. I am doing this now.

The walls of my tent are blue. It is possible for me, lying on my back on my bed, to reach up with my left big toe and snag a little silky thread which hangs from the roof liner and tug on it. My right foot is somehow just out of reach. I have concluded that this is owing to the angle of approach, and not to a disparity in leg lengths, although I know that my legs, like everyone else's, *are* of slightly different lengths; it just seems more likely that it's about angle. Yesterday I had reached the opposite conclusion. Then I changed my bed around so that the head end was the foot end, and now I'm sure it's about angle. I have developed this discussion as a defence against boredom. It doesn't work.

Some days I get sent on idiot missions to keep me sane. These missions impress upon me that this entire situation is irrational and incomprehensible, and that the only logical response to it is madness. I wonder how I will know when I go mad.

In half an hour I will get up and run to my station, where I will spend four hours attempting to stay alive and feeling guilty because I have not been shot.

In the meantime I read my letters. Two weeks ago, I wrote a little packet of letters home. I wrote to the Evangelist. I wrote to Ma Lubitsch and Old Man Lubitsch both at once, though I had to be very careful not to talk too much about Gonzo, who is doing something dangerous and secret which cannot be trusted to paper. I wrote to Dr. Fortismeer and I wrote short postcards to a lot of people I don't really care about, in the hope that one of them will care about me. I did not write to Elisabeth Soames because I do not want her to see me here, doing this. She belongs to Cricklewood Cove, and while she's there, so am I and so is Master Wu, and a little piece of my life before Jarndice will survive. Also, I am embarrassed about the "not getting shot" thing.

Old Man Lubitsch wrote back to tell me Ma Lubitsch has lost several pounds owing to worry, but she appended a denial in capital letters. She told me she has sent a food package, but it has not arrived. Dr. Fortismeer wrote, urging me to maintain good personal hygiene and stand tall in the face of adversity, and giving me news of home, which apparently is getting on jolly well without me. He enclosed a request from the university for money to build new facilities for the ladies' water polo team, about which he is very enthusiastic, and appended a cheery *postscript* that I should look out for any interesting examples of *foreign spice,* which I take to be a request for Katiri pornography, if there is such a thing.

Elisabeth Soames sent me a note via local military post to tell me she is also out here in the Elective Theatre. She is working as a journalist, writing a human interest story about the UN mission at Corvid's Field. She will be gone in a few days. She sent love. She did not suggest I visit, perhaps because I am a soldier or perhaps just because people in the Elective Theatre do not pay house calls.

The Evangelist wrote too, but only the date and the signature have survived the censor's knife. The rest of her communication has been removed with a razor blade, leaving me holding a limp carcass of eviscerated notepaper. It is a little spooky. It is a *zombie* letter. In the middle of the night it will rise from the grave and eat the other letters, starting with the headings. Then it will crawl out into the camp and begin its rampage, and some of the scraps it leaves behind will also reanimate. The undead paper plague will spread until nothing can stop it . . . bwha-hahaha!

I put the zombie letter away and shake out my shoes.

The fact that I have not been shot is preying upon me like a personal failing. I imagine that, back home, cake-baking ladies of a certain age, monitoring the progress of the conflict, are sitting around tutting over this as if I had farted in church or made free with the barmaid at the Angler's Arms. Missus Laraby and Miz Constance and Biddy Henschler and their friends, a fantasy bingo club of lorgnetted censure, are all sitting there, china cup and macaroon in hand, commiserating with one another and agreeing that I don't know how these things are done. Men like me are the reason why we haven't gotten home by Christmas. We lack the basic moral fibre which was so entirely a part of the men of their own generation that it was impossible for them to pass it on; they never knew how they did it or expressed in words that it must be done; rather, they *were* it and it was them and that is all anyone need say to convey the absolute failure which is me and all my ilk. And no, I will not be getting a care package full of cake, which was what they did for the real men of yesteryear, because in the first place I do not deserve it, and in the second because this war is taking place in a ludicrous far-off land where cakes go bad before the mail can deliver them (a consequence of the absence of fibre in postmen), and in the third place (no one ever needed a third place in the old days, two points of significant reason were enough back then, on account of the fibre) because the military machine had some bad experiences early on in this war with externally baked cakes, including cakes with messages on them which were not good for morale. There were cakes which said "I miss you" and "stupid war" and even, on one particularly radical gâteau, "Geopolitical cat's paw for entrenched interests, rebel!," a cake I personally saw with my own eyes when I was charged by George Copsen with its humane and most secret destruction in the name of discipline.

There were also cakes which contained instructions on how to fake sickness to avoid combat, and a vanishingly small but paranoia-inducing number of un-cakes which were sent by more unpleasant and violent disapprovers of the war effort, who sought to introduce poisons and even explosives into their baking, and thus strike a blow against the hegemonic cryptofascists. I have never seen any of these (cryptofascists, that is; botulinum poison cakes, alas, I can bear witness to) and don't know anyone who would own up to being one. The problem, no doubt, is that the cryptofascists of yesteryear were a better sort of cryptofascist who went out and fought and colonised and were a bit less crypto about the whole thing and said what they meant, whereas modern cryptofascists have *no standards.*

I put on my shirt. It is too hot. It is better than sunburn. I have a flak jacket too, in case I get shot. I have not been shot.

While I have not been shot *(Shame! Boo, hiss!)* that is not to say I have not been injured. Addeh Katir breeds injury. For an earthly paradise, the whole place is shockingly inimical. The fruit is beautiful and juicy and will, given a window of opportunity, lead a commando raid into your intestine which results in total evacuation. A local rodent has developed a taste for the rubber soles of our boots, and a variety of fire ant has taken to laying its eggs in the seams of servicemen's standard-issue trousers. All this before we contemplate the un-war which is going on all around and is possessed of an irrational and powerful volition all its own.

The oddness of it all seems to provoke oddnesses in us; the brutality calls out to our anger. The logic of un-war is strong. Certain actions demand certain responses, of which the simplest is "Shot at? Shoot back."

Of all the groups operating here, only one seems to be able to avoid those reactions—or maybe they are simply more perverse, more determinedly and convolutedly insane than everyone else; Zaher Bey's pirates for the most part do not shoot back. They elude, taunt and tease. They also steal as a way of counting coup—they will steal anything just to demonstrate that they can. They steal the traffic cones which we use to mark out our roads, and the little shining lights which sit on top of them. They hijack truckloads of boots and steal every single right foot, leaving all the left ones. They stole a consignment of flags and a lot of subversive cakes, and returned a solitary Battenberg with a note to the effect that it was rather dry. They penetrate defence-in-depth as if it was cling film. They mince through minefields and cut razor wire for no better reason than to stencil pornographic cartoons on our tanks and pinch our booze. This gives everyone the willies, because one day they may get serious and that would be bad. All the area commanders of all the forces in the region are united in wanting to demonstrate that no one steals from them with impunity. The first person to do this will gain an infinitesimal but possibly decisive measure of kudos.

A month ago a whole load of useful stuff—fencing, tyres, fuel, tentage and antibiotics—vanished from one of our supply dumps, so General Copsen packed me off with some soldiers to get our stuff back (I couldn't shake the image of myself knocking on a neighbour's door and asking for a miskicked football from the wreckage of their conservatory), and I chased the transponder signal from a beacon in the medical supplies pack for several miles across rough country. The trail led us to the outskirts of an abandoned industrial site five kilometres from the dump. The transponder was marching up and down a wall, trying to mate with everything it saw and kill anything which turned it down—or rather it was attached to the collar of a huge feral cat which was doing these things. I discovered this when I, intrepid detective, led my guys around the corner and ordered the cat to put its hands in the air and throw down its weapons, whereupon it jumped on my head and tried to rip my scalp off under the impression that I was a chew toy or a huge, armoured mouse. When this failed and it (thank God) did not find me physically attractive, it pissed on me and ran away.

The cat-bomb incident is important only in so far as it was the mechanism by which I met Tobemory Trent for the first time, as he sewed me up. This meeting caused me to mention, unwisely, that I thought Trent's job was admirable, and General Copsen immediately seconded me to him for a week. Tobemory Trent is a stretcherman.

Stretchermen are the doorkeepers of a hidden kingdom, a soft place where there are nurses. This makes them popular, of course, but at the same time they're gloomy people to think about, because the only way they'll let you into their kingdom is if you're in agony. No one wants to imagine they will ever make that spasmodic face and clutch at a spurting limb, or worse yet do the weird, happy thing people do when they're truly fucked and run around showing bits of bone to their friends and talking about how odd it is to have a hole in them until they bleed out.

My clock goes *beep*. That means I have to go and do this thing. I put on my flak jacket and go and do it.

THIS IS ME as a stretcherman, dismounting from a hot smelly medevac transport (that's a jeep with a cover on it) with a bunch of guys who have done this before. I have not been trained, particularly. I have just been given a medic's armband and told to take the back end because the front is the more skilled position. Being the front-end man requires that you:

1) know how to run with a man's head hitting your legs from behind,
2) be able to support the weight of a man behind your own back, and
3) can navigate the battlefield while doing 1) and 2) and being shot at.

I am sweating, partly because it's what everyone else is doing and I don't want to be left out. Like Tobemory Trent, I have left my shirt on. The idea is that you sweat and keep the moisture covered, so you only have to sweat once, as it were, and you don't carry on losing water. All I know about that is that I have a puddle around the waistband of my trousers and down my arse and I hope I do not get photographed with patches of damp around the buttocks by some overeager shutterbug hoping to "convey the moment." Becoming the posterchild for wet trousers has no appeal.

Away to the west, Green Sector is quiet and safe and there are probably guys getting bored and wondering what to do with the afternoon. They're likely doing the same at Red Gate, although we came through there a while back, and the soldiers gave me to understand they were not happy. Apparently the local commander is an idiot. I will have to remember to tell George Copsen about this when I get back. It's the kind of thing he likes to know.

Over to my right, in one of the contested zones, something huge is on fire, or more probably something quite small is hugely on fire. Smoke pours up and out and hides the blue sky and makes a shadow on the land below. Quite clearly it is Mordor, and there are orcs and monsters there, and the burning thing is

Mount Doom. It actually looks pretty cool, in a bad way. It also looks a long way off. Tobemory Trent, the Sage of the Field Dressing Station, ordered us dropped here a few moments ago, and is now tasting the air and (more important) paying heed to some secret testicle signal known only to front-end stretchermen. No one speaks. I, at least, have nothing to say. The back-end stretcherman's code is simple: obedience to the man at the front. In my case, this is Trent himself. He reaches a decision and moves towards the smoke in a narrow ellipse which will bring us around to it from the north and the higher ground.

I follow Trent down in the direction of Mount Doom, wondering which hobbit I am, and it seems to me that we cannot possibly get anywhere near the fighting. I can hear the gunshots and even, when the wind is right, smell them. I can hear and see explosions and so on, but they are all tinny and fake. Trent has deployed too early and in the wrong place. He picks up speed, and so, perforce, do I. The noises get louder. An armoured personnel carrier passes us at great speed, shiny and new and a bit urgent. I make a note to myself to request patrol duty when next General Copsen asks me if I feel I'm pulling my weight.

"Getting there," says Trent. He must be deeply moved to be so verbose. I do not know how he can tell. I suspect we will be running for quite a while, and wonder whether we might get the APC to pick us up and give us a lift.

When Trent demanded that the transport leave us here in the middle of nowhere, the other back-end guy seemed on the brink of committing a grave sin. He had the expression of someone about to *ask a question.* By this sign, I know that he is also new. The lieutenant in the transport, a man with exactly no hair and apparently made of ivory and parchment, just leaned over and threw him out of the door. Trent and the other front-end guy shared a look like "and this is the shit we have to work with nowadays," and we tumbled out into the sand. The transport roared away, and everything was calm. It mostly still is, although amid the (fairly) distant banging there's now a strange, domestic noise, a noise of pets. It goes *pitter patter babubudda-boom* (but that's not pets, that's small explosive munitions). *Lollop lollop.* Quite a lot of pets (*boom,* that one was a bit closer) and they are running all around, and just maybe they are carrying bits of change in their pockets or wearing bells, because there's just a whisper of *clinktinkle.* The pets should not be here. This is a dangerous place. I should not be here either.

I carry the stretcher. I follow Tobemory Trent.

We run around a corner, come over a rise and everything is much, much louder. We run into a small town where a lot of men are killing each other in a fairly energetic and random way. The smoke is suddenly not just nearby but all around us. Things scream past me which I realise are bullets and I completely forget to duck (Ma Lubitsch would be furious) but do not get shot. Tobemory Trent also does not get shot, although why this is I have no idea because he has not as much forgotten to duck as decided that since he doesn't know where the bullets are, moving his head is a lottery he can't be bothered to play. The *pitter patter* all around us turns out to be the sound, not of several thousand kittens entering a litter tray, but of masonry falling in chips and blocks from walls peppered with gunfire. The whole town is built out of egg timers, shedding sand from the top half into the bottom, and when the top half is empty the town will basically be a floor shorter than it was and much of it will fall over, probably in about eight minutes or so.

Trent leads the way along a small road which smells of latrines and leather and cooked meat and burning rubber and something else which isn't any of those things and which my animal instincts aren't at all happy about. For no especially good reason, no one is using this road as a shooting gallery, so aside from occasional through-and-throughs, it's about as safe as this town currently gets. The houses are pretty in a doomed way: sandstone or cement, and modern but with a traditional feeling to them which says yeah, sure, we used a crane and some prefabs to make this, but it's still the same kind of house we were making when the main construction material was mud. Every now and again there's a big boxy thing which must be a factory or a hotel or an apartment block which is made of the same stuff and seems to be leaning over the houses and muttering like a gawky teen about how this place is old and tiny and nothing cool ever happens here and why oh why isn't there a mall? A couple of these even have billboards on them advertising things, but I have no idea what, and this leads me to reflect that quite a lot of signage back home is also lousy with non-relevant noise and useless without text, and then some idiot starts bombing the town.

I know this because my legs feel like jelly and the buildings ripple and one of the billboards comes off on one side and half a smiling face rips through the roof of a dwelling place and exposes an empty kitchen with blood on the wall. And then there is a very loud noise, and Trent suggests we stop for a moment to consider our position and find out what the holy heck is going on, because the enemy here should not have artillery and any bombs falling on this town ought to be ours and they clearly ought not to be falling on it while we're in it. An old lady, or a dangerous insurgent dressed as an old lady, but probably just a middle-aged lady in rags who needs a bath and a few months spent in a place which is not a war zone, is waving pathetically at us to bugger off.

There is a flash up ahead, not a big one. It is a shell going off, clearly, between a hotel called Rick's American Casablanca (which is probably some kind of confused trademark infringement, but enough rights are being infringed here already that I'm not going to get worked up over intellectual property) and what appears to be a toyshop. Both of them have huge glass frontages which had not, until this moment, turned to sand. The flash is very bright and it stops me in my tracks, sort of fascinated, and the glass frontages bow and then collapse.

Trent hits me from one side and we fall together into the wall of a dismembered Laundromat. He counts. One. Two. Three . . . and a cloud of razors whispers by, a mist of broken glass which rakes the ground and tinkles off the awning struts and rips the fabric apart without slowing down, and the deflected splinters, some the size of fishfood and some like sideplates, drop around us from above.

"Close one," Trent mouths, or perhaps he is shouting and I am deaf. He jumps up and picks up the stretcher, and moves on into the main square, temporarily also the Hell of Shattered Men. Aline (irrelevant Aline, of the welcoming hips and the uncertain courage, whom I miss desperately at this moment but who mysteriously turns into Elisabeth Soames the last time I saw her, back in Cricklewood Cove, before she is occluded by a dying soldier from Paxton) would be annoyed by this description, because some of the corpses and near-corpses and dear Christ ought-to-be corpses here are female. The old lady/insurgent/average woman who wanted us to go has been transformed into a dead thing made of rags and bone.

There's a burning smell, and a creaking, and I realise there's a truck on fire—no, two, but one of them is already a furnace. A big guy brushes past me, some journo who has surprisingly dropped his camera and is making for the flames. There's screaming from that direction, but then there's screaming everywhere. The journo is yelling at his crew to *give a hand here, you arseholes,* and suddenly they get the idea, and there's a kind of news strike while they risk their lives for someone else's instead of for hard copy. Most of them look scared and a bit embarrassed about this, and finally the big guy has to be hauled away because the trucks are about to explode. They explode, but hardly anyone pays any attention. The journos all stand and stare at the people they have saved from death, completely unsure about what to do with them now.

Tobemory Trent weaves through Golgotha not like someone who has just been almost blown up, but like a man come home to a terrible but familiar monstrosity. He whips open his pack and does something brutal and necessary and a man shrieks and then says "Thank you," but then he can't stop saying it and it becomes a long burble *thankyou-thankyou-thankoo-ankooankooankoo.* Trent hits him in the head to knock him out, because drugs are precious and the guy's head isn't in any danger.

Somehow there are other stretchermen here among the pools of human juice, all long-limbed and grave and carrying, as we are, packs of bandages and basic splints and other things unmentionable to dispense relief. One of them is down, must have arrived just before us, a kid named Bobby Shank. I've seen him eating a few times, kinda waved, gotten a nod in return. Bobby Shank has a hole in the front of his head, but there is very little blood and he is still alive. That happens. On TV, if you get shot in the head, you die. Out here, sometimes you survive. Sometimes you even have a life afterwards. Bobby Shank is on his own stretcher, and his front man is strapping up a guy with a minor head wound so he can take Bobby's place at the back and carry him out. I look away. Bobby Shank will escape, but he will not be okay. Not unless a miracle happens, and the reason they're called miracles is that they don't. I glance over at Trent, who sees what I see and shakes his head to tell me I am right. And then he tells me to stop being a fucking tourist, and concentrate. He does not say it like he hates me, but more as if I've passed a test.

Somehow, the stretchermen collectively and individually knew that this was a place where they would be needed, and they split up and came here by a variety of avenues so as to minimise their own casualties and maximise their per capita efficacy. It is not relevant to any of them—nor even to me, because I'm here and we are doing this thing and we aren't leaving until it is done—that some tomfool a few kilometres away behind our fortifications has started bombarding this place while we are still in it. They will deal with that arsehole in due time and full measure. His sheets will be sewn with burrowing mites and his trousers seeded with fire ants. Unto him shall be dealt schoolboy pranks and humiliating revenges, and he shall count his hours a curse until such time as we relent, and by these signs the officers and men of this army of fools shall know this gospel: *Do not meddle with the stretchermen, for they are mad, and shall serve you according to a madman's lights.*

We give aid without hesitation, and do not discriminate. Everyone in this un-war treats all wounded. This has been agreed for ages, so sometimes I am working on men who scream in Xhosa or Russian. I put my fingers into a set of surgical gloves and then into a second set on Trent's instructions ("Some of these bastards have diseases other germs are scared of, man") and then I put my fingers into new and strange artificial orifices and chase rubbery arterial tissue down inside men's limbs and drag it back while Trent sutures and shouts that he isn't a fucking doctor, he's just a medic and we need to carry this guy out and we can't because there's no time; carry one out, lose four more, triage and triage again. We have dispensed relief for an hour, and I have aged one quarter of a lifetime, when thunder opens up and everything goes not white or black or even grey but blue: a dark, oceanic blue, and I do not get shot, but something else instead.

THUS to hospital, and smells of the Evangelist's study and the cellar at the Lubitsch house. Detergent and linen and elastic and powder and bleach and women working. Less convivial, also blood and sickness and effluvia unnamed but familiar and bad. None of these, currently, leaking from me. I open one eye and survey the dismal situation, and find it fairly good, and then very good, as a mechanical angel above me (almost enough to renew the faith I lost to the Evangelist's wood-beamed ceiling, this) pumps morphine into my veins. Gosh. Morphine is *way* cool.

My medical chart is something of a legend. The patient history is very nearly funny. The first person to be assailed by trouser-dwelling fire ants was me. The first person to discover that the gentle waters of the River Kanneh were home to a peculiarly belligerent kind of stinging weed was me. I was, by sheer misfortune, also the first person to be infected with an influenza imported from home on a bundle of letters. From there it got positively comedic: the rabid cat incident. I am a byword for misadventure and bizarre injury.

My present ills are a consequence of having been *blown up,* sadly by my own side. I say "sadly" because the friendly-fire aspect of the injury means that it cannot be fast-tracked or treated or even properly acknowledged, and there will be no citations, no promotions and emphatically no compassionate leave, because all this would involve the attribution of blame and the acceptance that what happened was erroneous and not in some way gloriously and brilliantly brave and strategically sound. Since our side has just blown up not only me, but also a supply train and half of a friendly local township, this cannot be permitted, and I am officially here owing to an *accidental weapons discharge,* which is usually code for "Idiot shot himself in the arse while cleaning his gun." In my case, of course, the piece of shrapnel in my arm argues that it was some other idiot who accidentally discharged his gun, several miles away, but no one is able to acknowledge that or they'll get fired, or (unlikely but seemingly not unthinkable) fired *upon.*

On the upside, the shell which exploded down the road from me was not made of uranium, and therefore the small raggedy chunk of it currently occupying space between my bicep and the bone of my upper arm is neither toxic (beyond being coated in airborne viruses and soil and dust and all the other crap it picked up between the point of detonation and its arrival in me) nor radioactive to any apppreciable degree.

Thus, while I have now visited the Hell of Friendly Shrapnel, I have not been shunted into the Hell of Heavy Metal Poisoning or the Hell of Internal Burns or the Slow Hell of Military-Grade Carcinoma That No One Will Talk About. I can expect to live and return to service in the Elective Theatre, where I will no doubt experience further time in the compounded, fractal hells which are the state of being there, namely the hells of Grit Up My Arse, Sandmite Bites, Endless Boredom and Constant Fear,

We Have No Idea What We're Doing Here and Baked Bean Muesli for Breakfast, this last being the inexplicable gift of the hell wardens known as Supply. Given that this is me we're talking about, I will not get shot, but I will get diseases, snakebites, sunstroke, skin-bloating due to rain, skin-cracking due to sun, toxic shock due to overapplication of skin remedies leading to bowel disorders, rashes and infected blisters. War is not hell. War is a chocolate box selection, an after-Christmas *Best of* compilation of hells. It occurs to me as I reach the end of this line of reasoning that morphine is wonderful stuff and I would like some more, and I press the little clicker which I know from previous adventures sometimes dispenses it, but nothing happens. Apparently my injury is not serious, or perhaps accidental discharge victims are treated with a sternness appropriate to their stupidity. It's not as if I've been (headshaking and tutting from the ladies of the cake bake) shot.

There is a woman at my bedside. She appears to be a nurse of some description. Her badge—which is clean and white like everything else about her—reveals that her name is Leah. She is beautiful. She misses the vein three times. Normally she would go to the other arm at this point, but it is by the nature of my injury not available. I forbear from telling her that there are seventeen people of my close acquaintance in this war who would have hit the thing dead on first time, so often have they injected into themselves the freely available heroin to which about one in three of the rank and file is addicted, although "addiction" suggests that there's something else they should be doing, and that is often far from clear. Are you addicted if there is simply no reason for you to do anything else? If you have not, since you took up heroin, had an occasion where it has interfered with your life? Or are you just fucked out of your mind and waiting to see what comes?

Despite being lousy with a needle (and this ought to be a hell all its own, but somehow isn't) she is beautiful. I would let her stick pins in me almost anywhere, at any time.

"I would let you stick pins in me almost anywhere, at any time," I assure her when she apologises. It comes out less sophisticated than I had hoped.

"Likewise," she says distractedly, making another hole in my unbandaged arm. I suspect it is starting to look like a bit of *pointillisme,* and this recalls to my mind the fact that monetary notes of various nations are often or possibly always created by *pointillistes,* for reasons I do not know, and I have the urge to go and find out.

"You'd let me poke you with a needle? That's very nice. Only I don't have a needle," I respond helpfully, and she blushes and it occurs to me that our conversation could have a rather obvious sexual subtext.

"Oh gosh, this conversation has a rather obvious sexual subtext. Did you know banknotes were designed by *pointillistes*? I mention it because you seem to have some talent in that direction." Someone is talking, and he sounds a great deal like me, but I wouldn't say something that crass unless I was medicated, which of course I am, because they are taking the friendly shrapnel out of my arm in an hour, and I am full to the gills with happy juice.

Leah gives a little howl of fury and then a cry of alarm and I pass out, which I understand later is because she has done something unhelpful with the needle. When I wake, she's still there, but the nervousness has gone from her. And it has taken with it the pain, or the original pain, although a new, dull ache has appeared and I have a hangover.

"I'm sorry," she says. "I hadn't slept for forty hours."

And she kisses me. It is not a sexual kiss, in the sense that she does not fling herself flat upon me and press herself against me and ravish my mouth with her slender, fascinating lips. It is however unquestionably and utterly an *erotic* kiss, above and beyond that I have lacked female company for seven months and can now, when I am not in agony, get turned on by the elegant lines of wooden chair legs and the sound of a floorboard sighing. It is erotic in the sense also that it is a thing of love, or the promise of love, or the offer of the possibility of love, and I am not aware of having done anything to deserve this. It is wonderful. And then it stops. She surveys the impact zone and seems pleased. I boggle at her (suavely, of course, not like a gaffed salmon being given the kiss of life by a mermaid, not at all), and she turns smartly and walks out. I fall asleep smiling, for the first time since I came to Addeh Katir.

"FUCKING fuckeroo hubabababafishwit *fuckit*!"

When I heard the door open, I hoped it might be a prelude to more acts of random affection. I kept my eyes closed, therefore, and languished in what I hoped was a subtle blend of need, manliness and puppy-like adorability. I was considering a small whiffling noise when my ear was assaulted by the first volley from this unwelcome substitute. It has pretty much kept going solidly until now, "fuckerang fuck-dammit," and so on, etc., etc. I never met a less imaginative vulgarist. After a while it just becomes noise. If he was saying "poot" instead—for example, "pootity pooting pootbuckets pooting papootipoot"—it would mean as much, and be worth greater consideration. Ah well.

I deduce from the sound of squeaking wheels and plastic sheeting that they have partitioned the room in the name of decency. Very flash this, in the Elective Theatre. Such niceties normally go out of the window, from which I further deduce that it is *his* decency and not mine which is at issue. Not that he seems to be a saintly sort of fellow, having used the F-word non-stop for eight minutes. Very coarse. I decide to imagine that he is, in fact, saying "poot."

"Poot you, poot *you,* poot everypooting pooter pootpoot*poot* motherpoot pootity pootastic aaa*poot*!"

Much better. And the more often he shouts "poot" at the top of his voice, the less attractive he makes himself, no doubt, to a certain splendid, elusive woman with a weak spot for stoical men-at-arms. I fall asleep again, if not smiling, at least smug. It's odd, though. He says these things without passion, as if he's just sort of running through them like a shopping list. Sometimes they are loud and sometimes they are quiet. That's all. I deduce that a bad thing has happened to this person, and I try not to get too close in case he is contagious.

They wheel him out in the morning, and he is still muttering. It is Bobby Shank. I feel like a total bastard. I also worry that there is a taxonomy of triage at work. Tomorrow they will bring in someone else, and he will scream, and then in the morning he will watch as they collect my still body and mark my chart with a big black X.

I worry about this until Nurse Leah comes back and smiles at me through the door, then steps through and blesses me with another brief, infuriating, mystifying kiss and slips away before I can call her to account.

LATER, a male nurse sits by my bed and explains that this is not common practice and that apparently I asked Leah to marry me in the recovery room and that whatever I said was so utterly brave and vulnerable that she wants very much to be asked out on a date. There is a merciless truth in anaesthesia, even more so than in wine. The nature of a man (or a woman) is exposed entirely by the astringent flood of Pentathol and its cousins. An actual date is probably impossible because we are in a war zone, and so she has written me a note, because she is aware that this will all sound silly, and is afraid to be there when I laugh at her or tell her I am already married. Would I like to have this note?

The nurse is called Egon Schlender. He is slim and disapproving and he comes from Gladdyston, and I do not know where that is and he does not tell me. He is protective and quite obviously he has been talked into this speech and he expects me to respond in a dishonourable way. I tell him I am not married. That there is no one waiting for me. That there is no lawful or social impediment to my making an honest woman of Nurse Leah, who is obviously his friend, but that I realise that the ravings of a post-operative idiot are not the basis for a sound marriage, which is a thing to be embarked upon solemnly and with due thought to the consequences and on the understanding that *to love* is an action, a verb, a thing of choice, and this can be promised and delivered where *in love* is a more tenuous and fragile thing which may come and go with the wind and the seasons.

I tell him that I really, really would like to take her out on a date, and that somehow it can be managed, and that yes, I would dearly love to see Nurse Leah's note.

Egon Schlender's face is very serious. He glances away behind me, thinking, and then he nods, and from his inner pocket he draws a small creamy envelope—by what arts this woman has stationery I do not know—and passes it to me. It smells of nothing so much as clean paper. There is no perfume on it, and I realise that this is because Nurse Leah wears none on the wards, even if she has any. She is constantly washing herself, constantly sterilising. The absence is her scent. Nurse Leah is the ambient smell of this place. But in the creases there must be a tiny whisper of her body, of the oils which are in her skin, of sweat. I snuffle it up, and just perhaps there is something there, a lingering mist of something floral, and of effort and care. Peach and latex.

The handwriting is small and neat. It is the handwriting of someone who does not consider themselves artistic, for whom clarity and purity of form are important. There are no frills, no extra strokes. The joins are fluid, but the letters are precisely separated by an instant's hesitation. The ink is black. The pen was not a ballpoint, but a fountain pen, and it must be one which she keeps for correspondence with home, because it would never survive the harsh use of nursing, most especially not here, in the Elective Theatre.

You asked if I would marry you. I did not know then, and I do not know now, the answer to that question. I do not know you, *which is one reason I want to go out on a date with you. Another is that I think if I don't have some laughs I will probably stick a scalpel in the senior medical officer the next time he asks me to triage his patients for him. You should consider the risks involved, however; even the fact that I am writing this letter to a man I have never formally met, and who asked me to marry him with the drip still in his arm, would seem to imply that I have lost my grip on conventional behaviour. Since I am also fatigued, furious, insomniac and having fantasies of violence against a harmless old lecher who is only trying to do his best in an impossible situation, it seems possible that I may be developing a light stress-induced psychosis, which, though harmless in the long term, may make me an even worse romantic bet than a man who, according to his medical chart, has been burned, run over, repeatedly infected by local diseases, assaulted by a rabid cat and finally blown up by his own side.*

With these minor reservations in mind, let me make it absolutely clear that if you ask me out I will say yes, which I hope will remove the element of self-doubt from your decision-making.

Leah

x

Egon Schlender watches my face throughout, his little, clever eyes reading me in turn. He only glances away to look over my head from time to time in what I take to be some kind of residual awareness that staring is either rude or faintly alarming. I do not put down the letter. I fold it along its pre-existing creases and put it back in the envelope, and Egon Schlender watches me for signs of what I will say and whether he is going to have to rip the drip from my vein and beat me to death with a blood rack in order to keep his friend's heart unbroken. His tapered fingers are tapping a slow, steady rhythm on his knee. I do not have a breast pocket, because I am wearing a hospital gown and not a jacket, so I cannot put the envelope anywhere except next to my skin. It rubs gently, the crisp edges occasionally snagging a hair or an old scar, and I am able by concentrating on it very hard to avoid weeping openly. When I have gotten used to the feeling of having it there (and there it will remain, one way or another, for ever) I look up at Egon Schlender.

"Would you tell Leah, please, that I said yes? That I said yes, yes, yes? That this is the most beautiful thing—that *she* is—I have ever seen?"

Egon Schlender stands up silently, although there is a strong sense of approval in his face, and walks out. And behind me I hear the sound of her breathing, and I realise that she has stood at the head of my bed throughout, and now she moves to kneel on the floor beside me so that she can stare at me eye to eye, and we stay like that for some time, her two hands on my good one.

I have a date in a war zone.

That's not bad going, actually, but now I need an Italian trattoria with check tablecloths and linen napkins. I need bruschetta (that's "broo-SKET-uh," not "brushetter," a slender piece of ciabatta toasted and brushed with garlic and oil and covered in fresh tomato and basil—the chunks inevitably fall off the bread and the olive oil runs over your lips and down your chin. The whole thing is delicious, deeply physical and delightfully undignified, and a woman who can eat a real bruschetta is a woman you can love and who can love you. Someone who pushes the thing away because it's messy is never going to cackle at you toothlessly across the living room of your retirement cottage or drag you back from your sixth heart attack by sheer furious affection. Never happen. You need a woman who isn't afraid of a faceful of olive oil for that) and Vino Nobile di Montepulciano (from the Cantine Innocenti, of course) and the view from the hills and all the trimmings. I need things which are in no way obtainable, and I need them so that the one good thing in the world will not go away. Fortunately, I have an edge, an old friend who has joined the hero club. If anyone can get me a bottle of plonk and a room with a view in a war zone, he will be it.

"WHO IS SHE?" Gonzo wants to know, as he sits at my bedside with his rugged health and his big bear shoulders rippling in his special forces jacket, and at that moment Leah appears to check my chart and tell him sternly not to wear me out, and to remind me that I am due for discharge tomorrow and not to screw it up. Gonzo's eyes follow her and check *her* chart and his hands-off-respectful look is a bit wistful, and when she marches out again without sparing him a second glance he pronounces her good.

"You want me to talk to some guys about some things?" Gonzo asks. "There's a place out past Red Sector which has an old castle. And a guy I know knows a guy who confiscated some silverware."

It turns out that between the loot secured in the course of liberating Addeh Katir from our fellow protectors, and the architecture of the cryptocommunist maharajas, I just might get a date after all, although Gonzo suggests I wait until the minefield is entirely laid out and the AA defences are properly entrenched, and then if there's a bombing raid we will get fireworks after dinner. The only hiccough is that although the fighting has moved on, Red Sector is still classed as a combat zone (unlike, to take a random example, the town where I was blown up, which is supposed to be reasonably safe), so we have to be ordered there. But Gonzo knows ways and means here as well, is an old hand at securing stern injunctions to do as he will, and puts together a mission profile with zero risk which requires the presence of a small commando team (Gonzo and his SpecOps chef, a team of heavily armed and lethal waiters and a command and control unit with a stove), an upper-echelon presence (me and a table for two, napkins officially classed as "flag patches, white linen, surplus") and a medical officer (Leah in a fetchingly close-cut paramedic jumpsuit with pockets in most intriguing places). Gonzo, as maître d', is pleased to inform me that there is space in the grill room at seven-thirty.

RED SECTOR IS HILLY and cool, and there's a small river which does not have anything unpleasant floating in it. Our light-armoured transport is basically a recreational vehicle pimped by Rambo. Leah sits on my knee, because there is no room for her elsewhere (Gonzo's calculations regarding gear and manpower were precisely calibrated, possibly to achieve exactly this), and her hair smells of heat and of her. Her hand balances on my shoulder. This proximity is making me extremely horny, and it gets no better when she leans back and stretches because she is cramped (or possibly because she, better even than Gonzo, knows the value of casual contact and accidental rubbings and touches, and she is well aware that her rear sliding over my thighs and her pale neck right there in front of me are causing an involuntary, embarrassing and deeply enjoyable physical reaction in my groin, to wit, a boner of truly splendid solidity which would be visible if she turned so much as a quarter circle and looked down, which she does not do, even when a gorgeous rose light paints the hills on that side of the car and she has to crane her neck to see it).

Behind us a big guy named Jim is driving another monster RV, this one fitted with a fifty-calibre machine gun, and behind the fifty-cal is a beefy, muscle-bound woman called Annabel by Gonzo and Ox by everyone else, and she appears to be speaking or yelling into the teeth of the wind.

I had believed, until earlier today, that SpecOps was a man's world, and no doubt it used to be, but Annabel/Ox is not alone in Gonzo's unit: there is also a pretty, long-limbed woman with cold eyes who is known mostly as Sally and sometimes as Eagle and who wears a khaki name badge reading "Culpepper" and when she arrived was carrying a long rifle over one long shoulder. Sally/Eagle rides next to Gonzo and occasionally makes course corrections, but mostly she scans the area with a pair of big spyglasses and draws Annabel's attention to little heat pockets which might need to be rapidly sprayed with fifty-cal shells whose velocity and spin is so incredible that a near miss will kill you as surely as a hit.

For "little heat pockets" read "people," although actually most of them so far have been weary, nervous sheep. A war zone is a bad place to be a sheep. It's not a good place to be anything, but sheep generally are a bit stupid and devoid of tactical acumen and individual reasoning, and they approach problem-solving in a trial-and-error kind of a way. Sheep wander, and wandering is not a survival trait where there are landmines. After the first member of a flock is blown up, the rest of the sheep automatically scatter in order to *confuse the predator*, and this, naturally, takes more than one of them onto yet another mine and there's another woolly *BOOM-splatterpitterslee-eutch*, which is the noise of an average-sized sheep being propelled into the air by an anti-personnel mine and partially dispersed, the largest single piece falling to Earth as a semi-liquidised blob. This sound or its concomitant reality upsets the remaining sheep even more, and not until quite a few of them have been showered over the neighbourhood do they get the notion that the only safe course is the reverse course. By this time, alas, they have forgotten where that is, and the whole thing begins again. *BOOM.*

The *first* corollary of this is that sheep are a nightmare if you're trying to construct a perimeter defence, because they can end up cutting a path right through it and leaving themselves in pieces as markers showing the cleared route to all comers. For this reason, many military officers now order a mass execution of unsecured sheep when fortifying a position, incidentally incurring the deep displeasure of local shepherds and creating yet another group of grumpy, armed persons who will shoot at anything in a uniform.

Knowing this, George Copsen has taken a pro-sheep position, in the vague hope that Baptiste Vasille or Ruth Kemner will begin the *ovicide* (which may or may not be the official word for a killing of sheep) and suffer the consequences. So far, it hasn't happened, and a kind of steely cold war of livestock has developed in which we drive sheep towards the other forces in the hope of triggering a slaughter, and they drive them at us with very much the same in mind. An unofficial book is being made on which area commander will snap first, and the betting heavily favours Ruth Kemner, who is apparently something of a scary lady.

The *second* corollary, which is more interesting in an academic sense, but utterly irrelevant in the real world, is that sheep surviving for a prolonged period in a heavily mined area will gradually evolve, and left long enough would develop into more intelligent, combat-hardened sheep, possibly with sonar for probing the earth in front of them, extremely long legs for stepping over suspect objects and large flat feet to distribute pressure evenly and avoid activating the fuse. A warsheep would be a cross between a dolphin and a small, limber elephant.

The sheep currently surrounding us have not yet had time to evolve physically, and in the meantime have evolved behaviours and coping strategies instead. They follow humans quite precisely, walk slowly and the flock unit has been replaced by a loose-knit affiliation of individual sheep carefully watching each other for signs of suddenly flying into the air and getting spread all over the place. Some have started walking in single file. Loud bangs no longer scare them, or possibly they have gone deaf, and there is a sharp, alert feeling about them which suggests they know exactly where they have just stepped and can retreat along their own hoofprints quite readily. The march of progress has reached even unto the sheep of Addeh Katir.

Just before Red Gate there is an actual Katiri village, or bazaar, or some muddled combination of the two. It is close enough to our emplacements to have fallen inside our defensive net, but far enough away that it has avoided becoming a target.

Its name is Fudin, a name to be spoken tonally, carefully and reverently, in the rippling language of Addeh Katir. Fudin is more than a name, it's a snatch of song.

Gonzo curls us into Fudin to pick up some extras for the feast, and also because the vaulted marketplace there is one of the few remaining things in the whole of Addeh Katir which points to what is buried in the ruins. It is striped like a Gothic cathedral, tiled like Babylon in rich blues and filled with pools and alcoves. It is also of course an outpost of the black market (possibly even a *festerance*), and Erwin Kumar and probably also our government would be jolly cross if they knew that it was here, operating under our protection. We have conquered this village (except that we haven't, because we don't, because we are at un-war and we don't occupy, we just sort of live in and around and provide staff and police) but it *belongs* to Zaher Bey.

This is the closest Addeh Katir has to a neutral place, and we wander, ignored by the shoppers. I smell bacon and cooked meat, then fruit, then something pungent and exciting I cannot name. The market is lit with candles and oil lamps which hang from hooks set into the tiles. The lanterns look as if they have been here since before I was born. They probably have. (Leah's shoulder fits perfectly under my arm. I can feel her against me, her fingers on my back. I stroke her hip very lightly, and she shivers.)

With a thunderous clapping of hands, a dark-eyed man in a glittering hat and a fine white shirt demands our attention. Having got it, he bounces forward and embraces us all at once, as if he has been waiting for us and only us for days, and where have we been? The shirt strains over his considerable belly and the nethermost button gives up the struggle. A slice of smooth brown skin is briefly revealed, startlingly naked. He smells of . . .

"Saffron! Yes! We have been saffron men since before the British!" he trumpets. "We were always saffron men. Our children are born with saffron hearts, our mothers sing the weights and measures to send us to sleep. There are no other true saffron men in Addeh Katir; Fudin is the place where saffron *wants* to be sold." He leans close and grins. "If you throw a box of saffron up in the air *anywhere in the whole of Asia* (except maybe in bloody Russia, which is a crazy mad place full of the children of bears and wanton women from the ice), that saffron will blow in the wind until it falls like rain here in Fudin, and I, Rao Tsur, will be standing outside with a box to catch it in, and welcome it home. We know the secret whispers of saffron; we know how to love it and keep it, and we sell it only to the deserving, always at a fair price . . ." He peers at Gonzo, as if unsure, and then his eye lights on me, and on Leah, and he erupts again. "Saffron is for lovers! There! These two, they are lovers, yes? Hmm?"

And at this point, because our delighted humiliation is not complete, it appears that Rao Tsur has a wife. She is lean, and beautiful in a mournful way. She throws up long arms and spreads wide immense hands. Her elbows bend and straighten, and she looks like an angry heron.

"You are an oaf! Yes, Rao, yes, you are. I am married to a buffoon. May you be forgiven for your clumsiness, so that the shame does not grow too much for me and kill me stone dead where I stand. Yes, stone dead. Yes. My mother (bless her dead and departed soul) was an idiot when she promised me to you. Oh, she said, any child of my friend Seeta and my friend Li will be a fine man, because she is wise and he is beautiful and both are loyal. Oh yes, she said, it's a fine thing I do now for my daughter. *Bah!* Do you hear me? *Bah!* And I, fool child, I looked at the broad-shouldered youth they showed me when it was time, and I saw the fire in his eyes and it lit me up like a tramp! Oh, yes, we were young then, and I thought of nothing but arching backs and sweat and the pumping, clenching ecstasy! I nodded, I agreed to my own doom, thinking with my crotch! Hah! But now look! He is fat! Fat, here and now, when the world is starving all around! How does he do it? Who knows? Not me, who have grown scrawny! Thin like a spider, a witch to fright the children, a stick woman to be broken by the wind. Oh, there was a time when I was fine, with a proud chest like a maharaja's pillow, all covered in silk. A chest to drive frenzies of lust, to start fights and make women tear at their hair. Hah! But now look"—and here she thrusts out for our inspection an impressive bosom, little weathered by time or hard living, and the muscles in her neck pronounce her fit and strong—"I am a waif! A wreck! And all because of you!" she adds to Rao Tsur, who is admiring the presented cleavage with some interest. "And *now,* when you should be selling saffron to feed your family and maybe, just maybe, restore to your ailing wife her former strength and beauty, though God knows her looks have departed under your wastrel management and she is dowdy and no doubt you mean to put her aside like a torn waistcoat, *now,* I say, you are offending these good people, because a blind man could see they are not lovers, not yet, and you have embarrassed them and maybe now it will never be! You may well cringe, husband, like a lardy, corpulent dog with a mouthful of your master's dinner! You have placed their love in jeopardy, idiot man, and what price saffron in a world where love is unsound? Eh? Eh? Bah!" And with that she collapses into a chair and scowls at him, drumming her fingertips together.

Rao Tsur looks at us, apologetic, and draws close.

"Acute embarrassment. I mingle my responsibilities. This ailing madwoman was placed in my care (curse my compassionate nature and my promise to my father always to succour the weak!) when I was a younger man, just starting in the world. She believed herself a hedgehog then, and spoke not a word. It was a simple thing to tend to her. A bowl of goat's milk and a warm box of straw and she was quite content. Alas! I meddled, for she was of such surpassing beauty that I fancied God, divine and high above, could not intend her to be thus for evermore. No, I thought, surely this creature has a higher purpose, an angelic destiny. (Not that I fancied myself a part of it, you understand, no, no, for Rao is modest, you see. No, a mere conduit to greatness, a *catalyst,* is Rao.) Thus, I coaxed her to the schoolhouse and there educated her in simple language and science, what history and art I knew, along the way demonstrating the fallacy of the hedgehog conceit. She took to learning as if born to it, and I rejoiced, thinking I had played my role in God's creation. Oh, yes, I was quite cock-a-hoop. But, alas for Rao! I unleashed a monster! She delights in the most foul-mouthed and lascivious pronouncements, and her delusions evolved along with her cognition! Her lusts now focus not on male hedgehogs, which are at least able to defend themselves, but on poor honest Rao! She believes herself my wife. And worse, she has acquired (through ceaseless acts of copulation with troglodytes and roadside peddlers) a brood of children more appalling even than herself! Unhappy Rao, fettered to a howling succubus and her demonic brats, forever punished for his presumption . . . and yet . . . in this rare instance one perceives she has uncovered a fragment of the truth, as a pig scratching in the earth uncovers, without comprehending, the cornerstone of a temple. You are not lovers! I have offended you! I have spoken out of turn (this hag's infections of the mind are virulently contagious) and I would make amends . . . perhaps a reduced price, if you wished to purchase a large quantity?"

THE ROAD goes by slowly, miles of hill country giving way to forests. I drift, lulled by the soft, easy pressure of Leah's rump against my lower body. She leans back onto me, perspiration diffusing through her clothes, a wicked, sexual marzipan smell, brushed with a sharp tar of hospital. She cannot fail to be aware that I am daydreaming of her, of her mouth and her buttocks. We are too close together now for such secrets. She lets her head rest against mine, and breathes out against my skin. There is a waft of this morning's mint toothpaste, and then I can taste her lungs; intimate exhalation.

We round a corner and the road becomes a dirt track and it

winds up a madly perfect woody hillside—maybe even a mountainside—to a temple-shaped sort of thing with minarets and a long jutting balcony facing west, and I realise that this is where I'm going. I'm having my date in Shangri-La. Leah gasps and yips, and Gonzo throws me a pure puppy grin like "Did I do you proud?" and I nod and laugh out loud at the sheer amazingness of it and smack him on the back, and we wind on up the snaky path.

We park in a forecourt strewn with actual gravel. Leah and I start trying to unload the gear and Gonzo sternly tells us to go get ready and if they're still fixing the place up when we get back, we can stroll a bit. He actually says "stroll like lovers" and Leah and I look hurriedly away from each other in case one of us is thinking no or maybe in case we're both thinking yes, because that would be too soon, too much, all crunched up before we've had a chance to enjoy courting. Leah nods at me and scurries off breathlessly to "get changed." The SpecOps waiters abduct my command table and Sally "Eagle" Culpepper vanishes to the top of one of the minarets and unlimbers her long gun and seems to disappear against the stonework. Gonzo draws me off to one side and produces of all things a camouflaged suit-carrier, from which emerges a dark suit in approximately my size and a shirt not stained with dust or blood. He shows me to an empty, dry little room with a cracked mirror and an orchid growing in through the window.

When I return to the long balcony, Leah is standing at the very end in her jumpsuit and I feel a bit awkward in my knock-off Armani, until she turns and her eyes light up and she seems to be sizing me up in a most pleasing manner. Then she reaches for the zipper on her jumpsuit and pulls it all the way down, and it drops off her shoulders and she peels it down over her chest and reveals a shiny, rippling gown which tumbles in a lean curve from white shoulder to well-turned ankle, because from somewhere, no doubt by girl magic, she has located a silk dress. Gonzo, master of all things, obtained for me a civvy suit, but not even he could manage *glamour.* Without his help, using only the secret communications of women, Leah has contrived to look like an Oscar winner. She wriggles. The creases fall out, and she steps from her jumpsuit, barefoot, and kisses me, then breaks away and whoops into the gathering dusk. A whooping woman in an evening gown is a woman to delight in.

Candlelit dinner for two at Maison Gonzo lasts until one in the morning. It is not actual Italian cuisine, but rather a wild blend of Asia and southern European, moistened with a wine-like drink bought from a friend of Rao Tsur, who makes it out of mango. We look at one another across the table, and our fingers touch when I pass the water jug and it is almost unbearable, and then there is dancing. Annabel (known to me now as Annie) sings jazz and Gonzo accompanies her on paper and comb. Big Jim Hepsobah is percussion, and there's a ring of steel around us, a one-hundred-metre hard cordon backed up by Eagle and her imaging gear and that scary gun—although Gonzo assures me, as he leads us to our accommodation for the night, that Sally's night goggles will not be pointed our way from now on. This is private time. He throws wide the door to a prince's chamber and hugs me, and departs to go do whatever reconnaissance he has promised in exchange for this date. There are two beds, but Leah has no time for my chivalrous notions and we tumble desperately into one. And that is all you need to know about that part. Sleep takes us sometime later, wrapped in rich musk and honeysuckle.

BOOTED FEET on stone, and clattering intensity. Gonzo, at speed and professional, and I wake because some part of me, even post-coital and even after a period of separation, knows the pattern of his urgency. I am standing by the time he reaches the bed, and he tosses me two bundles and Leah wakes smoothly too, because nurses know about crisis. I shake the bundles out as Gonzo vanishes again through the door, and realise that he was wearing a full moonsuit, and that we too are being put into biochem gear, and this means something very bad; it means that they or we have gone non-conventional, and since we don't have biochem (we have more terrible things, as I know well) it can only be them, and they have made a very serious mistake and this theatre is about to be the testing ground for Professor Derek's baby. That's a horrible idea and I want to be appalled by it but that will have to wait, because right now I am zipping Leah into her moonsuit and taping the tag down and she is doing the same for me in turn, and we are trotting, shuffling, galloping out of paradise and back to the convoy, and the suit smells of other people's armpits and latex and silicon and my own fear, and ever so slightly of Leah's body and mine.

"Chemical," Gonzo is saying, "sarin base, five kilometres. Wind?"

And Eagle says, "Thirty off," which means the gas will probably blow past us, because the wind is thirty degrees off true, true being the line between the gas contact and us. And then some bastard says:

"Second contact!" and it's Gonzo. The gas is on a broad front, and thirty degrees will clip us, test our moonsuit seals, and everyone checks their seams again and Jim Hepsobah in the other RV tosses some silicon to Annie and tells her to come inside, no one's going to shoot at us right now and if they do we're just gonna run like hell, and we career away down the road. Sally Culpepper is on the radio warning the units ahead of us and the rest of the SpecOps waiters are alert but basically pretty chilled out, because they maintain their own suits and they *know* there's nothing wrong with them. Leah puts her hand in mine and she is shaking, just like me, and she rests her helmet against mine and stares into my eyes and I know, I *know,* that as long as we look at each other like that, everything will be fine.

Everything is fine.

Until we get to Red Gate and Captain-idiot Ben Carsville.

Captain Carsville is a fantasist who lives war as movies. He's something between a running joke and a sucking chest wound. He made captain in peacetime, promoted over better soldiers because he looks good on a poster and he walks and talks the way a soldier should. He dodges and ducks under fire, scurries this way and that, panther-crawls and rolls and dummies. For the record, the best way not to get shot when you're under fire is to run as fast as possible in a moderately straight line towards the nearest cover and stay there. If you have to advance, then you leapfrog one another, each man doing this until you get to the target. Unless you are very, very close indeed to the person shooting at you, zigging and zagging just tires you out and gives him the opportunity to shoot at you for longer.

Ben Carsville is preternaturally beautiful in a profoundly masculine way. Looking at him makes you want to listen, rapt, to his perfect voice and his perfect wisdom as it proceeds from his perfect mouth. Sadly, when he speaks, his perfect tones are the harbingers of the perfect screw-up. Carsville grew up on war porn: films made by guys who had never seen real war, comics about men with names like Private Grit and Big Roy Solid. He was a cadet, and then he was a lieutenant on a police action which never really kicked off beyond a few riots and a car bomb which didn't go off. His only combat experience comes from some brief forays on the fringes of this war, "fact-finding" with visiting politicians. Ben Carsville thinks war is a sort of manly sport, and casualties are just what happens when you play.

He also thinks this gas attack is some sort of ruse. Gonzo and his guys have been taken in by the Enemy. They have been fed false data somehow, and now they are being used to convince wise and mighty Captain Carsville to abandon his position so that the Enemy can simply wander in, whereupon the Enemy will have some sort of party in which they will throw soft-boiled eggs at pictures of Ben Carsville and *mock him with their smiles.* He has, in accordance with his moderately weird perception of the situation, not given the order to his soldiers to suit up, and has not told the Katiris in Fudin what is happening.

Anticipating an assault on his position, he wants us to hang around to support his troops, and he intends, seriously, to send Gonzo & Co. back along our route to assess the threat. This does not put Gonzo in a cooperative and conciliatory mood. It puts him into a big, angry, SpecOps snit.

"Wind?" Gonzo demands.

"Twenty-five off," Eagle tells him, which is worse than it was.

"Time to contact?"

"Ten minutes."

"Calling it five hundred and forty seconds . . . mark."

This means that there's still plenty of time to get soldiers kitted up and even enough time to evacuate most of the Katiris, although they'll have to drive very, very fast on some fairly nasty roads. Gonzo is counting as we go through ID checks, counting as we get confirmation, counting as we approach the captain's position, counting as Ben Carsville still doesn't issue the order and counting out loud as he storms into the command tent with his rank insignia in one hand and the gas detector badge from his reconnaissance in the other. Gonzo stood in a cloud of gas and watched the chemical film react to the stuff. He knows he has not been misled or hornswoggled. He *has no time for this shit.* In fact, he knows exactly how little time he has, because he is counting it down out loud.

"(Four hundred and twenty-five seconds), Carsville, you are a fucking *arsewart,* what the *fuck* do you think you are doing? Are you (four hundred and twenty) out of your miserable fucking mind? There is a major, for real, treaty-busting, huge goatfuck disaster of a gas attack and you are right in the middle of it and you are wearing your (four hundred and fifteen) forgodsakes *dressing gown* and where the *fuck* did you get that, you mad-crazy *prick*? (Four hundred and ten) You unbelievable *idiot*!"

Carsville doesn't pay any attention to the language because Gonzo is special forces and Carsville knows he won't get anywhere with arguing about a few curses, but he leans back photogenically and demands to *know what those numbers are, soldier* and *what the hell do you know about it,* and when Gonzo lunges forward to grab him by the ears and beat him sensible, Carsville pulls a pistol from his dressing gown and flicks his thumb across the safety to release it. The outcomes of close combat with a loaded handgun are also distressingly unpredictable. Not even Gonzo can dodge bullets and while Carsville may be an idiot he's not a bad shot or even necessarily a bad fighter, so we all stand there like stalagmites while Gonzo mutters, "Four hundred oh oh, arsehole arsehole arsehole!"

Gonzo turns sharply on his heel as if Carsville has ceased to exist, walks out of the command tent and grabs the nearest grunt and tells him there's a chemical shitstorm coming down and to sound the alarm and tell the Katiris to evac and that he has at best three hundred and fifty-five seconds before this pleasant spot turns into a field of the dead. And Carsville, who has followed him out, points his gun at his own sentry and tells him to belay that order, and here we are again, only this time he's also telling Gonzo to get out of his moonsuit. Gonzo pulls the mask of the moonsuit up. Carsville shifts his aim and cocks the hammer, and everything is buggered up.

I step sideways, and say something like, "Gonzo, take the goddam suit off, man," secure in the knowledge that Gonzo is not about to do anything of the kind, because getting shot is one kind of bad, but getting gassed is quite another. Carsville cannot see my eyes, or detect the smooth current of information passing between myself and my oldest friend. He cannot hear the dialogue we do not speak.

Gonzo yells at me to shut up. I call him some unpleasant names. He takes offence, gets in my face and, when I won't give way, he shoves me. This puts me between him and Carsville, who lowers his gun slightly because I am on his side and he doesn't want to shoot me. Alas, I am suddenly very clumsy—*Oh, my stars and garters, what have I done?* I stumble into the captain. He discharges his weapon at the ground and I (with more than moderate satisfaction) smack Captain Ben Carsville's idiot mouth as hard as I can without breaking my hand, and crack his arm like a whip, so that it comes unstuck in some fundamental way and he drops the gun.

Carsville whimpers and the sentry goggles at me. My military career looks a bit rocky, because this does not even slightly qualify as a legitimate action, but if I am court-martialled I will go out saving a bunch of lives instead of ending them, and this has a certain charm. The military has dealt with this kind of court martial before. People get sternly reprimanded and thrown out with a promotion and a medal, and *let that be a lesson*! Leah is staring at me with wide eyes which have more than a little approval in them, and she hastens to reassemble Carsville's arm in what I suspect may be an unnecessarily painful way, because he passes out and therefore cannot give countervailing orders to his men, who snap into action as Gonzo tells them to move out. His tone implies that, having broken one arm today, I may suddenly have developed a taste for arms in general, but also is so honestly urgent that the threat is unnecessary and perhaps even unnoticed. Ben Carsville is bundled into his own staff car and driven away at speed. We get back in our RVs and charge on to Fudin.

The sad truth is that Ben Carsville has probably wasted too much time. Even with the company from Red Gate with us, there's no chance we can get them all out. It's going to be first come, first saved, and the rest will shift as best they can. I can't tell whether Leah has realised. Probably she has; she understands triage. Likely we will see a riot, a living mass of fear and anger composed of people no longer acting as individuals. We may have to shoot a few of them to save the rest. It's arguable whether we should attempt a rescue at all, but Gonzo has no time for arguable, and the decision is his, and no one here would quibble anyway.

It's possible that the people of Fudin will refuse our help. They may not believe us. They may choose to think we are lying when the alternative is cataclysm. We may have to leave again, abandon them to death because we are not credible, or the news we bring is too vast to be comprehensible in the time we have. We may fail without being allowed to try.

I've known this whole un-war business was stupid for a while. I've never liked it, but I haven't hated it until now. I am wondering whether Rao Tsur and his wife will greet annihilation with the same wit they showed in the marketplace; whether Mrs. Tsur will beg Jim Hepsobah to take her youngest son on his lap when there is no more space; whether she will stand like a pillar and hold her children while we depart; whether she will fling herself on us in a rage, or watch us struggle to save who we can with the eerie, patient understanding of imminent death; whether Rao will seek to reach an accommodation for the safety of his family, or whether we will see something darker and more horrible as he abandons them. Perhaps his love is a weak thing. Perhaps he does mean to exchange her for a younger model, or perhaps he simply values his own life over hers. Perhaps he will default, demand passage for himself alone, even try to bribe us. I think, if he does that, that I will kill him.

All these things and more I am prepared for in Fudin. I am *not* prepared for a stock car rally. But that is what I get.

Jim Hepsobah spins the wheel and brings us around the last bend into Fudin, and there are forty particoloured street-racers in a neat grid pattern, with families piling into them: goats and suitcases and children being loaded onto roofracks, and slender Katiri wives and tubby patriarchs and serious teenagers climbing aboard without hesitation or mishap. As soon as each car is filled it takes off, from the front of the grid, as if this were a Swiss taxi rank. Fudin is almost empty, which means that over a hundred cars have already left.

Each motor is driven by an energetic young person in a very expensive, personalised version of the suits we are wearing. Expensive, because tailored and cut to fit, and therefore figure-hugging and distinctly stylish. Their crash helmets are fitted onto the necks of their suits, so they look like science-fiction heroes or very rich technobikers from Silicon Valley, but each of them has a different pattern painted onto his or her back; they are a forest of dragons and courtesans and pirates. The word zings around inside my head: *piratespiratespirates.* Although there is more to them than yo-ho-ho. There is a deliberateness and a quiet centre. Pirate-monks, maybe.

They carry bags for their passengers, hold open doors for older ladies, and run around and zoom away, and they are managing this magic, this impossibly competent evacuation, with *music.* They clap, sing and stamp. Humanitarianism in four four time. The people of Fudin move with the beat (it's almost impossible not to) so no one trips and no one gets in anyone's way. *Load-the-roof two three four, get-in-the-car two three four, all-here? two three four, vavavoom two three four,* and another row of rescue wagons roars off the grid and now there are only thirty-two.

Standing in the middle of all this smoothly functioning chaos is a little bearded geezer with a round head and a glinting, challenging smile which would stand him in good stead in a toothpaste commercial aimed at moderately wealthy, moderately devout (moderately scandalous in youth but now moderately reformed) Asian gentlemen of good family. He is dressed in a pair of linen trousers and an open-necked shirt, over which he wears a leather jerkin. Around his middle is a red sash or cummerbund, from which depends a small collection of utilities and two items I can describe only as *cutlasses.* He is oddly and acutely familiar, but as he is at one and the same time directing refugee traffic, conducting an impromptu rhythm collective and speaking waspishly with a village elder who has taken it into her head that she will remain here, and since while he manages these small matters he is *also* fighting off the efforts of a scrawny, nervous grand-vizier-looking bloke who's trying to get him into a moon-suit, it's not easy to compare him with other memories.

Finally, he turns to the scrawny cohort and shoos him away, grabs the matron by one bony hand and, in the face of her delighted protests, sweeps her bodily from her feet. This bundle of femininity impedes him not at all as he bolts (fifteen seconds remaining by Gonzo's original count and at most sixty-five by the new one) for the hindmost car in the grid, which stands out from the others like a falcon among sparrows.

The car is not a street-racer. None of them, of course, started out that way, but this one even less so. Unlike its gaudy brethren, it is not a Honda Civic bursting with nitrous oxide systems and warranty-voiding gearbox enhancements or a roaring Focus tooled to go like a rocketship. It is not even a frog-green Subaru with a turbo and wide wheels like a sea lion's arse. It is a muted maroon colour, and it is as dignified as it is powerful. It looks distinctly bulletproof and the glass windows are smoked, but even so it's possible to see that this car has curtains. It also has a silver angel on the front end and the kind of engine they used to put in small planes. Quite possibly it will catch up with the front runners before it has to change gear. It is unmistakably a Rolls-Royce, but it is a Rolls-Royce the way Koh-i-noor is a diamond.

Into the unlikely evac vehicle goes the matron, hooting with laughter now at this scandalous chivalry, and a brief glimpse of the interior tells me that the car has an independent air supply. Once the hermetic door shuts, the passengers are safe and sound, and the vizier, who apparently doubles as driver, bundles himself aboard. With one last look to be sure the evacuation is complete, the bearded geezer glances at us and raises his hand to sign okay and possibly thank you, and dives into his car, which waits a heartbeat for the juiced-up Saab in front to make some space and then there's a noise like the old bull shaking his head at the young one ("No, son, we're not gonna *run* down and fuck *one* of those cows, we're gonna *walk* and *fuck 'em all*") and the Roller disappears from view in a cloud of its own dust. The convoy is moving like a gazelle herd, each individual weaving around the others, evasive, chaotic, purposive. Those immensely well-dressed personages have done Ronnie Cheung's tactical automotive course, or rather they have done one very like it. An advanced one for people who are intending to spend serious time in cars getting into trouble.

Gonzo stares after the Rolls-Royce. He has *heroismus interruptus.* He was ready, right then, to coordinate four or five hundred terrified civvies, lay down his life, kill for them, make a legend of disinterested soldiering. It's not that he resents what has happened, but he's having trouble changing gear. He was expecting to take charge. Instead he is struggling to keep up with a sexagenarian Mystery Man with an Errol Flynn grin who commands a legion of pirate-monk rally drivers and sweeps formidable older women from their feet in a cloud of cologne and Asian-Monarchic style. Deep in Gonzo's medulla oblongata, the lizardy brainstem which manages the most basic functions of living, part of him knows that this technique would work with equal facility on younger and more charming women, and knows this because Eagle Sally Culpepper has caught her breath and even Annie the Ox, utterly uninterested in men per se, has not stopped looking after the departing machines. Leah, forever blessed, is grinning, but her hand has not slackened in my grip and her delight is for the impish theatre of it all. Gonzo's inner reptile recognises a competitor. But, more important, he is now playing an unfamiliar game—follow-the-leader.

We rush headlong after the pirate convoy, and then—no doubt in obedience to some order from the enormous Rolls-Royce—the driver ahead of us makes a dogleg right across an area marked on our map as non-traversable. The whole cavalcade is streaming out into a snarl of underbrush and rubble and impassable ravines, the brightly coloured cars vanishing rapidly amid the crags. Their dust cloud whips away in the wind, the last Civic ducks down into a dip and they have disappeared entirely. I glance at the map. In that direction a few months ago lay a muddle of buildings, stony outcroppings and forest, a region part sparse conurbation and part mountain ("conruration?"), now riven through with burned, bombed-flat land and dried-out stream beds and air-dropped anti-personnel mines. If the road still exists, or the riverbed is solid, they might reach the mountains, or loop around to Lake Addeh and its islands. But whether that is what they will do, and whether we would be welcome if we tried to follow, we do not find out. Gonzo growls to Jim Hepsobah, and we let them go, following the road we know towards the uncertain safety of Command HQ.

PLASTIC HANDCUFF STRIPS and "Fall in two men, left right left right!" It is not quite the hero's welcome, but nor is it an actual firing squad, and since I arrived in the Elective Theatre I have learned that very few people share our perceptions of when they should be grateful to us. Gonzo's guys do not officially exist at all and therefore cannot be tried in a court martial without compromising national security. Leah is a civilian nurse, leaving only me for Carsville's wrath, which is fine by him anyway because I'm the one who messed up his arm. The fact that I was right to do so, that a lethal gas attack *was* in fact taking place, probably makes it worse. And thus my tickertape parade takes the form of two large military policemen with sidearms and blank faces. But Carsville too must be feeling the bite of disappointment, because there's a lack of enthusiasm about the MPs and they don't mock me or rough me up; they just clap me in irons in a mildly apologetic way, and manage not to pat me on the back or give me a hug.

Ben Carsville is not well liked, and his attempt to force his unit to commit gas seppuku has not improved his position with the men. Also, while I was out of line, my rank status is blurry and Carsville was wrong. Thus, Copsen's office not the stockade. General Copsen looks tense and distracted. There is a red phone on his desk and he has moved it to a convenient position, and this I take to mean that our considered response is right now being reconsidered. George Copsen is a man with a lot of other things to do, and this whole subplot involving one of his picked guys and some Ride of the Valkyries wannabe is ticking him off. There's serious things happening. For any number of years, the doctrine has been the same: we answer weapons of mass destruction with payment in kind, and ours are bigger than yours, so watch it. To do this now could change the face of the world, because General George didn't bother to bring any of the staples of unconventional war to this front. He left the deniable biologicals and the mislabelled chemicals and the acknowledged-but-downplayed nuclear deterrents at home, and brought his newest and his best: Professor Derek's baby. But when he uses it, people are definitely going to go apeshit and get nervous, and activate missile defences all around the world, because making the bad guys vanish entirely is going to put the wind up our friends and enemies alike. The world will change, just as it did on 6th August 1945. It's good to know he and his bosses are taking a couple of hours to chew it over, maybe even wondering whether it's a good idea.

Copsen waves at me to sit. He waves at Carsville to sit. He does not need this right now. He does not want us here. He has nothing to do until the phone rings, but by the same token he needs to be composed. He is in a very big, very lofty, very cold chair.

"Tell me," George Copsen says tiredly, "what you thought you were doing?"

I have no idea. I do not say anything. I stare back at him, voiceless. Gonzo would know what to say. Gonzo would be forthright. Gonzo would explain in manly tones and make it all okay with General George.

"I exercised my discretion as area commander," says Ben Carsville in manly tones. George Copsen's face goes quite opaque. He was not talking to Carsville. His anger was directed at me—at least for the moment. I have been irresponsible, and having shanghaied me and trained me and godfathered my admittance to the general staff, he is feeling betrayed and let down. He had it in mind to give me a paternal chewing-out before letting me go back to my tent to consider my faults. His game plan for this meeting was to let off some steam dressing me down and then accept Carsville's apology for bad judgement and parlay that into a let-off for me. Carsville would have done better to stay shut up. The notion that he might actually be unrepentant had clearly not occurred to General George, and it does not sit well with him.

"I understand that you . . . elected to disregard a gas alert?"

"Yes, sir."

"That seems like a curious decision, Captain Carsville."

"I considered it probably a ruse, sir."

George Copsen clambers to his feet and walks around his desk to get a clear view.

"A ruse."

"Yes, sir."

George Copsen has a certain look about him. It starts at his epicanthic folds and whispers down around his mouth. It invites clarification. It is familiar to me from a certain room with a particular piece of furniture. It is not a look you want to ignore or trifle with. But Ben Carsville, even now, does not explain. He lets his honesty shine through, and his earnestness and his loyalty. He has taken a decision as the man on the ground. His decision—and his reasoning—need no explanation. He is Ben Carsville. He is still wearing a silk dressing gown.

"You," says George Copsen, with some emphasis, "are a fucking liability. Lieutenant." And as Carsville boggles at him, General George makes a little flicking gesture, so to say "I'm done with you."

Lieutenant Carsville departs, pursued by bears.

George Copsen collapses into his chair and broods, and ignores me. He is staring at the red phone, daring it to ring. Finally he looks over at me and sighs.

"Screw-up," says George Copsen. I am uncertain whether he means the situation or me personally. It had not crossed my mind until this moment that I gave a damn for his opinion. It appears that I do. I feel wretched for ten seconds, which is how long it takes me to stand, shakily, and make my best salute. I stand there, offering my apology in the only way which is permitted. My arm aches, and while I am apologising to the man, I cannot actually think of anything I am sorry for. George Copsen looks into my eyes, measuring, and unlike Master Wu, unlike the Evangelist, he does not seem convinced by what he sees there. On the other hand, what he is looking for may not be a thing I wish him to find. We are standing like this, assessing one another and trying to figure out what we want from one another, when a shrill, old-fashioned bleating fills the room. George Copsen beckons me sharply, because being pissed off with me is a thing which belongs in the time before the phone rang, before the crisis went live again. He lifts the red telephone and says:

"Copsen."

Someone on the other end speaks, firmly and simply. General George either grows older or grows colder; it happens to him from within like a tall building being demolished or flowers growing in fast motion, and I realise that he is making himself into the cog, rather than the man. The saving grace of hierarchy—of the Government Machine—is this: George Copsen will execute the orders of his country, and in doing so he will kill thousands, maybe more. But it will not be his choice. It will be the action of a nation, a huge complex animal of which he is the tiniest part, albeit at this moment a significant part. *George* Copsen retreats and *General* Copsen emerges to take his place and keep him from going mad given what he will now do. This is a good thing for George. It may also be a good thing for the general, to be unhampered by his civilian self. Whether it is a good thing for anyone else is less clear.

The general squares his shoulders and begins running through his checklist. He activates my commission. I am now an officer in this war—and, as of a few moments ago, it *is* incontestably a war—with all the duties, rights and privileges pertaining thereunto. I will do what I have been trained to do. That is a little bit scary. I am assigned to Operations, which means that right now I am to go to the bank of screens on the far wall, and observe, and target, and relay my information to General Copsen (who moves from his desk to a command chair in the middle of the room) and to Colonel Tench and Brevet-Major Purvis, thus improving and refining our firing solutions, so that our use of weapons of mass destruction is accurate and irreproachable.

Together, we will make the enemy Go Away.

Chapter Six

Wheels, horror and flapjacks;
the End of the World;
Zaher Bey, at last.

THE ONLY PROBLEM concerns wheels. I was barely even aware of it, but Go Away Bombs have wheels on them. This is because each one is the size of a smallish car. We don't fire them as much as drop them, out of cargo planes. The wheels have been sitting in a crate in an airfield somewhere west of here for two months. They have gotten hot, and cold, and sandy, and dry, and then hot again. They are no longer the proud wheels we once knew. They are wonky. The technicians fit them to the bombs, and the bombs sit askew on them and don't roll in the smooth, oiled fashion the deployment crews were led to expect. They have to winch the bombs up into position. Fortunately, when the time comes to drop them, gravity will be to our advantage. The most advanced weapons in the history of warfare will be bobbled into the sky over the target like a bunch of elderly shopping trolleys being tossed into a river.

That's the one thing which slows down the attack. It slows it down by about a half hour. A little while later the first plane signals "Payload delivered" and our forward spotters relay the hit back to us via a digital feed. It is rather dull. The enemy outpost is situated in a shattered township. The bomb drops out of the sky and activates. There is no explosion, no ripple of pressure through the earth. A sort of viscous absence blooms. The enemy emplacements are erased, and air flows into the space, bringing dust. A perfect, smooth crater replaces the main square and the south-western quarter of the town, and two or three hourglass buildings which were leaning on each other are suddenly deprived of support and fall over. They do this slowly and without fuss. And that's it. It's a bit unsatisfying. In Blue Sector there's a mild tremor because the excision there runs deep and releases a little tectonic pressure. Five hundred kilometres away we create a waterfall and a lake where a bubble of Professor Derek's genius transects a river, taking out at the same time a bridge and two enemy special operations units proficient in torture (just like ours).

We sit back and wait for the next round of orders and the proud consequences of our strength. We have flexed big bold political muscles. We have stripped off on the international beach and showed pumped legs and crushing arms. We are totally the Big Dog. And all around the world, right now, people are saying "What the hell?" Analysts are being asked questions and speculating and talking hogwash. In Jarndice the news will break from the Junior Library outward in a circular wave, and then it will spread through mobile telephones and email and each of these individual missives will produce ripples of its own, so that shortly the courtyards will be filled with bothered, jubilant, appalled students thronging and wondering. Only we know what has happened.

We are still telling ourselves this, feeling a bit superior and waiting for the order to do some more demonstrative world-editing, when our very own Green Sector vanishes from the map. Our men just aren't there any more. The satellite image shows our emplacements wobbling and vanishing like a sandcastle being washed away by the tide. On channel seven (this is our channel seven, not the news channel) there is a nightmare. The spotter above that doomed little town where Tobemory Trent tourniqueted my arm and stopped me from bleeding out is now half a spotter, or possibly two thirds of one. His face is almost all there, but when he falls forward, you can see that he has been deprived of his left ear and the outermost inch of his head, and also his arm and hip. It's impossible to tell from looking at the screen whether he is still alive, or whether his body is just juddering by way of spooky reflex. Next to him is his partner, the sniper, who is most definitely alive, although that seems to be a temporary situation. The enemy has vanished the man's lower limbs but not the rest of him, and he is bleeding out. It does not look painless and humane, which I had somehow assumed it might be. It sounds a lot like every other kind of dying I have observed since coming here. Finally, because no one objects, I switch off the screen. The silence is almost worse than the noise.

George Copsen droops in his chair. When Richard P. Purvis goes to help him, General Copsen shrugs him off, then resumes his hunched position. From behind, I can see his shoulders clench and shudder, as if he has a fever.

A few moments later we learn that the same thing is happening everywhere. Not just in the Elective Theatre: everywhere. In cities. In countries far away and countries just around the corner. Somehow, without warning (although surely quite a lot of people somewhere knew this was possible, they just didn't see fit to share or were too proud to credit it) this nice little bush war has gone global. People are deploying weapons (weapons like ours) at the strategic level, which means missiles with intercontinental reach. The upside is that no one is using nukes or germs. The downside is that our supersecret weapon turns out to be absolutely the best beloved new toy of just about every advanced nation on Earth. Major cities are getting to look like Swiss cheeses, and the Swiss have developed a sort of ray gun based on the same principle and zapped everything they can reach to the east so the Russians know not to come at them. For reasons I have never understood, the Swiss still think the Russians are going to sweep down on the European fold and devour their babies. On this basis they have erased a corridor of populous farmland and a few lakes, just to show they really mean it. The Russians have responded by removing a piece of China they never much cared for, and everyone is now perforating the map so that it is getting to be a bit like a sheet of stamps. Serious commentators (people with no vested interest in war) are going on air live asking that this stop, right now, because there seems to be some danger of the world flying apart or falling in, so much of it has been vanished in the rush to show that *everyone* is the Big Dog.

George Copsen's command chair is dark grey, and it rests on a little raised platform. It has a remote control for all the TV screens built into the arm. It is the precise focus of every image in the room. The man sitting in it can turn his head, even shake it, and still see what is happening in stereoscopic widescreen. The speakers are set up for him too, so when he shuts his eyes, as he is doing now, it doesn't make it much better. We watch Trinidad sparkle and fold away into nothing. It is unclear why anyone has a beef with Trinidad, but the beef is well and truly settled. George Copsen murmurs something like "oh" although it might be "no."

We wait for orders, and it takes us a while to realise that we have been forgotten. The Elective Theatre has been closed down. There's absolutely no point fighting a proxy war when you're fighting a real one. This whole area was selected as a battleground because it was absolutely pointless. It just had people in it. The only reasons to fight here were social and political, nebulous things which for the moment do not matter. We are an army in the wrong place. No one cares to talk to us. They are busy fighting a real war with unreal weapons and wiping one another from the face of the Earth. It's a dream of power. Point, speak, and the thing which vexes you is unmade. It must be intoxicating; certainly, the men and women in houses of government around the world are hooked on it and reeling like drunkards.

From time to time we offer General Copsen food or drink, and once Richard P. Purvis suggests that he should address the men. The general does not respond. He does not drink the water on his left side, or eat any of the peanuts on his right. He sits, wrapped around himself, and every so often a little noise comes off him, a plaintive mew. He twitches. When I stand directly in front of him, I can see that he is not in fact curled into a foetal ball, but rather his eyes are fixed on the displays in front of him. I turn them back on. They are mostly blank, except for the one which shows this room. We all stand and look at ourselves on TV. This is me, watching me watching myself. This is my left hand waving. This is my right hand waving. This is me standing on one leg. George Copsen fumbles with his remote control, and we disappear.

Everyone in the room has a brief moment when they believe this is actually what has happened: that we too have been made to Go Away. Then we look at one another somewhat sheepishly and realise that he has simply turned the screens off again.

It is at this point that Riley Tench makes a very bad call. It's probably his duty, but it's the wrong thing to do. He tries to relieve the general. He stands in a suitably official pose, sort of manly in an asexual and impersonal way, conveying gravitas and regret, and according to whatever section of whatever rule, he informs his commanding officer that *he,* Riley Tench, has adjudged *him,* George Copsen, to be unfit to command by reason of psychological stress and collapse, and *he,* Riley Tench, for the good of the unit and by the power vested in him for this purpose, hereby assumes that role with due thought given to the gravity of the act and understanding that it may be later seen as mutiny by the assessing authority. Will George Copsen, General, accept that he is relieved in line with the protocols appertaining?

There is a longish moment of stillness and then George Copsen shoots him in the head. Riley Tench goes all over three monitors and Richard P. Purvis, who was standing in a kind of neutral way off to one side, quite possibly thinking that he wouldn't have chosen this moment to relieve his master.

And indeed, the general is not relieved. He's totally bugfuck homicidal and periodically catatonic, and that's the guy who's at the helm right now and will remain there until such time as we receive countervailing orders, amen.

. . .

For twenty-four hours, or thereabouts, we get a break. Not much happens. We have time to wash Riley Tench off our uniforms and then we have more time with no particular activity to occupy it. George Copsen ambles around telling grunts that the situation "will soon be resolved." This is probably supposed to be reassuring, but it isn't; it scares the bejesus out of everyone. The general's face is unshaven and pudgy, and shiny with old sweat. He looks as if he ought to be wearing a red flannel shirt and carrying a half-empty bottle of hooch. Every so often he goes and sits on a chair outside his tent and sort of zones out, glassy and slack.

I sit on my bed. I look at my letters, because they remind me of home and this has always helped before. Then I find the Evangelist's zombie letter, a frame of paper with nothing left in the middle, and I realise that home may no longer exist. I stare through the hole into space.

Gonzo wanders in and looks pretty freaked, and we drink some illicit (but excellent) special forces alcohol until Leah appears in my tent and sits down with her head resting on my chest, which makes me feel powerfully alpha male–ish. Gonzo looks a bit nervous and confused, and we all expect her bleeper to go off at any moment, but in fact no one is bringing in wounded right now because people are mostly either uninjured or non-existent. A few have had walls fall on them as a result of excisions, and some have broken limbs and cuts from the normal course of life when a whole bunch of armed men live in a smallish space and get bored and angry. For a few days everyone just coasts. This is post-traumatic stress, of course, but we don't call it that. We don't really give it a name or realise that we are doing it. Time spreads out and we see the world through a tunnel of grey. Our voices echo down it, so any serious conversation is impossible. We're in a kind of winterish Eden: not a place of innocence but exhaustion.

On the seventh day Gonzo takes matters in hand. He gathers his guys, sends them off to engage in certain necessary tasks and gets his project under way. The hero of a hundred secret battles rolls up his trouser legs and makes flapjacks.

It's a very strange thing seeing lethal men and women put aside the dagger of stealth and take up the spatula of home cooking; it wakes the sense of incongruity which has been slowly drugged insensible by months in this foreign place. Quite a lot of people come out to watch. Gonzo nods genially and goes back to treading the oats and the sugar. (This much flapjack cannot be stirred; you have to get right in there and churn it with your feet. Gonzo has established a footbath—legbath—at the entrance to his kitchen area. It is staffed by Egon and a pretty female nurse I do not recognise, but whose eyes do not leave Gonzo even as she labours over Annie the Ox's toes. For obvious reasons, anyone who joins the mixing party must have hygienic feet. The idea of hygienic feet suddenly appeals very much to all of us, so a queue is forming.) Someone in the crowd asks whether these will be *covert* flapjacks, and Gonzo says no, they will be ordinary flapjacks, but adds that it takes persons of courage and unusual skill to make flapjacks at a time like this. That gets a laugh. His mother's scowl flits across his face, and I can see her shaking her head, intangible hands reaching to restrain him. *No, schveetie, too much sugar, people will vomit.* But Gonzo, now as then, knows that the flapjack is a thing of desire rather than nutrition, and must taste like manna rather than a horse's nosebag. He does not stop with the sugar, and Ma Lubitsch huffs proudly and begins her three-point turn.

Most people in this situation would reckon to make a fair quantity of flapjacks, then a bunch more, until there were enough, but Gonzo is not most people, and in any case is working to an agenda which demands spectacle. He needs to cook these things all at once, in front of his troops (and we will all be *his* troops, if he can bring this off). The camp cooking facilities did at one time include a monster oven capable of doing this, but its gas supply was exhausted by a massive grill last month, and replacement cylinders have yet to arrive. Gonzo knew this when he chose to make flapjacks. It is part of the message he wants to send: we are still an army, and we will function like one; not everything which is not simple is actually hard; even hard things can be done fast; even things which seem impossible turn out to be doable. *We will survive.*

So Gonzo turns to the crowd (the smell of sugary oats has permeated tents and huts and fortified holes and guard turrets, and rumours of clean feet have gone even further, so there is now a crowd standing in curious contemplation of a bunch of commandos knee-deep and shoeless in pilfered oats and sugar) and sees two guys he is particularly looking for. He peers into the throng exactly where they aren't (Ma Lubitsch playing hide-and-seek: *dear me, zese old eyes of mine, I shall never find zem*) and innocently asks if anyone knows where to find Sergeant Duggan and Sergeant Crisp. No one says anything.

"Hell," says Gonzo, big dumb ox, chewing his lip and scratching, "I could really use some help." And he goes back to his stirring.

This puts everyone at their ease. This is not going to be some kind of weird oatsy inquisition. There will be no *auto des flapjaques.* This young man is not looking for scapegoats but for fellow flapjackers.

Sergeant Engineer Crisp and Sergeant Engineer Duggan don't say anything. That's partly because they're still kinda fuzzy on who they are; neither of them has spoken for three days, since the rest of their unit, over in Green Sector, vanished in the first retaliatory strike. Now, though, this seems to be holding up the show, and people nudge them.

That's you, mate. Man needs your help.

Oh, yes, right you are!

Score one to Gonzo: the crowd feels it has an interest in this project. The sergeants are shunted forward and they blink and stare up at Gonzo as he leans on the edge of his giant mixing bowl. MacArthur never addressed his troops from a mixing bowl—not even one made from a spare geodesic radio emplacement shell—and certainly de Gaulle never did. But Gonzo Lubitsch does, and he does it as if a whole long line of commanders were standing at his shoulder, urging him on.

"Gentlemen," says Gonzo softly, "holidays are over. I need an oven, and I need one in about twenty minutes, or these fine flapjacks will go to waste and that is *not* happening."

And something about this statement and the voice in which he says it makes it clear that it is simply true. One way or another, this thing will get done. Under a layer of grime and horror, these two are soldiers, and more, they are productive, can-do sorts of people. Rustily but with a gratitude which is not so far short of worship, they say "Yes, sir" and are about their business.

Having a task makes them part of Gonzo's new aristocracy, and very shortly there are people offering to help them out, and people clustering around Gonzo giving helpful advice, cooking tips, recipe suggestions and all manner of assistance. Gonzo starts giving orders of a more general nature, because (clearly) we will need somewhere to eat the flapjacks and somewhere to expel them later when nature takes its course, and the mess tents have been torn to shreds and the latrines are starting to get a bit funky through lack of attention, and these things need to be remedied. George Copsen is sitting under a sunshade outside the remains of his tent. He has shown no inclination to issue orders of substance since before he shot Riley Tench. Possibly it is his intention that no one should officially take over from him, so that his forces cannot be redeployed. Possibly this affable, lethal catatonia is a shield between us and the command structure. Possibly he is just broken. I half expect him to wander over to inspect Gonzo's flapjacks, but he doesn't. He has even stopped saying "Carry on" and "Soldier" as people pass. Through the sunshade the Addeh Katir sun is burning his face. His forehead is peeling.

Crisp and Duggan and their gang return with the fuel-less oven, and after some discussion and bitching and debate (in which they are gradually joined by a couple of mechanics, an ordnance technician and the quartermaster) they come to a decision. They submit plans to Gonzo and he listens, and the entire crowd listens with him, and finally he judges the plan acceptable and pleasingly insane, and sends them off to make it so. At this point he turns to the rest of the crowd and booms at them to form lines and prepare to divide the several cubic metres of flapjack into trays and cake tins and what all else. This he does in a way which suggests that they have been waiting for his order, and they are somewhat surprised to find that he is correct. Quite rapidly military discipline asserts itself, and by the time the engineers return and build a flapjack furnace, out of the old oven and a collection of flame-throwers all cobbled together to heat the radiator plates, there is a vast pile of random metalware filled and ready to cook, and shortly thereafter the furnace is fired up and does not explode.

Flapjacks happen.

ON WEDNESDAY we heal a gaping rift in international relations (at least locally) which feels pretty good. Baptiste Vasille (of the Joint Operational Task Force for Addeh Katir, and notionally an enemy) walks into camp, hands in the air, with a whole bunch of his men and announces that he has absolutely no intention of fighting us any more because our bit of the war has gone from absurd to actively silly. Vasille had no problem with absurd, but silly is something he won't stick at any price. He has had no communication from his masters and is reasonably confident that we haven't either. For all he knows, we few represent the entire surviving population of the planet, and he refuses (in a very French way) to be a bloody idiot about this and court the annihilation of the species over instructions which patently have nothing to do with today. Is that a cigarette? Baptiste Vasille will swear his eternal soul to our service for a cigarette. He has two hundred soldiers who would do more than that. For tobacco products, they will march on hell and put out the fire with their own blood. Of course they will. They are French. And Lebanese. And a couple of them are African. But no Belgians! Hah! . . . *Nom de dieu!* Flapjacks? Blood of Christ . . . Gonzo is a genius. He is almost French. Where should Vasille sign his name? Is there wine? Well, you can't have everything. Still, Vasille has some brandy. Only thirty cases, but still . . . You know that bitch? The Austrian? She's gone mad. Completely. Psychotic. Perhaps she always was. And she has her own little war going on, and a nemesis. Like Greek. Vasille knew a Greek girl once, in Thessalonika. She was special. A contortionist, *hein*? Those were the days. It was last summer, actually . . . How time flies. Does anyone have a lighter? Kemner. That's the bitch. Not the Greek girl, of course. The Austrian. Vasille quite likes Austrians, under normal circumstances. His brother married one. Nice girl. Never could get her in the sack though, too prissy. She (the Austrian, Kemner, a fiend from hell, *salope* . . . Mordieu, what a horrible thought! Who'd pay for that? Well, Kumar, of course, but *other* than him?) was the commander of the Addeh Defensive Initiative, yes? Bunch of crooks! Thieving weasel nations all in a row, and the Belgians at the heart of it, no doubt! Dealing with opium lords, dealing with mafias and mobski and triads and bastards and even Erwin Kumar, sure as milk. Yes, *milk*! Kumar is a stoat and a sexual deviant, and not in a good French way, but also he is a drug smuggler on an international scale, with the backing of the *merde* CIA from A-*merde*-ica. Of course, because they are the Cocaine Intelligence Agency, hah! Or was it the Russians? The Kokainum whateverthehell KGB stands for? Jesus, in the name of mercy . . .

Someone finally lights Vasille's fag. He holds it to his mouth as if he will devour it, then raises it like the head of a defeated enemy, and his men (and a couple of women) set up a roar of approval. The French have arrived, and it is a good thing, because they are different, and if nothing else was killing us, boredom was doing the trick.

Things are thus solidly ticking over on Thursday at about five in the afternoon, which is, as near as anyone can tell, when the world as we know it comes to an end. We had imagined, in so far as we had thought about this at all, that it had already taken place. We were wrong.

The guy's name is Foyle or Doyle, and he's got grit. His ribs are all bound up from some kind of blunt-force trauma, like maybe being exploded across the room, but he's out here lifting and hauling with the rest of us. We are building a reservoir, although it looks more like a beaver dam. A small river runs down from the hills and past the rear of our encampment, and where it hooks around a batch of harder rock, we are slowing it down. There will be a small lake, constantly filled at one side and constantly emptied at the other. Gonzo has decreed we should not be dependent on resources we cannot control. He is considering moving the base entire, but there are several thousand men here, and much of the equipment is not designed to be moved without air support. Air support is something we no longer have. Foyle (or Doyle) was a mechanic back home, and he thinks he could rig together a couple of the big trucks for this task, maybe one of the bridging tanks. He is telling me because I am Gonzo's Friend. Gonzo has many friends—Jim and Sally and Samuel P.—and they are also my friends, Leah's friends. But there is only one Friend here. The guy who can pledge Gonzo's word on his own. The guy who can anticipate him, who backs him, without whom he would occasionally trip over some human weakness or unseen glitch. Gonzo's practical side. His lesser half.

So Doyle, who goes by the alias of Foyle, but whose name (it now seems to me, as I consider his tags and my memory more closely) may actually be Tucker, is holding a long wooden stake against his chest, sort of under his chin like a violin. He is wrapping some twine around it and another stake resting against it, so that the two stakes together will make a giant V, and combined with the other stakes also configured in this shape will form the basis of a flexible breakwater, or water trap. The water will flow through them, they will accrue grunge and grime, and gradually they will become an obstacle, and this obstacle will generate a small pool. Tucker Foyle (I'm reasonably sure, now, that this is his name) grins and twines and doesn't stop yapping the while. And then something happens which is very strange and bad.

A streak of dapple and light scuds across the open space where we are working, and for a frozen instant we are at war.

Eyeblink: sunny day, men working, calm and business-like.

Eyeblink: darkness and screaming; the smell of guns and bloody execution; something zings by, a howling wasp. A were-wasp. It passes me and alights on Tucker Foyle.

Eyeblink: sunny day, men hesitating, rubbing their eyes. Combat flashback probably. Unmanly, perhaps. Not dangerous. A slow, humble recognition—we all had it. We laugh, reassured, we turn to one another to share the gag. Laughter evinces control. Mammals ho! We're conquering the world. No shadows. Just us.

Tucker Foyle slides slowly forward onto his spar. He has a bullet wound on his back, at the shoulder. This in itself would not be a terrible thing, but the impact has driven him onto the wooden spike resting under his chin. Tucker has been impaled. He is not dead. He will not die for several minutes, but die he will, and there is absolutely nothing we can do about it.

Dapple again. It comes from the same direction, and this time I can see it, rushing in across the compound, and with it the sound of incoming fire. It is a stripe of darkness, perhaps four metres deep and twenty or thirty long. All around me there is moderately ordinary life. Within the shadow, it's hell. Men duck or fling themselves flat, or die where they stand. When it has passed, they pick themselves up, emerge from cover and are afraid.

The shadow embraces us, and the world shifts. My nose gets it first: the scent of the nameless town where I was blown up. The air is filled with vaporised blood and the smell of people losing bladder control, and the rich stink of weapons fire and diesel. This is a battlefield smell. I'm already on the ground, which is good, because more wasps are buzzing by. I can feel the imprint of their passage. They come from one edge of the dapple, and they vanish at the other. From within it's hard to see out. There's fog and smoke and a lot of shouting and screaming—far too much for this little space. This is a portion of *somewhere else,* laid over *here,* except that it is unmistakably this place. I have not been transported anywhere. The world has changed around me.

Out of the fog stumbles a dying soldier. He's not wearing any uniform I recognise. It's a sort of hotchpotch of US WWII and British WWI, with just a dash of Vietnam and Gallipoli. Green trousers with braces to hold them up, but the braces are off his shoulders and he's wearing not a shirt but some kind of skivvies. He's got a helmet, but it's the wrong shape for this war, and made of steel. Must be from one of the mercenary outfits, but it can't be Vasille's—the Frenchman's men are better equipped. In any case, I can't ask this guy. He's been shot in the mouth. He stumbles away again, and disappears.

And then the war is gone, flickered away. I can see it rolling on through the camp. As it passes over our makeshift lake, the water fills with bodies and turns into a thick red jelly. The shadow passes on. The jelly stays, slick and dark and rotten. It breaks up sluggishly as fresh water piles onto it, undulating itself to pieces—but not fast enough, and the lake floods a bit before the bloody mess floats away downstream. An unidentifiable part of someone washes up against my leg. Absurdly, Tucker Foyle is unscathed. He has not been hit. He is still dying over there. This makes me angry. And then I hear behind me a low moan of awe and fear—not a single voice, but the combination of many. More is coming; I turn to stare it down.

The sky is black from one side to the other. The sun is hidden. A wave is breaking over us, a great black wall of this awful stuff. From within, the sounds of mayhem. This is not war. It is a caricature, an idea of war. A nightmare. The wave does not fall. I turn my face upward to see the top. Looking back down, I see that it still has not reached the camp. It is huge. It breaks. Shadow envelops us and we are smothered in war.

There is a whistle, and then a crack. And then another. A noise like a ricochet goes over my head, and there's a wallop of sound like a truck going by and we're all on the ground. The earth shakes. A hundred metres away, by the makeshift oven, a man dies (he's our pizza chef, named Jimmy Balene, although as of now no one is going to eat those pizzas because it is impossible to tell where the tomato paste ends and Jimmy's brain begins). Mud starts to fly everywhere. The attack is here, and there are people dying, but there's no enemy, just darkness, confusion and people getting dead. It's as if this were weather. Thursday's forecast: light cloud, drizzle until three, then showers of subsonic lead and howitzer shells, fog of war, lightening up later when a high-pressure zone pushes down from Green Sector, bringing mustard gas and mortars. Some hand-to-hand in isolated areas. Friday: fine, with incendiaries. This is impossible, and we cannot fight it. We can only run.

I find I have a duty. Soldiers like these do not run. It has been trained out of them. In any case, cut off from reinforcements, they have no clear idea of where to run to. They will hold in the face of this, and they will die. Unless someone tells them not to. Gonzo is de facto running this place, and that is fine. Gonzo, by acclamation, can build ovens and dig latrines. But he cannot order the retreat. Only one man can do that. Concurrent with this realisation, I begin moving towards the shabby little tent inside the compound where George Copsen sits in his mild homicidal catatonia, waiting for someone to try to relieve him, waiting for his masters to tell him to evacuate Addeh Katir, or maybe just for God to come by and tell him it's okay. In normal circumstances it's a brisk walk from where we are to General Copsen's chair. Under fire—even idiotic, unaimed fire—it is a very long way. There is a lead rain falling, horizontal and impersonal—forty-five-calibre precipitation. All around there are screaming soldiers with impossible injuries who seem unable to expire.

Lieutenant Ben Carsville, over by the showers, has mounted a stack of spare parts and is shaking his fist, and for no good reason he is still alive. And then I realise: this makes sense to Carsville. It's where he has always lived. This is like sunshine to the part of him which is batshit insane. The injured are scattered at semi-regular intervals around the place so that the howling they set up is audible wherever you go. And still there is no enemy, just this crazed, inimical storm. Something whines past my head, and I swat at it, realising a moment later that it was a ricochet. I fall on my stomach and crawl in the approved fashion (no knees on the ground, move using forearms and feet) to cover, although cover is impossible because the assault seems to come from everywhere. I am making good progress. In maybe an hour, at this rate, I will get where I am going. New plan. (People are shouting. Somewhere a scream reaches the precise pitch which makes your gut churn and all the hairs on your neck come up. Someone else is yelling "enemy" and maybe something else, but I cannot make it out. I'm not even sure it's a man.)

As I crawl, the whole thing breaks down into little cameos: flashes of clarity and survival and death. I scramble half-upright and break into a low, fearful trot, searching for friends, even for familiar enemies, anyone I have ever met apart from the Magnificent Carsville, who brushes past me and is now charging into the fog with a kitchen knife strapped to the end of an assault rifle as a bayonet. He seems oblivious to the fact that it will come off the first time he uses it, slip down the barrel without doing the target much harm and the tape will impede the action of his gun and cause it to explode in his stupid, handsome face. Of course he's oblivious to these things. They do not happen to screen idols. Carsville vanishes, and almost immediately there is a vast detonation in the fog—but it is not him, alas, for he weaves out again, cheering himself on, yawping about medals and glory and at last a real fight.

I have never seen anything less real in my life. I stub my foot on something, and it turns out to be a dead man I have never met. He looks like a prop: corpse number 8, gutshot, eyes open, almost peaceful. Also available: 9, eyes closed, limbs crusader-style; 10, head wound, bandaged. In his hand is the key to a jeep. I grab it, and his muscles are slack because he has only just died, perhaps when I trod on him. The jeep will make me a target, but it will also make me faster. Where is it? He had the keys in his hand, so he was close. Must have been. I look around. There. It was parked next to a tent, and the tent got shot up and is now actually draped over the top of the jeep, concealing it. (Napoléon used to ask his soldiers: "Are you lucky?" Yes, *mon Empereur,* I am, and let me remain so.) I take the jeep, and put my foot all the way down. It lurches, seems about to stall, then fires up and we roar away. I suppress the urge to pat it on the flank like a loyal horse. *Swoosh.* I career through fires and over corpses (I hope they are corpses). Twice I have to swerve to avoid a stream of sourceless gunfire. Then I arrive.

George Copsen sits where he always sits. He wears the same plastic smile. In his hands is his service sidearm. Very little has changed about him, except that he is dead. He has ended his own life quite neatly, efficiently and somehow gently, as if apologising for making a mess. There is actually not very much mess, all things considered. He is still warm, but sort of like coffee from an hour ago, rather than in any way which might suggest that he lingers. He smells of pepper. I look at him and back across the compound. Carsville has rounded up a small squad of men so scared they will actually believe he has a clue what he is doing, and they are charging at shadows, and occasionally one of them spins and loses half or two thirds of his face, and the others roar with rage and charge after the shooter. Perhaps because he is making their lives so much easier, the enemy snipers do not hit Carsville. If there are any; it feels more as if the bullets are ambient, drifting on the wind like pollen.

I look at the recently vacated shell of George Copsen. I know what he should be saying. I close my eyes the better to hear him say it. I wait, for a count of three. The general looks grave. He stands, just so, and clasps the back of his chair. Time to bug out, he tells me. We don't know what's happening and we can't defend against it. How bad are we hit so far? Maybe 40 per cent, sir. And getting worse. The general growls. We'll be lucky to get out of this with twenty, he says. Get your friend. Pass the word. Run. Scatter. Live off the land, go native, get across the border. Survive. Do not die, soldier, and that's an order. None of you. No more. Understand?

"Yes, sir!" I say loudly, Carsville-style. "I understand, sir! Immediately, sir!" And having delivered this order, the general staggers and stares at me, because he has been shot neatly in the head. He says no more, but sinks back into his chair and dies a hero. I take his gun, and I get back in the jeep and drive like hell.

The thing we were not trained for, the thing which no one back home ever gave any serious thought to, is losing. It was never expected we might be overrun. There is a drill for it, which we never rehearsed, and the drill is shit. It requires functioning infrastructure, alert and well-commanded troops. The drill is a drill made up by someone who expected to win, everywhere. I ignore the drill. Instead, I tell every soldier I meet that George Copsen has ordered the bug out. He has not invoked the plan. The plan is over. He says to flee, and do it now. Most of them just look at me blankly. It is assumed there will be artillery cover and planes. These things belong to the enemy now, although I still do not know who that is. I stop the jeep at the comms tent and record a message: "All units evacuate." It is the best I can do. I tell them to break singly or in groups, make for high ground and cover, radio one another if they find a safe place. I order them to live. I put the message on repeat, and listen as it booms out of the speakers around the base. Then I go back outside, to look for Gonzo and to find Leah.

Pale, fake-looking smoke curls around the tents in wisps, muffles the shouts and obscures the way. I skid the jeep between two empty sheds, thinking I ought to recognise them but I do not, and roar abruptly into a different kind of war. From one side of the road to the other, new landscape of destruction. Mortar shells are falling here, or maybe grenades. The shells whistle in like doodlebugs in old movies, hit the ground and wait a split second before going off. This is war with a sense of its own drama. It is phoney. (Shrapnel gouges a hole in the side of the jeep.) It is bloody dangerous. I duck down low over the dash and discover a compass in the footwell. Compasses are not standard issue, so thank God for the dead man and his grandmother, who sent him her husband's old compass from whatever war he was in. Thank you, Goody Hullabaloo, I'm sorry I trod on your boy, sorry he got shot and I did not. I career around a huge crater, then pile on the speed and ram the jeep through a barricade and into the eastern quarter of the camp. The mortars stop, as if turned off at the switch.

I drive on. There is a wrongness in the calm. I get the giggles, my own laughter very loud in my ears. I wonder if I have gone deaf from the mortars, if the only sound I can physically still hear is my own voice. I rev the engine, listen to the roar. It's very loud. And then, at last, there are enemies. If I had needed confirmation that this is not just any war, I have it now. The enemy are not men. They are shadows. They are a vision of the Other Side, made real.

The shadows are everywhere. They emerge from smoke, blend into one another, fade and reappear. I see eyes, hear breathing. I hear harsh words in an enemy language (it is no language I can recognise, perhaps not a real language at all, just the sound made by *foes*), and the clack of bolts being drawn back and weapons cocked, and then a hail of bullets tears the jeep apart and I am hiding behind it and holding my utterly ineffectual pistol and expecting, finally (very finally), to get shot.

I do not get shot. The jeep gets shot, again and again. Ronnie Cheung would shake his head and declare it *totally and irredeemably buggered in the back passage, boy, and do not tell me that there is no other place in which something can be buggered, because I am an old and evil man and if I say that there are further and more filthy ways to bugger something then you believe it and pray I do not explain myself, is that clear?* and I hear them approach.

They are careful. They are unhurried. In a moment they will find me. They move hopscotch style, one passing the other, each spending a beat covering, then skittering forward. I know this because I hear their feet on the earth: *clickclack* and then *clicker-clackershuffle,* which is the noise they make crossing over behind one another. It is possible that I will be spared if I am unarmed, but my hand will not let go of the gun, because it is also possible that I will be slaughtered if I am unarmed. The jeep creaks as one of them climbs onto it, and his knife whispers from his side. So this will be how it happens. I see a shadow against the sky, and the shadow looks down. I am uncovered. It comes for me.

Jim Hepsobah, from nowhere, opens up with a fifty-cal. How he got here, how they found me, is a mystery, except that this is a main road and they must travel down it to get out, just as I must, but what brought them here and now is a thing I will contemplate for evermore. He is standing on the weapons platform of the RV in which Leah and I rode to our date. Beside Jim's RV, Baptiste Vasille is in a small tank, and he and the bony bloke from my stretcher days are squabbling over whether it is better or worse than a French TV-9, although this does not stop them from filling the air with genuinely friendly fire and clearing a passage to me. A few years ago this rescue would have been illegal. Using a fifty-calibre weapon against a human target was forbidden by the Geneva Conventions, which meant that if you wanted to kill a guy with a fifty-cal weapon (such as, for example, a Barrett sniper rifle, now standard for marine and commando sharpshooters) you had to shoot his car and make it explode, because that was a perfectly respectable method of execution, whereas just blowing his head off was a war crime. This charming example of old world chivalry was struck off the books when I was at Jarndice—its demise was indeed one of the things

I protested against, and about which George Lourdes Copsen (deceased) questioned me in detail as I sat in an electric chair. Now I am delighted to feel the air throb with uncivilised fifty-cals, because without them I would be dead.

Shadowmen wilt and dive for cover. Annie the Ox is driving Jim's RV, and Gonzo has the second. Leah is riding shotgun with an actual shotgun clasped tightly in her hands. She picks off a couple of bad guys on the outside and snarls at them, and I swear for a moment that she has angel's wings. My lover. My furious, lethal woman. One of us should be dangerous. I am so proud it's her.

Egon Schlender leaps out and hauls me up and I realise at this time that I have been wounded, and I look down at my leg. For a moment I am weirdly hopeful, but once again I have not been shot. There is a slender spike sticking out of me, and by the feel of the nasty, audible grating which proceeds from it and buzzes up to my hip and down to my knee, and fizzes against my teeth, the damned thing is lodged in the bone. This bastard object is standard issue to men of Gonzo's profession. It is made of a ceramic material which is not readily detected by X-ray, and four or five of them can be strapped around the upper leg of the average man of action and thrown at targets of opportunity. They fly straight and will pierce some armour, because the sharp tip penetrates Kevlar weave and the blade edge cuts through the individual threads rather than trying to penetrate a mass of them as a bullet does. Unscrupulous individuals minded towards civilian wetwork rather than combat have been known to poison the blood grooves, but since I am still alive it is a reasonable guess that this is not the case with the one currently occupying pride of place in my thigh.

Egon loads me into the RV and yells to Jim that we're going to have to get somewhere so he can treat people, and I realise that almost everyone is hurt in one way or another: Jim is sporting a gash along his side and Annie has her arm in a makeshift splint, and Egon Schlender himself has some hastily stitched holes on the left side of his face. It's not surprising; it seems as if the air itself has started shooting at us. I look at Leah, please God—but she is only scraped and bruised and extremely pissed off and afraid. She checks my thigh and zaps me with a local, then there is a bright flash as she removes the spike. I can't feel the pain, exactly, but I am very aware that something alien is being dragged out of my leg bone, and not all the nerves are entirely asleep. She touches one on the way out and I say something manly, like *ow* or *mother.* She superglues me together (this is what superglue is actually for) and wraps the whole thing up with a bit of someone's dress shirt. I love her even more.

Gonzo leads us out into the countryside, and the farther we get from the camp, the less severe the fighting is. We drive on, and it's misty and cool and the wheels thrum beneath us and the sound of the engine and the road is tranquil. We stop, and people change places to get some rest, and Leah collapses onto my shoulder and falls asleep like a child. I hand my looted compass to Annie the Ox and she stares at me as if I have done a magic trick, then grins. "Well, damn," says Annie the Ox, nodding. "Not bad. Not bad at all." And she ruffles my hair. We move on. Sooner or later, someone will have to say "What the fuck was that?" But that time is not yet; by mutual consent, we're just leaving it alone for a while. Gonzo doesn't take a break; he's too wired.

When we slow for the second time, it is because Annie has seen something at the side of the road, drawn our collective attention to it. We brake and stop, and watchful Jim Hepsobah stands by, but there is no one here. We all saw, from a distance, a family walking single file. From close to, we see only stunted trees and broken earth and fog. We heard them, even caught a whiff of sweat and bandages on the wind, but they are gone now, and perhaps they never existed.

The next time it is Jim Hepsobah who spots them, a column of our guys disconsolately trudging westwards. They are gone before he can slow down, tricks of the light.

A bit later, soldiers appear as we pause to assist a lone woman with a baby, who turns out to be a slender boy with a bundle of rags, swaying his hips in a ludicrous counterfeit. He scampers away into the forest, shouting abuse, and there are bullets. The whole thing is petty, a moment of shock and almost of irritation. Someone is shooting at us. It's so rude. We shoot back until they stop. We move on.

Then a jeep draws alongside, very fast. A slender figure in fatigues, shivering with cold, eyes fixed on the road ahead and the horizon, sits alone at the wheel. Annie looks at Jim and Jim makes a frantic gesture and Annie and (perforce) Gonzo pick up the pace. Sally Culpepper has blood on her elegant eyebrows and she obviously didn't manage to grab a coat before she lit out. She won't answer when Jim calls her and for the longest time she seems to think we're like the ghosts at the roadside, and finally Jim steps from the machine-gun platform into the jeep next to her and she all but kills him, razor bowie whipping round in a blur. Jim does the smart thing, puts the outside of his arm up and takes the hit there, and Sally wrenches back and jolts and comes back to us, and Jim puts his arms around her as she drives, ignoring the gash on his arm as if it were a mosquito bite. Maybe it is. Maybe Jim Hepsobah is wearing chain mail under there. On the other hand, he's bleeding. Maybe Ronnie Cheung's hot iron filings and rough concrete blocks have made Jim Hepsobah immune to minor injuries. Or maybe it's just Jim Hepsobah, because he's in love, and isn't this exactly what I would do for Leah? Sally slows to a more manageable pace and I clamber up into the gun nest and we head on, silent, down the long dark road. I get to be a hero for a while. Then it's someone else's turn, and I go back down into the car, and Leah uses me as a pillow.

We speed on through the gathering night. Leah wakes and doesn't speak. I know she's awake because her breathing has changed, but her eyes are closed and she doesn't draw away from my shoulder, which is about the only good thing going on. Later, she asks where we're going. Gonzo glances at me. "Copsen ordered withdrawal," Gonzo says, and I look right back at him and say "Yes, he did," and Gonzo knows that I am lying. I'm not sure if he loves me or hates me for saving us all from a heroic (pointless) last stand. He knows that it was a necessary lie, but it is not something he would have done. Leah gets her answer from Jim Hepsobah.

Our destination is Corvid's Field, which is the name given by all the foreign forces in the Elective Theatre to the small flat strip of green grass and cracked runway which serves as the UN's gesture in the direction of Addeh Katir. The local name is long and musical and relates to a legend about monsters and magic and (probably somewhat later) Buddha. It has too many consonants and a precise intonation which of all of us—as far as I know, including Vasille's men—only Jim Hepsobah can get close to. He has an ear for melody.

"Twenty years ago, at least," says Jim Hepsobah, after a kind of drawing-in-your-memory pause, "there was a guy flew a small plane out of Corvid's Field. Back then it was still called Bravo Strip by anyone who didn't call it by the Katiri name, and people just about still came here as tourists. Guy's name was Bob Castle, but he played a decent game of chess and everyone who knew him called him Rook, which is the other word for a castle in chess." He glances back to make sure he's telling her something she already knows. Leah nods confirmation.

"So Castle—Rook—decided that was a pretty cool handle, and he painted a big black bird on his tail fin and changed his call sign, and he went right on flying his charters and taking backpackers on little pleasure hops and filling in the off-season with some more grey-area kind of stuff like medical supplies which may or may not have had a legitimate source. Those grey-area cargos he got from a local fixer called Harry Manjil, an Anglo-Chinese Katiri with messed-up legs. Maybe polio or something. Not sure. He was a little weasel geezer who could make you laugh in about a second and a half, and have your fillings out while you were doing it. And Harry had a gorgeous wife, about twenty years old, called Yvette, and Harry and Yvette and Rook used to spend every Friday night hanging out and playing mah-jongg with whatever girl Rook was dating, and drinking cheap hooch from Harry's still." Jim Hepsobah turns halfway in his seat, and glances around to be sure everyone is paying attention. He frowns.

"Rook never made a move on Yvette, and Yvette never made a move on Rook. It just wasn't a thing. I say this because people immediately think there's a whole *loooove triangle* aspect to this story, and that pisses me off, because you can get three people in a room without someone screwing someone else's spouse, and because these were good people and honourable people and this isn't that kind of weak-ass story. Are we clear?"

"No triangle," says Leah. "Gotcha."

"So one night Yvette comes to Rook in a fluster and she says Harry's gone, just gone, and she doesn't know where he is, and she thinks maybe he got taken by bandits or maybe someone he was doing business with wasn't into the right kind of business. And she thinks she knows where Harry was going and will Rook fly her around there so she can look down from on high and see if she can see anything? Like his car. Or him. Or something. Please? So . . . Rook says no. He says absolutely no. He tells her, go home. Harry will be back. But we are not going flying low over some criminal sonsabitches who are doing criminal sonsabitches–type business with Harry, because they will get nervous and shoot him, and us. And Yvette goes home. And Rook gets himself in his plane and he goes up and he looks for Harry himself, because he thinks Yvette is absolutely right.

"He takes himself a big old automatic rifle for personal security, and a couple of grenades for added personal security, and he goes out towards the mountains, which is where criminal sonsabitches mostly do business in this region. He goes out and he flies over a camp and he sees Harry's jeep all shot up, and he drops one of his grenades on the tents down below, because his friend is dead down there. Now, he knows what will happen next, but he's an emotional guy, this Rook, and he does what he thinks is the right thing. And the leader of these folk down on the ground is a huge bastard, a man called Nand. He comes out and he shoots Rook through the floor of the plane. Just plain lucky, or unlucky, or he just puts so many shells in the air that one of 'em has to do something, because Rook is flying so low. Rook knows he's all done, and he brings the plane around one last time. On the ground Nand is cursing him and shooting at him and blowing bits off the wings. He shoots up the cockpit pretty good. Rook takes a few more, but he keeps that plane level and going in a straight line, right towards this evil sonuvabitch who killed his friend. Gets so close he's staring Nand right in the eye. And then he pulls the pin on the second grenade and the plane comes down on the camp in a hail of fire. So Rook kills the ogre.

"But the thing is, Harry wasn't dead at all. He'd had his car stolen right out from under him, and a bunch of arseholes had ripped him off and tried to kill him, but he was fast and smart and he ducked away into the jungle. Maybe they would have gone after him, but Rook arrived about that time, and they got busy.

"So Harry was footsore, but he was alive. He came home to Yvette just like Rook had said he would. So when Harry made it rich, he bought up the strip and got people around to calling it Corvid's Field, because a rook is a kind of corvid, maybe the only good kind. Little headstone for a friend. And then Harry and Yvette packed up and went away and no one ever saw them again." Jim Hepsobah smiles a sad little smile. Leah sniffs.

"But . . . the local people, the Katiri farmers and traders and the pirates from Lake Addeh, they liked Rook too. And they say the birds of Corvid's Field fly around the strip each dusk, and they fly in formation like a little single-engine plane, and that's the spirit of Bob Castle, the Rook, watching over Corvid's Field and enjoying the sunset. And woe betide the man who steps out of line there, because Rook may not have any grenades left, but he still has a rifle and he's a mean shot." Jim Hepsobah grins like a Viking, and you can pretty much smell the aviation fuel and the cheap flyboy cigars, and you can hear Nand the bandit screaming as he sees those burning fragments coming down on him from the sky.

Leah asks if that's a true story, meaning "How much of it is a true story?" which makes me think of the Evangelist, and that, in turn, reminds me that Corvid's Field is the UN airfield Elisabeth was writing about for her newspaper, and is she still there? Did she go home? Is she alive? And I realise that Elisabeth does not know about Leah, and that Leah does not know about Elisabeth, and then that there is no reason why they should, because Elisabeth and I have never been other than friends and training partners.

Jim Hepsobah is about to answer Leah's question when the road in front of us explodes and the windscreen stars and shatters, and we are hurled not forward, but back, as Gonzo stamps on the accelerator and takes us around and alongside the crater, gunning the engine to make it over the rubble by the side of the road, and controlling the slewing and skidding as we leave the asphalt or tarmac or clay or whatever it is they use here. Ronnie Cheung's tactical driving course takes over, and everyone tries to throw the enemy, weaving in and out like a school of fish confusing a tuna. (It's hard to think of tuna as predators, because we eat them as sushi, but if you're on Mr. Bluefin's dinner list, he's as mean a sucker as you could ever know, and he is fast and damn hungry.) There are only four vehicles and one of them's a tank, so the effect is muted, but Mr. Bluefin in this case is a lousy shot, or more likely he's never seen coordinated tactical driving before. He shoots at where we are and he needs to be shooting at where we're going to be. He misses. We leave him behind.

Twenty minutes later: three figures beside a barricade of wood and rubble. Gonzo barely slows. He flicks his headlights to full, and I catch a glimpse of a couple of guys with an RPG (they are not *aiming* it at us, they just *have* one, like they're having tea and grenades) and a third figure in shredded coveralls. This third person, apart from the others, is tall and too thin, and wears an orange prisoner-suit and a gasmask. The gasmask is very strange because it makes the person in it look as if they have no head. The person waves, arms crossing and uncrossing. "Stop" the orange person is saying, or "Help" or possibly "Slow down so we can kill you and steal your car." And then they're gone—Gonzo has taken us over the middle of the barricade, and they haven't shot at us. Does that mean they weren't part of the outfit who blew up the road? Or does it mean that they were, but they don't fancy a real fight? I have no idea. I ask Gonzo, but he's fighting to control the car. He's had enough of this crap, and he's got the thing up to about sixty, which isn't bad on a road made of clay and asphalt patched with sheep shit. We leave the waving creepy person behind, and Gonzo keeps that speed up until we arrive at Corvid's Field.

THE UN FLAG is still flying over the control tower, sad and bleached. A couple of guys in blue helmets stand at the gates, covering us with their sidearms. The walls have been shot up some, and there's a dirty smear along one side of the tower where some kind of explosive has gone off and the tower has been patched but not repainted. Otherwise, they seem to have got lucky, although from this angle it's not possible to see the whole field. And on the runway *(Sing hosanna!)* there is a pair of elderly but serviceable cargo planes. They have no windows and the seating will not be comfortable, but between them, if we are permitted to use them, we can evacuate everyone.

One of the blue helmets walks out towards us, cautious. He's a brave little guy, probably Puerto Rican on secondment. It takes some chutzpah to leave your own gate and walk up to an armoured column—even one as ragtag as ours—and tell them to behave or face the consequences of your displeasure. That is what he is coming to do, and he knows—and he knows that we know—that those consequences are basically him being extremely stern and maybe his commander giving us a sound talking-to. Or, I realise, a blonde civilian with a too-long face coming out and stamping her foot—but Elisabeth is nowhere to be seen. I hope she has already gone home.

"Who the hell are you?" the UN guy wants to know.

"We're a travelling circus," Gonzo says acidly. "I'm the bearded lady and these here"—he points to Jim Hepsobah and Sally and me—"are my clowns." The UN guy doesn't think much of that.

"Fine," he says. "Take me to the ringmaster." And Gonzo says that's him too.

"Turn around," the UN guy says. "There's an armed camp maybe six or seven hours that way. They can help you better than we can."

"We need evac," Gonzo replies, "and so do you."

"Turn around," the UN guy says again. Gonzo looks thunderous and pissed off, and he's about to share his feelings when the gate opens and the other UN guy waves us in. Our guy looks pretty disgusted and steps out of the way. Gonzo throws him a little grin and we all cruise merrily past him, through the gates, and the last we see of him is a single figure trudging slowly back to his position. We don't pay him much attention, though, because by this time we realise how badly we have been fucked. We realise this because once everyone is inside the compound and outside their vehicles, soldiers who are emphatically not with the UN step out from the low buildings of Corvid's Field and point their guns at us, and unlike George Copsen's bastard squad at Jarndice, they don't bother to tell us we are prisoners, because that sort of speaks for itself. And after patting us down and disarming us quite thoroughly, they take us to their leader. Vasille makes a face: *merde.*

Ruth Kemner.

She has taken the small departures hall for her own. It is a high room with narrow vertical windows in frosted glass intended to let the light through but not the glare. There's a beaten-up luggage carousel by the door and a bar on one side, but the main event is at the far end under the sign saying *Embarquement* and the same in a variety of languages. Men stand in precise parade-ground formation, port arms. A moth-eaten red carpet has been laid out in strips across the floor, and a few rostra have been shoved together to make a dais. As in a place where a monarch sits—which is where the whole thing goes absolutely to the bad.

Ruth Kemner is sitting on a throne. It is not a very special throne, as these things go. It is the control chair of an assault helicopter welded to a metal frame, the whole thing draped over with a leopard skin which might have come from an actual leopard, but probably didn't. The setup looks like some seventies movie in which warrior women, played by bathing beauties, capture and threaten to execute a group of male castaways, before melting blissfully into the arms of the square-jawed and plucky chaps, who stand for no sapphic nonsense and know that every good girl wants a firm hand. It's ludicrous.

That's probably why she has added the two severed heads to the uprights of the throne. They lend her an undeniable air of not screwing around. Her eyes look completely ordinary, which is what eyes do, but the face in which they rest, the network of small muscles which are used, voluntarily and otherwise, to produce expressions and communicate mood, is broadcasting that she's dangerously psychotic. She sits forward, and she turns her head slowly so we can see that someone has taken a knife to her. They have attempted to open her throat, but they have failed, and there is a cut along her jaw which must have been painful and bloody, but which is now nicely stitched up. The surgeon has also put the lower half of her ear back, but it's not looking too hopeful. As she looks at us, her face is in precisely the same position as head number 2, and the resemblance is uncanny. Unless Ruth Kemner has a sister, she's gone and murdered someone who looks very like her, and used that person as part of the furnishings. It hardly matters which. Kemner has, as advertised, gone batshit. And from the old newspaper stand at the far end of the room her flunky brings out a muffled, furious figure, thrashing and bucking and roaring for a fair shot, or possibly for justice and freedom, and when they whip off his hood, we are all able to recognise Ben Carsville. If that scar is his work, it says a great deal for the unvarnished power of idiocy. It also explains why Kemner isn't dead, and foreshadows a very bad ending to the story of the most handsome soldier in the Elective Theatre.

Carsville sets his jaw and glances at the throne situation and the heads, and he obviously takes in the movie thing too, because he makes some off-colour joke. Ben Carsville, of course, is exactly the kind of man who would be able to win the heart of a libidinously frustrated Amazon queen. Unfortunately, Kemner isn't some busty trollop with a power complex. She *was* a respectable kind of mercenary soldier ("non-governmental military consultant") at the bloodier end of the spectrum. What she is now, after the things which have happened since George Copsen's red telephone rang and signalled the commencement of non-conventional hostilities in the new era, is less certain.

She looks at Ben Carsville with a chilly curiosity. Whatever sassy opening he used hasn't immediately had its effect. She doesn't slap him in an affronted yet alluring way; she doesn't stare moodily into his eyes. She regards him with a kind of scientific interest, as if he were a new species ready for vivisection. She nods at her thugs. They pick Carsville up with a lot of "hur hur hur" and Kemner leads us all out around the back of the departures hall.

When you walk a prisoner at gunpoint, there is one thing you do not do. You do not poke him with your gun barrel. Every second you spend in physical contact with your prisoner is a second he is aware of the disposition of your body, and is close enough to attack you—assuming he knows where the gun is—before you can pull the trigger. Olympic athletes leaving the starting blocks are too slow to fire a gun in the time it takes a trained soldier to push the barrel to one side once he knows where it is. A gun is a weapon of medium distance, not close combat. So you don't give him the chance to map out the situation, you don't let him feel how relaxed or how tense you are and you never, ever shove him with your weapon, because if you are a fraction off centre, and he allows the barrel to pivot him, you have just put the business end of your gun right past him and he can bite your nose off or use your gun to shoot the man in front or any number of other things which are not conducive to good penal discipline.

Kemner's men are good. They keep a fluid yet constant distance between us, they do not allow us to communicate and they do not rise to baits like stumbling, slight increases or decreases in speed or comments about their hair. They imagine, therefore, that they have communicated nothing to us about themselves beyond that they are in the position to kill us all, and have no intention of reversing roles. They are mistaken. The way they have deployed is extremely revealing. Our guards are moving in a mild curve behind us, so that we are caught in the focus of their field of fire if they should choose to gun us down—so much is to be expected. Around them, however, are other men whose eyes are turned outward. They watch the hills and the trees around, and they carry long guns. They are looking out, but also at everything which is not immediately within their sphere of control. In the control tower there is a sniper. These men are not pro forma. They are paying attention in a way which is unique to people who have recently been attacked and expect to be attacked again. And they are expecting attack not just from outside, but from *within the bounds* of Corvid's Field, which by rights should be their safe zone. Their fingers rest close to their triggers, and they are intense and even a bit twitchy. In other words, someone has given them a serious case of the willies. That information is worth something, but it slips away as we come in view of our destination, and my stomach lurches and all the hairs on my neck tingle as if there were a spider walking over my lips.

Corvid's Field has been hit by a Go Away Bomb. This place was not supposed to be a target—at least, it wasn't one of our targets—but on the other hand, what is supposed to be a target and what actually gets blown up (or Gone Away) are movable feasts in war. Beside the runway, concealed from the approach road by the bulk of the tower building, the ground slopes away in a smooth line, as if excavated in a single go by a very big, curved shovel. A large section of forest and a fragment of a wooden outhouse have disappeared, along with the latter half of a cargo plane. The plane has rolled back a bit, or been pushed, so that it's now a sort of open corridor out over the excision, which unlike all the ones I have seen in testing is not empty. Bubbling up from the centre there is water, or something looking very much like it: a silvery, frictionless fluid filled with bubbles. Little waves roll out from the middle, and a fine spume drifts over the surface, making crazy shapes like giants and gurning faces.

It smells wrong. A lake like this should send out a rich, warm scent of water. Even if it's a burst pipe or (less appetising) a sundered septic tank, there should be a strong smell to go with it. Looking at Kemner, I wonder about aviation fuel or chemical waste—it would suit her new persona very well to have a tame lake of fire behind her throne room—but there's not a whiff of either. There is no smell of anything at all—and yet there's a great quantity of whatever it is, bubbling away in front of us. Has the excision uncovered a well of naturally distilled water? Or saline? In the centre of the lake the surface heaves, a glassy bubble pushing up and then bursting to send a column of the stuff up twenty feet into the sky. Is Addeh Katir geothermically active? I have no idea. It was not included in the briefings we were given when we arrived. On the other hand, it probably wouldn't be. But a bad feeling is creeping up on me, above and beyond the obvious dread associated with the business of being in the hands of a grade-one loon; a sense of *Oh shit.* It is visceral and possibly—in the most literal sense—*existential.* I am worried about existence.

Kemner gestures, and Carsville appears in the aisle of the

truncated cargo plane. He is blindfolded, but his arms and legs are free. Piranha, I decide. She has found a breeding population of piranha, and she intends to feed us to them. Do they have piranha here? I have no idea. I know piranha are by origin South American, but on the other hand it would be quite like the imperial Brits in their day to have imported a few to add local colour. *What ho, Sergeant Daliwal, how are the fish today? Pukka, are they? Had enough goat? I swear, if I never eat goat again . . . The Italians eat it, you know, but they'll eat anything if it's got enough garlic. Can't fight, though, can they? Quality of man, Sergeant Daliwal, is what it's all about. Your lot know that. Why they signed up with us, of course. What's that? Anand lost another finger? Chap's careless. They're piranha, not bloody whelks.* It occurs to me that the man is probably an ancestor of Dr. Fortismeer. He is exactly the sort of person who would feel that a mountainous Eden was incomplete without ugly, ravenous fish in an ornamental lake. *Eat burglars, more fun than a haha! Aha, ahaha ha! Hah? Sort of a test project, y'see; if it goes well, we'll have a few more! Hah! Like to see the natives swim the moat then! Eh, Sergeant Daliwal, eh? 'Scusing your presence, of course, good man . . .*

Again, the possibility was not covered in my briefings. It will almost certainly have been in Gonzo's, if it happened, but now is not the moment to ask. Kemner's head flunky appears in the plane behind Carsville, and shoves him over the lip of the plane into the lake. Pirates again, I'm thinking, but of a very different kind. Plank-walking? Join or die, perhaps. Carsville shouts, flips and lands arse first and submerges. A second later, he is bolt upright, on his feet, sputtering, then he falls over. He is about thirty feet away, maybe a little more, and this time when he comes up, he flails wildly, striking the water. The piranha theory gains currency in my mind, but I don't believe it. My existential fear is in full flood. This is a *wrong* thing. It is an *anti-thing.* It has the quality of *not.* I am coming to believe, because I can see familiar debris, because of the shape of the excision and what might be the rear end of a delivery-system rocket shadowed in the centre of the lake, that this water is fallout from a Go Away Bomb. This stuff I am looking at is somehow not stuff I should ever see with my eyes. That would mean that Go Away Bombs are not clean and perfect after all, and that the wanton messing we have done with the basic level of the universe is not, after all, completely free and without consequence.

And then a hand reaches up out of the water and grabs Carsville by the shoulder. He falls backwards, under the surface, which heaves and billows as the struggle begins in earnest.

Ben Carsville fights for his life. He may be an arsehole—I may have had to hit him in the jaw to save his men from a gas attack—but he's not a coward (whatever that means in the real world). Nor is he a pushover. He surges up, and roars, and pummels at the person in the lake with him. This is a new Carsville, animated and furious, and actually quite impressive. He goes under, and comes up belly first, and he seems afraid, despairing and beaten. His opponent has him in an armlock, and is gradually ripping the joint apart. Carsville shouts and dives beneath the surface, reappears having somehow reversed the hold. He grins fiercely, then loses his grip. His opponent springs back, throws punches which start out scientific and grow more desperate. The two men flail at one another, cling together, grapple and throttle. They are well matched. Kemner has selected her executioner (or is it another prisoner?) with ominous appropriateness. It seems that neither one can defeat the other. Is that a draw? Or will she have them both impaled? Then finally, for a moment, the two men square off, eye to eye and mano-a-mano, and one of them lifts the other up, down, and holds his head below the surface.

This is the life of Benedict Anthony Carsville, as it flashes before his eyes. Most likely, as he struggles he is thinking about the toughness of his opponent's jacket, the strength of his arms. Possibly, as some men do in battle, he is worrying with terrible intensity about things like the smell of cows in the rain and the answer to last week's crossword. Be that as it may, this is what *ought* to go through his head:

He does not remember being born. No one does. Some people will tell you that they do. There are hypnotists who can help you recall it. They can also help you remember your time in the army of Rome, your life as an alien being in a far-off galaxy and what it was like to be a garden snail during the Renaissance. These recollections should be treated with the utmost caution.

He remembers his mother's orange trousers. They were made of stretchy velvet. She wore them the whole time. He remembers her hair, which was dyed, and the fact that it made him sick when he sucked it. He remembers his father, who had only one arm, and he remembers playing football with a balloon. The balloon took a very long time to do anything, so the game was a continuous exercise in frustration and delight.

He remembers the day they came and covered the playground in special rubberised tiles, so that it would be safer. They dug up the grass and the mud and replaced them with a scientifically proven composite which would reduce the chances of broken bones and scuffs. He watched the large, bored men going to and fro with rolls of underlay and stacks of special tiles. They laughed and stopped for tea, which was awful because he wanted to go on the swing. They fitted a governing device to the swing so that it couldn't go beyond a certain angle. He never really liked the playground after that, because it was just like being indoors. It smelled wrong. It was even and controlled. He waited for the new flooring to weather and split like the decking at his uncle's house, but it didn't. His father told him it was *biologically and chemically inert,* and he wanted to know what a "nert" was. His father thought this was funny.

He remembers kissing Lisa Crusky. She tasted in the main of snot, because they were only nine. There was an aftertaste of girl, which he wasn't sure was very nice. He remembers kissing her brother, Niall Crusky, and being beaten for it. He did not understand why, and actually still doesn't. Niall Crusky tasted exactly like Lisa, except without the tangerine ChapStick and the snot. After that day Lloyd Carsville insisted that his son wear grown-up clothes, in grey and blue. Benedict was the best-dressed, most uncomfortable child in school. As he got older, though, it started to look good on him, and he established that there were advantages to this. Girls—girls had soft parts boys did not, and he had discovered he was interested in those areas—became most aware of Ben Carsville's angel face and suited, conscious cool.

He was good at games. He was good at football, at hockey, at shooting and tennis and everything else. Everyone agreed he was a handsome lad, and always so well dressed. He was hot-tempered too, quick to pick a quarrel and quick to make friends. He was like a damned Greek, his uncle Frederick said, kind of admiring. Uncle Frederick worked with a lot of Greeks in the olive oil business. Most people found this funny and joked about the Mob. Uncle Frederick explained patiently that the Mafia was Italian and that in any case he actually did import olive oil. Someone had to.

He remembers his first great seduction; not his first time having sex (oh, yes, he remembers that, but it was unexpectedly drab) but his first *conquest.* It was on his nineteenth birthday. Gabrielle Vasseli was madly in love with him. Ben was madly in love with her older sister Tita, who was twenty-six. Gabrielle arrived in her sister's car, and Ben focused the full force of his charm on Tita for a few seconds as he held the door.

"Thank you, Miss Vasseli," Ben Carsville said. "Are you sure you won't come in as well?"

Tita Vasseli looked at him and Ben Carsville saw in her eyes, in the flicker of amazement and the involuntary swallow, that she was going to say yes. Ben was the rarest of things, a genuinely beautiful man. Good-looking men are commonplace, and beautiful women are not rare. Male beauty, capable of overcoming the stigma attached to it and undeniable, is one in many hundreds of thousands. Tita Vasseli wanted to possess this boy, to bathe in him, wash herself in him and have some of it rub off. At the very least, she wanted to bone him as he had never been boned before. She moistened her lips and sought a way to put this to him.

Gabrielle wrapped her arm around Ben Carsville's waist.

Tita Vasseli hated her baby sister for a full ten seconds. Then she recovered herself and felt a certain relief.

Ben Carsville didn't mind. He knew what he knew. If he never saw Tita Vasseli again, he would know it for ever. The answer was yes. He seduced Gabrielle in the meantime. Tita Vasseli went home, spent a few days trying to concentrate and finally admitted to herself that she was a spluttering kettle of sexual frustration liable to boil over, melt the kitchen counter, fry the ring main and short out the neighbourhood. Weighing the consequences, she coolly decided that the only way to deal with this situation in an adult fashion was to go full steam ahead with her first plan vis-à-vis Ben Carsville, *id est* the boning. She made the call. When Gabrielle caught Tita and Ben in bed together a month later, the wailing rattled the ceiling and the gnashing of teeth was ghastly to behold. Tita was abject but also quite pleased. Later that day she showed Ben something so obscene he almost passed out.

He enlisted out of boredom, and because, in his entire life, he'd never found anyone who could say no and make it stick. (Ben Carsville's life was not like Gonzo's: Gonzo was charming, and his relentless forward momentum made him irresistible. But he knew doubt. Ben Carsville did not. He knew only that from the day they covered his playground, the earth beneath his feet was smooth, conquered, featureless.)

In the service someone knocked out one of Ben Carsville's front teeth, and he had to have it replaced. He got a fine, elegant scar under one eye from a brawl over who jogged whose elbow at the bar. He was run ragged, reached the end of his physical capacity and then discovered more within himself. He glowed. And then it all sort of smoothed out. No war, no problem. Just more slow promotion—endless, inevitable, upward progress. He watched war movies because it was the only combat around. He watched *Apocalypse Now* two hundred and fifty times. He applied for and received duty as a peacekeeper in Africa. It was fine. The bad guys shot at him—but he was in a tank and wearing protective gear. Anyway, they never hit him. Once, out of curiosity, he stopped his armoured car and got out, walked into a fire zone, and took out a machine-gun emplacement by blowing it up with a grenade. He got a medal for bravery under fire, but in truth he had been neither.

He remembers coming to Addeh Katir. He remembers the sense of hope as he landed, the plane swinging out over green canopies of forests, over mountains like shattered glass and endless interconnected lakes. He remembers the people, open, suspicious and angry, abandoned and proud. This, at last, was a place which could say no in a great voice, and mean it. He fell in love.

Addeh Katir took three days to break Ben Carsville on its wheel. It wasn't remotely interested in his good looks. By the time he arrived, the Katiris had been living with Erwin Kumar and his bandit police and his foreign backers for more than a decade, and they were sick of it. Some of them—shepherds, probably, because Ben Carsville had ordered a mini-ovicide around Red Gate—took up arms and shot at his men. They fired bullets and arrows and darts and pebbles. Ben Carsville's command lost three men to pebbles in his first week. They were hit in the throat. The fourth one got lucky: he was hit in the eye and lost binocular vision, but didn't actually expire immediately. The unit medic patched him up, but while he was waiting for transport back to the main HQ it transpired the pebble was coated in resin from a vilely poisonous tree. Private Hengist started to scream. He screamed for seven hours until finally his lungs collapsed and he died. (Shepherds are the natural enemies of wolves and hunting cats. Like wolves and hunting cats, and like sheep, they are not interested in the Geneva Conventions or the Biological Weapons Treaty. They have a job to do, and they do it. Shepherds do not need to read Clausewitz to understand about total war, because they live with it all the time.)

Ben Carsville didn't care any more that Addeh Katir was a beautiful place. Nothing in his life had prepared him for this, ever given him any cause to believe the world contained no-win situations. He didn't care that Addeh Katir's people were vibrant and noble, traders and musicians and historians, with a gentle traditional religion and a powerful sense of community. He just wanted to be who he had always thought he was. He wanted to be bigger, stronger, more debonair, more dashing. It didn't really matter whether he was good at his job as long as he looked right. He was living in the war zone now, and he got his silk dressing gown out and he marched up and down his fence to show how in control he was and how he did not give a damn. He exhorted his men to greater efforts in personal grooming, tried to get them to understand that there were no chance encounters, only actions and reactions. They followed him for a while down this strange road. If his luck had been transferable, perhaps they would have followed him to hell. But Ben Carsville's luck was an intensely selective, individual thing. His unearthly beauty was dulled by dirt and anguish, but somehow it still worked. Snipers turned aside from him. They picked those nearby instead. When Ben Carsville walked his ramparts with a cigar, bullets zinged through the air to his right or left in case he was talking to someone. He could stand where he liked and do as he pleased. The other side was not interested in his death, but in his ruin. His reality began to diverge from everyone else's in marked, dangerous ways. Then he got punched out, taken down and disgraced by Gonzo Lubitsch and his smart-mouthed arsehole friends.

He remembers the plunge into Ruth Kemner's lake. He remembers the warm, sweet water and the strange sense of coming unstuck. He remembers going to climb out, and the ghastly, stomach-churning feeling of a hand dragging him down into the mud. An enemy. A monster. He struck out, found his target. He struck again, shook the water from his eyes and saw his man. He remembers being horrified, but he honestly does not remember why. It was important but not relevant. The man was inimical. The man was trying to take his life. He didn't need to know more. This was the moment where he would be what he wanted to be. He lunged: instinct, pure and bleak and hot.

Ben Carsville is fighting for his life, giving everything he has. He tries so hard. We watch, and we wonder if we will be next. The lake churns. Blood and bubbles. A figure staggers upright. I look. I do not know whether this is what I expected or not, and I don't know whether it is good or bad.

Ben Carsville spits blood and snot, coughs and marches back up the bank. Behind him, something man-like bobs in the water. Something dead and a bit sad. Carsville looks great, all cinematic and damp, and somehow more Carsville now than he ever was before. He glances at Kemner and starts to laugh. He sits down on the shore and cackles, and they come and wrap a towel around him, and leave him there. Apparently, he has walked the plank successfully.

They take us back inside and lock us up in what was, at one stage, the secure liquor locker for the airport bar. We are still handcuffed, so all they have to do is run a thick wire-cord rope between our hands and padlock it to the pins in the wall, and we're pretty securely detained. They slam the door like matinee villains and make a point of chortling as they walk away.

Gonzo looks at me, and I look at Gonzo. We were standing at the front, closest to the action, and so it's possible that no one else saw what we saw. If they didn't see it, they won't believe that we did. I'm not sure I do either. But for a moment, that moment when Ben Carsville stood eye to eye with his opponent, before he took him down and choked his mouth with the stuff in that unlikely lake, it looked as if that opponent was *also* Ben Carsville.

CHAINED to a wall by an implacable enemy. Situation: *v. bad, even horrible.* Special forces guys are trained for horrible situations, of course, and specifically for situations involving capture and terrible torture. They are schooled in resource. They are taught to be tough and ready. Nurses don't get that kind of training, but Leah seems to be managing pretty well; Egon isn't, so he's sort of hanging by his arms and weeping, and no one can pick him up or hold him and tell him it's okay, and in any case that would be a lie. Whatever happens when you get thrown into the lake, it clearly is bad. Ben Carsville isn't in here with us. He's outside with Kemner, a fully paid-up member of her jolly monster squad. Maybe the lake is just a huge pit of nasty brain-washing, psychosis-inducing gunk. Maybe it's a consequence of the Go Away Bombs and Professor Derek's genius-dumbarse physics. Whatever it is, Kemner wants to put us in it, one by one, and will enjoy putting us in it, and she is a crazy lady with a collection of human heads on her office furniture. This is enough for us to know that we need to escape.

The trouble is that although special forces guys are prepared for this, that essentially means keeping a positive mental attitude, being ready to take your chance when it comes and knowing how to resist torture for an extra half-hour of the really bad stuff. It does not make you able to walk through walls or bend solid steel with the power of your naked brain. Nor does it necessarily give you the ability to see the obvious, because it sort of concentrates you on a win/lose mind-set where winning is frustrating the other guy and losing is giving in to pain and injury. They can get their hands in front of them easily—just step through the cuffs, because they're yogi flexible—but then what?

Which is why this moment belongs to me. There is a very unsubtle, easy way to get loose from this prison. For all that he knows it's there, because he went to the same class I did on counter-restraint, it isn't the kind of thing Gonzo is liable to come up with. Gonzo is one of nature's winners, and this kind of victory is what you might call pyrrhic. It's not something you can ask Leah to do, and it's not something which would necessarily work for Jim Hepsobah or some of those other guys, because they've spent so much time bulking up and turning their hands into lethal weapons. It probably would work for Sally Culpepper, but it would also make her useless if we need a sniper somewhere down the line. So it's a perfect plan for me.

The thing is that although it is easy, it isn't going to be any fun. And so I take a few breaths before I do it, and I send up, for the first time, a sort of prayer, although it's rather hazy around the edges.

Most people, when they pray, have a notion of where the words are going. They have in mind God the Bearded, God the Robed, God the Absent Father sitting on a cloud going through his postbag. My prayer is in a blank envelope, left sitting at a bus stop. Anyone who is interested can pick it up and open it. Anyone, in fact, who wants to be God—to me, at least—can slip their thumb between the flap and the body of the envelope and crack the seal, and discover my one, solemn wish: *Dear Lord, I want to go home.* All they have to do, to get into my personal pantheon, is deliver the appropriate miracle. In the meantime, though, I'm working on the basis that the letter will sit there and get brushed off the back of the bench and into the gutter, and then a rainstorm will wash it into the sewer system where it will get sodden and mouldy, and the ink will fade and the paper turn to sludge, and my prayer will just fade away unread, as they mostly seem to. So I rest my left hand against the wall, thumb outwards. Then I stretch as far away from it as I possibly can. And then I hurl myself hard against it, the bone of my hip crunching against the small ones which make up my hand. This hurts, but nothing breaks. It takes a few minutes and several repetitions of the operation, during which everyone turns to stare at me in absolute horror, before something substantial snaps and I am able (after a few seconds of vomiting) to pull my broken hand out of the cuff and remove myself from the rope.

The pain is transcendentally awful. The sickly knowledge that I did this to myself amplifies it, makes it special. It rebounds off the understanding that I cannot stop, that I must go on, or suffer more of the same. Belatedly, I remember that there is a set of internal chi gong exercises which can be used (in advance, of course) to deaden pain. They are called the Nine Little Nurses, which Master Wu always found vaguely erotic, so that, when he explained them, there was a kind of wistful, naughty expression on his face, suggesting that in his younger years he knew at least three of them very well indeed. Not that there are actual nurses. Apart from Leah and Egon. I consider the possibility that Leah and Egon are illusions I created, moments ago, to help me through the pain, and then realise that I have been standing there, lightly holding my hand while everyone hopes like hell I don't scream or pass out, for a minute and a half, and that I am in the grip of some kind of weird psychological fugue, and it's time to shake it and go.

I shake it, and look over at Jim Hepsobah, who has a kind of placid energy about him which I figure I can usefully borrow about now. I take the quiet of Jim; a rugged, mountainous refuge of the heart. The fog sort of clears, or at least I can move again.

There is now only the door to deal with. It's not much of a door. It is intended to keep people out of the booze, not to keep anyone prisoner inside. (The pain from my hand is moderately appalling. I cling to the sense of Jim Hepsobah in my mind, and I review the mountain I have envisaged to symbolise him. It has streams. Cold, clear streams. I dip my hand in one, and clothe myself in Hepsobahish strength. Hepsobahian? Hepsobahic? Or would there be a contraction? Hepsoban? Part of me carries on with this important line of reasoning, and I let it, because while it's doing that it can't feel the pain. So.) If I had a hairpin, and I knew anything about locks, I could probably crack us out. I could, in time, kick the thing open, although the noise would almost certainly bring unwanted company. I contemplate the possibilities until I realise that Leah is trying to attract my attention with a growing urgency and, rather unfairly, exasperation. I go over to her.

"Turn the handle!" she says, and I open my mouth to object that no one would fail to lock the door, and then just to be sure, I go over there and turn the handle. The door opens.

Not that unfairly, then. To my Hepsobahian strength, I add

Leahian (there's another one ending in *h;* disaster!) perspicacity. Perspicaciousness. *Ow, ow, ow.* I look back at Leah. She grins fiercely, encouraging and imploring all at once, and I fall just a little bit more in love with her, then step out into the next room, which is the back of the airport bar. Around the corner I can hear someone mixing a cocktail. If it's a martini, he is butchering it. Barbarian. (Meaning "one who is bearded," and curiously not in origin pejorative. The Romans knew that people with beards could be sharp as a *gladius,* they just liked to distinguish smoothly shaven from hirsute . . . That sounds pornographic, doesn't it? Shaven? Yes, indeed. Mmm.)

I clamp down on my thoughts and extend Leah's smarts towards the cocktailista in the bar. By the sound of his footsteps, it is a man. Almost before I look, I know that it is Carsville, the new, dangerous Carsville, with added suave. I peer at him around the edge of the doorway. He has his back to me and he's brutalising a cheap shaker, James Bond style, making the wateriest martini this airport has ever seen. His face is unmarked, and he doesn't move like a guy who just fought for his life. No twinges, no hesitations, no gasps. He finishes his mix, and pours it out, spilling a fair bit. Then I lunge down behind the wall as he hops on the bar, briefly turning my way, and swivels on his backside as if this were some expensive penthouse in the city. I'm in no danger of discovery. His attention is all for who's watching: *Hey there, my name's Ben. Hi, ladies* . . . There are no ladies. They are in his head. (Shaven, no doubt. *Ow, ow, ow.* Hepsobah. The mountain has forests, and bears. Big, powerful animals. Slumbering. Waiting. Yes.) He ambles away towards Kemner and the others at the far end of the room. Halfway down, two of Kemner's men are on guard. Still nervous, even here. The willies, yes. I duck down again, watching the drips of ice-water martini splatter onto the floor.

And then I realise that someone has opened my prayer envelope, and taken at least partial steps to help me out. Praise unto Ben Carsville, idiot and monster, for he is an angel of the Lord—

even unawares. At eye level with me now, lying beside the cash register, there is a hammer. It briefly occurs to me to wonder whether this is for remonstrating with surly customers or correcting defects in the till, but even to me that is not the important thing. The important thing is that if I can get to it and get back out again without being spotted, it will be a useful study aid in my newly chosen specialist field of getting-the-fuck-out-of-here-ology. I crawl on my knees and my right hand along under the bar towards the hammer. Every shuffle makes a noise like a fire bell ringing and I can't imagine they don't hear, and every jolt sends a bright blue spike into my left eye, which for some reason is feeling the pain from my hand. I reach the hammer, and then I make an error of curiosity and open the fridge. Nine pairs of eyes stare back at me. The fridge stinks. Kemner is keeping her heads here so that she always has one ready to go on the throne. In the meantime, they rest on paper plates. UN soldiers, maybe a civilian doctor. I manage not to throw up, and close the fridge door softly. I find myself staring into my own eyes, reflected in the mirrored refrigerator. I look like hell, which is to be expected. I look like one of the poor bastards inside. Although there is a little mote in the surface of the fridge, a dint, which makes funny shapes if I move myself around it. And then I am not alone, which is a major shocker.

The face is above me, and it isn't really a face. It is a gasmask. It is poking through a hole in the ceiling. It isn't visible to the bad guys at the far end of the room because the bar has a canopy of stretched plastic with "KatiriCola" branded across it in probably actionable letters. The un-face sprouts from a pair of shoulders in an orange prisoner's jumpsuit, and in fact the wearer has the hood up as well. I am being spied on by an orange person! Orange-headed spies! I seem to recall a song about a man with an orange head. Sadly, I cannot remember the tune. I hum, very quietly so that Kemner's people do not come over and kill me. Laa dee dumm . . . *Ow, ow, ow.* The orange person—it is a male person, I can see stubble on his neck, and I can smell him—

manages to convey a look of alarm, which is pretty good going for someone with no facial features. It must be posture. Good old mammalian body language, functioning upside down. Still, I stop humming. The Leah and the Hepsobah parts of me are pretty sure this is not a good moment to be doing that. The person behind the mask considers me, and I look at his lenses and feel that I'm not getting the best of the arrangement. (Then again, there's a tiny crust of blood where the mask meets the hood, and when he moves, it is stiffly; he's injured. Perhaps I'd rather not see what is underneath, after all.)

I stare at the orange head. Is it considering betraying me? Should I take steps to eliminate it? But no. This is Kemner's secret foe, the sneaky one they're all worrying about. Oh. Oh yes. The waving crazy person by the roadside—the one who wanted us not to come here. At least he isn't saying he told us so. Isn't saying anything, actually, silent orange waving upside down gasmask person. We look at one another. I hum, but only in my head. I smell him again, and this time I smell blood and something sweet. Gangrene then. The orange person looks at my nauseous expression and nods. *Dying soon.*

After a moment the orange person traces with one gloved hand on the ceiling. Semicircle. Zigzag. He speaks in hieroglyphs. I understand nothing. Semicircle. Zigzag. A plan of attack? A clock. A pretty flower? He is Zorro. Yes. That's it! Zorro has come. The fox, with his mighty sword and whip, to smite the evildoers . . . Z for Zorro. I think about it. Ah. Semicircle. Zigzag. Not Z. U, N. He is a soldier. He was a prisoner. He will fight, because she keeps his friends in a drinks fridge.

Kemner has an orange enemy, or at least an orange not-friend. Which means that I have an orange maybe-friend. I wonder whether the face beneath the mask winked at me. It seems possible. I am tempted to get up and peer through the eyeholes. And then the figure shows me both hands (how it holds on up there is a mystery, perhaps it has orange friends? Or it is using its legs. Maybe it has long, orange toes. Ew.) and taps one wrist to indicate time, and then holds up both hands again, fingers spread. Ten. Ten minutes? Ten seconds? Ten o'clock? But if so, is that Zulu or local? The orange person slithers back up into the loft or the air duct or whatever it is up there, and I am alone with the hammer, and I realise that I can hear someone coming over to the bar. I have stared at the orange person for too long. Now I have to go fast, as if I weren't injured. Perhaps that was the point? Fast like a greyhound! Any time now. Yes. Right now.

And finally, because my internal Jim Hepsobah takes direct action, I move. It is agony like nothing else. My wrist is fine. Broken, but painless. My eye, which has nothing wrong with it, really hurts. *Ow, ow, ow.* It is made entirely of blue fire and my hand feels sort of muzzy as I round the corner to the lock-up. I have skittered, pell-mell, across the floor of the bar and around the corner, using the broken limb as if it weren't, and feeling the grating of bones and the general badness and not caring. And then I hand the hammer over to Jim Hepsobah (Gonzo looks hurt), who rips off his shirt to muffle the noise and proceeds to beat the rope out of the wall in about a minute. Everyone is free now, albeit unarmed and handcuffed. I explain about the orange person. Ten? Ten what? Gonzo thinks minutes. Tobemory Trent puts Egon down, and he and Leah set my hand as best they can and put it in a sling made from my shirt. Leah's fingers are warm on my chest, and I make her put her palm over my eye. It helps. A brief council of war is convened, during which everyone takes turns to hold Egon, because he is shaking and needs to be loved, and we are leaving no one behind, not physically and not spiritually, because we are who we are and that is how we're going to stay. Tobemory Trent moves around smashing handcuffs.

Assets: one wire-cord rope. One hammer. Two metal spikes. One irritated but unarmed SpecOps unit. Three medical specialists, a rear-echelon officer, assorted grunts with basic skills like driving, small-scale construction and stabbing people. Gonzo gestures to the wall. He holds a spike against it, and Jim Hepsobah swings. Stone falls away. And again, and again . . . A little light shows through. This room was not intended to be secure. He gestures to Sally Culpepper to wedge the door with the other spike. She does so immediately. And now things are happening very fast. Gonzo peers through the hole and is satisfied. He and Jim demolish a low, narrow stretch, and we crawl out one by one, finding ourselves behind some crates and other junk.

Gonzo is not there when I arrive, hopalong style, but as Egon is passed through, he reappears carrying a recently deceased bad guy over one shoulder and a rifle in his free hand. The first thing he drops on the ground, the second he passes not to Jim but to Sally, and he dons the undersized jacket and looted helmet of the dead man, and saunters away again. He vanishes around the corner, and I can hear him hailing someone, making a genuinely friendly noise. Gonzo likes everyone. He would really prefer that this person immediately see his point of view. He knows that won't happen, and so he grins affably (I know he does, though I cannot see) and hugs his new pal, and somewhere in the hug the surprised hugee discovers that he cannot breathe, cannot shout, and is now totally in the power of this strange man, and then he knows nothing more. In this situation, because Gonzo is pressed for time and can't afford any mistakes, the hugee will not awaken. Gonzo tosses the next uniform to one of his guys, a weird, plump little man called Sam who suffers from emotional (if not physical) priapism. Sam is a hound dog. He'd make a pass at a shop dummy. He shrugs into his borrowed clothes and vanishes after Gonzo, silent and serious, knife tucked away behind his forearm. Sam on business. Veeery scary. There is a muffled slicing noise, and Sam returns. There's no blood on his uniform, and none on that of the man he has killed. There is blood on his knife. What has he done? Something clever. Something vile. He drops the corpse, jolly, ever-so-slightly fat Sam, because even heavy training can't entirely defeat biology, and Sam is basically a fat man. The dead guy's mouth opens, and leaks.

"Back of the throat," Sam says, and Jim Hepsobah calls him a showboat. Sam shrugs. "Target of opportunity," he replies, and is gone again.

Eight minutes, give or take. Remaining issues: the sniper in the control tower. Evade or remove? Both are difficult. Summit conference behind the crates. Limited time before we are discovered.

At ten minutes on the dot, a grimy figure in orange tosses the sniper through the gaping windows of the tower and vanishes again. The sniper falls silently to the ground and hits, hard. He bounces, although it would be more correct to say that his body bounces, because he lands on his head and leaves most of it on the concrete. A few seconds later a plume of black smoke boils out of the tower. Kemner's guys come streaming out of the departures hall, and she runs out behind them yelling "Stop," which they don't. They run towards the tower to extinguish the blaze, so about ten of them are right next to it when it blows up. A second or so later several outbuildings and the remaining planes go up too. Corvid's Field gets loud and hot. I look around for dark clouds and dapple, but this is the ordinary sort of hell, man-made and reliable. Almost cosy. Kemner, with her remaining guys all around her, screams curses. Something screams back, bullets and rage, and the orange person emerges from a hangar and charges towards her, one leg twisted up and bullets going all over.

Kemner sees him. She doesn't do the sensible thing, or even the sane thing. She starts screaming and yelling and shooting, and runs towards him. They both get hit. Neither of them cares. Bloodspray and anger. They are doing their own personal, totally deranged *High Noon.* This is a very private thing. We leave them to it.

Gonzo grabs me by the neck and hurls me out into the road, and Sam the Killer and Jim Hepsobah lead us fast and low to the vehicle depot. Gonzo has Egon on his shoulders now, and he's running as fast as I am. Leah struggles along, but I cannot carry her. I am not Gonzo. My hand is broken. I drag her as fast as I dare and pray she will forgive me for not being bigger and stronger.

We reach the depot and we get our stuff. We run away. Kemner and the crazy orange person can have their last battle. We've had ours, and it's over now. It's not bold or heroic, but it's how you stay alive.

WE DRIVE for hours, just heading away. The orange person helped us considerably, but also blew up our way home on the runway. I hum, out loud, because Ruth Kemner is not coming to find me any more. Leah finds her medical kit and shoots me full of something nice. The sound of it all is still in our heads (don't mention heads) and the smell is in our noses. I watch the world go past outside, and realise where we are going. Gonzo is taking us to Shangri-La. Defensible. Perhaps even safe. But Addeh Katir is not the way it was. The whole landscape is grimmer and greyer, as if someone has dusted it with iron filings. There are buzzards and vultures in the sky, and even crows. The trees are dead. The sheep, most definitely, are dead; they have in fact been spread liberally around the place. Half of one gazes reproachfully from the roadside, mouth open in a despairing final "baaaa." The road is busted up. And by this time I have begun to realise that Professor Derek, like many other brilliant men before him, is a fucking idiot of the first water. The beauty of the Go Away Bomb was always supposed to be that it was clean—but this has the feeling of fallout. It has the feeling of aftermath. And it definitely feels like the kind of thing Professor Derek was adamant could not happen.

We ride through the grimy day. Occasionally we see people, or things which might be people, but they hide and we don't stop. Every so often we hear gunfire and explosions. Flashes of curiously bright colours, out of place, appear and disappear: Day-Glo green and gymnasium yellow flicker from around corners half a mile away, and then something goes *whump* or *kKRrrssst,* and then it's quiet. There's something familiar about those colours. We drive on. No one tries to kill us. We are in the eye of the storm, somehow. More glints among the trees, very unnatural pink. Far away, the sound of engines.

The road is gradually ceasing to be worthy of the name. A week ago it was a halfway decent piece of infrastructure, now it looks as if hailstones the size of footballs have been falling on it, and there are deep cracks and miniature ravines running through it. By the time we reach the mountains, it has given up and we're following a riverbed. The RVs and the jeep make more noise than we want them to, and the tank won't quite straddle the stream and either the left or the right caterpillar is constantly in the water, churning away and making a rut. We make Vasille drive at the back of the little convoy. The stream bed leads us around the back of the mesa (that's probably not what it is, or what it's called, but it's close enough that I've started thinking of it in that way and maybe that's a cowboy movie reference; maybe we're the gang running from the law) and it doesn't go conveniently up the mountain, it runs from a deep pool at the foot of a waterfall. There's a goat track which *does* go up the mountain. At least Vasille claims it's a goat track. There are nearly three times as many species of sheep as goats in this area, so the odds are against him. The point is that it's a path, of sorts, and there is a musty cave behind the waterfall just big enough to hide the RVs. The tank we leave in the open; it has a nifty anti-theft device now attached to a largish bomb. Vasille is not someone who gets caught the same way twice.

We climb. Slowly. Fearfully. We shoot at shadows, and once someone from down in the valley fires on us, and we all scurry for cover, and I think of Butch and Sundance, but nothing else happens. We hide for about half an hour anyway.

Halfway up, we come over a crest, all secret and seriously covert, and there are sheep. Not dead, but alive and not alone. There are shepherds too, armed and dangerous, Katiris from one army or another doing exactly what we are doing: running like hell from the most mad part of the world and looking for a place which is less mad. And here they are, and here we are, and there's lots of fear and guns and not much in the way of an exit strategy.

The tallest of them is also the leader, and he has a big, big handgun pointed at us, a Magnum or some other macho thing, and his friends all have AKs, probably Chinese AK-03s, basically the 74 model which everyone thinks of as an AK-47, plus a bottle opener and some extra seals to make them work better in the monsoon season. And this, right here, is a total goatfuck in the making, a big old mess of about-to-be-dead people. Gonzo and Jim Hepsobah are ready to go—they're doing casualty estimates in their heads—and Eagle Culpepper has recovered her functionality if not her sanity and is lined up on the leader, and every one of them is ready to shoot right back at us. We're staring into the eyes of universal casualties. It is entirely possible that we will be able to tell who wins the fight which is about to happen only by timing who dies last.

"Hugwughugwug!" says their boss man angrily, waving his gun around like it's a sceptre, although of course he actually asks us something perfectly sensible, he just asks it in his own language, which none of us can speak. His voice is liquid and lambent and beautiful. This does not alter the fact that he is very pissed off and upset. "Hug! Hugwug, hug wug wuggah ughug? Huuuugwuggah!" This last comes out a bit shrill as Leah slowly puts her shotgun on the ground in front of her. This is such a sensible thing to do that no one shoots anyone, mostly out of shock, and then we all continue not to shoot one another because it seems there may, possibly, be a way out of this. She walks slowly, prettily, across the gap between us and them, shunting a more-than-usually-suicidal sheep out of the way with her knee, which gets a big laugh. The Katiris do not stop pointing their guns at us, but nor does any one of them specifically cover her either. Leah walks until she's right in front of the leader, and his Desert Eagle is pointed at us over her shoulder. She leaves her hands by her sides, palms out, so as not to give anyone any mistaken impressions about subtle and terrifying *gong fu,* and she kisses him lightly on his right cheek, then on his left. As gestures go, it's unambiguous: let's all be friends. Then she turns her back and walks off to one side, and sits down on a rock, and looks at us all like we're being a bunch of total arseholes, which we are. This is also unambiguous, but it takes longer to work out because it runs counter to what you might charitably call the prevailing logic of the situation.

Leaderboy gets it slightly before Gonzo does, or maybe he just isn't a great card player, and he smiles cartoonishly, and very slowly and clearly holsters his gun and bows in Leah's direction, waits for her nod, and goes to sit with her. At this point there's a kind of general acknowledgement that no one wants to get annihilated here today, and a lot of weapons are lowered and put away and people embrace cautiously and laugh a bit and one of their soldiers even has a little cry. We say "Hooray" to them and they say "Hugwugwughug" to us, and we try to copy them and get it wrong, and everyone finds this enormously amusing, until one of the sheep wanders over to the left of where we're all leaping around and laughing and explodes with considerable emphasis, and we realise that we are doing all our hugwughugging on the edge of a minefield. At that point the whole business of whether we are allies or sort of neutral goes by the wayside, and we all fall into line and carefully tread in one another's footsteps while Gonzo, on his knees, pokes down into the soil with Sam's knife, and leads us through.

By the time we reach Shangri-La—us and the Katiris, both—we are thirsty and hungry, which is good because before we were just surviving—we didn't know about hungry any more. The castle is a ruin. Cracked walls and bullet holes. The long balcony is shattered and tumbled down, and the rolling meadows are a scrub. Fires are burning somewhere down in the valley. At the far end of the courtyard there's a row of tyre tracks—not ours. Someone has been here. Maybe is here. But they came here to hide, and they are not Ruth Kemner. In fact, I have an inkling who it must be. A Honda Civic with Day-Glo green paint and a whale-tail is parked just poking out from behind an outhouse. Day-Glo—like the flashes we have been seeing since we escaped from Corvid's Field. There's a pink Mitsubishi Evo against one wall. And off to one side, like a boarding school matron with her girls around her, the nose of a maroon Rolls-Royce. I think . . . I think we were invited to come here; even *escorted.* And so I walk to the main entrance and reach for the big, solid doors.

Which open, in advance of me, to reveal a glittering wall of knife blades and slender pirate-monks, and behind them a row of ceramic Glocks, and in the very centre of the scene a small, bearded figure with a glint of fire in his eye and a cutlass in either hand. He looks at us, and the Katiri shepherds behind us, and after a moment he smiles, thank God, and drops his hands, and the pirate-monks do the same, and he steps back and away and behind him we can see his few, flea-bitten, terrified refugees, and their families, and their animals. And as he smiles, some trick of the light reveals him to me, shows me how his face would look unshaven, and I recognise my old friend Freeman ibn Solomon, peripatetic ambassador to student debating clubs and cancan artist extraordinaire. He smiles.

"Welcome," says Zaher Bey.

Chapter Seven

Family history;
the sex life of Rao Tsur;
foals, monsters and dreams.

ZAHER BEY'S *nth* forefather was a Turkish Mameluke named Mustafa, a slave-soldier who served in Egypt until his particular genius in planning rather than personally inflicting massive casualties caused him to be raised above his schoolmates and made a general. Of this gentleman (who had lost an ear in his early career and wore a golden prosthesis in its place) no contemporary images survive, such being a violation of strict Islamic law as it was understood by Mustafa, but he is described by a contemporary diarist (freely translated) as a "chippy, murderous shortarse." His tenure as a general was quietly successful until 1798, when an army of Frenchmen led by a similarly chippy and shortarsed Corsican marched into Egypt in the hope of carving out a bit of the region and breaking the British stranglehold on India. Mustafa of the Golden Ear duly mustered his army and went out to meet the dastardly Frog, who despite having suffered an egregious defeat at the hands of Horatio Nelson still contrived to rout the Mameluke forces and capture the Bey himself.

Expecting only death and ridicule, Mustafa was pleasantly surprised to find himself an honoured guest, and even more delighted to discover that the reason for this was his hitherto injurious lack of vertical prominence. The Corsican, in turn, was much pleased to have created not a lifetime foe but a genuine admirer. Amid discussions about how exactly the victory had been achieved and what was to happen now, Napoléon and the Bey got blasted on a mixture of insanely strong coffee, French cognac and suspiciously fragrant pipe tobacco, and when the night was over (about a week later), Napoléon was sneaked through the British pickets to the coast by Mustafa Bey's scouts and returned to France to tell everyone about how he kicked some Anglo-Arab backside before heroically running home again. Mustafa Bey went back to his castle in the company of a formidable adventuress named Camille de la Saint-Vièrge, who shortly thereafter bore a son, the first of his get, and that son studied not only at the Mameluke school, but also with the British (on the basis that while it's always nice to study with the person who beat *you,* it's more practical to learn the trade from someone who handed *him* his hat with his teeth in it).

From these roots grew a seafaring family of Beys, international and sophisticated, fiercely independent and often at odds with their notional masters. These quibblings over chain of command might have made them natural Americans, save that Solomon Bey (1901–1947) eschewed all manner of religion after some time at the Sorbonne, and felt that the United States was by far the most devout nation on Earth. At the same time the Maharaja of Addeh Katir, Ranjit Rhoi—known as Doubtful Randy—felt an overpowering need for military men of good family, and invited Solomon, Zaher Bey's father, to create a river navy and a Katiri defence force for his Raj, a decision which the maharaja uncharacteristically stuck to, even when all else fell apart around him. Solomon perforce relocated his young, pregnant wife to an immensely beautiful hill fort just in time for the British empire to fall into horrible and bloody strife and remove itself from the subcontinent. Zaher Bey was born on a cloudy Sunday in June 1947, and orphaned on Wednesday the following week when representatives of a local crime syndicate decided to throw off the yoke of British oppression by killing Solomon and his recovering bride and coincidentally moving a huge shipment of opium from Afghanistan in the ensuing confusion. Zaher Bey was smuggled to London by an aide to Mountbatten, most likely with that great man's connivance, since very little escaped him at any time.

Thus came the Bey, swaddled in a goat blanket and bedded on a considerable fortune, to London, and in due time to Oxford University, where he raised some serious hell, drank and rowed for his college and was caught in flagrante with the daughter of the Dean of Balliol, all before taking an upper second class degree, which achievement is still regarded as something of a miracle by those who witnessed his blazing passage through Oxford's watering holes and comely undergraduettes. His companion and occasional bail bondsman was a slender Katiri scion named Nq'ula Jann, formidable polymath and intellectual snob, last seen driving the Roller at the evacuation of Fudin, and now charged with working out with all due speed what the hell is going on. These two, thus armed with a full education, returned to the Bey's native land with every intention of living soft and growing mighty fat. They arrived just in time for the removal of the last maharaja and the installation of Erwin Magnificat Kumar as puppet and president, whereupon they saw the way of things and the unpleasant nature of the new regime, and straightaway resolved to circumvent and vex it to the utmost of their considerable ability.

THE FIRST DAYS are very hard and strange. We find places to slump and even doze. There are people on every flagstone and in every alcove. Sally Culpepper and Jim Hepsobah make hammocks and sleep in them, high above the stone floor. I try this. It hurts my back. I wander at night and sleep in daylight, when there's room on the floor. The castle seems to come in three parts—Zaher Bey and his monks have the upper floor, near the temple spire; Gonzo's gang, including us, are in the entrance hall and on the blasted balcony; and the refugee Katiris are scattered through the interior of the building, although "scattered" makes them sound more sparsely distributed than they are. Leah and I revisit the room in which we spent the night. It is home now to three Katiri families, among them two injured men and an old lady whose rage causes her to spit and stammer. We nod respectfully as she tells us that our mothers were covered by wild dogs, and we do our best not to inhale the smell of blood and sweat coming from her nephew and his friend. The crone—although a few days ago she was probably a matron, maybe still is beneath the dirt and the exhaustion—bellows at us, and the nephew translates in a helpful monotone. He doesn't bother to stress any of the English words, just lays them before us so we can accuse ourselves at leisure.

"My sons. You took my sons. And for what? For what? They were my sons and I loved them. They were my only sons. I have no others. I have no daughters either, not any more. All gone. You took them. They are gone." And so he goes on, as if bored, and does not editorialise until she comes to a culmination, a long string of curses upon our seed, our land, our homes and our houses, for ever until the red blood of God washes clean the sky and judgement is issued in great gouts of fire. At this point he informs us that his aunt is angry. And he is angry too, of course. He lifts up his face to show us, but mostly in his eyes there's just emptiness, and he sees that we see it, and shrugs.

"I saw the land eaten," he says, as if that explains it, and holds his aunt in a gentle cage of arms and hugs until she weeps snot and saliva into his chest. As we go to leave, she breaks free of him and chases us in little lunges down the corridor, like a furious housecat. Leah leads me away, but the aunt persists, following in sharp jerks, as if dragged along by a lead. She sets up a new, gut-wrenching wail, and soon we are gathering a crowd of saturnine men and sullen women in our wake.

Our flight takes us to an inner courtyard, flagged and smooth. There is a well amid the wreck of a tiled fountain, and of course everyone who is not following menacingly behind us is sitting here, higgledy-piggledy, around and on top of one another, in box crates and bunk beds making up a great beehive town. As we enter, it gets quite still, and the aunt screeches hoarsely into the quiet. For the first time I am seeing the people of Addeh Katir from street level, not from the safe heights of an armoured convoy, and it occurs to me that they may be more forthcoming with their fury in this situation. One of the younger men moves to pick up a sort of stick, a farmer's tool good for threshing and minding animals, and beating enemies to death, and then there is a bellow of outrage from the middle of the courtyard, and everyone turns to look.

"Fornicatress! What is *that*?" A familiar figure is glaring in horror at a toddler in ragged blue pyjamas. If the child were eating raw meat, it could not merit such ghastly dismay.

"It's hideous! Unnatural! Where did it come from? No, no, don't tell me—this house is filled with likely men. I shall simply seek out the one who is broken and bleeding and know him for the idiot who took you to his bed. Or was it mine? *My* bed? And how did you birth it so quickly? Eh? Answer me that? No nine months for you, you unmarked harlot, no indeed, scant hours to produce another malignant brat! If I look around I will no doubt find the shell it hatched from. You're a demon, is what it is! A thing from the red inferno, where dwell incubi and satyrs and women with the legs of spiders, all coddled in a fetid mist! Oh, poor Rao Tsur, married to a sulphurous, rutting fiend! It wouldn't be so bad if she could cook, but as it is . . ."

"Imbecile! The child is yours, as you well know, and born two years ago. Yes, it was. Oh, for the love of . . . Must you declare your poverty of mind to the entire house? Yes, I see you must. You named him Jun, and gurgled at him like a river toad when you should have been attending to the spices. No customer was served for months but must admire the little thug. He spat at them. Vomited. Threw things unmentionable after them as they fled. A salesman like his father, yes, to hurl our clientele headlong, heaving, out into the road. Thus we live in penury and want. Yes. Penury and want. And, *oh, yes,* Rao Tsur, whose refined palate cares not for my kitchen's product any more than his empty heart has love for his enduring wife, the child is mine as well. We slept together, you and I. I say slept. In fact we copulated. Yes, you may well look abashed, it was no great matter. It barely counts. All that huffing and puffing and I swear I would have done better by myself!"

"Oh, indeed? Mistress of Onan, is Veda Tsur! Soloist! Luxuriant! And yet if I recall her spine was arched, presenting those unmentionable breasts to dread advantage, and from her open mouth proceeded such a racket as to sour milk and burst the eardrums of cats!"

"Hah! You admit it! You pounced upon me! Dark, your passions, Rao Tsur, when there was I, peaceably recalling my days of virtue. Oh yes, I'm sure I screamed! Quite likely, I called out for help! And no wonder, me being belaboured with that appalling cudgel you call a—" Her husband's eyes grow very wide, and Veda Tsur comes sharply to a halt. She has hit that naked space in a crowded place where every conversation stops at once and yours inexorably continues, slewing secrets into a loud silence. I once said "starkers from the waist down, of course, but no one noticed because of the feathers" in a lecture hall full of my professors. I'd been talking about dinosaurs and birds and evolution, but try telling that to a hundred hooting dons.

Veda Tsur shuffles. She looks at her feet. And she lets fall from her wide, welcoming lips a sort of girlish giggle of embarrassment. Rao Tsur too shifts uncomfortably. The Katiris stare. Short of a rain of frogs or the sun rising in the north, there's not much to top this, even now. Rao Tsur mumbles something like "Yes, well" and actually *cannot think of anything to say.* Awkwardly, he puts an arm around his wife and gathers up the wayward child which was the object of their debate, and quite a few others emerge from under boxes and blankets and scamper to complete the picture, until Family Tsur is fully assembled. And then, most impossible of all, Rao Tsur places a kiss upon the cheek of Veda Tsur as if they were just now stepping from a marriage service and he is afraid she will fly away if he does not occasionally soothe her and hang on to her. There is a frozen moment, then a snort from the aunt, and then the whole courtyard falls apart in a roar of laughter and cheering, like an explosion. It is the first laughter I have heard since the end of the world. (Nervous laughter and evil laughter do not count.)

Amid the laughter there is clapping, and the clapping becomes a rhythm, and the rhythm becomes a dance, and Rao Tsur by some strange coincidence is at this moment next to Leah. He seizes upon her, and Veda Tsur by way of revenge must have me, and Rao trumpets that she is making off with the hero of Fudin, and that just because I hit an idiot in the head and saved her life, she will now leave him for ever, and good riddance, faithless wench, may she bear me fine upstanding demon children. At which Veda asks tartly if Rao is not even now clutching that buxom doctor to his chest? And does he imagine she will gladly suffer his inexpert fondlings? She will run off with a handsome shepherd, and then where is Rao? Alone with his stupidity! And anyway, what nonsense! But even now they can't stop grinning at one another.

And so it goes, around and around, clap clap clapclap clap, *laLAHlalalaLAH . . . lahdahdahDEE-YA!* until a string is stretched across some empty cases and begins to *twang* and *zoom,* and a row of empty bottles goes *ping, pang, pong* and *pung,* and voices are making up the rest of the orchestra, *hmmhhhmm-aahmm, a-hooahomm,* and it's a regular rock-and-roll hoe-down, only with makeshift mandolins and xylophones, and not much in the way of skiffle until Tobemory Trent starts playing tortoiseshell and bone. And when the first dance is done, there is a brief moment for the aunt, in all humility, to kiss me on both cheeks in front of the whole crowd and pat my face and tell everyone that anybody who wants to pick a fight with *me* will answer to *her,* because if Rao Tsur, saffron merchant of Fudin, says I am a good man, and if Veda Tsur is content that my lady should dance with her husband, then that is good enough on any day for her, even if I had not—according to unimpeachable sources known to her personally—punched in the head a noted idiot in an effort to safeguard the lives of the people of Fudin. At which another great cheer goes up, and it is louder, for behind us is Zaher Bey, pint-sized titan and romantic lead, and sometime debater of the Jarndice Caucus club. And also, it emerges, funky-chicken instructor to the people of Fudin, the mysterious pirates of Addeh Katir and the remnant forces of the Combined Defensive Operational Force 8th Battlegroup, G.W. Lubitsch pro tem commander. So we get funky, together, and if anyone thinks Gonzo and Leah and Jim and Sally and I, or any of the others, is less than a friend, that person forgets about it, because we're all chums together, and drunk as well.

In the morning, the war comes back, like dandelion seeds.

THE EAST WIND brings it, winsome and inexorable. The wind flickers and jiggles excitedly, rolling over the hills and dusting the forest. It is friendly. It is obviously, appealingly soft. It is Disney Dust. For miles and miles, from here all the way to Lake Addeh, perky motes and japesome spirals flicker among the trees and fall into rivulets and streams with a noise like hot ash into snow. We stand on the long balcony and laugh, and nod good morning to one another. Today will be a good day. And then, as it draws closer, there is a sudden gust, and then another, pungent with animal smell, strange in the back of the nose and mouth, and there are birds, in their thousands, fleeing. No one kind predominates. They are not arranged in orderly flocks or even families. Swans lumber, geese flap, sparrows (or something very like them) flitter, all in one great avian mass of fear; one enormous, moderately cooperative exodus.

They crap on everything, evacuating their bowels the better to evacuate themselves. The second part of our war begins with a torrent of guano.

The Stuff rolls on towards us, and starts to change. It reaches the border of the lands we have defined for ourselves, the place of our safety, and divides around as if on a curtain rail. Wrapping around our border is a curdling shadow, from which proceed the cries of devils and the howling of the damned, or at least loud, unpleasant noises which make your hair stand on end and fill you (like a departing swan) with the desire to relieve certain internal pressures. All around me people are doing things of importance. Zaher Bey's pirate-monks are moving with determined efficiency, calming and reassuring, herding Katiri civilians further into the castle. Gonzo's guys—his core guys, Jim and Sally and Samuel and Annie—are rousing the others and bringing them up to speed. Leah and Tobemory Trent have gone professional, are talking triage prep and ad hoc transfusions, leaving me to watch the onset. I watch.

The Stuff is ragged and wispy. It is encountering some pressure or energy at our circumference, and responding to it. Things are happening at the meniscus: familiar shapes are appearing—armed men, vehicles, guns. They shimmer and collapse into one another, getting more solid. Some of them are ludicrous or awful. A small group charges across the border, Iwo Jima style, brothers in arms. They are too close together, weirdly awkward, and as they turn, I see that they are conjoined, all seven of them. The sergeant's hand on his corporal's back, urging him on, melds smoothly into the uniform and the spine. The soldier behind, supporting the sergeant, is merged with him at the hip. They struggle, scream and tumble, bringing down the others. They are an image to be seen from one side, not real men at all. They die, probably because they have not enough hearts between them, and slump to the ground, where a corpse-carpet is forming, the familiar exterior decor of modern skirmishing. I can hear the bullets whizzing, though there is as yet no one to fight. This is not an attack. It's atmosphere. It's war as a condition, war as furniture. We are under siege by a *notion* of war.

A monk, next to me, looks down in mute surprise as a bullet wound blooms on his chest. He dies calmly, maybe even affronted, but not appalled or screaming. The soldier next to him is different. He exhales a choking gas, a stink of battery acid, and with it part of a lung. He would scream, but this expression has been taken from him, so he just stares at me in horror, and I tell him I know, I know, it hurts, and you are dying. I know. I am here. He stares at me, and I cannot tell if he is thankful or if he simply cannot believe I am so damn trivial as to imagine that makes it any better. He dies while I am blinking.

A hand falls on my shoulder, rough and invasive. I slip it, twist. A flash of snaggled teeth and a whiff of halitosis. I hit out, block a weapon, push him away. He is gone. Shadowman. I crouch, ready. Nothing happens.

Up the hill, soldiers are attacking. Bad generalship, perhaps, but they are making ground. Vasille's tank opens up, and limbs fly, slapstick. Hah. But now the enemy has tanks too, rolling up the hill, commanders looking out the top, Patton-style, and when Gonzo blows the tracks off the first one, and Vasille splatters it across the landscape, it appears that Patton is fused to the tank from the hips, a man-tank chimera. Samuel P. throws up. No one laughs at him.

It's a game or a dream; wave upon wave, uncoordinated, endless; lethal but stupid. We fight. We die. We live. They go again. Nowhere is secure, nowhere is particularly under threat. Shadowmen flicker in corridors, half-complete, half-imagined; sometimes they kill someone, sometimes they loom and lurk and wait to be eliminated, like the guys in red shirts on *Star Trek* (the original one, not the later ones where no one was safe). In the infirmary there are extra patients appearing from nowhere. They cannot be healed. They just sit there and scream. Stretchermen we don't have bring wounded we never knew, each time putting them in the same spot. The first soldier in bed three (it's a packing case with a rug on it, but it's bed three) has a head wound. A moment later, another is laid on top of him and they are for a moment both there, one superimposed on the other, and then the first is gone—and with him the bandages Trent slapped on that cut—and instead there's a kid with a spurting leg, bleeding out, and then a moment later he has both injuries, and then he's dead, and then they bring in another one and it's a woman and then another, and another.

The sun comes out. The wind changes. We fight on. Shadowmen flail and die, and are not replaced. In the sunlight, in the ordinary world, they look pathetic: hulking, ugly brutes without advantages. Bullies. Bandits. Veda Tsur, spattered in grime and weeping, slams the last one to the ground with a copper saucepan, and Rao beats him, methodically, until he dies like a broken fly. He tried to take their children. Jun is clinging to his father's arm, adding his weight to every blow.

In good order, and because we are very angry and afraid, we counter. We sally forth. Sallying has gone out of fashion in recent years, because it doesn't work very well when you have gun emplacements, and anyway no one really lays siege in the traditional way any more; they blockade and they assail, but more usually they go house-to-house, because sieges kill civilians before they kill soldiers and this kind of thing is, broadly speaking, *bad.* It's okay to kill huge numbers of civilians *by mistake,* of course, but killing them *on purpose* is illegal, slap-on-the-wrist time. We sally because, hell, we've earned it. Vasille leads, Bone Briskett brings up the rear and in the middle are an improvised mechanised infantry of hyped Ford Focuses (Foci?) and armoured RVs.

The lower slopes are a charnel house. Everything is dead. We drive through. The forest is better. The first hundred metres or so is jellied and burned. After that, it's almost normal. The trees have been shot up a bit. One or two sheep have expired. We cruise. We do not get attacked. It rains, water. We dismount. We walk in the forest. It is nice. Leah and I hold hands. I transfer my gun to the other side and feel very protective. We lean against a pine tree and admire the flowers. We smell air which is not filled with awfulness. We live.

My radio clicks, once. It is the alert, but not the *enemy action* signal. It means *I have found an interesting thing, approach with caution.* The first click is followed by seven more in quick succession: one of the pirate-monks has the bearing seven position, to the south-south-east. We—Leah, Samuel and I—have five. We move downward.

The pirate-monk is standing at the edge of a forest clearing. He has chosen his location carefully, so as to be invisible to most of the clearing while able to survey it himself through a stand of bracken. We move up.

In the glade is a man, on a horse. He is tubby, and the horse is unkempt. His hair is matted and charred, and his arms are mired with sweat and grime. He is not a creature to inspire lust. The horse is brown or chestnut or one of those other technical terms horsepeople use to make it clear that they know stuff other people don't; the freemasonry of the hoof. "Horsepeople" is apt here, and this guy can choose his own damn nomenclature. Because he is not, in fact, a man *on* a horse. He is a man *and* a horse. A centaur, although . . . not. Centaurs, in stories, are natural horsepeople. They are born that way, made by Zeus or some other holy Fimo-kiddie, sculpted buff and ready to rumble. Deep voices and beards, testosterone stink. This one looks as if he has been welded or grafted. He looks like the compound wounded soldier in Leah's infirmary, or the tank commander who was part of his tank. He is not doing centaur sorts of things either. They are usually to be seen playing musical instruments or running about looking noble. This one looks confused, and he is digging a hole. He bends all the way over his front hooves, and lifts a shovelful of earth out of the ground. The hole is maybe a foot deep, but he has reached the maximum extension of what must be a curiously shaped spine. The next sweep of the shovel barely scrapes the soil.

He growls, and his front legs bend and he kneels, horse fashion. This is apparently uncomfortable, and unstable, because as he leans down to dig again, he falls over. He struggles for a while on his side, then rolls to his feet and starts again, and again. And then he throws the shovel away, and lays a slender, wrapped package in the hole. It is a person-sized package, if the person were small, or truncated. He picks up the shovel again, fills in the hole and stumbles away. He walks as if he is not used to having four legs: front left and back left move together, and he has to roll his weight onto his right like a sailor so as not to fall over, and then the reverse. He coughs, and spits a clot of blood onto a nearby fern. Perhaps his tubes are not properly lined up. It seems an uncertain proposition whether he can eat anything which will sustain him; which stomach does he use? What can it digest? We watch him wander off, and we are ashamed a bit that we don't offer to help. On the other hand, we haven't shot him either, which was a possibility, given that he was a completely impossible, alien object in the middle of a dangerous place at a dangerous time. That sort of thing usually gets shot at. Oh yes. Pillars of virtue over here. We don't look at one another.

The monk walks into the glade. Without fuss, and absolutely without disrespect, he digs up the package and unwraps it. His pirate-ness is in abeyance. Today he is just a monk, and very tired. Under a layer of oilcloth is a crochet blanket, and inside that is a child, or a foal. She is quite small. The transformation here has been less successful. She is—was—a horse with two legs, and arms ending in hooves. She clutches a small stuffed donkey. Her face is long and equine, with wide, black eyes. The monk nods, and buries her again, with his hands.

ZAHER BEY and Nq'ula Jann are taking council. I suppose, in a sense, it is a secret council to which everyone is invited. Zaher Bey is a wanted man, after all, and therefore his councils are perforce concealed things, but we are all allowed to know about it and contribute and listen in. Indeed, this is the essence of it. The question before the meeting is *What just happened?* and by and large we are in agreement that it's a jolly good question and one which needs answering before it happens to us. This has acquired a muttered urgency because—aside from the strange and the ghastly outside—there is a creeping rot within us too. It's more than a little bit difficult to recall the names and faces of the Gone Away. It can be done. It isn't impossible. It's just the difference between lifting the suitcase empty and lifting it full. And this invasion is, if anything, more horrible than the last.

This is where I first hear "Reification" in connection with the Go Away War, and I hear it because Zaher Bey is demanding to know what the hell it is. If I were not on guard against revealing that I had a rather large part in *What just happened,* I could tell him. Never let it be said that sociology is a useless discipline. Still, Nq'ula seems to have the concept well in hand.

"It is the making of an idea into a thing, Prince of Men," replies Nq'ula, *v. formal,* because this is not merely council, it is performance. Zaher Bey is turning a refugee plethora into an entity of its own: the Shangri-La Survivors, and in order to do that, he has to give them a stake. Gonzo offered flapjacks (and normality) in exchange for allegiance. The Bey is trading in *answers.*

Nq'ula lectures and theorises, and the Bey makes like he doesn't understand a word of it, which endears him to the rest of us. And if anyone has anything to add to what Nq'ula is saying, that's fine too, because we're all in this together, and two heads, or two hundred, are better than one. Nq'ula looks around, and notes that everyone is paying close attention. His friend makes a face suggesting that his explanation is not sufficient unto itself, so Nq'ula goes right ahead and unpacks it a bit.

"If you would be so kind, conjure before your mind's eye the image of a florid and uncouth man of the prehistoric wilderness."

Zaher Bey screws up his face and devotes himself to his task. There is a pause. Nq'ula taps impatiently. I look around. Exhausted though we are, everyone is concentrating on the shared image of our distant ancestor.

"If you are ready?"

"I am."

"Very good. What is most obvious about him?"

"Why is it, Nq'ula, that your explanations always involve me feeling like an eight-year-old?"

"Possibly, Prince of Men, it is the nature of learning."

"I think not."

"That, alas, is often the case." This gets a bit of a giggle. The Bey as intellectual underdog. "Leaving the long brown envelope of home truths sealed for the moment, however, let us return to our Cro-Magnon friend. So?"

"He appears to be naked."

"Indeed, Prince of Men. Indeed. And it is his nakedness which he even now seeks to mend."

"Are you sure? It appears to me that he is content in hoggish and unclean wallowing and lusty animalism. Yes, I am certain of it. See there, where his women gather. Are they not equally nude?"

Nq'ula allows himself to breathe out. He gives the impression that he is not a man who sighs at those above him, but that he is quite clearly a man who often wishes to.

"I had not mentioned his womenfolk, Prince of Men, lest their undress affright you."

"Oh it does, but they are at least more comely than that log of a penis which swings unlimbered beneath his belly."

This gets a big laugh, most especially from the scandalised village elder last seen being hoicked into the Bey's limousine amid a flurry of outdated undergarments. Now she eyes her hero with a wistful smile, content with hopeless admiration. Nq'ula rides out the giggling in good order and carries on.

"I had not hitherto observed it, Prince of Men, yet now I see the object of which you speak, and I must concur that it is far from easy on the eye. But returning to the women, do you not observe that they are cold?"

"The slender ones are shivering. The more curvaceous, I note, are yet insulated from the evening chill."

"Indeed. But even these register some trepidation at the onset of night and the concomitant drop in ambient temperature, for experience, that most harsh of magisterial reflections, causes them to believe that in the small hours of the clock—"

"Which they do not possess."

"Quite so, Prince of Men, for the technology of acquisition

of such commonplaces is the burden of this history, and thus I amend my description of their thought as follows: *in the deepest dark of the circadian cycle of which they, as primitive hunter-gatherers in tune with the ineffable wonders of the divine work and most specifically the unmeasured-but-measurable cooling of the air and earth during the primal night, are acutely aware,* they will be assailed during their slumber by feelings of discomfort related to cold. Are you appeased?"

"I am."

"Behold then, Prince of Men, as these ignorant domestics set about the prodigiously endowed master of the pack or herd—"

"Not 'pride'?"

"These are not your actual forebears, Prince of Men, but figments, and hence I do not dignify them by comparing them with lions, but rather consider them as dogs or cattle to be ruled, not venerated, by your good self."

"Ah. Very well. Shall we consider them as dogs, then?"

"I thank you, we shall. To continue: these rude females assail their mate with much wailing and shrieking, so that his aural equilibrium is quite undone."

"Do they also deny him that satisfaction of his feral desires which is so obviously necessary for his mental and libidinous good health?"

"We may assume that they do."

"Poor chap. I warm to our caveman, Nq'ula."

"Such was my hope, Bey of Addeh, for see: the wretched creature is about to bring us to the very climax and point of our discourse."

"Is he?"

"He is."

"How can you tell?"

"It is in his eyes."

"So it is. And under such trying circumstances too."

"Indeed, Prince of Men, it is the very *extremis* of his position which will cause his feeble cogitative apparatus to exceed the boundaries of normal function and discern a vital truth. His womenfolk demand warm dry weather, but it is cold and wet. They likewise assert their need to be protected from the many wild beasts which hunt the night, and from other packs which may be prowling nearby, but he can guard only one approach at a time, the others being as a matter of biology the ones to which he turns his back. From these insatiable desires he *abstracts* the notion of *shelter.*"

"Abstracts it?"

"Yes, Highness."

"Does he so?"

"He does. For the first time in history, Highness, a human creature descries a mental landscape of *concepts,* or *noosphere.* He has abstracted from the specific to the general, which operation causes him to perceive that along with the physical milieu with which he is familiar he inhabits a universe of mental things, and his action is simultaneous with the apprehension."

"What does he do?"

"He moves straightaway to the cliff face behind him, where is a cave occupied by some large animal. To this tenant he gives the thrashing of a lifetime, Highness. So much so that the animal . . . Shall we assume it is a hypothetical bear?"

"Very well."

"The bear immediately expires. Our hero takes possession of the cave for his pack, and they achieve *shelter,* thus *reified* in three rocky walls and a ceiling. Moreover, his epiphany lasts long enough for him to communicate it to his womenfolk, who instantly comprehend it and begin considering the *noosphere* and what other goods and services they shall now desire of him."

"This *noosphere* being, as it were, a great department store containing ideas."

"Requiring perhaps a little more effort than the act of shopping—"

"A contention which reveals instantly that you rarely shop, Nq'ula—"

"—but nonetheless accurate in the main."

"Hm. Dear me. I don't see that his situation is greatly improved."

"Social and physical pressure are ever the spurs of innovation, Highness, and we cannot waste our sympathy on this one individual merely because evolution demands that he be henpecked into his role as the spearhead of the first technological revolution. Presently, as you will observe, the caveman is clad in bearskin, thus obscuring from Your Highness's inner sight the ithyphallic object which so offended you at first—"

"I don't know that it was *ithyphallic,* Nq'ula, more pendulous—"

"In either case now mercifully and respectably concealed. He wields a bone club—"

"The reification of *defence* or *attack*—"

"Or possibly *thump,* Your Highness, these others being somewhat rarified for our caveman."

"Do you think he has a name by now?"

"It is unlikely that he needs one within his pack—which is becoming more a tribe—because he is the alpha male; he no more needs identification than does the sky or the earth. As the first modern man and the inventor of technology, however, it is perhaps fitting that he should be rewarded with an individuality."

"I concur. Yes, we shall call him John."

"So shall it be, Prince of Men. Observe, then: John's shelter is now lit and heated from within by a roaring furnace—though it is somewhat smoky as no one has yet reified their desire for fresh air in the form of a chimney—and filled with the hitherto unknown but pleasing odour of baked bear; shortly we shall see the arrival of assorted other tools and furnishings which eventually come together to create what we think of as modern life."

"These being further reifications."

"And the consequences thereof."

"Capital!"

"I am glad you approve, Prince of Men. Quite interestingly, however, capital is an *abstraction,* quite the opposite kind of thing: money is a system of tokens created to represent the transfer of *value.*"

"I am not sure that is as interesting as you seem to believe, Nq'ula."

"Then let us leave aside the study of economics and the illusion of currency, and proceed with our theorising."

And so they reach the end of this edifying part of the discussion. A shovel-faced pirate lady is drummed up from somewhere and puts on a pair of spindly spectacles (the kind which are made of flexible titanium and have no screws, so that you can sit on them and all that happens is the lenses pop out, affording you ten minutes' entertainment trying to slot them back in). Her name is Antonia Garcia, and Dr. Fortismeer, were he here, would say she was a fine figure of a woman. She is the holder of some incredibly involved qualifications and a species of religious calling which, in the course of missionary work in Addeh Katir, led her to the house of the Bey and thus to the revolution. She is science minister in the government without a country which Freeman ibn Solomon referred to as "an alternative," before he turned out to be a sneaky pirate king who drank my booze and probably caused my arrest and ultimately my presence here. She speaks and recaps what Professor Derek told me about the nature of the universe back at Project Albumen, and she doesn't seem to have any trouble working out Professor Derek's theory, although her guesses about some of the specifics of the Go Away Bomb are a little askew, and someone corrects her.

The whole place stops and turns. I get the impression that Professora Garcia doesn't often see a lot of correction of this kind, and I look around to see who was the source of the remark in question, before realising it was me. A moment later, before God and Gonzo Lubitsch and Zaher Bey, but mostly before Leah, because she is the one who must, must, must accept my confession and grant me absolution, I tell everything I know about such things, and where they come from and what they do and how there's no fallout of any kind, a claim which, as I utter it, I realise is patently absurd and untrue. And all this of course is high treason, highest treason, but against a country which no longer exists and has in any case forfeited all allegiance owed to it by blowing up the world, even if—as it now appears—it had plenty of help from its friends.

And actually, looking around, it's not all that hard to see what's happened, it's just hard to swallow—or it would be if we weren't sitting in the middle of it getting killed and seeing ghosts and burying the dead children of myths.

Consider the world, unravelled. The Go Away Bomb is a thing of awful power, a vacuum cleaner of information, sucking the organising principle, the *information,* out of *matter* and *energy.* Professor Derek assumed that either of these latter two stripped of the first simply ceased to exist. It seems that he was wrong. Matter stripped of information becomes Stuff, known to me recently as *Disney Dust* or *shadow.* It hangs around, desperate for new information. It becomes *hungry.*

Normally speaking, this informational part would be supplied by the *noosphere* (not John the caveman's department store, but rather the informational layer of the universe, the vast realm of which the department store is but a part), but of course we whisked away what ought to be there in the cause of war.

And as we have already seen, humans also have an information-y part. What has happened here, what is going on all around us, is that the human piece of the *noosphere*—our thoughts, and hopes, and fears—all these things are being *reified.* The human conceptual mishmash is becoming physical, replacing what is Gone Away with dreams and nightmares. Like the nightmare of war which rolled down on General Copsen's camp and then came here.

And like the little girl who wished she were a horse, and was immersed while sleeping in a storm of Stuff, and wakened to find herself transformed, hopelessly muddled with horsey parts and unable to breathe. Buried by a grieving, mangled parent walking on four legs instead of two.

"A world of dreams, Prince of Men," Nq'ula says, by which he means of course not pleasant daydreams, but the grimy rag and bone subconscious of our race.

Zaher Bey leans back and stretches. His eyes take in the shattered walls and the cold and the mud on the floor. They take in the broken windows and the bloody people all around him, reduced by a stupid, pointless argument to freezing nights and days of desperation. He looks at his battle-worn monks and his new allies, bloodied and torn. If I were him, if I were given to such things, there would be a knot in my chest and in my gut, and a terrible slow-burning anger would be transmuting my body from flesh to molten steel. And certainly there is a hint of that manner of man in the words he says now.

"Not my dreams, Nq'ula."

Chapter Eight

Piper 90; mimes and pornography; the Found Thousand.

I GREW UP with the Nuclear Threat. It lived on the corner of my street and it walked with me to school. Gonzo and I used to play with it when none of the other kids wanted to talk to us. We got so tired of playing Armageddon with that damn unimaginative Nuclear Threat that we implored it to learn another game, but it never did. Mostly it just sat there in the back of the classroom and glowered. And then one day we heard it was dead. Some people seemed pretty upset about this, but I was just glad I didn't have to carry it around any more. Kids are selfish.

Human beings can get used to just about anything, given time. They can get to the point where *not* living on the brink of being converted to fusing plasma at any time in an argument over economic theory and practice is a *bad* thing, a scary, uncomfortable, unimaginably dangerous thing. This is the gift of focus, or wilful denial, and it is something boys are particularly good at. Girls—at least where I grew up—tend to be more emotionally balanced and sane, and therefore find the kind of all-excluding concentration you need to care about dinosaurs, taxonomy, philately and geopolitical schemes a bit worrying and sad. Girls can grasp the bigger picture (i.e., *it might be better not to destroy the world over this*), where boys have a perfect grip on the fine print (i.e., *this insidious idea is antithetical to our existence and cannot be allowed to flourish alongside our peace-loving, free society*). Note carefully how it is probably better to let the girls deal with weapons of mass destruction.

In any case, we are almost offended when our doomed last stand comes to an end and we are rescued. We were doing so well. Granted, we had food rationing and medical shortages and nowhere to sleep; we were under sporadic attack by monsters (reified from the compounded nightmares of lots of different people and cultures), chimeras (people and animals twisted by Stuff), bifurcates (really creepy human-like things splintered off when a real person falls into a big vat of concentrated Stuff, such as happened to Ben Carsville) and other ills of varying sorts. We were, in other words, screwed. But we were on top of the situation. We knew we were screwed, and we had chosen the manner of our screwedness. We understood it and to that extent we controlled it. It was like the Nuclear Threat—while it was going on, we didn't have to think about any other kinds of screwed we might be.

And then we were *saved.*

We woke one morning, and there was a thunder in the valley and a great muttering, and something was rolling towards us which was much, much bigger than our castle. In fact, it was bigger than our mountain *and* our castle. The top of it was lofted way up above our heads, and it was broad and oily and smelly, and all around it was a cloud of strange, slick gunk. Where this gunk touched the puddles of leftover Stuff down on the valley floor, it sparkled and flashed, and then there was nothing there. Where the cloud of gunk met little wisps of Stuff drifting out of the forest, the wisps withered and fell to earth like rain. This big, remarkably ugly thing was *immune,* and there were people on it, and they were waving like they expected us to be glad to see them.

Resentfully, we acknowledged that we were. A man called Huster came to talk to us, very cautious, but when we let him in and he saw how we lived, he started to swear, and there was nearly a fight. Shangri-La was a mess, but it was our home.

No, Huster said, *you don't understand. We've been going for months now, and we've never found this many people still alive in one place. You guys are . . .*. He swallowed. His face was openly awestruck, and then he grinned. *I will be damned,* Huster said. *I will be damned.* And he laughed and laughed until someone brought him a beer.

We decided Huster was okay. And then we gathered up everything we had and went with him back to his rolling fortress, because ours was all done in.

I AM LYING on a tartan blanket on top of the man-made mountain called Piper 90; a vast industrial edifice stained black and striped by rain and grime. It looks like a cubist interpretation of a giant mechanical snail, laying out a silvery trail behind it: a power station on top of a hotel on top of an oil rig with caterpillar tracks. This is Huster's castle, and with it we are reclaiming the world. Or perhaps remaking it. The bits we find and join together do not seem to follow sequentially on our maps.

The blanket smells strongly of garlic sausage. This leads me to believe that one of Vasille's men has been using it. Only the French still have any garlic sausage. Their military ration packs were full of it: strange, freeze-dried, wind-cured, vitamin-enriched, pasteurised sausage, good for a hundred years. You can use it as a life preserver or beat your enemy to death with it, ski on it, burn it (the skin makes an excellent wick) or build fortifications with it. I have heard a rumour that, if combined in appropriate proportions with vinegar and certain human waste products, it can be transformed into an adequate explosive. Both disgusting and ingenious, if true, although it raises the alarming possibility of Vasille's men drinking vinegar and going off like fireworks, up and down the line. Perhaps there is a secret admixture contained in one of the seasonings they carry which nullifies the effect—I decide never to ask. The point is that you can put your sausage through the wringer, and when you're done you can still boil it up and eat it one-handed while you gesture expansively or hold a long gun steady with the other, and this, quite apparently, someone has been doing while lying on this blanket.

Through the extremely powerful telescopic sight of *my* long gun I can see Gonzo Lubitsch's familiar head as he rides out in front on a sort of kludged-together dune buggy. Like Piper 90 (although much, much, *much* smaller) Gonzo's ride is a bodger special, a lawnmower frame with the electrical engine from a milk float drilled onto it. This engine has an absolutely unfeasible amount of torque. Milk is an emulsion of butterfat in a water-based liquid, and the weight of a cubic metre of water defines the metric tonne; a milk float has to be able to carry an insane amount of weight, the kind which would kill your suspension and lay your chassis flat against the road. Strip away these encumbrances—and the monstrously heavy flatbed which is needed to maintain stability—and the humble milk float is a battery-powered rocketship with a whole lot of pent-up rage. Gonzo's dune buggy is unable to achieve lift-off only because no one has the time or the energy to put wings on it. If he needed to, he could fit spikes to his wheels and tow a tank.

Piper 90 is laying the Pipe. The Pipe contains the magic gunk which makes Stuff disappear. We spray the gunk (called FOX, for inFOrmationally eXtra-saturated matter) into the air, and it meets the Stuff and neutralises it. Behind us, the Pipe does the same thing, all the time, so that we are drawing a line across the world, making a strip of land which is safe to live in. FOX carries a load of junk information, so that Stuff which mixes with FOX becomes dust and air, and not monsters.

There was a moment, not long ago, when we thought Stuff itself might be a blessing in disguise; how wonderful to have discovered a substance which responds to thought. The end of scarcity and hunger. We allowed tiny streams of Stuff to stretch towards Piper 90 in the hope that we might mould them. But Stuff is nothing if not truthful, and the truth is that our strongest drives are not our most creditable. Our experiments produced swarms of tiny half-finished fiends and tortured flobbering wrecks, animated bread rolls and lethal candyfloss. We picked them off one by one, then sluiced the little rivulets with FOX to prevent a repeat.

It's important to remember that FOX itself won't stop monsters which have already been made. That's why I'm sitting up here with a rifle prepared to shoot anything with two heads which tries to swallow my friends. Still, FOX is more than a little bit vital. Also important to remember is why it's an aerosol. According to Huster, too much FOX and too much Stuff in one place at one time can go *boom,* and the *boom* in question is, while not revolutionary, respectably huge. It's more of a *BOOOMM-BADADA-THRUMMMM-mmm.* It is therefore best to use the FOX like a screen or a sandblasting tool, rather than a fire hose. A thousand kilometres back along the Pipe there's a hole in the ground the size of a football field which marks the spot where this fact came to light. Piper 90 has a matching scar, a big, black scorch mark along its southern face.

Gonzo sweeps wide to one side, and Jim Hepsobah and Samuel P. cross him. I keep Gonzo's head in frame at all times, but—since I don't want to shoot him, even accidentally—I don't let his noggin occupy the crosshairs. The point is to protect Gonzo while Gonzo and the others protect Piper 90, and Piper 90 gets on with the business of remaking the world. On three other ledges spread wide across the arc of Piper 90's east face (compass bearings are pretty arbitrary, but the sun still rises from approximately this direction, and it is the direction in which Piper is heading, and therefore it is unanimously declared east until someone can prove otherwise) Sally Culpepper, Tommy Lapland and Annie the Ox are also following the progress on the ground, also armed, and also looking for monsters.

Piper 90 has been attacked thirty-seven times in the last month. The broad metal armatures which support the aerosol nozzles are scratched and pitted. Bullets have been fired at them. Knives and even makeshift swords have slashed them. Bludgeons and clubs have thundered down on them. More unsettling, they have been chewed by large, impressive teeth. The northernmost arm has been crushed between the jaws of something big enough to be a great white shark, except that Piper 90, while parts of it started out as an oil platform, hasn't been in the water since before the arm was bolted on to its side.

Piper 90 isn't called that because it lays Pipe, by the way. That just happened. The superstructure around which this thing was built is a series of retooled oil platforms, and the original Piper 90 is actually just the first one of these. Its full name was Piper Nine Zero Bravo One One Uniform, which means, if you assume that each section of that designation could be either a number from zero to nine or a letter of the alphabet (as represented by the Alpha Bravo Charlie code beloved of gun nuts everywhere) that it was potentially one of 78,364,164,096 units. No one knows why any company on Earth could need that many possible serial numbers. Every model of mobile phone and video recorder has a number like this, most of them offering so many possible iterations of the technology that at the usual rate of product release—say, between three and fifty distinct products per line per year—the people making them will still have plenty of serial numbers left when humans are so highly evolved and so thoroughly integrated with their own technology that the idea of a phone as distinct from the organism is disturbing in the same way that carrying your lung around in your pocket seems a little freaky now. It may well be something to do with that boy-taxonomy-focus thing.

So Piper 90 has a totally dumb name, and it looks like the love child of a bulldozer and a shopping mall after someone has poured several thousand tonnes of yoghurt over it and left it out in the garden for a month. The people who built it were not worried about aesthetics; they were looking to make something survivable and strong. They took those oil platforms and they welded on huge, train-sized caterpillar tracks. They stuffed reactors from submarines in the basement to power the whole thing, and drive systems ripped out of aircraft carriers, and they synched the whole disaster together using matchbook maths, the gears from some defunct ultra-large crude carriers and a lot of duct tape. There are rooms, down there in the machine layer, which have nothing in them but huge toothed wheels going round and round, and even now there are people crawling through ducting and service tunnels and into dead spaces, just mapping the thing. There are bits of Piper 90 no one knows about because there simply wasn't time to work out they'd be there. You could hide a city in the gaps, below the city that's already bubbling away in the habitation section.

The whole catastrophe has a top speed of about a kilometre an hour, but no one is insane enough to make it go that fast. For something this size, on land, that is alarmingly quick. So Piper 90 trundles along at "barely noticeable" speed, and behind it there emerges a long, thick trail of Pipe, and around the Pipe our world is real again.

The Pipe runs all the way back to some distant laboratory, and along its path there are pumping stations, storage tanks, depots and maintenance caches, all demanded by people in some vestigial place of sanity where they have figured out what the hell is going on. Perhaps Professor Derek—accursed be his name and his seed in eternity, and may giant badgers pursue him for ever through the Bewildering Hell of Fire Ants, Soap Opera and Urethral Infections—is still alive and trying to clean up his mess.

Lots of people, given the choice, would leave Piper 90 and settle in one of the new towns which are springing up in our wake. There's rumour of a bright bulwark being constructed, a place called Heyerdahl Point, which is going to herald a new age of us being on top of the situation: back to real life. It's a powerful draw. Many of the survivors from our army have moved to the town of Matchingham, which is reputedly a serious hellhole. They claim it's like heaven. But Piper 90 is my favourite place in our small new world. Close to, you can see windows and lights and people wandering the glass-walled corridors and taking the slow, clanking lifts—they're mismatched; some are shiny executive things, some are old service elevators—from the ground floors to the roof. On the roof (a few levels below where I am now) there's a sort of park, a big open green space which doesn't have monsters in it. Children play in some of it; executives lounge in the rest.

So far, these executives are actually useful; *we* need people who can do quantities and manage resources, and *they* need everything to work. The profit motive is in abeyance—just—because we don't have surplus. And because anyone who gets caught making a buck on the back of human survival on this planet—if it still is one—is liable to be thrown down the top cooling tower into the steam vents. Liable, as in it's in the contract. All the organisations in the world which still existed at the end of the GA War and survived the first days of the Reification got together to make this happen. We're throwing everything we have at it. No messing.

Looking at the garden from up here, it's hard to tell the difference between the grown-ups and the kids, except maybe the children are better dressed. For some reason, the execs all wear chinos.

On the other side of Piper 90 is my apartment. Sally Culpepper is actually lying on my roof, and every so often Leah knocks on the ceiling and Sally clicks her radio and I click back, and Sally knocks on the floor and Leah knows that I'm fine, that I miss her and that I'll be home soon. We live in the top layer of the housing section, and the room looks out into the vast, bleak desert of the Unreal, which is what we call anything ahead of us or more than a few miles on either side. Our home is a strange, awkward shape. It is open plan (no spare materials for cosmetic walling) and shaped like two pieces of cake meeting at the pointy ends, or like the bars (but not the upright) of the letter *k*. The lower cake slice contains the bathroom, which is a metal tub with huge, heavy tubes going into it and some uneven stopcock taps. When I am off duty, I can sit in my bath and watch, through my picture windows, storms of matter being sundered and reconstituted, ghostly shapes and fires dancing or squabbling, temporary landscapes rising and falling with the prevailing wind. I think—I hope—that it's calming down out there. Maybe.

The execs all have the rooms looking the other way, back along the reassuring solidity of the area we have reclaimed. They gather each evening for a self-congratulatory cocktail party (although there are no cocktails) and stare out at the metal of the Pipe, at the post-industrial sludge we leave behind, and at the dry, dusty plains of the uncolonised Livable Zone. Farther back down the line, they can see something like soil, and twinkling lights. It makes them warm and they drink cheap white wine as if it were the good stuff (all of which is gone for the moment) and fuck one another in little cubicles no bigger than a wardrobe, because Pipeside rooms with a decent view are scarce and mostly given over to the orphanage and the hospital wards. That's why the execs running Piper 90 put hot tubs into the Stormside rooms (that and the fact that there's no space for them in Pipeside rooms anyway)—to encourage other people to live there. The rumour is that seeing the Unreal drives you mad, even from this distance (if that's true, a hot tub seems scant compensation, but since I don't believe it is, I feel I'm cheating the Man in a small, painless way; the execs believe they're putting one over on me, but know that I don't think so, and wouldn't have one of those cubbies for all the tea in Storage Bay 7A, and so everyone's happy).

The rumour is that the clean-up crews, even under the protective spray of aerosol FOX, are being saturated with Stuff, and we will have strange, dangerous children with unlikely destinies and curious names. The rumour is that we will never be allowed to live in the Livable Zone because we are tainted; the Zone will be pure, for real people only, and we're on the cusp now because we've been exposed for too long. The rumour is that they will exile us to the edges or make us disappear. Gonzo tells these rumours to each new recruit as he walks them out along the edge of the Piper roof terrace, and then waits for them to draw breath. Then he lunges at them and yells, "BOOOOGIE-BOOGIE-boogie-boogie!"

Anyone who does not actually pee gets the job. It's all hog-wash, most likely—the kind of myth you get at times like this—but it's true that there are things out there. And it's true that they are terrible.

Last week the monsters looked like buffalo. They were huge and brown, and they stank. They came out of the north-east like a bass drum, and they brought a cloud of choking dust. They stared and bellowed and charged at Piper 90, gored it and slashed at it. We shot them from a distance, one by one, and they died easily. Jim Hepsobah thought they had probably been real buffalo at one time. Not any more; they were bigger and heavier, with hoofed feet like lead and horns which bent and scissored. They could jump, too, almost like flying. The dreamshape of an angry cow. But animals are okay, really. Stuff makes them more like what they are, maybe, or bigger and badder, but an animal is not all that creative. A buffalo wants to be meaner than other buffalo, meaner than a wolf pack, or he wants to be able to get up a cliff face which is in his way. That's not much. Human thoughts are the problem. Stuff bonded to a human can be more complex, more weird and more awful.

For the most part, a human mind is not a concentrated thing. A mind at rest is a mind considering a hundred things with only the faintest intensity, and Stuff touching it ends up making biscuits, agendas, fleeting images of past times, random smells. No problem. They go into the great muddle of the Unreal, and mostly they just fade away. A mind under stress, afraid of dying, is a different thing. That kind of mind is *very* concentrated, and it makes far more vivid impressions. It can make monsters. Birds like flying piranhas, shadowmen with smooth faces like eggshells which somehow see you anyway and turn towards you like snakes. Or perhaps these are the product of more than one person;

perhaps these things are made when nightmares blend together in the moment of creation. I do not know, or care. I know they are awful.

The week before, when we crossed a small stretch of brackish water, it was mermaids—although actually there were men and women both. They were slender and greenish, and they came up out of the water on the crests of the waves and climbed the outside of Piper 90 with long monkey fingers. Wide fishy mouths with too many teeth gaped open and swallowed in short order two technicians and the entirety of Delta Team. The mermaids had soft fluting voices and they gabbled nonsense which sounded like real speech: "Ho there, Foster! The lady wearing postulates; is it laudable or trout?" And while you stared at them and wondered what in all the hell that meant, another one was sneaking up behind you on its single, snailish foot, and biting out the back of your head to slurp the brainstem, which is apparently what they eat. We fought them to a standstill by the side of the clothing depot on B deck, and threw the remains over the side. I think Samuel P. had a mind to keep some tail fin for steaks, but Leah confiscated it and sent it back down the line. Maybe they were human, she said, maybe they weren't, but we'll ask the scientists first and eat them later, if that turns out to be appropriate.

The new monsters—fresh from some pool like the one at Corvid's Field, or after a storm brings horizontal, unreal rain and everything for miles around is drenched in Stuff—are hard to take down. They seem not to understand the rules: get shot in a vital spot, die. Perhaps they simply don't have enough experience of reality to recognise what's happening to them, and so their bodies just repair themselves (if there's enough spare Stuff around or in them) and up they get, snarling and leaking and ready for round two. There was a slug-thing a while back which took hours, because we absolutely could not find its brain. Gonzo solved the problem by setting it on fire, and the countryside stank for days.

In truth, the obvious ones are not the bad ones. The worst are the subtle ones, the seemingly unchanged ones which are all unnatural inside—or maybe they're not unchanged at all, but new. My nightmares always used to have real people in them, so no doubt there are plenty of things running around out there looking like human beings, colliding and merging with one another and finally becoming something solid enough to obtrude upon our notice. But it's the ones which you know, somehow, are ordinary men and women gone askew, which are the saddest and the strangest. Perhaps because of what happened to poor Ben Carsville, killed by something split off from himself, bifurcated in that pond of bloody Ruth Kemner's, they make me shudder. At a level beneath words, I know that they are *wrong*. I have known this for ever—we all have—but most particularly since the business with Pascal Timbery and Dora the dog.

GONZO AND I were scouting, maybe three miles ahead of Piper 90. We do this because there are still obstacles in the world, still cliffs and ravines and scarred little towns. Towns we go through, or near to, in case there are survivors, and mostly there are. Cliffs and ravines we go around, because Piper 90 is not a hot rod. We haven't seen a city yet, most likely because they're all Gone Away. Sometimes it's clear we're uncovering what was there before, and sometimes it seems like it's either brand new or jumbled up from somewhere else. I don't know how that works, and I don't much care, as long as we can live.

We came upon a place the size of Cricklewood Cove (another nightmare, to come upon one's own home rendered awful) and Pascal Timbery was sitting outside a grocer's shop, rocking and smiling and waiting for us. The grocer's shop was full of sprouting veg, the inmates taking over the asylum. There were potatoes in there with spindly legs like spiders, and I absolutely wasn't going to think about that in case it was the literal truth. Or became it.

"Welcome!" Pascal Timbery said, and, "You took your goddam time!" But he was smiling. He had a couple of spare chairs—they were deckchairs, actually, one red and white, one blue and white, and his, which was green and white—and we sat down. Pascal Timbery had his feet flat on the ground, as if he were scared the whole place might tilt under him and tip him into the sky. He waited until we leaned back in our chairs.

"It was bad," Pascal Timbery said. "It was really bad. But you're here now. So it's all all right." And he choked a little bit, not like hysteria but like happiness, as if someone were getting married.

Gonzo passed him a chocolate bar, and he sort of enveloped it, didn't even seem to bite it, just shoved the whole thing into his face and swallowed, and there was a bit of brown spittle on the corner of his mouth, and his tongue picked that up, and that was Gonzo's chocolate bar all done. Pascal Timbery didn't say anything like "Thank you" or "That's good" but it seemed to make him happier. Sometimes these survivors can't say thank you, or really anything like it, because if they do they just come apart at the seams.

So Piper 90 checked in, which is to say Sally Culpepper and Jim Hepsobah checked in from a position a shade to our right, and Annie the Ox and Tobemory Trent called in from somewhere to the left, and Samuel P. was watching all of us from the high tower and relaying what he saw to a few more guys with long guns and we were fairly well covered, and we told Pascal Timbery that there'd be rescue on the way any time now, and could he see that big old rotten tooth of a thing coming around the hill? That was Piper 90. And Pascal Timbery said he could, and finally he said thank you and started to cry, which was a big relief to all of us, and got up out of his deckchair and hugged us, which was moderately snotty and disgusting, but nice too.

We found him a room in the south tower, and he said could he possibly have a garden allotment rather than a hot tub, and the execs said yes, and he said he'd be glad to work the rest of the garden too, and they said that would be okay as long as he took orders from Bill Sands in the horticulture department, and we settled him in. He burned his old clothes and bought a huge number of cigarettes, and that was all good. He went to the park and stared at the kids and the execs and wept a bit more, then stood looking back down the Pipe and admiring the sunset, and that was all good too. He made a few friends—another refugee called Fabian, a maintenance worker from Piper 90 called Tusk (I have no idea what kind of a name that is, but he went by Larry and had a dog called Dora) who handled the roses and a young widow called Arianne. Arianne had the strangest hair: it was thick and resilient, and she wore it short in a sort of helmet. It made her look all the time like a backing singer for one of those groups with a lava lamp fixation. Larry Tusk flirted with her and she flirted back in a very polite way, as if neither of them wanted to do anything about it but they were no way going to be so rude as to say so. Pascal Timbery didn't flirt with anyone; he just smiled his little light smile and petted the dog. And these three sat around and stared at the horizon, and worked in the garden until it was dark, and then after hours they consulted the maps, and they got into ghost geography.

"This here," Pascal Timbery would say, pointing at a shallow space off to one side of Piper 90, "this was Ollincester. Population fifteen thousand Light industrial. They made prefab pizza boxes and linens." Pascal Timbery was obsessed with memory. He was never going to let those people fade. He wanted to know about all the places that weren't there any more. And they would take a buggy, and go out with one of the teams, and stand in the space which used to be the town hall, and walk through it.

"Here, there used to be a fine example of nineteenth-century panelling. They had a painting by Stanhope Forbes *here,* and the council chamber *here* was famous for a ceiling mosaic. Here's a postcard." And here, truly, would be a picture of some grotty civic chamber and Pascal Timbery would point out that it was probably the most ugly example of the kind known to man, but he didn't care. He just wanted to remember. And they'd walk through the whole non-existent town, remembering places they'd never been which weren't there any more. Step for step. And gradually more and more people went along, as if it were a church service. This is the world, *in memoriam.*

But no one ever saw Pascal Timbery eat. In all that time we never did, except when he ate Gonzo's chocolate bar in one go. It seems stupid now, but we never wondered about that. If we thought about it at all, we imagined he must have been injured during the Reification—maybe he couldn't swallow properly; maybe his jaw was broken and he leaked. Maybe he'd eaten things which a right-thinking man normally wouldn't eat, and now he was ashamed to eat in front of people. That was a matter for him. There were a whole lot of people round about then with a whole lot of weird problems, the kinds of problems which would have been uncommon or even alarming back before the Reification, but which now seemed just about ordinary.

And then one day Larry Tusk couldn't find his dog. Just couldn't find her. Went walking around the place, calling hither and yon, with a little scrap of biscuit and some cheese. That poor scrawny little dog loved cheese, even the ghastly schlop they made on Piper 90, even Rory Trevin, who was a cheesewright back in the real world, but what the hell was he supposed to use to make the stuff now, when the buffalo were evil and a cow was a distant memory? When even the grass could turn around and bite you with sharp, angry little mouths? So Larry Tusk went a-walking, and as he passed Pascal Timbery's room he heard a familiar yip, and he figured the dog was stuck in there and Pascal didn't know. So in he went. And there, on the bed, was Pascal Timbery, with a great bloated tummy, and from this bulge there came the barking of the dog.

Larry Tusk went crazy. It actually wasn't about the dog. It was about this *thing,* lying there on the bed, a thing which looked human and talked human and hugged human, but which could open up and envelop you like a snake. Pascal Timbery made a noise as if he were trying to speak, maybe to say something like "I'm really sorry I ate your dog," which might or might not have been a good thing to say, and surely it wouldn't have been the most tactful sentiment at that time. But Larry Tusk didn't give him any opportunity to discuss the dog-eating or the whole business of Pascal Timbery being a monster from beyond the fireside. The thing with the distended stomach was *other,* and Larry Tusk wasn't having any of it. He just up and hit Pascal Timbery in the head with a fire extinguisher, and kept going until Pascal was basically a smear. And then he stuck his hand into Pascal Timbery's corpse and pulled out Dora the dog, all smeared in yuck and most unhappy at the strangeness of it all. We found him in Commissary 3, feeding her little bites of meat which were worth a week's pay to him, each and every one.

Sometimes, the nightmares look like people.

On the upside, the dog was fine. Dogs don't fret. She hadn't liked being swallowed and kept in a stinky, airless little place, of course, and she doesn't like darkness to this day—Larry leaves the light on for her. But broadly speaking she was just happy to see Larry again and delighted to be bathed and fed the best food Larry could get his hands on, and for everyone to be so pleased to see her. On the downside, it raised a question no one was prepared for about the Unreal People and what they were. Because we had *liked* Pascal Timbery, and if someone ordinary and mad had eaten Dora the dog, and Larry Tusk had beaten them to death with a fire extinguisher, that would have been murder, albeit provoked. And the thing is that for all that Pascal was a monster, he was clearly a thinking, feeling monster, and that made him at least most of the way to being a person. And if he'd come clean about his dietary requirements, well, maybe something could have been done. Although we might just have killed him out of fear. I'm not saying Pascal Timbery was wrong to hide what he was. I'm saying that if he hadn't, things would have gone differently.

That night we sat in the Stormside pub and argued about

whether the whole thing was more or less awful and imponderable than the fact that the world had come to an end nearly a year ago and most of the people we had ever known were dead. And as we sat there concluding that whichever of these things was worse, both were irredeemably awful and would shadow our lives for ever and ever until the last syllable of recorded time (pubs are not good places for this kind of conversation) there arrived a lumpy, water-stained parcel containing an elderly cherry pie.

A cherry pie is not something which ages well. It is ephemeral. From the moment it emerges from the oven, it begins a steep decline: from too hot to edible to cold to stale to mouldy, and finally to a post-pie state where only history can tell you that it was once considered food. The pie is a parable of human life. But this pie had been subjected to the kind of abuse which no pastry of any kind should have to put up with. It had been tempest-tossed. It had been a brave pie, but ultimately an ordinary one; it was not a pie of steel. It had split and withered. The filling had smeared the outer skin with red, sugary juices; this pie was a casualty. The only thing to be done with it was to put it in the ground with other brave pies and give it honour, and say a prayer for its humble and unselfish shortcrust soul. And that prayer would be well deserved, earned in battle and paid for in confectiony suffering, because this pie, fallible and ultimately unequal to the mighty task set before it—a task beyond what is achievable by mortal pies—bore a message from far away. The letter which accompanied it had run and bleached. Whatever was written on the paper was long vanished. But the pie itself was made of sterner stuff: it read simply "For Gonzo" and underneath "From Ma." The parcel was stamped with the just-legible frank of Cricklewood Cove post office, and dated just a few weeks before.

Cricklewood Cove had survived the Go Away War.

That night I took Leah out into the roof garden and proposed to her. She said yes. We're doing the deed next week.

Tonight, washed of garlic sausage and clad in my finest, I'm going to Matchingham with an L-plate on my chest, and Gonzo and Bone Briskett and Jim Hepsobah (and also, at my insistence and because I value my life, Sally Culpepper and Annie the Ox) and all the boys are going to get me horribly drunk and celebrate my last days of bachelorhood.

Gonzo completes his sweep on the milk-buggy (no monsters, no refugees, just grass and trees) and Sally Culpepper calls time. Stern duties involving makeshift ales and moonshine await us. Good soldiers all, we know how to obey orders.

MATCHINGHAM IS A SORRY excuse for a town. In fact, it is not a town at all but a collection of ramshackle houses and hotels and hostels and hostiles which has sprawled together into a sort of disurbation, stretched along the Jorgmund Pipe like towns used to stretch out along a road or a river. It has exactly nothing going for it except that it is the biggest place for a thousand miles in any direction which isn't actually moving along on giant caterpillar tracks, and it is notionally possible to make money here so as to go back along the Pipe to a real town (there are supposed to be real towns, even cities, growing up back west) or even buy a small-holding in the new agricultural areas around the Pipe, and make some sort of life. Every town like Matchingham ever in history has had this kind of *raison d'être,* and few are the people who have actually made it out and done these things. It's like the lottery. Everyone knows someone who has won something. No one actually wins themselves. Somehow or other, the big break, the dream, stays out of reach; people here just get older and greyer and a tad more bitter, and eventually they're not around any more and no one asks why. It is the kind of place where people know how to smash a glass and use it in a fight without getting sliced to ribbons.

It is therefore not the kind of place anyone has a great deal to say about. Matchingham has less history than a Styrofoam cup, and the closest it gets to a cathedral or a historic centre is a grimy cruciform monument on the way in, an advertisement for a blasphemously themed strip club. Matchingham isn't even a feeder town. There's nothing for it to feed.

We are on the back of Gonzo's buggy, destined for a bar called the Ace of Thighs, and from the name you would guess it is in the bad part of town. You would be wrong. Matchingham doesn't have a nice part of town, but if it did, the Ace of Thighs would be in it, and the way you know that is that the name of the bar is a word game (not actually a pun as such, but getting that way), and this kind of elevated humour is restricted to Matchingham's golden elite.

We cruise along the main street, and it's reasonably clear how the good folk here spend their time. The female half dances nude for the male half (with a statistical variation to account for less common orientations) or wrestles in a variety of convenience foodstuffs or performs in cinematic fantasies with simple, pithy titles. Some of the inhabitants engage in unmediated physical commerce of an ancient and simple sort. The porn shops of Matchingham observe a strict progression of obscenity, beginning with an almost fluffy eroticorium (catering either to tourists, if Matchingham ever had such a thing, or to the two or three women here who think of sex as a leisure activity), and moving from the modest HARD CORE! to the more self-aggrandising X-TREME HARD CORE!!! to various delights identified by jargon at least as impenetrable as Isaac Newton's Second Law. The pale, as it were, beyond which one may not go, is a small shop with a faded handwritten sign and quite a lot of dust in the window. It stands just past an emporium sporting a neon outline of a woman swallowing the head of a Sucuri anaconda (the distinctive markings are surprisingly well rendered in lilac tubing) while being beaten by attendant cowboys with what appear to be starfish. It seems that the people of Matchingham have attained, with their limited resources, a jaded expertise in perversity I had assumed was found only in wealthy university towns. Even for this population of mining-town Caligulas, the little boutique to the left has gone too far with its simple sign: EXPLICIT EROTIC MOVIES—*WITH A STORY!!!!*

Faced with this disgraceful banner, men cross to the other side of the street. Collars turn up and eyes slide away from the dusty exterior. Respectable prostitutes turn up their noses like Salem nuns. Shame! Narrative! Outcast, unclean! A bored and profoundly ugly teenager sits at a desk within, waiting for the first heavily disguised patron of the night.

Beyond this vileness lurks the Ace of Thighs, a sprawling pyramid to the dead god of desire. There's a little alleyway in between the bar and the storyporn shop, and the name of the road actually changes, so the Ace of Thighs is not part of the sliding scale of sin which comes before. It is the beginning of a fresh new innocence, which runs from here to a bend in the road ("Wash the woman of your choice!") and on into darker fantasies better left unplumbed. A vast papier mâché rendering of a set of meaty female legs is bolted to the side of the Ace of Thighs, a playing card strategically covering the most relevant area. It looks as if a giant strumpet sat down on the building after a tough night, and the wall yielded under her weight, throwing her backwards into the club. Her thick, poster-painted ankles are swollen around her stilettos, the westernmost of which hovers over the crossroads like a diamanté barrage balloon. If I go in the main door, I will be eye to massive eye with the fallen woman, and I have no doubt the great orb will be glassy and bloodshot, and the whole place will stink of her boozy breath. This is the least feminine place I have ever been. Only men think this way, and precious few of them at that.

There's a queue. The guys are big, cattle-shouldered men in blue cloth caps and working men's jeans or cotton trousers. After a moment I realise that it isn't a queue, it's just kinduva huddle, either a fight about to happen or a drug deal or some other thing we don't need. So we walk along the rope line—there actually is a red carpet too, although it looks as if it maybe was ripped from the corpse of a dead hotel—and the bouncer looks me over, pronounces us good enough (Samuel P. seems to know the guy) and we go in.

Curious, I probe the dark corners of the Ace of Thighs with my eyes. There are many of these (corners, not eyes)—the building is designed to provide maximum raunch, after all—but actually once you accept that this is an awful place, it's not that bad. It's clean, in the sense that there is no visible dirt and no obvious bodily effluvia. The velvet couches do not have many cigarette burns. The waitresses are efficient and non-judgemental, distinguished from the dancers and hostesses (and, in a fit of inclusiveness, also hosts) by a severe and defiantly unsexy uniform which accentuates how available the entertainers are. Nudity by implication.

Gonzo hails the nearest waitress, and summons a few hostesses and hosts to distribute themselves around and flash bits of skin and bore us with made up stories of medical degrees and sexual longings, and generally scam us. This is part of the fun. We sit at a round (red leather) table with bounteous (red velvet) chairs and gold trim. A woman perches on the arm of my chair and declaims that I'm the lucky boy. The muscles in her face barely move as she smiles. Her name, apparently, is Saphira d'Amour. She says it like *da mor,* which would mean "of death." If you want love, you have to find the letter *u* in there somewhere. Saphira and I do not form a close natural friendship even by the standards of strip club *politesse,* and eventually Annie lifts her bodily and drops her on Samuel P., who is delighted. It emerges instantly that they are the same age, give or take a few years; that they attended different schools with the same name; that they both hated mathematics and institutional lunches; and that neither of them completed the full educational experience before being sent to a borstal. How strange and powerful is the synchronicity of romance in the Ace of Thighs! This calls for a drink. Samuel P. spends another impossible sum of money on Saphira's neo-champagne, and she professes herself terribly pleased. Perhaps she actually is.

Meanwhile, something is odd. There's a distinctive and utterly inappropriate scent underlying the badger-gland perfumes and tarpit aftershaves in here. Greasepaint. It doesn't take long to find the source, because they are standing by the bar and there's a kind of circle of awestruck anticipation around them made up of assorted toughs and brawlers waiting to see who will take the first bite.

There are ten or so of them, tall, short, thin, fat, and all white-faced and black-clothed, and surely about to die. Not white-faced like skin pigment, but white-faced like wearing full stage make-up. They are clowns. Worse than that. They are *mimes.* As I approach the circle to say that maybe we should just leave quietly and of course this will be something they are quite good at, being what they are, the mime-in-chief spins to the bar and leans over it, and under the eyes of seventeen of the most dangerous men in Matchingham, he orders a glass of milk.

In sign language.

This involves *miming* milking a cow.

The whole bar is so stunned by this that he does not immediately die. The barman, very much to his own surprise, locates a carton of the white stuff (THIS MILK BELONGS TO MARBELLA, IT'S FOR MY SNAKE, OKAY?) and pours a half-pint into a glass. Ike—on his chest is a narrow conference badge which reads "Ike Thermite"—gets into a brief Three Stooges thing with the mimes next to him about who's buying. He concludes it by stamping sharply on the foot of Mime A, while at the same time sharply twisting the nose of Mime B, so that A lurches back and B folds over, and the two of them meet midway and bounce off each other, jolting other mimes in a kind of robotic, mechanical pratfall which culminates in every single mime knocking into every other in a circle, until the penultimate mimes on each side of the circle jolt A and B again and their left and right hands respectively fly up in perfect unison to present Ike Thermite with a bill each, and he pays. It's brilliantly done.

It is probably the last thing they will *ever* do. Half a dozen thugs are trying to figure out when is the appropriate moment to break into this baroque suicide attempt and do some actual killing, but the tempo is off and they simply can't get to the threshold required for homicidal violence. Ike knocks back his milk and makes a silent sigh. Then he collapses onto his chair and puts his feet up on an imaginary footrest. They do not waver. His control is absolute. The half-dozen thugs make a mental note that, when they kill him, they will not kill him by hitting him in the stomach, because that would be long and boring. They will kill him by ripping his head off instead. Still his feet do not wobble. He shuts his eyes and gives every appearance of going to sleep. No one moves. He commences to snore silently; his chest heaves and his lips flutter, all with nary a sound. Some alteration of posture suggests he has farted. His mouth crooks in a satisfied, post-flatulent smile. Someone snickers, and suddenly there is a collective realisation that the moment has gone. Somehow, Mr. Thermite and his greasepaint pals are going to live. No one is going to kill them today; tomorrow, if they come back, this bar will tear them apart as if they were candyfloss. Tonight, everyone's just going to go back to what they were doing. Ike Thermite feels the tension drain away, and he hears the sound of a room full of bastards and minor felons getting on with their lawful business. After a moment, when all their backs are turned and they are settled to their large yellow ales, he swings his feet slowly to the floor and opens his eyes.

"Hi," he says. "I'm Ike Thermite." He extends a single gloved hand. I shake it, and he takes it back to light a roll-up. "And we," he adds, "are the Matahuxee Mime Combine." He nods. Several members of the Matahuxee Mime Combine nod too, in unison. The others follow suit, and finally I'm surrounded by a small sea of nodding clown faces. It is not a memory I will treasure. I look away, and my retinas are blasted by a glimpse of Marbella doing her thing with a boa constrictor. Clearly, this is not the act with the starfish promised by the place two doors back along the road, because 1) there are no cowboys, 2) the snake is from Madagascar rather than South America, and 3) while it is notably obscene, it does not actually send me mad to watch it.

I nod back at the Matahuxee Mime Combine, and Ike Thermite smiles broadly, and Jim Hepsobah claps Ike on the back and says any man who is arsehole enough to order milk in a dive like this one is a man indeed. I was not aware of this verse in Kipling's poem, but sure, if Jim says, it must be so. The mimes are adopted into our company, and they come to our table in a long line, each with a beer or a drink with a cherry or a clear spirit, unsmiling, like the Charge of the Existentialist Brigade.

Ike Thermite raises his glass.

"To the man of the hour," he cries. Two of his buddies stand up and mime this, but they are by now seriously drunk, and the whole clock-face thing devolves into farce and they sit down again, howling with silent laughter.

I ask Ike why it is that he is allowed to speak.

"It's like Trappists," he says.

Sixpence none the wiser.

"Trappists," Ike Thermite says, because we are now friends for life, owing to beer and male bonding and women in sequins breathing throatily on us like inexpensive Lauren Bacalls (Lauren in that movie with Humphrey Bogart where she was just heart-stoppingly, rudely sexy, rather than in the ones where she was cool and beautiful and somewhat reserved).

"Trappists are monks," Ike Thermite says redundantly, with owlish precision. "They take a vow of silence. They have one person who's allowed to talk, so that the others don't have to. Like an appointed voice? It has to be someone who isn't going to be corrupted by speaking—someone who's so deep in the thing that silence is irrelevant. Someone whose inner silence is so damn profound that just actually saying something isn't going to disturb it."

"And that's you?"

Ike Thermite nods.

"I am totally serene," he says.

I do not comment on this directly, because I cannot think of anything I could say about it which would not be unkind.

"Y'know," Ike Thermite says, "it would be nice if you would pretend to buy my bullshit just a little. Otherwise I feel kind of small. Oh dear." This last because a very small mime with glasses is even now poking his finger pugnaciously into the chest of the nearest bouncer and telling him something very impolite by means of a universally recognised piece of sign language.

"I'll deal with this," Ike Thermite says, and falls over. After a moment he snores. It is not a mime snore. It is a loud, ugly, chainsaw snore, with drooling.

Annie the Ox slips into his place and eyes me firmly.

"Right then, Tiger," she says. "That lady over there is going to dance for you in the most vulgar possible way, which you and I will both enjoy without really giving a damn one way or the other, and then I'm going to take you home and give you back to the nearly-wife before this gets gnarly, okay?"

Annie the Ox is an angel of mercy with size-ten feet.

From somewhere across the room comes the sound of a mime getting beaten up.

LEAH AND I get married in the old church by the Soames School. It's a long way from Piper 90, so we have to take almost all our holiday in one block, and even then we won't get much of a honeymoon. I don't care. She walks through the doors of the church and all I see is light. She smells of jasmine and clean lace. The church smells of old-fashioned furniture polish. Everything is so shiny. The pews, the candlesticks and even the air seem to be glowing. The altar rail is made of gold, which is curious, because I distinctly recall it being an iffy tinted oak. Leah is so bright that I am concerned that she has inadvertently set herself on fire during her journey down the aisle, and only Gonzo's firm reassurances from somewhere nearby prevent me from rushing to the font and putting her out.

Assumption Soames sits in the back and I swear she cries, quietly, over an embroidered kneeler. Elisabeth is still missing. I'm terribly worried about her but very glad she isn't here. Zaher Bey, in his Freeman ibn Solomon drag, sits behind a pillar and grins at everyone. A clump of soldiers and oily-rag men occupy the middle of the church, openly amazed that two of their number are actually doing this extraordinary thing. Old Man Lubitsch reads a poem he has written. It is very moving, even though no one except Ma Lubitsch speaks Polish, so we have no clue what it means. At some point we kneel and are tied together with a bit of embroidered silk, and then the vicar says we're married. It seems a bit easy for such a momentous thing, but everyone claps and cheers, so it must be true. I look round and realise that I am now all shiny too. An enormous number of people want to hug me. Assumption Soames holds me at arm's length, and buries her tiny face in my chest for a moment, and wishes me long life and simplicity. Then she flees and is replaced by Zaher Bey, and the last I see of Elisabeth's mother is the ragged end of her shawl floating in the doorway of the church.

We spend our wedding night in an empty house in Cricklewood Cove. There are many of these. The Reification was a bad time here. Things came up out of the creek with muddy eyes, and the incidence of kuru was awfully high among the townsfolk. Some bandits passed through a few months before contact was re-established, and took several families away with them for purposes unknown. The house we are in does not have an unhappy history—it was for sale when the Go Away War began. It's not a grave, just a sweet little two-bedroom with an insignificant kitchen and a log stove. Leah and I make love on the sofa and fall off onto the floor. Laughing, she drags me upstairs to a preposterous four-poster bed with pink lace and heavy curtains. In the morning a discreet lady from around the corner arrives to make us breakfast, then vanishes again with a sad, soft smile.

In the evening we set off back to the giant metal snailshell which is our home. The break makes Piper 90 strange for both of us, because we see it from the outside, and start to think too much. Things have changed since we first arrived: the place has tamed and evolved, but it has also become unfamiliar in odd, unsettling ways, like the blind spots in your eyes after you look at the sun.

Now, Huster is leaving.

In the beginning, just after Piper 90 arrived and rescued us from certain death, we were somewhere between a mad dictatorship and a sort of daffy anarcho-syndicate, a cooperative venture in self-salvation and heroism. Huster (he has no other name I ever heard) was Piper's captain, her pilot, her master: a grizzled old fart who had managed an oil platform and knew engineers and tolerances and red lines and tipping points, and who got on well with just about anyone. Huster had never been military because he had some fever or ague as a kid which rendered him infirm—the kind of infirm which works thirty hours without a break and can arm-wrestle a bear. His word was law, and the various bean counters—really quartermasters—bowed to him and were glad of him, because they could see what he was about, and from an intellectual distance they respected it. They were survivors too, and content to facilitate and function and be part of his show. He'd fought wars of attrition against rust and salt water and hurricane winds, and drunkards with pneumatic tools, and just about every form of screw-up you could name. He understood about what was going to work and what never had a chance.

Huster was technically some species of ambassador, but it was never clear for whom or to whom—"us," I suppose, and no one really bothered to ask who that was and who it might not be. He was just the right man in the right place, and that was so obvious that no one argued about it. He never exactly gave orders or speeches, he just went ahead with the driving and let us get on with our thing—it's not as if anyone had any doubts what the task was, after all—and when something tricky came up he wandered around Piper 90, from the roof garden to the engine level, and he talked to people. He had a sort of permanent council, composed of someone from our group (former soldiers, oily-rag men), someone from the general population (mostly a sepulchral woman named Melody with a gimlet eye for bullshit) and the Bey, to represent the Katiris, plus anyone else who wanted to come and hang around and talk, and who wasn't a pain in the arse. Quippe might have called it a demarchy, except it was more a kind of consultative absolutism, and Sebastian would have said it was fine for a generation but the moment you had new blood it could turn on you like a scorpion and eat your brain, at which Quippe would have been diverted into a discussion about whether that was actually something scorpions did.

And then about three months ago Huster got the call. He went to a meeting back along the Pipe—all the way back, I think, where the first pump was switched on and the first section was laid on the first piece of solid earth—and they retired him. A more enlightened style of management was called for, apparently, more *centralised,* so that opportunities for *efficacy maximation* could be *cross-competenced* by a *meritocratically upgraded leadership group.* Huster, while he was a *good on-the-ground man,* was not in possession of the necessary secondary skills to be a *full-active co-decisionist within the frame of the Re-visioning Taskforce,* and therefore, while he would retain an analytical input to the *forward-impetused directional committee,* he would not, in fact, be invited to continue in his executive capacity at Piper 90, which was a position now requiring experience in *global, holistic, trans-disciplinary interactions* and *pseudo-leveraged quasi-financial exchanges,* and a full understanding of the management of a large collective entity with reference to dislocated populations with concomitant instabilities.

In short, Huster was fired, and our friendly quartermasterish execs were replaced with a skein of—there was no other word—

pencilnecks. These pencilnecks were led by Hellen Fust and Ricardo van Meents, who seemed far too young and far too clean to have achieved anything which merited their promotion to this job. I am at this moment formulating a sketchy taxonomy of paper-pushers of this kind, and I have tentatively labelled them as type C: young and hungry, sharp elbows, excised conscience. They held on to Huster's council, but they called it the Advisory Panel, as in *advise,* as in *don't have to listen to.*

So now Huster is leaving. The big guy is taking his stuff and going away someplace. His consultative role means getting ignored in committee, and he hasn't bothered to show up for a meeting for two weeks. Maybe there's a town out there which can use him. Maybe this place, Heyerdahl Point, needs a troubleshooter. Maybe he'll just homestead and find a lady friend and have a parcel of oily-rag rugrats. Be that as it may, he's had it with Piper, and God bless her and all who sail in her, but not him, not any more.

Huster wanders from table to table in the Club Room, which isn't really all that much of a club or even that much of a room: it's the hull of a small ship pressed into service as a part of Piper 90's lower reaches, and across the bilges or the hold or whatever you call the bit of the thing no one goes into, someone long ago laid bare boards and plates and slats, and then by magic there was furniture and a bar and people day and night, because Piper 90 never sleeps. The Club Room has never been so full, nor so sad. Huster is our collective mother, our ruler and our voice of reason and our final court of appeal. And now he's getting a new family and we're being left behind. Jim Hepsobah snuffles into a tall beer, and Sally strokes his arm to say it'll be okay in the end. Tobemory Trent mops at his one good eye; Samuel P. is making wagers on cat races.

"You okay?" Huster says to me when his royal progress brings him to my corner.

"We'll get by, I guess."

"Yes, you will."

"What about you?"

"Oh, I'll be fine. Be nice not having the cares of the world on my back for a bit. Really nice, actually." He considers it. "Yeah." He claps me on the back, and I tell him to look me up, and he says the same applies, and that's it. Huster walks away and then there are people between us. He's gone. I offer a thoughtful salute with my beer glass, and hear a sigh. Zaher Bey is leaning against the wall behind. He gazes after Huster and slumps dejectedly into a chair. I've never seen him do this before. The Bey does not flag. He jump-starts. There is no end to his energy. He rubs his palms down his face and looks exhausted.

"It's starting," he says. "I thought it would take longer."

"What's starting?"

"The . . . I don't know what you would call it. Not rot, exactly. The not-right things are starting again." He shakes his head.

"Because of Huster?"

"No. No, no. That's . . ." The Bey waves his hand generously, and I wonder briefly whether he's plastered. "That's a consequence. Huster is my canary. Yes?" Yes. I know about canaries. If you're mining for coal, you keep a canary in a cage so that if you hit a gas pocket, the bird will die before you do, and you have time to get out. Assuming that you don't explode. Actually, in modern times the canary has been supplanted by an electrocatalytic sensing electrode, but quite a lot of people still call the unit after its avian predecessor.

"So what's starting?"

"What was the first reification?"

"No one knows."

"No. Not our kind. The old kind. The making of an idea into a thing."

"Shelter? Thump?"

"Yes." He sighs. "I didn't mean that either. I had a thought." He ponders. His beer is finished. It is also disgusting. The beer in Piper 90 is made in a huge tank on the other side of the engine room, warmed by the nuclear reactor—everyone makes jokes about it glowing in the dark, but that isn't true because the radiation would kill the yeast. I'm almost sure it would, anyway. The beer is not toxic so much as it tastes of oil rig. I get him another one.

"You remember when I was just Freeman ibn Solomon?"

"Of course."

"We had whisky!"

"We did, indeed."

"And there was a girl with the most curious hair."

"Yes," I agree. He laughs.

"You see? Even I miss the old days, and my old days were dreadful. And I don't believe we should miss them. I think we should . . . *strike out*!" He thumps the table. "Make a new world! Not the old one all over again. But . . . people are scared." He shrugs.

"So what was your thought?"

"Oh. I don't know. I thought . . . What is this thing, this Jorgmund? How did it begin? What is FOX? Who controls it? How is it made? Jorgmund knows, and no one else. So I asked again, what is Jorgmund? Not the Pipe. *The Pipe* is an object which brings relief. But Jorgmund is not only that. Is it a government? A company?" He shrugs again. "It is both. And what is its purpose? You might say 'to reclaim the world,' but that is *our* purpose. Jorgmund is *a machine for laying, maintaining and defending the Pipe.* That is its only task. Its only priority. In fact, that is the only thing it can see. It is blind to us. It does not even know that we exist, except in so far as we impinge upon that purpose. If the Pipe could be constructed by monkeys and guarded by dogs, Jorgmund would be content with that. More content, actually, because it would be cheaper. Humans are simply not of interest to Jorgmund. We are gears. Jorgmund sees the world, and the Pipe, and anything which gets in the way. Nothing else."

He's looking at me as though that should be enough. I don't understand. He rolls his hands over one another, slow and fluid, reeling in his thoughts. Then he nods.

"Imagine," the Bey says, "that your wife was trapped in the mud in front of Piper 90, and she could not escape. What would Huster do?"

I shiver. "Stop the rig."

"Yes. But Jorgmund would not. It would not see her. Jorgmund would roll on over her because the only thing it understands is the Pipe. Huster wouldn't let that happen."

"I don't think Fust or van Meents would either."

"Almost certainly not. But are you as sure of them as you are of Huster?"

I try to be. I fail. They just might take a little longer.

"No, I guess I'm not."

"So: they stop the rig. Your wife is saved. Piper 90 is a day behind schedule. No problem for Huster or for us. But Jorgmund doesn't understand: oh, there's a good *reason* for the delay, but when the annual report is processed, it's still a delay. Fust and van Meents are replaced with someone whose priorities are closer to that of Jorgmund. And then the person who replaces them is replaced later for the same thing . . . Do you see? Sooner or later you arrive at someone who is not human, not really; someone who is just a cog. And at what point along the way does the executive in charge of Piper 90 let it roll on over someone?" He wobbles his hand in the air, flutters the fingers. "How long before the Pipe is more important than a life? Or a home? Or a river which feeds a village? How long before the *convenience* of the Pipe is more important than these things?"

"I don't know. Maybe never."

"But Jorgmund *already* thinks that way. For Jorgmund, everything is judged by that one criterion: *How did the day advance the Pipe?* That's it. Only the people within the structure can temper it, and those who do will naturally be selected out."

"Maybe."

The Bey shrugs. "I didn't see it at first, when it happened to me. I thought I was fighting against greedy, evil men. And then I began to realise that they were just ordinary men, but that what was happening inside them was very strange. They were behaving as if they were evil. As if they hated us. The consequences of their actions were horrible. They deposed a just ruler—not a brilliant man, but a perfectly good, sensible one—because he would not give them money he did not owe them. They invaded his country and burned it and cast its people out into the wilderness, then installed a madman on the throne and called him a statesman. He plundered the wealth of the people and took the daughters of Addeh for concubines and outlawed their brothers who protested. So we rose up, and we fought him, though mostly we just stole from him and bilked him and made him angry. And then this poor nation was invaded *again,* by a hundred different armies, and they ate our food and diverted our rivers and we starved and thirsted and died in the crossfire. In the space of two decades they took a prosperous land which was waking to the modern world and transformed it into a battlefield of blood and burning trees. And all the time I could not understand *why.* There was no human reason for this. There wasn't enough money, enough gold or oil or diamonds or rare earths, in all of the mountains or the lakes of Addeh Katir to pay for any of this. It was futile. It made no sense. Only an idiot would engage in such a battle."

Zaher Bey's voice is catching just a little. He's not shouting or declaiming, but there's a terrible intensity in what he says, a dreadful inspiration.

"An idiot or a machine. The All Asian Investment and Progressive Banking Group was a *machine for making money.* And Addeh Katir was refusing to pay. It didn't matter that the outlay was greater than the debt. We could not be allowed to default. That would have ground the gears and shattered the engine. It can go in only one direction. So it rolled over us. Do you see? *It rolled over us.* And this will be the same."

I'm not sure. It makes sense, but it's also rather dark. There are so many things which would have to go wrong. And so many people who would have to be lazy, or wicked. It seems far-fetched. Zaher Bey shrugs and finishes his beer, tilting it all the way back so that the foam slides into his mouth, and throws out his arms.

"Enough! I am a pessimistic old man at a party. Blah, blah, blah! Enough! I shall teach these young ones to dance, or I shall die in the attempt. Where is the band? Make music! Let the revels commence!" He leaps to his feet and raises his voice. "I am here! I am Zaher ibn Solomon Bey, Freeman of Addeh Katir, and I am the Prince of the Funky Chicken, Sultan of the Ineffable Conga!" A rousing cheer goes up, and he plunges into the throng. And somewhere there actually is a band, and he locates them and works out a tune which will satisfy him, and he grasps Huster by the arm and creates a cancan line, right there in the middle of the room.

I come home late, but not as late as Leah, who is working the late shift at the infirmary. She shuffles into bed as the sky is going pale and presses her cold nose against my back.

"I love you," she says.

I love her too. I think I say it, but perhaps I just make a little grunt. Either way, she is content. The pressure of her nose does not abate.

HUSTER LEAVES. We wave him off, and we go on with life. I don't think about Zaher Bey's worries for a while. No immediate catastrophe comes calling, and Hellen Fust makes some good decisions, a few things get tightened up and a couple of minor spats are sorted out rather well. She has a winning smile and a practical manner. She's not Huster, but she's not an idiot. She'll do. Van Meents keeps a lower profile, but he's no dead weight either. So I begin to think maybe the Bey was just maudlin drunk, which can happen to anyone, even heroes, and there's no question in my mind that's what he is. A genuinely good man. I don't see him very much, because Leah and I are busy kludging together some furniture and making a home up in our weird little

V-shaped apartment (one of Rao Tsur's friends sends us some dried flowers and Veda herself appears with a charcoal sketch of Shangri-La she did from memory, in a frame made of fan belt and the offcut from some decking), but occasionally I glimpse him riding out with one of the teams or talking to people in the roof garden. The rest of the Katiris sort of fade away: they don't find jobs in Piper 90, and they don't settle up the line. They're around, you can hear them and glimpse them, but they keep themselves to themselves. I figure maybe they're just trying to find a bit of quiet and be them for a while. I work, and play, and sleep, and the food on Piper 90 gets a bit better, and somehow a few months slip past me.

Until we come on the Found Thousand, and I get in over my head—again.

IT BEGINS with a piece of string and a stick. More accurately, a piece of twine. The twine and the stick are interlinked in a simple-yet-effective style to make a snare. The snare is occupied by a small, strange thing like a bald rabbit with the head of a fish. It hisses at me as I go near. I back away. It tries to bite Samuel P. instead. He shrugs, unlimbers his gun, and converts it into a slick, ichory smear: BANG.

The shot doesn't echo. It sort of whispers away into the trees around us, giving the impression it is going to cover a lot of ground. Everyone looks around—everyone being me and Gonzo, and Annie and Bone, and Tobemory Trent.

"Sam," says Gonzo, "if we are ambushed in the next twenty minutes by anthropophagous plants or by giant fish-rabbits looking for their horrid young, I am going to let them have you. In fact I will serve you to them on a plate made of banana leaves. I will put a white napkin over my arm and I will carry you into their dining room with an apple in your mouth, and I will offer to carve you. I will recommend a full-bodied red wine, because I suspect your meat will be gamey or even smoked, and I will bow until my nose touches the vile, gobbet-covered carpet of their lair and wish them *bon appétit,* and then I will walk out and consider myself richer and the world a better, less arsehole-ridden place." Sam just stares at him, because this sort of discourse is not his daily fare, and Gonzo sighs. "Sam," Gonzo says, "don't do that again."

We move on.

The forest is tropical; it is pungent with funk and perfume. It smells like the dressing room of an exceptionally expensive and environmentally conscious prostitute. Turn your head one way, and your nose is teased by a fine scent of sherbert and musk. Turn the other way, something trufflish and blatantly rude slips into your mouth and makes you swallow. This is a *basic* place, all reproduction and hunting and raw meat. It is like a woman who once visited Caucus to talk about the New Russo-Slav Feminism. She arrived at dinner in the sort of dress your mother would wear, with a Peter Pan collar and Shakespearean sleeves, but she was wearing it open to somewhere just below her ribs. She smoked vile black cigarettes, and when she moved—which was often, because she spoke with her hands and her shoulders and with everything she had—her very white, very round bosoms (quite clearly not *breasts* or *knockers* or even *tatas,* but the genuine, incontestable *bosoms* of a curvaceous forty-nine-year-old woman who isn't wearing a brassiere) sallied forth individually or together to view the scene. It was my strong suspicion then, as it is now, that she took Sebastian to her bed that night and nearly killed him.

Svetlana Yegorova would have loved this forest.

We push through the undergrowth, all of us feeling that we are undressing someone we shouldn't be. We aren't exactly hiding, not after Samuel P.'s clarion call shot; we just go cautiously, as you might in the new world. We check in with one another, covering our backs. We retain a knowledge of where we might defend ourselves, where we might fall back, and where not to get stuck. And then we round a corner and there is a clearing and a small fortified village with little neat houses crouched behind a stone and wood stockade. It is—and this is not usually the case with fortified settlements in the new world—pretty. The houses are solid and strong, but they are also quaint. I find myself looking for bric-a-brac in the windows. People who live in lovely small houses inevitably feel the urge to line their windows with primary school paintings and china dogs from the seaside. The rich woodwork and weathered stone vanishes under strata of postcards, biscuit crumbs, carpet fluff and cat hair.

No bric-a-brac. But that's hardly surprising. These houses are recent, and it's not as if there's been either the time or—as I look at them—the leisure to assemble that kind of crap. These houses are scarred and pocked. They have seen hard use. They have been shot at, bludgeoned and burned. Little pig, little pig . . . Was the first version of this village made of thatch? How many householders got roasted by the local bad guys (perhaps adult rabbit-fish breathe fire) before they managed to put this place together? Because the more I look at it, the more I realise that this is a *defensible* village, and it has *been defended.* Those little ripples in the grass have grown up around sharpened pegs protruding a few inches from the soil. No fun at all charging the walls over a field of those. You'd want very heavy boots, or caterpillar tracks. Shoes or tyres would be pierced, with obvious consequences. There is a safe path, but it curves and winds in on itself. Plenty of time for the defenders to pick you off if there is need. And once you are inside the wall—no mean feat—there are no sight lines except from the roofs. The houses create a winding maze of streets around the centre of the village. You'd pay for every metre.

Real go-getters, then. Real survivors. People who have had it rough and come through. *Our* kind of people, in fact. Gonzo is grinning widely as he threads his way to the gate and bangs on it. It makes the kind of dull noise which very, very solid things make. He bangs louder. There is a small door set into the main one, a Judas port. In the Judas port there is a viewing slot. It opens, and someone views us. Then she speaks.

"Go away."

"We're not bandits," Gonzo says. "We don't need supplies. We're not looking to move in either. We've got some good news." He's almost embarrassed, and you can hear it in his voice.

"And who are you?" she says.

"My name's Gonzo Lubitsch," Gonzo replies, and in for a penny, in for a pound: "I'm here to rescue you. We can take you to a safe place. No monsters. We're making the world right again."

There is a sort of choked snort from the other side of the door.

"Is that so?"

"Yes!"

She chuckles.

"We have a safe place, Gonzo-Lubitsch-I'm-here-to-rescue-you," says the lady behind the grille. "We don't need yours. So why don't you walk back down the path, and run back through the forest, and go rescue someone else? We won't hold it against you. We'll be fine. Thanks, though."

She shuts the grille firmly, though not rudely, and not all of our polite knockings can draw her back again. We hang around for a while feeling stupid and then go back to Piper 90.

Hellen Fust and Ricardo van Meents are not pleased.

The problem is a small one, but it comes at a key point. The village is in a strategically and logistically important location. To the south, there's a stretch of water tentatively identified as a major sea. To the north, the land becomes rugged and mountainous, so that while we could build the Pipe through it, we couldn't actually take Piper 90 up there, so we'd have to slow down and do it at one remove, the leading end of the construction moving farther and farther from our base of operations, becoming more and more exposed, until a midway point where Piper 90 would move around to the far end and all work would have to stop until contact was re-established, some five weeks later (one kilometre per hour times twenty-four hours times seven days times five weeks is eight hundred and forty kilometres), putting us way behind, even without factoring in the extra distance and the fact that the final route of the Pipe would be inaccessible, unmaintainable and indefensible.

Piper 90 is going through that village, one way or another. And since Piper 90 is a large heavy thing made of steel, and it is wider than the whole of the town, that pretty much means the village will cease to exist.

The Advisory Panel is asked if there's any way around this. Hellen Fust comes all the way down from a meeting in the top level. She asks, politely, if anyone has a remedy for the situation. She asks most particularly of Zaher Bey. He doesn't answer. He just sits and glowers from beneath his brows, and contemplates her as if she is a moderately noxious insect.

"I don't see any alternative," Hellen Fust says.

"It's very upsetting," Hellen Fust says.

"If there were a more *holistically appealing* way of dealing with the situation which was satisfying to everyone, I'd be the first to advocate it," Hellen Fust says.

"But without that I'm going to have to recommend that we continue as planned, and inform these people—with regret—that we're going to have to *relocate* them," Hellen Fust says.

"You mean we should just roll right on over their homes," Zaher Bey says abruptly. Hellen Fust looks at him as if he's being insufferably rude. The Bey looks across at me. His dark, angry eyes rest on mine. I look away.

Huster could not have solved this either, I am telling myself. He would have had to make the same choice, although maybe he could have persuaded those people it was for the best. Perhaps the difference, in the end, is that Hellen Fust does not go out to the village to tell the inhabitants what is going to happen. She sends us instead.

"I APPRECIATE you've had some bad experiences," Gonzo says persuasively. "A lot of people have. But we're here to make it all okay again. You don't have to be afraid. We'll take care of you."

"We don't need taking care of," says the woman behind the grille patiently. "We can take care of ourselves. We are alive, after all."

Gonzo is soft-pedalling. He wants to make this their choice, so that he doesn't have to be a stormtrooper. It's not working for him. Perhaps the woman—her name is Dina—perhaps she is used to smooth-talking men at her door. Or perhaps she can hear in Gonzo's voice the tension and the regret, and she's torturing him a little before giving in to the inevitable. Gonzo waves me over. *Take charge,* he is saying, and more quietly, *do the deed.*

Because my honour is negotiable, and his is not.

I take his place in front of the grille.

"Hi," Dina says chirpily. I smile at her. I sit down on the ground and look up at the doors, and she has to stand on tiptoe (I know this because I can see her eyes drop out of sight and then hop back into view as she looks for me again) to see me.

"Your houses look pretty solid," I say after a bit.

"Yes. They are."

"Taken a beating too."

"They have."

"What kind of thing?"

"Lots of kinds."

I was hoping to get more out of that line of questioning, to be honest. After a second or two of silence, Dina continues.

"Shark things. With legs."

"Nasty."

"Very."

"And some soldiers."

"Real ones?"

Dina sighs.

"Mostly, it's been desperate people. They see what we have and they think they can just have it. We show them otherwise."

"Yeah. I'm sure." Just as I'm sure they can't stop Piper 90, when it comes. The stone I'm sitting on is quite comfy. I shuffle on it, using the roughness to scratch an itch on my leg.

"We wondered, when you came, whether you were real. Or whether you were new."

"New?"

"Made. It's what we call the people who weren't born, who were just made up or who are split in half so that there's two of them. Or more."

"More?"

"There was an old man from over in Gondry turned out to have four whole people running around in his head. One of 'em was a dangerous bastard. Others were just scared. We call that kind of person *new.*"

"Have you seen a lot of them?"

"Yes, I would say that we have."

"We've seen only a few."

"How did that go?"

So I tell her about Pascal Timbery and Larry Tusk's dog, and the fear.

"But you'd be safe from all of that, with us."

"So you say."

There's a pause.

"I know this region pretty well," Dina says. "I was thinking about it last night."

Oh crap.

"You can't go south, because of the water."

"No."

"And I guess you could go north. But it would be hard."

"Not impossible."

"Really?"

"Probably."

"But the truth is, you're coming through my town. Aren't you?"

"*I*'m not. I mean, if it happens, I'll be there. But I'm not . . ." I'm not the one who wants to roll on over you. I just deliver her messages. "You'll be safe. It'll be all right. Better. We really are doing a good thing."

"Oh," says the woman behind the grille, and her voice sounds sort of strange and weak, which is normal for persons being rescued and fills us all with a kind of relief, but also sort of lost, which isn't and doesn't. "Oh well. In that case, if you promise we'll be safe?"

"I do," I say. And when that isn't enough for her, I say the words, slowly and out loud, so everyone can hear. She sighs again.

"Then come on in."

And she opens the door.

We walk into the village and I know something—everything—is more wrong than right. Dina is small and spry and somewhere between thirty and sixty, with greyish hair tied back like a hippie's. Around her there are men and women in all shapes and sizes, in all kinds of clothes scavenged and pieced together. Over by the fence there's a huge man like an ape, with a bearskin around his waist and a bristling beard. His eyes are sharp and dangerous, and he stares at me all the way until I pass behind a wall. Without a word, Dina turns and leads us through the narrow streets, under the watchful eyes of the people on the rooftops, and into the main square. And that is where the wrong becomes clear. Gonzo stares. Samuel P. lifts his hands and leaves his gun very well alone. Sally Culpepper steps just a little closer to Jim, and Jim doesn't do a damn thing, just stands there and waits to see what will break.

"You promised," the woman reminds me, and yes, I did.

Tobemory Trent turns his head to take in the whole thing,

and then he steps with his left foot turned out, and lets his body carry him all the way around. One step, two, three, four. Back to where he began. His gaze takes in the men and women around us, and the children, and then it flicks over them to the others huddled in doorways and peering from around corners: the strange haunted eyes and the curious hands and all the other little things like scales and fur—these are dream people, fake people, people made real from someone's thoughts. Reification people. They are the *new.*

Oh crap.

"How many of you are there?" I ask at last.

"One thousand and eight," she says.

"And how many of those . . . ," I begin, staring at Dina. She pushes her hair back from her ears. They have little points, like an elf's. "How many of you are . . . *new*?"

"All of us," she says.

Crap-a-doodle-do.

ZAHER BEY is thumping the table. I have never seen him so angry. I have never really seen him angry at all. To whatever extent I have considered it, I have imagined that his anger would be cool and sophisticated, possibly barbed. It would be witty, trenchant and terribly effective. It is none of these things. His hand, with round fingers and very pink nails, hits the tabletop again. Hits it very hard. The coffee cups are jumping a little and the noise he is producing with each impact is a sort of bone-deep *BUH!* rather than the soft *pmf!* which people use for emphasis, or the *toctoctoc!* you sometimes hear when a Teutonic public speaker wants to call the room to order.

BUH! BUH! BUH! (And *sscluttertinkledonkdonk!*—that's the coffee cups.)

It's not a noise of debate. It's a sound of fury. It's what you get when you horrify someone.

Hellen Fust convened the council as soon as she heard my

report, and she and Ricardo van Meents are sitting at the top of the table in a shiny new executive meeting room. It is a very grown-up place. It makes you feel very professional, very wise and very realistic. In this room you can't cavil at necessity. It has ugly prints on the wall and coffee from a Thermos, but the Thermos isn't a solid, portable one with smooth sides; it is got up to look like a classic coffee jug. I went to pour myself some, and got scalded as the hot coffee squirted in a thin stream at right angles to the lip. Hellen Fust took it away from me and unscrewed the lid, turning it a couple of times so that the little arrow on top pointed straight ahead. She gave it back to me. The coffee came out in a broad gush, due north. I felt like an idiot. And then they started.

"I think we can all agree that this is a very significant moment," Ricardo van Meents said, fingers flat on the table like a frog's. He rolled his thumb against the reflective surface, making a print, then scuffed at it with his sleeve. He didn't say anything else. Hellen Fust nodded. And then she began to speak, although it didn't feel like a speech. It was a series of things which had to be said before a thing is done, like the last rites before the hangman's trapdoor opens. It was an execution.

Hellen Fust used what might be thought of as the basic five-step text for announcing an act of atrocity; she didn't embellish or call on anyone's patriotism, and she didn't spew invective at the enemy or froth at the mouth. She was actually very reasonable. It was just that once you followed her reasoning all the way to the end, you found youself somewhere you didn't want to be. It went like this:

1) She told us who we were and who she was. She regretted that the responsibility for this situation was hers, and she thanked us for seeking to lighten her burden. She admitted that she was tempted, but averred that in the end, command is not shared. *Translation: this is not your decision.*

2) She reminded us of the exigencies placed upon her, and upon us, by the terrible situation in which we found ourselves. She recalled to our minds the dreadful fact that the population of the world was a fraction of what it should have been. The trust of the remnant population—of all our loved ones far away—was vested in us. *Translation: no one has the right to shirk what must be done.*
3) She pointed out very gently that the villagers were not human. They were, by their own admission, *new.* They were consequences of the Go Away War, with strange powers and strange appetites which could not be detected or guarded against. They were not safe. And if they should infiltrate us, it was not clear whether this would jeopardise our survival as a species—could they breed with humans? Would they try?—but the risk was very high and the consequences appalling. The precautionary principle must be applied. In this, we stood at the gateway of our race, and we must close the door. *Translation: these people are not people. They are un-people. Worse, they are pretend people. They will come for us, if once we trust them, and we will be destroyed.*
4) She hung her head and allowed sorrowfully that this upset her personally very much. She had a PhD in sociology and was well aware of the perilous antecedents of such announcements. And yet, here she stood. She accepted the difficulty of the situation, and she believed that the majority of people—real people—would feel the same way as she did. Of course, that could not be allowed. The panic which would ensue at the notion of a colony of unreal people would be awful. This must remain a secret, for now. *Translation: if they knew what we were doing, they would thank us out there. We keep it from them so that they may rest easy. We have the backing of the people, even if they do not know it.*

5) She hoped that in future times, when this moment was discussed, it would be seen as a necessary sacrifice for the good of all, and she enjoined us to see it that way even now. We were fighting to survive. They were—however friendly they might seem—the enemy. *Translation: if, which is denied, what we do now is wrong, history will understand it as a wrong chosen* in extremis *to prevent a greater, and God bless us, every one.*

And then she said, quite simply, that the village was to be razed, and the inhabitants taken into custody for study. Given the nature of the settlement and those who lived there, however, resistance of any kind should be treated as extreme hostility. Better safe than sorry.

And it was into the silence following this pronouncement that the noise of Zaher Bey's strong, soft palm striking the table came clamouring like an ambulance bell. He has continued to thump the table with greater and greater emphasis for some moments, and now, finally, he boils over into words:

"No, no, *no, no, NO*!"

His face is suffused, and his chin is tight with fury. Having captured the podium by main force, he holds it by erudition and outrage. He begins by cataloguing all the instances of mass murder and genocide he can think of, all the atrocities in the name of necessity that he can come up with. And then, into the silence this generates (because these events demand silence, in acknowledgement) he starts to throw personal abuse at evil-doers in general and Fust and van Meents in particular. They are roaches. They are parasites. They choose to crawl when they should cry out for their humanity, beg for a breath of life to make them whole. They are weak. They are wretched. May they be forgiven for countenancing the return of this kind of monstrosity into the world; may they be forgiven by some god or other, because that same deity will be well aware that such pardons will not be forthcoming from Zaher Bey (ibn Solomon ibn Hassan al-Barqooq, of the lake of Addeh and the mountains called Katir, most precious of lands and mother of peace). Then he turns on me.

"And you!" the Bey says, finger shaking. "You of all people! We took you in, didn't we? When you needed a place to hide, to shelter? And you were our enemy. But we took you in. So now—and by your own admission you promised these people—*people*—that they would be safe—you're prepared to let them die, kill them yourself, because you haven't decided yet whether they're real or not. Of course they're real! And you made a promise! So what's it worth?" And he throws a wad of paper at me, and we watch as the leaves tumble and drop to the ground. "Nothing!" says the Bey. And he stalks to the window and looks out.

In the silence which follows I think about that. And then I find that I am speaking. My voice is low, but it carries.

"He's right," I say.

I am standing. Everyone is looking at me. It is one of those moments, like the one in Crispin Hoare's study, where I seem to have any number of options but in fact there is only one. I could, for example, stop there and slide back into the shadows. I could try to calm the Bey, build a bridge between the parties—something which would ultimately play into the hands of Fust and van Meents. But the Bey is right. This is bad. It is a clear, horrible thing and it is wrong. I don't know whether the people of the Found Thousand (which is what we have been calling them to one another; Hellen Fust won't say it because un-people can't have names) can be at peace with us. I don't know what they're really like—whether we're going to discover that they all live exclusively on a diet of small children with a dash of puppy juice (if they do, maybe we can find a baby substitute; as to puppies, I like them, but if the price of avoiding genocide is a hundred or so puppies a year going into a kind of monster version of Tabasco, I'm good with that). What I do know is that I won't be a part of this. I have discovered a line in myself which I am unwilling to cross, and therefore to my own great surprise, I rip the Piper 90 badge from my shoulder and toss it onto the table. Hellen Fust starts to say something. I hold out my hand to cut her off.

"I quit," I say. "This is wrong. *Fuck you* for thinking that it isn't, and *fuck you slowly* for asking me to do it. This is not how you make a safe world. This is what got us here in the first place." I look across the room at Zaher Bey, and see in his eyes a fine, bright hope and a moment of pride. I nod, and he nods back. Well, yeah. Damn right.

And I walk out, thinking that Leah will understand and that I'm *so* unemployed and that it's going to be a very lonely walk home. Until I hear a strange noise behind me, a *pitterpatter* as of ducks in anger, and I realise that Jim, and Sally, and Tobemory Trent have all also torn the badges off, and Gonzo is here, and we are all walking out together. And as the word spreads, so does the sound of fabric ripping and voices raised in discontent, and by the end of the day everyone in our gang has quit, along with a whole bunch of other people, and everyone in Piper 90 is on strike.

It is a mystery of human mathematics that—however you may transect a population, whether you decimate it or cut it clean in half, whether you pick out the obvious troublemakers or collect at random some fraction of the whole—once you have set apart your chosen group, you will find among them at least two persons of otherwise gentle and accommodating mien who know in their blood and bones how to organise a strike. You need only cry the words "Aaaaaaaallll OUT!" on the factory floor and lead with confidence, and by the time you reach the outer gate there will be a woman from catering marching beside you leading the chant ("Two, four, six, *eight*! Down with prej'dice, down with *hate*! What is it that we won't a-*bide*? Comp'ny men and *gen-o-cide*!") and a milk-faced bloke in a knitted jumper handing out placards and telling the pickets where to stand to cause maximum disruption. By the time you get to the Club Room (*ex officio* HQ of the Piper 90 Strike Committee) there's an open meeting ready to go, and milk-face has collated your grievances into an agenda and drafted a motion.

Baptiste Vasille and his boys have shown up to provide security—apparently they have done a certain amount of counter-strike work in the past, very much against their personal political convictions, he informs us stoutly, but one must make a crust, to be sure, and please put this hat on so that you're less obvious, it's always the figureheads we go after (pardon, *they* go after) first. Everyone from our old unit is here, and mutinous with it. The curious thing is that almost everyone feels ambivalent about the Found Thousand. Many people in this room are deeply suspicious of them—and they may be right. The point, as Tommy Lapland announces to a rapt audience of civilian refugees, is that we don't go out and annihilate people just because we don't trust them. That's how you tell the bad guys from the good guys. And finally Larry Tusk gets up on the stand (two packing cases roped together which until two hours ago were doing duty as a table) with Dora the dog in his arms, and clears his throat.

"I don't know much," Larry Tusk says, and then has to repeat it because he didn't have his megaphone on. "I say, I don't know much! I wasn't ever much for talking and I'm not now, either." Dora the dog snuffles at the megaphone, and there's a rousing cheer for the plucky canine comrade. "But you all know where I come from on this and what I did to Pascal Timbery." Larry Tusk lowers his head for a second. He liked Pascal Timbery. When he can remember Pascal without remembering cutting Dora from Pascal's insides, he misses him, and he's not ashamed to tell you that over a glass of something, if you care to listen. "Now, that's all well and good. It's done, and I can't promise I'd do different now. But the thing is," and he has to stop because there's another round of applause, "the *thing is,* what I did, I did on the spur of the moment. I came upon it all sudden-like, and I up and cut him open and saved Dora because she was all I had. I killed *my friend* because I was afraid and I was shocked and he was attacking something I loved. Well, that's one thing. But this here is another, and it's a whole *other* kind of a thing. What they're talking about is taking people—*people,* same as Pascal—and crushing their homes and handing them over to some science fellas likely the same as those who did all this in the first place—not that they didn't have all our help, and don't you forget it—because we're afraid. And I don't know about you," says Larry Tusk, "but I don't fancy being that person and I won't have it in my name. I won't be afraid half my life and ashamed the other half." And before he can sit down, Dora the dog yips sharply into the megaphone, and such a cheer goes up that the walls vibrate and Dora becomes overexcited and barks some more, and the motion is carried on a sea of indignation. Piper 90 will not give itself to this. Not today, not ever. No, no, no, no, no. Which ultimately is how all revolutions start.

I look around for Zaher Bey but cannot find him. This is his victory, as much as anyone's. But perhaps he and the Katiris are having their own celebration, or perhaps they are working. But the open meeting is turning into a party (no one has work tomorrow), and on my shoulder there is a cool hand, and on my cheek a kiss. Leah is with me, and she is proud. I can do anything.

IT TAKES Fust and van Meents thirty hours to get a bastard squad in from elsewhere. We block them and obstruct them, we stand in front of them and make them crawl ahead of Piper 90. We will not start the fighting, if there's going to be fighting. There is a red line on our map at the edge of the forest. If they try to come past us there, this will get bad. I take Leah's hand on one side, and Annie the Ox's on the other. We are the human chain. We will not break. We will stand, and if they want to come through, they must come through us. In fact, our pacifism is called somewhat into question by Vasille's concealed tank and selection of small explosive devices we have been scattering in our wake. The strike committee is very much in favour of non-violent resolution, but there are problems with pacifism in a situation where the soldiers of the enemy are being launched upon a particular, short-duration task. They can roll over you and apologise later, when the deed is done. Passive resistance is a long-term game of sacrifice, and it works against humans, not machines.

The lead bastard is a hundred yards away from us and coming on strong when Tobemory Trent emerges from the forest with a jaunty smile upon his face.

"Let'em through," he says.

We stare at him. Trent can barely contain his laughter.

"Seriously. Let'em through. It'll be fine." And so we do. We turn and walk towards the village in tandem with its putative destroyers. When we reach the pickets, we get the joke.

In the main square and everywhere there are traces. There are signs of heavy trunks being dragged and wheels spinning. Rubber has been laid by squealing tyres. A wide dirty track has been created at the back of the village, leading out and away into the unreal world beyond, where we will not go. It is all very familiar. This place has been evacuated by an army in small city cars, perfectly coordinated and swift. In my mind's eye I can see the riot of colour, the deep burgundy of the Rolls-Royce amid the Subarus and Skodas, and the cheerful singing of the pirates and their leader as they steal the Found Thousand from under the eyes of the system. Fust and van Meents stamp furiously through the wreckage. They are looking for something to persecute or yell at. It's not rational, but it's predictable. Most people would do the same.

"In there," says Hellen Fust, "I heard something." Ricardo van Meents, for some reason wearing desert camo, marches into the house.

The scene is weirdly familiar. I consider it: an armed force in fruitless pursuit of the Bey and his scoundrels. Searching an empty house. An old scar on my scalp is itching. *Oh.* I watch Ricardo van Meents with something approaching sympathy. Visible inside the doorway for a moment, just under the lintel: a flicker of angry, bottlebrush tail. Van Meents doesn't notice.

I close my eyes for a moment and count to three. I wait until I hear the sound of an expensive executive screaming as a sexually frustrated, rabid cat falls on him from above. I wonder briefly whether it is the same cat, imported for this purpose. And then I start to laugh.

Ricardo van Meents comes running out, wearing on his head a furious feral tom with one ear and no nose to speak of. Hellen Fust glares at me, then stalks after him. I am so fired. But since I quit anyway, that's hardly a problem.

That night we pack our things and leave Piper 90. We roll back along the Pipe, sleeping in our cars. We just keep going for days through the patchwork landscape, along tributaries and back to the main Pipe, until we come at last to a noisome little bar on the edge of a collection of shacks masquerading as a town. A sign reads "Exmoor welcomes you." This seems unlikely. It is more probable that Exmoor doesn't like your face but has decided for the moment not to hit you with an axe handle. This place, at last, is somewhere we can stop and wonder what we have become.

We park up and stretch, and we stare around us at this ugly little place. There's a strong smell of pigs and a nasty-looking bar at one end of town. Sally Culpepper, who has in some measure understood for months that the end must come, and who understands further that with people like van Meents and Fust in charge there will always be a need for actual competence in the form of contractors, sits us in the saloon and puts the beers on the table and tells us that we are, as of now, the Haulage & HazMat Emergency Civil Freebooting Company, head office tbc, and we can call her "sir." And Jim Hepsobah lifts her up in his arms and then onto his shoulders, and we mourn our lost jobs by dancing on the pool table (amid a collection of alarming stains) and around this ghastly, nameless dive we're in, until the barman starts swearing at us with such depth and natural talent that we all stop to take note.

ZAHER BEY'S LETTER ARRIVES by means unknown and unimaginable, left resting against the door of the Nameless Bar along with a basket of weird-looking fruit and the first decent cheese I have seen since the Go Away War. The paper is rough, and the words perfectly formed. It is the handwriting of someone who has learned the Roman alphabet as a second script, and as a consequence makes his words reverently, like a visitor in a house with a pale carpet.

> *Dear Friends,*
> *My profoundest apologies for not saying a proper goodbye. Nq'ula was most adamant that our departure must come as a surprise so that the greatest possible time might elapse before pursuit could be fielded by those we must now regard as enemies. He begs me to convey that there was no lack of trust in this insistence, but that it was rather a gesture of respect for your honesty, and for your belief in the great project of which we were all a part: the creation of a better world. Even my people were ignorant of the full scope of our plan. I longed to discuss the matter with you, but dared not assume your complicity in deceiving those who must remain ignorant of my design. This posture deprived me of the opportunity for farewells which I wanted very much to make— and at the same time I could not hope to enlist you or*

to offer you the hospitality of my hearth, wherever it eventually may be. Rest assured, the House of the Bey will always open its doors to you.

The people of Addeh Katir and of the Found Thousand will now embark on a great adventure. We will strike out beyond the embrace of the Pipe, and we will see what can be achieved, and how we are changed, by living with a world which can reveal us to ourselves or assail us with our fears. The Found Thousand tell me it is not so hard. And surely it cannot be more dangerous than to exist within the compass of Jorgmund's grasp, and risk casual annihilation or disenfranchisement by faceless persons "up the line." I beg you to consider: "What is this thing called Jorgmund, and what may it become? What is its power, and the source of that power? What is my place in the pattern?" And if ever the answers should cease to please you, seek us out, and be assured of welcome.

Rao and Veda Tsur in particular have asked me to send their love, and with it I enclose my own, in the hope that you will not find it a hollow thing. More practically, I enclose also some of our better local produce, by way of a tiny bribe. The dairy is lost to us, of course, and it will be some time before the goats recover from their journey enough for us to milk them, but this is a taste of what we will achieve, and to what we aspire. Zaher ibn Solomon, of the family of Barqooq, will take pride in his people's cheese. I should think the Golden-Eared Bey may be spinning like a top in his vanished grave. On the other hand, I am now the leader of the only rebellion in the new world, which may serve to reduce the number of rotations per minute.

In anticipation of another meeting, I remain,
Your Friend,
Zaher ibn Solomon al-Barqooq Bey,
Freeman.

We ate the cheese, one mouthful each, and gorged on the fruit. We even shared some with Flynn the Barman, for which he swore an oath of eternal friendship in terms which made my hair stand on end. And then we put the letter away in a box behind the bar: the secret escape route, the last resort. Two weeks later Sally Culpepper's phone rang. Some mayor of somewhere had a spillage of something, and there were brigands on horseback.

We took the job. We did it well. We got another.

From then on it was just life; each single day is short, yet when you come to count them you find that time's strange process has forged them all together into years. We found places to live, we painted fences and front doors, and the seasons abraded the paint and we did it all again. Samuel P. proposed to Saphira one Christmas, and she turned him down. He tried again twelve months later and her uncle set the dogs on him. Tommy Lapland found a grey hair in his pubic region and rushed to the Nameless Bar to show us all, in the process exposing his legendarily ugly member and causing Tobemory Trent to remark that he'd never before been sorry to retain one eye. Sally Culpepper got sterner and more beautiful, and moved in with Jim. Baptiste Vasille built a greenhouse and made wine which tasted of ash and fishbones. We told him it was delicious and breathed a sigh of relief when he drank a great deal of the Premier Cru and reversed his tank over the vines. Annie the Ox started collecting puppet heads. She had a cat, a dog, a monkey and several bears. But her favourite was an elephant head with bent tusks made of hempcloth. On its face was a sad little smile, as if it missed the taffeta savannah and the rolling burlap grasses of home. We never asked what they meant to her, because some things were private, however weird and unsettling it was to see her set them out in a little head-huddle over her bed. So all in all we ate and drank and loved, and passed time living the ordinary lot of people doing people things, and then one day the Pipe caught fire and the lights went out in the Nameless Bar and Gonzo Lubitsch put his big new truck into gear for the first time.

Chapter Nine

Meet Mr. Pestle;
the miracle of fire;
an act of heroism.

THE NEW truck still smelled of plastic, but now it smelled of trucker as well: of too little sleep and a lot of coffee, of paying attention and hurrying. There was a feathery smear on the windscreen where the pigeon had bounced off the cab, and Gonzo had already spilled Flynn the Barman's espresso into the cupholder. Try as we might, though, we couldn't quite get rid of the smell of pig. It stuck to the seats and hung in the air, and from time to time you tasted it in passing if you were eating a piece of chocolate and were rash enough to open your mouth. Give us a few days of bad terrain and no showers, and this truck would be so entirely baptised in us that you couldn't imagine anyone else wanting to go near it, but that whisper of the wallow seemed as if it might be there for ever. I moved my feet along the dash, trying to jam my heels into the handle of the glove box, and they slipped. I lifted them back up and tried again. No good. Our old truck was just that little bit smaller, I could get purchase on the dash and wedge my spine into the seat, but this monster was more luxurious and I wasn't quite tall enough.

Drowned Cross was a day behind us, and for all my misgivings we'd come through the Border without as much as a single monster charging from the gloom or dropping out of a tree. The road had been empty from one end to the other. Once I saw a shadowy figure off to one side, and another time a bird or a bat flittered past the truck, but that was all. The route might as well have been cleared in advance. Even Bone Briskett seemed to feel we'd made good time, and he'd slackened his breakneck pace so that the drivers could breathe a little easier, and told us we were nearly there. Dick Washburn put his head out of the tank and pointed ahead down the road as if he were in command, and Bone's tank suddenly developed a mysterious gearbox problem which bounced him around and shook him up until he went back inside.

We came back into the solid world a little while later, and almost straight into Harrisburg, which was a no-fun town in a completely different way from Drowned Cross. It wasn't much of a burg and there had probably never been a Harris. It was a collection of little concrete boxes for people to be kept in while they were waiting to go on duty. You could see it in the bargain-basement architecture: those neat roads and regulation fences and heartless little prefabs, laid out as if they were a real town with shops and boutiques and cafes and a future, and not just a place of preparation and storage whose tomorrows were inevitably violent and sad. This town was a body bank; the adults were the current account and the kids were on deposit, just waiting to be spent at need.

Harrisburg's only reason to exist was on a muddy rise just beyond the tarmac square which served as the city centre: a big fat storage facility where they kept things no one who lived in Haviland City or New Paris would want to be anywhere near. Bone Briskett's tank rolled up to the gates, and a couple of guys in suits and standard-issue sunglasses came out and looked at him. Bone glowered back and gave them his ID. The standard-issue guys huddled. Bone growled, and the pencilneck popped up next to him and yipped, and they waved us through. The convoy peeled off to one side and we were escorted through to a vast, empty hangar with a lot of soldiers and standard-issue guys around it, and in the middle of this enormous space there were ten objects arranged in a ring. Each of them was a lash-up, a thing about seven feet tall and bolted together in a hurry.

Gonzo sucked air between his teeth.

Between the crossed arms of the standard-issue guys, we could see that each charge was made up of two big containment tanks yoked together. One tank was yellow, in a loud, friendly way which nonetheless was not reassuring. The other one was red, the kind of red which means it's best not to get near it rather than the kind which says come in and have a smoke and a fairy cake. The yellow tanks were marked with the word FOX. The red ones had hazard stamps on them, and STUFF in black. These things, put together the right way, make what you might term an idiot bomb. It makes a very large bang, but you have to be stupid to want one.

Gonzo jumped down out of the truck, and sauntered over to have a look. The standard-issue guys didn't like that, so there was a great deal of cock waving, which went like this:

Gonzo: So these are our babies?

Mr. Standard Issue: Step away from there, please, sir.

Gonzo: Gotta tell you, no one said anything about FOX . . .

Mr. Standard Issue: Step *away,* sir!

Gonzo: Ex-queeze me?

Mr. Standard Issue: We are required to keep the tanks secured. Sir.

Gonzo: Yeah, well, not from me. I'm the guy who—

Mr. Standard Issue: Yes, sir, also from you.

Gonzo: Uh . . . Sparky? This thing and I need to get to know one another, and you're in the way.

Mr. Standard Issue: My name is Lipton, sir.

Gonzo: Good. Well, Sparky, in a short while now I will be leaving with this appalling crap, and my friends and I will take it off somewhere and use it to do this thing which you may or may not be cleared to know about—

Mr. Standard Issue: (*tetchy*) I'm fully cleared for the mission, sir.

Gonzo: —but which you absolutely do not have the stones for. And the thing is that while you were still learning your ABC of exploding cigars, these people you see here were building the Jorgmund Pipe, and generally saving the arse of the planet . . .

Mr. Standard Issue: I'm aware of who these people are, sir.

Gonzo: And so the question is not whether you have yet had permission for me to approach that catastrophe of demolition over there, because that is the whole point of it existing. The question is whether you or any of these governmental *protozoa* is qualified to be anywhere near it. And the answer, unless you can show me a diploma or some relevant experience, is absolutely no fucking way. So step back, stand down and let the dog see the rabbit, okay?

Mr. Standard Issue: (*leaning close and lowering his voice*) Now you listen to me, you cowboy fuckstick. Mr. Pestle will be here in five minutes to release the goods to you. If you approach these tanks without clearance, I will drop the hammer on the remote detonator right now, as per my standing orders, and we will all end up as dust in the wind, which is seriously poetic but isn't how I expect you want to spend the rest of your day. So why don't you park your attitude in your oversized compensator back there and we'll all wait for the authorisation code, all right?

Gonzo: (*also leaning close and reaching into his coat*) What, this detonator?

Mr. Standard Issue: (*clutching at his left pocket*) How? Ungh! (*The word "ungh" should be taken to mean that Gonzo, by means of this deception and now armed with the location of the remote, has punched Mr. Standard Issue in the throat, gently enough that the guy's just really unhappy rather than dead, and abstracted the object in that pocket, which is a scary-looking slab of plastic with a red button on it.*)

Gonzo: (*whistling tunelessly as he wanders over to the nearest tank*) Hello, little lady! Ain't you a fine figure of a woman? (*Because for Gonzo, anything which may explode at any moment is clearly a girl.*)

Gonzo's massive testicular superiority thus established, he caressed the nearest bomb in a moderately obscene way, and the rest of us climbed out of our trucks and started figuring out how best to lift and stow them. The soldierboys had a forklift, but forklifts don't have a whole lot of suspension and there was no way you wanted these things jolting around. In the end we rigged a set of A-frame pulleys with turntable waists, and we lifted them with actual muscle and sweat so we would be able to feel anything going wrong before it happened.

Mr. Pestle made his appearance as we were loading up the last truck, and he did it with aplomb. He was a genial old gaffer with weightlifter's shoulders and a neat patch of silver wire on his head, and he was craggy with a man's experience. His shoes were two-tone leather like a gangster's in a movie, and they made little noises as he walked: *tink* for one and *tonk* for the other. He threw an arm around Gonzo, and slapped him thunderously on the shoulder with one gloved hand. He was letting us know he wasn't Dickwash, that he was the real thing; that he had the right to tell us what to do, and just maybe he did. There was a faint scar along one side of his face, by the hairline, which might have been shrapnel, certainly wasn't a facelift. Mr. Pestle had a voice like a town crier.

"I'm Pestle, call me Humbert! Pestle like mortar, mortar like in a wall! Ain't that ever a regrettable name? If my mother was alive, God rest her, I'd have her walk behind me and explain herself to every Jack and Jill—especially every Jill! Dead these many years, the old monster, and tongue-lashing the Almighty in heaven or the Devil in hell, depending on her ultimate destination. So you're the guy? Gonzo Lubitsch, man of action? And these here are your deputies! Ha! Ha? Cowboy joke, you're too young . . . And this lady must be Sally Culpepper, who handed Washburn his papery backside and won you people a contract I'd like a piece of myself? Richard"—and by this he meant the pencilneck, probably the name Dick belonged to some crusty upper-echelon SOB and so Dick Washburn was Richard to his superiors, because there can only ever be One True Dick—"neglected to mention you had legs like the Queen of Sheba. Poor dumb animal never stood a chance, did he? Ha!" And he wrapped an arm around Sally too, with a respectful nod to Jim Hepsobah, because Humbert Pestle was not a genial old gaffer at all, he was a silverback, a pencilneck *in excelsis,* and he could read a personnel file and play you like a tuppenny whistle. Pestle nodded to the standard-issue guys, then turned back to us, as a group.

"Ladies and Gentlemen of the Free Company, we have exactly no time at all. You are near as dammit on schedule and I mean for you to stay that way, so let's get this thing started before it's too late to do it at all. Unlikely though it may seem I have a few things to tell you which may actually help. When I was a young man," Humbert Pestle said, "we used to call it 'the Dope.'"

Maybe it was that one word which turned the trick: "the dope" is sniper slang for anything which helps you acquire and hit a given target. There was something about him too, a sniff of gunmetal beneath the fluff. Humbert Pestle gestured, and we trotted towards a pale green door in the far wall. He waited until the last of us was through before he came in himself.

BURNING FOX WAS A MOST fearsome thing. If it came into contact with live Stuff, it would ignite it instead of neutralising it, and that Stuff would ignite more Stuff, and pretty soon the unreal world would be on fire. And the unreal world was wrapped around the Livable Zone like the doughnut around the jam.

At the same time, FOX fire was very rare. You had to get it very hot, for a long time. So this could be an accident, but if so it was a particularly odd one, and if it wasn't then that was something else to watch out for.

Humbert Pestle leaned on the table at the front of the room. I noticed he'd taken off only one glove. It wasn't cold in the briefing room, but he was a respectable age. Or maybe he had a prosthetic, because he was careful with that hand, held it close to his chest as though it were fragile. He flicked on an overhead projector and there was a map, with lines of elevation and the clear, sharp boundaries of a cluster of buildings.

"This is the place. We call it Station 9," Pestle said. "It contains our major reserve of FOX and a small back-up FOX generating system. And this is the fire." He pulled a second layer of plastic down over the first, and a great, uneven patch of red swallowed the building, going orange over some storage huts and verging on yellow in the centre. "And this is the storm which is arriving in about twenty hours." And over the top he laid a pattern of pressure and wind which would fan the flames and lift anything escaping straight to the Border and beyond.

"Ladies and Gentlemen, please!" And when we looked at him, he said it again: "Please . . . Go down there and *put that fucker out.*" Humbert Pestle had lived a life. He knew how to swear and make it stick. And one by one we looked at him and nodded, and Jim Hepsobah looked at Sally, and she nodded too. *Yes, sir.*

Jim Hepsobah stepped up and talked about approaches, and Annie the Ox joined him like a maiden aunt talking tea and cake, but she was talking explosive yield and necessary detonation overlap and minimum functional vacuum. Conventional explosives wouldn't get the job done for burning FOX, hence the ten scary objects in our trucks outside. We'd set them in exactly the right place, detonate them in exactly the right sequence, and the blast would suck the air away from the fire and blow out the ordinary part of it, and the sudden combination of FOX and Stuff would do the same to the unconventional part. So all we had to be was brave, fast and perfect.

Okeydokey.

There were two serviceable roads, here and here, and we could have either of them or both of them to ourselves. And we had no time, none at all. Even without the storm winds coming, pressure in the Pipe was so low it was effectively offline in a great arc from Sallera to Brindleby, and there was word of a vanishing. It was unconfirmed but probable: a little place called Templeton, maybe three hundred people gone. Bad at any time, but very bad now because maybe the two were connected.

I'd been to Templeton twice—once on a job, and once with Leah for shopping, because Templeton was one of those rare places which traded with the people from the Border. It was right out on a finger of the Livable Zone, a valley spur which came off the Pipe and nestled in the crook of a lake. The borderliners came in their nimble cars and hefty 4 × 4s and traded unlikely fabrics and new spices. Risky living, to stay ahead of the Stuff and remain unchanged, and even more so, to come within reach of a town. If the folk there decided you were *new,* anything could happen. But now Templeton was gone, and you had to ask yourself whether maybe they'd had a little too much to do with the Border, and it had taken them. I shut my mouth very tight and tried not to feel sick at the idea of Templeton shucked from its shell and swallowed like Drowned Cross. Pestle drew his face down and a little bit of the old, cold bastard was briefly visible within; if Templeton *was* gone, then there was going to be a reckoning this time. You didn't come into his bit of the world and pillage and plunder and steal his people out from under him. He leaned forward again and rested both hands in fists on the table (the plump, naked one squashed around the fingers but held at the knuckle: *a little boxing at the alma mater, old fellow,* and the muscles under his jacket heaved a little; the prosthetic didn't give at all). He asked if there were any questions, and there weren't, that was all there was. He looked around the room, nodded to Gonzo, and walked out, his shoes making that weird little noise again, one going *tink,* the other one *tonk.* We looked after him, and Jim Hepsobah walked up to the front and growled.

"What the fuck are you all staring at? Is it your first dance? Bring back my company! Get in your suits, get in your trucks and *let's do this thing*!" And somehow that plugged us all back into ourselves, and we dived for our hazmat moonsuits and hit the trucks at speed and were gone in a rattle and a roar. I glanced in the mirror as we pulled out. Pestle was nowhere. The standard-issue guys were gone. Harrisburg was a ghost again, but just maybe, in the high window of a building by the gate, there was the shadow of a silverback.

I drove and Gonzo slept. Jim had chosen the southern route, and Bone Briskett's convoy moved us swiftly but cautiously along well-kept roads. No one wanted to risk a smash with ten makeshift FOX bombs in close proximity.

I wondered about Templeton, and whether it was possible what people said: that the vanishings were the *new* people, the Found Thousand showing their real face. I wondered about Zaher Bey—a most unlikely bogeyman—but I'd never been in his bad books. Only on his good side. If it was true; if the Bey was leading an army of vengeful horrors, then there was another war coming, and I would fight. Or maybe it was already here. Maybe the Found Thousand were just striking back. Who knew what we'd been doing, on the quiet and in the dark? Men of Gonzo's old profession slinking out beyond our fences to strike the enemy before they had the chance to become a threat.

I just couldn't see the Bey as a monster.

I wondered if that was because he was my friend, or had been.

I wondered that for three hours, and then Gonzo woke up to take his turn at the wheel. I stared at the unfamiliar ceiling of our new truck and wished for our old one, and worried some more until the sound of the road under us made me drowsy, and the little corner of the moon I could see through the window disappeared behind some clouds. I dozed, and in the patches of wakefulness when Gonzo braked a little harder or the wind played a higher note around the sheer edges of the cab, I thought about fire.

THE MIRACLE OF FIRE is that it dies. It is a chemical and sometimes an atomic reaction, the collapse and recombination of things at their most fundamental level. Without it, we could not exist, and yet if it persisted past the point where it wanes, nothing would survive. Thus, the saving grace of fire is that it has limits and can be extinguished.

At least, very small fires can be. Others, one must simply outlive. We are so proud of our mastery of the element; we unleashed the broken atom in 1945 and thought ourselves quite significant, but a bad forest fire will release in ten minutes all the energy which consumed Hiroshima, and produce heat four hundred times greater than our most sophisticated firefighting units can control. Fire was our first magic and our first science, and we have harnessed it hardly at all.

Like an empire, fire must expand. It consumes the land it stands on, so it cannot rest. Thus it can be contained in two dimensions, though not reliably in three. A firebreak of preemptively burned ground will cage a blaze, and eventually, if the job is done well, it will fade and expire like a lonely bear. Also, flames need oxygen and enough ambient heat to sustain ignition. This is the fireman's triad: drive away the air for long enough, cool the fuel and abate the heat and your job is done. And thus our plan: the blast from our explosives would kill the flames themselves, blow away the oxygen and then draw in cold air from all sides. The reaction would consume much of the fuel, so that—we believed—the whole process could not begin again. This was less like conventional firefighting than it was surgery.

I wondered how it would look, this FOX fire, and how it would smell. I asked myself how hot it would be, how long we would be able to operate, even in our suits. I wondered whether that heat would stop the bombs from working, or set them off too soon. I thought of a towering plume, a great, white jet roaring like a geyser from the ground, fed by barrels and buildings, sucking in more air and spreading, flashing over into stands of trees. I thought about blackened grass and smoking soil, and the layered nature of fire: first, the clear gases which are not yet burning, which roost below the flame; then the thin bright line above it where those gases catch; and finally the incandescent cone which reaches up and out, orange or white or green, depending on all the badness in the mix.

And then I realised I was not dreaming. I was simply looking, staring, through the glass at the thing itself.

Station 9 was a circle of buildings like a hill fort, and once upon a time they'd been all sleek and *we're-in-control,* towers and domes and cylinders. Now, though, they were the stamen of a thick, many-petalled flower, grey and magnesium-white and blazing. Even this far out, I could feel the heat through the windscreen. The temperature around the main storage area was reaching levels it really didn't oughta, and the whole thing would shortly melt, tear and sluice down into itself. Little leaves of dirty fire were twisting away into the sky. If those leaves carried to the Border—and the wind was coming up, blowing that way even now—then we'd have failed, and more than failed.

Half a mile from Station 9 there was a broad circle of road, a turning place, with a patch of smoking grass in the middle. Bone Briskett stopped off to one side with his tank pointed at the fire as if he wanted to shoot it. We lined up the trucks in a row, facing the enemy. Five target zones on the edge of the blaze; ten primary trucks, each with a bomb and paired so that one could go wrong and the pattern wouldn't be upset; and ten more trucks in support, filled with lifting gear, decon chambers and medical bays and additional moonsuits. The suits are good for five hundred degrees—for a while, anyway—but the radios don't work in heat like that for very long, and the days of GPS came to an end on the first day of the Go Away War. There were triangulation towers around Station 9 which would tell us where we were, but they needed line of sight to be reliable and we wouldn't have it, so we'd memorised where we had to be. Every single one of us can work from a map with nothing more than a memory and the ground beneath his feet, or hers. This is what we do. We stared at the fire and waited for the word.

All around us, Bone Briskett's soldiers waited too, in suits of their own, most likely wishing for a stand-up fight over this, any day. Humbert Pestle had decreed that we should have our escort all the way to the edge of hell. *No harm in being safe,* he'd said, and *it only takes a few people to save the world, but it never hurts to have some guys on hand to carry them out afterwards.* You couldn't argue with him; he just smiled and did what he did, and you felt better for knowing he was there. I looked at the soldiers closest to me and wondered if they'd lied about their ages to enlist.

The growl of the engines was too quiet to hear over the noise of the fire.

"Hoods," said Jim Hepsobah over the radio, and we checked our masks and suit seals.

"Locations," Jim said, and we sounded off where we were going.

"Deploy in two minutes. Time to detonation, twelve hundred seconds from the go," Sally Culpepper said. And we waited.

Twelve hundred seconds. Three hundred to enter and reach the target area. Six hundred to set and secure the bomb. Three hundred to get out again and reach safe distance. No radio detonators because they might be triggered by interference on the site. I checked my suit again. It was big and ungainly and made of impermeable fabric and some kind of metallic sheath. It had a coolant layer, and when you switched it on it filled with air. You could stand in a gas cloud and puncture the suit, and the air would flow out rather than in for long enough to keep you alive. No one had ever tried it with Stuff, because no one wanted to be the first.

"One minute," Sally Culpepper said.

Gonzo looked at me and grinned through his faceplate. We were going through the middle with Jim and Sally, setting the bomb closest to the blaze. The most dangerous, the most important.

Gonzo's favourite thing. And then at some point Sally Culpepper said "Go" because everyone surged forward at once.

We ploughed in. Bone Briskett charged his tank through the main gates, and they *spanged* and *popped* and his tracks crushed them, bent them flat. Tobemory Trent and Annie the Ox went off to one side, and Samuel P. and Brightwater Fisk spun off to the other. Gonzo and I and Jim and Sally (first in, last out, no matter where and what) rolled over the busted gates, and our tyres chewed them apart, because they were heated up and soft, and we headed for our target. We were going inside the secondary depot of Station 9, just this side of the main holding area, which was currently holding the flames like a crucible—but not for long. We roared the trucks right in across the executive parking lot and the yellow and black tarmac which said ACCESS ONLY, and then through the red trapezium reading RESTRICTED, and the paint on the bonnet started to blister. Then we crashed through the corrugated doors and into the depot, and it was like coming in out of the sun. The depot was filled with vapours and heat shimmer, but it wasn't as hot as outside. Two loads of Bone Briskett's men hurtled in after us and spread out to the sides.

Jim Hepsobah half swung, half jack-knifed his truck in a slewing turn which brought his bomb as close as could be to the X (there was no actual X) and stopped, leaving a trail of rubber on the floor and saving us twenty seconds. We stepped out into a hot, bad place. Bone's boys, looking like wasps in their armoured military suits, went out around us in a circle, like anyone would be crazy enough to attack us now, while we were doing this. They had big, special-manufacture guns which would work in these conditions, flanged and water-cooled and stacked with ammunition which would kill a man but leave a FOX tank unharmed. Probably.

Off to one side there was a row of black boxes, man-high and bound up in a tangle of hoses. *FOX generator, back-up, one.* Nothing to say how it worked. No magic wands or fairies flitting around it, no choirs of angels. If anything, it was sinister, like a row of six coffins linked together for a mass embalming. No lights on: good. If the thing isn't running, there's no danger of it feeding the blaze. We can just blow it away. One problem the less, and high time we caught a break.

The ground was thrumming. The whole structure was vibrating with the sheer power of what was going on on the other side of the wall. Twenty feet to the crucible. Seven feet through the crucible to the flames and the more-than-flames. Thirty feet from the most destructive force in the world, held in by a crumbling cup of not-very-strong stone and dust. No time to screw around then. Hoist, pulleys: Jim Hepsobah took the strain, and Sally steered with nimble arms, and all of us heard one another's grunting over the radios, but that was all—no chatter, no questions. We knew the job; we knew one another. Conversation meant misunderstanding.

"Position set," Sally said, because it was. Time: four minutes fifty seconds and counting. Fastest ever, anywhere, by anyone. Jim Hepsobah stepped forward to adjust dials and set the timer, and then something went *plink.* I turned to see what it was, and I saw, and I felt the world turn to ice.

There was a man in here with us. A slender, ordinary man in black, almost priestly—or monkish perhaps. He was sweating, because it was way too hot in here for a human being. At around forty degrees, the human brain starts to flake out. Core body temperature can go up only a couple of degrees before you forget what's going on and start to die. This guy was not starting to die. He had not lost his concentration. He looked, if anything, slightly bored. In one hand he carried a length of chain with a hook on the end. He was about five eleven, had some Asian ancestry somewhere and his arms and legs were loose like a marionette's. He had a really posey little moustache, two half-inch barbs like the bad guy in a black-and-white film. He bowed.

"Good evening," said the moustache guy. "My presence here is a regrettable necessity. This will be over soon." And with that cursory introduction, he started killing Bone's boys.

Now understand, Bone's boys were not a bunch of slacker kids with guns. They were not just standing around waiting for Mr. Moustache to sink his hook-and-chain arrangement into their soft parts. They were armoured soldiers with modern weapons, some of the best troops the world had to offer. They fought. They took positions, created a kill zone, found firing solutions. A triangle-base volume of air (a pentahedron; you don't see many of those) maybe six feet in height became instantly uninhabitable. When he slipped past that, they dumped the guns and went hand to hand with carbon-fibre batons and ceramic knives. They were young and fast and strong, and they knew how to fight without getting in each other's way. There was a lot of karate and some Silat and the occasional bit of Iaijutsu going on, and none of it was amateur. Bone's boys were good. They were so good, they very nearly slowed him down.

Moustache stepped through them, fluid and measured. He was not particularly quick. He was simply exactly where he wanted to be. By the time they had compensated for one movement, he had made another. Contrary to popular wisdom, it was almost exactly *not* like a dance. A dancer works with rhythm and display. The body moves as a series of separate parts, finding beauty in harmony. A dancer wants to express something rather than conceal it. Moustache did none of these things. He did not move his body extraneously, or any part of it in isolation, and he was not showy. He killed without suddenness or excess force. He stabbed you just enough to make you die, not enough to get his hook caught up on your ribs or your spine. He killed ergonomically, so that later, when he was reporting to his evil moustache boss, he would not have an uncomfortable twinge in his shoulders, would not have to go to the evil moustache doctor and ask for some time off to get rid of his RSI. And occasionally, when he wasn't quite perfect, his chain-and hook weapon went *plink*. It was the only energy he wasted.

In my ear Jim Hepsobah was broadcasting while he worked, *Hostile, say again, hostile! We are under attack!* But the interference from the fire was bad, and only broken phrases came back. The others were either setting their explosives or fighting for their lives, maybe both. It mattered, but it wasn't relevant. We had our own job to do.

Moustache removed the hook from some kid whose name I never had time to ask, and stepped towards us.

Gonzo went to meet him.

Things happened.

I had never seen Gonzo fight at full stretch. I had never realised how scary my best friend was. Gonzo stepped towards Moustache, moving in a straight line (hard forms; closest distance between two points, close with the target and strike, and keep doing it) and scooping up a short steel bar along the way. Encumbered by the suit, Gonzo was not as graceful as Moustache. He moved like an ice shelf. Moustache stopped. He didn't like what he was seeing. And then he slid forward into a new stance, and the hook started to move around his body on its chain. *Whirr, whirr, whupp.* And again.

Gonzo was at full speed when he hit Moustache's blurring shield. His steel bar caught the hook perfectly and he wrenched back on it, hard and unsubtle, which was not what Moustache was expecting. Moustache had a choice: follow the wrench and risk grappling, or release the weapon and take the opportunity to strike. He must not have fancied grappling with a big man in a flabby suit, because he chose the second option. The hook spun away, and Moustache launched a hand high, twisted, slammed Gonzo with a foot like a rivet gun, *kerchunk!,* then stepped back along a different line so that Gonzo's blinding riposte with the bar blurred through empty air. So. One up to Gonzo, but not for nothing.

Moustache came back in, which proved to be a mistake because Gonzo was waiting for it. The bar slammed into his chest, and something broke. Moustache rolled out, taking Gonzo's leg on the way, a single shot to the muscle of the calf which must have deadened it, because Gonzo staggered and had to hop to regain his balance. Moustache scuttled over to his right and scooped up his hook again, and instead of going after Gonzo, he came after us. Specifically, he came after the FOX bomb. His hand whipped out and flicked once, twice, like a man fly-fishing, and the hook sailed over my head and into the machinery of the bomb. It sliced through a hose, and hit the gubbins and gaskets. It stuck. Moustache pulled, and it came free. Something went *plink.* It wasn't the hook. It was the bomb. As Moustache reeled in his weapon, something sprang after it: a length of tubing and some bits of metal. *Plink.*

Through the terrible howl of fire only thirty feet away; through the suits; through testosterone and fear and my own breathing, I heard that damn thing break, and I moved. I moved, and Gonzo moved with me, perfect mirrors. I lunged for the loose, flapping conduit, the magnetised metallic gooseneck which was connected to the Stuff tank on the bomb. I lunged, and I got it. And Gonzo, more human, less sensible, shunted Jim Hepsobah out of the way, so that both of us were dead centre of the target when the thing happened, and all the best-laid plans went thoroughly agley and the situation was, as Ronnie Cheung would have said, bollocksed from here to Buddha's colon.

Above us, the valve on the Stuff tank shattered. The Stuff inside raced down the magnetic tube and flooded out. We stood, together, under the waterfall, and who knew what was happening? The Stuff was interacting with us, bonding with us, doing whatever it did, and I'd have horns and a tail and Leah would never kiss me again. But there was no time. Five minutes exactly, and so we had five more to rig the back-up and not let everyone down, and that's what I shouted into my radio as I spun out of the stream and raced for our truck. Moustache stared. Maybe evil moustache men didn't have friends who'd do that for them, or maybe he hadn't imagined that anyone who wasn't an evil moustache man would accept falling through a stream of Stuff and carry on with their mission. Whatever—Moustache was distracted. Almost absent-mindedly, Gonzo bowled the steel bar through the air, and Moustache clocked it about a half a beat too late. It sank a few inches into his temple, and he fell straight over onto his back. He didn't even shudder, he was just gone. Don't care. Not important.

I reached the doors of our truck and hauled them open, then glanced over my shoulder. Gonzo was staring at me through his visor, and he seemed to be all right. Maybe the suits had kept us safe, maybe the presence of so much leaky FOX had made it all okay, neutralised it. Maybe all that time on Piper 90 had made us immune. And maybe there was a special retirement farm for old dogs where all the rabbits were too fat to run away and an eccentric millionaire hired professional masseurs to stroke them every evening in front of a log fire. Jim Hepsobah wasn't moving and neither was Sally Culpepper. They were all petrified. Oh, bloody hell, maybe they were *petrified.* I screamed at them, a rageful yawp full of command and desperation.

"Four minutes and twenty seconds and then we're fucked. I don't care if I have got fucking horns and a tail, do this and you can cut them off me, but stop standing there like a fucking bikini parade and move the bloody bomb!" I had become Ronnie, but Gonzo at least was hit between the eyes by it, moved alongside me in a heartbeat, and he almost lifted the damn bomb without the hoist. Then Jim and Sally were there and we had three minutes and that's impossible, but we were doing it. We were over target but under deadline—we knew that because we were alive. And staying that way, yes. We didn't have time to stop and pick up the wounded, but thank God, Moustache wasn't the kind of guy who left any. Gonzo's suit had dissolved along one arm, and his skin must be burning, but he didn't slow. We fled.

"New bomb," Sally was saying. "New bomb in place! Evacuate *now,* repeat *now.* Confirm by solid tone *only,*" because each handset can send a single note for Morse or to test a channel, and seconds later it came back, a series of tones blending into a chord, and we knew they could hear us and they were alive. We set the timer for ninety seconds and jumped back in our trucks. At ninety seconds we were passing through the searing heat outside, and the tyres were actually skidding in the melted surface of the road. Eighty seconds, and we skidded over the gates and dragged a piece with us for a moment, and we could see the other trucks and the rest of Bone's boys way out ahead of us. The radio channel lit up with questions and demands: *What the fuck? What enemy? Jesus, put your foot down* and Jim Hepsobah like a minister: *Shut up and tell me it's done!* And it is. All charges set. One minute to detonation, and Gonzo nearly turned the truck over getting us around the curve of the hill.

We tucked in under the brow, twenty trucks and as many tanks and armoured vehicles, paint scorched and wheels melted, and we hid and hunkered down, and waited.

"Three seconds," Sally Culpepper said, and I was sure she was wrong.

Then the sky went white above us and I squeezed my eyes shut, and even so I could see the shadow of the hill against the white of the fields beyond, and the image of a steering wheel. The trucks shook and shuddered, and one of the tanks on the very outside of our huddle flipped over.

When we looked around the hill, Station 9 was gone, and in its place was a black, smoking ruin, and no fire.

Good feeling.

Chapter Ten

Homecoming;
some slight confusions regarding fidelity;
a new experience.

IT IS the day after, and the world is new. Everything is clear and crisp, and the colours are very bright. I am alive, and so is everyone I love. This simple fact amazes me, and makes me giggle, so that Gonzo, who is not a giggling sort of a person, pointedly ignores me as we drive along. I feel brand-new, washed and somehow reconnected. My memories and my present are all shook up and have fallen somehow the right way around. I am me. It's terribly exciting, and I giggle again.

Gonzo has sustained a minor (heroic) injury. I have none. Despite all the funny looks and the obvious concern, I am unscathed. I have not grown demonwings or turned green or become a monster. In fact, I suspect this very immunity is what is making everyone so nervous. I am the guy who took a gazillion volts through the palms of his hands, and they earthed in the soil at his feet without as much as making his hair stand on end. I am the woman who fell from a plane and walked away unscathed. It happens. Not often, not reliably and not when you want it to. But miracle escapes do take place, and I have had one. So, in truth, has Gonzo, although his arm is angry and bruised and burned, and his ribs are taped up and he looks like a thundercloud. Gonzo is always angry after being afraid, possibly to distract you.

So, a day of rest. By tacit agreement, Gonzo is taking me home.

Heaven's gates are getting on a bit, and the wood has peeled around the top. I painted them years ago in response to Leah's need for a white fence, but neither of us liked the effect, so we chipped and scraped the paint off and let the moss grow. Now, wind and sun and water have contributed to the mossy assault, and the remaining glossy white has rolled up and flaked. Shove the gates roughly and a little snowfall of dry paint tumbles to the ground. Gonzo batters them open with an accustomed hand, and they bounce to a halt in the rut left by previous shuntings, *winging* and *wanging* as the ripples of the impact exert torsion on their fabric and test their remaining strength. Sometime soon they will break, and I will have to get new gates. Perhaps I should buy new gates now, and leave them in the open for a while before I put them up so we never actually have new wood at this entrance.

Climbing back into the driving seat, Gonzo dances the cab through the narrow gate. It's actually delicate, what he does to sneak the thing between those posts without scraping the cab or knocking down my uprights. He sort of shimmies it through. He takes the long drive slowly, concentrating, and I know every bump. There's the twin dips first, rainwater puddles made worse by taking a car over them while they were wet. Then there's the channel, an iron watercourse set into the road and preceded by a drift of gravel. It makes a hump, and on the other side there's a dip where water flowing along the upper lip has washed away the soil. The whole thing produces a combined height differential of several inches. Gonzo takes the cab over it one wheel at a time, and we rock gently. After that, the puddles, the dip (where a dirt track from the old contruction days crosses the drive), the footsteps (which I will tell my children, when we have some, are the footsteps of giants, because they have grown in magnitude since I carried Leah through a rainstorm and lost my left boot to the suction) and the lintel, where a single slab of stone marks the entrance to our forecourt. Gonzo takes them all gently, preserving my history as well as ever I could.

Any moment now she will open the door. She will not fling it wide because boldness is sometimes rewarded with a travelling salesman or someone late and lost upon the road. Once it was a burglar, although that is a charitable description of the creature who approached her, a creepy, wheedling sociopath with more than theft on his mind and a sack of convictions for crimes murky and unpleasant; but Leah is not some troubled urban incapable. She can take care of herself, and she knocked him on his back and waited with him until the gendarmes came and carted him away.

So she will open the door just a crack, to be sure there's no disappointment in store. She will peer. She will see the truck, but it will be unfamiliar—something she already knew from the foreign engine noise and the sound of the tyres on the lane. So she will look through the tinted windscreen, and she will see us, or perhaps not until we open the doors. And then she will be unleashed, and throw wide the big front door and walk down, not quite scampering, to meet me. Arms about me, no deep kisses because the heart must be satisfied first, and her eyes will pick out any new scratches on me. I have been away for over a week. Leah is a member of the Free Company. Sometimes she rides out with the rest of us, medic and shift driver, but she hates to watch me in action, so often she works from the house, fielding calls and quartermastering. When we are separated, we count hours. When we are together, we never do. Tonight there will be drinking and celebration, and finally to bed, to hold and to have and to be had.

The porch light is on because it gets dark suddenly up here: the sun hits the mountain ridge behind us and a shadow rises from the valley, bringing on night like a blindfold. You don't realise, until you have lived somewhere where this happens, how long twilight is or how much of it relies on reflections from the landscape all around. No twilight here, to speak of—just a dusky glimmer off the peaks and the smell of trees in darkness. We got the place cheap because it's on the fringes of the Livable Zone. Look down the valley to the very end, and you can see into the Border and what lies beyond.

When the grateful nations—mayoralties by then, but they hadn't acknowledged yet how small they had become, and Jorgmund was barely born—were handing out space, they parcelled land according to a complicated system of pluses and minuses so that everyone could have a bit to call their own. Land in the city was at a premium, and you could just about get a share in a new apartment block with your allocation. My bonuses from the Pipe were pretty hefty, and if we hadn't needed a place to live we could have bought ourselves a plane or a diamond the size of your fist. But we did.

We looked at Tallacre Lofts, which was the sort of Boho of the new world, a long agglomerated mess of construction, quasi-random and intricate, designed to make a home in not very much room. Tallacre sites were typically on the edge of town but well inside the Livable Zone and so thought to be a safe, secure, inexpensive place to be. We walked around one: default beige and *lifestyled* interior (I have no idea what that means) and cream leather sofas, and you had to look hard before you could find the stitching where someone had reconstituted the hides of a lot of smallish sheep from the war zones. There was a built-in kitchen and a little balcony looking over New Paris (which was being built by a company from what had been Grand Cayman in the teeth of furious opposition from the French) and recessed lighting and a power shower. Everything matched, and the lines were cool and enduring. It was a great flat. Leah was weeping by the time we got in the car. She hated it so much she could barely move. Every muscle in her body was rock hard, and her hand gripped mine on the gear stick. The flat was mean and empty and it was a coffin waiting to bury her. She hated everyone who told her it was a good place; she wanted to burn it down, to make them swallow the damn couch.

I promised we would never have to live anywhere like that. I told the agent we'd get back to him. He urged me to be quick. I waited half an hour, then rang back and told him we had a better site in mind. I said it with a ringing certainty, and I heard him freeze, heard him wonder where the hell I was going and how could he get there too. Then I cradled the phone and held my wife as she shuddered, and wondered what the hell I was going to do now.

We lived on friends' sofas and in their lofts and woodsheds. We slept in the parking lot of the Nameless Bar and got so cold we nearly froze. And then, two weeks later, Jim Hepsobah walked me along a mountain a couple of hours out of Exmoor and told me he was building his place twenty miles further along the Pipe, but he'd had to toss a coin to decide. In the evenings you could see the storms beyond the Border, but that didn't worry Jim and he didn't reckon it'd worry me. We'd both been a lot closer than that. You couldn't see the Pipe running behind the escarpment at the back of the plot, pumping its good juju into the air all around. There was silence and dew, and birds. Probably badgers, Jim said, if you knew where to look. And then we sat there and didn't talk, and after a bit I borrowed his phone and called Leah, and she and Sally Culpepper came over from Jim's plot and Leah and I called the local guy and said this was ours, and he fell over himself trying to get it all done because no one wanted these old isolated places on the Pipe and the Border, not now, and maybe not ever again. So we got about a gazillion hectares or acres or whatever it is thrown in, useless and pretty and full of badgers. The house is part log cabin and part stone manse, and it's part Frank Lloyd Wright A-frame and part Bauhaus, and the gates are flaky. That's what heaven is. A place where none of that matters.

And now the door is opening a little, and now a lot, and then she comes out in a bustle and a swirl, and we are climbing out of the truck. But something is wrong, and more than wrong. She comes down the steps and across the forecourt, but her trajectory is off along the gravel, and when she takes flight, she lands squarely on Gonzo and clings to him, and stares into his eyes rather than mine. It is Gonzo she has missed, and Gonzo alone, and she glances over at me with moderate curiosity only when she has drunk him in and patted him in a familiar way and grabbed him along various dimensions to be sure it is all still there. Then, to my endless horror, she sticks out her hand as if we've never met. And I, idiot that I am, shake it, and Gonzo looks relieved and pats her on the hips, and she leads us into the house.

Gonzo is screwing my wife. More than that. He has stolen her love. It is in this weird and awful manner that I am learning of a long-running affair, a thing of months and years. I am being replaced. I *have* been.

I follow the lovebirds indoors, wondering why I don't want to kill them. I ought to want to. It is my genetic and cultural right—not to do it, but at least to feel the desire. Perhaps it is simply too enormous, and the affair itself too much an enormity, and I cannot see the edges of my anger because I am so far within. Perhaps, but seemingly not. Mostly what I feel is a desire to melt away and vanish, to un-be. I am a needless thing, and I am embarrassing only myself. Gonzo and Leah seem unbothered.

Inside, she has redecorated. It's odd. She has (understandably) removed all my things. They are probably in the garage, stuffed into a vagabond's kettle and a red hanky on a stick. She has replaced them, not with new, but with old. My comfy armchair, ragged and tumbledown and had from an artist's studio in Berlton, in which I used to sit and in which on more than one occasion we have made precarious love, has gone. In its place there is one of those weird wicker things which look infinitely more cosy than they are, which creak when you sit on them, and smell of grass in damp weather. Gonzo slumps into it and reaches, blind, for a pair of furry indoor boots which wait alongside. At some point they have been chewed by a dog, which is mysterious because we don't have one. But Gonzo does have one. A faithful hound comes lolloping in from elsewhere (a room which ought to be the kitchen, but it appears in fact to be a den, a plush Gonzo-space of spice and sandalwood, off-limits without special invitation to women of any kind).

In my mind I can see one home—mine—and with my eyes I see another. This corner is empty because the ghastly vase we put in it broke—but it's not empty. There is a set of shelves jammed into it, covered in old sporting trophies and yearbooks from the Soames School, all bound between hard covers to preserve them. Here there was a little occasional table (although it was really a perpetual table, in that we never moved it or thought about putting it away) on which were Leah's photographs from her nursing days and my pictures of us. Now, there is a faux-mahogany tallboy displaying garish red and gold china, slightly chipped. At one end, a ghastly stuffed toy wearing a T-shirt saying "Love Me Like a Bunny, Baby!!!" is scrunched up against the wood. I seem to remember Gonzo winning it from one of those machines with a claw which supposedly reaches down into the box and retrieves a prize, but which actually rummages around limply before dropping anything heavier than a weaselfart and coming up empty. It took him seventeen goes, I think, and then he won the bunny rather than the cow. The cow was wearing a shirt which said "Got Horn?"

Leah brings beers, and we talk inconsequences until I can't stand it, and I excuse myself and stand on the veranda wondering what on Earth to do. Should I storm out? Confront them both? Confront them singly? Talk to Leah in a forgiving, husbandly way, or with wrathful, god-like disdain? Could I manage either? I have no idea.

Inside, Gonzo is telling her about the day, the accident, the *plink* and the fear. I can't hear the words, but I know the tone, the awestruck "How in the hell we lived, I'll never know," and then his voice deepens, and I know he's telling her about the torrent of vile, impossible crap which fell on us and what happened or didn't happen. She glances out at me, pale with worry. I see her lips move in a question: "Is he . . ." And I turn away before I can see her ask if I am okay, because no, I am not okay, I am in hell.

Perhaps that's it! Perhaps I have not been betrayed; I have been cast away. Perhaps I was transported to a parallel world in that moment. A vast rift of energy and broken matter threw me, Buck Rogers style, into a realm unfamiliar and fearsomely strange. Except that I know it didn't. I just got damp. And so I weep because it seems like the only thing to do, and after a bit I can feel Gonzo's eyes on me through the window, but when I look round, he is climbing the stairs to bed. To my bed, no doubt. The big one made from giant slices of local trees and sanded by hand in the forecourt. My marriage bed. And then, in the doorway, there is Leah, and I wait for her to say something to make it all all right. Perhaps we are in some weird, impossible plot, an undercover operation by trained professionals, and they have asked her to play this role to defray suspicion, because Gonzo, Special Operations Gonzo, is being put into play against some threat to the world. I will be the ace in the hole, the secret, and Gonzo will be invulnerable because of me and this bizarre deception.

Leah looks at me but she does not explain. Worse, her face is filled with a terrible sympathy. She knows what I am hoping for, but she cannot give it, cannot offer me anything at all. Except pity. And this she does, in a breaking voice, as she steps close to me and kisses me lightly on the cheek.

"I'm so sorry," Leah whispers. "There's a bed in the den." And she goes inside and follows Gonzo upstairs.

I sleep in a Zedbed in my own unrecognisable house. I sleep quite well, which is infuriating. The following morning Leah brings me toast. She smells of jasmine and Gonzo. I find reasons to be busy until ten, when Gonzo and I climb into the truck. We are taking it to see Malevolent Pete the mechanic before we rejoin Sally and Jim. All trucks in the company pool must be approved and frequently serviced by Malevolent Pete. It is our law. And I cannot help feeling that Gonzo wants some us-time, which is definitely in order.

Leah waves us off.

I have decided two things: the first, that it is impossible for me to hate two people I love for loving one another (quite untrue); the second, that I am less frightened of talking to Gonzo about this than I am of hearing it from my wife. The conversation I have with Gonzo will be hurtful and there will probably be shouting. The one I have with Leah could twist my ribs apart and burst my heart like a water balloon. And so I wave through the passenger-side window at Leah, and she waves back at both of us, biting her lower lip. Gonzo takes us out of heaven and back into the world. The feeling of relief is the worst good feeling I have ever had.

Pete's garage is in a town called Baggin. It's a frontiersy kind of place, gunslinging and macho but basically okay, and they make their own branded cigars there for added grit. The town smells of tobacco all day and all night, and the western end has a brewery too. Baggin is about a day away along the Pipe, but there's a short cut: a more-or-less stable road through the Border, takes about two hours. Gonzo and I have pretty much waltzed through the worst thing that can happen to you in terms of Stuff exposure, and we're okay, so it's just a question of dangerous men out there, and we're officially dangerous too. The weather forecast is fine, anyway—good winds driving the Stuff away from us. So the fork in the road gives Gonzo no pause, and he takes us into the Border. He doesn't have to glance my way. He knows what I would say. He must also know that I am trying to frame my questions, get away from my (hate, horror, fury, screaming hideous gut-eating devils of pain) emotions so I can ask what's going on in a clear, gentle way, as between men of good character and intent. And so it must come as a surprise to him—as it does to me—when it boils out of me at the fifty-mile marker when I spill my drink.

Slick, sickly goo glugs down over my stomach, and I can feel it soak the material and prickle against my skin. It is loathsome. It feels vile. It feels like yesterday. I hate it.

But instead of yelling about the fizzy sugar stuff on my shirt and trousers, I turn on Gonzo and I yell incoherently at him, and then it all comes out. Everything I love, he has taken, and he is my friend, but there are some sacrifices he should not ask, how long has it been going on? Does Leah love him, or have I been perpetrating some terrible sexual inadequacy I have no notion of? Did I skip a lesson at the Soames School? Doze off during a lecture on erogenousnesses vital to the maintenance of faithful relationships? Or was there a class on post ethical friendship which I somehow did not attend? What, in short, does Gonzo William Lubitsch think he is doing sharing mattress-whoopee with *my wife*?

And it is only when I say these words, which are after all magic words, that Gonzo seems to pay any attention at all. It is at this point that he half-turns to look at me with a kind of sick curiosity. I say them again in case he has not understood. And Gonzo flinches. This result pleases me, and I say it over and over and watch him shrink like the lying sod he is, until finally I am raw enough that I pause to gulp some air, and he says:

"So. You want a beer?"

Which is the most weirdly comforting thing I have ever heard. Of course I want a beer. Clearly, he has an explanation. He is unfussed by what he has heard. This whole business is some ill-conceived prank gone wrong, or yes, that strange undercover operation I could not be warned of in advance. It is a test, and I/we have passed, and George Copsen, who is not dead at all, will now appear from behind the curtain to make sense of everything. Gonzo reaches in the back for the beer, must have stashed some there before we left the house. I am still feverishly seeking Copsen's hiding place, and I conclude that it must be extra-dimensional: Professor Derek has been at his tricks again, in some even more remarkable way. And indeed we have crossed into some kind of weird, inappropriate place, because when

Gonzo's hand emerges from behind the seat, he is holding not a beer but a decent-sized gun. It is a handgun in workman-like grey, and he does not offer it to me but compounds his error by pointing it at my head.

In fact, he does not point it *at my head.* He just generally points it at me, but when I look into its one good eye, and catch the glint of the nominally soft-nosed (but actually irretrievably solid and lethal) slug in the chamber, all I can imagine is the thing going off and my brain sluicing backwards onto the expensive upholstery. And hence I think of it as *at my head,* despite its being aimed loosely at my torso.

Twenty hours ago Gonzo was a cartoonish hero-lout, a perpetual boychild with the body of a Hercules. He drank beer from the bottle, liked his steaks and his women raw, and would have stepped without hesitation between a puppy and a speeding truck for no better reason than a fuzzy sense of the way things oughta be. This Gonzo is a new deal: a nervous, glazed bastard with designer shades and a greasy, half-regretful expression which tells you he doesn't really care a damn. This Gonzo is not your friend, he's just this guy you met a few times; granted, you like one another, but in the final analysis, if there's a shark in the water he hopes you get eaten whole, and that you're fat enough to satisfy the fish or stick in its salty white throat and choke it with your masticated leg. This is a guy who will kill you on the off-chance that sharks cannot vomit.

"Get out of the truck," Gonzo tells me. He waves the gun, eyes mostly on the road. His peripheral vision will tell him if I move, those old biological hardwirings spotting muscles and hinges moving relative to one another and producing the basic response: he'll fire the gun. And so I stay extremely still. The gun wobbles anyway, and for a moment it is pointed down and a little behind me. Now, instead of imagining my head bursting open, I see what will happen if he discharges the gun in that direction: the slug penetrating the enormous fuel tank, stimulating the stored chemical energy into a bright gasp of heat. For a fraction of a second the whole thing will look like one of those weird little static globes the hippie scions had at Jarndice, and then it will look like the beginning of a model sun. We will not actually witness this, because our eyes will be burned from their sockets and our brains will follow them into oblivion before ever we have a chance to apprehend the mechanism by which we die.

Thinking this, I am willing or even eager to leave the truck. It seems this will resolve what has become a rather twitchy situation. I feel somewhat hard done by; it is I, after all, who has been grievously wronged. Gonzo is guilty (and if I had any doubts on that score, they have rather faded away) and by rights ought to be contrite. Although perhaps that is how it goes: anger is easier, after all. I must have sinned against Gonzo in the past. Everyone distractedly injures their friends from time to time. I wonder briefly which of my unknown transgressions so deeply offended him as to bring us here. It must have been a howler. Or perhaps he is in love with Leah, and she with him, in the tradition of *weak-ass romance* Jim Hepsobah so abhors. I remember Leah's apology last night, her discomfort. "I'm so sorry." But not sorry enough to repent, to abjure. No. There is more to this. Please, God, it is more than it seems.

In this brief meditation I have lost the opportunity to assail Gonzo in a fast-moving truck while he is driving with one hand and holding a pistol in the other, and this is not entirely a matter for regret. He speaks again:

"Get out."

All Gonzo needs to do to achieve my departure is stop the truck, or at least bring it to a speed where I won't splinter anything more vital than the grommets on my shoelaces when I hit the ground running. I tell him so. It is possible that I am unclear. For answer, he points the gun at my body and pulls the trigger more times than I would have thought possible.

At long last, I get shot.

I wonder briefly whether it counts if you get shot by a friend instead of by an enemy, and then I realise that those definitions have now become confused.

The experience of repeatedly getting shot in the gut at close range is pretty much as advertised. The only thing is I don't pass out. Having finally gotten shot, I am damn well going to live the experience. I am thrown from the truck, Gonzo's boot striking my chest above the entry wounds, exquisite pain. I catch the wind, billow like a kite. My back bends limply forward until my spine is at maximum arc, my arms are out beyond my shoulders and head, the new orifice in my stomach creased, agony beyond nausea. I am totally and utterly one of those weird images by Warhol: *Silhouette of a Gunshot Victim,* silkscreen print, one in a series intended to mimic the fractional motion of twenty-four frames of cinematic film. I am printed in black on yellow, reproduced as a T-shirt. I am this year's Che Guevara. A single second separates me from the asphalt.

I do not pass out.

I strike like a break-dancer doing one of those impossible belly flips. I bounce. My eyelashes brush the ground, frail antenna sensing so much: dry, dry road, dust and gravel, a kernel of wheat, the slight tackiness of the surface. I smell oil and heat, desert grass and something cloying and rich which I cannot name. Then I am standing upright, flying in that position towards the accelerating truck. The pain rides my shadow, my angel's wings. Bones have broken somewhere, I know it, but I am totally unable to say which ones. My legs touch the road, pass through the surface, fall into the ground. The earth is too soft to support my weight. It is candyfloss. I am a titan. Only if I lie down can it hold me, the greater surface area compensating for my remarkable weight.

I lie down, but I do not pass out. It seems to me that it would be okay to do that now, because the bouncing is over, but I have forgotten how. There ought to be a darkness waiting, a coma, perhaps a merciful death. If these things are present they are on strike or lazy, or I'm a second-class passenger and the unconsciousness car is currently occupied by premium travellers.

I lie with my face pressed to the uncomfortable heat of the asphalt and a small stone pricking my ear. It annoys me more than I can say. And as if this wasn't bad enough, now I am hallucinating. A person in a top hat is screaming at me to wake up, which is ludicrous because I am awake and fully aware of this awful mess. The person shakes his head and actually goes as far as to slap me to get my attention. He slaps like a girl. Hah! I have been shot. Mere slapping cannot harm me! I feel no pain. I tell him so. He has big round eyes like a cow. Perhaps he *is* a cow. Most likely, a friendly cow has come to sit with me while I die. He is not weeping on my face, he is licking it with bovine simplicity. He is desirous of conversation or a biscuit, or maybe he just wants to help a fellow mammal. A comradely cow. I wonder if it will make him sad when I expire. Perhaps I should wait a bit, until he is gone. Shall I wait, Comrade Cow? Yes, the cow says. Wait. Wait.

I wait. It is cold here, in the sun. I shiver. The cow wraps me in slender arms (my hallucination, my rules, *nyahh*) and lays me in her cow lap. All cows are girls, or at least, all cows with laps. Boy cows have no available lap space, owing to their masculine construction. Wait, says Comrade Cow. Just wait.

I lie there in this damned uncomfortable position for seven hours, nine minutes and eight seconds. I know this because I count them. Comrade Cow sits with me all the way through, does not stop talking that entire time, and does not let me fall asleep, which I would love to do. I become a Cow-ist (to rhyme with Mao-ist and Dao-ist). I live for Comrade Cow. And then finally a bulbous, carrot-shaped silver Airstream bus appears in my field of vision like a road-going whale, and from its belly—via the mouth or driver's-side door—out jumps Jonah, and starts shouting and giving orders, although he is very fat and appears to be wearing a sarong, and they roll me over onto a stretcher and do magic things to make me better, but these, alas, I do not get to observe, because when Jonah sees that I am fully conscious he starts swearing and they fill my body with a fearsome, blue-white cold which proceeds from my hand to the rest of my body, and I realise, from the sudden lack, that the pain has been with me all the time.

I pass out.

Chapter Eleven

The wrong afterlife;
the Devil;
all the fun of the fair.

WHEREVER I AM, it is the good kind of place. Well, small caveat: it is conceivable that I am dead, but *other* than that, it is the good kind of place. There are fields. You might term them pastures, although there are no actual cattle (poor Comrade Cow is lonely, somewhere), and hence no cattle related by-products which might make you unwilling to run barefoot through them. These are fields of the sort envisaged as eternal rewards. In the distance there are mountains, but they aren't mountains like my home—my old home—they are bigger, bluer and snowier, and as a consequence of this, looking at them doesn't hurt. Nothing does, actually, which is jolly welcome. And there are shepherdesses. If you visit a museum almost anywhere in the world, you see shepherdesses like this; the fantasy is hard-wired into the lechers of our race. These shepherdesses are on the blowsy, wistful end of the filthy dream spectrum. They are, to be honest, nymphs. They titter, and they move in a way which can be described only as flitting. (Flitting is a form of locomotion which involves running on tiptoe, wiggling and bouncing, and having your clothes very nearly fall off.) They are winsome, albeit in a knowing way which suggests practice. When I look at them, they look back from beneath heavy lashes. When I look away, they pout. If they suspect I am able to see them in the corner of my eye, they stretch languorously, and make little whimpering sounds as of a person with a pleasant itch which needs careful scratching. It appears that I am a pagan.

I come to this understanding slowly, and it is primarily based upon the realisation that there is almost nothing about these ladies to suggest that they are virgins. Christian myth is not top-heavy (unlike nymph number twelve) with wanton heavens. In a good solid Christian story these girls would be covered up and singing hymns. That is emphatically not the case. These are women of blissful sexual emancipation (what the Evangelist would call, publicly, *low moral character*). If they sing at all, they are singers, not of hymns, but of the throaty, wicked kind of song where the chanteuse concludes her performance wearing nothing but a smile. Sadly they are also, damn the scruples I learned from Old Man Lubitsch and Aline and all the rest, *lacking.*

Don't get me wrong: you can't fault your nymph on deportment or diaphanous robes, and they have erotic intermittence absolutely nailed to the carpet. But get past the natural desire to grab a handful of Elysian backside and perform a bit of strenuous quality testing, and there are significant lacunae in their interpersonal skills, starting with a vocabulary which extends only a few hundred words beyond "Ooh, la *la*!" And though it is difficult to concentrate here—by reason of the pan pipes, the stretching and what appears to be a rolling Miss Nearly Naked competition—I am peripherally aware that "Ooh, la *la*" is not an expression often seen in classical Greek. The thought occurs to me, fuzzily, that I am spiritually misplaced. I am dead, but by some error—of a type with which I am extremely familiar—I am in the wrong afterlife, and while it is reasonably picturesque and full of (pretty but ill-educated and also curiously *French*) nymphs, I should really be getting along. I grasp a passing shepherdess by the least erogenous protruding part and attempt to secure some relevant information.

"Excuse me? Where am I?"

Titter.

"Am I dead? Is this my afterlife?"

Snort, giggle, bounce. The bouncing is interesting. I am

distracted by it. She wanders off. I pull myself together, secure another one.

"I *really* need to go. This is lovely, and you're all, really, very attractive, but I have things to do and places to be and I'm basically not your epicurean afterlife sort of person, I'm more the wild beauty, the thundering rivers and vast oceans sort of person. This is all a bit agricultural. So if there's a door . . . ?"

Tee hee.

Grandmother Wu's voice, in my head, suggests that this is a very special hell for intellectual, caring men. You can get your ashes hauled, get fed grapes and eat pastry all you like, for ever, but the whole thing will eventually drive you into a coma of self-loathing and ennui which will destroy your mind and turn your self-respect into a razor in the soul. If that's the case, by the way, the Immortal Judge has sorely overestimated my integrity, but for the moment I'm still trying to get out of here.

"Anybody? I *really* want to get out of here!"

My wish is, in some measure, granted: I catch fire. This is not really what I was hoping for. It's immediately recognisable: extreme discomfort and intense heat spreading from a point of initial ignition around the ankles upwards to my thighs and belly. I'm being burned at the stake. The invisible, intangible stake. Marvellous. Without the stench of burning and any sign of actual fire about my lower limbs, however, I conclude that this must be the onset of my translation to another inappropriate spiritual world of less pleasing aspect such as the Christian hell (returning to my roots, alas) described so forcefully by James Joyce in *Portrait of the Artist,* which the Evangelist read to us every year at Christmas time. So: to hell, thrashing in agony, because I have fallen down on my face. The nymphs pay me no attention at all as I writhe on the ground, which causes me to ponder the possibility that they are not true individuals but spiritual automata, and while I am thinking this, someone catheterises me, an intervention guaranteed to attract the attention of the patient. Thus, my journey across the infinite cosmos of the soul takes the form of me wincing and saying "ow," and by the time I open my eyes, I have missed limbo and pandemonium and possibly the glimpse of heaven I was supposed to get to torment me for eternity, and am in hell.

Hell is smaller than I expected. Indeed, it appears to be a long, narrow motel room. The infernal prison of Lucifer Morningstar is upholstered in a cheap hessian wallpaper. There is also a bed, which does not seem to be a surgical table or other torturer's tool, although there is a drip in my arm and another in a place more intimate about which you already know. If there is a part of me which does not hurt, it's being very quiet about it. The only properly hell-ish things about it are a strange, nauseating sense of motion and the dim awareness of hissing and gasping voices, or possibly a large river or ill-tuned radio set, nearby: *whoossh-shweeddogga-dogga-dogga-shweee,* and so on.

The Devil—for surely no one else would think to catheterise a ghost—appears to have let himself go a bit. His stomach is proudly rounded, and protrudes like a single vast breast implant over the belt line of a green-and-purple sarong. His face is demonically out of focus.

"Hi," the Devil says. "I thought you were a goner." And he smiles, revealing imperfect but cheerful teeth. My spiritual certainty recedes. Nowhere have I ever heard of Satan taking the form of an avuncular hippie. No doubt he could. It just seems inefficient. This is not a form ideal for offering blandishments or inciting fear. It isn't even particularly reassuring. It's just a guy who could use several years on a cross-trainer and a diet of lettuce so that he can view his ankles without the aid of a mirror.

"My name's K," he says. "Pleased to meet you. Don't talk just yet. You've still got plenty of resting up left in you. Tomorrow we'll see about getting some whole food for you." But this last is already from a great distance, because now that I am awake again, conscious and possibly alive, I feel a great urge to sleep.

I sleep. I dream good dreams about being a kid, about Cricklewood Cove and Ma Lubitsch's goulash and Old Man

Lubitsch's bees. I dream about Elisabeth and Jarndice, and Aline. I do not dream about sex, which means that the bit about Aline is quite short. I dream of educated nymphs playing poker and talking politics, and investigating crimes in a city covered in greenery and bioluminescent lights, where domesticated bison pull the trains (I am the mayor, but for all my power I can't stop people from wearing red hats, which of course makes the bison belligerent and causes accidents every day). I dream about being a crab, which is less tedious than it sounds. I dream I am a playing card, but no one will tell me which one, and I cannot crane my neck to see.

I dream someone is burning bacon, and when I wake up, I find the Devil—K—swearing amid a cloud of giddy bacon-smoke, working at a portable stove at the far end of the room. Mercifully, I am no longer attached to a bag by a thin piece of tubing protruding from my genitals, or I would probably be embarrassed. Indeed, even my drip seems to have gone. K looks back over his shoulder and waves. It's not immediately obvious whether he does this because he knows I am awake, or because he can't see me through the incinerated pig. I feel a moment's guilt at being present for the death rites of a pig, because Flynn the Barman's pigs did such sterling service not so long ago when we needed them.

K waves again, and this one is definitely for me. At his side stands a girl in batik, wearing the expression of one who told him the pan was too hot. She has short dark hair cut aggressively flat around one side. She marches through the fog of pig and stands in front of me.

"Hi," she says. "I'm K."

I must look confused. I thought K was the fat geezer. Some bloke with a dry mouth says this out loud.

"No," she says. "I mean, he is. But I'm *K*." As if that makes it all clear. My K—the original and still the most enormous—sheds his apron with a slightly despairing gesture and chucks the bacon remnant into a bin. He opens a narrow window near the stove, and instantly the smoke whisks out and the unmistakable sound of the road bores in. Yes. The silver whale. I am aboard Jonah's bus. Jonah's bus is my hospital, which is Satan's hell. Satan's hell is a camper van. K, somewhat troublingly, is not the same as K. I gurgle a bit. Frege is not the ideal companion for a man recently ventilated. K the corpulent shuts the window and shoots his companion a cross look.

"Don't do that to him, love. He's been shot. He's addled enough as it is," and to me, "I'm K. She's also K. We both—many of us here, actually—have the same name. Not that we're all the same person, you understand. We just use one signifier to encourage random reassessment of the nature of our relationships. We don't like to make assumptions, yeah?"

"Except K likes to assume he can cook," the girl says savagely. "And he can't cook."

"I haven't demonstrated the ability to cook," K murmurs placidly, "but it's inaccurate to say that I can't. Perhaps I'm just waiting for the right moment."

"The right moment."

"Yes," says K, airily, "possibly I am waiting for a moment which is tactically advantageous. I will suddenly leap upon the raw food and render it cordon bleu in a fit of remarkable efficacy, and in doing so, I will change the world for the better." He smiles.

The girl arches a sceptical eyebrow and does not speak. It is the more sceptical because of the way her hair is cut, which is most probably why it's cut that way.

K (the fat one, not the sceptic) demands a moment of communion with his patient. He fusses over me. He consults something which looks a bit like a medical chart, except that it is clipped to a piece of orange Perspex which used to be a drinks tray in a bar called *Viva Humperdink!*

"How do you feel?" he says.

"I don't know."

"Okay," K says, and apparently ticks a box on the chart

which says "Don't know." "Basically," K says, "you're doing amazingly well. You had a lot of cracked and broken ribs and so on, and they're . . . well, they're broken, but they're not dangerous. Both of your ankles are sprained, but not badly, which is frankly a bit miraculous. And you have bruising all over you, and of course you've been, you know . . ."

This one, I do know.

"Shot."

K nods.

"But you're going to live."

Oh.

"How did you find me?"

K looks uncomfortable.

"Thank Dr. Andromas," he says, and ducks behind the chart. Apparently Dr. Andromas isn't a topic he wants to dwell on. "Is there anything else you want to know?"

There are several questions I do not ask. I do not ask them because I have studied the *gong fu* of Isaac Newton. Assumption Soames, insurrectionist and secret heretic, required that her students grasp Newton's Laws at an early age, so I was familiar with them even before Master Wu appointed Newton a *sifu* and a person of consequence. On the ostensible basis that every righteous soldier must know his enemy, the Evangelist stalked and purred from the back of the classroom to the front—a teacher you cannot see but know is there is infinitely more imposing than one you can measure with your eyes—and pounced on dissenters and doodlers and demanded they recite the blasphemous catechism of the alchemist and sorcerer.

So: *A body continues in its state of rest or uniform motion in a straight line unless acted upon by a net external force.* And here I am, continuing in my state of rest. This is the Law of Inertia, something of which I have a great deal at the moment. Although I may also, *pace* Albert Einstein, be in motion—the jag of the wheels and the hiss of air around the bus strongly suggests it must be so.

Next, the awkward one, which is frankly slippery as a fish and wriggles away from your comprehension as you reach for it: *The alteration of motion is ever proportional to the motive force impressed, and is made in the direction of the right line in which that force is impressed.* It comes out windy because it is naturally expressed neither in Latin nor in English, but in the murky cant of mathematics known as algebra. To the uninitiated, this law is so much noise, like the whistling around the bus. I am a master mason of both these temples. I speak not only algebra but also the language of the many-wheeled heavy transport. I know from the sound of the tyres that we are on an A-class road in medium repair, but that we are nowhere urban, because I can hear the dust and random gravel of the desert. I know that the bus needs a service, and that we are travelling at around sixty miles per hour, and that there is at least one vehicle of similar disposition close to us on the right. I know also that our front right tyre is somewhat bald and that its opposite number needs some air.

These things I know because I have kneeled at the feet of mechanical wizards and seen their secret texts. From my other initiation, the backhanded educational magic of the Evangelist, I know that Newton's Second Law is rendered as $F = ma$, Force is equal to mass times acceleration. Force is measured in *Newtons,* and the everyday utility of this law can be assessed from the fact that almost no one knows that. On the other hand, almost nothing with cogs or an engine would work without it.

It is Newton's Third Law—the one which Assumption Soames used to manipulate the world—which concerns me now: *For every action, there is an equal and opposite reaction.* Push an object and you will go backwards unless you brace yourself to offset the reaction. No force flows in one direction only. Now, a normal person, waking in an unknown bed, decatheterised and enveloped in the smoke of burned and carcinogenic breakfast biomass, would naturally ask a string of questions beginning with "Where am I?" or "How long have I been out?" or other questions more personal and vastly more dangerous. But I have been in this place before. The *gong fu* of waking from serious injury is also known to me. Questions like that lead in a given direction, or rather in two. They lead from the sickroom to the corridor and thence to the real world beyond, with all its demands and calculations and income tax returns and moral obligations; to weddings and women you love and to attendant catastrophes; and they lead backwards in time to the moment of injury and any matters bearing upon it, such as being blown up or sudden revelations of horrible conspiracies. Newton's Third Law is to be approached with caution.

Newton's work on gravity led to the discovery of the Lagrange point, a place where opposing forces cancel one another out, and a body may remain at relative rest. This is where I am right now; the forces in my life confound one another. Better, for the moment, to be here and now, without history or future. A man in need of breakfast. So that is what I am. I accept everything they say, and I wait while K (the batik-wearing sceptic, not the corpulent Lucifer) seeks out nutritious stuff which has not been immolated. And I set my eyes and my feet solidly on a path of painless emptiness for as long as it may last, because for all that I am on the mend in body, there is a dark place in my mind and in my heart which needs a little time before it may be stretched and probed and exercised, and before it is allowed to have an equal and opposite reaction. Because I sense something in it and around it which is alien to me, something boiling and hard, and it occurs to me, as I carefully turn my back upon it, and leave it in its ring-fenced, oxygen-tented, shadowed place, that this unfamiliar thing inside me may be *rage*.

I EAT BREAKFAST. I hobble around. Days go by during which I ask no questions and make a point of not answering any either. I do this not aggressively but vaguely, leaving anyone who tries to draw me out with the feeling they learned something, and that next time I will surely open up and let them know it all.

I do not let anyone know it all, least of all myself.

And so I eat and fugue and wander and listen to the chat, and sleep in K's Airstream and listen to his deep, basso breathing when my chest twinges and I wake for a while. And through the days I sit with him, riding shotgun, even driving, watching the road go under the wheels and listening to the tyres. K does not ask any questions. Sometimes K turns up and she wants to know everything, which is almost as restful, because I can barely begin one prevarication before she runs off at a tangent and supplies me with another. There is a maze in my head, and I grow it out and up, and the monster in the middle fades away. This is a good thing. It works well. Until we come to Rheingold, and all the fences come crashing down.

We go to Rheingold to meet up with a few more folks who are part of K's loose-knit caravan, some guys K says I will totally love. Rheingold will get a circus, and we'll all hook up and then travel on and around and just live, which I gather is what K and his friends do.

Rheingold is not *in* the Border, exactly—but on a bad day, when the wind blows strongly from the north-west, and the pressure dips over Lake Barbarella, the Border can just about embrace it, swallow it whole, and everyone goes down into the cellars and waits to see what will be there when they come back up. Rheingold is like Hurricane Alley, with monsters.

In the manner of people who live on the edge of disaster, the lady townsfolk are very correct and proper, and not in the least fond of surprises or loose behaviour. Their job (self-appointed but no less legitimate) is to make sure that Rheingold persists, remains itself, and imparts to the next generation a sense of belonging. They are the walls of Rheingold. Like Ma Lubitsch, another bulwark against the capricious world, they set great store by trifles and commonplaces, and they hew to a church of Regular Meals.

The men here, by contrast, are crusty, loud and bombastic.

Their job (self-appointed but no less real) is to carve out a space in which their mothers, daughters, wives and sisters can make the town. They do this by the energy of their actions, the strength of their backs and their convictions and a great deal of shouting. They construct and maintain and occasionally knock down and rebuild the town. They do manly tasks and they hunt or farm, till the soil and maintain livestock, and they fortify and watch over Rheingold in case it is attacked by something ludicrous or dangerous or insane.

And yes, there are broad-shouldered, termagant women, swinging a pick with the boys, and slender, spiritual men rolled around compassionate hearts waiting at home for them, or for some macho fellow with a lumberjack moustache who prefers the physical company of men to the alarming recesses of the female anatomy. There are boys who like boys and girls who like girls and all the variations in between. This world being what it is now, no one gives a pinch of orange tummyfluff who shares whose bed, as long as the whole thing is done in the appropriately formal style and nobody gets hurt.

We arrive, and there is a careful exchange of assurances. Folks in places like Rheingold are not careless in welcoming new people. There are rituals and testings to be observed, earnests of security and mutual humanity to be given on both sides. Rheingold does not wish to vanish, and K and his friends have no intention of ending their days as the gristle in a cooking pot. K goes out in his best sarong and his most unthreatening sandals, and with him goes K (a slender accountant with pale eyes) and K the batik sceptic, and they explain carefully that they are just passing through, carnival players, and they'd happily set up outside the town on the north side and maybe a little trade and respectable good times might be available to such of the good people of Rheingold as might wish to enjoy them. If (and only if) this meets with the approval of the elders of Rheingold, K will summon one or two other persons of his persuasion and acquaintance, who might add colour and verve to the show.

The Rheingolders, for their part, emerge slowly, open-handed, respectful. They smile widely so that we can see they don't file their teeth to cannibal points, and they all find excuses for taking off their shoes (small stones, itches, hangnails, broken soles and such) so that we will know they have toes instead of talons. There is a great deal of nodding and handshaking and back-slapping, and it is gradually established that no one has reversible knees or double-jointed thumbs or dorsal fins. At that point there is a certain amount of beer.

While the amber peacemaker flows among the men, K (the sceptic) wanders off and goes shopping, and chatting to the old women and young mothers of the town and getting a haircut, in a performance calculated as an earnest of intent: *See, I need grooming products. Yea, indeed, I need grooming. Will none among you style me? I am a mammal, just as you are, and I need close contact and the nits picked from my fur.* And after a while, the ladies of Rheingold take her in and give her cakes and ascertain that she is stepping out with a (quite fictional) young man named K (although she goes as far as to confide that his real name is Clifford, and that he is a recent arrival in the caravans) and that she intends to marry him as soon as time and decent convention permit, and that she is very much in love and not a little frustrated by the delay, because of course she cannot move into his Airstream, nor he into hers, until the formalities have been observed. This display of monogamy and right-thinking behaviour gives the lady Rheingolders an opportunity to wax earthy, to giggle and primp and to suggest in low voices that there must be ample places in a caravan where two young people of good character might divert one another to at least a degree of satisfaction, surely? *Teehee* and *yes,* says K, there are, but it's *hardly* the same and *one so wishes,* etc., and yes, the ladies of Rheingold reply, quite true, and how *desperately* romantic it is, and the only person, my dear girl, quite the *only* person to cut your hair is Dame Lisa, and it so happens she will be here at four and why don't you stay and have some more cake until then?

Dame Lisa arrives amid great ceremony and is ushered in, and pronounces K's hair just lovely, of course, but my poor child the *ends,* but my, how *daring* that cut! Just *splendid* on one so young, thank *goodness* you've no chest to speak of or I should feel *all outshone,* and K, howling with inner hilarity, avers that a woman of Dame Lisa's proportions need never be concerned that anyone, anywhere might ever be more *feminine* than she, and for good measure she goggles wretchedly at Dame Lisa's formidable cleavage. This display of abject beta femaleness results in K's immediate adoption as chief temporary protégée of the klatch, and she is eventually sent back to her Airstream reeking of three different perfumes and with her hair arranged to give her a rakish yet classic frontierswoman look. She has, along the way, secured promises from every matron, maiden and crone to come along and see the circus, and bring as many male relatives as they can legitimately muster. Indeed, there is already competition among the younger girls as to who will bring more young men and thus impress the wild, romantic, respectable, comfortably flat-chested, soon-to-depart and monogamous gypsy. As a consequence of this absolute female enthusiasm and the accompanying opportunities for respectable-yet-steamy-boy-Rheingolder-on-girl-Rheingolder-action, the issues of permissions and debates in council become moot. And thus the circus comes to town.

We have circled our wagons and made camp at a convenient yet non-intrusive distance from Rheingold, and it is morning on the day after our arrival. From out of the shady purple in one quarter of the sky comes a lonesome bus, ancient and sputtering diesel, with metal showing where the paint has flaked away. It is something of the order of a twenty-six-seater, and it is about as far from the smooth contours of K's Airstream as you can get and still have wheels. Saggy tyres skid and squirm on the road, bulging perilously because there's hardly enough air in there to keep the rims off the asphalt. The engine pops and bangs and little clouds of soot emerge, still burning, from an exhaust pipe which hangs pathetically between the rear wheels on a length of what appears to be stocking elastic. This wreck-in-waiting draws level with us, and almost everyone scurries back from it. The bus is painted a patchy blue, rusted away around the edges, and it has been savaged and snapped. This is not so much a bus as a dying warrior. And in each starred, dusty window a weird white face is pressed against the glass, white of skin and black of eye, contorted in a spooky sneer or a wild grin or an open howl: Munch's painting replicated over and over.

The doors open, and the driver hops down from his seat. He waves and grins.

"Hi!" says Ike Thermite. "I'm Ike Thermite," in case anyone has forgotten, "and *we* are the Matahuxee Mime Combine!" He springs lightly to the ground, and behind him come the mimes, all popping joints and pins and needles from the journey. A moment later he is whisked away by K and K and carried shoulder-high around the buses. I am alone with the mimes.

We look at one another. No one says anything. It's like sharing a lift to a funeral. After a moment I wave at them, a bit hesitantly. One by one, they wave back in a perfect imitation. My uncertain wave starts with the nearest one, is picked up by the next before it can fade, and ripples away to the back.

And then, just as the wave starts its return journey, there is an odd little commotion. The mime on the far side spots something on the horizon, shudders and hides behind the next one in. The mime being used for cover looks sharply in both directions and dashes for K's bus. The revealed mime scurries behind the next in line, who also declines the honour and hurries away, leaving the little man crouched, bandy-legged, peering around an obstacle which isn't there. He spins and dives behind mime number four, who stares in horror into the haze and remembers a pressing engagement elsewhere. And so too with the next, and the next. A few seconds later the petrified mime is peering into my face and we are the only two people around. Slowly a single shaky finger extends, and then an arm, and the mime points back along the road. Huge, round eyes like a puppy's make a silent appeal.

Okay, already. Hide behind me.

I look in the direction indicated by the pointing finger. There's a small dust cloud now, and at the business end of it another vehicle: a covered military surplus truck which has seen better days, with a couple of bullet holes painted on the side and some weird scratches, and dings pretty much everywhere. The canvas section has been replaced with wood, panels reclaimed from some old-style restaurant or stately home, and a sort of caravan has been constructed. Daubed in foot-high letters along the side is MAGIC OF ANDROMAS. The painter knew more about carpentry than pigment, because the pigment has dribbled, and the whole thing looks less like a gypsy wagon than a scary melted waxwork. I glance around at my concealed mime, and find him gone. The *Magic of Andromas* stops exactly parallel to K's Airstream. The driver's door opens, and grey dust like graveyard sand trickles out onto the ground. A scuffed black patent-leather shoe touches the ground. It makes no noise.

Dr. Andromas gets out of the truck. He wears a top hat with a fine piece of gauze or mosquito net dangling lankly to his neck. Beneath it his face is white, with a tiny villainous moustache, and he wears a pair of aviator goggles over his eyes. His entire body is wrapped in a black cloak, which makes him look like a mummy or a sickly giant bat. For all that, he's not as tall as I am. It feels very odd, and somehow dangerous, to be looking down on him.

"Dr. Andromas?"

The doctor looks at me for a long moment, and then shrugs past on business of his own.

You have to worry about someone even mimes find creepy.

IT IS lunchtime, but the mimes are not eating. They are standing in a long, regimented line, absolutely still. They are not rigid, they are relaxed and ready, but motionless. Corpse quiet, expressions painted on, they attend Ike Thermite's commandments. Ike walks along the line, serious for the first time in my brief experience. And then he turns his back on them and spreads his arms like a bird. The Matahuxee Mime Combine follow suit, slowly. Ike brings his arm around and opens an imaginary door. He steps forward into an imaginary world. He tucks a non-existent chair under an intangible table. He invites them in.

The mimes cross the threshold one by one. Not one of them touches the door frame or puts a hand through a wall. There are too many of them to fit into the first room, and they get stuck, crowding around the entrance, jammed up together. Ike opens another door and goes farther into his imaginary space, brings the front half of the Matahuxee Mime Combine with him. The rest of the mimes fall into the first room, which is apparently a kitchen. They do the chores. They wash. They clean up. They step around one another, vault over non-physical furniture. They cook. In the next room there's some heavy DIY going on. Mimes saw and chop, scrub the floor, clean the windows. They dodge flailing arms, lift bowls of soup in either hand, tightrope-walk along the edge of sofas, squabble, fight, duck and dive. Straight-backed and fluid, they do all these things in utter quiet, save for the occasional group sigh. Ike watches. This is the kata of the greatest mime in the world.

I am hypnotised, sad, thrilled and suddenly terribly homesick. I came here to talk to Ike Thermite, say hi, talk about old times, but suddenly I am not sure that I want to. I am very glad when K comes to give me a job. As I depart, the mimes are starting to practise their clown work: mops, umbrellas and plantain bananas are being passed out in solemn stillness.

Five minutes later I am swinging a sledgehammer to knock metal pins into the ground. These pins will hold up the main tent, so there are quite a few of them, and this task is vital and important. A lot of other people are doing the same thing, but these pins are given to me. It is a pleasantly percussive task.

There is a method to the execution of the task, a technique.

The hammer is wickedly heavy and hard to control. Only a strongman could lift it and hammer in a series of separate actions for longer than a few moments. Only an idiot strongman would actually do it, and there are surprisingly few of these. The process of building a body which *can* lift a vast amount in an unscientific way is most often also the process of learning that the other way is easier. The trick is in Newton's Laws, of course: move the hammer and let its momentum carry it up, then divert it when it has the maximum kinetic energy but the minimum momentum, and bounce it off the metal pin or stake in such a way that the *re-action* can be used to complement the initiation of another upward arc. Much the same principle applies to the single-edged sword-form of Master Wu's Voiceless Dragon style.

In any case, I have familiarised myself with the heft of the hammer, with its balance and bounce, and with its pitfalls—it becomes slippery in the heat, it does not always bounce true, and unlike a sword it is heavily biased towards the business end. I have set up the pins in a long row. And now, prepared and quiet in my mind, I move along the line in a single unbroken motion. It begins with Snake Concealed (the weapon hangs behind the trailing leg, so that it cannot easily be seen, and the enemy must either accept this or seek to alter his position accordingly—the pins unwisely take the first option) and moves on to Stirring the Cauldron (a twisting motion which starts the weapon moving, preparing the first attack).

I flip the hammer up (Horse Rears at the Moon), and then I step forward. Parting the Hair (downward strike) followed by Cloud Hands (rolling motion) and back to Stirring the Cauldron. There is a little shuffle here which Master Wu insisted was called Walk Like Elvis, but Elisabeth asserted, not without some justification, that this was unlikely to be the original name. Still, I Walk Like Elvis. After three or four spikes have gone in smoothly, I add Cut Across a Thousand Troops (a swirl where the weapon makes a full one-hundred-and-eighty-degree arc, positioning me between two pins and at ninety degrees to my starting vector) and follow it with Wheels of the Master's Cart (rolling the hammer on one side, then the other) before taking the last six in quick succession (Babbling Brook and Parting the Hair bound together in succession), and then turning (Monkey's Dance), hammer still in motion, and driving them all another six inches into the hard ground. Thus returned to the beginning, I stop. My arms are not tired, but my heart is beating quickly, and my scabs are hurting. There are lines of pain aching through my chest, and little globes of heat inside the flesh where the bullets were. Still, job done—in perhaps three minutes. K told me it would take half an hour. Hah! See how my skills are transferable!

As I turn to go in search of pies, I see a figure standing by the canteen tent. Ike Thermite is watching me. His eyes are round. Of course his eyes are always round. They are painted on. Still and all, somehow he is broadcasting considerable surprise, or so it seems. By the time I reach him, he is grinning.

"Tent pegs?" he says.

"Yeah."

"Usually," says Ike Thermite, in the tone of one imparting a secret, "usually, we put the ropes around the pins before we hammer them in."

Bugger.

But at least he does not want to talk about Matchingham, or ask me about my wife, and for this I feel an overwhelming gratitude.

THE CIRCUS is a thing of many parts. It is a cakebake, a display of acrobatics (and mime), a sheepdog trial and a magic show. The sheepdog trial is something of a surprise. Amid the noise and haste, a lanky black Scotsman with a voluminous beard hurtles up on a quad bike; two Border collies, dappled, eager and curious, sit on the platform at the back. In a wheeled chicken-wire box are several Indian runner ducks. The collies are called something like Mnwr and Hbw, and the man himself—another K, of course—speaks for the moment only in sharp, irritated growls and yaps. The Indian runner ducks have no names, or at least no names they share with us, and are here to represent sheep. They have many of the characteristics of sheep without actually being sheep. They are fabulously stupid. They cannot fly. They gather together and, given the opportunity, dither and fall over each other. They are protected from moisture by a natural oil which permeates their outer covering. A short amount of time spent in their company is enough to make you want to kill them all out of frustration.

K (the Scotsman) flings wide his arms.

"Hello, ladies and gentlemen, my name is K, and I will be your ringmaster this evening!" (Except it is actually "Hah-lo, leddies 'n' djentlemenn, ayem yer ringmasster thus evven-ung!") And he launches straight into an explanation of the strong-eye and the weak-eye dog (the first being a dog whose face implies that he is a duck-eating psychopath, a creature of action who will stop at nothing to achieve his goals, suitable for starting animals moving at speed and cowing them into stillness, and for lethal action in the heat of battle; and the second being a gentle-hearted creature doing a job, friendly and mostly non-violent, good for repairing rents in the flock, precise manoeuvring and charity work), then shows a few bits of black-belt duck herding, before segueing into a ringing denunciation of the Highland Clearances. Impressive that rage at this ancient political sin can survive the disintegration of the Highlands themselves, and pass, unmitigated, into the new world.

The mimes take their turn. In empty air they create a house, a street, a town, a nation under a capricious god. They rush around the world (backdrops depict ancient Gone Away places of mystery, like Venice and Delhi) in great confusion, an endless parade of slapstick and acrobatics against a scenery of sorrow and loss. The Matahuxee Mime Combine share a universe with us. They are mesmerising; they flip, bend, whoosh and custard-pie one another in a kind of restful quiet. They are sort of anti-Nietzschean clowns, who restore the ordinary simply by existing; a gentle remedy for the insidious forgetting which afflicts us. And then, out of nowhere, they create Dr. Andromas.

One moment Ike Thermite is engaged in a slapstick routine in the middle of the stage, and the next the mimes have apparently grown tired of him, and carry him off. There is a great clap of thunder, and everything goes dark, and there is Dr. Andromas, like a beggar king-in-waiting. He is dressed in a dusty tail-coat, a pair of disreputable trousers and fine, pointed shoes. His topper turns out to be an opera hat, with a folding skeleton inside which can be compressed for ease of carriage. One side of the skeleton must be loose or broken, because every so often Dr. Andromas's hat flinches and sinks on the left, and the good doctor removes it and punches it back out and flops it once more into position. His face, unveiled for the occasion, is white and startled, and he has waxed his preposterous moustache into tiny, pinprick points. He has fine androgynous features, the kind you look at and immediately think you recognise. I try picturing him without the moustache. I don't know him.

Dr. Andromas introduces himself (gestures grandly to a banner bearing his name in self-important letters), and the mimes lean on things all around him and giggle silently. He capers stiffly, loses his hat, finds it and draws from it in quick succession two carrots and a lettuce, slightly gnawed. He ponders these, apparently unsure where they can have come from, and leaves the hat sitting on the table behind him while he goes to confer with a mime on the other side of the stage. A rabbit scuttles out of the hat in pursuit of the carrots. The audience goes wild. Andromas turns around, and the rabbit bolts for the hat. Andromas lunges for it but misses, then jams his arm into the topper, and pulls out three metres of orange silk, a sink plunger and the shapely leg of a young woman. This last is sharply withdrawn, and a slender arm emerges and slaps him across the face. He recoils and jams the hat in a panic onto his head. A moment later he sighs and takes it off again. The rabbit is back.

At this point Dr. Andromas steps up a gear. He passes the rabbit to a very young Rheingolder, who takes it with some misgivings until the rabbit parks itself firmly on her lap and falls asleep. Dr. Andromas silently requests from the gentlemen of Rheingold a simple favour: might he have the loan of a gentleman's watch? (Asking for the watch involves a great deal of careful gesticulation and the miming of cogs. It gives the clear impression that pompous Dr. Andromas believes he is dealing with imbeciles who don't speak mime like any proper person.) The townsfolk of Rheingold recognise without difficulty that they are invited to dislike this persona, and they laugh at his popinjay manners and his battered dignity, and Andromas preens and assumes that this is all down to his massive comic talent. It's a contract, and everyone is behaving quite according to their assigned role. The audience is thus perfectly prepared for The Trick.

The Trick follows a predictable pattern. Dr. Andromas takes the watch, and wraps it for safe keeping in a green pocket handkerchief. Then he gives a genial, reassuring wave and smashes the little green cloth bundle repeatedly with a wooden mallet. Several hundred people giggle and gasp. The owner of the watch winces and chuckles tolerantly and silently wishes himself elsewhere. His wife clutches at his arm with nervous good humour. Everyone knows it will be all right. But a look of dismay passes over the doctor's greasepainted face. He looks in the handkerchief. He rattles it, and—somewhat alarmingly in the context—it goes *tinkle.* A single stray cogwheel falls out and rolls across the table. Dr. Andromas freezes. He raises one hand in a conjuring sort of a way, and then drops it again. He rattles the handkerchief. *Tinkle.* A sickly little grin appears on his face. He trots over to the side of the stage and talks urgently to one of the mimes. The mime shrugs. More mimes are called in, and the discussion grows animated. Ike Thermite is hurriedly brought out and does a creditable double-take when informed of the problem. Wrathful Ike despatches a mime to give Andromas a sound bollocking. The Rheingolders cheer and chuckle. Dr. Andromas makes his way to the front of the stage.

Andromas composes his face—impossible moustache and all—into an expression of the most profound regret. He clasps his hands. He is beseeching Rheingold in general, and the owner of the (currently deceased) watch in particular, to be merciful. He gestures to the table, the rabbit, to all the good things he has done. He gives the audience to understand that, in all his years, he has never made such an error as this. But he has, today, experienced the first pang of senility. He has blanked. Possibly tomorrow, when the pressure has abated, he will recover himself. Right now . . . he has forgotten the second half of the trick.

And he opens the handkerchief, and pours a stream of sand and cogs and glass fragments into his open hands.

There is absolute silence. It isn't, of course, the silence of horror, although it's sort of bleeding in that direction. It is the silence of demand: *Make it okay,* Ike's audience is saying. *This was funny and now it's scary and you have to make it be okay.* Ike Thermite steps forward and whispers sharply in the doctor's ear. An ultimatum, apparently—Dr. Andromas looks around for salvation. The mimes desert him. Alone in the middle of the stage, Andromas fretfully wraps the pieces up and makes a few passes over them, but nothing happens. The mimes silently dismantle the scenery. They take the Alps away, and Loch Ness, and everything else, and the lights all go out except for the one which picks out Dr. Andromas like the accused on the witness stand. And finally he cries, on his knees, and this has turned out to be a very other kind of show from the one everyone was expecting. It is, on the one hand, *quite clear* that Dr. Andromas doesn't know how to put it all back together, and it is, on the other, *very unclear* whether this means the watch or the world, or whether there is a difference. An awed, awful quiet settles on the people of Rheingold. There is a sniffle from one of the sturdier matrons and a murmur of mourning from the men. Dr. Andromas is the bearer of an awkward truth. Andromas himself rubs desperately at his moustache until it droops. His huge girlish eyes open very wide, and he allows a single tear to make its way down his face.

And just as Dr. Andromas falls down onto his face and his hat drops off to reveal not the balding pate I had somehow expected but a lush crop of messy hair cut sensibly short, the rabbit abandons its cosy perch and hops back onto the stage. And of course it is wearing a watch around its neck. Yes, *that* watch. The lights come back, and the mimes are sitting among the audience, and behind the stripy fabric of the circus tent, which is drawn aside, the scenery is all set up: the old world, in a single panorama, mixed with the new: the waterfall at Alicetown, the Westery Mountains, where what must at one time have been a great lake or an inland sea falls over a cliff into something which may have been the Indian Ocean. The first wonders of the age. The crowd erupts with relief and delight. Noise like thunder. Bright light. Joy.

At which point a thing happens to me. The chain of mental dominoes is very simple; the results are not. Complexity arising from simple properties: this is called *chaos.* The name is very apt. I am drowned in chaos. The woman in front of me claps, vigorously. She whoops. She moves her head. She has a lace band tied round a smart ponytail, and from it a sweet wash of jasmine rolls up and over me. Jasmine. And lace. Leah, in the church in Cricklewood Cove. And immediately thereafter, Leah with Gonzo. Cordite, pain and asphalt.

All the walls come down inside my head. I am betrayed, murdered, rescued, healed and bereft. I have saved the world and been rewarded with five shots in the chest, booted out to die in mid-air on a dusty road. I am toxic waste. I have known heaven, and now I am in hell, and there are mimes. And if there is one thing I will do, before I die in truth, it is this: I will find Gonzo Lubitsch, and I will know *why.* I will know *when,* and whether they felt guilty, or whether they laughed at me. I will make him tell me everything. I will make *them* tell me. Gonzo and her. Her, and Gonzo. I will ride the wind and arrive like a storm, and I will compel answers. I am almost screaming, and my eyes are filled with power and heat. I must be wrapped in boiling shadows. The world must surely be responding to this, making physical my fury, dripping acid from my skin. Although, if so, the man in the seat next to me is taking it remarkably well.

I will avenge. I will have recompense, oh yes. I will.

I am about to surge to my feet. I am about to run out and steal a truck or a bus, and charge off, chase them down. I will travel across the world, if I have to. I will go on for ever. I am inexorable. I am wronged. I am Nemesis, meting out just deserts. Any second now, I will begin. Any second now.

Except that I can see only one conclusion to that course. The road has a logic of its own, a violent, inexorable pressure towards some kind of fearful reckoning. If I chase Gonzo, I must catch him. If I catch him, I must confront him. We will fight. It will end when one of us is dead. Perhaps I will have to kill Leah too. And these are not *my* footsteps; *Gonzo* is the man of action. It is Gonzo who rushes in head first, who leads with the chin, gets back on the horse, takes no prisoners.

I am not Gonzo Lubitsch.

And so, when movement comes back to my limbs and I flee the circus tent into the dark, I do not steal K's bus and charge off in hot pursuit to who knows what bad end. I walk out into the night with a fire in my gut, and I do what Gonzo Lubitsch, in his whole life that I know of, has never really done.

I think.

Chapter Twelve

Wise man's counsel; Jim and Sally at play; Crazy Joe Spork and the Sandpit of Truth.

RONNIE CHEUNG might seem like an odd sort of mentor. You might reasonably expect, as I stand there, hallucinating in the dark outside the Rheingold circus tent, that I would be visited by Master Wu, or by Old Man Lubitsch. If I were in the business of choosing my spiritual guide, I probably wouldn't choose Ronnie. On the other hand, it seems that I, some part of me at least, *would* choose Ronnie, because that is who I end up talking to. Not the real one of course—rumour has it he survived the war but I've no idea where he is. This is a sort of ghost.

We all carry a multitude of ghosts around with us: impressions of other people, strong or weak, deep from long acquaintance or shallow with brevity. Those ghosts are maps, updated with each encounter, made detailed, judged, liked or disliked. They are, if you ask a philosopher, all we can ever really know of the other people in the world. It's usually best not to ask philosophers anything, precisely because they have the habit of what in the Persian language is called *sanud:* the profitless consideration of unsettling yet inconsequential things. Be that as it may, Master Wu and Old Man Lubitsch—even in portable form—are both too wise for this moment. There is a level of enlightenment to which it is painful to confess your failings. To admit to either of those elders that I have failed in my life, been so incompetent as to be cuckolded and shot within hours of saving the world (partially), is too much. To be forgiven by them would be to suffer another wound.

Ronnie Cheung, on the other hand, is familiar with screw-up. His advice is of the harsher sort, and it is spoken with the gentleness of a man replete with his own failings and conversant with shame and victim's guilt and all the rest. Ronnie Cheung is the kind of Buddha you can imagine meeting in a bar, the kind who will save your soul and then rob you blind at the pool table. He is the sort of saint who will smack you repeatedly about the head and neck with a codfish if that's what you need to get back on track. My subconscious chooses him, so it is Ronnie's ghost-in-the-head which marches up to me to hear the whole sad story and give advice.

The night is cool. An indecisive moon is hanging above the circus tent while a murmur of approbation filters out through the canvas backdrops. I sit on a stump and stand up again, then sit. Then I stand up. We like to believe we are complex creatures, but sometimes we just get perfectly balanced between conflicting drives, and we dither. Up, down. Up, down. I'm a dog caught between a piece of steak and a comfortable chair. It's tearing me apart. Up, down. Down. Hmm, no. Up.

"Bumhole. You are giving me a pain. I will not say where. The location of the pain you are giving me is so vile and intimate it would turn your man-parts to water even to contemplate it. I am not in the least bit joking."

Ronnie's voice. It's not that I'm hallucinating. I know perfectly well he isn't there. And yet I know also what he is saying and where he is standing, and how his big ugly fingers make a casually obscene gesture.

"Come on then. Out with it."

And out it comes, all of it, in a great awful blurt, delivered without mercy or self-concealment to the empty air, and Ronnie—who isn't there—paces impatiently.

"Oi," he says, when I am finished and hanging my head. "You want to know what I think?"

"No."

"Bollocks. And I'm telling you anyway."

"Go away."

Ronnie, who is intangible, hits me extremely hard in the nose. It doesn't hurt exactly, but a cold rush washes over my face where his fist makes landfall. It makes me shiver, and little fizzy things happen in my brain. It sort of clears out the fluff.

"Bumhole, I am not here to amuse myself. I can do that with my own two hands and a jar of Swarfega. I am here because you, in your tiny wisdom, are seeking me, in mine. All right? So stop being a tosspot and pay attention."

I pay attention, but in a surly way which conveys that I am only doing so to please him. I do not want his advice. I do not want anyone's advice.

"The question is whether you were listening to your Uncle Ron all those years ago when he whispered salient truths in your ear, or whether you were in fact jerking off. Do you recall my tactical driving course?"

"Yes."

"Do you recall every last detail of it?"

"I don't know."

"Almost certainly not, because I am a fountain of wisdom and you are a twerp. However. What I am about to impart to you was not in the basic course. I do believe that you took the advanced. Did you?"

"Yes."

"In the advanced we consider longer-range missions with better opportunities for planning. In other words, strategic and logistics-based driving missions. And in that context we talk about the value of local knowledge, understanding your enemy's objectives and theatre-wide intelligence. We talk about the minimum threshold for planning. Without a decent picture of what is happening around you, any decision you make is for shit. Still with me? Making sense?"

"I don't know."

" 'Yes, Ronnie, you are!' "

"Yes, Ronnie, you are."

"All right then. So, you are fucked. Am I right?" Ronnie Cheung waves to indicate that I should respond.

"Yes, Ronnie, you are."

"Yes, I am. You are fucked. You are desirous of getting unfucked. Unfucking is considerably more difficult than fucking. The Second Law of *ther-mo-dynamics*—because if you were thinking *even for a minute* that you are better educated than I am and therefore superior, Bumhole, you were mistaken—does not look with kindness upon unfucking. The level of fuckedness in a system always increases unless something acts on it from the outside. Worse yet, Bumhole, you do not *own* your own fuckedness. You do not appreciate the fullness of the fucking which has happened to you. You cannot hope to *amend* your situation without knowing what it is."

"I do know."

"I do not think that you do."

"I do!"

"Then by all means, Bumhole, explain to me why you are not dead—indeed, why you are positively chipper—when you were recently shot in the digestive tract; why your best friend of many years seems to have been conducting an affair with your wife so secret that you never had an inkling, yet so astoundingly absolute that he has moved into your house, exchanged your furniture for his own and bought a bloody dog; and how he was able to do all these things for years when you have been living with your missus all that time."

"I don't know."

"Ah. Well, then perhaps you might want to find out. And while you're at it, you might want to ask who in all the world might want to damage the Jorgmund Pipe and why; and what name we give a man who wears black, appears from nowhere and cuts his way through a moderately competent fighting force as if they were made of yak butter. You might probe the origin of the mysterious phone call which advised you—presciently, I think we can now say—to avoid this job as if it were a dose of Mongolian Sausage Rot. And since you are a loyal student and friend of dear old Wu Shenyang, you might also give some thought to whether this black-clad sanguinary *fucker,* who pushed you and your former chum under a shower of the most awful and corrosive muck since the Goss brothers stopped singing, and who tried to cut your head off, is related by some chance to the *other* black-clad, sanguinary *fuckers* who may or may not have murdered your teacher and set his house on fire. All of which begs the question of how it is, Bumhole, that you were not warped, twisted and buggered in the eyeholes like anyone else would have been when you were drenched in a shedload of ontologically toxic goop, and whether your current problems derive in some measure from this close encounter with the poisoned lifeblood of the world. Am I right?"

I nod.

" 'Yes, Ronnie, you are!' How will you do these things?"

"I don't know!"

"Fuck me, Bumhole—which now I come to think of it is a very strange invitation and you should ignore it—but you don't know much, do you?" And this is so transparently accurate that I lose the surly and just want a hug.

"No, Ronnie. I really don't." And at this Ronnie Cheung peers at me a bit more closely.

"Balls," he says at last. He slumps next to me on the stump and lights a dog-end from behind his ear.

"Your situation, Bumhole, is a mess. You know nothing. You cannot go over the top in that condition or you will die. You may have noticed that you have escaped death not once but three times in the last little while. Everyone around you is playing for keeps. *You* are playing with your sister's doll's house or—God help us—your own tiny winky. *They* are on home ground. *You* are in enemy territory. Pay close attention, Bumhole, because this is the burden of my song: *you were set up.* Is that clear? If someone knew enough to warn you—by phone, personally—then what has happened has in some measure happened *according to a plan.* We may assume that this plan does not especially favour you. We shall therefore regard it as an *enemy plan.* That being the case, you need to know about it. You need the *cui bono?,* which is to say *who benefits?* You need maps and charts; you need weather reports and field intelligence. You need these things because everybody else *already has them.* You haven't got a prayer until you know what's going on."

"How much of it?"

Ronnie Cheung shrugs.

"All of it, for preference."

"I don't care about all of it. I just want to know my bit."

"Bumhole," says Ronnie Cheung, taking a deep drag on his gasper and tilting his head back to examine the sky, "what in all this ever gave you the impression that anyone was paying attention to what *you* want?"

And then I can still smell his dog-end, but he's not there any more.

From the dark, behind me, comes a gust of wind, and with it just a faint flavour of greasepaint.

"Well," says Ike Thermite softly, "that is quite a story."

RHEINGOLD is fading away behind us and Ike Thermite—who is, despite making his living by painting his face and falling over imaginary roller-skates, *very* smart—has asked me to drive. I can look in the rear view mirror of the little bus and see, past the bobbled fabric seats and the rounded windows plastered with the traces of tour stickers and smears of greasepaint, the horizon receding behind me. There's no chatter in the bus. The mimes—obviously—are quiet. Some of them are sleeping, like scary whiteface children; they make little snuffling noises and one of them murmurs "Buster! Put that down!" and rolls over to drool onto his spare beret. The rest just sit and watch the scenery or the middle distance. When we pass anything of note—a truck stop or a lonely house or even a lamp post shining down on a little mountain of rubbish and disregarded newspapers—their heads turn in unison to watch it go by, their wide black eyes and pudding-bowl haircuts tracking the patch of light until it slips past the hind edge of their window and fades into the dark. I am driving a colony of owls.

The road ahead of us is straight and clear, and there's not much in the way of a speed limit out here, nor much of a police force even if there were. My only limitation is the engine of the Matahuxee Mime Combine's bus, and while the bus was essentially dead when it arrived in Rheingold, it has since been loved-up by K of the sarong, who knows the Blacksmith's Word (new edition) and speaks fluently the language of the camshaft. He opened the bus's bonnet and whispered with his hands, was covered in spurting black stuff and hydraulic fluid and miserable, grainy water, and pronounced it sound but grievously abused. He and K—the latter very fetching in a boiler suit, poster girl for gender-bending lust—stripped, lubed and serviced it, an operation requiring many richly erotic rubbings and cleansings and complex tête-à-têtes. They sorted out the ignition sequence, dealt with the plugs and the alternator, and several other matters of high occult wisdom. They then lectured Ike Thermite for a few moments on the right way to take care of a motor vehicle, as exemplified by exactly not what he had obviously done to this point, and scurried off for some post-maintenance coitus. I hadn't even realised, until that moment, that they were lovers.

Ike Thermite says nothing to me until Rheingold is a faint whisper of sodium orange bravely gleaming on the far side of the horizon line. He lets me get some distance from the place of my awakening so that, although I have not escaped my demons, I have at least left behind the place where last they made themselves felt. And then, in the secure, hypnotic darkness of the road, Ike Thermite suggests that the steering pulls a bit to the left. After a moment I tell him that I think K sorted that out, and he says well, maybe. And we don't say anything for a bit.

And then Ike Thermite says that he's known K for some time and likes him very much, but has always secretly suspected that he was as mad as a box of frogs.

To this I reply that I have, knowing K only for a short time, reached very much the same conclusion, but that I can't pin down the precise point at which K's version of what is departs from everyone else's, and Ike Thermite suggests that this is because everyone else is also a bit mad, but in more overtly acceptable ways. I feel able to agree. We giggle a bit at the idea that K is just the most cheerily obvious of a planet of loons, and Ike shares with me his small supply of chewy fruit sweets, which he seems to have secured from one of the ladies of Rheingold on a promise of greater delights when next he passes through. I hadn't really thought of Ike as a babe-magnet up to this point. The notion of a mime having sex is somehow fundamentally *wrong.* I tell him so, and this sets off another round of helpless giggling, and one of the wakeful mimes lurches over and signs to me firmly, and somehow rather waspishly, that I need to concentrate on the driving.

And finally Ike Thermite says:

"That is quite a story."

I almost ask "What story?" but don't, because I realise in time that this would be the single stupidest question ever asked in the history of the world.

"Yes," I say.

"Seems like you have some things to do."

"Yes."

Ike Thermite nods. It's not the freaky mime nod, it's a contemplative human nod. "Where are you going first?"

This is a very good question. I want to talk to Leah. I can't. I don't know yet what I can tell her. Maybe I can talk to Jim Hepsobah. Maybe Sally Culpepper would broker a meeting. Maybe Sally would talk to Egon and Egon could talk to Leah. Or maybe Gonzo has pronounced me a monster, a slayer of men and a bad egg, and my friends are not friends any more. I put my trust in the solidity of Jim Hepsobah and in Sally Culpepper's wit. They will know what to do.

"That way, towards the mountains," I tell Ike. "I know someone." And please, let it be true.

"We have an itinerary," he says. "We have engagements."

I nod.

"It so happens, however, that they are mostly over there in a general sort of way. And none of them is pressing." He pauses, looks at me.

"What about the others?" By which I mean, what about K and K (the lovers) and K (the Highlander), and the sheepdogs, and the Indian runner ducks, and the assorted other Ks presently taking down the circus tent and due to join us tomorrow or the day after.

Ike shrugs. "They can manage without us for a bit."

Ike Thermite is offering to go out of his way to help me. Honest faces lie. What do mime faces do? Mime faces are pale and strange. They mock you. I do not answer.

Ike Thermite rubs his eyes. I can hear the grit in them.

"Ask yourself a question," he says. "Looking around you, do you see anyone who strikes you as a basically joyful person? I mean, is there anyone on this bus who habitually wears red or orange? Yellow? Blue? Any colour other than black?"

There is not. But K and his lot are many-coloured. They are perky even.

"K," Ike Thermite says, "used to be a medical professional. Then, because he was promoted, he became an administrator, and finally he became an executive. He worked for the System. He lived and breathed it. He was very good at it. He was married, and he had a family. And one morning he woke up and he realised that he hadn't seen them for two months. He didn't know, even, which city they were in. They might be in the main house in New Paris, or in the apartment in Constantinopolis, or in the pool house at Tavistock Villas. So he started checking his personal in-tray, which was about four feet high. He found some bills and some junk mail and some cards for his birthday the year before, and finally he found a letter from a lawyer telling him they'd all been killed in a crash. Apparently it was quite a big one—in all the newspapers and so on. But he hadn't known they were travelling and he hadn't been watching the news, because it wasn't part of his professional life, and his job demanded he put his personal stuff in a separate part of his mind and switch it off. Which he did, because that was the *right* thing for all of them. He was being a professional. Maybe he was doing it in order to be a Dad, but that's something else, that's personal motivation, and he wasn't supposed to be thinking about that on the clock. So. Turns out he'd missed the funerals because he was doing what he was supposed to be doing, *being professional.* Now . . . you might expect me to say that he quit on the spot. He didn't. And if he had, you might say he'd had some kind of nervous breakdown. Which he didn't.

"What K did—what Joel Athens Lantern did, because that was K's name once upon a time, and I can tell you that because no one of that name exists any more—was file a request for some personal time and go back to work. Because that was what he knew was the professional thing to do—and if he wasn't a father any more, or a husband, the least he could do was be a good professional. He had all these patterns in his head for behaviour. Ways of being, each with its own little set of priorities and responses. But he'd somehow swallowed all of them under his professional hat, and now that was all he had left. So he defined himself by work. And then, a little bit later, he was so appalled by that decision—how cold, how not-human it was, how it was an anti-Dad decision—that he walked out of his office and got onto the first bus which would take him, which was this one, and wandered off into the world and never looked back. He called himself K from then on, and gradually he got a few other people to do the same, so that they would always have to stop and think about the people and the personal relationships and the context in order to understand which of them you were talking about. It's confusing, so they *have* to use their heads and examine everything. They can't be tricked by labels. In other words, K is called K so that he never becomes mechanical again, so that he has to consider his humanity every time he speaks to someone."

Ike Thermite sits back in his seat and flaps his hand, dispersing the tension as if it were a sweet wrapper stuck to his forefinger.

"What I am telling you," he says, "is that you are surrounded by people who know what it is like to have a bad day. And we will help you, because we choose to."

At which I feel very small, and I say "Thank you."

We drive on. The road feels open now, not closed, and the mime mobile is strong with torque and freshly cleansed spark plugs. The wagon of Dr. Andromas appears in the mirror behind us, and Ike Thermite, unlike his brother mimes, seems to derive some satisfaction from its presence.

"Who is he?" I ask Ike, because K wouldn't tell.

"Andromas?"

"Yes. And why did he help me? Why is everyone afraid of him?"

Ike Thermite ponders.

"You've got the wrong idea about Andromas," he says at last. But try as I might, I cannot get him to tell me any more.

IT WAS in former days the practice of James V. Hepsobah (Sergeant), during the quiet periods between missions, to remove the hair from his head by means of a sharpened edge. He had seen at first-hand the inutility of flowing locks in the combat zone, when his personal mentor and senior officer, Gumbo Bill Faziel, was sucked head first into the business end of an aircraft engine after leaping from a plane during a mismanaged political assassination, with the consequence that Gumbo Bill came to be spread over fourteen villages and towns in a fine ochre-coloured layer, and the plane itself tumbled from the sky like a swingball cut off from the centre post. Gumbo Bill may or may not have been the greatest covert military operative of the late twentieth century, but no one could have faulted his fine coiffure until the moment when its in-theatre failings became horribly apparent.

The peculiarities of his life being what they were—night boat rides and tropical camps and free-fall insertions—Jim often had to do his depilation in places which were not fully equipped for barbering. As a consequence of this, he established an inflexible method for the task: he would first smear his head with a plant extract which, while possessing many of the nutritive and hypo-allergenic properties of the more expensive commercial products, smelled not of sandalwood or spice, but rather of leaf mulch and wet fur, and thus would not give him away when the wind changed during an operation. Second, while the balsam was working on his scalp—opening the pores and making the fine fuzz of hair stand on end—he would test his crescent-shaped boot knife for sharpness and occasionally stroke the blade with a special stone to achieve a proper razor finish. Next, he would hold the handle of the knife lightly but firmly in the three bottom fingers of his right hand (*aikidoka*-style), rest his index finger on the spine of the knife and cradle it in the palm of his left. Finally, using his two thumbs as guide rails, he would move the whole stable and predictable parcel across his scalp from front to back, allowing the skin and bone to dictate the movement of the blade. In four long, slow strokes, he would complete his task, and not waves nor clear air turbulence nor minor quakes could make him draw blood. Bone Briskett once saw Jim shave in a typhoon, or so he claims—but Bone is an inveterate teller of tall tales and regards any man who is voluntarily bald as a lunatic.

When Sally Culpepper told Jim that they were dating—Jim not being quick enough on the uptake to suit her in this context—she also took control of his shaving regimen. Sally ordained that—unless they were in the field—Jim would use a soap which did not smell like a muskrat's armpit, and would allow her to perform the task, as watching him gave her the willies. When they moved in together, and while Sally waited for Jim to read and act on the next set of orders regarding their relationship (i.e., the trip they will shortly be making to some manner of church or civil place of ceremony and pomp), she added a further guideline that she would perform this function twice weekly, in the living room, to whatever music most suited her mood, and that Jim would wear a suit for the occasion. The precise motivation behind this decree was occult. I had not in honesty wished it clarified, in case there was sex involved. It explains, however, what I see as I walk in through the front door of the house they share.

Jim and Sally do not lock their door. In the first place, there's no one hereabouts to make trouble. In the second, they have little enough to steal. In the third, anyone who could threaten either of them in any serious way would not be deterred by a door. It is a rule among the Haulage & HazMat Civil Freebooting Company that you only pitch up at sociable hours—these being flexible—but also that you damn well do pitch up rather than not. If it's a bad moment, you'll know. If it's not, you're welcome, the beer's in the fridge.

Jim Hepsobah is wearing a pinstripe. It's not a grey pinstripe; it's a very dark brown, with red. It's positively Nathan Detroit. It's the suit Humphrey Bogart is wearing in all those black-and-white movies where it simply doesn't occur to you to ask. He lies back in a genuine barber's chair, and one half of his head is covered in foam. A big white napkin or towel (it's made of untextured cotton; people do make towels from that stuff, but nobody ever actually got dry with one) is draped over the top half of his body to catch the drips, and his eyes are closed in deep, sensuous bliss. It's disturbing (intimate) but not nearly as disturbing as the next bit.

Sally Culpepper stands behind him. The razor she holds is

like a wire or a glass filament, and her strokes are deft and slow. Not one bristle will escape her. She is doing not only Jim's head, but his chin as well. She is wearing a barber's coat and has her hair slicked back in fine vintage style. The coat comes down to mid-thigh, and under it she is wearing stockings. I am unable to say what else she may or may not be wearing, because as soon as I realise that I am looking at Sally Culpepper in what might loosely be termed a state of undress (although in fact actual nudity would be considerably less filthy, less fascinatingly and blazingly lewd) I spin round and face the other way, so that, as I address them both, I am in fact backing into the room and blushing—or, I very much fear, flushing.

I stammer for a moment, because my eyes and my mind, by that much-beloved phenomenon of image retention, can still see Sally's legs—thighs—moving as she stepped around Jim, crossing and uncrossing, whispering past one another in those endless stockings with their purple trim and crosshatched net. Images of shadow and skin, deeper mysteries than mere legs, unresolved in that one glance but now inevitably untangled by the more primitive and unashamed parts of my brain, burn themselves into me. I do not want Sally Culpepper specifically, but her body, glimpsed in this moment of playful desire, is the flag my own has chosen to remind me that I have not ceased to be sexual, or romantic, that my urge to have monster sex has not vanished simply because I have been abandoned and shot. Indeed, perhaps the reverse is true. Until now I have simply sat on that part of myself, or maybe it has been asleep.

Not any more. It's probably a good thing I am at this moment standing with my back to them.

Ludicrous as my behaviour is, and fabulously uncool, it may well save my life, because it is so plainly not an attack that it apparently tempers Jim's first reaction upon seeing me, which is to reach beneath the napkin (or towel) on his lap and produce a very real, Al Capone–looking gun. I pray, heartily, that Sally Culpepper is not going to put the knife to my throat. The combination of danger and sex would probably leave me irretrievably perverse. Mercifully, she does not. Instead, I hear some distracting rustlings and swooshings, and when Jim Hepsobah tells me to turn, I find him standing on his feet and her a bit behind him and to the left, wearing a pair of chequered trousers with braces, and a white shirt. This is the rest of her barber's outfit, I suppose, and the braces do fascinating things which I cannot entirely ignore, but the danger of my—for example—grunting with lust when I open my mouth to speak is gone. Sadly, the danger that Jim Hepsobah will shoot me remains.

Jim glowers at me.

"Who the hell are you?" he demands. He says it flat. There's no doubt he means it exactly the way it sounds.

It's not the question I was expecting. It catches me somewhat between the eyes. To begin with, this is Jim talking—after Gonzo, the first man to whom I would give my trust, my buddy—but at the same time, it's not Jim, or not *my* Jim. This is the Jim Hepsobah strangers see: a big powerful man with a talent for war. Sergeant Jim: do not mess. This man is asking me, in defiance of a decade-plus of shared history, who the hell I am. It's a mismatch. He *knows* who I am. He was there. Although, quite apparently, he does *not* know. At the same time it is, on a level far beyond the one where Jim is asking it, a bloody good question. If I am not Gonzo Lubitsch's best friend and trusty wingman; if I am not Leah's husband; if I am not these two things by which I have defined my life, who am I? "Victim" is not an identity I particularly covet. Vice president, i/c strategy and planning, Haulage & HazMat Civil Freebooting Company, of course—but not if Jim doesn't know me any more. Reluctant soldier. Former ideological anarchist (with reservations and the understanding that it was only for the sex). Student of the School of the Voiceless Dragon (now defunct). Lonely child in a sandpit. It seems, in fact, that I am not very much of anything any more. I have gone as if I never were.

It occurs to me that I may be in the bull's-eye of some kind of irony. Perhaps the noxious Stuff at Station 9 (slipping over my suit, into the cracks, touching my matter, infiltrating and co-opting me, *yuck*) has reacted with my guilt at being George Copsen's right hand in the operations room long ago. I started all this. Now I am living it. Sort of. Perhaps, by some trick not yet understood and by my own subconscious needs, I have Gone Away. Or half-gone, so that I can (and the taxonomist within is making a note for Grandma Wu of this new and exciting variation) experience the Personal Hell of Living Your Own Life from the Outside. People have forgotten me, and the world has rushed in from all sides to fill the gap I have left. Leah is chaste, Gonzo is innocent. I am my own ghost. The situation is not irretrievable.

It's a lovely idea.

It's a comforting lie.

I'm starting to see the truth. The truth is worse.

I look at Sally Culpepper—last hope. Her face is clean and cold. There is not one flicker of recognition in her eyes. If this were anyone else—if it was Samuel P. and Tommy Lapland, say, coming down the steps of some ghastly bordello and pulling iron on me on sight, I might believe that they were scared to talk to me, or guilty, and this was a dodge. Not Jim, who never backs away from the unpleasant, and never in front of Sally. The shame would kill him, to dissemble in the face of responsibility. And not Sally, in front of Jim, who must only ever see her perfect and composed. She cannot realise that it's her imperfections he loves: the bump in her arm where she broke it as a kid, the moment when she laughs mid-sip and snorts beer from her nose—which is why he doesn't propose. He is afraid of blemishing her.

"Sorry," I say. "My mistake. I'm leaving now."

And I back out, arms in the air. The Al Capone gun follows me to the door.

What the hell.

"James Vortigern Hepsobah," I say, and it goes right into his face from all the way across the room, "you need to ask that woman to marry you. She's your beating heart and every drop of blood in your veins, but in the small dark hours before the dawn she worries maybe she's not enough. So stop being a prick and do the thing."

And I walk out into the front garden having done at least that much.

IN MOVIES it's cool to be the Man With No Name. You get all manner of female attention and you're somehow more dangerous than everyone around you. You have no past, and a mysterious destiny awaits you. All very exciting. But I've never wanted a destiny. I was happy with having a life. And while, in movies, having no identity is a noble grief which brings profundity and romance to the hero, in real life it's just a cold, sad place with no horizon. Plus also, if my life were a movie, my dog at least would remember me. When all about me were staring at me in blank incomprehension, and some piece of well-chosen Sibelius was emphasising my pain, the simple, loyal canine would trot out of my old house and demand to be a part of my adventures, for good or ill, and no doubt would save my life in the last reel. Of course, I don't have a dog. Gonzo has a dog.

All of a sudden I think I understand Annie the Ox's puppet head collection.

I go back to the mime mobile. Ike Thermite doesn't remember me from the Ace of Thighs, when I ask. He remembers a whole bunch of us, but not me in particular. I don't tell him that I'm wondering if I've Gone Away (revised version) and I don't speculate on the Other Possibility either. Instead, I ask him if he would mind taking a detour from his itinerary to go see Malevolent Pete. Pete may not remember me either, but this is completely normal. Pete does not acknowledge customers as anything other than annoying people who bring him work which shouldn't need to be done and pay late. But Pete has my one remaining friend boarding with him, and I want to go see her, touch her (to make sure she's real) and ask her to come along. Otherwise I will go mad.

The thing which sets Malevolent Pete aside from humanity as a whole is his tininess. It's not that he's especially short. There are many short men who are also nice, and many who are not afflicted with what the French call Napoléon's syndrome and the descendants of the Golden-Eared Bey refer to as Mustafa's colic. They go about their business and have no urge to dominion or empire, probably because they have been raised successfully to believe that being short is an advantage, predisposes one to be an acrobat, looks better on celluloid, fits into Italian sports cars, and doesn't bang one's head when having sex in the lower bunk bed. Malevolent Pete is otherwise. He has made his loathing of height into a definition. He is not so much short as anti-tall. He stands out in a group of people because he is belligerently, loomingly short. He brings his anti-tallness to everything he does; his lean, agitated face is a map to the town of Bad-Tempered Git. He is obsessed with measurement. Specifically, with measuring his own superiority. There are no errors in Pete's garage. He has analysed them into extinction. He kept lists and tallies, re-organised and re-examined, performed complex genealogical investigations of failure, and fired two hundred and thirty-one assistant mechanics in four years.

In Pete's garage there are no compromises and no substitutions. He releases your vehicle when it is ready, or not at all. He warns you not to slip the gears unless you want a new box in a month, and if you bring the thing in stripped, he will take the keys from you in a way which makes you feel like you're grounded and in disgrace. He tuts better than any other person alive. He does not embellish his bills—they are exacting, and written in perfect unjoined print. Each letter is the image of the others of its own kind, no bigger, no smaller. No deviation is possible, let alone permitted. The workshop is clean, except in those specific areas where oil and grease are tolerated and necessary, and these are marked with yellow and black chevrons. Safety procedures are followed. Hard hats are worn. Pink and blue slips make their way to you inexorably through the system to Purchasing and Tallies respectively, while the *goldenrod* pages (this is the proper name of the yellow slips, and therefore the name used in Malevolent Pete's garage) go through Pete's in-tray to his self-invented filing system, which allows him to backstop, check and recheck everything, and also monitor his employees and their working patterns by checking the time stamps on each one. The last time Pete was audited he sent two suits back to Haviland City holding their slide rules and whimpering, because he caught two errors and a fudge in their calculations in the scant forty-nine minutes they were there.

Pete may or may not be God's own mechanic. He never swears, and he absolutely will not cheat. He is perfection as viewed through the lens of precision. On the other hand he thinks *caritas* is a branded cola. God comes in a variety of flavours, but almost all of them would be offended by something about this hatchet-faced little squirt with his blunt certainty and his sneering ungenerosity. To Malevolent Pete, there is one hell, and this is it: that he lends us these vehicles we own, and we take them away and do irresponsible things like drive them through muck and dust, and he has to take them back all dinged up and make them work so that we can torture them again. That we pay for this service is not relevant; Pete would have work whatever the circumstances, his fame is ubiquitous in the Livable Zone. The point is that we make unnecessary problems for him, which are measurable on a graph showing Reasonable Wear & Tear vs. Actual Necessary Repairs. We are reckless, one and all, and he is like a triage doctor in a war zone, patching men up so they can get injured again. Except that these are trucks, big dumb lugs, and they are far more important and vulnerable than a man could ever be. Narrow eyes survey me from his narrow face, and a precise amount of speculative disapproval is unwrapped and prepared for use. *Disapproval, anticipated,* x 1 from stores.

"What do you want?" Narrow mouth moving just enough to form words, main hand still making notes, because time is, if not money, at least time, and there's no point wasting it. Indeed, there's probably paperwork for non-chargeable units. Pete would be an impossible boss. He hires no one who is not utterly subordinate. If ever I am king of the world, I will make sure, absolutely sure, that there is not one single Pete in my government. If Pete cared about anything other than trucks and precision, he'd be a monster. As it is, he's just an elemental of the internal combustion engine.

"I ride with Gonzo. Shotgun seat."

"Never seen you."

"I try not to get in the way." And this appears to be the right thing to say, because Malevolent Pete nods in a way which suggests I have been degraded from Threat to Nuisance, and Nuisance is a broad category which includes Paying Customer. He parks the pen. I show him my company badge, one of the few things recovered by K from the sad little bundle of bloody rags which were my good shirt and trousers, in the aftermath of Gonzo's radical reconceptualisation of my outfit and my body. STAKEHOLDER, it says, because I am. Stakeholders are permitted access to company equipment. It's in the charter. Pete knows it. So now I am downgraded still further to Legitimate Nuisance, and we're all friends, to whatever extent Malevolent Pete accepts that classification. His left hand, which has been idly tapping the bench near a big wrench (*hand-to-hand combat, for use in,* x 1), snaps to his side as he stands up.

"What do I call you?" he demands, not asking my name but what name he's going to use on the paperwork, because Malevolent Pete does not need superfluous information in his life. The formalities are obeyed. He cannot be reproached. I think about it, and since I'm currently not anyone in particular, and it seems to be in vogue, I tell him "K," and he writes down Kaye as a surname. I do not correct him, and he does not check. We walk together to the main workshop.

"Number thirty-seven," I remind him, and he nods without answering.

Our old truck—*my* truck—is in bay 37. It is big and ugly. Not even Pete's garage can get the thing entirely clean. The dirt is part of the paintwork. The pipes are not chromed. I found it—"her"—in a burned-out barn when we were still working out of Piper 90, and spent the whole summer taking it apart and putting it back together. The seats are leatherette, and they have holes in them from where someone has driven a ballpoint pen through the fabric. There are little scribbles around the edges, in the shape of flowers and faces and human genital organs. There's no tape player and no air-con, but there's a rifle clip over the wheel and the engine absolutely will not quit until you have got where you're going.

Annabelle, the truck. My last old friend in the world.

I sign Pete's chitty (press hard; blue and pink and goldenrod must be clear, and Pete has added carbon paper so that he has a white copy for me and a clear copy for his new microfiche system), and he walks away without saying goodbye or thank you. Pete does not do customer relations. I run my fingers over the steering wheel.

Voiceless Dragon *gong fu* is a soft style. The relaxed muscles and receptive mind allow you to follow your opponent's movements, react to his tensions before his strikes are executed. You strive to retain contact, learn him, understand him, so that you own him. Experimenting with this doctrine during Ronnie Cheung's advanced tactical (and strategic) driving course, I established that it is possible to learn an inanimate object too, so that you can—for example—read the road through the wheels of a vehicle, know the surface and the conditions. It's what I was doing in K's Airstream. It is infinitely easier if you know the vehicle concerned. At that point the steel and rubber around you is an extension of your body into the world. Feel that? That's a pebble on the left wing. Wind speed? Twenty to twenty-five, coming from (assuming the battered chrome mandala on the front of the truck is zero degrees) bearing oh three five. Right now, in the garage, there's a man leaning on the rear fender, and it's probably Ike Thermite. It's not Pete, whose touch is angular and invasive; it's someone quiet and subtle, someone who flexes and listens with his hands. An acrobat or a scholar. Ike Thermite is both, of course. Wu Shenyang would have liked him.

Ike opens the passenger door.

"Where we going, cowboy?" He's found a mime to drive his bus, a woman named Lianne who specialises in a sort of combination of tightrope and dance; they roll her along poles and ladders as if she were a beach ball, and she emerges at each end looking fuddled and swaying, and then some accident propels her back along another pole, another impossible, gravity-defying tumble. It's great for slapstick routines. Lianne has fabulous balance and depth perception, and is almost totally impossible to rattle. Exactly the sort of person you want to entrust your driving to. In the meantime, Ike is coming with me. It's weird, having him sitting there in my seat while I sit in Gonzo's. I feel a vertiginous, cliff-edge lurch: the strange, inverted desire to do the worst imaginable thing. In the case of a cliff, of course, it's to jump; here it is to become like Gonzo, to reach for a gun and pepper him with bullets. I shunt it back into the mad and bad section of my subconscious, where it belongs.

I rev the engine. Annabelle growls tunelessly, like a bear hibernating on a bassoonist.

"Home," I tell him. "Cricklewood Cove."

Ike Thermite looks at me curiously. Once again, he's got that face going on, the one which says there's things happening here he ought to know more about. I probably ought to know too.

"You've been there?" I ask him.

Ike Thermite shrugs. "Heard of it," he says.

I take Annabelle off the leash.

IKE THERMITE and the Matahuxee Mime Combine have some kind of pilgrimage to make. Apparently a very well-considered mime once lived in Cricklewood Cove (to whatever extent mimes are ever well-considered), and when he died his dependants established his home as a small museum. Mimish artefacts are cased in glass and revered as relics of the Master. Bunsen burner and retort (for the making of greasepaint); soft shoes; sewing machine (it's hard to get good baggy pants these days); a wall of photographs of great moments. The Master shaking hands with the King of the UIK. The Master dancing the samba with two princesses. The Master doing "Climb Wall, Step in Something" for the Thai ambassador, who finds this hilarious. The Master in his one and only film, *The Quiet Life,* in which he plays a sombre assassin who just wants to be funny. Ike Thermite assures me it is fascinating, and a little sad. It is also the only museum in the world where there is no audio tour.

I am amazed that I have never been there. Ma Lubitsch took us to every museum in town when I was a kid. Ike Thermite points out gently that the Master was, at that time, still alive.

Ike walks off, a little bandy-legged (Annabelle's bench is stout and durable but hardly comfy), followed by a long line of polo necks and berets and respectful nodding. They're like a little army, very self-possessed and serious. Their weirdness doesn't upset them. They are who they are.

Lucky them.

So here now is the corner of Lambic Street, where the old ironmonger's used to be, and here is Packlehyde Road. On my left, about two hundred yards away, is the Soames School. Off beyond a way is Doyle's Walk and the house at the end is the Warren, where Elisabeth lived when she wasn't sleeping at Wu Shenyang's. (And exactly how that came about would be a mystery to me if I hadn't met the *other* Assumption Soames, the real one, to whom the wretched old buzzard we knew as the Evangelist was a mask which allowed her to teach tolerance more effectively and prepare us all for the roads less travelled and the cannibals of life. Assumption must have been delighted to discover Master Wu, a crazed old coot packed with life skills and wisdom, on her doorstep, tutoring her daughter.)

In the other direction is the Lubitsch house. The original donkeys have gone to a better place, without fences or yapping dogs or Lydia Copsen to torment them with her inappropriate style choices. Old Man Lubitsch never said so, but I suspect they met their end during the Reification, when Cricklewood Cove was cut off (literally cut off at the southern end, where the sea poured into the shallow excision and made a new beach alongside the cinema) from the rest of the world. Food was scarce, and donkey eats well when the cupboard's bare. Gonzo believes that they died naturally, and are buried by the roses. And indeed, in a sense, they did, eaten by an apex predator in hard times.

Before the wedding, I had high tea with Gonzo's parents for the sake of Auld Lang Syne. Cricklewood Cove had seen some excitement in the long months of the Reification: brigands had come out of the hills, looking for things to eat and things to trade, but above all things to steal and people to kill; fearsome beasts had roamed the highways and mauled the mayor; Assumption Soames had led a small army against rumoured cannibals, but none had been found; and even since the Cove had been back on the map, there was word of vanishings—a place called Heyerdahl Point had apparently disappeared, been—so the breathless would have it—eaten entire by monsters. But everywhere was like that. The Cove was a refuge. It was simple and safe, something I very much needed amid the bustle of everyone getting ready to marry me. Old Man Lubitsch, craggier and spikier, muttering about monsters and brigands and the parlous state of the world, and building a big black bee house for special bees, would not come in from the cold. Ma Lubitsch smiled and took him a scone on a plastic plate.

I can't go to the Lubitsch house yet. It's not time. And I can't face the Evangelist either, still not knowing where Elisabeth may be. Her body was never recovered from Corvid's Field, but that proves nothing. Four billion people disappeared without trace back then. It's ludicrous to blame myself for this ignorance. I do, anyway. So the only other place is along Packlehyde Road to the edge of the new sea, to the Aggerdean Bluff and my parents' house.

Some memories are greyscale; paint-by-numbers. If you examine them in your head, your mind hurriedly glosses everything, fills in the spaces with tints and shades. If you turn your head too quickly, you catch yourself daubing the walls to match what you know was there but cannot actually recall. Others are all sensation, all colour and no detail. The living room of my parents' house—in memory—is a cool airy blue, with a dark oak fireplace and modern oil paintings in driftwood frames. It's like a living room cut into a glacier. In the same memories my father is a deep voice from an upward direction, a moving wall of woollen trouser and leather brogues. He is a source of unexpected swoops and presents wrapped inexpertly in newspaper. My mother is brown corduroy and a nurturing spoon. Her hands are cool upon my forehead, soothing my fevers, making magic on bruises and knocks. Neither of them, in my infant recollection, has a face, and actually that hardly changes as I get older. I can remember how I feel about their expressions, and what kind of expressions they are wearing, but in none of the images I have of them can I see a still image, a snapshot, of their faces. I am concerned I will not recognise them. And if I don't, how will they possibly know me, absent these many years?

I climb the hill on foot. My borrowed boots are a bit large, and my left heel is getting a blister on it. When I walk, I push my toe all the way forward into the boot. My heel comes down a half-centimetre or so from the back, and slides across the insole. For some reason a little patch just off-centre catches against the fabric. It is a slide-rub, the skin dragging and making an elongated patch, slowly filling with clear fluid. Tomorrow, I will resent it. Right now the sensation of the disconnected skin, rough and stretchy and no longer a part of me yet still connected, is a bit disgusting and a bit fascinating.

I remember this hill. It is a deceptive bugger. It is rippled, legacy of long-ago terraced agriculture. Just when you think you've done the hard bit, the hard bit begins again. The house is very dark up there. Perhaps they are not in. I climb. The blister stretches.

A car winds by. (Is it them? Will they recognise me? Stop and pick me up? No.) Another memory, of two slender shapes in the doorway of the house, graceful arms waving me off. Good luck. I remember thinking (child surly) that they were gladder to see me go than to return, that they enjoyed their unencumbered time. I remember Gonzo drawing me away to the playground or to school, consoling, endlessly creative. I remember unconditional gratitude. I know, from this distance, that he was lonely too. At the time it seemed like compassion.

Go out and play. That, I remember. Cricklewood Cove was a place so safe I could be left alone. There must have been a childminder or a nursery club. I don't remember them either. I remember my parents as beautiful shapes waving from the porch, arm in arm. I remember them stepping gingerly through Lego. And yet they are the kind of memory you paint in. I have to strain to recall their faces. That happens too. The face of someone you have known all your life clouds as you look at it, and you realise that you remember *them,* for who they are and what they mean, far more than you remember what they look like. The mind plays tricks to stop us knowing how disconnected we are.

Another car goes by, executive swish. It could be theirs. It is not. Endless, my expectation of rescue.

Top of the hill. On the flat, the blister is surprisingly painful already. I soften my left knee, stiffen the ankle and foot a little, and keep walking.

There is no one on the veranda, no light on in the kitchen. No surprise.

The gate is dry. The catch is rusty. The metal has not been oiled; I can feel roughness in it through the wood. Voiceless Dragon style: keep contact, let your softness tell you where your enemy is going, when he will stop. Resistance is information. The gate resists, a tiny thorn of decaying metal snagging the hinge. I lean into my arm, and the rust breaks. The tiny flecks of my enemy tumble to the ground. The gate swings open.

The front door is painted black, glossy wrought-iron black. The key is where it should be, under the statue of the goddess Diana—a bit racy for Cricklewood Cove, now that I see it as an adult, with one breast bare and a very short toga covering her hips as she runs.

Key turns in the lock; it's quiet. I always have to shout to attract attention when I come in. Although I also seem to remember them being there, waiting. Well. They could hardly do that this time.

"Hi! I'm home! Just me. Hi." The words fall flat on timber and paint.

There is no one here. The house is empty. It smells of empty, of old sheets, of resin leaking from wooden heirloom furniture, and dust. I walk down the hall, feeling that the walls are contracting around me, knowing it for a child's perspective. The hall isn't shrinking. I am larger. The hall was a grown-up place, where doors were answered and post delivered and exotic guests were welcomed (although I don't know who, now that I think about it), and where I was relinquished to Gonzo's care each morning and handed back by him later, or the following day. By the time I went to Jarndice, they were so rarely here. I used the back-door key, lived my own, sovereign life. In the intervening time we have somehow never spoken. There was no rift, just distance and time. I know they survived the war. I heard it somewhere, I think, or perhaps I just realise that I have not grieved, and from that I deduce their continuance.

The glacier room has huge windows and a great, throne-like chair. I remove the sheet and look at it. I remember it another colour, as if seen at dusk, a golden glow upon it. The shoulders and back of the chair are bleached from direct light. The room is filled with ghosts. Ghost legs. Ghost cocktails. Ghost parties. What parties? I remove some more sheets. I do not know the other furniture, just this chair. The one which is visible from the window. Have I sustained a head injury at any time, to forget my own life here? In the far wall there is a door. It leads to my father's den, mysteries of maleness. Will I find him in there, skin like parchment, dead these many years? Or making love, passionately, to a new wife? Is that why I haven't heard from them? I open the door with caution onto the panelled snug, balance to go down two steps, because the den was excavated to make it warm in the Cove's occasional chill, and for privacy besides.

The door opens onto a cupboard, bare and cold. Only the door is familiar—imposing, ornamental and false.

Rebuffed, I walk through the kitchen to the back, open the cellar door, which leads down to my old apartment, where Theresa Hollow made love to me the night of the great cannibal dog slaying. A narrow stair leads not down, but up. The room at the top is a sort of ghastly boudoir, filled with old-lady trophies.

I do not know this house.

It becomes increasingly obvious—painfully obvious—as I wander through it. I know it the way a stranger does, a passer-by or a curious child: I know it from the outside, its public spaces and the rooms in easy reach of the windows. I may have looked in. I have never inhabited it. And yet I remember my house behind this door. And where, in my home with Leah, this was clear evidence of infidelity, of terrible betrayal, here it simply cannot be. Impossible to imagine Gonzo has seduced my parents too, however great his successes. They have not divorced me and taken up with him. They have not remodelled the house to make the point to me. This was never my house to misremember. Points in evidence: the people who lived here had no children. Their home has no pencil marks on the frame of the kitchen door, no torn carpet or scratched paint. There is no room which might have been mine, no bunk bed, no cluttered, dingy bedroom where the young me might have sulked and sweated his way to adulthood. And the pictures of the inhabitants are not pictures of my parents. The names on the old letters in a tin box are not familiar, let alone familial. This house has a history, and I am not in it.

My chest is very tight. My eyes are itchy, sandy in their sockets. I can feel the pulse in them. I wonder if they will rupture. I turn, and turn, and turn, or perhaps the house does, or the world. Did I dream a life? Did I, perhaps, make it all up? Yes. Yes! That must be it. My real life is so drab or grim that I have created a fresh one from scratch. I have lost my grip. I am weeping on the landing, precarious. My mother—if she existed—would tell me to be careful, and when this did not penetrate my awful grief, would sit below me on the third step down, and hold me in her arms and wait to be sure I did not fall. I have no mother. The step is empty. Like the house. Like, in fact, every place I go. *Gonzo Lubitsch, I believe I hate you.*

I roar without words, until my lungs are empty too. I laugh, and the sound of it is loud and unsettling, which encourages me, and I laugh louder. Then I cry, and the two become one. Quite deranged, sobbing and whooping in the dark of a burglarised manse. Deranged? I ponder. Yes! That would explain everything! My alternative life unfolds before me.

> Behold the madman! His name is Crazy Joe Spork, a tinker and Freeman of the Open Road! Crazy Joe once served his country bravely, but went a bit far into the dark and lost his marbles, hence his sobriquet. Now he sees all authority figures with loofahs instead of heads! Crazy Joe was discharged from the army for washing his craggy thighs with an officer's toupeé (still attached!). Alas, this same disability rendered him quite unfit for civilian life. After some unhappy incidents he became a drunk and a jailbird, and his medals were forgotten—sold, in fact, for

low-grade hooch. More recently, asleep one night against the fence of the pumping station where he makes his home (the breezes from the air-con vents are warm, the soldiers keep him safe from mountain lions), he heard a grand kerfuffle and charged to investigate what he took to be a thief making off with his moonshine. But no! Baser villainy was afoot that night, and some fragment of the decorated veteran resurfaced. Slipping through the blasted gates, he found a crew of heroes boldly struggling to save the world, set upon by a dastardly bandit! No slouch is Joe, for all his bathtime confusions, and taking charge he led them to a hallowed victory. Sadly, even as his broad shoulders laboured to achieve their goal, his traitorous, malfunctioning brain was spontaneously inventing a long and glorious history with his new chums, which fantasy unfortunately brought him into conflict with the man whose wife he had inadvertently appropriated! Shot in self-defence was Crazy Joe Spork, and quite right too, tumbling from a moving vehicle even as he lunged with murderous intent for his rival's spongy head. Injured but too tough to die, he wandered to and fro, and thus came he to this old house, with which he has no connection beyond the wild visions of his imagined world, but onto which he projected a childhood by turns idyllic and neglected, with parents whose faces were appropriated from a mail-order advertisement. What will he do, confronted with proof of his own madness? Broken on the wheel of truth, his strange fixation lies in pieces in his lap. Will he heal? Perhaps crawl up from his distempered pit and find a proper job, buy nice clothes and settle with some kind lass of lardy middle, who will care for him and bring more Sporks into the world? A colony of bucolic brats and a spreading wife, possibly some contented pigs, would be a fitting end for this good, unchancy man. Or is it Loofahland henceforth for Crazy

Joe, and acts of ever-greater violence until at last he stands, picked out in the spotlight of a police helicopter, shaking one enormous fist? "Put your hands in the air, Joe, and give yourself up! Father Dingle's here, your old headmaster!" But Father Dingle's pabulums are of no interest to Joe; he roars his King Kong fury at theology's finest and the consolation of Mother Church. An elemental, downtrodden and misunderstood, he wants only revenge of gruesome stripe. Has he hostages? Perhaps. Or bombs. It hardly matters. "Joe, your mother wants to talk to you!" The negotiator's trump card is a disaster, fatally misdealt: Crazy Joe Spork hates his mother, consequence of long years spent locked away in the closet for sins against her endless list of fatuous commandments. Bellowing irrelevantly that he will not eat his sprouts, he whips a vast and improbable gun from beneath his tattered coat and blazes away, killing dozens; is, without delay, perforated and transformed for the most part into a red mist by the thousand rifles all around. His head tumbles to the ground and rolls wetly to the feet of Police Captain Malone.

"Garn," says Captain Malone, "that's a bad 'un, right enough." And he heads home, red-headed (though not in the same way as poor Crazy Joe), to eat with his Irish wife and freckly rugrats. Over tea and sausage, he teaches the children to say "eejit" and "Pawdraig" and is well satisfied with his day.

Deep breaths. In halfway. Stop. Fill your lungs, from the diaphragm. Stop. Out halfway, pushing with the belly. Stop. Empty your lungs. Stop. Stop laughing. Yes. Stop crying. Repeat.

I am curled in a ball on the landing, and I have leaked tears into the carpet. And this grief, this immense, inconsolable upset, takes me inevitably to the place I need to go, to the sandpit where I met Gonzo. At first I go there only in my head, recollection triggered by this same horrid sense of alienation and distress. Since that time only this has hurt so much. But shortly I am there in the flesh as well, a tallish, thinnish man with wayward hair, standing in a public sandpit in the middle of the night—the day has moved around me as I screamed and rocked in the empty house. I am observed from a respectful distance by some teenagers who are perplexed to find their trysting ground and occasional drugstore invaded by a tearful nutjob, but who—as I remove my shoes to run my toes through the sand—draw a little closer in the hope that I will do something dreadful or disgusting which will be worth talking about.

The sand is rougher than I remember. Perhaps they have refilled it with a different sand, a cheaper one. They must have done. The old sand was imported. The beach it came from probably does not exist any more. It was white sand. This is yellow. It holds more moisture, for longer. My toes are cold.

Across the sandpit and thirty years distance, near enough, I spy the infant Gonzo. He has taken possession of a rough circle about twice his own height in diameter. He has rolled around on it to make it flat, then carefully and meticulously smoothed the dimples made by his protruding joints with his flat-soled shoes. The arena is ready. Missing, however, is an opponent. In the sand Gonzo can draw his battalions and sculpt the terrain; he can render the world exactly the way he wants it. What he cannot do is replace the missing element. His shoulders droop, and he lets his face fall into shadow. Older brothers are supposed to be immune to accident.

They had The News two weeks ago, and the funeral on Friday: Marcus Lubitsch is dead. Gone for a soldier, killed in a dry country, laid to rest half a mile away with honours and the acrid smell of gunpowder as his friends sent him on his road. The smoke made Gonzo's eyes water and the bang made him flinch, for which he feels guilty. Marcus did not flinch at anything—not even the shot which killed him. Some part of Gonzo still feels that if he had just been nicer to him, Marcus might have come back alive, instead of dead. He tried to say this to his mother on Wednesday afternoon, and she shouted at him to be quiet and then apologised (something she has never done before) and wrapped him in enormous arms and shuddered all around him. Gonzo's tears disappeared entirely in his mother's tidal wave, his hugest howlings dwarfed by hers.

Marcus Maximus Lubitsch: earthbound god, companion, gap in the landscape; Gonzo's instinct is to re-create him. In his mind he carries Marcus and all the things they have done together. He can still hear his brother's voice, knows roughly what Marcus would say and do in any given interaction. So he can still play with Marcus, even though he knows he will never play with Marcus again. He can share his bereavement with Marcus, hear his brother's voice telling him it will all be all right soon, taste the blandishing ice cream of sibling bribery. This is what he wants to do, desperately.

But Gonzo, at the same time, has begun to appreciate that there are things in the world other than himself. He senses that continuing to play with Marcus is somehow wrong. When his brother was put in the ground, certain things became not-right which had always been perfectly okay till then. For example, on the day before The News came, Gonzo had a tea party whose attendees included two aliens, a talking mouse named Clarissa, Marcus in his tank (all soldiers have tanks and drive them everywhere they go) and three former kings of Scotland in various states of decapitation. There was nothing odd or unsuitable about this. His mother provided cake for all of them, but insisted that the mouse, the aliens and the kings have magic, invisible cake, and that Gonzo and Marcus share one tangible slice between two. In the event, Marcus pronounced himself not hungry, so Gonzo ate the whole piece.

After The News, though, this wasn't possible any more. Marcus was perfectly able to be in several places at once before he died, but it is somehow part of the process of his dying that this is no longer the case. Gonzo—lacking the words to express his understanding—believes this is because Marcus, alive, could be brought up to speed when he came home on what he and Gonzo had been doing while he was away. Marcus, dead, is complete and unalterable. He will never recover these absentee experiences. They are therefore some kind of theft or trick. Pretending to be with him now diminishes his death and as a consequence the preciousness of his life. Refusing temptation, Gonzo is bereaved twice.

However, he knows what to do. After The News had been imparted and everyone cried—which was awful—there was The Conversation. Old Man Lubitsch took Gonzo on a long walk, perhaps the longest walk they have ever been on together, longer even than the time they went to the very top of Aggerdean Bluff to look at the sea and stare into the mansion, through its grimy windows at the ghostly tented furniture and solemn rooms. Gonzo's father told his son to grieve without reservation or embarrassment until he could grieve solemnly and inwardly, and then finally to hang up his tears and wear them only occasionally, as befits the true men of the heart. Grief is not a thing to be ashamed of or suppressed, he told Gonzo. Nor yet is it a thing to cherish. Feel it, inhabit it and leave it behind. It is right, but it is not the end. Old Man Lubitsch could barely bring himself to say the last word aloud.

Gonzo considered this, and then announced that he had some questions, but that he didn't want to ask silly questions or bad questions and he didn't know which ones these might be. Old Man Lubitsch said that there were no questions Gonzo could not ask, here, with his father, at such a time. So Gonzo unburdened himself of the key issues arising from the matter, in no particular order: Why did someone kill Marcus? Would they now kill Gonzo? How would Gonzo, without Marcus, play various games they had played together? Could Gonzo have Marcus's enormous hat with antlers on? Should Gonzo dedicate himself forthwith to the speedy eradication of those responsible, by deed, accident or omission for Marcus's death? If he did so, would he still have to hand in homework? Who would walk with Gonzo to school? Would Ma Lubitsch make him a new brother? Please could it not be a sister? Was Ma all right? Did what had happened to Marcus hurt a very great deal? Was it Gonzo's fault at all? Did Gonzo's parents still love him, even if it was? Would there be cake at dinner this evening? Was Marcus in heaven, as the Evangelist asserted, or was it possible he was haunting the Lubitsch house and looking after them all for now and evermore? And had Marcus, as he had at one time intimated he might, purchased a puppy for Gonzo, and would the puppy still arrive or was it in some way made moot by the death of its sponsor? Was Gonzo's father all right too?

And Old Man Lubitsch replied that these were, for the most part, excellent questions. He answered them at some length, with considerable patience and exactness, so that it emerged that Gonzo, much-loved younger son, might well eat cake; was not responsible; must indeed continue to go to school; would not get another brother or alas a puppy, but was on the plus side not in danger of being shot; need not give his life over to the business of horrible revenge; and could indeed have Marcus's hat. The question "Why?" Old Man Lubitsch deferred to another day (along with the discussion of pain and mortality, to which he professed himself at this moment unequal, saying that he did not know for certain and would therefore be required by the dialogue to speculate on Marcus's feelings at the instant of his death). And to these good answers he added that none of them would ever be able to replace Marcus, and should never seek to do so—but that Gonzo must, while knowing that, and like all of them, *try to make new friends.*

Gonzo stares across the sandpit. It is a wasteland. He can see no one he wants to play with. If he cannot find a friend, he will start to cry again. His grief will catch up with him. It stalks him, jumps on him in idle moments. Gonzo already has puffy cheeks and raw, red eyes. Hurriedly, he takes his father's advice.

He *makes a new friend.*

A boy (of course) his own age. Smaller. As alone as he is. Someone to share his burdens, racked—as children can be, for no discrete reason—with dreadful sadness. Cautious, as Marcus urged Gonzo to be from time to time, in curious contradiction of his own bold (careless?) fate. Someone to watch Gonzo's back. We settle down to play, and it emerges that I am not quite as good at this as he is but good enough to keep him on his toes. In fact, this is almost definitive of me: in all the areas where Gonzo wishes to excel, I am just close enough behind to push him harder. In those he chooses to ignore, I am often quite talented. I am his foil. His sidekick. His Jiminy Cricket. Someone who will always take the blame, carry the can, own up, speak the truth, pay attention in class. A repository for dull virtues and a haven in times of trouble. Judicious, clever and sensible where he is headlong, intuitive and rash. Gonzo splits himself down the middle, and knows that he will never be alone again.

This sandpit is not where we met. It is where I was born—or, rather, made. I am Gonzo's invisible companion, his friend in adversity, co-conspirator in mischief, refuge in dismay. Insepara-ble, complementary, we made our way and fought each other's battles and offered a shoulder to cry on or a word of advice in difficult times. I am the man he chose, at every turn, not to be, though sometimes he pillaged me for aid and assistance, when sheer bravado and brilliant improvisation were not enough. And it occurs to me: how is this different from how it was a week ago? Everything I remember is true—except for the very edges of Gonzo's imagined history of me, like the house on Aggerdean Bluff and the parents I never had—and everything is false. And Leah . . . Leah is true too, up to a point. But I won her for Gonzo, it seems—and if I am honest, he saw her first; proposed to her while I was unconscious. A truly headlong moment. And maybe she loved him before she loved me. It must have come as a terrible shock to him to turn and find me there beside him in Station 9, the secret keeper of his dreams made real, his minority opinions given life. You don't expect to have to compete with yourself quite so directly. And yet that was the first time we had ever been in full agreement. Protect Jim. Do the job. Save the world.

The moment when it happened, that ghastly *plink* and everything gone awry. Cold, terrible liquid rained down on us, demanding instruction, finding Gonzo's fractured noosphere, his revisions and indecisions resolved by never making a serious choice—whichever option he did not like, he gave away. On one side the hero, the fearless man of action; on the other . . . me: second fiddle, weedy sidekick, junior scout—and every so often older, wiser head. We were deluged together in the raw, unbalanced Stuff of the universe. Inevitable consequence:

My own little reification.

I was made flesh, and in the process taken from him. I was never supposed to be *real.* How terrifying to confide your every doubt to an imaginary companion, to bequeath to him every alternative, and then one day to turn and see him standing before you. Gonzo must be feeling so hollow inside, with me spun out and separated from him. It must be quiet and empty in there.

And that, of course, is how I survived being shot. Freshly minted, *new,* I wasn't real enough to die.

I HAVE FALLEN to my knees, rather self-consciously, because it seemed appropriate. Now I am wondering why. The sand is giving up its dew to my trousers, and some of it has filtered through the fabric and is making my skin itch. I wonder whether there are sand mites. The teenagers are watching with great interest. In the narrative logic of men collapsing to the ground in transports of horror, I should now throw back my head and scream at the top of my voice, a bellowing of pain and inconsolable rage. They peer at me with hopeful anticipation.

I get up, and something falls or scuttles down my left leg. I shake it. I leave.

There's a general feeling among my audience that I haven't delivered on my early promise. Silence and a minor palsy afflicting one lower limb do not constitute a full performance. They would have liked to see some groaning, possibly some violent fitting, and a finale involving invisible demons and shouted profanity culminating in a drug-induced coma. With a sharply critical air, they go back to assessing one another for possible sex.

I walk to Packlehyde Street, and pass through the streetlamp light to the Lubitsch house. And then, before I can think better of it, I bang on the door.

Chapter Thirteen

The mathematics of love;
bees of good and evil;
Gonzo's injuries.

I HAVE NOT considered the time of day, or night. The house is not wakeful. I stand between the two brass lanterns outside the Lubitsch storm porch and I can hear the hall clock through the door, and I realise that it is after midnight. They will assume some emergency. I should come back tomorrow. On the other hand, I have already woken them. I can hear Ma Lubitsch's careful, full-footed tread on the stairs, and behind her the tango patter of Gonzo's father. Old Man Lubitsch wears slender, suede-bottomed slippers, neat around his small feet. His wife wears sandals, even in winter, because her feet get too hot in the furry boots her son brought from the city that first winter home from Jarndice. If the weather is cold enough that she has to cover up, she wears woollen socks, and on each foot the thong of the sandal pulls the fabric tight over her (enormous) big toe. Socks which are not well made will shortly tear at the seam or fray over the edge of her nails, and often she has to take a purchased sock and graft onto it a lower section of her own manufacture, so that from the ankle upward she wears a grey, ho-hum sort of sock, but from there on down she is a riot of colour, wool from a dozen tail ends and unravelling jumpers pressed into service.

Either she has become a tad more frail this year or the season has been harsh, because this is what I see as the door opens a crack: a foot like a loaf of bread in a Father Christmas costume, and behind it an-other with purple toes and chartreuse heel. The brass lanterns come on, and a deep, suspicious voice says "Yes?" except it is a more like a "Eeyehh-iss?" and I realise that I am too ashamed to lift my eyes. Ashamed about what, I do not know; but the fact that I exist at all must surely be a horror to them, and yet here I am seeking something from them, be it sympathy or support or even information about Gonzo and his intentions, and these things I have no right to ask. But then again this is my refuge in time of trouble. Nowhere else but here did I ever get disinfectant on my grazes or buttered toast after falling in the creek. I cannot help it if I am a monster. This is my home.

"Who is that?" Ma Lubitsch says insistently. "My husband is here," she adds, in case I am contemplating an attack upon her virtue. "He has arranged to defend me!" And I am quite sure that he has, by simple force or some baroque design. Perhaps the brass lamps are wired to the electrical main, and he can cause lightning to arc between them. Perhaps he has just obtained a shotgun. These are troubled times, and Cricklewood Cove has surely seen her share of marauders and the rest.

Hangdog, I linger, head down. Obviously I must flee—this was a mistake. In fact, the matter of my continued presence bears examination. The way lies open behind me for an inglorious bolt into the dark, surely less ghastly than saying the words out loud to these people: I am the product of your son's mourning, all grown up, and tried to make off with his wife, shot and yet still crawling home to haunt him and extract a reckoning, of whatever sort (and that, now that I think about it, is something I should consider in the light of recent revelations). Infinitely less unpleasant to blurt out some apology, wrong house, so sorry, bit drunk, and vanish for ever. Perhaps I could go and live with the Found Thousand, among my own kind. Perhaps they have room for a confused man with a fictional past.

But something has happened to my feet. They are glued to the ground. Part of Old Man Lubitsch's home defence system, perhaps, shortly to be followed, unless I explain myself sharpish, with a bolt of purging electrical fire and a sudden jolt of heat as I am turned to vapour. And yet I am still here. I can lift one foot. I can lift the other. I can in fact jump up and down. (Oh, marvellous. I am continuing my lunatic act, this time for the benefit of Gonzo's parents. Ideal.) But backwards, it seems, I cannot go. Or no, not *cannot,* but *will not.* And that is an absolutely extraordinary idea. I will not go back into the dark. I will raise my head. I will be seen.

And then I have *been* seen. I am looking into the face of Old Man Lubitsch as he elbows his way around his wife (a task requiring both arms), and it is hard to say which of us is more amazed.

Gonzo's father has not aged so much as he has acquired topography. His skin is folded, refolded, counterfolded, until it is almost smooth. Deep subduction lines have appeared around his mouth and eyes. His face is all over rock and water, with a fine spray of lichens on the lower slopes, and I observe him as he does me. His eyes widen, then contract, then narrow: recognition, confusion, suspicion. Then, as I flinch back, and half-turn to escape his dismissal, his gnarly arm shoots out and fingers tested by generations of bees clamp around my wrist. His hand stays me, then draws back; dabs at me once, twice, ever upward as if gathering pollen; finally folds around my shoulder to reposition me. He pulls me closer to the brass lamp on the left, then turns me away again for the other aspect. Unabashed, he reaches up and squashes my cheeks, then hauls down hard upon my shoulders so that I must bend my knees or lift him from the ground, and when I do bend, he touches my face as if sculpting it, to and fro. His skin is like brown paper. At last he steps back, mission accomplished, and still he has no idea what to think or what to do. He mutters to his wife: *Ul-li-ye-na?* And I realise it is her name; Yelena Lubitsch. She huffs at him, "Silly man," and steps aside.

"Come in," Ma Lubitsch says. She does not ask why I am here or who I am. Whatever else, I am a young man in a bad place, and the current has thrown me up upon her strand. Yelena Lubitsch does not shirk the responsibilities of such occurrences—and nor yet does she base her decisions upon swift examinations on doorsteps, between swinging brass lamps, in the middle of the night. "Come in," she says again, more forcefully because I am standing with my mouth open like a dog unsure whether he wants to be in the garden or by the fire, and without the sense to draw conclusions from the gathering clouds. And finally, when I still stand there, she makes a "tcha" sound which I recognise as meaning that all men are idiots, and all young men most especially so (and God has cursed her with a husband *eternally* young), and she plucks at my sleeve with a fraction of her strength, and brings me firmly across the threshold into her house. There's a new smell, like honey and coal and furniture polish. Not unpleasant, but strong.

"Boil the kettle," she says, and it's only when I look round and find that Old Man Lubitsch has already gone that I realise she is talking to me.

THE OLD IRON KETTLE is where I remember, hanging like a benevolent bat above the stove. This kettle is a miracle provider, an endless source of cooking water, but also bathwater, medical water and when necessary veterinary water as well. At the same time it is a peril. Not a big peril, but a deceptive and painful peril nonetheless. There's nowhere in Ma Lubitsch's kitchen to cool it down. It sits on the stove when it's being used, and it goes back on the hook when it's dry, and as a consequence there is a kettle code relating to procedures for taking it down again without getting burned. This code is not written. It is a part of the landscape. I follow the code without thinking.

First, check there are no toys, animals or small persons underfoot. Check your back, so that no one blunders into you. Second, remove from the hidden hook beside the stove the raggedy towel (double-stitched and padded with sand and clay) which hangs there. Wrap the towel around your hand. Third, reach up and test the weight of the kettle, in case some tomfool (Gonzo, probably) has hung it up with water in it. Repeat step one, then bring the kettle down and, without setting it on the stove because cold water poured onto the iron base will spit if it is hot, fill it from the tap. Note: do not overfill it so that the resulting cauldron is beyond your strength. Fourth, lift it back onto the stove. Finally, replace the raggedy towel on its hook so that the next user knows where to find it.

Job done, I turn and find Ma Lubitsch watching, eyes shadowed by the high line of her cheeks. I notice that even her forehead is fat.

Ma Lubitsch says "Hnuh" or "Nyuh" to indicate that I have not offended against the kettle code. Then she shoos me out of the sacred space into the hall and waves at the living room, where her husband has lit a fire in the grate and is waiting for me. I hesitate. She shoos me again and commences her three-point turn.

WE HAVE SAT in silence. We have considered one another, and the strange portents that we are. We have done all the hesitating we can do. And so I have simply asked about Gonzo, and have they seen him lately, and Old Man Lubitsch sighs and nods and scents the storm in the wind. Or has been scenting it for days.

"They came together," Old Man Lubitsch says. "Gonzo and Leah. Yelena was delighted. They came out of the blue, and they stayed in the guest room. Why? I always have to ask why. Were they pregnant? They didn't need money, surely. Looking for a house? But no, not that either. He had a new job, he said. A special job. He was going to make the world a better place. A safe place. He was very proud. But underneath he was something else. Something else."

Firelight draws zigzags across the ridges on Old Man Lubitsch's face. He expands and contracts with the flames. The room smells of pine smoke.

"Gonzo is not a diplomat. He cannot say one thing and think

another thing. He cannot lie to his mother because he loves her, and he cannot lie to me because—I'm not saying he doesn't love me, it's just different between mothers and sons and fathers and sons—because I am an old fart with sharp eyes and he doesn't have the practice. And he was lying with every part of him. Lying like shouting. *Everything is okay, everything is wonderful. Look how happy I am, look how I am at ease.* Bah." Old Man Lubitsch picks up the poker and pokes. He starts quite gently, shunting one stray log farther from the hearthrug. The log is round and bent like a banana, so each time he rolls it over, it rolls back again. Old Man Lubitsch pushes harder. The poker slips, the log hesitates, then rolls back, and without warning he is stabbing at it, bashing it, and the fire crackles and sparks alarmingly. I wait quietly until he stops and puts the poker back on the stand. Old Man Lubitsch goes on.

"He had a bandage on his arm. Around the edge it was grubby. An old bandage. Bruises and burns. Leah went to take it off. Tender, the way that she is. He was angry. He was so angry, and afraid, and ashamed." Gonzo's father broods. "Gonzo is a good man. We laid down the rules to him when he was a child: we told him what men do and what they do not and he understood. Marcus . . ." Old Man Lubitsch stutters on the unfamiliar name. "Marcus also. He taught his brother what it is to be the right kind of man. So there was no violence in his anger. It's not that he was restraining himself, you understand? It is not in him to lash out, to hit someone dear to him." And in a funny way this is true, although there are scars on my chest to make me feel different, however the Sandpit of Truth has changed my perspective on all that with the shooting and the kicking me from a truck at speed. "So Gonzo had this rage, this horror, and he did not know what to do with it. I saw it only in his mouth. He was so still, so calm, but his mouth gave him away. I thought he would vomit, or scream. He just sat there, absolutely stiff in his chair—that chair"—and here Old Man Lubitsch indicates a very ordinary lounger with velour cushions which shows no evidence of being a place of trauma—"and he asked her quietly please not to do that right now. She took her hands away so fast . . . I wished he had shouted. It would have been easier. The bandage was quite old. She had tried before. She does not know why he refuses. How was he hurt? Was he burned? Cut? What is this injury, and what does it mean to him? It hurts her, and she cannot ask. She can only offer herself, as she always does, and be refused, and absorb it and try again. I think, eventually, it will kill her.

"And he . . . he is afraid of her kindness, that it will break something in him, some resolve. He is afraid to be loved, because he is unworthy. He is too ashamed. But also he is angry. So angry, because he is hurt in some way which he thinks is unfair, and he is like a child, he does not know why. And this new job will make it all better. It will make him good again. Make him clean. Make the bad thing *go away.*"

Ma Lubitsch sets a cup beside me; when she wants to, she can move like a cat. Ma Lubitsch is very good at being the woman she is. Her weight has made her graceful; her bulk has made her strong. She has brewed a smoky tea, because it is after midnight and we need the sharpness, and she has poured a spot of milk into it to make it smooth. In Ma Lubitsch's house only she is the arbiter of how you take your tea. She judges by eye, and she awards Darjeeling or Lapsang Souchong or Assam or Pekoe as the moment requires. She gives no quarter to received proprieties of milk and sugar. She picks the vessels too, little cups on hot summer days, thick mugs for winter. Tonight we have some I have never seen, thick with glaze and chipped to reveal the terracotta underneath. Emergency mugs, for moments of desperate need.

"I spoke to James," this being Jim Hepsobah. Old Man Lubitsch will not acknowledge the contraction. Jim is always James to him, as if Jim's strength is too great to be contained in a nickname. "Or rather I tried. He was polite. He made small talk. He is . . . *very* bad at small talk. He passed me to Sally. She lies well. She lies with omission and elision and prevarication and misdirection. She was cheerful. What could possibly be wrong? She was very unhappy." Old Man Lubitsch sighs.

"And now, you," he says. "With that face, in the middle of the night. And you are the opposite. You want to run away, as if we will attack you. You expect to be rejected. And yet you have done nothing wrong. Every part of you is certain. You have done nothing wrong. You are angry too, but you are not guilty. Why? Who are you? And why are you here? You are not here to keep secrets. If you wanted to lie, you only had to walk past the door. So. What has my son done to you, that he is running so far and so fast?"

I cannot answer straightaway, but there is no need. There is no time in this room. The fire will burn for ever—Old Man Lubitsch tosses another log on it, and pine sap puffs and steams and burns—and the tea will keep flowing. This is the heart of the world, and I am safe. I draw my thoughts together, and I tell my tale. I do not try to separate my memory from Gonzo's or to make judgements about what *actually* happened in a given room. The past is memory, and no two persons' memories are alike. I know my story, and I tell it as it was for me. I do not skimp when the moment of my genesis arrives. I do not prevaricate. I make the position clear. *I am Gonzo's shadow. I am his imaginary friend made real. I am* new.

Ma Lubitsch's eyes widen, and she draws back, then catches herself and growls. After a moment she leans forward and pokes me tentatively in the arm with one fat finger, watching closely to see if anything happens. When nothing does, she settles into her chair again. Old Man Lubitsch simply nods as if just now understanding something he should have realised ages ago. Neither one of them seems terribly upset at the idea of having a bifurcate in the house.

"I am a monster," I tell them, in case they haven't understood.

"Are you?" Old Man Lubitsch wants to know.

"Yes."

"What is the most monstrous thing you have done?"

Well, now that he mentions it, I can't recall the last terrible crime I committed. Participated in the Go Away War, perhaps. But human people did that. Gonzo did.

I suggest that being a monster is a matter of fact, rather than action, and Old Man Lubitsch says "Bah."

Since that seems to be all they have to say about it, I carry on with my story.

SUNRISE on the Aggerdean Bluff is cold. The wind off the ocean is wet, and the air is rich with salt and weed. The waves are quiet and slick, the colour of the sky, so that the horizon line is impossible to find except where the sun is resting on it, white behind a cloud—a world in monochrome after the warm colours of the living room. Old Man Lubitsch is wearing his preposterous fur hat, which is even more like a rat than I remember. Ma Lubitsch is bare-headed, but the bottom half of her neck is wrapped in a tweed scarf, and it climbs at the back so as to take in the lower part of her ears. Her thick coat is the colour of pea soup. When the sun cuts through the cloud, it lights her up golden, and in those brief moments you can see that she was beautiful, still is beautiful. I realise that this is what Old Man Lubitsch sees all the time. His Yelena.

We spent the first part of our walk peering through the doors of the house on Aggerdean Bluff. I offered to let them in, but when we opened the door it seemed like a pointless intrusion. Should I walk them around the house and show them the things which were never there? *Here* is where I didn't sleep? *This* is where a mother I never had never made me breakfast on a stove which never existed? I have no appetite for it, and fortunately nor do they. I lead the way down the hill to the sandpit and show them the game. This is where Gonzo was. There was the ice cream van. You were here. Yes. And Ma Lubitsch remembers the day—of course she does, she remembers every day of that awful month separately and completely—and nods as I flatten out the sand. Yes, this was Gonzo's game. And mine. She smiles, old love and old pain.

Through Cricklewood Cove, still in shadow, sky dark on the far side. These are my streets. They are still gloomy, but now there are shapes in them, and early risers are brushing their teeth and going to and fro, visible through their windows. We walk more quickly because our silence is oppressive. We've had our air, and there are conclusions to be reached. And breakfast to be had, of course. In half an hour the bees will wake, and then by turns the rest of the Cove, and Ike Thermite will be looking for me.

In the hallway that smell again: winter fires and nectar and a bitter bar across the back of the mouth. There's something animal in it too, something doggy maybe. Perhaps Ma Lubitsch has adopted another stray, a cannibal dog left over from before. (I picture her ruffling its massive head and disciplining it with a smart tap on its thick black nose. "Tcha! No eating! Eating guests is bad. Ju-uuust the play . . . Who's a *good* dog? *You* are! Yes!" And the vast head and scrap of tail waggle as the animal makes plain its willingness to be her eternal servant in trade for her belief—broadly applied and absolutely improbable—that there is good in everyone and everything, and a little pie and friendship will find it out.) But that's not it, not quite, this elusive flavour in the air. Perhaps it's just a house smell: rising damp, old furniture and good food.

"You came here to find him," Ma Lubitsch says abruptly. I am sitting back in my chair by the fire, and she has produced fresh cold juice and bacon fried to make it crisp. You can pick this bacon up in your fingers and pop it in your mouth like a sweet, or sandwich it between layers of brown bread with mayonnaise. Served with Assam and scalded milk, so that there's something toffeeish in every swallow.

"I don't know," I tell her.

"Tcha." Ma Lubitsch is used to people not knowing. That's what she's there for. To know, on their behalf, until they know too; to be grumpy at them until they use their heads and figure it out. "You came because of what you are and what he is. Of course you did. And you know what he is doing now."

I have no idea. And yet of course I do. Something big and stupid, to wipe clean the slate. Something ineffably Gonzo, with fireworks and fanfares, to restore himself in the eyes of the world. Something *heroic*. And there is no one there to dig him out when it goes wrong. Gonzo is flying solo. He needs help. He needs a second opinion.

Whatever else I am, I am not the sort of person to leave a friend in the lurch. I am, by definition, the other sort. By Gonzo's definition. I could choose to become a different kind of person. I don't want to. I've met those people. I don't like them.

I have given myself away—in the face, or the sigh, or something: Old Man Lubitsch nods to himself and says his own personal version of "tcha," which is a sort of "hihnf." It is a noise of confirmation.

"He has a job in the city," Old Man Lubitsch says. "They came for him. Executives, in person. They made him feel very good. Very important. It was uncomfortable. Yelena was not happy. Gonzo should not need these men to believe in himself, but he did. Without them, he was like a puppet. Slack. Leah also was not happy. She would not say why she was unhappy, but it was the job, of course. She was unhappy with what they asked of him. She was unhappy because he agreed to it."

"A dangerous job."

"Perhaps. But also a bad one."

All this is making Ma Lubitsch impatient. It is man chat, needlessly precise. She raps her husband on the arm, flaps at him to be quiet.

"You must help my son," she says. "It is who you are. Afterwards, there will be time for the rest. You can be angry with him then. But for now it doesn't matter. Gonzo needs you."

Ma Lubitsch understands the mathematics of love. Love is merciless. Love does not count costs, only value. I came here because of a relationship I remembered with two people I had never met. I did not expect them to acknowledge me, to return my affection. I did not expect to find, in this house, family and its attendant responsibilities, but I have. And so I will do what I have always done. I will find Gonzo. I will save him from himself. I will be a friend, in spite of all of it. Where is Gonzo? He has gone deeper into whatever *enemy plan* is at work.

> Very cosy, Bumhole. Fraught with charm and personal growth. Now, could we return with some dispatch to the matter of *cui bono?* Because while you are having a group hug, you may be reasonably certain that your unfriend out there—whom we shall term the Evil Mastermind, Bumhole, so as to keep matters clear for your tiny brain—is occupying himself with further nefarious doings, most likely on present showing to be in the nature of mayhem and death. Am I right?

Yes, Ronnie, you are.

Simultaneous with this realisation comes another, even less welcome. I am standing. My eyes are moving and my limbs are light. Something is wrong. I listen. *There:* that silence was not a silence. It was the gap between two very faint sounds. Another. *Tahhh . . . pahhh . . . [pause] . . . tahhh . . . pahhh . . . [pause]* . . . The noise of footsteps, very quiet.

I move to the breakfast tray and cover my fingers in bacon fat, then transfer it to the hinges of the door. Wait. Don't hurry. Listen . . . now. The person is not in the hall. He—or she—is upstairs. More, the next step is . . . now, which is the perfect time to open the door. It glides on bacon fat and more ordinary greases, Old Man Lubitsch's home maintenance at work. I slip out into the hall. In the kitchen there are harmless domestic items which might be pressed into service as weapons. I should have asked Old Man Lubitsch about his home defence. Perhaps it is a big stick. I would like a big stick right about now.

The kitchen is on the north side of the house. It is still dark. The hallway is light. Move quickly.

Kitchen door. Open it. Step through.

A bee buzzes past me, a glinting, metallic bee with sharp wings. Like every other bee in history, it imagines it can pass magically through glass. Unlike every other bee, this one is right. The window breaks. This is not one of Old Man Lubitsch's bees. It is another sort. The window shatters. I keep moving, or rather my body keeps moving: it ducks, smoothly and unfussed, weaves around and about, and my hand slaps wood as I vault over Ma Lubitsch's kitchen table. Stout construction, it barely notices my passing. More bees float past, angry about something. One of them is a bad navigator, buries its head in the larder door. It is a most curious bee, with five sharp points. A shuriken bee, very rare. Very *specific.* Five spikes around a central hub, you flip it like a Frisbee or a playing card. Kill with it. *Tool of butchery,* indeed. My body is still moving; I twitch the shuriken bee out of the larder door, send it back the way it came, slip away as more bees fly into the shadows of the kitchen. Real bees would never do this, they like light and sun. Old Man Lubitsch's bees converged on bulbs and glowing rods. These bees are evil bees, bees of darkness. *Fear the evil bee.* I do. But I cannot hide from it for ever. I cannot leave Gonzo's parents to face the Evil Apiarist alone.

For a moment there's a single figure silhouetted in the corridor. *Bad ninja! You are revealed! Your teacher will hit you with a bamboo stick for this behaviour. If I don't get you first.* I bowl a copper pot at him and whip away again, using available cover. In this case the available cover is the kitchen wall. Thus, he knows I must come through that doorway. He will assume I must come from right or left. I wait. The softest of steps, one, two. Deliberately loud enough to hear. I am invited to gamble. Come from the left, and maybe he will guess wrong, maybe he will not be fast enough to adapt. Ho, ho, ho. He has a weapon of some sort, sharp. He will be holding it horizontally. Both my options are bad options. Don't gamble. The house always wins.

This is my house.

I step back, bounce off the lip of the kitchen counter and catch the door frame. I slither through the doorway at head height, feet first, my hands hinging me and the lintel a brief caress on my hair as I pass. The apiarist is all in black, and he has got pollen on him from climbing Old Man Lubitsch's trellises to reach the upstairs window. He carries a formidable thingummy with beak-like blades at each end. My feet slide over the top of it, take him in the chest, and he staggers. I land badly, try to roll back into the kitchen. The ninja springs back to his feet, whirring. If only I had some Tupperware. Must be some in the kitchen. Too far.

Damn.

He doesn't kill me because he misjudges how winded I am from falling on (as it appears) Old Man Lubitsch's leather umbrella stand. Instead, the blunt bit of the thingummy hits me in the shoulder. White light. Pain. *Idiot. You're fighting like Gonzo.* I'm not sure whose voice it is. It's right.

The ninja flourishes his beak-like thingummy, slashes at me. I roll away. My arm is useless. It's not broken; it's just switched off. Left hand only then. Slow. Relax. Think. He is strong, but I am skilled. The only enemy is timing. The only danger is fear. Master Wu's garden, endless hours of practice. Elisabeth Soames's mute approval as she helps me out of the fish pond. The thingummy blurrs. I step. None of my limbs comes off. The thingummy wheels away to one side with a clatter. I hit the ninja in the nose with my elbow. He hits me back. We tumble out into the garden. Real fights are undignified. Only true masters make them look effortless. I am not one. He pokes me in the eye. Master Wu would be disappointed. This is not how it's done. I can't find the quiet place in my head from which to fight. But hey, it's my first time.

The ninja hits me again, gets to his feet and snaps into a sort of "ready" posture while he tries to decide which way to kill me, and then there comes a quite remarkable noise. It goes: *WHACKLUTSCHSCHslutchscludderpankpank.*

The ninja stops absolutely still. He makes a sort of sad little sound of his own, a child-like reproach. And then he falls forward on his face. Ike Thermite is standing behind him, with a plank. It looks like a fence post.

"Was that right?" Ike says. "He was attacking you. So I hit him." He waves the plank. It appears to have a couple of nails sticking out. Spare fence posts are piled against the side of the house, ready for deployment. This is probably not what Old Man Lubitsch had in mind for them. "Is he going to be okay?" Ike Thermite says. "Because I only really wanted to knock him out."

The ninja has two largish holes in the back of his head. There is white stuff coming out. He shakes.

"I saw all the planks," says Ike Thermite cheerily. "Gosh, there are a lot of planks. But I couldn't decide which one. And then I thought, what the hell are you talking about, it really doesn't matter which one. Only I think perhaps it does. Yes? Because this one has nails in it . . ."

The ninja stops moving. The smell of blood is rather acute.

"Oh dear," Ike Thermite says. There is brain matter on his shoe. "That's quite unpleasant." He drops the plank and passes out.

I have been saved from death by a specialist in physical theatre. This is bad. Sadly, it is not the worst thing about this moment. The worst thing is that the dead man has five friends—or at least colleagues—standing in the azaleas.

Ma Lubitsch throws a bucket of perfumed furniture polish out of the living room window. It mostly lands on Ike Thermite. A healthy dose of it splashes on me. If this was an attempt to wake Ike and unleash his dreaded Mime Powers, it does not work. Ike stays down. I have nectar goo on my trousers. If it comes to a fight—and it will—I'm going to be all sticky. I hear a voice, surprisingly calm and very dignified.

"May I have your attention, please?" says Old Man Lubitsch. "You are on private land. You are not welcome. You were not invited. You have offered violence to my house. I would like you all to leave."

The five remaining ninjas look at him. I turn to look too. Old Man Lubitsch is standing next to his beehives. He is standing, in fact, next to the large black hive he was building the last time I came to Cricklewood Cove. It is tall and oddly shaped, ugly where the others are uniform little whiteboard houses. Clearly, he feels it represents some sort of threat.

The ninjas don't. They step forward. Old Man Lubitsch shrugs. He reaches up and pulls the lid off the hive. And then, demonstrating that sanity has absolutely passed him by today, he gives it a solid kick.

The noise which emerges from the big hive is a deep Harley-Davidson growl of warning. Quite apparently, the occupant is a mutant bee. Gonzo's father has raised a single, furious, man-size bee with teeth like razors. It is a guard bee. Even the ninjas pause. The nearest one is about eight feet from me, and from Ike Thermite. He looks as if he doesn't like the idea of fighting a giant bee very much.

Old Man Lubitsch kicks the hive again. It explodes.

It doesn't actually explode, of course, but the phenomenon is remarkably similar. There is a noise as of war in heaven. A black shadow crosses the face of the sky like the end of days, racing out from the hive in a circle which expands until it covers all of us. We are struck by a thousand tiny impacts, like a shower of gravel: bees landing, swooping, tasting.

I do not watch the rest of it. The bees from the black hive—Africanised *Megachile pluto,* most likely—recognise us by the smell of nectar goo as fellow (if weird-lookin' and useless) members of the hive. The ninjas are therefore aggressors of some sort who must be dealt with. The last thing they see before the vengeance of the bees is Old Man Lubitsch, shrouded in inch-long black insects, stepping towards them with a garden rake.

"You would have hurt my wife," Old Man Lubitsch says through the sound of the hive.

But when I turn away, because death by bee is a ghastly thing, and death by rake not much better, it is not his wife I see, but mine.

LEAH's hiding place is upstairs, between the guest room and the airing cupboard. A false wall makes room for a corridor, and the corridor leads to a small space under the eaves like an artist's garret. Old Man Lubitsch built it during the Reification. He and Ma Lubitsch hid there when Cricklewood Cove was overrun by bandits, and then they hid a young man there when the bandits were defeated and a hanging mood took the town. Currently, Leah shares it with a family of cats who moved in unofficially. She explains that the cats were here first. They are nice cats. Leah likes them. She misses her dog, but the dog went with Gonzo. She stayed behind. Gonzo insisted. It was too dangerous. So here she is, sharing space with La Gioconda (the mother cat) and Sunflower, Waterlily, Adoration (which is short for Adoration of the Magi) and Flea. She named the kittens after paintings, but realised that she didn't know the proper names of very many. She declined to name Flea after an approximation of the title of a painting. Flea is called Flea because she can jump right up in the air. She was so bored up here (Leah, not Flea), but Gonzo insisted she must be safe. From whom she does not know. He wouldn't tell her anything. The cats walk on her face in the mornings to wake her up. She must look terrible.

"Leah," I say, but she has more to tell me, more she needs to say, things of great importance. She pauses, then begins. The room gets very cold at night, so she's quite glad to have them around then, and of course they need her to protect them from owls. Owls are a great hazard to kittens. Owls eat more kittens in a year than dogs do in ten. Dogs chase cats, they don't eat them. Owls eat anything. Fortunately, the owls are scared of Old Man

Lubitsch's mutant bees, so the kittens are safe in the garden. Leah washes them in nectar shampoo, which makes them furious (and very cute) and the bees sort of hover over them and scowl, not that they can scowl, but they do. Leah was listening through the floor last night, all night, she has bags under her eyes this morning, even kitten maquillage doesn't leave her this harrowed normally, she heard and understood and she had no idea what Gonzo had done, he just told her that I was *new* and made out of him and not to say anything to anyone and I was leaving. She has no idea what to say to me.

Since I don't know what to say either, we sit there and look at one another in silence for a while.

Leah looks depleted. She draws strength from the mountains, but primarily from love. She takes delight in love. This passage has injured her in the place from which she draws her strength. My instinct is to hold her. I offer her my hand, and she looks at it with deep uncertainty. We are sitting opposite one another. To take it, she must shuffle forward. She does, but she takes a grip on me which is opposed, so that her palm faces me while her fingers wrap around mine. Thus far and no farther. Her palm is like one of Ike Thermite's invisible walls. I want to storm the fortress. I might. She might respond. And then what? In Gonzo's house, with his parents standing guard, to cuckold him and take her away? "What is the most monstrous thing you have done?" Oh! I know! I know!

So. We sit opposite one another. My back hurts. I have never been able to sit comfortably on the ground, even at my most flexible. When I was at Jarndice, and I could—by dint of constant practice in the Voiceless Dragon forms—do the lotus position from cold and come within seven inches of the box splits (that's the ones you do by opening your legs to the side rather than pushing one foot forward and one back), even then the business of sitting on the floor was an agony. Aline found it a cause for annoyance. Furniture was bourgeois when good people had none. Comfortable furniture was almost certainly counter-revolutionary. (This was the army which George Copsen's Government Machine so desperately feared.) When my hips start to hurt too, I shift position, which is difficult because I do not want to let go of her hand. I wince.

"Are you all right?"

"I love you."

Bugger.

She stares at me. In for a penny.

"I love you. I have always loved you. I remember your letter, in the hospital. I remember asking Gonzo to find us somewhere to have a date. He got me a suit. You had that amazing dress, from nowhere, by magic. We made love in the castle, all night. And when I smell jasmine I think of you, of getting married and of how you hated the city, so Jim Hepsobah helped me find a house in the mountains. I remember carrying you over the threshold and falling over, and we just lay there and laughed." The only time I have ever been comfortable on a floor. Leah is shaking her head, her whole body twisting one way and another in denial. She has not let go of my hand. We are welded together by pain. "Leah, please . . ." But please what? And because I don't know, I apologise. I tell her I am sorry. My outburst was inappropriate.

She looks at me sharply. Certainty. I have sealed my own rejection. Leah loves a man who would never be concerned with inappropriate. Leah loves a man who would have brushed her objections aside and held her, and been slapped if need be. Leah loves a man who does not do stalemate.

Gonzo.

And what am I? Where does Gonzo finish and where do I begin? We were both there. I ask her outright. *What am I to you?* And then I wish I hadn't.

"Suppose," Leah murmurs, and she will not look at me while she destroys me, "suppose Gonzo had been hit on the head. Fallen off the roof. And suppose his brain was damaged. He changed. Couldn't remember things. Suppose he needed my help to recover, to be who he was. Suppose this had nothing to do with Stuff and monsters. He was just hurt. He would need me. More than ever. Need love." She shrugs. She is indifferent. Clinical. It's a lie. She is making it true. "This isn't different. Not between me and him."

Leah, the nurse, looks at me and sees an injury. I love her. She thinks I am aphasia with feet. I tell her I am not.

"Do you remember asking me to marry you?"

Of course. It was on the roof garden of Piper 90.

"No," she says, "the first time."

In the recovery room. I know I did it. I could lie.

I cannot lie.

Leah nods.

"I'm so sorry," she says. "This must hurt so much."

Yes.

"But you and me . . ." She is still going. Determined. "You remember loving me. But do you love me right now, this minute? Do you feel it? No. Your business," Leah says, "your thing is with Gonzo. Not with me. We're strangers."

Yes. You're a nurse. I'm a disease.

"I'm so sorry."

I feel agony. But I have no idea if I feel love. I don't have a great deal of experience sorting memory from the present. Is this love? Is that? What about this sort of squidgy feeling there? She might be right. Agony is not love. Not by itself. Unless love comes in various flavours and textures, and this is the one which hurts. That might be. Perhaps love is like hell, and every one is different.

There is water in my eyes. She will not release my hand. We sit. She waits for me to sob out. So. My thing is with Gonzo. We're strangers. Saying it makes it true. My Leah would never do this to me. And damn you, Gonzo, anyway. You couldn't be bothered to dream a dream girl for me too. If you had, we wouldn't be here.

Leah has a question. She is waiting for me to struggle back to myself. I nod.

"Gonzo . . . used to joke about Sally." Joke. Yes. Of course he did. About how he spent the night with her. About the things they did. All a joke.

"Just kidding around," I tell her. It might even be true.

She lets me go. I leave.

IKE THERMITE is lying on the sofa in the living room, and Ma Lubitsch is filling him with cake and some kind of murky grey infusion she makes from her window boxes, and which (like me) has no name. Her husband is in the garden, burying ninjas. He is assisted by the Matahuxee Mime Combine, which might or might not be a good thing. I go out and help.

Corpses are dead weight. Ha ha ha. Old Man Lubitsch has a technique. He shoves a board under one cold shoulder, and shoves it with his rake. The mimes, armed with poles and sticks from the garden, shove as well. The friction between the corpse and the board is less than that between the corpse and the grass, so the corpse stays where it is and the board goes most of the way underneath. If the corpse starts to slip, mimes rush around and brace it. Then Old Man Lubitsch runs to the other side and kicks the corpse until it is almost entirely on the board. Finally, he clamps little barrow wheels to each corner, and he has a corpse on a go-cart which he can drag around to the west paddock, now redesignated the ninja disposal area. The kicking part is the most effortful, but quite apparently also the part which he most enjoys. I do not intend to take this pleasure from him, but he clearly feels I need to kick something, so I get the last one to do myself. We slide the ninja off the board into a pit, and cover him. I sit down on a stone and moan. I wail—not tears, just a heart-deep noise of rejection. The Matahuxee Mime Combine all stand around looking awkward. Old Man Lubitsch puts a rough hand on my shoulder, but that makes it worse. I cannot face his approval, not now. I have done the right thing, in spite of myself. I stare at everything. It's too bright.

Old Man Lubitsch squats down beside me.

"She needed a safe place," he says. He looks away. I think he's guilty.

I want to tell him that he does not have to apologise for sheltering his son's wife in a strange time. Instead, I make some sort of dry sound. He seems to understand what it means. We sit for a while. I hope he won't say anything else.

"It's never easy," Old Man Lubitsch says. "You did right."

Didn't mean to. Meant to, couldn't stick to it, failed to be evil. Not the same.

"You did right," Old Man Lubitsch says again. We sit. He stares straight ahead, seeing something private and very distant.

"You look like him," Old Man Lubitsch says.

Like Gonzo?

"No," Old Man Lubitsch says, "not like Gonzo." And there is a tremor in his voice. The mimes have filed out of the garden, and we are alone. I don't turn to see his face, because I don't think I could stand it if he was crying.

"Not like Gonzo," he says. And he gets up and walks away, leaving me alone.

Something happens to my mouth then. It twists and opens, and my eyes make water, and from my throat and belly come deep, raw noises. It's like crying, the way wine is like water.

Strange, slender arms surround me. They are strong and warm. The black wings of a theatrical cloak wrap around me to keep me warm. Dr. Andromas. The arms rock me, and the gloved hands soothe my hair, and I rest my face against the odd goggled head. Dr. Andromas is a lumpy person to hug, but very giving. Oh yes. Comrade Cow is Dr. Andromas. Gives good hug. But why did you cry on me, Doctor? Do you cry for all your patients?

Dr. Andromas rocks me, and my wounds begin to heal. Again.

"I'm sorry," I tell Dr. Andromas's upper arm. "I'm sorry."

Perhaps, from within the gauze, there is a whispered "shush."

The narrow shoulders stretch and the hands crawl a little farther across my back, settle again to hold me tighter. The only person who can do this for me, right now, is a stranger.

I HAVE decided that I need to go to Haviland alone. Gonzo has gone to Haviland. Dickwash came from there. The *enemy plan* is there, whether that is where it nests or just a place along its route. I must go, and go quietly. I cannot do this if I am being followed around by a small army of neo-Marceauists in berets. I need to ask questions in discreet rooms. The Matahuxee Mime Combine is not a covert operation. It is, especially for a completely silent group of people, stunningly loud. And so I have suggested to Ike that—for the moment—we must part company. I'm a little surprised at how hard this was. Ike has become a friend.

Ike, though, is not the problem.

Dr. Andromas turns to peer at me, then looks back at Ike. Ike shrugs. Andromas makes a sort of irritable wiggle, as if to say I'm an idiot but that doesn't change anything. What it apparently doesn't change is the doctor's intention to come with me to Haviland City.

"It's no good," Ike Thermite says. "Don't look at me."

"He works for you."

Andromas rolls his eyes at Ike, who sighs.

"Andromas," Ike says, "works for Andromas."

"I'm going alone." Ike nods. Andromas doesn't. Andromas just stares into space, like a cat being told to get off the bed. He gazes at the horizon as if I'm talking about someone else. I wave my hand in front of his goggles.

"Hey! Alone!"

Andromas nods. Yes. I am going alone. Andromas is just going in the same direction at the same time. He is not following. We are fellow travellers. Coincidence is wonderful, Hesperus is Phosphorus, no cause for alarm. I glance back at Ike. Ike is wearing the same face: this isn't his problem, there's nothing he can do about it, why am I talking to him? I'm surrounded by a benevolent conspiracy of idiots.

Andromas fluffs his cloak and cocks one arm with the elbow, so that the fabric covers the lower part of his face (already covered, of course, by his gauzy mask, and when did I stop finding that alarming and weird?), and stalks forward. Then he stalks off to the left and makes a full circle around us. Then he cocks the other hand and stalks back the way he came. He will disguise himself. He will be invisible, like the wind in the trees and the shadow of a tiger in the moonlight. No one will notice him.

Apart from *everyone in the world who isn't actually blind.*

Perhaps I can lose him on the road.

"Don't get in the way," I tell him. Andromas nods happily and bounces off to warm up his truck. Annabelle—trucks should have proper names, not silly ones like *Magic of Andromas*—is waiting. I look back at Ike.

"I'm sorry," I tell him. "I just think I should do this myself."

Ike grins.

"I'm a mime artist," he says, "not a superman. What could we possibly do but get in the way? But if you need us, Andromas will know how to find us. And K, of course."

My shock troops. I can't lose.

"And Andromas might surprise you."

Yes. That much is almost certain.

There's a fruity noise somewhere between a klaxon and a trumpet. Andromas—who isn't coming with me, wouldn't dream of it, just going in that direction—is eager to be off. I climb into the cab. The Matahuxee Mime Combine stand in a long line outside the Lubitsch house and wave, each a little out of synch with the next. From the porch Gonzo's parents look on. We have already said our goodbyes, and the physical evidence is sitting next to me on Annabelle's bench: a bundle of clothes, a Tupperware container and an envelope. The clothes are a mixture—cast-offs of Gonzo's and a few of those mysterious items which accumulate in a big house over the years (the canary waistcoat is my favourite; I cannot conceive of any circumstance under which I would wear it) and two pieces of slick black fabric—a ninja outfit in my approximate size for the confusion of my enemies. It smells ever so slightly of bees. I put it down sharply and open the envelope. Money. Not a fortune but some, and thus infinitely more than I had before: *facilitating* money. And last a card, with two words written on it in Old Man Lubitsch's awful scrawl—the name of one of the executives who came to take Gonzo away for his important new job. A familiar name. *Richard Washburn.*

Hello there, Dickwash.

The Tupperware tub is simpler. It is the old kind, a milky basin and a tight-fitting lid, the latter moulded with a flimsy tab at one corner to help you get it off again. The tub contains a sandwich—home-made bread jammed with more chicken, bacon, lettuce, tomato, egg, cheese and mayonnaise than any right-thinking loaf would ever willingly attempt to contain—and a bottle of home-made fizzy pop. There is even an apple and a little pot of honey.

Ma Lubitsch has made me lunch, and with it she has packed her love.

Chapter Fourteen

Working the System;
the paper trail and Mr. Crabtree;
I get my arse kicked.

THE PLAIN WHITE," Libby Lloyd says definitively. She flicks her hair.

Libby Lloyd's shop is in the glitzy part of Haviland, which is all of it except the bits which most Havilanders don't think of as the city proper, like the slums and the outer metropolitan area. It wasn't hard to find. I ditched Annabelle at a truck stop after the drive and took a bus into the centre, then asked the nearest tourist where the best shops were. She consulted a little guidebook and said that the good deals were over to the west of the square. I thanked her and went east. Andromas pottered along behind me for a while, then ducked into a doorway to look at glittering rows of rings and necklaces. I expected him to pop up again, but he didn't. Perhaps he's invisible, or perhaps he has a short attention span. In either case, he's not bothering me. I look back at Libby Lloyd.

"I like the stripes."

"The stripes are very popular among the senior executives." Subtext: surely you aren't one.

"Ideal," I tell her briskly. Subtext: then why on Earth are you showing me this other crap?

Libby Lloyd reassesses. She does not know me, so she has assumed that I am not important. On the other hand, I'm in her insane little shop in Haviland Square buying unpleasantly tight sports gear. More, I'm buying top of the line, and I'm not scared of the Big Dogs. A new customer. A new executive. Possibly unmarried. She tosses her head. It's a full-service effort. One hand goes to her fringe, catches it lightly. The other rests on her stomach, emphasising its flatness and drawing attention to the elegant curve of her bust. She twists her neck sharply. Blonde hair spreads like a parachute and spins around her, light and feathery and infinitely strokable. It falls around her in a haze, and she fires a smouldering look at me for just a heartbeat before smoothing it into something professional and cool; you'd swear you hadn't seen it. Libby Lloyd makes more money in a week than I have ever seen in one place. Money is not the issue. The issue is *access.* Running the most exclusive sports boutique in Haviland is still being a shopkeeper. It's not being part of the System, and Libby Lloyd wants In. I know this because in Haviland everybody who isn't In wants In, and everybody who is In wants to keep them Out. Pencilneck Heaven. A brief conversation via the electric telephone with K (the original and still the best) filled in my sketchy understanding of life here. Essentially, K said, the more ludicrously you behave, the more they will assume you have the right to.

I pay cash. Subtext: your pathetic bill means *nothing* to me! *Bwahahaha!* Libby Lloyd flutters. It's a large bill; if this is just walking-around money where I come from, then she really does need to know me better. I hesitate going out of the door. Libby Lloyd preens. This is where I ask her if she's busy later, because I'm going to this party and I don't know anyone in town.

"I wonder," I say brightly.

"Yes?" Subtext: anything at all.

"Who makes the best suits in Haviland these days?"

Disappointment tempered by patience. Subtext: you will be mine.

"Royce Allen," she says firmly. "He's just across the street. Come in and see me when you pick it up." She smiles and bats her lashes at me. I swear I feel a breeze.

. . .

THE BAG FROM Libby Lloyd's is a passport to greatness. It has a gold colophon on a shiny white background, and with it under my arm scruffy clothes are simply not an issue. I have already bought. I am spending. I have money. Respectable clothing is what I will come *out* of Royce Allen's with, not what I need going *in.* The door across the road opens before I can knock.

I spend five minutes pottering around admiring Royce Allen's off-the-peg stuff while his nervous assistant follows me to and fro, nodding when I make little noises of discontent and explaining that (while everything I see is of the highest quality in all respects) the bespoke work is vastly superior. I try on a shirt. It makes me look like a god. I suggest that it's a little tight under the arms. Yes. Definitely pulling . . . what sort of thread does Royce Allen use in his seams? It feels coarse. The assistant assures me that the thread is the finest baby hair and angora rabbit, the softest known to man. I sigh. It must be the fabric then. A pity. No, no, the fabric is a cotton picked by child slave labourers who wash and moisturise their hands every hour so as to prevent their fingers from roughing the fibres. They bleed, of course, but their blood contains chemicals (owing to a strictly controlled diet) which actually add to the luxuriant mellowness of the weave. The blood is as a matter of course hygenically bleached out with a mineral cleaning agent made from crushed diamond and virgin's saliva, which adds lustre and radiance, and also gives the finished shirt the toughness of ballistic nylon.

I explain sorrowfully that all this discussion has left me with a dry throat. It is now my intention to return later, or possibly next week, having refreshed my mucous membranes. I am politely disinclined to discuss the matter further. I am so polite as to be almost rude. I cough gently, to remind Royce Allen's assistant that the absolute last thing I want is further chat, because—possibly owing to the amount of time I spend on the phone firing people and arranging the fate of millions—my larynx is in such terrible agony. He summons a minion (Royce Allen's shop is awash with minions coming and going clutching swatches and fabrics, and occasionally, from the fitting rooms, there comes the voice of the great man himself: "Freddie! Get the blue flannel for Mr. Custer-Price, please, he needs to see it against the checks," and Freddie—or Tom, or Phylis, or Betsy, or someone—scurries over and looks the other way so that Mr. Custer-Price is not embarrassed in his partial nudity) and the minion brings a tray of drinks. I hover over the expensive Scotch and then the Armagnac, but finally settle on a glass of rich red claret. I put it near my nose and nearly pass out. It smells of old houses and aged wood and dark secrets, but also of hard, hot sunshine through ancient shutters and long, wicked afternoons in a four-poster bed. It's not a wine, it's a life, right there in the glass. I sip it. Fire and fruit wash over my tongue.

"Oh, that's actually not bad." Calumny. I sit. The assistant relaxes a little and asks if I would mind waiting while he fetches Mr. Royce Allen, in person. I decide that I wouldn't. I sip again. I really wouldn't.

Royce Allen is a hearty fellow with sausage fingers and the obligatory tape measure around his neck. He is not so much unctuous as balsamic. He eels out of the fitting rooms and glad-hands me and confides that he's been hoping I'd come by ever since he heard I was coming to Haviland. He was concerned that I'd been seduced by that clothbutcher, Daniel Prang. I swear that the false glamour of Prang never appealed even for a second, and he adjudges me not just a powerful man but also—and this is rare, sir, very rare—a man of taste. Daniel Prang (confides Royce Allen) began as a very excellent cobbler; had he stuck to gentlemen's shoes and boots, all would have been well. The original Prang shoe was a splendid thing, a brogue with fine slim lines and a steel and silver slash across the back of the heel, with a unique crest designed for each customer so that a gentleman's footprints were instantly recognisable to his friends. Sadly, after a few months, the cleats tended to come loose, and one was forever stopping to *examine one's sole* (ahaha, just my little joke, sir, but you see, yes, well of course you do).

In those good old days Royce Allen himself bought shoes at Prang's, and his crest was a camel passing through the eye of the needle, very droll indeed. Alas, Mr. Prang has upset the natural balance of things by venturing to make gentlemen's clothing, and it is not a task for which life has equipped him. Royce Allen is delighted that I have the natural acuity and good sense to reject the Prang suit with its modern lines, and determines that I shall have only his best work. He thus dispenses with all the moderate fabrics (read: cheap) and whisks me straight to the last table by his den where he keeps the ones which empty banks and consume the wealth of nations. I ponder, he measures. I cannot decide between the alpaca and cuttlefish (honestly) and the Mylar-silk (very good in summertime), and—since I'm never going to wear them—I order one of each. Royce Allen licks his lips and applauds my boldness. The first fitting will be in three weeks. Royce Allen's assistant brings me another glass of the red lest my throat should again be giving me trouble after this exertion, and hovers with the bottle in case I need to make any more difficult choices regarding shirts. While we're in the mood, I toss a couple of the superb off-the-peg jackets on the pile (for casual wear, Mr. Allen) along with some *At Work By Allen* jeans and some slacks and a pair of *Foot By Allen* shoes. Royce Allen is so delighted that he throws in a pair of socks. I give him my entirely fictitious address in the nice part of the city and ask if I can pop back in later to pick up the off-the-peg stuff. I've got squash in an hour at the Club (I don't know which club yet, but everyone else obviously does, they nod and bob reverently) and Royce Allen says of course. We shake hands, for which I put down the glass on the sales counter, and the assistant moves forward to grasp it before it can become a hazard. Alas, alack, how *do* these things happen? I have stepped back into the space he was intending to occupy. Silly me. Perhaps I am clumsy, or supremely confident, or drunk. Certainly, I couldn't have intended this outcome: the remainder of the bottle (I will linger in the oenophile's Hell of Corked Vintages for a thousand years) glugs massively over my shirt and down my back.

There is absolute silence. I worry for a moment that the assistant has actually died or gone mad; he's frozen in place. Then he straightens, murmurs "I'm most terribly sorry" and walks into the back room to gather his things. He does not wait to be told that he's fired. I hope it's a drill. I hope he's going to go and sit in a bar until Royce Allen calls him and tells him to come back to work, the client is gone. I doubt it.

Royce Allen sighs.

"What a muddle," he says. "Going to the Brandon Club, you said?"

"Yes," I tell him sadly, "I was."

"Well, you can't go like that," says Royce Allen. He shrugs. "Take the casual now," he says. "You can pay for it when you come for the first fitting. If you don't like it, we'll shove it on the dummy and you can call it a loan, all right?"

I couldn't possibly, but you must, no, Mr. Allen, sir, I insist, blah blah. We out-polite one another for a while until he puts his foot down and I walk out of his shop wearing a fortune and carrying a change of clothes, and with two glasses of his wine inside me. I'd feel guilty, but he'll be fine, and he'll make an extra 5 per cent this year just telling the story to gentlemen in the fitting room. How I Was Took by a Felon, by Royce Allen, and I'd do it again, sir, because that's how we are in this shop. Oh, no, sir, to be honest, I think we'll have to go up a grade, that fabric doesn't do you justice.

I get in a taxi, and tell the driver to take me to the Brandon Club.

BUDDY KEENE lends me a racquet. He has five, in a thick sack, and he uses a different one depending on mood. His name

(Bartholomew Keene) is printed in gold on the bag. Tom Link and Roy Massaman put me on to him by the water fountain: Buddy has too many damn racquets, man he'll set you up. And he will, because Royce Allen's craft is all over me, and that's as much a passport as Libby Lloyd's whites. The stripes cause a bit of a murmur when they come out.

I stand in the gallery and watch, and chat. The Brandon Club gallery, overlooking the courts, has ferns and fig trees in little pots at inconvenient intervals, and supremely uncomfortable chairs made from bamboo. Anyone spending any significant amount of time here will develop expensive back pain, and the club has a health spa which is particularly good at dealing with injuries sustained from sitting all day in a lounger. The walls are painted off-white (because true white makes the guests look ill) and there's a great deal of glass. The point appears to be that you could only possibly pay what you pay to be a member here if you are very rich, because anyone with less money would demand better service at the price.

From Buddy and his friends—who rotate on and off the court, so that one of them is always talking to me in a somewhat wheezy voice and mopping his underarms—I learn that Haviland City is filled with excellent bars; that it is (like ancient Rome) constructed on a string of hills, the precise number of which no one can quite recall. I learn that the market (this being the stock market, not the local produce market, although in fact the produce market is of course a subset of the other) is low at the moment owing to a string of vanishings and the recent fire on the Pipe (Old J.P.), but that certain people confidently expect it to rise shortly when these matters are resolved. (Resolved how? Just *resolved.*) I learn that Haviland City is now the centre of operations for Jorgmund, although the old head office remains out along the Pipe (the Silver) a way, where it all began. These things are moderately interesting, but not what I came here for. I wait. Sooner or later, they have to ask me to join the game. And they do. Buddy Keene, red from the neck up and dripping sweat from his earlobe, gets down on one knee. Would I like a shot at the title? I give Buddy a bit of polite surprise. Oh no. No, I'm waiting for Someone. Buddy catches hold of the capital S. His eyes light up. Is it a babe? Babes who play Brandon Racquets (the club's own variant, which has few or no rules about physical contact) are hot. They are hot racquet babes. They get physical. Yeah!

"No," I murmur, infinitely bored, "I'm here to see Richard."

"Richard?"

"Washburn."

"You mean Dick?"

"I call him Richard."

"He prefers Dick."

"How ambitious."

This is easy. No one here is telling the truth. Every single one of them is living for every other. They do things because they must be seen to do them. These are type D or even type E pencil-necks vying for an upgrade. They're here to lose a bit of identity, to become more the Right Kind of Guy. The rules they know are their own rules, and someone who breaks them without fear must be playing on the next level up.

I look at my watch. It's not expensive. They stare. I tap it.

"Piece of crap. Won it off a guy."

"You bet for that?"

"That . . . and his job." They all suck air sharply, and Roy Massaman takes a little step back.

Yes, tiny men. I eat what I kill.

"Anyone know where Richard is? I'm due on a call at five. I'll see him later."

"He's going to the party this evening."

"Good. I'll see him there. Is that the board thing?"

"Uh, no. There's a board thing?"

"If there isn't, I've come a long way for nothing. So where's Richard going to be?"

And of course they tell me. Anything to help a fellow out.

Particularly if you suspect he may be your next boss. Buddy Keene is looking at me, little wheels turning in his head. Think, Buddy. Take a risk. Grift.

I toss Buddy his racquet. We'll do drinks, okay? And yes, they all say happily, we'll do drinks. I step out into the corridor, and I walk away. He might not come. He might not have anything to offer. And then, heavy footsteps, the flat clatter of someone trying to lose speed in training shoes.

"Hey," says Buddy Keene. "Wait up."

Goodness me, whatever can it be?

"You're coming to our office? Here in Haviland?"

"Seems that way."

"Well . . ." Buddy Keene smiles an ingratiating smile. "There's a meeting of the Planning Horizons Committee in an hour. Would you like to sit in, unofficially?"

Yes, Buddy. That would be just ideal.

JORGMUND has the big building on the left, with the annexe. The big building on the right belongs to the mayoralty. It is not as big as the big building on the left, which is topped with the circular snake logo, and has a couple of extra floors to drive the point home. The mayoralty had permission to go taller, but since Jorgmund was doing the construction, they somehow never got around to asking for those extra levels.

We are on one of the middle floors, and Buddy Keene has explained to everyone that I am *absolutely not here,* and given them to understand that I am a bigwig from back along the Silver. He says this with the absolute conviction of someone who wants to be first in line for promotion when I ascend, and his avarice is incredibly persuasive.

Buddy Keene, with a smile on his lips, opens his first red folder and slaps it down on the table in front of him. "Right," he says. "Let's rule the world." Everyone grins. I assume that he is joking. A few minutes later I realise that he is not, or not entirely.

They aren't actually ruling the world, but they're planning for Haviland City, and what goes for Haviland goes everywhere else in Jorgmund's domain, which is everywhere.

Everything in Jorgmund is governed by the Core. The Core is the final authority, the yes or the no. Naturally, everyone wants to get into the Core. This is made more difficult by the fact that no one knows who else is in it. (Buddy Keene is almost 100 per cent certain that Humbert Pestle is in the Core. That means Dick Washburn has the ear of the Core—if such a thing can be said to exist—and hence that I am going around telling everyone that I'm one better than the guy who knows the guy who is almost certainly one of The Guys.)

Between us in this room and them in whatever corporate Olympus they occupy, there is the Senior Board. The Senior Board is composed of people who would very much like to be in the Core, and who therefore go out of their way to demonstrate how ruthless and commercially minded and efficient they are by going through the proposals of the Planning Horizons Committee and kicking out the weak, kittenish ideas and retaining only the fanged, pit bull ideas. Everyone here (except me) can name the Senior Board, list their hobbies and their weaknesses, knows how they like to be called and what their favourite drink is. Dick Washburn is tipped as surefire Senior Board material, as long as the Lubitsch Project comes out well.

"That was a bold initiative," I murmur, and there's a great deal of nodding and harrumphing. "Did anyone see the projections?"

"They're huge," says Buddy Keene.

"Really major," says a woman named Mae Milton.

They look at me to see if they've said the right thing. I realise they have no idea what it is.

The Lubitsch Project. I turn the words over in my head. I don't like them. I don't like the fact that it has a name rather than an incident number or a nickname, or that they've heard about it in a place with the word "planning" in the title. I don't like it that the name attached is Gonzo's, in particular. This wasn't about the Free Company. It wasn't about Jim Hepsobah and his expertise, or Sally Culpepper and her negotiator *gong fu*. It was and is about Gonzo, in person. *You were set up*. Yes, Ronnie, we were. And yes, indeed. Who profits?

Buddy Keene is talking about house prices. Apparently, they're on the rise, and many employees are asking for higher salaries to cope with the difference. Buddy Keene suggests that Jorgmund encourage them to move to the fringes of town where property is cheaper. This will entail new construction (Jorgmund has a large construction arm) and better transport (supplied by Jorgmund Rail & Road). The longer commute will take a chunk out of employees' days, of course, but this will leave them with more disposable income during their remaining leisure time. The alternative is to pay them more, have them live in a more expensive neighbourhood and feel underpaid, beginning a cycle of disaffection which can only be bad for the company. Additionally, people who spend more time with their families develop attachments and retire early, sometimes have children, and require day care and leave, whereas people who work long hours do not develop such strong outside attachments; they swim in the company water and think it's the whole world. Day care and recruitment are expensive, and thus to be avoided. Since it is the major real-estate owner in Haviland City, Jorgmund could lower rents and sale prices, but this would mean taking a loss in a sector which is at present growing well. That kind of option is available to the Senior Board, but not to Planning Horizons.

Buddy Keene minutes the recommendations from the committee and puts them in an orange envelope. He sets the orange envelope in a tray marked "Action Up" and moves on to sanitation and water. This is, if anything, more problematic than housing. I nod my way through it and wish I hadn't come. *The Lubitsch Project*. Damn, damn, damn.

"How was it for you?" Buddy Keene asks, when it's over and I can stop nodding.

"Fascinating, Buddy," I tell him warmly. "Really great. I owe you." And this is the right thing to say. Buddy Keene nods back. Service rendered, debt accepted, between guys who want to be Guys. The members of the committee make polite goodbyes and wish they'd seen me first.

I am shaking hands with Mae Milton when I hear a rustling behind me. An old man in a maroon V-neck is collecting the Action Up tray and putting an empty one in its place. I did not see him come in, and I realise now that there is a low concealed door, like a servant's entrance in a country house, just behind the chairman's place at the top of the table. Over his heart there is a narrow metal badge: "Robert Crabtree."

"Hey," says Mae Milton, "it's the boss man!" She grins.

I look at him. Clearly, she's making with the funny. Milton holds up a warning hand.

"Don't be deceived. Mr. Crabtree is our secret master, right, Robert?"

Dark eyes rise slowly from his cart and peer at me from beneath heavy, folded lids.

"I just move the paper," he says firmly. In the world of Mr. Crabtree, moving the paper is a trust. You don't make jokes about the paper. On the other hand, Mae Milton is moderately charming, and even Robert Crabtree is not immune. She offers him a broad, genuine smile. It occurs to me that Mae Milton will not last long as a pencilneck if this is how she carries on.

"Mmph," says Robert Crabtree. He moves the corners of his mouth a bit to indicate that he's seen the smile, and wheels the cart around me. Mr. Crabtree has seen a hundred of my kind come and go. He is not impressed. By next year I will be promoted or fired. I will be erased or eulogised, and the only memory of my presence on this floor will be my initials carved into the back of a cubicle door in the executive women's washroom. Fair enough. But Robert Crabtree is important. I don't know how, but Mae Milton has shown me something significant, if I have the wit to grasp it.

I wave to her and wander after him. He makes no objection. I watch him walk the halls of Jorgmund with his cart, piling up orange envelopes. No one speaks to him. No one even really looks at him. He's just there, cog in the machine. Finally he walks into a big round room with an expensive table in it. Some ferns (what is it with ferns?) make his passage to the head of the table more difficult, and he's almost blocked by a display case with some high-echelon bric-a-brac inside.

"Senior Board room," says Mr. Crabtree. He looks around as if seeing it for the first time. More likely it's just the first time today. He sneers a bit at the bric-a-brac. Mr. Crabtree does not approve of fripperies. They get in the way of the paper. He dumps the whole cartload on the table, and lines the envelopes up so that they're in piles, ready to go. Waiting for him is a smaller stack of yellow envelopes stamped "Forward to Core." He takes them, and moves off down the corridor again. *Maps and charts,* Ronnie Cheung said in the dark outside K's circus. Know your enemy. Follow the paper. I follow. Mr. Crabtree is my guide in a strange land. *So, Robert, where are the maps and charts? Just curious, don't want to be a bother.*

"Pleased to meet you," Robert Crabtree says, without looking up. I glance around. He is talking to me. He is saying goodbye.

We are coming to the edge of the building. At the end of this corridor there is a window looking out over Haviland City and a small, half-size construction clinging to the side of the Jorgmund office. Robert Crabtree pushes his cart into a small service lift and turns to face me. There is only room for him.

"Core," says Robert Crabtree flatly. The doors close.

I listen to the lift. It goes down a long way. Probably, it goes to the top floor of the other building, the one nudging up against Jorgmund. It might go to an office in this building which looks out over their roof. I stand at the end of the corridor, gazing out at the city, hoping no one sees me and thinks to ask why I am here. Ten minutes later the lift doors open again. Robert Crabtree emerges. His cart is covered in green envelopes marked

"Execute." He looks at me for a moment, wondering what the hell I am doing waiting around for him. He decides he doesn't care.

"If you're going to follow me like a bloody baa-lamb," Robert Crabtree says abruptly, "you can put your hand on the front there, because otherwise the buggers fall off and get creased and there's no end of bother."

I hesitate. He takes my hand in his clumsy arthritic grasp, angry already, and settles it painfully hard on the front of the trolley. He wraps my fingers around the sharp-edged envelopes using his palm, because his own fingers don't bend that well, and we make his round. We deliver thirty executive decisions. We are messengers of God, invisible, inevitable, ignored.

When we're done, I go to the party to find Dick.

PINEMARTIN HILL is long and green. It is a genuine hill, quite a steep one, although the road runs along the side of it. Presumably part of the charm is having a view which tumbles away at your feet. The street lights are old-fashioned. There's a big modern house on the left full of happy people having fun—a stilt house. My car pulls up by the topiary. It isn't really my car; it was booked for someone else, but I stole it and its impassive chauffeur, and if the person it was booked for figures out what happened, he or she will almost certainly invite me to use it until I get settled in. The Brandon Club were so delighted to have my patronage that they gave me a free room for the night and a spa treatment, so I went to sleep for an hour while a matronly woman exfoliated me and talked about her family. Dressing, I chose the second shirt, the one softened in the mouth of a trained and perfumed albino hippopotamus and made entirely of pigeon's wool, because it goes better with the shoes than the one stitched with baby hair. The cuffs gave me some trouble until I remembered that the button isn't supposed to wrap your arm like an ordinary shirt, but to clasp the two parts of the sleeve together like a cuff link. Smooth.

The door to number one five four is open, and a lot of people are shrugging out of coats and shedding scarves. Jorgmund's children—or maybe its myrmidons—do themselves well enough for clothes and rocks. I go in. The hallway curves round into a wide open living room with an alpine vibe, and, sure enough, beyond the garden terrace there's a long drop to the ground. The decor features muted colours with lush, unmatched furniture, and low tables occupied by little bits and bobs of stuff like armadillo shells—used as olive bowls—or pufferfish skins with gilded spines, which have no discernible purpose and are very sharp. It's a model of a home.

In any given situation there are myriad forms of attack. (Actually, there aren't. A myriad is ten thousand in the Greek arithmetical system, which was based on their alphabet and made Archimedes' life impossibly difficult. If he'd had decimals, he might have done remarkable things, and we'd all be driving flying cars and heating our bathwater with home fusion, or perhaps speaking Latin and living in the ashes of the Graeco-Roman Nuclear Winter; in any case, there are usually *several* ways of dealing with any given situation.) I could walk up to Dick Washburn and stick out my hand. Buddy Keene and Roy Massaman and Tom Link would all be there, and Dick would almost certainly have to take it. But I have worked hard to make Buddy & Co. think of me as a big fish, even a man-eating shark, and I might still need that. If I let them see me right next to Dick—if I walk up to him and shake his hand, Gonzo-style—reality will assert itself. I will be in direct conflict with Dick's dominance, and he's had longer to bruit it about and can actually back it up by firing people and buying expensive things. In a direct, mano-a-mano hard-form conflict, I will lose. By the criteria of Haviland City, Dick Washburn is infinitely bigger and meaner than I am.

I could seek an introduction, but since I've given the impression that I already know Dick Washburn, that might confuse people and lead to the same unfortunate awakenings as option one. Fortunately, I am devious. The problem of how to say hi to a powerful, confident executive you have never met but whom you are supposed to know is a very difficult one. I have considered from all angles and decided that there is almost no way to do it which doesn't make you look smaller than he does. Having this problem both sucks and blows. Thus, I have arranged for it to be Dick Washburn's problem.

This is the room, from above. It is irregular but roughly oval. It is lined with tables and chairs for receiving. Later tonight it will be cool and dark, and smell of cigars and spilled mojitos. The carpet will hold the marks of a hundred pairs of elegant shoes, and the lead crystal glasses will carry traces of designer lipstick and executive DNA. The writing desk, pressed into service by the entrance to the breakfast room, will still have perfume on it, because the woman with the penetrating laugh is leaning all the way forward to adjust her interlocutor's tie and (her mother taught her this when she was seventeen) she sprays scent into her cleavage before she goes out. Right now, though, the room is bustling and alive. If you speeded it up, you would see twisting patterns like clouds and pressure lines, and at the very centre of the biggest one is Richard Washburn, Esquire. His presence defines the play of forces in the room; the flutter of his wings causes tremors by the bar and tidal waves at the chaise longue in front of the patio doors. On most nights Richard Washburn is the eye of the storm. But today he is not alone. There is something wrong, a perturbation in the smooth carriage of his life. Another weather centre, a zone of high pressure, small but very hot, is moving across the shag-pile floor. Perhaps it's a tornado. Perhaps it's the beginning of a hurricane. Will it bounce off him, or swallow him up? Most likely it will swell his power, increase his domain, but it just might be a danger to him. Whatever, he cannot ignore it. Which is why he is, even now, moving through the throng towards me. He sticks out his hand and prepares to say hi in a big, dominant way.

And then Dick Washburn's eyes widen. I can feel the change

too; I know roughly what's happened before I turn round. If my presence here is like a tropical storm closing in on Dick's island paradise of warm weather and regular rainfall, this is like the arrival of Moses at the Red Sea. The flow of wind and water slows, then stops altogether. A momentous thing has happened. And behind me there is a strange, familiar noise. It is the sound of shoes with little metal cleats tapping on the wood boards of the hallway.

"Hi, Humbert," Dickwash says a bit squeakily. "So glad you could come." I wonder if Humbert Pestle has ever shown up to one of these soirées before. I wonder why he is here now. Maybe Dickwash is up for promotion. Maybe Humbert's about to eat him alive.

"Richard," Humbert Pestle says jovially, "I wouldn't have missed it for worlds. But I'm taking you away from your guest." Not guests, plural, just me. Humbert Pestle sticks out a muscular hand. The other one (the possible prosthetic) is tucked, genial old-fart style, into his trouser pocket. This makes him uneven and a bit rumpled, but his clothes are so perfect (no doubt Royce Allen cut and stitched every bit himself, from the purest milk-washed brontosaurus foreskin) that he just looks terribly relaxed. Which he is.

"I'm Pestle, call me Humbert—"

I recognise the line from his briefing at Harrisburg, and give him the next bit: "Pestle like mortar . . ."

He stares for a moment then says, "Mortar like in a wall—"

"And ain't *that* ever a regrettable name?"

Now I have Humbert Pestle's full attention, and the power of his gaze, when he switches it on, is like a weight on my chest. There is absolute quiet, except for someone, somewhere in the room, who chooses this moment to finish a sentence with the words "ludicrous cocksucker!" and then goes very quiet and hides behind an urn. I'd feel sympathetic, but I'm busy exuding bonhomie and harmless, cheeky, up-and-coming pencilneckhood.

Dick Washburn changes colour a few times, and looks as if he may faint. I remember belatedly that Humbert Pestle is an *Übermann,* a major player. He probably doesn't hear his own material parroted back at him, ever. Probably the last guy who did that is now a janitor, with only one eye, and speaks in a series of burps because Pestle-call-me-Humbert tore out his larynx. *Breathe.* Check the exits. Too much mouth too soon, and now it's over. But Humbert Pestle lets out a huge bark of laughter and claps me on the back. "You're damn right," he says. "You are absolutely right." His craggy eyes peer at me, sparkling.

"I need a drink, young Richard, so why don't you show me to the bar? And then I need a proper introduction to this gentleman because he reminds me of a kid I used to know—with an awful name." Still chuckling, he leads the pencilneck away as if this were his house and his party, and when he reaches the bar, with its tiled surround, his shoes make that weird little *tink, tonk,* which I take to mean Daniel Prang's signature footwear has shed its cleat, as Royce Allen told me it would.

"Balls of steel, man," says Tom Link.

"Epic," agrees Roy Massaman. They make that annoying sun-god worship gesture you used to see in movies about California, hands up in the air, bowing at the belly. I look away, hoping to see something I can pretend to find interesting and thus leave them behind. I am looking clear across into the garden, where Dick Washburn's swimming pool is lit with dark pink underwater lights. I have never seen that before. Granted, I haven't seen a private pool in twenty years either, but somehow I just assumed it was a natural law: pool lighting is plain, or bluеish. The pool has deep purple shadows and looks like a venue for insane flirting and trysting rather than actual swimming. Doing your laps in it would be a bit prim, sort of like wearing an anorak to a toga party. The garden doors are—for the moment—closed, but there's enough steam coming off the water that it's apparently at a pretty good heat, and there are those elongated metal mushrooms with gas burners in them making it warm out there, so sooner or later, when the drink is flowing, the daring and the beautiful will presumably strip down and jump in. And at the very edge of the pool, on the far side from the house, is the ghostly figure of Dr. Andromas, sitting cross-legged on the diving board.

Just discovering him like that, in plain sight, scares the shit out of me. There's nothing supernatural about his being here. He has come in over the wall. Presumably he has followed me here. And he's on my side (or I'm on his, perhaps) but still, Dr. Andromas is just *wrong.* He is the most unnatural man I have ever met. Also, if he chooses to come in here and advertise our previous acquaintance, my best-laid plans will look a bit like chopped liver. No one else has noticed him yet (I can tell because there is no screaming) but the moment Sippy Roehunter decides it's time to show the board members what she's got, or Dan deLine gets a hankering to bare his musculature for the benefit of the Jorgmund Ladies' Lacrosse Team, it will be hard for anyone to ignore a top-hatted H. G. Wells–looking lunatic sitting in the lotus position on the edge of Dick Washburn's giant pink sex pool. I will him to disappear. It doesn't work. I grind my teeth. This doesn't help either.

"You okay?" Tom Link is concerned.

"I'm fine. New bite plate. Leaves me a bit rocky in the evenings." Cosmetic dentistry excuse, all men together. Link nods. Damn those orthodontic torturers and their perfect smiles. Andromas appears to be fishing for imaginary fish. Or maybe real ones, who knows? But he's using an imaginary rod.

Wallop. Something hits me between the shoulder blades. It's about the size of a human hand, but it seems to be made of rock, and it is powered by some kind of pneumatic press. It doesn't hurt, but it shocks me, and my muscles all freeze up.

"Hey there, stranger! Let's talk turkey!" Humbert Pestle. I hope he really does want to talk turkey. If we're going to roister now, if he's got some line-up of corporate houris we need to check out while drinking some faux-frontiersman drink he got to like back in the day, he's going to kill me. He's about twice my weight and he spends way too much time in the executive gym. On the other hand, if he's going to fall into the mystery of *who is this bright young executive and why haven't I seen his file,* I may be able to find out where he and Dick Washburn fit into the screw-up which has become my life, and maybe what he intends for Gonzo, my idiot brother, progenitor, pal and would-be murderer.

"Let's walk the parapet," Humbert Pestle says, and then glances at Dick Washburn. "You do have a parapet, don't you?"

"Only the terrace," says Dick. And he points out to the pool, and Dr. Andromas. Everyone looks.

"Now that is a pool, Richard," says Humbert Pestle after a moment. "Pink as hell." I open one eye (apparently I had shut both at some point) and find that Andromas has gone. Of course. "Can we have the terrace a moment, Richard?" And Dick Washburn says of course, and it turns out there's a magic button which makes the glass opaque. Very space age. Humbert Pestle makes a noise which might be "I haveta git me some o' those fer mah own place" or it might be "Boys and their toys" and then points me out onto the terrace. We walk out. It's cool, but warmer than I expected because the steam from the pool is hanging over the terrace.

"You made me laugh back there," murmurs Humbert Pestle gently, "and that is a rare, rare thing. Now maybe that's because I rule too much with a rod of iron or maybe it's just I have a low sense of humour and so do you. But I don't know your face, young sir, and so I have to ask you where you heard me say that before we get to the meat."

Direct, of course. Naturally he is direct. Look at him. He's got a big cigar in his free hand and shoulders like a door. This is a man who believes in frontal assault. All right then. Answer the question, but dodge the truth.

"At a briefing, few months back."

"What briefing?"

"On the Lubitsch thing."

"Oh," says Humbert Pestle, nodding. "That briefing. Yeah. I figured." And I realise that I have made a very large mistake. I realise this because I am not a total idiot, despite how it might occasionally appear, and because Humbert Pestle hits me like water from a fire hose. I fly backwards. I don't know where he hit me. It doesn't matter. If it's broken, I will find out. If it's not, I can worry about it later. I roll. He's fast, though. He catches me just as I'm coming up. I slip the punch, but the kick gets me and I go into the air again.

There are fights, and there are fights. The first kind is dialogue: boxing matches, sparring, even rhinos' mating fights. It's all dialogue. Am I better? Am I faster? The second kind—and it's not that the first kind can't go this way if someone doesn't like the way a point is expressed—the second kind is about erasure. It is the urge behind the gun with which Gonzo shot me, and behind the Go Away Bomb. It is the desire that the enemy not be a consideration any more, ever, that the world no longer contain them. Humbert Pestle is fighting this kind of fight right now, and he will kill me very thoroughly if I don't stop him. The thing is, I don't know how.

Pestle fires off a few jabs at me with his good hand. He has the other one wrapped around his body now, tucked behind his back. Warning: that means he has a weapon. He came prepared. He intends to surprise me with it. Or alternatively he wants me to believe that, to pay undue attention to the missing hand. It's easy to get knocked unconscious because the other guy is waving a broken bottle, and the sharp edges are hypnotic with the promise of laceration, and then the other hand is just a blur of one, two, three, good night. So, I don't get distracted. I don't assume. *Move. Evade.* The enemy attacks in arcs and straight lines. Your body has joints. Use them. I rock, bend, twist. My arms stop moving like windmills and start to make themselves useful. I do not try to block directly. Ronnie Cheung might be able to do that. Gonzo might. I can't. I guide the heavy hand past me, step so that the attacks are in the wrong place. *Move.*

Step. Brush. Twist. Yes. He cannot touch me. I remember this. One opponent is not hard. He has limited options. And he's still hiding that hand.

But Humbert Pestle is watching. He is watching with a kind of anticipation. And as I get the better of his one-armed attack, he starts to pay more attention. He watches my feet. I chop and change my evasions, looking for the best one: Nine Palace Shuffle; Five Element Foot; Walk Like Elvis. *Walk Like Elvis.* He breathes out faster, as if he's hungry. *Walk Like Elvis.* His face twists in a little sneer, or maybe a smile. Humbert Pestle meets my eyes and now he is definitely grinning. He is not smiling at me. We are not friends. We are un-friends. He is smiling at my Walk Like Elvis as if it is the last kitten in a litter he was intending to drown. He *recognises* it. And like a nightmare, he gets bigger and badder just as I'm on top.

His left hand comes around out from behind his back, and it's not a prosthetic at all. It's just that it's made almost entirely of knotted bone. It's like a club. Ronnie Cheung's hands were big and solid. They were as strong as you could possibly need, and obviously they maintained some utility as tools for eating and carrying stuff. More important, Ronnie had made a choice about how far down the road of becoming a human killing machine he was prepared to go, and allowing his training to warp his body to the point where he was in some measure *only* suited to that task was exactly where he drew the line. Ronnie was all in favour of necessary violence, but he was as a consequence particularly venomous about the other kind. *I do not train ninjas,* he told Riley Tench, and it was a statement of his creed. But you heard stories. One of those stories concerned the Iron Skin Meditation.

The idea is that you forge your whole body into a weapon. For example, you take an ordinary hand and you use it to hit stuff. You start with sackcloth filled with wool, then with sawdust, then with wire wool, then iron filings. Then you just use a wooden board. Then a stone. You just keep hitting. When you can do that, you heat the stone until you can cook an egg on it. And you keep hitting. You do this until pain becomes a thing of memory and your hand is broken and remade and finally it is a solid weapon with which you might punch your way out of a bank vault or splinter someone's ribs with a single blow. There are various ways of describing this kind of behaviour. One would be "single-minded." Another would be "stark raving mad." "Single-minded" is quite revealing, actually, because to do this to yourself requires a negation of everything else it is to be human. It's about becoming a *thing* with a single purpose, whereas people are usually a bit more generalised—hence Ronnie never bothered, or wanted to, or really considered it. Also, Ronnie was not stark raving mad.

Humbert Pestle has engaged in some variant of the Iron Skin Meditation. And he is about to hit me with the consequence.

He doesn't. He suckers me with his other hand. I even saw it coming. And *now* he comes after me with his left. *Of course* he's left-handed. The object (can't think of it as a hand, somehow it's too alien) comes towards my head. I duck, guide the punch past me and, since the opportunity is there, I hit him back. It gets even less result than I was hoping for, and all I was hoping for was a breathing space. It hurts me more than him. Like Ronnie, he has been struck so many times there's not much left in the way of capillaries to break.

I feel the breeze of his monster fist go past my face. Then it comes back, a sort of bear hug, or maybe a lobster's claw. It ruffles my hair and makes a kind of dizzy *thunk* noise where it grazes my skull. I see stars and hear Tweety Birds. I tap him in the eye, which he doesn't like. Can't Iron Skin your eyeballs, so it fills with tears. Why is he doing this? Who is he, that he can? And—hell. I as good as told him who I was, if he knows about Gonzo, and almost everyone tries to kill me once they know that. *An enemy plan implies an enemy planner, Bumhole, or had this not occurred to you?* Humbert Pestle moves rapidly to the top of my list of suspects. Now if I can just stop him from murdering me . . .

We fight.

It's uneven, because all I'm trying to do is stay alive and maybe get back to the party, where he may not feel able to pursue his present line of argument, and all he's trying to do is open my skull like a grizzly with a honeycomb. At some point he hits me properly with the Iron Skin hand. I don't know when. I assume the fight has lasted about an hour by this point, but realistically it must be about three minutes. He hits me at less than full force, and not in the head. Nothing actually breaks, but I feel my ribs bend inward, spring out, and my lung protests and I can't breathe. Cramp? Serious damage? Work through or die. I retreat, choking. I know nothing to beat him. I am faster, but he's tireless. I can't lock his arms—can't afford to grapple at all, when even a passing strike with that hand could knock me out. He's a fortress. Master Wu should have taught us the Ghost Palm. If Pestle's using the Iron Skin, I should have my own special magic power. Where are my laser eye beams? *Concentrate.*

I lash out with my fist, and when he blocks (scythes his forearm across as if he can smash my hand off; maybe he could) I roll my arm and step inside his guard. My elbow catches him in the face. I keep going, and my hip and shoulder hit him too. It's like walking into a wall. I skip out, try to deaden his leg, and he leans into the blow, nearly catches my foot. Just to rub it in, he extends that same leg into my shoulder like a piston, curls it back down to the ground. I dodge around him, suppressing the urge to rub the arm. He doesn't move his feet, just follows me with his head, wraps himself up like a spring. Or a snake. He uncoils, and his hand—the bad hand—strikes me somewhere on the torso. Insane wisdom, counter-intuitive, sends me forward into the blow. It saves my life. The power is expended too soon, there isn't the snap to make it a punch, it's more like a push. My feet leave the ground.

Pestle's expression of interest has gone, which can't be good. His face is below me, dwindling rapidly. My chest hurts. Shouldn't I be touching down? I think of Master Wu's fountain, long ago. Will I land in the pool this time? That might not be so bad. Perhaps people would come out and see what was happening. Pestle is following me, rather slowly. He knows something I do not. *Again.* Perhaps I am headed for the shallow end or the edge of the pool (nasty domestic accident waiting to happen there). I look down to check on it, and I see the bad thing. Beneath me there is only air and darkness. I have flown over the edge of the parapet. *A body continues in its state of rest or uniform motion in a straight line unless acted upon by a net external force.* I fall away from Humbert Pestle, which somehow surprises me: he is so big and dense, he ought to have his own gravity. I see his empty, bored face looking down and I know I have dropped out of the light and into the shadow. I have been erased. And now I am going to hit the ground very, very hard.

Something catches my foot and pulls me in towards the concrete stanchions of the terrace. Marvellous. I will not hit the ground after all, I will slam sideways into the wall. Perhaps I will lose only half of my brain, but with whatever I left behind in Gonzo's head that will be only a quarter, which seems unlikely to be enough.

Fire in my leg. Why do people always set me on fire from the ankle? Cheats. But I have not hit the wall. Fingers like wire-cord rope have clamped around my foot, and while my head swings perilously near the concrete, I do not touch. My knee hurts. My chest hurts. But I am not dead—again.

With a grunt of effort, Dr. Andromas reels me in. He is suspended in a cat's cradle of rope and pitons. He is presently, like me, upside down. Once he has stabilised the situation, he does something to a small box thingummy and we unwind slowly to the ground, whereupon Dr. Andromas grabs me by the lapel and says "You *idiot*!" with some heat, and rips off his aviator goggles and his moustache, and kisses me hard on the mouth. And it is only now, after all this time, that I realise that Dr. Andromas is a girl, and more specifically, that Hesperus is Phosphorus and Clark Kent is Superman, and Dr. Andromas is Elisabeth Soames, late of Cricklewood Cove.

She pulls back from the kiss, swears like a fishwife and half carries me down the hill to the *Magic of Andromas,* which is parked under a tree. I fall into the passenger side, and she speeds us on our way. She looks at me.

"Idiot," she says again, exasperated. But she says it almost as if I have done something right.

THE *MAGIC OF ANDROMAS* is neither fast nor inconspicuous, but it appears that no one is looking for us. Humbert Pestle has thrown me from the parapet and gone inside to drink and be merry, and no one at the party will miss me except maybe Buddy Keene. Elisabeth Soames weaves us through Haviland's night-time streets. She has, for the sake of form, put her (now that I think about it, abjectly unpersuasive) false moustache back on, and her hat, and I am hunkered down trying to look like a stage prop. This would be uncomfortable even if someone hadn't just tried to kill me with his Improbable Iron Fist of Death. At last she ducks us around a corner into an underground garage, and leads me by the hand through what appears to be a service door into a damp tunnel and up some stairs to the roof, where a string of pigeon coops have been transformed into some manner of dwelling place. From all of which I deduce that in the matter of Elisabeth Soames, as in so much else, there is some missing history to be discussed.

"Yes," Elisabeth says. "There is." And then she doesn't. She leans back against the wall of the pigeon coop (this is coop number three, which makes up her living room: a couple of futons and some throw cushions, a two-bar electric fire fed from a cable spliced into the mains feed under our feet and a few pictures hanging on the wall) and stares at me.

"I have gone mad," she says at last. "I have come to the end of my tether. You are not you. But you are." Well, yes. I know that feeling. She shakes her head a bit, and rolls half forward and draws me across the room to sit next to her, and clings to me like the last bit of driftwood after the wreck. I stroke her between the shoulder blades. I scratch her back. She squirms so that a particular bit of spine can be attended to, and then we stop moving because everything is in its perfect place, for however long that lasts. The memory of a clock makes a noise like *tock tick*.

"I've missed you," she says quite sensibly into my chest. I don't know quite how to take this, because while I know her, I don't really see how she can know me. Perhaps she has mistaken me for another person, some cousin of Gonzo's she happens to know, and my plunge from the jaws of death to the slender, delicious lips of rescue was a sort of benign error. It's a mistake anyone could have made. She shouldn't feel bad about it, but it might be as well to get the confusion sorted out before anything untowards happens, such as more kissing of me by her, or other actions which might complicate an already-Byzantine situation. I suggest this tentatively, and she stares at me.

"Yes," she says at last, "it really *is* you." And she begins her story.

Elisabeth Soames was born to Assumption and Evander John Soames in the Chinese Year of the Rat (I already knew this, but before I can object, some small part of me realises that much of what I have believed I knew turned out to be untrue, and that if I start complaining I may not get the story in full and indeed may not get hugged any more, and the hugging is very nice, in part because it seems to be as important to her as it is to me) and was an only child. She enjoyed skipping and making sandcastles, but rarely visited the sandpit in the children's enclosure of her local park as Evander Soames was very much against violence of any kind, and one of the other children played an involved war game in the sandpit, a strange, sprawling, constantly evolving fantasy instigated by his older brother. Evander Soames petitioned the local authorities to have this practice banned in the code of conduct for the playground, but was outvoted, and therefore directed his energies inward. A total ban on the playground was enforced on his daughter until he died. His lady wife found ways to give Elisabeth access to other sands (at the beach and at friends' houses) and social interaction (which would in any case have been somewhat tempered by her position as headmistress at the Soames School for the Children of Townsfolk, a burden for her daughter roughly equivalent to being the offspring of a plague carrier).

In consequence of her father's diktat against the sandpit, Elisabeth came to question his wisdom as it emerged from his mouth and concluded that, although Evander Soames was a very intelligent man, he was not always forthcoming with balanced argument, but rather preferred to deploy his intellect in pursuit of his own goals (she expressed this at the time as "Daddy makes things up which are true but not how he says they are," which is as accurate a summation of academic hair-splitting as you could wish for). When he expired in his own bed from a variant brain disease most usually associated with unconventional cuisine, Elisabeth mourned him as young children mourn: deeply, sporadically and without the awful sense of her own mortality which such death implies to adults. She also took herself straightaway to a nearby house inhabited by an elderly gentleman of Chinese extraction and demanded that he instruct her in the full range of violences and counter-violences which his extensive experience could offer. Wu Shenyang initially refused this request, but Elisabeth had considerably more experience with getting around old men than Wu Shenyang did of denying small girls, and she shortly ensconced herself in his living room and was immersed in the Way of the Voiceless Dragon. Her studies were facilitated by her mother's grief, which took the form of community service (however backhanded) and which found the sight of her only child a powerful reminder of the infuriating, beloved dead. Mutual loss and mutual affection kept them orbiting one another at a precise distance which only great upset could overcome, and if this seems like a small madness drawing fuel from pain, it kept them from far larger ones and allowed them to be together for short periods of comfort and reflection without becoming maudlin, vengeful, jealous or any of the other irrational things which sorrow can enforce quite unfairly on those who love one another very much.

One great upset was the young man who was her first love, a bewildering muddle of brashness and familiar grief who stole her heart without ever bothering to check his pockets, used her wisdom but not—to her enduring fury—her body and then ran away to war and fell in love with a nurse. (Here Elisabeth pauses to look at me sharply. Her face is set in the expression I used to associate with a dressing-down, but which, looking at it with twenty years' worth of human experience, I recognise as fear. I squeeze her lightly. This was apparently the right thing to do, at least as far as she is concerned, although it is, like everything else, painful. Humbert Pestle's fingerprints are on my bones. I squeak. Elisabeth stares for a second, and then wordlessly draws back, and demands that I remove my shirt. From coop number two she retrieves a small package filled with ointments and cotton wool, and she begins to dab at me.)

On hearing of the engagement, Elisabeth Soames, from a grim hotel room, sobbed vile words and gut-wrenching envies to her mother, and Assumption averred that things might yet turn out well, and in any case the boy was simply too mixed-up to be worth the full measure of regret. With this observation Elisabeth was reluctantly forced to agree: he never finished anything, never concentrated on anything, he wanted everything and the introspective aspect of him she admired contrasted unfavourably with a brassiness, even an arrogance, which she found deeply unattractive. (She pours something on my ribs which is very cold and smells dreadful. If there are any pigeons in here, they're getting treated to a very fine selection of noises of alarm and discomfort. Her hands smooth this stuff into my skin, and my aches start to go away. I feel warm and prickly. I try not to; it's producing moderately inappropriate physical reactions. I haven't been hugged or touched in this way for some time—or perhaps *ever*, depending on how you look at it—and I've just escaped death.

These things cause untold amounts of what can only be described as *horn.* Elisabeth either doesn't notice or doesn't mind. Her fingers slide around my side, where it hurts most. They are very gentle, so I don't faint.)

In any case, she has more important things on her mind. Shortly after she went away to study, Wu Shenyang—never a surrogate father, but a person whose suppleness of mind made a true friendship possible across decades of impossibly different experience—was killed by fire and treachery. He had as much as warned her such a thing was possible. Elisabeth, knowing better but steeped in the culture of feuding schools which is the cinematic heritage of *gong fu,* expected his senior students to leap from the woodwork and snatch her up to join the cause of rooting out his enemies. Nothing happened. Offended, she determined to do the job herself, or at the very least locate the missing seniors and ask them why they weren't pursuing due revenges. She realigned her studies towards this goal, and obtained qualifications as a journalist to allow her to travel and investigate. The moderate support available to her from Evander Soames's estate allowed her a certain leeway in filing stories. She roamed, and searched, and heard whispers: there was a man called *Smith.* He had asked about Wu Shenyang. He had enquired in many places. The tone of his enquiry had left most people eager to forget him. Smith was sinister. He frightened you, and he allowed you to know that this pleased him. He had a way of seeing where to apply pressure, how to bring you to heel. Smith could be friendly, but never nice. Smith was a hard man, and he had chosen his alias because he didn't care if people knew it wasn't his real name; he just wanted to be sure he left no trace. If anyone knew anything about the death of Wu Shenyang, it was this wicked, terrible Smith. Elisabeth set out to find him.

Smith was elusive for such a big man. She would find his tracks, follow him to a hotel or a bar, to a private house or a shop, and she would hurry there to find him gone. Smith could walk into a lobster pot and leave by the back door. He knew the back alleys of the worst part of every country on Earth. Elisabeth got to know them, too. She drank pale beers in a cellar in Phuket and sipped fermented mare's milk in a town in Mongolia. She paid small amounts to border guards—*for your son's schooling, mon Capitaine, because I hear he is a most excellent boy, no, please, I will wait in line . . . well, but if you insist . . . no, no, let there be no debts between us, we are family, your wife taught me to shop for melon*—and smiled with cherry lips at gullible men. She went to baby showers in Idaho and played darts with working men in working men's clubs, and she asked questions in quiet corners and pauses in conversation, and most often she had to claim she'd been misheard. Most often, no one had heard of the Voiceless Dragon, or believed in ninjas (which is a word which can be confused with: ginger, injured, fringes, hinges and many others which might crop up in a casual conversation) and so Elisabeth went on her way smiling, and was not seen again. But every now and again, in quite unlikely places, she would be drawn aside or shushed—*I don't talk about that; I know him; what would a girl like you . . . promise me you won't say I said.*

She was following Smith through the conflicted, dangerous maze of Addeh Katir when the Go Away War broke out and the world was changed for ever. She hid and fought and stayed alive, until her meandering brought her into contact with the Pipe at a town called Borristry. She worked as a cook, a cleaner, a fruit picker and a magician's assistant, and finally fell in with a group of travelling mime artists of dubious reputation and curious skills led by a chortling troublemaker named Ike Thermite. Under Ike's mangy wing and in the guise of Dr. Andromas—she had no desire to bring down destruction on the Matahuxee Mime Combine—she continued her quest.

Finally, in Conradinburg, in a yellowing pinewood absinthe den amid the ice, she heard a tale from a whimpering old man with no family and nothing left to lose. His name, when he remembered it, was Frey, and long ago he'd been a servant of the Clockwork Hand. Frey wore fingerless gloves, smoked with his left and ate with his right. He wore a fur coat against the cold, and it smelled even worse than he did because the furrier and the tanner between them had failed to get the stink of rot out of it before it was stitched. Elisabeth breathed through her mouth and drank vodka in small sips to ward off the reek, and Frey gave up a most secret history in exchange for another round and a tin of shag.

She came home, and finally ran across Smith again in a place called Harrisburg, only to find him looking to acquire the services of one G. William Lubitsch. Alarmed, she broke a lifetime rule and sent Gonzo a message: *Don't take the job,* but of course the warning made no difference at all. Since Smith had—she was now reasonably sure—engineered the demise of the Voiceless Dragon, and since Gonzo was—sometimes—a part of the school, she followed the Free Company to Station 9 to keep an eye on him. So she saw the ninja, and the moment of my creation, and later the moment of my assassination as well.

"That was bad," Elisabeth Soames says meditatively. Watching your first love attempt to murder part of himself and toss the wreckage from a moving truck. Yes. I suppose it was. Good old Comrade Cow.

She is looking at me with a kind of intensity. The moustache is gone again, thank God, vile little rat-fur thing that it is, and her face is very pretty. Dr. Andromas's costume, once you know it is occupied by a woman, is quite fetching, and a little bit daring. The shirt is a narrow, deep V. White skin and dark eyes. If I breathe through my nose, I can smell liniment. If I breathe through my mouth, I can taste her, somehow, still on my lips. I choose my mouth. We do not speak. It's one of those moments when things could go in any direction. I have missed a few of these in my life, always through ignorance or indecision. I don't know how this one will go. I don't know how I want it to go.

"There is an old tradition," says Elisabeth Soames at last, "regarding rescues of this kind." She leans towards me until her face is all I can see. The electric fire is very hot on my bare left side, so that her body makes a heat shadow, a cool place. On my chest—still tender, still prickly—I can feel the cotton of Dr. Andromas's shirt, and beneath that I can feel Elisabeth Soames. She is slight, feathery, and the resilience of her body commands attention. She continues.

"The rescue-er and the rescue-ee are recovering from their ordeal, you see, and the rescue-ee goes all weak at the knees and says something like 'But how can I *ever* repay you?' and the rescue-er jumps on the rescue-ee and doinks him lustfully and with great attention to detail. It is taken as non-binding owing to the stressful circumstances of the initial lunge, but certain liens and possibilities are established with a view to more thoughtful and long-lasting consummation at a future time, when the present danger is abated. I am wondering," she says, "whether you intend to honour this fine old—" But exactly what "fine old" it is she does not get to say, because I grab her and stop her mouth with mine, and her hands are busy and avid. She wraps herself around me, strong, long limbs, and if any pigeons remain within earshot after my earlier noises of agony, they take off and hide on the next rooftop until we are done.

This is quite some time.

And later, when we are covered in a medley of blankets and rugs and drinking hot chocolate heated over the two-bar fire, Elisabeth looks at my arm and says "Huh."

"Hm?"

"You've got a mark."

"Where?"

She shows me. There is indeed a strange shape on my shoulder, the bruise made by Humbert Pestle's shoe. And in the centre there is a pattern, almost a brand: the imprint left by the engraved crest which forms his heel. From this angle it looks like a new moon, or a bowl of soup with a spoon in it. I have seen it before. It is a pestle sticking up out of a mortar.

Glinting in the sad light of Drowned Cross as we raced across the main square: not a cuff link or an earring or a key fob. Humbert Pestle's missing cleat.

He was there. And more than that. Monsters do not make day trips.

"Who is he?" I ask. "Humbert Pestle?"

"I don't know, exactly," she says. "I know who he's *been.*"

"Who?"

"Smith," Elisabeth says.

Smith. Smith is Pestle and Smith is the enemy of Master Wu. Pestle is Smith and Pestle can walk through me as if I am nothing. Sifu Smith then. Sifu Humbert. Master of the ninjas, also sometimes called the Clockwork Hand Society. Plotter. *Enemy planner.* The man who sends ninjas out to do his bidding, to kill Gonzo's parents, to attack him during world-shaking blazes. Saboteur. Murderer. *Cui bono* no longer. Now, the question is *why?*

"Tell me about him."

She does.

IMAGINE A HOUSE with a white front and high, arched windows. It has three floors and is covered in wisteria and grapes, like a house in a French storybook. It is an old house, a house built when such houses were merely respectable, rather than staggering, and the family who own it now owned it then. They are still only respectable, so they own no other houses, no jets and no yachts (unless you count the inflatable dinghy resting on its side in the garden shed). The house itself is in need of some minor repairs—the west wall could do with some fresh whitewash and the guttering leaks in wet weather, showering the kitchen garden with great gouts of water, flattening the tomatoes. It hardly matters. The sound does not penetrate the thick walls, and the tomatoes are immune to such indignities.

Once upon a time, a boy lived here, in this splendid house, a boy with a most unfortunate name. He kept his things in a great oaken trunk he had from his mother, bound up with iron bands. When he went to school—which was seldom—he emptied the trunk of some of his treasures and left them in safe places around the house, in nooks and corners and on shelves, and a very few under the floorboard in the back of his cupboard. When he came home again, he went around each room and gathered up his things, and put them all back in the trunk so that he would know he had them.

On the occasion of his ninth birthday, the trunk contained: a paper crown; a calico cat; an Aston Martin car like the one James Bond had, with a red button on the bottom which made a metal plate shoot up at the back to deflect bullets (he had never seen the film and couldn't understand how James Bond got out of the car and pushed the button when he was driving, but grown-ups were forever making their own lives difficult and so he didn't worry very much about that); an old book in a language he could not read; a fossilised frog; a plastic soldier some ten inches high, complete with full pack and cyborg eye (through which, if you opened the panel in his skull, you could descry things a very long way off—they were supposed to look closer, though they tended to look smudged owing to a quantity of jam on the lens); drawings of dragons and animals seen at the zoo; a compass in metal and glass given him just that morning by his father; and a vast collection of invisible goods which he alone could describe or enumerate, but whose values exceeded the tangible items by an order of magnitude.

The house itself was no less wondrous. Through the wide wooden door, each room was a separate mystery wherein a young man might discover strange countries. The living room had a vaulted ceiling where—in the dusk—gargoyles could be seen flying from roost to roost. The den, used by both his father and his mother in the winter months for long, whiskied evenings in front of the black-tiled fireplace, was populated with gnomish metalworkers making legendary swords and lethal pikes. If he was good and quiet, and nimble when required, they had no objection to the tiny human child watching and learning as long as he swore (with hand on heart and one foot on an iron peg) never to reveal their ways. In the kitchen, between bags of taters and onions on a string, the stove whispered to his older self surprisingly accurate advice on romance, winning him willing compliance from a certain girl and surprising sensations hitherto unknown. This was a house of marvels.

In the third of the long, hot summers which the world endured around that time, the boy with the unfortunate name (his father was old Caspian Pestle, of Tennessee, and his mother a stick-like woman from the East, so far in that direction as to be near enough west, instead) came to man's estate, and went out of his home town to make his way. He toiled as a soldier in a far-off jungle (this being the custom of his nation and his father's people, and a noted part of the process of making a child into an adult fit to vote; sadly, it also stripped Humbert Pestle of a number of society's preconceived notions of morality, as war is apt to do) and then as a student in a place of learning (this being a new necessity in the world just then). On returning, he found that his father had evicted his mother from the house on the grounds of his desire to install a newer replacement, and they fought. He informed his father that this was the action of a weasel, a phoney and a cheat. Caspian Pestle received this information without argument, even going as far as to add to the list the descriptions debaucher, Lothario and libertine. This recognition—coupled with an aggressive lack of repentance—drove Humbert into a fury. He discovered a moment later that he had struck Caspian Pestle backhanded. He did not recall doing so, but he found himself not unhappy with the decision. Leaning on the sofa which the child Humbert had envisaged as a pirate vessel, Caspian invited his son to depart. He did.

Humbert Pestle travelled, and joined a reputable firm, and worked to forget his irksome paternity. He found that while the old man faded rapidly from his mind, the house remained very much alive within him, and dreaming of it caused him considerable pain. He aged somewhat, and was promoted, fell in lust and out of it, fought in dojos and occasionally in bars and alleyways to assuage his anger, and grew bored and disenchanted with everything he had. And then, on a Monday in October—while I was struggling with university admissions—he chanced to encounter his mother's brother, Mr. Eliard Rusth.

Mr. Rusth (to rhyme with must) was a small, densely constructed person with a bald head. He wore a long jacket and a short collar, and his eyes regarded the world through circular glasses. These gave him the look which snowmen acquire the day after their construction, of being partly dissolved and cavernous. He asked Humbert whether he wished to be a man of small consequence or whether he would care instead to play upon the grand stage, and Humbert Pestle replied that if he had a choice, his preference would be for the latter. Eliard Rusth said that he wasn't here to talk about preferences. If preferences were all Humbert could offer, Eliard Rusth was in the wrong place and would now remove himself.

Humbert Pestle rephrased his reply in stronger terms.

Greatness, Eliard Rusth said, was not achieved by acting on one's own account. Fortunes could be made that way; professions could be conquered. But greatness required that one set aside one's own desires and become the instrument of destiny. And this, he explained, was the purpose of the Society of the Clockwork Hand. To be the instrument of destiny. The Clockwork Hand was a mechanism: once set in motion, it could not be stopped, not by time or force of arms or diplomacy. Members obeyed their instructions without question, whatever they might be, and the Master of the Hand, freed from all mundane considerations, listened in silence for the music of the great wheels of destiny.

A year later Humbert Pestle went by train and car to his father's home, the house of marvels where he grew up, and burned it to the ground. As it transpired, the house was occupied, which Humbert Pestle, watching from the great lawn, came to realise only when he spied a figure limned in fire at one of the upper windows. (Opening a window in a burning building is inadvisable. This was immediately demonstrated quite practically, and the figure—male, elderly but still strong—was consumed entirely in a wreath of fire and fell from view.) Humbert Pestle, watching these events, had expected to find in himself a great tearing and commotion. Instead, he found that all his commotions were stilled. This was a thing so huge that it implied a hidden meaning. It was too vast to be anything but part of a huge and remarkable pattern. And as Humbert Pestle stared at the flames, he believed he could see the edges of that pattern. He could hear it moving. The sound was a measured beat, an endless whirring. It was not yet a piece of music, but he knew it would be in time.

In consequence of this enlightenment, Eliard Rusth shared with Humbert Pestle the Iron Skin Meditation and the more conventional *gong fu* of the Clockwork Hand (whose name itself derived from the perfect progress of the universe as if steered by a mechanical armature) so that his student's experience as a commando was overlaid with a subtlety of technique and a terrifying endurance which allowed him, over the course of time, to advance within the Clockwork Hand to the position of *Sigung,* the most exalted of equals.

The ascent of Humbert Pestle to the leadership of the Clockwork Hand would not have been a catastrophe—save for a particular hereditary enemy of the Hand now eking out a living as a small-time instructor of the risible Voiceless Dragon style (whose tenets included a starkly *discordant* insistence on the value of a single human life) in a town almost too small for the name—had not the world suddenly collapsed upon itself in a great spasm and the lazy ascent towards *unity* come fundamentally unstuck.

The Go Away War and the Reification were a great chaos which brought an end to everything we knew. By accident or subconscious design, we destroyed the pattern of our lives, reduced our species to tiny pockets of survival and engendered a world whose very fabric responded to our thoughts. Humbert

Pestle, silver at the temples and tough like a yew tree, survived the cataclysm but was appalled by the havoc that it wrought. Seeing in his mind the cogs of the great progress scattered willy-nilly all about, Pestle longed to put them back in the clockwork and make it run again. Nor was he alone. We all of us looked at the turmoil around and were afraid, and instead of going out to meet it and sniff it like good mammals, good *primates,* we got cold feet and fell back upon our cold blood; like lizards on a cloudy day, we wished ourselves back in the comfort of our holes; we wanted our finite horizons of predictable problems and predictable joys.

Humbert Pestle wandered through the chaos in despair. Discord was everywhere. The sense of destiny he had acquired in the Clockwork Hand was broken. And then one day he witnessed something which filled him with hope, something great and terrible, and Humbert Pestle looked at it and heard the first notes of the music he had been searching for. With that music sounding in his mind, he set about the creation of something great, around the remainder of the old financial system and the Society of the Clockwork Hand. He called it Jorgmund, and it would circle the world in its grip. The blood of Jorgmund was a thing called FOX, which could usher out the new and restore the old.

ELISABETH SOAMES coughs. She has been speaking for a long time. I pass her some water from the plastic bucket in the corner. She has wrapped the bucket in blankets because it is a dreadful colour, a sort of chartreuse. The result looks a lot like something you would find in a Bedouin hut if the Bedu shopped at Ikea. She sips at the water and presses closer to me.

"What did he see?" I ask.

"I don't know."

It is the heart of all of this. It is the engine in Humbert's machine, his *enemy plan.* Jorgmund. FOX. Gonzo. All of a piece.

Find the connections. Find out why. What does Jorgmund want with Gonzo? Old questions: *What is this thing called Jorgmund? What does it want? What is my place in the pattern?*

"I need to see the Core," I tell Elisabeth Soames. She does not say "Are you up to it?" or "If they catch you . . ." (which would be another rhetorical ellipsis, of course, and thus far, far beneath her). She seems to review everything which has happened, and herself and me, and weigh it all, and in that light she opens her eyes again, and she nods once, sharply.

"Okay."

Chapter Fifteen

Empires and rooftops;
pussy willow;
the face of my enemy.

UNTIL RECENTLY, the great Empire of Sartoria—the continent of style whence come all manner of dinner suits, morning coats, Edwards, Ascots, Lichfields, smokings and casuals—was marked on my personal map as a small island just to windward of the Useless Archipelago. It was populated with skilled but pointless individuals disconnected from the ebb and flow of living. An hour spent with Royce Allen has disabused me of that notion. Tailors are vital. Royce Allen is a receiving and transmitting station for news and storm warnings of various kinds, and a voice of stark truth to those whose importance is such that they generally hear none. Men of his profession have been quietly saving the world for years.

"No, sir, the chartreuse is a disaster. It makes you look like the Wampyr. As in the Undead. Yes. A cartoonist's dream, sir. No, not pale and aristocratic, I fear, though one can see how you might imagine that, but more on the deliquescent side of things. On the whole, sir, the pink. If you absolutely must, sir, then the russet, but it has to my mind a hint of the dung heap about it. Yes. Oh, and regarding the economy, sir? Parlous. Yes, I am aware of your new proposals, sir. They are, if you will forgive me, worse than that burlap sack your missus was wearing on the telly last night. Yes. Mass unemployment in days, I should imagine. Well, might I propose that you just leave bloody well alone, sir—let the housing market settle and the banks get over their alarm, and pop in in a week for another fitting? Very good. Now, as to footwear—might I venture that you've been taking advice on this topic from the defence secretary, sir? Only these would appear to be Cuban heels."

The items I am currently wearing come from a different stable. The same expertise has been applied to their making, the same exacting standards, but the intent behind their construction is less benign. The trousers are double lined: the inner layer is a sheer silk which instantly clings to the leg; the outer one is coarser, and slides over the silk without catching or making a noise. The final layer of fabric is not strictly black, but mottled midnight-on-anthracite—night-time camouflage. The jacket is the same. It tugs a little over the shoulders because I am an inch or so larger about the torso than the previous occupant. This is a suit intended to facilitate mayhem and violence in silence.

I'm wearing a ninja outfit. When I put it on there was a single, enormous bee corpse in the crotch. I didn't scream because I am a man of action and a serious person engaged in serious business. Also because Elisabeth Soames was watching. I did, however, pick it up by one huge wing and drop it with a sardonic smile into the wastepaper basket in pigeon coop number one. And my whole nether region went cold as ice. This was probably a good thing. Until then I had been watching Elisabeth Soames wriggle into her own ninja gear (at some point one of them has run afoul of her and been denuded; I don't know whether this was post-mortem and I don't necessarily want to) and thinking that maybe this could wait until I'd taken her back to bed. It's time to concentrate. I long to contemplate her in a vastly more tactile and rewarding fashion, and this would be a bad idea. Bad, bad, bad. I growl out loud. She turns round.

I drag my eyes upward, and find her face. She is looking patient. It does not look like the kind of patience which comes naturally, but the kind you adopt by choice. I mumble something. She kisses me chastely on each cheek, looks into my eyes.

"Ready?"

"Yes."

And we go out into the early dark.

Elisabeth's rooftop is only a few storeys high, and there's an iron fire escape hanging down from the building above. She has at some point tied a rope to the bottom; she drags it down, and we climb. It's a long way—this place has fifteen or more floors. We climb past windows and kitchens and feuding families; we eavesdrop on lovers and catch fragments of television shows. We climb. I begin to realise how she maintains that greyhound physique. When we get to the top, she leads me over an obstacle course, made all the more exciting by the fact that it is ever ascending, until we are at least twenty storeys up. And then her movements change, she grows cautious and I know that we are close.

This new roof is slippery, canted slightly towards a distant drop. The ninja shoes had little crampons for this kind of thing, but my donor had small feet. Girly feet. I hope he was a man. I don't want to be wearing a dead girl's clothes. At the far end of the rooftop there is another wall, and this one is vast. It goes up and up, maybe seventy floors above us. Fortunately, there is a lift, like a window cleaner's hoist. We take it all the way. The little electric motors whine and complain, and the wind blows us all over the place. In movies people have fights on these things. You just wouldn't. You'd sit there politely, talk about your favourite place to eat in the city below, maybe exchange names. You'd wait until you got to the top or the bottom and get off, then either fight in the knowledge that you had the ground under you and you'd die of violence rather than gravity, or reckon to resolve your differences over a coffee and a sandwich in the fortieth-floor bar. That model City of Lights down there is only a few seconds away by the direct route. These planks are strong enough to stand on, to sit on. But they flex when you walk. There are cracks. The planks are screwed into the frame, but one of the screws has worked loose and another is broken. Window cleaners have nerves of steel.

The roof of the Jorgmund Company, their neon logo shuddering in the wind above us. It's freezing up here. Elisabeth puts on Dr. Andromas's goggles to protect her eyes. I don't have any goggles so I put up the ninja's hood and squint. It doesn't help very much. The wind is a kind of localised hurricane, a circling snarl created by all the buildings. In daytime it would be scary. In the dark it is disorientating, misleading. You could press against it to get away from the edge, and walk clear off the other lip thinking you were still right up against the first one. Elisabeth knows the way; if you traced it on a graph, it would be a curve or part of a spiral. Up here, right now, it's a straight line across the roof to the other side. We pass under the signage and I can hear it creak. The torsion on the bolts must be tremendous. I wonder how often they have to come up here and change them, or check them for shearing. And then she clips a couple of bits of nylon around my chest and hooks us together, and we jump off.

I am acquiring a profound dislike of falling. Even in the arms of Elisabeth Soames, with her sweat still on my skin; even with the shriek of the little winch paying out a line; even knowing that we will never hit the ground, that everything is taken care of, I hate the lurch in my stomach and the wicked clawing of the air. Air should be a soft thing, a coddling thing, a breeze which wakes you in the morning, ruffles your hair and wafts the scent of summer in your face. It should bring tea. It should not rip like an angry dog at your clothes and graze your face with abrasive claws. We fall. Just enough time for a chat with my invisible life coach.

So, Bumhole, how are we in our little self?

Bit busy, Ronnie.

So one observes. Pneumatic bit of crumpet too.

Please never, ever say that again.

Are we in any danger of finding out the Why behind all this, Bumhole? Because those of us in the gallery are developing a profound desire to break some heads.

I tried that. He's too strong.

Might be too strong for you, Bumhole. Might or might not be too strong for me. However, that's not the point, is it? You aren't supposed to be stronger. You're supposed to be cleverer. Old Wu's *gong fu* is beloved of smartarses the world over. Use your noggin.

How?

My thinking? Shoot the fucker in his Iron Brain. Absolutely guaranteed to mess up his day. But then, I'm a practical sort.

Would that count?

Well, Bumhole, he'd be dead, wouldn't he? And you'd be alive. Which is definitely a species of victory, especially if you are directly responsible for the variance.

I think . . . I think that's not what Master Wu would do.

Ah. Now, there, Bumhole, you have me. Predicting the old fart was a game we used to play endlessly and without success. If you can do that, you'll have passed me by. Now, may I suggest, relax your legs, stiffen your core muscles and place your tray-tables in the upright position for landing. And move your head so you don't hit that limber bit of totty in her elegantly formed nose. You have arrived at your destination.

Bye, Ronnie.

The winch slows us, and we touch down almost without a sound. Elisabeth Soames is pleased: she has estimated the distance and the weight to a fine margin. Geek fu is strong in this one. She looks at me curiously.

"Were you talking to yourself back there?"

"Taking advice from an old friend."

She smiles.

"I do that. I talk to Master Wu and my mother and . . ." She hesitates. "Well, you, actually, now that I think about it. Or mostly you. Hm." She frowns, then brushes this little oddness away like a cobweb. "Come on." She slips away, soft-footed and sure. She has done this before.

Elisabeth leads the way to a curious dome or pagoda, and next to it a very ordinary door set into an equally ordinary concrete box. A rooftop door. It is padlocked. Elisabeth Soames taps the hinge sharply, and the pin falls out into her hand. She lifts the door against the catch. It opens just enough for us to slip through. She slips it back and pockets the hinge pin. I wipe away the water in my eyes and look around.

We are on a gantry, a floating walkway. There is a network of them, metal grilles suspended above insulation, fibrous tiles, cables and hoses. There's even an emergency mini-Pipe system. This is the gut of the building, the gasworksish bit which doesn't mesh with the idea that everything just happens, smoothly, at will and on demand. All this is hidden so as to convey perfection without achieving it. The gantries are here to allow access when imperfection becomes too obvious to ignore. Elisabeth sets off at a swift, smooth pace. We follow the gantry for thirty metres, then it curves away left and we go right and over to a bright spot, where light filters up from the room below. More gantries converge here. If you mapped them, this place would be a node, a multiple crossroads where weary plumbers meet tilers and gaffers, drink stale tea from vacuum flasks and exchange sandwich quarters and oily-rag gossip. I look around. Yes. At the juncture of our gantry and the next there is a smooth spot, worn shiny by years of arses settling, wrapping legs around the stanchions—and there, underneath the railing, someone has scratched an obscene graffito, a ludicrously long male sexual organ chasing a pair of rudimentary breasts. It looks to have been done with a screwdriver, too big for the task. There are scratches where the artist lost traction and the tool skidded away, taking a narrow slice of plastic paint and ruining the integrity of the image. Below us there is a single piece of grillework. A vent.

Elisabeth lies on her stomach and slips her fingers slowly through the holes in the vent. She breathes in, heaves and makes a noise like "uhh-hhhhp," very soft. The vent comes away in her hands. So now, technically, it's an *aperture:* a hatchway. Elisabeth mouths: *Down here.* She doesn't tell me to be careful. She knows me.

She braces against the gantry, and lowers me through the hatch.

I AM standing in a lounge sort of thing, with sofas. The lights are on. My remaining Royce Allen jacket drops beside me. I look up. Elisabeth smiles slightly, encouraging, as if I'm taking baby steps. She points to herself (Do I imagine that she is very specific about pointing to the left side of her chest, where the heart is? Or is that just because she's twisted around to hang out over the hole and see me?) and mouths: *I'll be watching.*

She hoists herself up and out of the way, so I can't see her face any more, just her shoes. She wiggles a leg at me: *Get going,* or perhaps *Move it, you sexy beast!* which would be very gratifying. In either case, I obey. I remove the ninja hood. It's all very well being invisible, but it also takes away your hearing and makes you just a little bit less sensitive to noises and feelings. I put on the jacket. Now I'm not a scary ninja guy. I'm just a bloke in the office on an all-nighter. I hope.

I bend, touch my front teeth to the door handle. (Vibration in a corridor means footsteps; faint vibration is most easily felt with your teeth against metal; closest metal to reach with your mouth is a door handle; ludicrous but effective. Don't believe me? Try it.)

My incisors have nothing to report. I listen, just in case. Silence. I open the door and step through into the corridor. Above me I hear a soft sound of cloth on metal. Elisabeth is following.

It's dark, but not completely. Exit lights glimmer every five doors. I'm about midway along a windowless corridor. The way to my right is slightly lighter. Someone home, perhaps. I head in that direction, softly softly. I walk the way Gonzo used to on patrol, not on tiptoe, but putting the front outer side of the foot down, rolling back onto the heel. It's almost as fast as ordinary walking, but quiet. My ribs complain. Of course they do. Ribs are whiners. I tell them so. There's a noise now, a cranky, creaky noise, small rubber wheels. Mr. Crabtree, right on time, regular as . . . (don't say "clockwork," not here, not now: to name the Devil is to call him . . . *Humbert Pestle.* Shhh! *Humbert! Pestle!* . . . I go back to my simile) regular as a German train. If Crabtree sees me, he may sound the alarm. On the other hand, Robert Crabtree is a very specific sort of person. His job is not security, it is paper. He may reason that if I am here, I must be meant to be here. He may show me wonders. Risk and reward.

Follow the paper. Not Ronnie's voice. Not anyone's but mine.

All right. I stand and wait. Mr. Crabtree slouches into view. He stops. He looks at me.

"Unh," says Mr. Crabtree.

He looks down.

"You're in the way," he says irritably. I should know better. I am halfway to being a paper man myself. I have walked the paper path with him already today. I hasten to make space for the cart. He rolls past. I follow.

Mr. Crabtree shuffles along the corridor and through into a conference room. Bottles of water sit on the table, notepads and glasses at each place. Pencils have been sharpened, ready.

"Core Committee," Crabtree says. The lack of unnecessary furniture meets with his approval, or at least it means that there are no objects to get in his way and arouse his ire. He shuffles forward.

The chair at the head of the table is bigger than all the others, and there are two trays in front of it. The green APPROVED tray is empty. The yellow tray is full. They must be meeting tomorrow.

Robert Crabtree tuts. He walks to the head of the table and puts the new tray down, shifting the other one inward. Then he bends slowly, reproachfully, to the lower shelf on the paper cart, and fetches up a bundle of green envelopes. He takes the older set of yellow envelopes and opens them, transfers their contents to the green envelopes from his cart. Then he puts the green envelopes in the APPROVED tray and puts them back on the cart. The proposals and recommendations from the Senior Board (in the yellow envelopes) have become actions and policies, as if by magic.

"What are you looking at?" says Mr. Crabtree. I become aware that I am staring.

"Is that . . . ," I begin. Robert Crabtree stiffens. He knows what is in my mind. This is a short circuit; it must be a mistake. But it is Robert Crabtree's job—his vocation. It is everything he is. His life.

"Standing order," he says. He scowls. I have suggested he doesn't know his job. Worse, I have implied he might interfere with the paper in an inappropriate way. He might *tamper*. I have genuinely, deeply offended him. I took his manner to be low-level irritation, and perhaps it is. It might just be chronic pain from his withered hands. Now, though, he moves sharply, jaggedly, and his jaw is set. He has a slight underbite which makes him look like a boxer. Beneath his folded eyelids his pupils are very small. I have called his identity into question, slandered his good name.

Robert Crabtree slams the last recommendation into an EXECUTE envelope and tosses it onto the cart. Our friendship is over. He barges past me. I follow him back to the sorting room, and he turns on the threshold and glowers at me. I open my mouth to apologise, although there's really nothing I can say: it is as if I had casually accused a priest of spitting in the communion wine. He shuts the door in my face.

Well. I am in the belly of the beast. Not the moment to regret.

I move on, into the next corridor. I am thinking about Humbert Pestle, about how a man like that could run a company which was effectively running itself. He could do anything he wanted. Use it for anything he wanted. So what does he want? Destiny, of course, but that covers a lot of ground. *Greatness.* Likewise.

A murmur—conversation? Prayer? Humans. I slow, move closer. There is a door ahead, light visible around the edges. I press my face to the hinge. The door is a good fit, but not perfect. I look through into the room beyond.

Ninjas, like lethal kindergartners, kneeling on the floor.

They sit in rows, maybe a hundred of them. They are quiet. At the front a whipcord-thin man is murmuring a formula, and the congregation is repeating it. Ninja om, maybe, or their version of the paternoster—*Our Father, who kills in silence.* On the wall there are pictures. Photos and paintings. Ninja heroes. The newest one is familiar, a huge-shouldered man brandishing a club-like fist. His stomach is covered in fat, but beneath the rolls vast abdominal muscles flex. Humbert Pestle.

The guy at the front shouts, and two ninjas from the front row leap up and attack him. He punches one, very fast, and intercepts the other's attack and breaks his arm. It makes a noise like gristle. The injured men bow and sit down again. I feel ill. I consider setting the building on fire—a bright, scouring blaze to clean this place to the stones and put its occupants out of my misery, and then I remember Master Wu and I feel guilty for considering it. It's not me. Not that I can't think those thoughts (demonstrably) but the other way around: choosing not to accept that kind of idea as an actual option is what defines *me* as distinct from *them.*

Pestle is Smith is Sifu Humbert. Ninjas are crazy. I knew these things already. I leave the ninjas alone—perhaps they will hospitalise one another. I debate internally whether hoping that each of them suffers a catastrophic groin strain or bruised testicle during the course of normal business is a *them* sort of thought, and decide that it's not. I spend a moment dreaming of ninja hernias.

The corridor splits, at right angles. (Is Elisabeth still above me? Or above and to the side? The gantries are unpredictable. Perhaps she is a room away, or squinting down from the junction, willing me to move one way or the other.) To the left, I would be heading back along the wall of the ninja temple; to the right, to the main body of the building and the Jorgmund offices. No doubt there are secrets there too, but they are not my secrets. They are secrets like the Colonel's Secret Blend of herbs and spices and the one true recipe for Coca-Cola (now that there's no actual cocaine in it); how to make a lightbulb which lasts for a hundred years or a white cloth which never stains or frays. Secrets, but not dark ones.

I go left. The left-hand path is also the *sinister* path. The cannibal's road. In my heels I can feel the occasional *boompf* from the temple beside and, a few steps later, behind me. In my toes I can feel nothing. This end of the building is quiet.

Quiet, but not calm, and not restful. There's nothing different about the way it looks, but it *feels* different. Sixty steps back that way, this building is the kind of place a guy like Buddy Keene has his office in ten years' time—vapid, flashy, with a desk made for after-hours sex, and a lamp which gives a decent source of illumination as he leans over the intern to look down her dress. Up here it's cold. There's no lust in these walls. Maybe it's the orientation of the building. During the day one side of a skyscraper soaks up more heat energy than the other. If you're in the northern hemisphere that's the south side, which is why an apartment with a south prospect is more expensive. This is the night side, then, grey and cold. Except that I know that isn't it. This corridor is . . . *watchful.* I tell myself that yes, of course, Elisabeth is watching. But this is not her attention I feel. It is not kindly.

The hairs on the back of my neck are prickling. I keep checking my dead zone, the space directly behind you where an attacker is in a prime position to strike and there's almost nothing you can do about it. I wave my hand through it, step slightly off-axis. Shadows twist at the far end of the corridor, little beads of darkness crawl over one another. Stare into the dark for long enough, and you see shapes. Good old human eye—if we were squid, it probably wouldn't happen. (Squid have better eyes than we do; there's no blind spot. I wonder briefly whether this means they have no need for image retention and therefore would be immune to television. Thousands of squid families, sitting at home at night watching a single bright spark zing across a black screen, wondering what all the fuss is about.)

The ceiling creaks above me. Elisabeth? Or someone else. Although, if Elisabeth has been caught, it was done in absolute silence. Ninja style. Really *good* ninja style. Do they have someone like that? Someone who is to stealth what Humbert Pestle is to combat? A ghost. Maybe the ghost is standing behind me. Maybe that's why I feel so naked. *He's behind me right now.*

I turn fast, scythe my fingers through the air, flow sideways, kick, step away to the wall. Nothing happens except that I feel like an idiot. The shadows at the end of the corridor continue to boil.

All right then. That's where I'm going.

It's probably my nose doing this to me. Your nose can do all kinds of clever things; the trouble is, we're so unused to accepting olfactory assistance that we tend to misinterpret it. Assumption Soames told me that she could smell something *wrong* on Dr. Evander John when he came home from Cricklewood Fen; she assumed it was a stinky swamp plant or something the dog had rolled in. It faded away after a few days. When the good doctor got kuru and died, she realised she'd been smelling his recent diet in his sweat. So I pay close attention: what am I smelling?

Faint perfume. Faint cologne. Cigars, a while ago. Human smells—skin, sweat. All old. Beneath them industrial cleaner.

Polish. Bleach. Blood, very faint—the ninjas' first aid station, maybe, back by the temple. Rubber, iron, fresh paint. Something else, old and familiar, out of place.

Ahead of me is a doorway. More than a doorway. A double door, framed in lustre and marble.

It looks like a boardroom door. On the other hand, the Core Committee Room is back that way. This is something else. I go in.

No, I don't. I start to take a step but I can't. In my head alarms are screaming, dive klaxons are whooping. My right foot peels itself halfway off the floor and stops, then slowly falls back. My body locks in place, retreats with painful caution. My head looks at the carpet. It is predictably unpleasant and hard-wearing. Office carpet. And yet it looks very clean. Everywhere else there are trolley tracks: a hundred days of Robert Crabtree, to and fro. Not here. My body stares. Then (without asking me for permission) it gets down low to the ground and stares fixedly ahead at . . . not quite nothing. *Something.* I smell dried flowers and carpet and that out-of-place note which I can't place. Yes, *place.* Exactly. It's too cool and too urban here. That smell belongs in forests and mountains. My body allows me back into the driving seat, but not without misgivings. *Pay attention.*

In front of me there is a fine, silver thread, like a cobweb. I don't touch it. I sniff. Yes. That scent, like almond and play-dough and solvent. I used to smell it from time to time in Addeh Katir, when the combat engineers were coming in. And before that, in the armoury at Project Albumen. With just my eyes, I follow the thread to the wall. It's stuck to the plaster with a minute drop of clear glue. So. I follow it the other way. It vanishes into a vase of pussy willow. Very authentic, except that spiders don't carry adhesive around in a little tube, they make their own. I peer a little closer. Yes. There is a shape in the pussy willow, like one of those mean, two-pronged signs in upmarket parks which say PLEASE KEEP OFF THE GRASS. This one does not say PLEASE KEEP OFF THE GRASS. It says instead FRONT TOWARDS ENEMY. The letters are embossed or moulded onto the grey-green metal casing, along with (I know this, though I cannot see it) a similar piece of wisdom on the back which reads: REAR—OTHER SIDE FRONT. If the gossamer line is broken, a switch trips inside the device, and it explodes. The casing turns into shrapnel, and anyone inside its radius turns into something which looks like jambalaya, except that the head parts sometimes look like shrimp. Every time I see one of these things, I think of how it must be to have one of them go off nearby, to have those idiotic words fly towards you and then through you; to be killed by Times New Roman font.

Somewhere there is a keyhole into which you can put a key and disarm the thing. I do not have a key. On the other hand: a landmine in an office block. I'm in the right place.

I look at the line. It is very slender. It is alone. I peer at the carpet. No pressure pad. So. Deep breath. In, out. I step over the thread. I don't die. I go through the door.

The room beyond is not a boardroom. Or not only a boardroom. Boardrooms are rooms to show how important you are. This is an *operations* room. It is a place where you do important things. This room is lined with maps, papered with graphs. Item the first, old business: a family tree of the Jorgmund Company. At the top, the Core, in its own bubble. Depending from the bubble, the Senior Board and its sub-committees; the Executive Branch with its various teams and specialists, and on the far left, the Clockwork Hand Society, co-equal, separate except for a small area of overlap marked H.P. Below the Clockwork Hand there's nothing. It is self-contained. All around the family tree are displays showing that all of these various committees are vital to the continued good health of the firm (and hence the world) and run by terribly competent people who are essentially irreplaceable. (Apparently the ninjas don't really feel the need to submit reports. It's reasonable. If you can kill a man with a paper clip and inflict horrible pain using only your finger, the corporate hierarchy is pretty much prepared to assume no one else could do your job.)

The charts are fresh and laminated. They have been amended with markers, adjusted to show even more spectacular profits and accomplishments. Pins have been shoved heedlessly through into the soft wood behind. Ribbons stretch across charts—predicted and actual profit, objectives, needs, acquisitions, outlays.

And enemies.

On a glass gallery-stand in the middle of the room, enemies. Master Wu, in a grainy picture. He is holding tea in one hand, and he looks old and sad. His other hand is out of frame, but I suspect it holds apple cake. Someone has scraped an X in red felt-tip across his face. They have started at the top right, above his ear, and stabbed down hard to his chin, pressing over his eyes and nose. The pen was held left-handed. The second stroke starts top left, and drives bottom right. It is angry, vindictive. The place where they cross is almost black. The end of the second stroke has a little tail, as if the author was shaking. Or as if his hand was clumsy. Or both.

On the board with Master Wu are other pictures. One small one looks like a blurred image of Dr. Andromas; next to it there is a clearer, but much older, picture of Elisabeth. On the other side, Zaher Bey. Someone dislikes the Bey intensely, because there are quite a lot of photos of him. There is a new picture of me, taken by some sort of security camera at Station 9. I look surprised and a bit fatter than I would like. And finally there is Gonzo, looking moody. I don't recognise the picture. Perhaps they took it while he was here. He is an enemy, but at the same time not. There is red ink down one edge of his picture, but it's a wiggly line, ever so slightly smug. A Latin teacher's correction: not *agricola,* but *agricolam.* From the picture emerges a red, greasy slash, a problem-solving arrow. A Go Away arrow. It points from Gonzo's upper right canine to the Bey's left eye. It is, in the grand old phrase, a line of death. Fear this line and what it may mean.

Beyond the stand there is a table, and on the table there is a file. It has all manner of stamps on it meaning that no one should read it, ever, and if they do they should do so only after putting out their eyes. I look around at the room. I sit down and start to read.

HUMBERT PESTLE, friend to all mankind; I suspect he was avuncular or even *headmasterly.* Gonzo the hellraiser has always had a sneaking respect for headmasters, as long as they were someone else's. And remember, this was a new Gonzo, naked in the world, his cynicism and his second thoughts embodied in me, asleep in K's Airstream and presumed dead, all those miles away. His psyche must have looked like a diver after a moderately bad shark attack. He had survived, but you could see the bones. His brain was limping and his ego hurt like hell. More, he was filled with a secret terror, a 3 a.m. anguish, confided to Leah at the last minute and from her to me as an earnest of trust and a demand for help: he feared he had somehow lost part of his capacity to love his wife. The hero could feel passion but not domestic bliss. He was terrified that he might lose her too, that she would hate him, that she must already be disgusted. He needed to act, to regain his self-respect and wash away this taint.

Gonzo was suggestible. This was anticipated. The plan anticipated everything—except me.

It's all in the file.

The room in which Humbert Pestle seduced Gonzo to the Dark Side was dressed for the occasion.

Humbert Pestle: Mr. Lubitsch.

Gonzo: Mr. Pestle.

(*Handshake, mighty muscles straining, mutuality of testicular steeliness tested and acknowledged.*)

H.P.: We're not children in this room.

Gonzo: I should say not.

H.P.: I hope you're well.

Gonzo: (*who clearly isn't*) Yes, sir. Tip top.

H.P.: Only I have a problem, Mr. Lubitsch, and it's a big one. It's more your kind of problem than mine, these days. It's a young man's problem, and I am an old fart.

Gonzo: I wouldn't say that.

H.P.: Fercrissakes, Mr. Lubitsch, I am an old fart. I am powerful and dangerous and sexually potent. I do not have a problem with my old-fartness. Let's not get into how I am in the prime of my life. I know I am in the prime of my life. I am also an old fart. Okay?

(*Beat*)

Gonzo: What can I do for you, Mr. Pestle?

H.P.: I would like you to look around this room and tell me what you see.

(*Gonzo looks. What he sees is a forest of maps and pictures. Drowned Cross. Miserichord. Horrisham. Templeton. He is looking at the Vanishings. He has never seen them laid out like this before. They seem to make a sort of pattern around the Pipe.*)

H.P.: What do you see, son?

Gonzo: I'm not sure. The Vanishings.

H.P.: Let me help you out.

(*Humbert Pestle turns on an overhead projector. It is an old one, with sheets of transparent plastic and wipe-clean pens. It is the kind Ms. Poynter used to sketch the erogenous zones in biology, a moment Gonzo remembers with burning intensity as he has had frequent cause to recall it since. Humbert Pestle knows this, because he has done his homework, or rather someone has done it for him. He knows that Gonzo likes this particular model of OHP, that it makes a hum he finds, without realising it, reassuring and just a little bit sexy. Ms. Poynter was a babe and reputedly also a serious love machine, and Gonzo once, during a particularly vexing test, found her leaning down to study his answers, and caught a glimpse of what he could only assume was a breast. This projector is inextricably bound up with Gonzo's early orgasms. Today, though, Humbert Pestle projects not erogenous zones but something quite the opposite. He shows Gonzo that the Vanishings could be taken as a fence, a scar around the Pipe and the people who live within its benevolent fog.*)

Gonzo: I don't—quite—understand.

H.P.: Well, Mr. Lubitsch, it's like this. We have encircled the Earth, and we have created a little area of civilisation and safety and good commerce. But all around us there is a wild place of monsters. You are personally well aware of this. There are things that look human, and things which don't, and they want to eat us all up. Our house is made of bricks, so they can't just huff and puff us into the open. But they can chisel away. They can strangle us. And that is what they are doing. Every finger we put outside a certain distance from the Pipe, they cut off. And that distance is shrinking, Mr. Lubitsch. It takes less time to make a town vanish than it does to build one. We are encircled. We are under siege. And we are losing.

(*Humbert Pestle is a better orator than Dick Washburn. He does not attempt the rhetorical ellipsis overtly. He does not trail off, awed by the awfulness of the awesome thing he is trying to convey. His ellipsis is tacit. He does not say "And if we lose . . ." He knows Gonzo will say that to himself, and your own ellipses are infinitely more persuasive than someone else's.*)

Gonzo: That is—well—that is quite a problem, Mr. Pestle.

H.P.: Yes, Mr. Lubitsch. That is quite a problem. It is a real problem in the real world. A grown-up problem. This is why I asked—because I know damn well that the answer is yes—if we were all adults here. Because we're in a very adult place right now. We have no time for niceties.

(*Beat*)

H.P.: May I ask you a question?

Gonzo: Of course.

H.P.: If you could do something about it—something only you had a really good shot at—would you do it?

Gonzo: Yes, I would.

H.P.: Even if it was basically a bad thing? A wrong thing?

Gonzo: How wrong?

H.P.: Wrong. A bad thing. But . . . effective. One bad thing to stop more bad things from happening.

Gonzo: (*he considers*) Sometimes you have to do those things.

H.P.: Sometimes you do.

(*Beat*)

H.P.: But not always, of course.

(*Humbert Pestle removes from a folder an image of Zaher Bey and places it on the table between them.*)

H.P.: I believe you know Zaher Bey. He has made his life with the monsters.

(*Gonzo nods.*)

H.P.: The Found Thousand, Mr. Lubitsch. The unreal people. They want our world. They want our lives.

(*And Gonzo, of course, knows first-hand that this is true. Because I tried to take his wife.*)

H.P.: I need to have a talk with this good gentleman. I need him to come to me to discuss this situation. I need to have a free hand at those discussions.

Gonzo: I see.

H.P.: Now, the Bey won't come out to play. But I have reason to believe that if you went and asked him, he might reconsider. You knew him in the Reification, I gather.

Gonzo: Yes, I did.

H.P.: He trusts your word, Mr. Lubitsch. If he has your assurance of his safety, I believe he would come.

Gonzo: And then you would talk to him.

H.P.: You would not be required to be part of the conversation, Mr. Lubitsch. Only to bring him to me.

(*And Gonzo knows, really, that he is being invited to weasel. His responsibility is sharply bounded. Get the Bey. Bring him to the place. That is all he will have done. This is the seduction of Humbert Pestle's proposition: the idea of limited consequence. The dark deeds which will be done after Gonzo hands over his trusting companion will be someone else's burden. He cannot know, not really, that they will take place. Humbert Pestle—a very respectable man—is requesting a specific task of him, a noble task. He has no reason to doubt. And even if these dark deeds are done, would that be so bad? Certain prices must be paid, after all. We're all grown-ups here.*)

Gonzo: All right, then.

Because this was always the plan. Humbert Pestle sent Moustache the ninja to set the Pipe on fire, dispatched Dick Washburn to hire the Free Company to put it out. He had Moustache wait and try to kill us, knowing the ninja could not possibly succeed. He sent men to kill Gonzo's parents and Leah. All to destabilise Gonzo, to make him so angry that Pestle could throw the blame at Zaher Bey and let fear and panic make it stick. *The Found Thousand are coming! The enemy is at the gate! Fight them! Kill them! Hesitation is death to those you love.* And then offer this grimy solution, a sordid, appealing little deal to take away the fear. *Leave it all to Humbert.*

Pestle must have been thrilled when he heard about me. The ideal whip to drive Gonzo with. The perfect cat's paw. *They want our lives.*

Gonzo will bring the Bey, and Humbert Pestle will kill him. I cannot allow it. It will damn Gonzo, of course. He will not recover from having lent himself to such a thing. He will become, gradually, a pencilneck, and he will lend himself to more and more until finally he is no one I know. But more, I cannot allow it because the Bey is not really trusting Gonzo. He is trusting the portable Gonzo he carries in his head, the image of the person who brought him to Caucus and hung on his every word; of the castaway who washed up on his shore with a broken hand and confessed his part in the Go Away War, and who became part of the Bey's extended family in Shangri-La. And that person is not Gonzo Lubitsch. It is me. If Gonzo delivers Zaher Bey to Humbert Pestle, he will do it in my colours.

That is the least awful thing I read in Humbert Pestle's secret file.

I AM in the corridor again, and I have not been blown up. I am walking back the way I came. I do not remember leaving the room. I know that I wanted to. I also wanted to be sick, but I think—I hope—that I managed not to do that. I am full of answers, but I don't understand them. I still don't know the *why.* And I no longer know where to look. I have seen the Core. I have seen the file. I just don't get it.

Maybe I'm ignoring the obvious. Perhaps Pestle is *insane.* He seems to be: set the Pipe on fire to recruit Gonzo; risk the entire world for a chance to kill the Bey. And somewhere in there cause the Vanishings as well, if his cleat is anything to go by. The scales are not balanced, but maybe Pestle just hates Zaher Bey so much (and *why?* again) that he doesn't care.

I have gone the wrong way somewhere. Elisabeth is tapping on the ceiling, *tra-tratratra.* This way.

I don't go that way. I have seen something. In for a penny. One more room. The door is half-open, and there's a soft light coming out, maybe a television screen or a computer. I look in.

The man sitting at the desk is huge. I do not immediately recognise him because he is so still. He is lit from a single monitor screen, a pale blueish luminescence which casts long shadows over his face. Always before when I have seen him, he has been speaking with his whole body, using his physicality for all it's worth. Now he sits, slack, in this chair in this featureless box. His eyes are open, and he is looking straight ahead. It seems at first that he is dead. If so, he has gone into rigor in place; they will never be able to get him out of the chair without bolt cutters (the dirty secret of undertakers). On the other hand, with the muscle he has, I'd expect him to be more contorted. He should be all wrapped around himself, like a spider in the rain. He is not. If anything, he's like a sleeper. If I lean my head, I can see his chest move slowly, in and out. Humbert Pestle is not dead. He has been put away. This is how he is when he is not the Boss. When he has no purpose. Humbert Pestle is a type A pencilneck, and this is what he is when there is no work to be done.

I think of Robert Crabtree and of the maps and graphs in the operations room, of the secret file and Humbert Pestle's vacant eyes, and now I *do* understand. At last, in the cold light of the screen, I see the face of my enemy.

Chapter Sixteen

Fear and marine biology;
just like old times;
it all goes wrong.

FEAR is an emotion with many shapes. It can be a thing of jolts and shudders, like an electric shock, or it can be like the tendril of cold night air which reaches you in your bed when all your doors and windows should be closed. It can come in the shape of a well-known footstep in the wrong place at the wrong time, or a foreign one in a familiar room. But all fear is connected, a susurrus which plays around you in the dark and brushes against your skin, pushes the hair back from your face like an uninvited guest, and slips away before you dare to open your eyes. Also, fear is *sneaky.* It establishes a foothold and sits, content. While you confront it, it is small and weak, and looks back at you with timorous eyes, so that you wonder how it could ever stir you for more than a moment. Turn your back, and it waxes, casting giant shadows and flickering in the corner of your eye, leaning lingeringly on the creaky floorboard. It inflates and bursts, propelling fragments of itself to the far corners of your mind, where they grow again until you are inundated, and you drown.

I am not afraid as I stare at Humbert Pestle. He is there, in front of me, and he does not see me. It's like seeing the wolf padding through the forest: you know it is there, it's just an animal, and it's not coming your way. Good. I slip out, and down the corridor, and Elisabeth's *tra-tratra* guides me to the grille. I am not afraid as we climb onto the roof and head back the way we came. I am not afraid in the moonlight as we winch ourselves back up, yard by yard, away from Pestle and his vacant gaze.

And then, once we are over the Jorgmund building, with its snake badge in silly neon, I make a mistake. I start to pick up the pace. I am impatient, and the longer we are exposed like this, the greater our risk. The consequences of discovery are very grave—no sense in taking more chances than we have to. I trot. He saw me. He will send men. They will follow, and they will catch Elisabeth, and it will be *my fault.* The trot becomes a run. Elisabeth is ahead of me, and they will take her and erase her and it will *all be my fault.* Then they will come for me, and do terrible things, and I will die and be *gone,* extinguished, after so little time to be at all. The sky yawns above me, and for a second it is a chasm into which I may fall, an impossible depth, and I am looking not up into it but down onto it, and the threads of gravity and atmosphere which tie me to it are very slender and I am very, very small.

Fear is not rational. A moment later the run becomes a sprint, and a panic, and I am afraid of everything I have ever been afraid of. I am afraid that I will be hauled up on charges for terrible crimes I have not committed, or that I have, and I will be an outcast and a pariah, and Old Man Lubitsch will shake his head and turn away, and be appalled. I am afraid that Elisabeth will despise me, leave me, attack me, and I will not know how to stop her without killing her and then I will be a murderer. I am afraid of falling, of fire, of torture and monsters and infestations of spiders and wild dogs and cancer and the End of the World (a proper one, without a sequel) and everything else I have imagined in the small hours between two and four, when unreasonable, improbable waking nightmares can attain solidity and bulk.

I overtake Elisabeth, grab her hand and drag her along with me, plunge and weave across the rooftops. She calls to me to stop, *stop,* and when I do it is because we have arrived, and I dive through the open door and into the pigeon loft and begin to pack. We cannot stay, cannot stop, not now, never again, until this is done. Fear has given way to *horror.* It is the animal in me, seeing the thing which is my foe, and that thing is not like me. The face of my enemy.

In the sea, there are creatures like this. *Physalia physalis* is an individual, but it is also a colony. It is a floating sack of gas composed of a million little polyps, of four different kinds. Some of them digest and some of them sting, and some of them are for breeding, and some for keeping the others from sinking down into the sea. I met a sailor once, a woman from Redyard, who had been stung by one. She said it was like being scraped with hot wire, and she screamed and drank down brine, but the worst part was being tangled in the tendrils of the monster, brushing against them and recoiling into more, and gasping, and *swallowing* them, being wrapped about and snuggled and invaded by something alien and awful which had no eyes and yet knew she was there.

The gas bag was barely as big as her head. It could no more consume her than it could get up and dance—but it was trying, oh yes, and if she sank, then she would die, and her assailant would devour her slowly, gram by gram. She had weals upon her arms and neck, livid scars like the marks of a whip or a brand, and she favoured one hand. The doctors said her survival was a miracle, that she must have a giant's heart. She spoke as if she'd been smoking with every breath, her larynx coarsened by scars. When they pulled her out of the water, the thing came too, all blue-grey and appalling, half-liquid. On dry land it couldn't move—no muscles at all. They unwrapped her from it and she spasmed away across the deck, but she wouldn't let them throw it back. She made them keep it, and when she was well, weeks later, she burned it in her yard and vomited for two straight days. She didn't drink; alcohol, she said, gave her dreams of polyp arms about her, and made her wake up screaming. Her husband put his thick, dry hands on her shoulders and stroked gently at the places where she was marked, and the revulsion faded from her as she relaxed against him.

Jorgmund is like that. It is one thing, made from many. It does not think; it exists and it reacts and it expands, and that is all. The people who work for it are like the polyps, neither entirely individual nor entirely subsumed. They carry the monster in their minds, and they cannot see the whole. They give themselves to it, time-share, and slip into the body of the beast when they prefer not to be human. The ninjas are the stinging cells, reaching out and destroying enemies, killing food. Of all of them, Humbert Pestle is the greatest and the worst. He has made himself one with the machine, the monster. He sees it, and it does not appall him. He carries it in his head all the time, to the point where it is impossible to say whether he still exists separate from the thing.

I feel as if I have overturned a stone, expecting insects, and discovered that the stone itself is nothing but a vast mass of bugs.

IN ACTION MOVIES the hero can explain the danger in a few cogent sentences, and (aside from a token person who later gets eaten or has to apologise) everyone immediately accepts the reality of what he says and understands its significance. Monkey reflex is churning in me: flee, seek advantage, fight. Hit small, soft things with your hands. If you want to kill something big and tough, you need a stick with a rock on the end, or a sharp piece of bone. And I want to kill it, just as badly as it wants to kill me—or the Bey, or the Found Thousand, or anyone who sees it for what it is. Everything must function in a way which is compatible with Jorgmund. Anything which does not, may not persist. Evolution is not fuzzy or kind; DNA does not negotiate. This thing is like that: too basic, too young, too simple of its type to permit difference.

Elisabeth Soames does not quibble. She gauges me with rapid glances. She hears the words which do not come out, apprehends the ideas foaming behind them. She tosses our belongings into a bag, turns out the lights in the pigeon loft and unplugs the electric fire, then leads me rapidly away. She does not look back at the place which has been her home for twenty months or more. She does not allow herself to miss it. Her hand tightens in mine, just a little, as we drop down below the roof level, and we leave the cosy, ramshackle building behind.

WE TAKE the main road, along the Pipe. I drive. We have left the *Magic of Andromas* under wraps in Haviland. It is conspicuous where Annabelle is anonymous, just another big, creaky truck. If we are lucky, they believe I am dead. They won't find my body, but there are many reasons why that might be so. Perhaps jackals have devoured me, or starving children of the street. Perhaps I rolled or crawled, broken, to the road, and was flattened by a succession of buses. Maybe—and I am particularly proud of this one—my body has been washed into a storm drain and is slowly leaching into the city's water.

"No," says Elisabeth Soames, as I continue in this vein, "enough. Enough and more than enough." Because I have been sharing these brilliant thoughts with her for several hours, and she has winced and gagged her way through quite some few of them in that time.

Humbert Pestle's file had a map. Quite close to Haviland, innocuous and ordinary, there's a side turning which looks like a farm track. Turn down it and follow it, and the track becomes a lane, and then a wide, lazy road. The buildings are signposted as a synthetic milk plant. This is Jorgmund Actual, where FOX is made (I haven't told Elisabeth yet what I know about that, the darkest of Humbert Pestle's secrets, the black coffins burning at Station 9), and the Pipe begins and ends. The head and tail of the serpent. It is where the Bey will be. It is more than that. It is where I must go, where everything will finish.

For the moment, though, we need a place which is known,

where we can meet our allies, such as they are, and if they come. So I have called Flynn the Barman's private number and rented a room (something I have never dared to do before, lest I overhear him and Mrs. Flynn romping on the pool table or making whoopee in the master suite) at the Nameless Bar.

The desert is very much the same as it was. Deserts do change, of course. They go through subtle alterations, become more arid or more lush, favour one sly, pink-eared animal or another. It's just very hard to tell. Deserts are like a nearly bald man having a haircut. The difference is absolutely crucial from within, but to the rest of us it's still a dusty scrubland with little in the way of plant life. Tonight it's cold. There's a fine mist and a wind off the mountains which smells of snow. By contrast, the smell of pigs, warm and bilious, wafts along the road to greet us.

THE NAMELESS BAR is quiet. Not silent, but not loud. There's no chatter of conversation, no sound of glasses being clinked. The windows are clear and bright through the mist, but there's little sign of people passing in front of them. I wonder whether it is empty. We made our calls on the way, from a rest stop by the main Pipe. The bar should be full. If no one has come, then this is over before it begins. Elisabeth presses lightly against me. I am not alone. She at least is here, and going nowhere. Two against an army. Fine. Then the door opens, and there are Sally and Jim. Then they fall back a little, and a smaller woman steps between them: Leah.

I couldn't ask the Free Company to come here. I couldn't tell them what was going on and expect them to believe me. So I wasn't going to. Elisabeth Soames is made of tougher stuff. She knew exactly how to make it happen, who would listen to me, who owed me and would feel it. *She* called Leah, told her who she was, and that she was with me, and what was happening and what Gonzo was really doing and how he'd been set up. For good measure she told Ma Lubitsch the same story, and Ma Lubitsch has a soft spot for Elisabeth Soames, who she considers to be, despite the evidence that Elisabeth is an itinerant magician-revenger who lives in a pigeon loft, "a nice young girl from *Crick-elvud Cowff* and *very vell brought up.*" Ma Lubitsch bent Leah's ear on one side and Elisabeth bent the other, and Old Man Lubitsch had to intervene so that Leah could say anything at all, and when she did it was very simple, and likely what she would have said before if she could have got a word in edgewise, which was: *Yes.*

So Sally and Jim were interrupted once again by visitors from our house—Gonzo's house—though thankfully this time they were eating. Leah laid it out for them, and Jim rumbled and Sally stared, and then they got up and collected their emergency bags, the ones they have kept packed every day and night since Shangri-La, from just inside the bedroom door. Jim rubbed his bald, naked head and put a hat on, and all three of them went to round up Tommy Lapland and Samuel P., who were gadding about in some place very like Matchingham. These four dragged Tobemory Trent out of a wine-tasting, and Annie the Ox and Egon Schlender from a baby shower, and so it went on until they had the whole gang assembled and ready for the job at hand, although none of them knew precisely what that was.

Jim Hepsobah gives me a look from toe to top, and finds nothing to suggest that I am actually evil. If Leah trusts me; if Ma Lubitsch (who has had words with James V. Hepsobah on the subject of his tardiness regarding marriage) accepts me, that's good enough for Jim. Sally is cooler. She is the backstop, the sniper, the plug-puller and the outer perimeter; being the deal-maker also makes her the deal-breaker in time of need. But even Sally nods to me shortly, and then the three of them bring me into the Nameless Bar, and I find myself in front of the people I know as well as I know anyone, and they have never met me before.

Annie the Ox is the first one I pick out of the crowd, her face serious and measured. She is actually holding a puppet head (I think it's the elephant), which she does only on the most significant occasions. Seeing my gaze on the thing, she glances down and goes to hide it, then straightens and puts it firmly on the table in front of her. *Make what you will,* she says with her eyes, and I reply with mine very much the same.

Tobemory Trent, speaking of eyes, is watching from a bar stool. Long spider legs and rootish hands around a tankard, Trent looks more like himself than he ever has before. Or maybe I am just seeing him with my own eyes for the first time. And then the Free Company gives way to newer, stranger friends. Next to Trent is K (the shepherd, not the sarong-wearing original), who despite his tweeds might have been raised in the same house; he's wearing an identical expression of patience and hanging thunder. Beyond K are several other Ks, well known and less so, and beyond them, a sea of mimish faces, expressionless beneath matching white make-up.

What the hell do you say? I ought to be getting better at it. "Hi, I'm . . . *oh, bugger* . . ." (Note to self: must get a name.) "And it's really good to see you all here this evening, because . . ."

Lynch me now. It'll be kinder. I clear my throat. Everyone looks at me. Whatever I was going to say sticks and then goes right out of my head. These people are going to risk everything for me, but I can't give them as much as a greeting. I could weep, if I could make any sound at all.

The noise which saves me is quite possibly the most awful noise I have ever heard. It is a high scream of porcine affront, a vast, ear-splitting yowl of shock and alarm which vibrates the glasses and rattles the windows. It sounds for all the world like murder in one of those old black-and-white mystery movies where the heroine's chest was all covered up but could at least be brought to the viewer's attention by some serious heaving, and many a career was made by impressive lungs.

Flynn the Barman leaps up and charges for the back door, which slams open to reveal a figure in a raincoat and a fanciful pirate's hat.

"Sorry!" cries the apparition cheerfully. "K's strong-eye dog has just terrorised your pigs and they seem to be running around in circles. The dogs are being hosed down; they got stuck in the wallow, which apparently upset the pigs even more. Still, no harm done, medals all round, not that pigs really care."

Ike Thermite waves at everyone, even the mimes, who look back at him and think whatever thoughts mimes do think when considering the one of their number who is permitted speech. And behind Ike there is a small, disenchanted old man with leather skin and a fighter's frame, weathered but undefeated, and possessed of a deep well of vile temper.

"Those are not pigs," this person says firmly, "those are the gate-keepers of the Hell of Flying Shite. It is not enough that I have been dragged from acts of considerable obscenity in a place we shall not name with women whose sole object in life was to make my final years a great celebration of my dwindling sexual resources; I must also be showered in pig poo. Thus, we shall not discuss the charmingness of the day or the cool night breezes any more than we absolutely have to, Mr. *Ike Thermite* of the *Matahuxee Mime Combine;* we shall proceed to the main event, eftsoons and right speedily, with all due dispatch, lest I become bad-tempered and profane. Now," he says, "where is this bumhole we're so excited about?"

I step forward through the crowd, pushing people out of the way, and I hug him. His chest, beneath his flannel shirt, feels like metal plate covered in uncooked veal. Ronnie Cheung has aged well, but he has aged fully, and even stone is eroded by time and water. After a moment, he speaks.

"Bumhole," he says, "you are standing on my corn."

I HAVE made up my own five-step plan for public speaking, loosely adapted from Hellen Fust's let's-have-an-atrocity speech. It is intended to be brief, but as I start speaking I find that I have quite a lot to say and that all of it is relevant, so the story grows in the telling and the speech in the making, and Elisabeth spirits a glass of something sharp and wet from the bar to moisten my tongue.

I tell them who I am and where I come from; I tell them about Marcus Maximus Lubitsch and the foreign field, and Gonzo's game and his sorrow, and about how he made a new friend. I tell them about getting shot. I do not look at Leah as I talk about the hard surface of the road. *This is who I am, what I am. That's all there is.*

Then I go back in time and tell them things they already know about the Go Away War and the Reification, and how Zaher Bey gave shelter to a small group of desperate people, and fed them, and how we'd have died without him and his people, or maybe drowned in a sea of Stuff. *We have a debt.*

And because I cannot hold it in any longer, I tell them the last of Humbert Pestle's awful secrets, the worm in the apple of the world. It goes like this:

Once upon a time there was a boy named Bobby Shank. Bobby was near-sighted and not too bright, but he had good intentions and an empty bank account, so it came to him that he might do worse than sign up for a tour with the forces. He was a lousy shot, but he had a strong back and a willing heart, and he was good-natured and maybe a bit too stupid to be scared. He dug earthworks in Addeh Katir and toiled and tramped and carried things back and forth until Riley Tench assigned him permanently to the medical corps. And finally he happened to be in a certain street in a combat zone mostly by accident when his own side started shelling the place and a big, improbable window shattered, and the fragments flew about like rainbow insects with scalpel wings.

One of those fragments hit Bobby Shank in the head. It was not thick, but it was long and *very* sharp, and because it struck dead on, the force of the blow was transmitted along the length of it and it behaved much as if it had been a spear. It penetrated Bobby's skull and went into his brain, where it broke into several pieces which each performed distinct and unlikely surgery. The first one deflected upward and partially severed Bobby Shank's higher functions from the rest of his brain. Bobby couldn't actually see anything any more, not in real time. He could look at something and *remember* having seen it, tell you all about it. But he was not, for example, going to be playing any football anytime soon. Similarly, he couldn't smell either, but he could recall smells from about a minute ago, and at the moment what he could mostly smell was blood, which he rightly deduced was his own. He tried to scream, but this proved impossible because the second piece had deflected off the skull and gone sort of up-left, arriving at Broca's area, which deals with speech, and turning it instantly into porridge. Bobby's mouth began making sounds, long strings of word-like noises. The third piece was either the cruellest or the kindest, depending on how bleak you take your mercy. It went into his brainstem, occasionally dropping Bobby Shank into total unconsciousness, and was working slowly inward so that he would eventually die. Bobby was a stretcherman. Tobemory Trent should probably have declared him dead-at-scene, but he didn't because stretchermen didn't get left behind, not ever.

After a few days they shipped Bobby Shank back home and he lay in a hospital, drifting in and out of the world. They tried using ultrasound on the third piece of glass, because otherwise he was going to die anyway, and they broke it up real good, along with the other pieces they'd sort of hoped to leave well alone. That turned out to be a mixed blessing, because the shards went into the part of him which had long-term memories and took a lot of them away. Bobby Shank forgot that he had a name, he just lived in the last five minutes. In a way it was a success, because now he'd never been anything other than what he was, a kind of dream of white walls and nice smells, slowly decohering and fading away, until Bobby was a short circuit, just a brain registering what was in front of him, and not really being aware of itself at all. He smiled more and swore less, which was nice.

And then the lights went out, and half the city was swallowed by a very large Go Away Bomb, and the machines switched off, and Bobby Shank got hungry. He crawled out into the street. I figure it must have taken him about an hour to make it that far, maybe a little more if he got knocked out or distracted by the pretty patterns on the first-floor carpet. Where he thought he was going, or even if he understood that he was moving at all, I have no idea.

Bobby Shank, who didn't know that he was Bobby Shank, crawled along Hornchurch Street, looking for pancakes. He could smell them, and while he didn't remember them, some part of him knew that was what he wanted. A miracle, he found them. He crawled into the living room of a lady named Edith MacIntyre, and when she'd finished screaming at this hairy wreck of a human life and realised that he was a gentle, suffering thing, she fed him very slowly and rocked him, because her family were all missing and more than likely Gone Away.

Over time, Edith MacIntyre's home became a hostel and a meeting place. Travellers drifted in and stayed for a few days, and talked to one another around Edith's big old breakfast table, and they worked for their keep or paid in food. It was warm and safe, and what remained of Bobby Shank liked it very much indeed. He stayed—not that he was in any shape to run away—and he sat in a chair on the veranda and got monstrously fat.

The storms came to Edith MacIntyre's place that winter, and a lot of people got turned into something strange, and a lot of houses were surrounded by chimeras and talking dogs. Half-imagined food stank in the gutters and spiders like fists skittered across roads made of gold and mud and ice. But nothing happened to Edith MacIntyre's house. When the storms came down, the Stuff trickled through the roof and into the living room, and when it fell to the floor it was water, or dust. Anywhere near Bobby Shank, Stuff just became like whatever he was looking at. Because Bobby Shank couldn't imagine anything else. He didn't have desires or dreams. He just had what was in front of him, and precious little of that.

And then one morning a man with a most unfortunate name chanced to come by and rest up with Edith MacIntyre. When he saw Bobby Shank, it was like he was looking at the face of God. He was hearing the music, he said. Edith MacIntyre didn't like this man very much, with his great bear shoulders and too-loud laugh. She'd had a husband like that, back in the day, and he'd been a bastard too.

A week later Humbert Pestle came back and stole Bobby Shank away, and Edith MacIntyre never saw him again. She worried about him, but after a little while she was too busy with the business of staying alive to think about it.

The station on the Jorgmund Pipe consisted of Humbert Pestle and Bobby Shank and an old sewage pump, working in a little place called Aldony. It didn't take long before they were ready to expand. Bobby could turn as much Stuff into anti-Stuff (Humbert Pestle didn't have a catchy name for it yet) as you could bring within a few feet of him. It didn't have to be there for more than a second. It just touched Bobby's tattered remnant of a mind and changed right away. And that was fine for a few months. He found the Clockwork Hand again—or they found him, the fifty or so who were still alive—and he had the beginnings of an empire. All good. Until Jorgmund got a bit bigger, and Humbert Pestle had to go looking for more like Bobby Shank. That was harder than it seemed. Very specific, strange things had happened to Bobby Shank. Humbert had to make do with approximations.

He found a woman in Bridgeport who'd been in a coma for twenty years. She was no use. Her brain didn't do anything at all.

He found a kid from Belfistry who'd broken his neck. That was a disaster. The kid made monsters and houris and terrible, giant slugs. They flickered and raged and then vanished again; his mind was all over the place.

He found an elderly man from the Punjab who was afflicted with some manner of disease. This person was quite promising until blood came out of his nose and he died. Humbert Pestle had to keep looking, but wherever he looked, he couldn't find another Bobby Shank. So he looked into his heart and listened to the music, and he knew what he had to do. He had to *make* people like Bobby Shank. After all, this was for the future of the human race.

At first he used bandits. There were plenty of them, ordinary people gone savage and angry, preying on those who'd stuck it out and living, like Ruth Kemner and her gang, in ghastly halls which stank of executions and stale beer. He got fifteen like that. Some of them he just locked away until the EEG readings went like Bobby's. Others he did things to, sharp, messy things. They didn't last long, not like Bobby, but they worked. They produced. But not fast enough. The new towns were springing up faster than he could increase his production.

That's when he went to Heyerdahl Point with the whole of the Clockwork Hand, and turned it into Drowned Cross.

He took the people of Drowned Cross, and he worked on them until he had five hundred Bobby Shanks in five hundred black boxes with hoses coming out. They still didn't last very long, but they lasted long enough. And when they were all used up, he took another town, and then another. Most recently, he took Templeton. Soon enough, he'll take another one. That's how Jorgmund saves the world. It uses people up. Feeds the princess to the dragon.

I tell them all this, and I tell them that I'm going to stop it. I don't know how I can do it without them but I will, because I care about Gonzo and I care about the Bey and I care about those however many poor broken people in boxes. I don't care if I am a monster, if what I am is the opposite of what they are. I won't sit by. No, no, no, no, no.

My hand is hurting because I have been hitting the bar for

emphasis. I don't recall deciding to do that. I look down at it because it is throbbing. And then I look up at the sea of faces, and no one says a word. God. I've completely blown it. They think I'm totally insane. They despise me. It's a bust. I'm sorry, everyone, I have completely screwed the pooch.

Ronnie Cheung raises one hand to shoulder height, and then he drops it, hard, onto the table next to him. The ashtray jumps. He raises his hand again, and brings it down. Ike Thermite follows suit, and Elisabeth, and Leah, and then Jim and Sally and Tobemory Trent, and Baptiste Vasille is shaking his fist and shouting something in French, and the thrumming roar of sound washes over me like an ocean. They do not hate me. They are not laughing.

They are applauding.

I did something right.

Samuel P. is lying on his stomach on my left side, and I can smell him. It's surprisingly pleasant. Because he is wearing a frame of foliage on his body and pretending to be a small tree, Sam's body odour is essentially grass and soil, with just a whiff of bracken. Beneath that, there's a bass note of armpit, which I try to ignore. Any smell like that contains small bits of actual skin, and I don't want to think about having Samuel P.'s pits in my lungs. But funky though he is, Sam is very good at this kind of thing—"this kind of thing" being your professional-grade sneaking.

On my other side is Elisabeth Soames, wearing her ninja outfit again, partly because it's suited to sneaking and partly because it might afford the enemy some confusion if we get caught and she's wearing one of their uniforms. I'm wearing mine, with a pair of decent shoes. The last-ditch plan is to pretend that we're escorting a prisoner, then cause mayhem. Elisabeth Soames pointed out that this didn't work well in *Star Wars* and can reasonably be expected to fail in the real world, which is somewhat more demanding in the field of cunning plans, and Samuel P. tried very hard to pretend he hadn't been thinking of *Star Wars* when he proposed it. The trouble is that although it's a lousy last-ditch plan, it is also our only last-ditch plan.

The rest of the plan is quite good, and if it works the way it is supposed to, we will do very well, and we won't need the lousy part. On the other hand, it almost certainly won't work like that, because plans don't. It will twist, creep, change, swivel and mutate, until finally we're flying on sheer bravado and chutzpah, and hoping the other guy thinks it's all accounted for. You don't make strategy so that there's one path to victory; you make it so that as many paths as possible lead to something which isn't loss. At least you do unless you want to die.

In broad-brush terms (because the minutiae are surprisingly boring), Jim Hepsobah and Annie the Ox will lead a small body of the Free Company (temporarily re-militarised, and therefore referred to by one and all as the *Uncivil* Freebooting Company) up to the main gate and *blow it up*. This will draw a considerable amount of negative attention in the form of people shooting at them (the guards here are soldiers rather than ninjas, although they may *also* be or include ninjas, because that's rather the point about being a secret assassin; you don't go around telling everyone) and cause those in charge of the facility to pay closer attention to the main entrance and somewhat less to a small area of fence at the side where Samuel P. and I, along with Elisabeth Soames, will be doing our sneaking. The frontal attack will withdraw into the treeline, sucking in pursuers who will run into certain obstacles and quite a lot more members of the Free Company. This diversionary force will then coax the enemy away from us and into a bizarre world which will almost certainly cause them to doubt their sanity.

On the far side from our position, K (the fat one) and his circus of history have deployed such of their son et lumière as can be used out of doors to create chaos and confusion, something K is by nature extremely good at. The forested hillside will be covered in wacky mirrors, enormous jack-in-the-boxes and automated pie-throwers loaded with bags of chilli powder (inhaled or just drifting into your eyes, this is almost guaranteed to cause agony and incapacitation). There will also be Indian runner ducks in vast quantity, and some recently acquired geese with foul tempers. The sheepdogs, Hbw and Mnwr, cannot be permitted to join the fun in case they get shot (also because Hbw would probably develop a taste for disembowelling and Mnwr would instantly defect). This is called "making full use of all resources," and comes under the subheading "ludicrous crap which may or may not work, but which we know about and they don't." Amid the fun, however, there will be a wrinkled and foul-tempered unarmed combat instructor with years of experience in making people wish they were dead. Ronnie Cheung has specifically requested this assignment on the basis that it is a job for a mean-minded and obnoxious person of questionable moral character.

Less far-fetched, the panoramic backdrops from Ike Thermite's stage show have been erected randomly around the place under cover of night, repainted and positioned to appear to be or to conceal local landmarks. The big generator (usually used to light the circus) has been set up to emit broad-spectrum squawks which will make radio triangulations almost impossible. Since there is no longer a GPS network (satellites did not respond well to the reallocation of mass and gravity occasioned by the Go Away War, and quite some number of them drifted away or fell to earth), this should blind our enemy quite effectively, at least for a while. K's people and the mimes themselves will be several miles away at go-hour, providing medical support for anyone who can be got out to them, and creating the appearance that we are all elsewhere by means of sequential costume changes.

With Humbert Pestle's security forces thus distracted, we will enter the compound, rendezvous with the remaining members of the Free Company (under the leadership of Tobemory Trent, Tommy Lapland and Baptiste Vasille) and free the remaining undamaged prisoners from Templeton (the file says there are seventy-one, a tiny fraction of the initial population, but that doesn't make them not worth worrying about), locate the Bey and inform him of his peril, nab Gonzo and get them all out before Humbert Pestle can change into his evil pyjamas and come a-hunting. Ideally, when Humbert does shed his jolly japester-cum-corporate-silverback guise and get serious, he will have to come out of the building he is in, at which point Sally Culpepper will shoot him. This last was not Ronnie Cheung's suggestion but mine, because for all that Master Wu might not approve, I don't have the right to be squeamish about it when other people are risking their lives for me. Ronnie, however, made a sort of approving noise through his nose as if to say it was more sensible than he would have expected from a bumhole like me, especially an imaginary bumhole with a talent for seeing both sides of the fight.

It's not a bad plan. It has the benefit of simplicity, coupled with some elements which are unconventional (ducks, for example, are not often part of a covert intrusion and extraction scenario, and nor are pie-throwers). I could wish for more, but this is what we have to work with. Improvised mayhem has a long and chequered heritage going back to the time when weapons did not come with user's manuals, and a stick for herding goats was just as often a stick for beating your neighbour to death with if he looked at you funny. The fact that some of our weapons are weird and silly doesn't mean they won't work. We hope.

I look across at Elisabeth Soames. She looks back. I am afraid for her. I don't want to see any of the things which may shortly happen happen to her. I have not insulted her by asking her to remain behind. Even if she weren't at least as capable as I am, she loved Wu Shenyang very much, and while most people here are concentrating on the other awful things Humbert Pestle has done, I know that in her mind the destruction of that overstuffed cosy house and all the amazing things in it—the wind-up gramophone, the ugly porcelain ornaments, the ancient Buddhas and the awful yet splendid weapons on the walls, the photographs, and worst of all Master Wu himself—is as high and fresh a crime as all the others.

She takes my hand and squeezes it.

There's a pale, slender moon shining down on the buildings below, making them look clean and soft. Jorgmund Actual is huge. It's adapted from one of Piper 90's cousins and set deep into the ground. Down there is a well, a cauldron of FOX waiting to be pumped out under pressure, filled all the time from the manufactory a hundred yards to the west. (I can't think about FOX any more without shuddering. Time was when it gave me a warm glow. Now I feel sick.) The Pipe emerges from the station like a huge worm, bending at right angles and burrowing immediately into the hillside. That's not where we need to be. Our first stop is the main control centre, two buildings over (looks like a shoebox; even has the little rim a third of the way down the side). I look at Samuel P. and he nods, mouths a countdown. I look back at Elisabeth, and she smiles fiercely then apologetically lets go of my hand. I miss her immediately.

The night explodes.

I RUN low, like the hunchback. There are no bells to lament, but there are whistles, klaxons and people shouting, and also small-arms discharges and things going *b-boom!* Jorgmund Actual is on fire. Hah! Payback is good. I zigzag like Ben Carsville, and Elisabeth and Sam zigzag around me. We are a fishball, a confusing shadow. We are invisible. Then someone sends up a flare or uses some kind of phosporus weapon, and everything is like day. Disaster. We're completely exposed, trying to disappear behind a shrub the size of a television set. I wait for the chatter of guns and the inevitable pain. I know, courtesy of Gonzo, what it is like to get shot. And now I am real enough to die. I wish I had had a chance to take Elisabeth to dinner and eat bruschetta.

Please, dear Lord. Tomatoes and basil, and plenty of green olive oil. A prayer for the antipasti.

Nothing happens. There's no one looking, or they're stupid, or they were blinded by the flare. Maybe the ninja outfits are working in our favour. It doesn't matter. We survive.

The fighting moves away from the main gate, and from us, and redoubles. There's a loud sound, a joyful cry of "HELLO, THERRRE!" and then startled, undisciplined gunfire; the first jack-in-the-box has been set off and the guards are starting to realise that they are in for a very strange evening indeed. Another flare goes up, and I can see the jack peeping out of the trees and wobbling, to and fro, before someone hits it with a grenade. Then there are screams—not of serious injury, but of alarm and pain. Chilli powder in the wind. Somewhere, right about now, Ronnie Cheung is kicking someone sharply in the unmentionables, and the geese are being whipped into a frenzy.

In my head the map from Humbert Pestle's file. This is Hut 1. It contains machine parts. As we pass by, I kick the door in. This is part of the plan: we won't be able to avoid triggering alarms as we move through the compound, so we are going to trigger *all* of them. If you can't be silent, you hide yourself in a forest of sound. I glance inside the hut: machine parts. So far, so good.

Samuel P. falls flat on his face. He becomes a bush amid the flowers (this is a corporate facility; at some point it has been landscaped just a little). Elisabeth and I flatten ourselves against the wall. A guard. Two. Professionals then, to ignore the grand kerfuffle going on beyond the fence on the other side of the enclosure (do they believe they are guarding a synthetic milk plant?) and carry on with their rounds. They are wary, but they are not looking for a commando rhododendron. They walk past Sam. He rises silently behind them. A man falls. The other turns, and Elisabeth hits him in the side of the neck, once, twice, three times, catches him as he goes down. She is gentle. I envy him just a little. We put them both in Hut 1, amid the spares. It's fine if they wake up and make a ruckus, as long as they do it in three minutes, not right now. It'll add to the fun.

Past Hut 7 and across the roundabout (more flowers). Jorgmund Actual is dressed up as the main office of Lactopolis Inc., glossy and dressed in pink and baby blue, with modern glass. Very corporate. Very ironic. I'm not laughing. The building is large—huge even. Parked boldly in front is a familiar maroon Rolls-Royce. The Bey. We look at one another, shift up another gear. The hardest part will be inside.

Ahead of us four guards, well-armed, armoured. They disappear as we draw close: Vasille's team is faster than we are. He waves. Baptiste Vasille is totally delighted with this situation. Typical Frenchman. (In the hills around the plant another Jack goes up: "IIIII'M JACKOOOO!" and then a boom and more chilli powder, and furious ducks and geese. Strobe lights, shouting, confusion.)

The accommodation block, for visiting milk executives. The glass is armoured and the doors are locked (as expected). Vasille's group has a circular saw to cover this situation. The noise is very loud, a shrieking, grinding wail. On the other side of the enclosure Tobemory Trent's team sets something on fire and more alarms go off to cover us. Perfect synchrony. We go inside. A guard arrives at a run, and one of Vasille's men shoots him in the head. He is the first person I know we have killed, and I feel bad about it. Gonzo wouldn't. Gonzo is a secret soldier, a pro. Perhaps that's part of what I was to him: the luxury of regret. The guard doesn't bleed very much; the bullet is still in his head. He leaks.

Past the lobby everything is calmer. The floor is made of marble. There's a fountain, and some very stylish seats in artful circles around coffee tables. A row of very old bonsai trees rest under glass. This place is expensive. Five-star. I feel underdressed—a terrible faux pas. At any moment the maître d' will arrive and request that I retire to my room and change into something more suitable. Not relevant. I shake my head to clear it, follow Elisabeth. (I worry all the same: unease of any kind is a warning. No matter that the fear was spurious. The warning is not. Something is wrong.) Samuel P. leads us down a service corridor.

Hallways and stairs and endless lounges with upmarket carpets. The diversion is working—the guards are elsewhere or not paying attention, or other things less pleasant. First floor. Second. Third. (Something is wrong. I don't know what it is. Something about the guards.) Guest accommodation. Vasille opens one door after another on the left, Samuel P. the right. No. Nothing. Keep moving—next set of doors. Find the Bey. No. No. No again. (Something missing. Something *wrong.* Guards but not guards. Booby traps? No. Not that. No pussy willow. Use your nose . . . no. Not that. But something is wrong.)

Samuel P. slams open a door and there are five of them, big lads with guns. Two of them are sitting. Vasille dives into the room, they all fall together in a huddle. His men pile in after, a Belgian and a Spaniard, all flying fists and arms. We follow. It's a short fight. I don't even hit anyone, just duck and then my opponent is gone. Not hard. Easy. (Too easy. These men are competent but no more. They are soldiers. Humbert Pestle has had no hand in their training. Too easy. I wait for the shoe to drop. It doesn't.) I look at Elisabeth. She knows. Her eyes are lit with nervous energy. Not fear but anticipation. The hard part is yet to come. She knocks on the main door.

"Hello?"

The door opens a crack. Zaher Bey, greyer, leaner and warier, in a bathrobe. And then it flies open and he whoops, and does a little dance, and Vasille is shushing him and saying now's not the time, *mordieu*! But the Bey is prancing around Vasille.

> It's been so long, so long, so long! How good to see you. Oh, yes, of course, quite right, I shall be totally silent, silent like the mouse, or better! Hah! The flea which whispers past the mouse's eagle eye (if such a thing he can be

said to possess, being a mouse and not an eagle): in either case the epitome of stealth. What? When? Immediately! Now! . . . Oh, yes, I see. Indeed. Shshsh . . .

He is quiet at last, or rather he is for a moment, then murmurs that *we should probably go. I have made something of an error of judgement, yes, indeed. Of trust* . . . And then his eye is upon me, and he peers, and sees . . . something. I extend my hand. He takes it, and there is familiarity for us both.

"Zaher Bey," he says, probing.

"We've met," I tell him, "but you wouldn't remember; it was a long time ago."

Zaher Bey holds on to my hand, feels the grip like a butcher with a joint, then his eyes take in my shoulders and my stance, my expression. He pushes against me, and I yield, soft-form style. "Ah!" he says. He draws me back the other way, turns his body, and I follow, butterfly-light. Our hands move a few inches, no more. He stares. "Yes. I see. I see, I see. I am an idiot that I didn't see it before, when he came. You are he and he is you and neither of you is who you were . . ." He smiles at my dismay. "Years with the Found Thousand. One becomes used to recognising the *new*."

Which is as far as we get before Vasille and Samuel P. slap an armoured coat upon him and remove his bathrobe (white is not a good colour for escaping). The Bey is revealed in a pair of strikingly elegant silk pyjamas, handily maroon (to match his Rolls-Royce, no doubt), which is the next best thing to black at night. In these rooms, with their lush mahoganies, he will blend in even better than we do. Success, stage one. (But still something is wrong.)

Back down to the main level (lots of stairs again, the Bey surprisingly spry, good for him; we're all panting. Damn, you have to be in good shape for this stuff. I'm sweating. Samuel P. smells like one enormous groin. It's the thing which limits his effectiveness in special operations: you can always find him if you know how. On the other hand, on longer missions he starts to smell like a jungle cat, carnivore breath and matted fur. He blends right in, as long as he's in a jungle or on a plain. In an office block, less good.

"Where's Gonzo?"

The Bey doesn't know. He was brought here, then imprisoned. There was a big man with an easy laugh and eyes like a porcelain doll, perfect and empty. *Pestle.* (Where is Pestle? I can't hear the fighting outside any longer—does that mean we've won? Or lost? Is Jim Hepsobah in a cell, or dead? I glance at my watch. Fourteen minutes to the hour. When the big hand hits twelve, the generator will be switched off; we will have radios for one minute. Preset signals will be exchanged to signify the state of play. Or they won't, if we're already screwed. (We're not. Not yet. I don't think. But we're walking a ledge. Something, somewhere . . . Damn. Crispin Hoare told me that—among Pont's other impossible tricks of genius—was the ability to remember great sequences of numbers, letters, words, playing cards, names . . . anything. And when he couldn't remember, he didn't say "I can't remember," he said "The information is coming to me *now*" and snapped his fingers, because that created positive reinforcement and you remembered. I try a variation. I know what's wrong . . . *Now.* Except that, annoyingly, I don't. Also, I have slapped myself on the forehead like a five-year-old. Everyone looks at me.)

"Nothing . . ."

Marvellous.

Swiftly down the main hall to the back, out of the fire doors. Open space and yes, there are fireworks still going off. I glance at the time: twelve minutes to the hour. Fine. Keep moving. The fire at the gate is out. The noise of geese is diminished. The ducks have apparently either run away or been shot. Samuel P. takes the Bey away—escape now, one objective achieved. The Bey argues but not much. This isn't his show, it's ours, and he's not in a position to know the score. Good. One less thing to worry about.

We kick open the door and go into Generation Centre 1. And stop.

This is the house that Humbert built. It is a huge room filled with regular, dark shapes, and each of those shapes is an isolation cylinder, a special life-support system for one person who has been broken on the wheel of Humbert Pestle's destiny. I look, and I see four rows of five, set apart from the rest. And then I look again, and I see that each dark shape in the middle distance is in fact a group like this one. Hoses and pumps, dials and buttons. This is a place where people feed the machine. In the great colony-organism that is Jorgmund, this is the gas bag that keeps the whole thing afloat, and strong. These are the Vanished, in boxes. This is the sacrifice which keeps the world the way we'd like it to be, allows us to ignore the changes we have wrought. It's like tying a virgin to a rock. The dragon takes her and goes away, and set against the fate of a nation, what's one virgin here or there? Nothing. A black box with a light on, and the slow, gasping wheeze of a ventilator for the ones who can't breathe by themselves. *Vvvv . . . gaahhh . . . Vvvv . . . gaahhh . . .* Otherwise, it's quiet.

This is not what we came for. We have to go through this. Six minutes to the hour. We walk. *Vvv . . . gaahhh.* Every so often there's a shudder as one of the dreamers kicks and shakes—autonomic reaction, spasm of old muscle. Maybe a heart attack. None of them perceives the world any more. None of them knows anything other than the grey interior walls of their coffins. A big hose brings Stuff from a pool or a lake, or a reservoir. The Stuff rolls past them, and changes into FOX. And Royce Allen's clients live the good life. We all do. Most of these people will die in the next six weeks. The remainder will carry on for as much as a year, then one day they'll just shut down and Humbert will throw them away like so many used gearboxes.

"Don't get too close," Elisabeth murmurs. "That's still Stuff in there." If we get too close, we might upset the process, make something instead of FOX. Could be good, could be bad. Isn't in the plan. Leave it. We'll do something for these people, though. Something. If we can. (If I get close to the Stuff, will I make something which would show me what's bothering me? Pass on. Not worth the risk. Pass on.)

I pass on.

We trot down the main avenue between the boxes full of people, and we emerge into a place which isn't quite as bad. Metal doors, stone walls, strip lighting. Guards on the floor. Holding cells. Tommy Lapland applauds from a chair by the guards' room.

"Did you get him?"

"We got the Bey."

"Gonzo?"

"No."

Tommy nods. Bad news, but expected. Gonzo is deeper in. Of course.

"Seventy people in the cells. Trent's taking them out the way you came in."

The radio pops to life. On the hour. Jim Hepsobah:

"Rustic." That means Jim's alive and well. "Flambeau." All proceeding smoothly. "Islington." No sign of Humbert Pestle. The others respond. All according to plan. (No sign of Pestle. No sign of Gonzo. I hope that's coincidence. I doubt that it is.) Jim Hepsobah says "Dolphin," which means "Find Gonzo or don't, but get out soon." And then the radio goes flat again. The generator is back online.

Baptiste Vasille shrugs. It's very much a French shrug. It says "Well, what did you expect?" and it says it in a way which suggests the world is essentially English, and hence a bit awkward and silly.

"Control Centre," Vasille says.

Yes. Of course. On the map it is marked as a second building like this one, with an operations room controlling every aspect of the facility and the super-secure offices of management. The holdfast within the fortress. Pestle's file says the warehouse part is empty—not enough donors (this is the term he uses for his victims, very sanitary, very *voluntary*) to fill it right now.

In ten minutes Jim Hepsobah will switch off the generator and pull everyone out. Sally Culpepper will put away her long gun and give up on the Pestlehunt, and we will run and hide and claim to have been drunk in a bar all night, and it was two other fellas and anyway they hit me first. We have exactly that long to get in and out. Vasille and Tommy Lapland grin. It can't be done. We've done it before. Just like old times.

We go do it.

THE BAD ELF of disaster is riding my shoulder as we get to the big doors. It is screaming in my ear as we go through them. *Too easy, too fast, too inviting.* I think of Professor Derek's architectural traps at the old Project Albumen, and I wonder if we will just be frozen or melted, rendered down and sluiced away. It is dark inside, and quiet. Not quiet like empty. Not even trying. Quiet like expectant, like waiting for the show.

The lights come on.

And there, in front of me, is exactly what's wrong.

Ninjas.

In all this time I haven't seen a single ninja. Now I know why: they were all here. Waiting. Row upon row upon row. It never occurred to me there might be so many of them. In front of them is Humbert Pestle, in a pair of casual slacks and a white shirt looking every inch a gentleman. And yes, of course, beside him is Gonzo, proud, stupid and only now waking up to the possibility that something is seriously messed up. Only now, as two more ninjas bring in Zaher Bey, and behind us the refugees from Templeton are herded through the doors, sad and afraid and totally at a loss, to have salvation stolen away from them at this last instant. Idiot plan. Idiot me. All my fault. All Gonzo's too, but he's still catching up, so I can carry the can for us both.

He turns to Humbert Pestle, and a brief conversation takes place which I cannot hear but which goes approximately like this:

Gonzo: What are they all doing here?
Humbert: Rescuing you, among other things. Sweet, isn't it?
Gonzo: (*heroic*) I do not understand. I am a strong man and a stout warrior, but I am a bear of very little brain and long words confuse me.
Humbert: Idiot.
Gonzo: Release my friends and we'll say no more about it.
Humbert: No. Look, you're not getting this, are you? I am . . . evil! Yes! Eeee-vil! Bwah-hahaha!

Gonzo's face at this moment is a picture. If the situation were not so dire, I would frame it. I want to nod. Yes, Gonzo. He is a monster. Yes, he has betrayed you. Yes, all of this and worse yet—everyone else saw it coming a hundred miles away. Then Humbert Pestle gestures, and they bring in Leah. She looks unharmed and not in mourning but very cross. Thus, a trick. Leah has been decoyed here. *Gonzo needs you, come at once!* Ma and Old Man Lubitsch left safe at home, saved up in case more leverage is needed.

If I were still inside Gonzo's head, this tactic would work admirably. I would doubt and dither, and the moment would be lost. But Gonzo Lubitsch, in pure form, does not do stand-off. He moves straight from shock to attack, so quickly that even Pestle is surprised. Gonzo's fists strike him, hard and fast, and they do not stop. Elbow, knee, knee, knee . . . It is a pounding, a ceaseless assault. Pestle gags. Gonzo strikes again, and again. The ninjas do not move. I don't understand . . . I do understand. This too is part of the evening's entertainment. They were expecting it. Leah was not brought to restrain Gonzo. She was brought to provoke him. And because, like the rest of us, she has defied the machine and must die.

Pestle's head comes up sharply as if he has been woken from a sound sleep and only now realises that he's being attacked. There's blood on his face. Gonzo hits him in the nose, and it breaks, in as much as there's anything left of it to break. Pestle shakes snot and spit, dyed red, from his mouth, and rolls the next punch off like a dog shedding a cobweb. Then he hits back. Gonzo blocks. He puts his whole body into it, hard style, turning as he does so. Wallop. They lock like that for a second, eye to eye, and then Gonzo bounces away as Pestle's heavy hand reaches for his head. It's his right hand, of course, so big that Humbert Pestle could actually grab Gonzo and hold him the way I'd hold an orange. Bambambam. More blows, Gonzo like a dervish, striking the upper body. Pestle grins again, smacks Gonzo in turn. Ow. Gonzo staggers back, kicks out, Pestle slips the kick, and around it goes. The ninjas watch without speaking. They've seen this dance before, and they're not interested. Hard form versus hard form. Pestle is bigger and stronger. Sure, he's old. He's not that old.

The end comes a moment later. Gonzo and Pestle are bound up together, straining and barging. It looks much less scientific than it is. Then Gonzo breaks a bit too slowly, and Pestle yells with delight and brings his huge, clubbed hand around in a mighty arc for Gonzo's head. Gonzo throws up his arms to ward it off, and turns into the punch to punish it.

Two sharp snaps, and Gonzo goes white. His arms are broken between the elbow and the wrist. Pestle kicks him and he sprawls away, gasping. Man down.

And then he turns to us. Me, Elisabeth, Tommy Lapland, Baptiste Vasille. A second later Vasille is wearing a row of spikes in his arms and legs. He sinks down, groaning. Tommy Lapland falls to the floor at the same moment. A thrown billy club clatters to the ground beside him. Leaving just us two.

Pestle walks towards us. The ninjas straighten a little, pay attention. We're the main event. *Killing us,* in fact, is the main event. Pestle is fifteen feet away and grinning hungrily. He's looking from me to Elisabeth as if he can't decide where to start.

I smell something.

I feel better.

It's ludicrous.

I'm going to die but I don't mind because I smell something which reminds me of good times. What *is* that? Then Elisabeth smells it too—and her face goes absolutely still. And suddenly she grins, wide. A tiger's grin. Humbert Pestle, stalking towards us, stops in his tracks.

Greasepaint.

The refugees behind us look a lot less grey and wan than they used to. They look almost *avid.* Around their eyes and lips they have traces of white make-up, and they are wearing black, in fact they are wearing black polo necks, with a few overcoats and things thrown in. Not refugees at all. Substitutes. *Ringers.* The Matahuxee Mime Combine. And then a figure steps from their midst, slender and sprightly.

"Hello," says Ike Thermite. "My name is Ike Thermite." He smiles. "And *we,*" he adds, "are the School of the Voiceless Dragon."

HUMBERT PESTLE roars something furious which sounds like "No" and charges towards us. His huge, dreadful fist thunders at my head. And Ike Thermite's narrow fingers brush it to one side and his shoulder hits Humbert Pestle and drives him back, and all around us the Matahuxee Mime Combine are making a fighting wedge, a slender knife where each person supports and protects the next, and the ninjas are having a really bad day. The students of Wu Shenyang have a great deal of pent-up aggression, and while they don't generally believe in that sort of thing, they are prepared to make an exception today in honour of the Clockwork Hand and most especially those who burned Master Wu alive in his own home. Of course, no one knows exactly who those people were, so they're content to assume that the person they are presently hitting very hard was solely responsible. Elisabeth Soames dives for the steps leading up to Leah Lubitsch, and a second later it rains unwary members of the Hand. I look for Gonzo. It's like one of those movies where a hundred bad guys attack the hero one at a time; the only danger is that he may get out of breath hitting them. I am liquid. I am steel. I hit people.

There's a guy with a pole. He thrusts it at me. I slide past it, and he tries to use the broad side. I roll under it. He twists. I twist too. He flies past me, and now I have the pole. I glower at him. Run away, little man. I am on a job here, saving a friend. If I weren't, we'd be pursuing that conversation in terms you would not enjoy.

He decides to fight someone else. I glance around.

Down by the door, four ninjas pursuing Zaher Bey find themselves confronted with a prune-faced bloke aged about a hundred and nine. They laugh at him. Ronnie Cheung turns on his heel and drops his trousers to expose his ugly, wrinkled arse. The ninjas freeze. It isn't just the sheer gall of this action; Ronnie Cheung's arse is a startling sight, and where it cleaves there are suggestions of unspeakable mysteries, hirsute awfulnesses best left unexamined. Ronnie smiles over one shoulder at the ninjas, removes his left leg from his trousers, and kicks the nearest one in the throat. Then another. The third and fourth realise their mistake and rush him. Ronnie kicks up with his other leg, wraps his trousers around the head of the smaller one, and drags him down into the path of the other. Then his bare leg scythes onto the fallen guy's head and it breaks open. The fourth ninja tries to run away, and Ronnie punches him in the back. The ninja lies on the ground, thrashing.

I decide I can safely leave Zaher Bey with Ronnie for the time being and turn back to the fight.

Ike Thermite is going toe to toe with Humbert Pestle. Pestle is impervious; Ike is untouchable. It's a draw. Master Wu obviously didn't teach him any Secret Internal Alchemies either. I had this crazy hope, for a moment.

Ike hits Humbert with a combination. It's a blinder. Pestle

takes it in his stride, and Ike has to dodge fast and low. He's in terrific shape. He can't do this for ever. Sooner or later, something has to give.

Something does. Humbert Pestle lashes out, and Ike Thermite is slow. He absorbs the blow, flies across the room and lands in a heap. Pestle follows, smashing through the fight around him as if it were a garden hedge. One mime and one ninja are clubbed to the ground. He doesn't care. He wants Ike. He stands over him and slowly raises his left hand up, his right on Ike's head. In a moment he will exchange the two, palm for fist, and Ike will break open and die. Pestle's shoulders ripple as he begins the strike.

Someone hits him with a broom handle.

It's a very ordinary broom handle. It's light and strong and not a terribly frightening thing. It breaks on his head like balsa. Pestle drops Ike and turns around, wrath-of-God slow. Scary as hell.

It's only as I glance down at the fractured broom in my hands that I realise who was dumb enough and brave enough to do the deed.

Oh *bugger.*

Dodge. Twist. I am air. I step, skip, shuffle. Elvis Walk (defensive, agile) becomes Lorenz Palace Step (random directions making up a usable pattern of attack), and on and on. My hands blur and slap, stroke and twist. Humbert Pestle lunges. I gouge his eye. He roars and strikes down. I savage the muscles in his arm. He kicks, and I punish the joint, lock it, stress it, let it go and whisper away into the space next door as he slams into where I was. I do all these things and it is not enough. Somewhere over there Ike Thermite is broken, out of the fight, and Ike was infinitely better at this than I am. Ike was a senior student. It's not enough.

He hits me. It's not a full strike, just a love tap. It picks me up and winds me. No time. I roll. I feel his foot stamp on the ground. Keep moving, don't tense; breathe, live. I move. Blind Man's Sword: a sequence to use when you cannot see, a system of deflections and evasions which appear to imply knowledge of the enemy's movements. Bluff. It works. I move again. He is stalking me, moving smoothly and fast. He is too big to be that fast, or maybe too fast to be that big. I can see. I wish I couldn't. A thumb fills my vision, and I duck, move away off-axis. It's a feint. A kick lands in my chest, and I feel my ribs flex. All the air comes out of me. I see colours, black and white and grey and red all at once, then purple and yellow together, laid over each other, then other colours without names. I dodge the follow-up, turn my shoulder and shunt him back, just as Ike did.

I'm going to lose.

I stare up and around in desperation. Where is Sally Culpepper and her gun? Elisabeth is on the gallery. She has Leah behind her, safe for the moment. I meet her eyes.

And I see her.

I see Elisabeth Soames in every moment that I have known her. Every frame of every minute. Elisabeth with cake. Elisabeth stamping her foot. Elisabeth as Andromas. Elisabeth kissing me. Elisabeth, as revealed by a single, white, little-girl sock protruding from the end of a sofa. And I see her, a million years ago, in Master Wu's house, asking about the Secrets. About the Iron Skin meditation.

There aren't any of those.

But there are. I am fighting one. Therefore . . .

I will make one up.

And he does. It is a good secret. It is so good, it could almost be real.

I will make one up.

You sneaky, underhanded, cheeky old sod.

Align the chi . . . Feel the ocean . . . You will storm the strongest fortress.

I look at Humbert Pestle. He is unbeatable. He is impregnable.

He is *mine.*

In that moment I place my absolute trust in the hands of a

dead man who wore sandals in winter and asserted a belief that the Chinese space programme was unfairly disadvantaged by the position of the Moon. This is perhaps a slender thread from which to hang the future of the world. Like spider silk, it is strong enough to do the job.

I slow down. It's not about fast; it's about where I need to be, and where he needs me not to be. I step lightly. It's not about power; it's about timing. Humbert Pestle chops at me, but I am not there. He strikes, but I am outside his centre line and the blow has no strength. Well, it snaps my head back and it hurts, but that's all it does. I crack his hand as he withdraws it. He tenses. I slide past his guard and slap him. It doesn't hurt him, but it is extremely embarrassing. I have just girly-slapped him in front of all his ninja kiddies. I have no respect. So *nyah.*

He slashes at me. He tries to catch me with a fist coming up as I go down, but I am already turning away, and he looks for a moment like some guy posing at the beach, arm bent and tensed, massive bicep straining. Hey, Bluto, where's my spinach? *Nyah nyah nyah.* He breathes. I breathe with him. His elbow catches me on the way back and nearly stuns me, but the follow-up is in the wrong place, because I am in the right one. I stamp on his instep. Something snaps. He's tough enough to ignore it, but it hurts anyway. The rhythm of his breathing is broken as he holds in a grunt of pain.

I touch Humbert Pestle, and I *listen* to him. I let my hands rest on him as I stroke aside his terrible punches. I taste the air as he exhales. I learn him. I understand the way he moves. I know where he is strong, and where he is not. He is a fortress. But he is not invulnerable. I breathe out. I breathe in. Humbert Pestle works through his pain. It is irrelevant. He breathes out. He breathes in.

Now we move in concert. I mirror him, step with him. I stick to him, slip and slide and duck and dive. His mace-hand goes over my head with a terrific *woosh.* It frustrates him. He stalks me some more, and finally he is following me. He does not know it. He thinks he is setting the pace, but he has fallen into a rhythm. It is syncopated and abrupt. It varies. But it is a pattern, and I know it intimately, at a level beyond mistake. I can break it. He cannot. He doesn't realise he has to. I could strike now, hit him endlessly—but there's no target. He has made himself into a weapon, an armoured monster. There's no point. I breathe out. So does he. I breathe in. So does he. We are locked together.

We fight some more. We breathe. The thing is, I am a littler guy than Humbert Pestle, and I'm using a lot less energy. I don't need as much oxygen. His heart rate is going up. He's starting to feel tired, and he doesn't like it. He doesn't understand. I can see it in his face. He's cross and just a little nervous—he should not be feeling this way. Not so soon. He does this kind of exercise every day. He's pretty much the hardest bastard in the world. He may not be a young kid any more, but he's in tip-top shape. He can't be tired. Push through it. It's the enemy.

I breathe. He breathes. He throws a combination so fast I can't imagine being able to block it. I don't have to. I was never going to be in its path. I was already leaving the target area when he decided to launch it. I slap him again because this man is trying to kill me, so I don't feel bad about messing with him. His ninja kiddies look shocked and unhappy now. They're watching him, all of them, even while they fend off the Voiceless Dragon School and keep this area clear. Come on, Humbert! Snap him like a twig! He is weak! What's the hold-up?

No pressure.

Humbert Pestle is fifty-five. That means his maximum safe heart rate, notionally, is around one hundred and sixty-seven beats per minute. I can see the vein in his neck walloping away. He's at around one seventy now. I breathe. He is still with me. We're still in this weird mirror dance. He throws a couple more punches, but they're weak and slow. There's not enough oxygen in his blood. He should back off, but he won't. It's not who he is. Weakness is an enemy. Fight through it. I look at him. It's time. I slip a punch and come round in front of him, and I look into his eyes and sigh.

I put everything I have into it. I give him my grief when I heard about Master Wu. I give him poor mad George Copsen's horror at destroying the world, and every stupid death I saw in the Go Away War. I give him Micah Monroe and the soldiers who didn't make it. I give him the foal-girl we buried in Addeh Katir. I give him the crazed cannibal dog in Cricklewood Cove and Ma Lubitsch's endless mourning. I give him my broken heart when Leah shook my hand.

I breathe all the way out, long and slow, and the noise which comes from me is a sadness which could kill you. And Humbert Pestle breathes out with me. He takes my sorrow. He thinks that sigh is me giving up. He draws back his hand for one killer punch.

His heart tops one ninety.

I uncoil and hit him in the chest. I feel the force travel through him from sternum to spine. I know him. I could draw his organs on his skin.

His heart stutters, cramps and stops.

Humbert Pestle staggers. He clutches at his shirt in absolute horror and falls to the ground.

Ghost Palm of the Voiceless Dragon Style, fucker.

Humbert Pestle dies.

The ninja kiddies freeze. Each and every one of them has that Tupperware feeling.

Epilogue

After.

PINE SMOKE and the smell of snow; Cricklewood Cove in wintertime. Elisabeth is with her mother for the next few hours, and Leah has taken Gonzo's parents off on some vital jaunt. There is a very strong directive inherent in this curious circumstance. Gonzo and I are to get together and *talk*. We are to *sort things out*. Otherwise, we will *brood* and be *unmanageable*. This is not an acceptable outcome.

The Battle of Jorgmund Actual was two months ago. On the whole, given that the plan was a failure and the enemy ambushed us, it was a roaring success. It helped that Ike Thermite and K are devious beyond all reasonable expectation, and that Master Wu laid his ninja trap deeper than his own grave. Laid it, in fact, in me.

Humbert Pestle died. Jorgmund did not. You can't kill a machine.

On the other hand, you can *own* one.

The ownership of Jorgmund is vested in the Clockwork Hand. The Clockwork Hand is controlled by the present master. That master is chosen by acclamation, or by combat, meaning that the present master of the Hand and chairman of Jorgmund Inc. is, well . . .

Me.

I thought about trying to do good with it. I sat in the Nameless Bar and we all discussed it drunk, and sober, and half asleep, and perky with Flynn's coffee. I almost persuaded myself it could be done. I could turn the monster around. And then Elisabeth wandered over and dumped the Spawn of Flynn in my lap. He looked up at me through a field of snot.

"What do you think?" I said.

"The lady with the flower on her back is having a baby," said Spawn of Flynn, "but you're not to tell anyone."

Sally Culpepper went bright red. Jim Hepsobah choked on his coffee.

"The coughy man is the daddy," the Spawn of Flynn added.

I wound Jorgmund up. I marched into Dick Washburn's office and dumped the entire sordid truth on his desk, without omission. I told him and Mae Milton to break the company up and do good things with the bits. Sally and Jim's baby didn't need a world with a thing like that in it. We made the whole thing public too, and I put the Clockwork Hand to writing letters to all the relatives of the Vanished. Most people didn't want to believe it, but they'll come around. The last of the FOX will dry up in about six months. Already the pressure is slackening, and the unreal world is coming closer to ours. People will have to choose how to live.

Jim Hepsobah and Sally got married. Gonzo was best man. I sat at the back. A surprising number of people nodded to me. Old Man Lubitsch gave the happy couple a beehive, complete with lethal bees. Ma Lubitsch gave them socks. I smiled. Gonzo's father smiled back. *Well done, boy. Well done.*

Ike Thermite and the Matahuxee Mime Combine have resurrected Master Wu's school in Cricklewood Cove. There never was a master mime who lived there. Ike thinks he's extremely clever for slipping that one past me, and he probably is.

Nq'ula Jann, having figured out Humbert Pestle's dastardly plan, showed up with a vast number of Zaher Bey's pirates to rescue everyone. When it was established that we'd taken care of that ourselves, the rescuers got drunk and sang songs about shepherdesses.

Rao and Veda Tsur demanded that they should be godparents to Sally and Jim's child.

Ronnie Cheung took one look at Elisabeth's mother and announced to her face that there was a sack of bones he wouldn't mind rattling. She hit him with a ladle. Their third date passed without sex, but Assumption has given her daughter to understand that on no account is she to show up unannounced tomorrow morning.

So now here I am, knocking on Gonzo's door and feeling five years old.

He opens the door and lets me in. His right arm is still in a cast. The left one, it turns out, was only cracked. We walk into the living room and sit in front of the fire.

"So," Gonzo says. And that's all.

Well, don't look at me. This is the most awkward moment of my entire life. What do you say to a man whose brain you have stolen? To someone who shot you in the chest and shoved you out of a truck? What does he say to you, now that you have saved his life and the world?

We say nothing for some time. Then we talk about how well everyone's doing and how weird the world is going to get. And then we dry up, because you can't make small talk with someone you've known for ever when there's an elephant in the room. And yet it all seems so clear. What's to say?

"You know I don't have a name yet?"

"You're kidding me . . ."

"Well, you never gave me one, so don't look at me like I'm the idiot."

"That's true," Gonzo says. "I never did." He ponders. "Are you . . . going to do more of that?"

"Of what?"

"Derring-do."

"I don't know."

"I'm not," Gonzo says definitively. "I'm done. I want to be . . . I don't know. But I want it. I need to be quiet for a while."

"Oh."

"So . . . if you want . . . you could be Gonzo Lubitsch."

I think about it.

"No. But thanks."

Silence. We stare at each other for a while, measuring.

"We could pretend," Gonzo says at last, "that we finished this conversation."

It's an interesting idea.

"We could," I tell him cautiously.

"We wouldn't have to actually talk about it all."

"No . . . Yeah, exactly."

"Hm." He trails off.

"We'd have to have a pretty good story, though. In case we were questioned."

"That's true." He muses. "I suppose we could say that I started by saying I'm sorry I shot you. Because that's a good opening line."

"Or that I'm sorry . . . I don't know exactly. I'm not sorry I exist. But I'm sorry I didn't realise sooner what was happening. I didn't mean to try to take her from you."

"You think we should start with that?"

"It sounds a bit flaky. But you know what I'm getting at."

He nods.

"I think we should tell them," says Gonzo Lubitsch, "that I said I was sorry for shooting you."

"Okay."

And then he throws himself at me, wraps me in his heavy arms and shakes on my shoulder, and I am murmuring things like "It's okay, it's all right" and I have to sit him down and rock him.

I honestly don't know what we say to each other. It goes on for hours, and at the end of it I'm not sure if we are friends or brothers or anything except me and Gonzo. I don't feel easy around him. But the thing is done, and from here it's all about forwards.

. . .

ZAHER BEY gets out of the car. The sun is setting over a huge green forest. Below us, in the valley, water flows and there are birds. Something huge is stalking through the trees, making them shake. A moment later something smaller squeals sharply, and then stops. In the distance there's a walled town, high towers and pale houses. The wind carries a murmur from its streets.

"The Found Thousand," Zaher Bey says.

The world we knew is gone for good this time. The new one is beautiful and dangerous. It is *us.* I sit with Elisabeth and Zaher Bey and watch the stars come out overhead.

"Are you ready?" the Bey asks.

Elisabeth breathes out onto my cheek. We both answer him at once.

"Yes."

ACKNOWLEDGEMENTS

Authoring may be solitary, but this author at least cannot function in a vacuum. The first person I must thank, now and ever, is Clare. I started this book in January 2006 while we were planning our wedding; the deal was done in 2007 on the day we moved house—which meant that Clare moved house and I went to meetings where everyone was nice to me. Without her keen eye and her laughter, this book would make less sense and be less funny and I would be a very lonely fellow.

I have, as is customary, borrowed from (read "pillaged") every story I have ever loved to write my own, but I must bow especially to P. G. Wodehouse, to Sir Arthur Conan Doyle, and to Alexandre Dumas. It's not what they did, but how they did it.

In the forest of the booktrade, I am guided by the inestimable Patrick Walsh, without whom I would be eaten by bears. Jason Arthur at William Heinemann and Edward Kastenmeier at Knopf rein in my more incomprehensible moments and gently but firmly insist that I get the thing done right. All those involved in designing, setting, presenting and selling the book have pushed the boat out in wonderful and bizarre ways, which makes the whole thing even more exciting than it already is.

Over the years, I have received from my parents—by osmosis, as it were—a master class in writing and surviving the novel; this in addition to the whole business of how to be a person.

Thanks to everyone who participated in the Great Title Hunt. Good titles are rarer than snarks and twice as slippery as Gussie Fink-Nottle's newts.

Lastly, I have stolen bits and pieces of real people to make my characters, and I have put them together to work the action without thought for where they came from. There simply is not one portrait of a real person in this book—although, if you look carefully, you may find your own nose above someone else's moustache. To all those anonymous donors, thank you.

Well, now. On to the next one.

Nick Harkaway

London, 2008

ALSO AVAILABLE FROM

VINTAGE CONTEMPORARIES

THE BRIEF HISTORY OF THE DEAD

by Kevin Brockmeier

The City is inhabited by those who have departed Earth but are still remembered by the living. They will reside in this afterlife until they are completely forgotten. But the City is shrinking, and the residents are clearing out. Some of the holdouts, like Luka Sims, who produces the City's only newspaper, are wondering what exactly is going on. Others, like Coleman Kinzler, believe it is the beginning of the end. Meanwhile, Laura Byrd is trapped in an Antarctic research station, her supplies are running low, her radio finds only static, and the power is failing. With little choice, Laura sets out across the ice to look for help, but time is running out. Brockmeier alternates these two storylines to create a lyrical and haunting story about love, loss, and the power of memory.

Fiction/978-1-4000-9595-7

THE EGG CODE

by Mike Heppner

Olden Field is a solitary computer hacker, whose ultimate purpose is the destruction of the Gloria 21169, a monstrous router that has taken control of the Internet. Motivational speaker Derek Skye finds himself sickened by the advice he spews to his legions of fans. Meanwhile, his ex-wife, Donna, fabricates folklore to assist those looking for guidance in our troubled times. Her friend Lydia Tree-Mould is determined to see her talentless son, Simon, achieve celebrity, so she bullies her complacent husband into getting Simon his big break in a company advertising campaign. As only the most accomplished fiction can, *The Egg Code* brings them together with a host of others in a sweeping, comic, wildly entertaining narrative. In this audacious literary debut, Mike Heppner concocts a brilliantly realized, impeccably structured meditation on the value of information in our information-saturated time.

Fiction/978-0-375-72725-2

TOO BEAUTIFUL FOR YOU
by Rod Liddle

Dumped by his mistress, Dempsey weeps on his wife's shoulder, wondering how best to kill himself so at least seven people will try to stop him. Eddie miserably sneaks off to sleep with his wife's mother—a rather unpleasant situation from which he can't seem to extricate himself. And Christian, despite a terrible train accident and medical disaster, must just make it to Uttoxeter before he is caught in a horrible lie. Disturbingly funny, psychologically astute, and sharp as a knife, this collection of stories reveals the dark heart of human compulsion.

Fiction/978-1-4000-7813-X